A former police reporter for the *Los Angeles Times*, Michael Connelly is the author of sixteen acclaimed and bestselling novels. His novels have won an Edgar Award, the Nero Wolfe prize and the Anthony Award. He lives in Florida with his wife and daughter. Visit his website at www.MichaelConnelly.com.

By Michael Connelly

The Lincoln Lawyer
The Closers
The Narrows
Lost Light
Chasing the Dime
City of Bones
A Darkness More Than Night
Void Moon
Angels Flight
Blood Work
Trunk Music
The Poet
The Last Coyote
The Concrete Blonde
The Black Ice
The Black Echo

The Concrete Blonde

Blonde

The Last Coyote

Michael Connelly

The Concrete Blonde
First published in Great Britain by Orion in 1994

The Last Coyote
First published in Great Britain by Orion in 1995

This omnibus edition published in 2008
by Orion Books Ltd
Orion House, 5 Upper St Martin's Lane
London WC2H 9EA

A CIP catalogue record for this book is available from the British Library.

ISBN 978-1-4072-1623-2

Printed and bound in Great Britain by
Clays Ltd, St Ives plc

www.orionbooks.co.uk

The Concrete Blonde

Michael Connelly

This is for Susan, Paul and Jamie, Bob and Marlen, Ellen, Jane and Damian

The house in Silverlake was dark, its windows as empty as a dead man's eyes. It was an old California Craftsman with a full front porch and two dormer windows set on the long slope of the roof. But no light shone behind the glass, not even from above the doorway. Instead, the house cast a foreboding darkness about it that not even the glow from the streetlight could penetrate. A man could be standing there on the porch and Bosch knew he probably wouldn't be able to see him.

'You sure this is it?' he asked her.

'Not the house,' she said. 'Behind it. The garage. Pull up so you can see down the drive.'

Bosch tapped the gas pedal and the Caprice moved forward and crossed the entrance to the driveway.

'There,' she said.

Bosch stopped the car. There was a garage behind the house with an apartment above it. Wooden staircase up the side, light over the door. Two windows, lights on inside.

'Okay,' Bosch said.

They stared at the garage for several moments. Bosch didn't know what he expected to see. Maybe nothing. The whore's perfume was filling the car and he rolled his window down. He didn't know whether to trust her claim or not. The one thing he knew he couldn't do was call for backup. He hadn't brought a rover with him and the car was not equipped with a phone.

'What are you going to – there he goes!' she said urgently.

Bosch had seen it, the shadow of a figure crossing behind the smaller window. The bathroom, he guessed.

'He's in the bathroom,' she said. 'That's where I saw all the stuff.'

Bosch looked away from the window and at her.

'What stuff?' ·

'I, uh, checked the cabinet. You know, when I was in there. Just looking to see what he had. A girl has to be careful. And I saw all the stuff. Makeup shit. You know, mascara, lipsticks, compacts and stuff. That's how I figured it was him. He used all that stuff to paint 'em when he was done, you know, killing them.'

'Why didn't you tell me that on the phone?'

'You didn't ask.'

He saw the figure pass behind the curtains of the other window. Bosch's mind was racing now, his heart jacking up into its overdrive mode.

'How long ago was this that you ran out of there?'

'Shit, I don't know. I hadda walk down to Franklin just to find a fucking ride over to the Boulevard. I was with the ride 'bout ten minutes. So I don't know.'

'Guess. It's important.'

'I don't know. It's been more than an hour.'

Shit, Bosch thought. She stopped to turn a trick before she called the task force number. Showed a lot of genuine concern there. Now there could be a replacement up there and I'm sitting out here watching.

He gunned the car up the street and found a space in front of a hydrant. He turned off the engine but left the keys in the ignition. After he jumped out he stuck his head back in through the open window.

'Listen, I'm going up there. You stay here. If you hear shots, or if I'm not back here in ten minutes, you start knocking on doors and get some cops out here. Tell them an officer needs assistance. There's a clock on the dash. Ten minutes.'

'Ten minutes, baby. You go be the hero now. But I'm getting that reward.'

Bosch pulled his gun as he hurried down the driveway. The stairs up the side of the garage were old and warped. He took them three at a time, as quietly as he could. But still it felt as if he were shouting his arrival to the world. At the

2

top, he raised the gun and broke the bare bulb that was in place over the door. Then, he leaned back into the darkness, against the outside railing. He raised his left leg and put all his weight and momentum into his heel. He struck the door above the knob.

The door swung open with a loud crack. In a crouch, Bosch moved through the threshold in the standard combat stance. Right away he saw the man across the room, standing on the other side of a bed. The man was naked and not only bald but completely hairless. His vision locked on the man's eyes and he saw the look of terror quickly fill them. Bosch yelled, his voice high and taut.

'COPS! DON'T FUCKING MOVE!'

The man froze, but only for a beat, and then began bending down, his right arm reaching for the pillow. He hesitated once and then continued the movement. Bosch couldn't believe it. What the fuck was he doing? Time went into suspension. The adrenaline pounding through his body gave his vision a slow-motion clarity. Bosch knew the man was either reaching for the pillow for something to cover himself with, or he was –

The hand swept under the pillow.

'DON'T DO IT!'

The hand was closing on something beneath the pillow. The man had never taken his eyes off Bosch. Then Bosch realized it wasn't terror in his eyes. It was something else. Anger? Hate? The hand was coming out from beneath the pillow now.

'NO!'

Bosch fired one shot, his gun kicking up in his two-handed grasp. The naked man jerked upright and backward. He hit the wood-paneled wall behind him, then bounced forward and fell across the bed thrashing and gagging. Bosch quickly moved into the room and to the bed.

The man's left hand was reaching again for the pillow. Bosch brought his left leg up and knelt on his back, pinning

3

him to the bed. He pulled the cuffs off his belt and grabbed the groping left hand and cuffed it. Then the right. Behind the back. The naked man was gagging and moaning.

'I can't – I can't,' he said, but his statement was lost in a bloody coughing fit.

'You can't do what I told you,' Bosch said. 'I told you not to move!'

Just die, man, Bosch thought but didn't say. It will be easier for all of us.

He moved around the bed to the pillow. He lifted it, stared at what was beneath it for a few moments and then dropped it. He closed his eyes for a moment.

'Goddammit!' he called at the back of the naked man's head. 'What were you doing? I had a fucking gun and you, you reach – I told you not to move!'

Bosch came around the bed so he could see the man's face. Blood was emptying from his mouth onto the dingy white sheet. Bosch knew his bullet had hit the lungs. The naked man was the dying man now.

'You didn't have to die,' Bosch said to him.

Then the man was dead.

Bosch looked around the room. There was no one else. No replacement for the whore who had run. He had been wrong on that guess. He went into the bathroom and opened the cabinet beneath the sink. The makeup was there, as the whore had said. Bosch recognized some of the brand names. Max Factor, L'Oréal, Cover Girl, Revlon. It all seemed to fit.

He looked back through the bathroom door at the corpse on the bed. There was still the smell of gunpowder in the air. He lit a cigarette and it was so quiet in the place that he could hear the crisp tobacco burn as he dragged the soothing smoke into his lungs.

There was no phone in the apartment. Bosch sat on a chair in the kitchenette and waited. Staring across the room at the body, he realized that his heart was still pounding rapidly and that he felt lightheaded. He also realized that he felt nothing – not sympathy or guilt or sorrow – for the man on the bed. Nothing at all.

Instead, he tried to concentrate on the sound of the siren that was now sounding in the distance and coming closer. After a while, he was able to discern that it was more than one siren. It was many.

ONE

There are no benches in the hallways of the US District Courthouse in downtown Los Angeles. No place to sit. Anybody who slides down the wall to sit on the cold marble floor will get rousted by the first deputy marshal who walks by. And the marshals are always out in the halls, walking by.

The lack of hospitality exists because the federal government does not want its courthouse to give even the appearance that justice may be slow, or nonexistent. It does not want people lining the halls on benches, or on the floor, waiting with weary eyes for the courtroom doors to open and their cases or the cases of their jailed loved ones to be called. There is enough of that going on across Spring Street in the County Criminal Courts building. Every day the benches in the hallways of every floor are clogged with those who wait. Mostly they are women and children, their husbands or fathers or lovers held in lockup. Mostly they are black or brown. Mostly the benches look like crowded life rafts – women and children first – with people pressed together and cast adrift, waiting, always waiting, to be found. Boat people, the courthouse smartasses call them.

Harry Bosch thought about these differences as he smoked a cigarette and stood on the front steps of the federal courthouse. That was another thing. No smoking in the hallways inside. So he had to take the escalator down and come outside during the trial's breaks. Outside there was a sand-filled ash can behind the concrete base of the statue of the blindfolded woman holding up the scales of justice. Bosch looked up at the statue; he could never remember her name. The Lady of Justice. Something Greek, he thought but wasn't sure. He went back to the folded newspaper in his hands and reread the story.

Lately, in the mornings, he would read only the Sports section, concentrating his full attention on the pages in the back where box scores and statistics were carefully charted and updated each day. He somehow found the columns of numbers and percentages comforting. They were clear and concise, an absolute order in a disordered world. Having knowledge of who had hit the most home runs for the Dodgers made him feel that he was still connected in some way to the city, and to his life.

But today he had left the Sports section folded and tucked into his briefcase, which was under his chair in the courtroom. The *Los Angeles Times*'s Metro section was in his hands now. He had carefully folded the section into quarters, the way he had seen drivers on the freeway do it so they could read while they drove, and the story on the trial was on the bottom corner of the section's front page. He once again read the story and once again felt his face grow hot as he read about himself.

TRIAL ON POLICE 'TOUPEE' SHOOTING TO BEGIN

By Joel Bremmer, *Times* Staff Writer

As an unusual civil rights trial gets underway today, a Los Angeles police detective stands accused of having used excessive force four years ago when he shot and killed a purported serial killer he believed was reaching for a gun. The alleged killer was actually reaching for his toupee.

Los Angeles Police Detective Harry Bosch, 43, is being sued in US District Court by the widow of Norman Church, an aerospace worker Bosch shot to death at the climax of the investigation into the so-called Dollmaker killings.

For nearly a year before the shooting, police had sought a serial killer so named by the media because he used makeup to paint the faces of his 11 victims. The highly publicized manhunt was marked by the killer's sending of poems and notes to Bosch and the *Times*.

After Church was killed, police announced they had unequivocal evidence proving that the mechanical engineer was the killer.

Bosch was suspended and later transferred from the homicide special unit of the LAPD Robbery-Homicide Division to the Hollywood Division homicide squad. In making the demotion, police stressed that Bosch was disciplined for procedural errors, such as his failure to call for a backup to the Silverlake apartment where the fatal shooting took place.

Police administrators maintained that the Church killing was a 'good' shooting – department terminology meaning not improper.

Since Church's death precluded a trial, much of the evidence gathered by police has never been provided publicly under oath. That will likely change with the federal trial. A week-long jury selection process is expected to be completed today with the opening statements of the attorneys to follow.

Bosch had to refold the paper to continue reading the story on an inside page. He was momentarily distracted by seeing his own picture, which was on the inside page. It was an old photo and looked not unlike a mug shot. It was the same one that was on his department ID card. Bosch was more annoyed by the photo than the story. It was an invasion of his privacy to put his picture out like that. He tried to concentrate on the story.

Bosch is being defended by the City Attorney's Office because he was acting in the line of duty when the shooting occurred. If any judgment is won by the plaintiff, the city taxpayers, not Bosch, will pay.

Church's wife, Deborah, is being represented by civil rights attorney Honey Chandler, who specializes in police abuse cases. In an interview last week, Chandler said she will seek to prove to the jury that Bosch acted in such a reckless manner that a fatal shooting of Church was inevitable.

'Detective Bosch was cowboying and a man ended up dead,' Chandler said. 'I don't know if he was merely reckless or if there is something more sinister here, but we will find out in the trial.'

That was the line that Bosch had read and reread at least six times since getting the paper during the first break. Sinister. What did she mean by that? He had tried not to let it bother him, knowing that Chandler would not be above using a newspaper interview for a psych-ops outing but, still, it felt like a warning shot. It let him know more was to come.

Chandler said she also plans to question the police evidence that Church was the Dollmaker. She said Church, the father of two daughters, was not the serial killer police sought and that they labeled him as such to cover up Bosch's misdeed.

'Detective Bosch killed an innocent man in cold blood,' Chandler said. 'What we are doing with this civil rights suit is what the police department and the district attorney's office refused to do: bring forward the truth and provide justice for Norman Church's family.'

Bosch and Asst City Atty Rodney Belk, who is defending him, declined comment for this story. Along with Bosch, those expected to testify in the one- to two-week case include –

'Spare change, pal?'

Bosch looked up from the paper into the grimy but familiar face of the homeless man who had staked out the front of the courthouse as his turf. Bosch had seen him out here every day during the week of jury selection, making his change-and-cigarette rounds. The man wore a threadbare tweed jacket over two sweaters and corduroy pants. He carried a plastic bag of belongings and a Big Gulp cup to shake in front of people when he asked for change. He also always carried with him a yellow legal pad with scribbling all over it.

9

Bosch instinctively patted his pockets and shrugged. He had no change.

'I'd take a dollar, you know.'

'Don't have a spare dollar.'

The homeless man dismissed him and looked into the ash can. Yellowed cigarette butts grew from the sand like a crop of cancer. He put his yellow pad under his arm and began to pick through the offerings, taking those that still had a quarter inch or more of tobacco to smoke. Every now and then he would find a nearly whole cigarette and make a clicking sound with his mouth to show his approval. He put the harvest from the ash can in the Big Gulp cup.

Happy with his findings, the man stepped back from the ash can and looked up at the statue. He looked back at Bosch and winked, then began to rock his hips in a lewd mimicry of a sexual act.

'How 'bout my girl here?' he said.

The man then kissed his hand and reached up and patted the statue.

Before Bosch could think of something to say, the pager on his belt began to chirp. The homeless man stepped back another two steps and raised his free hand as if to ward off some unknown evil. Bosch saw the look of deranged panic spread on his face. It was the look of a man whose brain synapses were spread too far apart, the connections dulled. The man turned and scurried away, out toward Spring Street, with his cup of used cigarettes.

Bosch watched him until he was gone and then pulled the pager off his belt. He recognized the number on the display. It was Lieutenant Harvey 'Ninety-eight' Pounds's direct line at the Hollywood station. He put what was left of his cigarette into the sand and went back into the courthouse. There was a bank of pay phones at the top of the escalator, near the second-floor courtrooms.

'Harry, what's happening there?' Pounds asked.

'The usual. Just waiting around. We got a jury, so now the lawyers are in with the judge, talking about openers.

Belk said I didn't have to sit in on that, so I'm just hanging around.'

He looked at his watch. It was ten to twelve.

'They'll be breaking for lunch soon,' he added.

'Good. I need you.'

Bosch didn't reply. Pounds had promised he would be off the case rotation until the trial was over. A week more, maybe two, at the most. It was a promise Pounds had no choice but to make. He knew that Bosch couldn't handle catching a homicide investigation while in federal court four days a week.

'What's going on? I thought I was off the list.'

'You are. But we may have a problem. It concerns you.'

Bosch hesitated again. Dealing with Pounds was like that. Harry would trust a street snitch before he'd trust Pounds. There was always the spoken motive and the hidden motive. It seemed that this time the lieutenant was doing one of his routine dances. Speaking in elliptical phrases, trying to get Bosch to bite on the hook.

'A problem?' Bosch finally asked. A good noncommittal reply.

'Well, I take it you saw the paper today – the *Times* story about your case?'

'Yeah, I was just reading it.'

'Well, we got another note.'

'A note? What are you talking about?'

'I'm talking about somebody dropping a note at the front desk. Addressed to you. And damn if it doesn't sound like those notes you got from the Dollmaker back when all of that was going on.'

Bosch could tell Pounds was enjoying this, the stretching it out.

'If it was addressed to me, how do you know about it?'

'It wasn't mailed. No envelope. It was just one page, folded over. Had your name on the fold. Somebody left it at the front desk. Somebody there read it, you can figure it from there.'

'What does it say?'

'Well, you're not going to like this, Harry, the timing is god-awful, but the note says, it says basically that you got the wrong guy. That the Dollmaker is still out there. The writer says he's the real Dollmaker and that the body count continues. Says you killed the wrong guy.'

'It's bullshit. The Dollmaker's letters were carried in the paper, in Bremmer's book on the case. Anybody could pick up the style and write a note. You –'

'You take me for a moron, Bosch? I know anybody could've written this. But so did the writer know that. So to prove his point he included a little treasure map, I'd guess you'd call it. Directions to another victim's body.'

A long silence filled the line while Bosch thought and Pounds waited.

'And so?' Bosch finally said.

'And so I sent Edgar out to the location this morning. You remember Bing's, on Western?'

'Bing's? Yeah, south of the Boulevard. Bing's. A pool hall. Didn't that place go down in the riots last year?'

'Right,' Pounds said. 'Complete burnout. They looted and torched the place. Just the slab and three walls left standing. There's a city demolition order against it but the owner hasn't acted yet. Anyway, that's the spot, according to this note we got. Note says she was buried under the floor slab. Edgar went out there with a city crew, jackhammers, the works . . .'

Pounds was dragging it out. What a petty asshole, Bosch thought. This time he would wait longer. And when the silence grew nervously long, Pounds finally spoke.

'He found a body. Just like the note said he would. Beneath the concrete. He found a body. That's –'

'How old is it?'

'Don't know yet. But it's old. That's why I'm calling. I need you to go out there during the lunch break and see what you can make of this. You know, is it legit as a Dollmaker victim or is some other wacko jerking us off? You're the expert. You could go out there when the judge breaks for lunch. I'll meet you there. And you'll be back in time for openers.'

Bosch felt numb. He already needed another cigarette. He tried to place all of what Pounds had just said into some semblance of order. The Dollmaker – Norman Church – had been dead four years now. There had been no mistake. Bosch knew that night. He still knew it in his guts today. Church was the Dollmaker.

'So this note just appeared at the desk?'

'Desk sergeant found it on the front counter about four hours ago. Nobody saw anybody leave it. You know, a lot of people come through the front in the mornings. Plus we had change of shift. I had Meehan go up and talk to the desk uniforms. Nobody remembers jack shit about it until they found it.'

'Shit. Read it to me.'

'Can't. SID has it. Doubt there will be any lifts, but we have to go through the motions. I'll get a copy and have it with me at the scene, okay?'

Bosch didn't answer.

'I know what you're thinking,' Pounds said. 'But let's hold our horses till we see what is out there. No reason to worry yet. Might be some stunt cooked up by that lawyer, Chandler. Wouldn't put it past her. She's the type, she'd do anything to nail another LAPD scalp to the wall. Likes seeing her name in the paper.'

'What about the media? They heard about this yet?'

'We've gotten a few calls about a body being found. They must've gotten it off the coroner's dispatch freek. We've been staying off the air. Anyway, nobody knows about the note or the Dollmaker tie-in. They just know there's a body. The idea of it being found under the floor of one of the riot burnouts is sexy, I guess.

'Anyway, we have to keep the Dollmaker part under our hat for the time being. Unless, of course, whoever wrote it also sent copies out to the media. If he did that, we'll hear about it by the end of the day.'

'How could he bury her under the slab of a pool hall?'

'The whole building wasn't a pool hall. There were storage rooms in the back. Before it was Bing's it was a studio prop house. After Bing's took the front, they rented out sections in the back for storage. This is all from Edgar, he got the owner out there. The killer must've had one of the rooms, broke through the existing slab and put this girl's body in there. Anyway, it all got burned down in the riots. But the fire didn't hurt the slab. This poor girl's body has been down in there through all of that. Edgar said it looks like a mummy or something.'

Bosch saw the door to courtroom 4 open and members of the Church family came out followed by their lawyer. They were breaking for lunch. Deborah Church and her two teenaged daughters did not look at him. But Honey Chandler, known by most cops and others in the federal courts building as Money Chandler, stared at him with killer eyes as she passed. They were as dark as burnt mahogany and set against a tanned face with a strong jawline. She was an attractive woman with smooth gold hair. Her figure was hidden in the stiff lines of her blue suit. Bosch could feel the animosity from the group wash over him like a wave.

'Bosch, you still there?' Pounds asked.

'Yeah. It looks like we just broke for lunch.'

'Good. Then head over there and I'll meet you. I can't believe I'm actually saying this, but I hope it's just another wacko. For your sake, it might be best.'

'Right.'

As Bosch was hanging up he heard Pounds's voice and brought the phone back to his ear.

'One more thing. If the media shows up out there, leave them to me. However this turns out, you shouldn't be formally involved in this new case because of the litigation stemming from the old. We are just having you out there as an expert witness, so to speak.'

'Right.'

'See you there.'

TWO

Bosch took Wilshire out of downtown and cut up to Third after he made it through what was left of MacArthur Park. Turning north on Western he could see up on the left the grouping of patrol cars, detective cars and the crime-scene and coroner's vans. In the distance the HOLLYWOOD sign hung over the northern view, its letters barely legible in the smog.

Bing's was three blackened walls cradling a pile of charred debris. No roof, but the uniforms had hung a blue plastic tarp over the top of the rear wall and strung it to the chain-link fence that ran along the front of the property. Bosch knew it hadn't been done because the investigators wanted shade where they worked. He leaned forward and looked up through the windshield. He saw them up there, circling. The city's carrion birds: the media helicopters.

As Bosch pulled to a stop at the curb he saw a couple of city workers standing next to an equipment truck. They had sick looks on their faces and dragged hard and deep on cigarettes. Their jackhammers were on the ground near the back of the truck. They were waiting – hoping – that their work here was done.

On the other side of their truck Pounds was standing next to the coroner's blue van. It looked as though he was composing himself, and Bosch saw that he shared the same sick expression with the civilians. Though Pounds was commander of Hollywood detectives, including the homicide table, he had never actually worked homicide himself. Like many of the department's administrators, his climb up the ladder was based on test scores and brownnosing, not experience. It always pleased Bosch to see someone like Pounds get a dose of what real cops dealt with every day.

Bosch looked at his watch before getting out of his Caprice. He had one hour before he had to be back in court for openers.

'Harry,' Pounds said as he walked up. 'Glad you made it.'

'Always glad to check out another body, Lieutenant.'

Bosch slipped off his suit coat and put it inside his car on the seat. Then he moved to the trunk and got out a baggy blue jumpsuit and put it on over his clothes. It would be hot, but he didn't want to come back into court covered with dirt and dust.

'Good idea,' Pounds said. 'Wish I had brought my stuff.'

But Bosch knew he didn't have any stuff. Pounds ventured to a crime scene only when there was a good chance TV would show up and he could give a sound bite. And it was only TV he was interested in. Not print media. You had to make sense for more than two sentences in a row with a newspaper reporter. And then your words became attached to a piece of paper and were there all the next day and possibly forever to haunt you. It wasn't good department politics to talk to the print media. TV was a more fleeting and less dangerous thrill.

Bosch headed toward the blue tarp. Beneath it he saw the usual gathering of investigators. They stood next to a pile of broken concrete and along the edge of a trench dug into the concrete pad that had been the building's foundation. Bosch looked up as one of the TV helicopters made a low flyover. They wouldn't get much usable video with the tarp hiding the scene. They were probably dispatching ground crews now.

There was still a lot of debris in the building's shell. Charred ceiling beams and timber, broken concrete block and other rubble. Pounds caught up with Bosch and they began carefully stepping through to the gathering beneath the tarp.

'They'll bulldoze this and make another parking lot,' Pounds said. 'That's all the riots gave the city. About a thousand new parking lots. You want to park in South Central these days, no problem. You want a bottle of soda or to put gas in your car, then you got a problem. They burned every place down. You drive through the South Side before Christmas? They got Christmas tree lots every block, all the open space down there. I still don't understand why those people burned their own neighborhoods.'

Bosch knew that the fact people like Pounds didn't understand why 'those people' did what they did was one reason they did it, and would have to do it again someday. Bosch looked at it as a cycle. Every twenty-five years or so the city had its soul torched by the fires of reality. But then it drove on. Quickly, without looking back. Like a hit-and-run.

Suddenly Pounds went down after slipping on the loose rubble. He stopped his fall with his hands and jumped up quickly, embarrassed.

'Damn it!' he cried out, and then, though Bosch hadn't asked, he added, 'I'm okay. I'm okay.'

He quickly used his hand to carefully smooth back the strands of hair that had slipped off his balding cranium. He didn't realize that he was smearing black char from his hand across his forehead as he did this and Bosch didn't tell him.

They finally picked their way to the gathering. Bosch walked toward his former partner, Jerry Edgar, who stood with a couple of investigators Harry knew and two women he didn't. The women wore green jumpsuits, the uniform of the coroner's body movers. Minimum-wage earners who were dispatched from death scene to death scene in the blue van, picking up the bodies and taking them to the ice box.

'Whereyat, Harry?' Edgar said.

'Right here.'

Edgar had just been to New Orleans for the blues festival and had somehow come back with the greeting. He said it so often it had become annoying. Edgar was the only one in the detective bureau who didn't realize this.

Edgar was the standout amidst the group. He was not wearing a jumpsuit like Bosch – in fact, he never did because they wrinkled his Nordstrom suits – and somehow had managed to make his way into the crime scene area without getting so much as a trace of dust on the pants cuffs of his gray double-breasted suit. The real estate market – Edgar's onetime lucrative outside gig – had been in the shithouse for three years but Edgar still managed to be the sharpest dresser in the division. Bosch looked at Edgar's pale blue silk tie, knotted tightly at the black detective's throat, and guessed that it might have cost more than his own shirt and tie combined.

Bosch looked away and nodded to Art Donovan, the SID crime scene tech, but said nothing else to the others. He was following protocol. As at any murder scene a carefully orchestrated and incestuous caste system was in effect. The detectives did most of the talking amongst themselves or to the SID tech. The uniforms didn't speak unless spoken to. The body movers, the lowest on the totem pole, spoke to no one except the coroner's tech. The coroner's tech said little to the cops. He despised them because in his view they were whiners – always needing this or that, the autopsy done, the tox tests done, all of it done by yesterday.

Bosch looked into the trench they stood above. The jackhammer crew had broken through the slab and dug a hole about eight feet long and four feet deep. They had then excavated sideways into a large formation of concrete that extended three feet below the surface of the slab. There was a hollow in the stone. Bosch dropped to a crouch so he could look closer and saw that the concrete hollow was the outline of a woman's body. It was as if it were a mold into which plaster could be poured to make a cast, maybe to manufacture a mannikin. But it was empty inside.

'Where's the body?' Bosch asked.

'They took what was left out already,' Edgar said. 'It's in the bag in the truck. We're trying to figure out how to get this piece of the slab outta here in one piece.'

Bosch looked silently into the hollow for a few moments before standing back up and making his way back out from beneath the tarp. Larry Sakai, the coroner's investigator, followed him to the coroner's van and unlocked and opened the back door. Inside the van it was sweltering and the smell of Sakai's breath was stronger than the odor of industrial disinfectant.

'I figured they'd call you out here,' Sakai said.

'Oh, yeah? Why's that?'

''Cause it looks like the fuckin' Dollmaker, man.'

Bosch said nothing, so as not to give Sakai any indication of confirmation. Sakai had worked some of the Dollmaker cases four years earlier. Bosch suspected he was responsible for the name the media attached to the serial killer. Someone had leaked details of the killer's repeated use of makeup on the bodies to one of the anchors at Channel 4. The anchor christened the killer the Dollmaker. After that, the killer was called that by everybody, even the cops.

But Bosch always hated that name. It said something about the victims as well as the killer. It depersonalized them, made it easier for the Dollmaker stories that were broadcast to be entertaining instead of horrifying.

Bosch looked around the van. There were two gurneys and two bodies. One filled the black bag completely, the unseen corpse having been heavy in life or bloated in death. He turned to the other bag, the remains inside barely filling it. He knew this was the body taken from the concrete.

'Yeah, this one,' Sakai said. 'This other's a stabbing up on Lankershim. North Hollywood's working it. We were coming in when we got the dispatch on this one.'

That explained how the media caught on so quickly, Bosch knew. The coroner's dispatch frequency played in every newsroom in the city.

He studied the smaller body bag a moment and without waiting for Sakai to do it he yanked open the zipper on the heavy black plastic. It unleashed a sharp, musty smell that was not as bad as it could have been had they found the body sooner. Sakai pulled the bag open and Bosch looked at the remains of a human body. The skin was dark and like leather stretched taut over the bones. Bosch was not repulsed because he was used to it and had the ability to become detached from such scenes. He sometimes believed that looking at bodies was his life's work. He had ID'd his mother's body for the cops when he wasn't yet twelve years old, he had seen countless dead in Vietnam, and in nearly twenty years with the cops the bodies had become too many to put a number to. It had left him, most times, as detached from what he saw as a camera. As detached, he knew, as a psychopath.

The woman in the bag had been small, Bosch could tell. But the deterioration of tissue and shrinkage made the body seem even smaller than it had certainly been in life. What was left of the hair was shoulder length and looked as if it had been bleached blonde. Bosch could see the powdery remains of makeup on the skin of the face. His eyes were drawn to the breasts because they were shockingly large in comparison to the rest of the shrunken corpse. They were full and rounded and the skin was stretched taut across them. It somehow seemed to be the most grotesque feature of the corpse because it was not as it should have been.

'Implants,' Sakai said. 'They don't decompose. Could probably take 'em out and resell them to the next stupid chick that wants 'em. We could start a recycling program.'

Bosch didn't say anything. He was suddenly depressed at the thought of the woman – whoever she was – doing that to her body to somehow make herself more appealing, and then to end up this way. Had she only succeeded, he wondered, in making herself appealing to her killer?

Sakai interrupted his thoughts.

'If the Dollmaker did this, that means she's been in the concrete at least four years, right? So if that's the case, decomp isn't that bad for that length of time. Still got the hair, eyes, some internal tissues. We'll be able to work with it. Last week, I picked up a piece of work, a hiker they found out in Soledad Canyon. They figure it was a guy went missing last summer. Now he was nothing but bones. 'Course out in the open like that, you got the animals. You know they come in through the ass. It's the softest entry and the animals –'

'I know, Sakai. Let's stay on this one.'

'Anyway, with this woman, the concrete apparently slowed things down for us. Sure didn't stop it, but slowed it down. It must've been like an airtight tomb in there.'

'You people going to be able to establish just how long she's been dead?'

'Probably not from the body. We get her ID'd, then you people might find out when she went missing. That'll be the way.'

Bosch looked at the fingers. They were dark sticks almost as thin as pencils.

'What about prints?'

'We'll get 'em, but not from those.'

Bosch looked over and saw Sakai smiling.

'What? She left them in the concrete?'

Sakai's glee was smashed like a fly. Bosch had ruined his surprise.

'Yeah, that's right. She left an impression, you could say. We're going to get prints, maybe even a mold of her face, if we can get what's left of that slab out of there. Whoever mixed this concrete used too much water. Made it very fine. That's a break for us. We'll get the prints.'

Bosch leaned over the gurney to study the knotted strip of leather that was wrapped around the corpse's neck. It was thin black leather and he could see the manufacturer's seam along the edges. It was a strap cut away from a purse. Like all the others. He bent closer and the cadaver's smell filled his nose and mouth. The circumference of the leather strap around the neck was small, maybe about the size of a wine bottle. Small enough to be fatal. He could see where it had cut into the now darkened skin and choked away life. He looked at the knot. A slipknot pulled tight on the right side with the left hand. Like all the others. Church had been left-handed.

There was one more thing to check. The signature, as they had called it.

'No clothes? Shoes?'

'Nothing. Like the others, remember?'

'Open it all the way. I want to see the rest.'

Sakai pulled the zipper on the black bag down all the way to the feet. Bosch was unsure if Sakai knew of the signature but was not going to bring it up. He leaned over the corpse and looked down, acting as if he was studying everything when he was only interested in the toenails. The toes were shriveled, black and cracked. The nails were cracked, too, and completely missing from a few toes. But Bosch saw the paint on the toes that were intact. Hot pink dulled by decomposition fluids, dust and age. And on the large toe on the right foot he saw the signature. What was still left of it to be seen. A tiny white cross had been carefully painted on the nail. The Dollmaker's sign. It had been there on all the bodies.

Bosch could feel his heart pounding loudly. He looked around the van's interior and began to feel claustrophobic. The first sense of paranoia was poking into his brain. His mind began churning through the possibilities. If this body matched every known specification of a Dollmaker kill, then Church was the killer. If Church was this woman's killer and is now dead himself, then who left the note at the Hollywood station front desk?

He straightened up and took in the body as a whole for the first time. Naked and shrunken, forgotten. He wondered if there were others out there in the concrete, waiting to be discovered.

'Close it,' he said to Sakai.

'It's him, isn't it? The Dollmaker.'

Bosch didn't answer. He climbed out of the van, pulled the zipper on his jumpsuit down a bit to let in some air.

'Hey, Bosch,' Sakai called from inside the van. 'I'm just

curious. How'd you guys find this? If the Dollmaker is dead, who told you where to look?'

Bosch didn't answer that one either. He walked slowly back underneath the tarp. It looked like the others still hadn't figured out what to do about removing the concrete the body had been found in. Edgar was standing around trying not to get dirty. Bosch signaled to him and Pounds and they gathered together at a spot to the left of the trench, where they could talk without being overheard.

'Well?' Pounds asked. 'What've we got?'

'It looks like Church's work,' Bosch said.

'Shit,' Edgar said.

'How can you be sure?' Pounds asked.

'From what I can see, it matches every detail followed by the Dollmaker. Including the signature. It's there.'

'The signature?' Edgar asked.

'The white cross on the toe. We held that back during the investigation, cut deals with all the reporters not to put it out.'

'What about a copycat?' Edgar offered hopefully.

'Could be. The white cross was never made public until after we closed the case. After that, Bremmer over at the *Times* wrote that book about the case. It was mentioned.'

'So we have a copycat,' Pounds pronounced.

'It all depends on when she died,' Bosch said. 'His book came out a year after Church was dead. If she got killed after that, you probably got a copycat. If she got put in that concrete before, then I don't know . . .'

'Shit,' said Edgar.

Bosch thought a moment before speaking again.

'We could be dealing with one of a lot of different things. There's the copycat. Or maybe Church had a partner and we never saw it. Or maybe . . . I popped the wrong guy. Maybe whoever wrote this note we got is telling the truth.'

That hung out there in the momentary silence like dogshit on the sidewalk. Everybody walks carefully around it without looking too closely at it.

'Where's the note?' Bosch finally said to Pounds.

'In my car. I'll get it. What do you mean, he may have had a partner?'

'I mean, say Church did do this, then where'd the note come from, since he is dead? It would obviously have to be someone who knew he did it and where he had hidden the body. If that's the case, who is this second person? A partner? Did Church have a killing partner we never knew about?'

'Remember the Hillside Strangler?' Edgar asked. 'Turned out it was stranglers. Plural. Two cousins with the same taste for killing young women.'

Pounds took a step back and shook his head as if to ward off a potentially career-threatening case.

'What about Chandler, the lawyer?' Pounds said. 'Say Church's wife knows where he buried bodies, literally. She tells Chandler and Chandler hatches this scheme. She writes a note like the Dollmaker and drops it off at the station. It's guaranteed to fuck up your case.'

Bosch replayed that one in his mind. It seemed to work, then he saw the fault lines. He saw that they ran through all the scenarios.

'But why would Church bury some bodies and not others? The shrink who advised the task force back then said there was a purpose to his displaying of the victims. He was an exhibitionist. Toward the end, after the seventh victim, he started dropping the notes to us and the newspaper. It doesn't make sense that he'd leave some of the bodies to be found and some buried in concrete.'

'True,' Pounds said.

'I like the copycat,' Edgar said.

'But why copy someone's whole profile, right down to the signature, and then bury the body?' Bosch asked.

He wasn't really asking them. It was a question he'd have to answer himself. They stood there in silence for a long moment, each man beginning to see that the most plausible possibility might be that the Dollmaker was still alive.

'Whoever did it, why the note?' Pounds said. He seemed very agitated. 'Why would he drop us the note? He'd gotten away.'

'Because he wants attention,' Bosch said. 'Like the Dollmaker got. Like this trial is going to get.'

The silence came back then for a long moment.

'The key,' Bosch finally said, 'is ID'ing her, finding out how long she's been in the concrete. We'll know then what we've got.'

'So what do we do?' Edgar said.

'I'll tell you what we do,' Pounds said. 'We don't say a damned thing about this to anyone. Not yet. Not until we are absolutely sure of what we've got. We wait on the autopsy and the ID. We find out how long this girl's been dead and what she was doing when she disappeared. We'll make – I'll make a call on which way we go after that.

'Meantime, say nothing. If this is misconstrued, it could be very damaging to the department. I see some of the media is already here, so I'll handle them. No one else is to talk. We clear?'

Bosch and Edgar nodded and Pounds went off, slowly moving through the debris toward a knot of reporters and cameramen who stood behind the yellow tape the uniforms had put up.

Bosch and Edgar stood silent for a few moments, watching him go.

'I hope he knows what the hell he is saying,' Edgar said.

'Does inspire a lot of confidence, doesn't he?' Bosch replied.

'Oh, yeah.'

Bosch walked back over to the trench and Edgar followed.

'What are you going to do about the impression she left in the concrete?'

'The jackhammers don't think it's movable. They said whoever mixed the concrete she was put in didn't follow the directions too well. Used too much water and small-grain sand. It's like plaster of paris. We try to lift the whole thing out in one piece it will crumble under its own weight.'

'So?'

'Donovan's mixing plaster. He's going to make a mold of the face. On the hand – we only got the left, the right side crumbled when we dug in. Donovan's going to try using rubber silicone. He says it's the best chance of pulling out a mold with prints.'

Bosch nodded. For a few moments he watched Pounds talking to the reporters and saw the first thing worth smiling about all day. Pounds was on camera but apparently none of the reporters had told him about the dirt smeared across his forehead. He lit a cigarette and turned his attention back to Edgar.

'So, this area here was all storage rooms for rent?' he asked.

'That's right. The owner of the property was here a little while ago. Said that all this area back in here was partitioned storage. Individual rooms. The Dollmaker – er, the killer, whoever the fuck it was – could've had one of the rooms and had his privacy to do what he wanted. The only problem would be the noise he made breaking up the original flooring. But it could've been night work. Owner said most people didn't come back into the storage area at night. People who rented the rooms got a key to an exterior door off the alley. The perp could've come in and done the whole job in one night.'

The next question was obvious, so Edgar answered before Bosch asked.

'The owner can't give us the name of the renter. Not for sure, at least. The records went up in the fire. His insurance company made settlements with most people that filed claims and we'll get those names. But he said there were a few who never made a claim after the riots. He just never heard from them again. He can't remember all the names, but if one was our guy then it was probably an alias anyway. Leastwise, if I was going to rent a room and dig through the

26

floor to bury a body, you wouldn't find me giving no real name.'

Bosch nodded and looked at his watch. He had to get going soon. He realized that he was hungry but probably wouldn't get the chance to eat. Bosch looked down at the excavation and noticed the delineation of color between the old and newer concrete. The old slab was almost white. The concrete the woman had been encased in was a dark gray. He noticed a small piece of red paper protruding from a gray chunk at the bottom of the trench. He dropped down into the excavation and picked the chunk up. It was about the size of a softball. He pounded it on the old slab until it broke apart in his hand. The paper was part of a crumpled and empty Marlboro cigarette package. Edgar pulled a plastic evidence bag from his suit pocket and held it open for Bosch to drop the discovery in.

'It's got to've been put in with the body,' he said. 'Good catch.'

Bosch climbed out of the trench and looked at his watch again. It was time to go.

'Let me know if you get the ID,' he said to Edgar.

He dumped his jumpsuit back in the trunk and lit a fresh cigarette. He stood next to his Caprice and watched Pounds, who was wrapping up his skillfully planned impromptu press conference. Harry could tell by the cameras and the expensive clothes that most of the reporters were from TV. He saw Bremmer, the *Times* guy, standing at the edge of the pack. Bosch hadn't seen him in a while and noticed he had put on weight and a beard. Bosch knew that Bremmer was standing on the periphery of the circle waiting for the TV questions to end so he could hit Pounds with something solid that would take some thought to answer.

Bosch smoked and waited for five minutes before Pounds was done. He was risking being late for court but he wanted to see the note. When Pounds was finally done with the reporters he signaled Bosch to follow him to his car. Bosch got in the passenger side and Pounds handed him a photocopy.

Harry studied the note for a long time. It was written in the recognizable printed scrawl. The analyst in Suspicious Documents had called the printing Philadelphia block style and had concluded that its right-to-left slant was the result of it's being the work of an untrained hand; possibly a left-handed person printing with his right hand.

Newspaper says the trial's just begun
A verdict to return on the Dollmaker's run
A bullet from Bosch fired straight and true
But the dolls should know me work's not through

On Western is the spot where my heart doth sings
When I think o the dolly laid beneath at Bing's
Too bad, good Bosch, a bullet of bad aim
Years gone past, and I'm still in the game

Bosch knew style could be copied but something about the poem ground into him. It was like the others. The same bad schoolboy rhymes, the same semiliterate attempt at high-flown language. He felt confusion and a tugging in his chest.

It's him, he thought. It's him.

THREE

'Ladies and gentlemen,' US District Judge Alva Keyes intoned as he eyed the jury, 'we begin the trial with what we call opening statements by the attorneys. Mind you, these are not to be construed by you as evidence. These are more or less blueprints – road maps, if you will, of the route each attorney wants to take with his or her case. You do not consider them evidence. They may make some highfalutin allegations, but just because they say it doesn't make it true. After all, they're lawyers.'

This brought a polite titter of laughter from the jury and the rest of courtroom 4. With his southern accent, it sounded as if the judge had said lie-yers, which added to the glee. Even Money Chandler smiled. Bosch looked around from his seat at the defense table and saw that the public seats in the huge wood-paneled courtroom with twenty-foot ceilings were about half full. In the front row on the plaintiff's side were eight people who were Norman Church's family members and friends, not counting his widow, who sat up at the plaintiff's table with Chandler.

There were also about a half dozen courthouse hangers-on, old men with nothing better to do but watch the drama in other people's lives. Plus an assortment of law clerks and students who probably wanted to watch the great Honey Chandler do her thing, and a group of reporters with their pens poised over their pads. Openers always made a story – because, as the judge had said, the lawyers could say anything they wanted. After today, Bosch knew, the reporters would drop in from time to time but there probably wouldn't be many other stories until closing statements and a verdict.

Unless something unusual happened.

Bosch looked directly behind him. There was nobody in the benches back there. He knew Sylvia Moore would not be there. They had agreed on that before. He didn't want her seeing this. He had told her it was just a formality, part of the cop's burden to be sued for doing his job. He knew the real reason he didn't want her here was because he had no control over this situation. He had to sit there at the defense table and let people take their best shots. Anything could come up and probably would. He didn't want her watching that.

He wondered now if the jury would see the empty seats behind him in the spectators gallery and think that maybe he was guilty because no one had come to show support.

When the murmur of laughter died down he looked back at the judge. Judge Keyes was impressive up there on the bench. He was a big man who wore the black robe well, his thick forearms and big hands folded in front of his barrel chest, giving a sense of reserved power. His balding and sun-reddened head was large and seemed perfectly round, trimmed around the edges with gray hair and suggesting the organized storage of a massive amount of legal knowledge and perspective. He was a transplanted southerner who had specialized in civil rights cases as a lawyer and had made a name for himself by suing the LAPD for its dispropor-tionate number of cases in which black citizens died after being put in chokeholds by officers. He had been appointed to the federal bench by President Jimmy Carter, right before he was sent back to Georgia. Judge Keyes had been ruling the roost in courtroom 4 ever since.

Bosch's lawyer, deputy city attorney Rod Belk, had fought like hell during pretrial stages to have the judge disqualified on procedural ground and to get another judge assigned to the case. Preferably a judge without a back-ground as a guardian of civil rights. But he had failed.

However, Bosch was not as upset by this as Belk. He realized that Judge Keyes was cut from the same legal cloth as plaintiff's attorney Honey Chandler – suspicious of police, even hateful at times – but Bosch sensed that beyond that he was ultimately a fair man. And that's all Bosch thought he needed to come out okay. A fair shot at the system. After all, he knew in his heart his actions at the apartment in Silverlake were correct. He had done the right thing.

'It will be up to you,' the judge was saying to the jury, 'to decide if what the lawyers say is proven during trial. Remember that. Now, Ms Chandler, you go first.'

Honey Chandler nodded at him and stood up. She moved to the lectern that stood between the plaintiff's and the defense tables. Judge Keyes had set the strict guidelines earlier. In his courtroom, there was no moving about, no approaching the witness stand or jury box by lawyers. Anything said out loud by a lawyer was said from the lectern between the tables. Knowing the judge's strict demand for compliance to his guidelines, Chandler even asked his permission before turning the heavy mahogany altar at an angle so she would face the jury while speaking. The judge sternly nodded his approval.

'Good afternoon,' she began. 'The judge is quite right when he tells you that this statement is nothing more than a road map.'

Good strategy, Bosch thought from the cellar of cynicism from which he viewed this whole case. Pander to the judge with your first sentence. He watched Chandler as she referred to the yellow legal pad she had put down on the lectern. Bosch noticed that over the top button of her blouse was a large pin with a round black onyx stone set in it. It was flat and as dead as a shark's eye. She had her hair pulled severely back and braided in a no-nonsense style behind her head. But one tress of hair had come loose and it helped affect the image of a woman not preoccupied with her looks but totally focused on the law, on the case, on the heinous

31

miscarriage of justice perpetrated by the defendant. Bosch believed she probably pulled the hair loose on purpose.

As he watched her start, Bosch remembered the thud he had felt in his chest when he heard she was the lawyer for Church's wife. To him, it was far more disturbing than learning Judge Keyes had been assigned the trial. She was that good. That was why they called her Money.

'I would like to take you down the road a piece,' Chandler said and Bosch wondered if she was even developing a southern accent now. 'I just want to highlight what our case is about and what we believe the evidence will prove. It is a civil rights case. It involves the fatal shooting of a man named Norman Church at the hands of the police.'

She paused here. Not to look at her yellow pad but for effect, to gather all attention to what she would say next. Bosch looked over at the jury. Five women and seven men. Three blacks, three Latinos, one Asian and five whites. They were looking at Chandler with rapt attention.

'This case,' Chandler said, 'is about a police officer who wasn't satisfied with his job and the vast powers it gave him. This officer also wanted your job. And he wanted Judge Keyes's job. And he wanted the state's job of administering the verdicts and sentences set down by judges and juries. He wanted it all. This case is about Detective Harry Bosch, who you see sitting at the defendant's table.'

She pointed at Bosch while drawing out the word dee-fend-ant. Belk immediately stood up and objected.

'Miss Chandler does not need to point my client out to the jury or make sarcastic vocalizations. Yes, we are at the defense table. That's because this is a civil case and in this country anybody can sue anybody, even the family of a –'

'Objection, Your Honor,' Chandler shouted. 'He is using his objection to further try to destroy the reputation of Mr Church, who was never convicted of anything because –'

'Enough!' Judge Keyes thundered. 'Objection sustained. Ms Chandler, we don't need to point. We all know who we are. We also do not need inflammatory accent being placed on any words. Words are beautiful and ugly, all on their own. Let them stand for themselves. As for Mr Belk, I find it acutely annoying when opposing counsel interrupts opening statements or closing arguments. You will have your turn, sir. I would suggest that you not object during Ms Chandler's statement unless an egregious trespass on your client has occurred. I do not consider pointing at him worth the objection.'

'Thank you, Your Honor,' Belk and Chandler said in unison.

'Proceed, Ms Chandler. As I said in chambers this morning, I want opening statements done by the end of the day and I have another matter at four.'

'Thank you, Your Honor,' she said again. Then, turning back to the jury, she said, 'Ladies and gentlemen, we all need our police. We all look up to our police. Most of them – the vast majority of them – do a thankless job and do it well. The police department is an indispensable part of our society. What would we do if we could not count on police officers to serve and protect us? But that is not what this trial is about. I want you to remember that as the trial progresses. This is about what we would do if one member of that police force broke away from the rules and regulations, the policies that govern that police force. What we are talking about is called a rogue cop. And the evidence will show that Harry Bosch is a rogue cop, a man who one night four years ago decided to be judge, jury and executioner. He shot a man that he thought was a killer. A heinous serial killer, yes, but at the moment the defendant chose to pull out his gun and fire on Mr Norman Church there was no legal evidence of that.

'Now, you are going to hear from the defense all manner of supposed evidence that police said they found that connected Mr Church to these killings, but remember during the trial where this evidence came from – the police themselves – and when it was found – after Mr Church had been executed. I think we will show that this supposed

33

evidence is questionable at best. Tainted, at best. And, in effect, you will have to decide if Mr Church, a married man with two young children and a well-paying job at an aircraft factory, was indeed this killer, the so-called Dollmaker, or simply was made the fall guy, the scapegoat, by a police department covering up the sin of one of its own. The brutal, unwarranted and unnecessary execution of an unarmed man.'

She continued on, speaking at length about the code of silence known to exist in the department, the force's long history of brutality, the Rodney King beating and the riots. Somehow, according to Honey Chandler, these were all black flowers on a plant grown from a seed that was Harry Bosch's killing of Norman Church. Bosch heard her go on but wasn't really listening anymore. He kept his eyes open and occasionally made eye contact with a juror, but he was off on his own. This was his own defense. The lawyers, the jurors and the judge were going to take a week, maybe longer, to dissect what he had thought and done in less than five seconds. To be able to sit in the courtroom for this he was going to have to be able to go off on his own.

In his private reverie he thought of Church's face. At the end, in the apartment over the garage on Hyperion Street. They had locked eyes. The eyes Bosch had seen were killer's eyes, as dark as the stone at Chandler's throat.

'. . . even if he was reaching for a gun, would that matter?' Chandler was saying. 'A man had kicked the door open. A man with a gun. Who could blame someone for reaching, according to police, for a weapon for protection. The fact that he was reaching for something seemingly as laughable as a hairpiece makes this episode all the more repugnant. He was killed in cold blood. Our society cannot accept that.'

Bosch tuned her out again and thought of the new victim, entombed for what was likely years in a concrete floor. He wondered if a missing-person report was ever taken, if there was a mother or father or husband or child wondering all this time about her. After returning from the scene he had started to tell Belk about the discovery. He asked the lawyer to ask Judge Keyes for a continuance, to delay the trial until the new death could be sorted out. But Belk had cut him off, telling him that the less he knew the better. Belk seemed so frightened of the implications of the new discovery that he determined that the best tack was to do the opposite of what Bosch suggested. He wanted to hurry the trial through before news of the discovery and its possible connection to the Dollmaker became public.

Chandler was now near the end of the one-hour allotment for her opener. She had gone on at length about the police department's shooting policy and Bosch thought she might have lost the grip she had on the jury in the beginning. For a while she had even lost Belk, who sat next to Bosch paging through his own yellow pad and rehearsing his opener in his head.

Belk was a large man – almost eighty pounds overweight, Bosch guessed – and prone to sweating, even in the overly cooled courtroom. Bosch had often wondered during the jury selection if the sweating was Belk's response to the burden of weight he carried or the burden of trying a case against Chandler and before Judge Keyes. Belk couldn't be over thirty, Bosch guessed. Maybe five years max out of a middle-range law school and in over his head going up against Chandler.

The word 'justice' brought Bosch's attention back. He knew that Chandler had turned it up a notch and was coming down the backstretch when she started using the word in almost every sentence. In civil court, justice and money were interchangeable because they meant the same thing.

'Justice for Norman Church was fleeting. It lasted all of a few seconds. Justice was the time it took Detective Bosch to kick open the door, point his satin-finished 9mm Smith & Wesson and pull the trigger. Justice was one shot. The bullet Detective Bosch chose to execute Mr Church with

35

was called an XTP. That is short for extreme terminal performance. It's a bullet that expands to 1.5 times its width on impact and takes out huge portions of tissue and organ in its path. It took out Mr Church's heart. That was justice.'

Bosch noticed that many of the jurors were not looking at Chandler but at the plaintiff's table. By leaning forward slightly he could see past the lectern and saw that the widow, Deborah Church, was dabbing tears on her cheeks with a tissue. She was a bell-shaped woman with short dark hair and small pale blue eyes. She had been the epitome of the suburban housewife and mother until the morning Bosch killed her husband and the cops showed up at her house with their search warrant and the reporters showed up with their questions. Bosch had actually felt sorry for her, even counted her as a victim, until she hired Money Chandler and started calling him a murderer.

'The evidence will show, ladies and gentlemen, that Detective Bosch is a product of his department,' Chandler said. 'A callous, arrogant machine that dispensed justice as he saw it on his own. You will be asked if this is what you want from your police department. You will be asked to right a wrong, to provide justice for a family whose father and husband was taken.

'In closing, I would like to quote to you from a German philosopher named Friedrich Nietzsche, who wrote something a century ago that I think is germane to what we are doing today. He said, "Whoever fights monsters should see to it that in the process he does not become a monster. And when you look into the abyss, the abyss also looks into you . . ."

'Ladies and gentlemen, that is what this case is about. Detective Harry Bosch has not only looked into the abyss, but on the night Norman Church was murdered it looked into him. The darkness engulfed him and Detective Bosch fell. He became that which he served to fight. A monster. I think you will find that the evidence will lead you to no other conclusion. Thank you.'

Chandler sat down and patted her hand in a 'there, there' gesture on Deborah Church's arm. Bosch, of course, knew this was done for the jury's sake, not the widow's.

The judge looked up at the brass hands of the clock built into the mahogany paneling above the courtroom door and declared a fifteen-minute recess before Belk would take the lectern. As he stood for the jury, Bosch noticed one of Church's daughters staring at him from the front row of the spectators section. He guessed she was about thirteen. The older one, Nancy. He quickly looked away and then felt guilty. He wondered if anyone in the jury saw this.

Belk said he needed the break time alone to go over his statement to the jury. Bosch felt like going up to the snack bar on the sixth floor because he still had not eaten, but it was likely a few of the jurors would go there, or worse yet, members of Church's family. Instead, he took the escalator down to the lobby and went out to the ash can in front of the building. He lit a cigarette and leaned back against the base of the statue. He realized that he was clammy with sweat beneath his suit. Chandler's hour-long opener had seemed like an eternity – an eternity with the eyes of the world on him. He knew the suit wouldn't last the week and he would have to make sure his other one was clean. Thinking about such minor details finally helped relax him.

He had already put one butt out in the sand and was on his second smoke when the steel-and-glass door to the courthouse opened. Honey Chandler had used her back to push open the heavy door and therefore hadn't seen him. She turned as she came through the door, her head bent down as she lit a cigarette with a gold lighter. As she straightened and exhaled she saw him. She walked toward the ash can, ready to bury the fresh cigarette.

'It's okay,' Bosch said. 'It's the only one around as far as I know.'

'It is, but I don't think it does either of us good to have to face each other outside of court.'

He shrugged and didn't say anything. It was her move,

she could leave if she wanted to. She took another drag on the cigarette.

'Just a half. I have to get back in anyway.'

He nodded and looked out toward Spring Street. In front of the county courthouse he saw a line of people waiting to go in through the metal detectors. More boat people, he thought. He saw the homeless man coming up the pavement to make his afternoon check of the ash can. The man suddenly turned around and walked back out to Spring and away. He looked back once uneasily over his shoulder as he went.

'He knows me.'

Bosch looked back at Chandler.

'He knows you?'

'He used to be a lawyer. I knew him then. Tom something-or-other. I can't remember at the – Faraday, that's it. I guess he didn't want me to see him that way. But everybody around here knows about him. He's the reminder of what can happen when things go terribly wrong.'

'What happened?'

'It's a long story. Maybe your lawyer will tell you. Can I ask you something?'

Bosch didn't answer.

'Why didn't the city settle this case? Rodney King, the riots. It's the worst time in the world to take a police case to trial. I don't think Bulk – that's what I call him, because I know he calls me Money. I don't think he's got a hold on this one. And you'll be the one hung out to dry.'

Bosch thought a moment before answering.

'It's off the record, Detective Bosch,' she said. 'I'm just making conversation.'

'I told him not to settle. I told him if he wanted to settle, I'd go out and pay for my own lawyer.'

'That sure of yourself, huh?' She paused to inhale on her cigarette. 'Well, we'll see, I guess.'

'I guess.'

'You know it's nothing personal.'

He knew she would get around to saying that. The biggest lie in the game.

'Maybe not for you.'

'Oh, it is for you? You shoot an unarmed man and then you take it personally when his wife objects, when she sues you?'

'Your client's husband used to cut the strap off the purses of his victims, tie it in a slipknot around their neck and then slowly but steadily strangle them while he was raping them. He preferred leather straps. He didn't seem to care about what women he did this to. Just the leather.'

She didn't even flinch. He hadn't expected her to.

'That's *late* husband. My client's late husband. And the only thing that is for sure in this case, that is provable, is that you killed him.'

'Yeah, and I'd do it again.'

'I know, Detective Bosch. That's why we're here.'

She pursed her lips in a frozen kiss which sharply set the line of her jaw. Her hair caught the glint of the afternoon sun. She angrily stubbed her cigarette out in the sand and then went back inside. She swung the door open as if it were made of balsa wood.

FOUR

Bosch pulled into the rear parking lot of the Hollywood station on Wilcox shortly before four. Belk had used only ten minutes of his allotted hour for his opening statement and Judge Keyes had recessed early, saying he wanted to start testimony on a separate day from openers so the jury would not confuse evidentiary testimony with the lawyers' words.

Bosch had felt uneasy with Belk's short discourse in front of the jurors but Belk had told him there was nothing to worry about. He walked in through the back door near the tank and took the rear hallway to the detective bureau. By four the bureau is usually deserted. It was that way when Bosch walked in, except for Jerry Edgar, who was parked in front of one of the IBMs typing on a form Bosch recognized as a 51 – an Investigating Officer's Chronological Record. He looked up and saw Bosch approaching.

'Whereyat, Harry?'

'Right here.'

'Got done early, I see. Don't tell me, directed verdict. The judge threw Money Chandler out on her ass.'

'I wish.'

'Yeah, I know.'

'What do you have so far?'

Edgar said there was nothing so far. No identification yet. Bosch sat down at his desk and loosened his tie. Pounds's office was dark so it was safe to light a cigarette. His mind trailed off into thinking about the trial and Money Chandler. She had captured the jury for most of her argument. She had, in effect, called Bosch a murderer, hitting with a gut-level, emotional charge. Belk had responded with a dissertation on the law and a police officer's right to use deadly force when danger was near. Even if it turned out there was no danger, no gun beneath the pillow, Belk said, Church's own actions created the climate of danger that allowed Bosch to act as he did.

Finally, Belk had countered Chandler's Nietzsche by quoting *The Art of War* by Sun Tzu. Belk said Bosch had entered the 'Dying Ground' when he kicked Church's apartment door open. At that point he had to fight or perish, shoot or be shot. Second-guessing his actions afterward was unjust.

Sitting across from Edgar now, Bosch acknowledged to himself that it hadn't worked. Belk had been boring while Chandler had been interesting, and convincing. They were starting in the hole. He noticed Edgar had stopped talking and Harry had not registered anything he had said.

'What about prints?' he asked.

'Harry, you listening to me? I just said we finished with the rubber silicone about an hour ago. Donovan got prints off the hand. He said they look good, came up in the rubber pretty well. He'll start the DOJ run tonight and probably by morning we'll have the similars. It will probably take him the rest of the morning to go through them. But, at least, they're not letting this one drown in the backup. Pounds gave it a priority status.'

'Good, let me know what comes out. I'll be in and out all week, I guess.'

'Harry, don't worry, I'll let you know what we've got. But try to stay cool. Look, you got the right guy? You got any doubt about that?'

'Not before today.'

'Then don't worry. Might is right. Money Chandler can blow the judge and the whole jury, it's not going to change that.'

'Right is might.'

41

'What?'

'Nothing.'

Bosch thought about what Edgar had said about Chandler. It was interesting how often a threat from a woman, even a professional woman, was reduced by cops to a sexual threat. He believed that most cops might be like Edgar, thinking there was something about Chandler's sexuality that gave her an edge. They would not admit that she was damn good at her job, whereas the fat city attorney defending Bosch wasn't.

Bosch stood up and went back to the file cabinets. He unlocked one of his drawers and dug into the back to pull out two of the blue binders that were called murder books. Both were heavy, about three inches thick. On the spine of the first it said BIOS. The other was labeled DOCS. They were from the Dollmaker case.

'Who's testifying tomorrow?' Edgar called from across the squad room.

'I don't know the order. The judge wouldn't make her say. But she's got me subpoenaed, also Lloyd and Irving. She's got Amado, the ME coordinator, and even Bremmer. They all gotta show up and then she'll say which ones she'll put on tomorrow and which ones later.'

'The *Times* isn't going to let Bremmer testify. They always fight that shit.'

'Yeah, but he isn't subpoenaed as a *Times* reporter. He wrote that book about the case. So she served paper on him as the author. Judge Keyes already ruled he doesn't have the same reporter's-shield rights. *Times* lawyers may show up to argue but the judge already made the ruling. Bremmer testifies.'

'See what I mean, she's probably already been back in chambers with that old guy. Anyway, it's no matter, Bremmer can't hurt you. That book made you out like the hero who saved the day.'

'I guess.'

'Harry, come here and take a look at this.'

Edgar got up from his typing station and went over to the file cabinets. He gingerly slid a cardboard box off the top and put it down on the homicide table. It was about the size of a hatbox.

'Gotta be careful. Donovan says it should set over night.'

He lifted off the top of the box and there was a woman's face set in white plaster. The face was turned slightly so that its right side was fully sculpted in the plaster. Most of the lower left side, the jawline, was missing. The eyes were closed, the mouth slightly open and irregular. The hairline was almost unnoticeable. The face seemed swollen by the right eye. It was like a classical frieze Bosch had seen in a cemetery or a museum somewhere. But it wasn't beautiful. It was a death mask.

'Looks like the guy popped her on the eye. It swelled up.'

Bosch nodded but didn't speak. There was something unnerving about looking at the face in the box, more so than looking at an actual dead body. He didn't know why. Edgar finally put the top back on the box and carefully put it back on top of the file cabinet.

'What are you going to do with it?'

'Not sure. If we don't get anything from the prints it might be our only way of getting an ID. There's an anthropologist at Cal State Northridge that contracts with the coroner to make facial recreations. Usually, he's working from a skeleton, a skull. I'll take this to him and see if he can maybe finish the face, put a blonde wig on it or something. He can paint the plaster, too, give it a skin color. I don't know, it's probably just pissing in the wind but I figure it's worth a try.'

Edgar returned to the typewriter and Bosch sat down in front of the murder books. He opened the binder marked BIOS but then sat there and watched Edgar for a few moments. He did not know whether he should admire Edgar's hustle on the case or not. They had been partners once and Bosch had essentially spent a year training him to be a homicide investigator. But he was never sure how much of it took. Edgar was always going off to look at real estate, taking two-hour lunches to go to closings. He never seemed to understand that the homicide squad wasn't a job. It was a mission. As surely as murder was an art for some who committed it, homicide investigation was an art for those on the mission. And it chose you, you didn't choose it.

With that in mind it was hard for Bosch to accept that Edgar was busting ass on the case for the right reasons.

'What're you looking at?' Edgar asked without looking up from the IBM or stopping his typing.

'Nothing. I was just thinking about stuff.'

'Harry, don't worry. It's going to work out.'

Bosch dumped his cigarette butt in a Styrofoam cup of dead coffee and lit another.

'Did the priority Pounds put on the case open up the OT?'

'Absolutely,' Edgar said, smiling. 'You're looking at a man who has his head fully in the overtime trough.'

At least he was honest about it, Bosch thought. Content that his original take on Edgar was still intact, Bosch went back to the murder book and ran his fingers along the edge of the thick sheaf of reports on its three rings. There were eleven divider tabs, each marked with a name of one of the Dollmaker's victims. He began leafing from section to section, looking at the crime scene photographs from each killing and the biographical data of each victim.

The women had all come from similar backgrounds; street prostitutes, the higher-class escort outfits, strippers, porno actresses who did outcall work on the side. The Dollmaker had moved comfortably along the underside of the city. He had found his victims with the same ease that they had gone into the darkness with him. There was a pattern in that, Bosch remembered the task force's psychologist had said.

But looking at the frozen faces of death in the photographs, Bosch remembered that the task force had never gotten a fix on common physical aspects of the victims.

There were blondes and brunettes. Heavy-set women and frail drug addicts. There were six white women, two Latinas, two Asians and a black woman. No pattern. The Dollmaker had been indiscriminate in that respect, his only identifiable pattern being that he sought only women on the edge – that place where choices are limited and they go easily with a stranger. The psychologist had said each of the women was like an injured fish, sending off an invisible signal that inevitably drew the shark.

'She was white, right?' he asked Edgar.

Edgar stopped typing.

'Yeah, that's what the coroner said.'

'They already did the cut? Who?'

'No, the autopsy's tomorrow or the next day but Corazón took a look when we brought it in. She guessed that the stiff had been white. Why?'

'Nothing. Blonde?'

'Yeah, at least when she died. Bleached. If you're going to ask if I checked missing persons on a white blonde chick who went into the wind four years ago, fuck you, Harry. I can use the OT but that description wouldn't narrow it down to but three, four hundred. I ain't going to wade into that when I'll probably pull a name on the prints tomorrow. Waste of time.'

'Yeah, I know. I just wish . . .'

'You just wish you had some answers. We all do. But things take time sometimes, my man.'

Edgar started typing again and Harry looked down into the binder. But he couldn't help but think about the face in the box. No name, no occupation. They knew nothing about her. But something about the plaster cast told him she had somehow fit into the Dollmaker's pattern. There was a hardness there that had nothing to do with the plaster. She had come from the edge.

'Anything else found in the concrete after I left?'

Edgar stopped typing, exhaled loudly and shook his head.

'How do you mean, like the cigarette package?'

'With the other ones the Dollmaker left their purses. He'd cut the straps off to strangle them, but when he dumped the bodies we always found the purses and clothes nearby. Only thing missing was their makeup. He always kept their makeup.'

'Not this time – at least in the concrete. Pounds left a uniform on the site while they finished tearing it up. Nothing else was found. That stuff might've been stashed in the storage room and got burned up or looted. Harry, what're you thinking, copycat?'

'I guess.'

'Yeah, me too.'

Bosch nodded and told Edgar he was sorry he kept interrupting. He went back to studying the reports. After a few minutes Edgar rolled the form out of the typewriter and brought it back to the homicide table. He snapped it into a new binder with the thin stack of paperwork from the day's case and put it into a file cabinet behind his chair. He then went through his daily ritual of calling his wife while straightening up the blotter, the message spike and the message pad at his place. He told her he had to make a quick stop on his way home. Listening to the conversation made Bosch think of Sylvia Moore and some of the domestic rituals that had become ingrained for them.

'I'm outta here, Harry,' Edgar said after hanging up.

Bosch nodded.

'So how come you're hanging around?'

'I don't know. I'm just reading through this stuff so I'll know what I'm saying when I testify.'

That was a lie. He didn't need the murder books to refresh his memory of the Dollmaker.

'I hope you tear Money Chandler up.'

'She'll probably rip me. She's good.'

'Well, I gotta hit it. I'll see you.'

'Hey, remember, if you get a name tomorrow, give me a beep or something.'

After Edgar was gone Bosch looked at his watch – it was five – and turned on the TV that sat on top of the file cabinet next to the box with the face in it. While he was waiting for the story on the body he picked up his phone and dialed Sylvia's house.

'I'm not going to make it out there tonight.'

'Harry, what's wrong? How did the opening statements go?'

'It's not the trial. It's another case. A body was found today, looks a lot like the Dollmaker did it. We got a note at the station. Basically said I killed the wrong guy. That the Dollmaker, the real one, is still out there.'

'Can it be true?'

'I don't know. There had been no doubt before today.'

'How could –'

'Wait a minute, the story's on the news. Channel 2.'

'I'll put it on.'

They watched on separate TVs but connected by phone as the story was reported on the early news show. The anchor reported nothing about the Dollmaker. There was an aerial shot of the scene and then a sound bite of Pounds saying that little was known, that an anonymous tip had led police to the body. Harry and Sylvia both laughed when they saw Pounds's char-smeared forehead. It felt good to Bosch to laugh. After the report Sylvia turned serious.

'So, he didn't tell the media.'

'Well, we have to make sure. We have to figure out what's going on first. It was either him or a copycat . . . or maybe he had a partner we didn't know about.'

'When will you know which direction to go?'

It was a nice way of asking when he'd know if he had killed an innocent man.

'I don't know, probably tomorrow. Autopsy will tell us some things. But the ID will tell us when she died.'

'Harry, it wasn't the Dollmaker. Don't you worry.'

'Thanks, Sylvia.'

Her unequivocal loyalty was beautiful, he thought. He

then immediately felt guilty because he had never been totally open with her about all the things that concerned them. He had been the one who held back.

'You still haven't said how it went in court today or why you aren't coming out here like you said you would.'

'It's this new case they found today. I am involved . . . and I want to do some thinking on it.'

'You can think anywhere, Harry.'

'You know what I mean.'

'Yes, I do. And court?'

'It went fine, I guess. We only had openers. Testimony starts tomorrow. But this new case . . . It's sort of hanging over everything.'

He switched the channels as he spoke but he had missed reports on the new body discovery on the other channels.

'Well, what's your lawyer say about it?'

'Nothing. He doesn't want to know about it.'

'What a shit.'

'He just wants to get through the case quickly, hope that if the Dollmaker or a partner is still running around out there, that we don't confirm it until the trial is over.'

'But, Harry, that is unethical. Even if it is evidence in the plaintiff's favor, doesn't he have to bring it forward?'

'Yes, if he knows about it. That's just it. He doesn't want to know about it. That makes him safe.'

'When will it be your turn to testify? I want to be there. I can take a personal day and be there.'

'No. Don't worry. It's all a formality. I don't want you to know any more about this story than you do already.'

'Why? It's your story.'

'No it's not. It's his.'

He hung up after telling her he'd call her the next day. Afterward, he looked at the phone on the table in front of him for a long time. He and Sylvia Moore had been spending three or four nights a week together for nearly a year. Though Sylvia had been the one who spoke of changing the arrangement and even had her house for sale,

48

Bosch had never wanted to touch the question for fear that it might disturb the fragile balance and comfort he felt with her.

He wondered now if he was doing just that, disturbing the balance. He had lied to her. He was involved in the new case to some degree, but he was done for the day and was going home. He had lied because he felt the need to be alone. With his thoughts. With the Dollmaker.

He flipped through the second binder to the back where there were clear plastic Ziploc pouches for holding documentary evidence. In these were copies of the Dollmaker's previous letters. There were three of them. The killer had begun sending them after the media firestorm started and he had been christened with the name Dollmaker. One had gone to Bosch, prior to the eleventh killing – the last. The other two had gone to Bremmer at the *Times* after the seventh and eleventh killings. Harry now studied the photocopy of the envelope that was addressed to him in a printed script of block letters. Then he looked at the poem on the folded page. It also had been printed in the same oddly slanted block script. He read the words he already knew by heart.

I feel compelled to forewarn and forsake.
T'night I'm out for a snack – my lust partake.
Another doll for the shelf, as it were't.
She breathes her last – just as I squirt.

A little late mommy and daddy weeple
A fine young miss 'neath my steeple.
As I tight the purse strings 'fore preparing the wash.
I hear the last gasp – a sound like Boschhhhh!

Bosch closed the binders and put them in his briefcase. He turned off the TV and headed out to the back parking lot. He held the station door for two uniform cops who were wrestling with a handcuffed drunk. The drunk threw a kick out at him but Harry stepped outside of its reach.

He pointed the Caprice north and took Outpost Road up to Mulholland, which he then took to Woodrow Wilson. After pulling into the carport, he sat with his hands on the wheel for a long time. He thought about the letters and the signature the Dollmaker had left on each victim's body, the cross painted on the toenail. After Church was dead they figured out what it had meant. The cross had been the steeple. The steeple of a Church.

FIVE

In the morning, Bosch sat on the rear deck of his house and watched the sun come up over the Cahuenga Pass. It burned away the morning fog and bathed the wildflowers on the hillside that had burned the winter before. He watched and smoked and drank coffee until the sound of traffic on the Hollywood Freeway became one uninterrupted hiss from the pass below.

He dressed in his dark blue suit with a white shirt that had a button-down collar. As he put on a maroon tie dotted with gold gladiator helmets in front of the bedroom mirror, he wondered about how he must appear to the jurors. He had noticed the day before that when he made eye contact with any of the twelve, they were always the first to look away. What did that mean? He would have liked to ask Belk what it meant but he did not like Belk and knew he would feel uncomfortable asking his opinion on anything.

Using the same hole poked through it before, he secured the tie in place with his silver tie tack that said '187' – the California penal code for murder. He used a plastic comb to put his brown-and-gray hair, still wet from the shower, in place and then combed his mustache. He put Visine drops in his eyes and then leaned close to the glass to study them. Red-rimmed from little sleep, the irises as dark as ice on asphalt. Why do they look away from me, he wondered again. He thought about how Chandler had described him the day before. And he knew why.

He was heading to the door, briefcase in hand, when it

opened before he got there. Sylvia stepped in while pulling her key out of the lock.

'Hi,' she said when she saw him. 'I hoped I'd catch you.'

She smiled. She was wearing khaki pants and a pink shirt with a button-down collar. He knew she did not wear dresses on Tuesday and Thursday because those were her assigned days as a schoolyard rover. Sometimes she had to run after students. Sometimes she had to break up fights. The sun coming through the porch door turned her dark blonde hair gold.

'Catch me at what?'

She came to him smiling still and they kissed.

'I know I'm making you late. I'm late, too. But I just wanted to come and say good luck today. Not that you need it.'

He held on to her, smelling her hair. It had been nearly a year since they met, but Bosch still held to her sometimes with the fear that she might abruptly turn and leave, declare her attraction to him a mistake. Perhaps he was still a substitute for the husband she'd lost, a cop like Harry, a narcotics detective whose apparent suicide Bosch had investigated.

Their relationship had progressed to a point of complete comfortableness but in recent weeks he had felt a sense of inertia begin to set in. She had, too, and had even talked about it. She said the problem was he could not drop his guard completely and he knew this was true. Bosch had spent a lifetime alone, but not necessarily lonely. He had secrets, many of them buried too deep to give up to her. Not so soon.

'Thanks for coming by,' he said, pulling back and looking down into her face to see the light still there. She had gotten a fleck of lipstick on one of her front teeth. 'You be careful in the yard today, huh?'

'Yes.' Then she frowned. 'I know what you said, but I want to come and watch court – at least one day. I want to be there for you, Harry.'

'You don't have to be there to be there. Know what I mean?'

She nodded but he knew his answer didn't satisfy her. They dropped it and small-talked for a few minutes more, making plans to get together that night for dinner. Bosch said he would come to her place in Bouquet Canyon. They kissed again and headed out, he to court and she to the high school, both places fraught with danger.

There was always an adrenaline rush at the start of each day as the courtroom fell silent and they waited for the judge to open his door and step up to the bench. It was 9:10 and still no sign of the judge, which was unusual because he had been a stickler for promptness during the week of jury selection. Bosch looked around and saw several reporters, maybe more than the day before. He found this curious since opening arguments were always such a draw.

Belk leaned toward Bosch and whispered, 'Keyes is probably in there reading the *Times* story. Did you see it?'

Running late because of Sylvia, Bosch had had no time to read the paper. He'd left it on the mat at the front door.

'What'd it say?'

The paneled door opened and the judge came out before Belk could answer.

'Hold the jury, Miss Rivera,' the judge said to his clerk. He dropped his girth into his padded chair, surveyed the courtroom and said, 'Counsel, any matters for discussion before we bring the jury in? Ms Chandler?'

'Yes, Your Honor,' Chandler said as she walked to the lectern.

Today she had on the gray suit. She had been alternating among three suits since jury selection began. Belk had told Bosch that this was because she didn't want to give the jurors the idea that she was wealthy. He said women lawyers could lose women jurors over something like that.

'Your Honor, the plaintiff asks for sanctions against Detective Bosch and Mr Belk.'

She held up the folded Metro section of the *Times*. Bosch could see the story had caught the bottom right corner, same as the story the day before. The headline said CONCRETE BLONDE TIED TO DOLLMAKER. Belk stood but did not say anything, for once observing the judge's strict decorum of noninterruption.

'Sanctions for what, Ms Chandler?' the judge asked.

'Your Honor, the discovery of this body yesterday has a tremendous evidentiary impact on this case. As an officer of the court, it was incumbent upon Mr Belk to bring this information forward. Under Rule 11 of discovery, defendant's attorney must –'

'Your Honor,' Belk interrupted, 'I was not informed of this development until last night. My intention was to bring the matter forward this morning. She is –'

'Hold it right there, Mr Belk. One at a time in my courtroom. Seems you need a daily reminder of that. Ms Chandler, I read that story you are referring to and though Detective Bosch was mentioned because of this case, he was not quoted. And Mr Belk has rather rudely pointed out that he knew nothing about this until after court yesterday. Frankly, I don't see a sanctionable offense here. Unless you've got a card you haven't played.'

She did.

'Your Honor, Detective Bosch was well aware of this development, whether quoted or not. He was at the scene during yesterday's lunch break.'

'Your Honor?' Belk tried timidly.

Judge Keyes turned but looked at Bosch, not Belk.

'That right, Detective Bosch, what she says?'

Bosch looked at Belk for a moment and then up at the judge. Fucking Belk, he thought. His lie had left Bosch holding the bag.

'I was there, Your Honor. When I got back here for the afternoon session, there was no time to tell Mr Belk about the discovery. I told him after court last night. I didn't see the paper yet this morning and I don't know what it says, but nothing has been confirmed about this body in regard to the Dollmaker or anyone else. There isn't even an ID yet.'

'Your Honor,' Chandler said, 'Detective Bosch has conveniently forgotten that we had a fifteen-minute break during the afternoon session. I should think that was ample time for the detective to fill in his attorney on such important information.'

The judge looked at Bosch.

'I wanted to tell him during the break but Mr Belk said he needed the time to prepare his opening statement.'

The judge eyed him closely for several seconds without saying anything. Bosch could tell the judge knew he was pushing the edge of the envelope of truth. Judge Keyes seemed to be making some kind of decision.

'Well, Ms Chandler,' he finally said. 'I don't rightly see the conspiracy that you do here. I'm going to let this go with a warning to all parties; withholding evidence is the most heinous crime you can commit in my courtroom. If you do it and I catch ya, you're gonna wish you never took the LSAT. Now, do we want to talk about this new development?'

'Your Honor,' Belk said quickly. He moved to the lectern. 'In light of this discovery less than twenty-four hours ago, I move for a continuance so that this situation can be thoroughly investigated so that it can be determined exactly what it means to this case.'

Now he finally asks, Bosch thought. He knew there was no way he'd get a delay now.

'Uh, huh,' Judge Keyes said. 'What do you think about that, Ms Chandler?'

'No delay, Your Honor. This family has waited four years for this trial. I think any further delay would be perpetuating the crime. Besides, who does Mr Belk propose investigate this matter, Detective Bosch?'

'I am sure the defense counselor would be satisfied with the LAPD handling the investigation,' the judge said.

'But I wouldn't.'

'I know you wouldn't, Ms Chandler, but that's not your concern. You said yourself yesterday that the wide majority of police in this city are good, competent people. You'll just have to live by your own words . . . But I am going to deny the request for a continuation. We've started a trial and we're not going to stop. The police can and should investigate this matter and keep the court informed but I'm not going to stand by. This case will continue until such time that these events need to be addressed again. Anything else? I've got a jury waiting.'

'What about the story in the newspaper?' Belk asked.

'What about it?'

'Your Honor, I'd like the jury to be polled to see if anyone read it. Also, they should be warned again not to read the papers or watch the TV news tonight. All of the channels will likely follow the *Times*.'

'I instructed jurors yesterday not to read the paper or watch the news but I plan to poll them anyway about this very story. Let's see what they say and then, depending on what we hear, we can clear 'em out again if you want to talk about a mistrial.'

'I don't want a mistrial,' Chandler said. 'That's what the defendant wants. That'll just delay this another two months. This family has already waited four years for justice. They –'

'Well, let's just see what the jury says. Sorry to interrupt, Ms Chandler.'

'Your Honor, may I be heard on sanctions?' Belk said.

'I don't think you need to be, Mr Belk. I denied her motion for sanctions. What more's to be said?'

'I know that, Your Honor. I would like to ask for sanctions against Miss Chandler. She has defamed me by alleging this cover-up of the evidence and I –'

'Mr Belk, sit down. I'll tell you both right now; quit with the extracurricular sparring because it doesn't get you anywhere with me. No sanctions either way. One last time, any other matters?'

'Yes, Your Honor,' Chandler said.

She had one more card. From beneath her legal pad she pulled out a document and walked it up to the clerk, who handed it to the judge. Chandler then returned to the lectern.

'Your Honor, that is a subpoena I have prepared for the police department that I would like reflected in the record. I am asking that a copy of the note referred to in the *Times* article, the note written by the Dollmaker and received yesterday, be released to me as part of discovery.'

Belk jumped to his feet.

'Hold on, Mr Belk,' the judge admonished. 'Let her finish.'

'Your Honor, it is evidence in this case. It should be turned over immediately.'

Judge Keyes gave Belk the nod and the deputy city attorney lumbered to the lectern, Chandler having to back up to give him room.

'Your Honor, this note is in no way evidence in this case. It has not been verified as having come from anybody. However, it is evidence in a murder case unattached to this proceeding. And it is not the LAPD's practice to parade its evidence out in an open court while there is a suspect still at large. I ask that you deny her request.'

Judge Keyes clasped his hands together and thought a moment.

'Tell you what, Mr Belk. You get a copy of the note and bring it in here. I'll take a look and then decide if it will be entered in evidence. That's all. Ms Rivera, call in the jury please, we're losing the morning.'

After the jury was in the box and everybody in court sat down, Judge Keyes asked who had seen any news stories relating to the case. No one in the box raised a hand. Bosch knew that if any one of them had seen the story, they wouldn't admit to it anyway. To do so would be to invite certain dismissal from the jury – a ticket straight back to the jury assembly room where the minutes tick by like hours.

'Very well,' the judge said. 'Call your first witness, Ms Chandler.'

Terry Lloyd took the witness stand like a man who was as familiar with it as the recliner chair he got drunk in every night in front of the TV set. He even adjusted the microphone in front of him without any help from the clerk. Lloyd had a drinker's badge of a nose and unusually dark brown hair for a man of his age, which was pushing sixty. That was because it was obvious to everyone who looked at him, except maybe himself, that he wore a rug. Chandler went through some preliminary questions, establishing that he was a lieutenant in the LAPD's elite Robbery-Homicide Division.

'During a period beginning four and a half years ago were you placed in charge of a task force of detectives attempting to identify a serial killer?'

'Yes I was.'

'Can you tell the jury how that came about and functioned?'

'It was put together after the same killer was identified as the perpetrator in five killings. We were unofficially known in the department as the Westside Strangler Task Force. After the media got wind of it, the killer became known as the Dollmaker – because he used the victims' own makeup to paint their faces like dolls. I had eighteen detectives assigned to the task force. We broke them up into two squads, A and B. Squad A worked a day shift, B took the nights. We investigated the killings as they occurred and followed the call-in leads. After it hit the media, we were getting maybe a hundred calls a week – people saying this guy or that guy was the Dollmaker. We had to check them all out.'

'The task force, no matter what it was called, was not successful, is that correct?'

'No, ma'am, that is wrong. We were successful. We got the killer.'

'And who was that?'

'Norman Church was the killer.'

'Was he identified as such before or after he was killed?'

'After. He was good for all of them.'

'And good for the department, too?'

'I don't follow.'

'It was good for the department that you were able to connect him to the murders. Otherwise you'd –'

'Ask questions, Ms Chandler,' the judge interrupted.

'Sorry, Your Honor. Lieutenant Lloyd, the man you say was the killer, Norman Church, was not killed himself until there were at least six more murders following the establishment of the task force, is that correct?'

'Correct.'

'Allowing at least six more women to be strangled. How is that considered successful by the department?'

'We didn't allow anything. We did the best we could to track down this perpetrator. We eventually did. That made us successful. Very successful, in my book.'

'In your book. Tell me, Lieutenant Lloyd, had the name Norman Church come up at any time in the investigation before the night he was shot to death while unarmed by Detective Bosch? Any reference at all?'

'No, it hadn't. But we connected –'

'Just answer the question I ask, Lieutenant. Thank you.'

Chandler referred to her yellow pad on the lectern. Bosch noticed that Belk was alternately taking notes on one pad in front of him and writing down questions on another.

'Okay, Lieutenant,' Chandler said, 'your task force did not catch up with a supposed perpetrator, as you call it, until six deaths after you started. Would it be fair to say you and your detectives were under severe pressure to catch him, to close this case?'

'We were under pressure, yes.'

'From who? Who was pressuring you, Lieutenant Lloyd?'

'Well, we had the papers, TV. The department was on me.'

'How so? The department, I mean. Did you have meetings with your supervisors?'

'I had daily meetings with the RHD captain and weeklies – every Monday – with the police chief.'

'What did they tell you about solving the case?'

'They said get the thing solved. People were dying. I didn't need to be told that but they did anyway.'

'And did you communicate that to the task force detectives?'

'Of course. But they didn't need to be told it either. These guys were looking at the bodies every time one showed up. It was hard. They wanted this guy bad. They didn't need to read it in the papers or hear it from the chief or even me, for that matter.'

Lloyd seemed to be getting off on his cop-as-a-lonely-hunter tangent. Bosch could see that he didn't realize he had walked into Chandler's trap. She was going to argue at the end of the trial that Bosch and the cops were under such pressure to find a killer that Bosch killed Church and then they fabricated his ties to the killings. The fall-guy theory. Harry wished he could call time out and tell Lloyd to shut the hell up.

'So everyone on the task force knew there was pressure to find a killer?'

'Not a killer. *The* killer. Yes, there was pressure. It's part of the job.'

'What was Detective Bosch's role on the task force?'

'He was my B squad supervisor. He worked the night shift. He was a detective third grade so he kind of ran things when I wasn't there, which was often. Primarily, I was a floater but I usually worked the day shift with squad A.'

'Do you recall saying to Detective Bosch, "We've gotta get this guy," words to that effect?'

'Not specifically. But I said words to that effect at squad meetings. He was there. But that was our goal, nothing wrong with that. We had to get this guy. Same situation, I'd say it again.'

Bosch began to feel that Lloyd was paying him back for having stolen the show, closing the case without him. His answers no longer appeared to be grounded in congenial stupidity but in malice. Bosch bent close to Belk and whispered, 'He's fucking me because he didn't get to shoot Church himself.'

Belk put his finger to his lips, signaling Harry to be quiet. He then went back to writing on one of his two pads.

'Have you ever heard of the FBI's Behavioral Science Division?' Chandler asked.

'Yes, I have.'

'What do they do?'

'They study serial killers among other things. Come up with psychological profiles, victim profiles, give advice, things like that.'

'You had eleven murders, what advice did the FBI's Behavioral Science Division give you?'

'None.'

'Why was that? Were they stumped?'

'No, we didn't call on them.'

'Ah, and why didn't you call them?'

'Well, ma'am, we believed we had a handle on it. We had worked up profiles ourselves and we didn't think the FBI could help us much. The forensic psychologist helping us, Dr Locke from USC, had once been an adviser to the FBI on sex crimes. We had his experience and the department's staff psychiatrist helping out. We believed we were in good shape in that department.'

'Did the FBI offer their help?'

Lloyd hesitated here. It seemed he was finally understanding where she was headed.

'Uh, yes, somebody called after the case was making a lot of press. They wanted to get in on it. I told them we were fine, that no help was needed.'

'Do you regret that decision now?'

'No. I don't think the FBI could've done any better than

61

us. They usually come in on cases being handled by smaller departments or cases making a big media splash.'

'And you don't think that's fair, correct?'

'What?'

'Bigfooting, I think it's called. You didn't want the FBI coming in and taking over, right?'

'No. It was like I said, we were okay without them.'

'Isn't it true that the LAPD and the FBI have a long-standing history of jealousies and competitiveness that has resulted in the two agencies rarely communicating or working together?'

'No, I don't buy that.'

It didn't matter if he bought it. Bosch knew she was making her points with the jury. Whether *they* bought it was the only thing that mattered.

'Your task force came up with a suspect profile, correct?'

'Yes. I believe I just mentioned that.'

She asked Judge Keyes if she could approach the witness with a document she said was plaintiff's exhibit 1A. She handed it to the clerk, who handed it to Lloyd.

'What is that, Lieutenant?'

'This is a composite drawing and the psychological profile we came up with after, I think, the seventh killing.'

'How did you come up with the drawing of the suspect?'

'Between the seventh and eighth victims, we had an intended victim who managed to survive. She was able to get away from the man and call the police. Working with this survivor, we came up with the drawing.'

'Okay, are you familiar with the facial appearance of Norman Church?'

'Not to a great extent. I saw him after he was dead.'

Chandler asked to approach again and submitted plaintiff's 2A, a collage of several photographs of Church taped to a piece of cardboard. She gave Lloyd a few moments to study them.

'Do you see any resemblance between the composite drawing and the photographs of Mr Church?'

Lloyd hesitated and then said, 'Our killer was known to wear disguises and our witness – the victim who got away – was a drug user. She was a porno actress. She wasn't reliable.'

'Your Honor, can you instruct the witness to answer the questions that are asked?'

The judge did so.

'No,' Lloyd said, his head bowed after being chastised. 'No resemblance.'

'Okay,' Chandler said, 'going back to the profile you have there. Where did that come from?'

'Primarily from Dr Locke at USC and Dr Shafer, an LAPD staff psychiatrist. I think they consulted with some others before writing it up.'

'Can you read that first paragraph?'

'Yes. It says, "Subject is believed to be a white male, twenty-five to thirty-five years old with minimal college education. He is a physically strong man though may not be large in appearance. He lives alone, alienated from family and friends. He is reacting to a deep-rooted hatred of women suggesting an abusive mother or female guardian. His painting of the faces of his victims with makeup is his attempt to remake women into an image that pleases him, that smiles at him. They become dolls, not threats." Do you want me to read the part that outlines the repetitive traits of the killings?'

'No, that is not necessary. You were involved in the investigation of Mr Church after he was killed by Bosch, correct?'

'Correct.'

'List for the jury all of the traits in the suspect profile that your task force found that matched Mr Church.'

Lloyd looked down at the paper in his hands for a long time without speaking.

'I'll help you get started, Lieutenant,' Chandler said. 'He was a white male, correct?'

'Yes.'

'What else is similar? Did he live alone?'

'No.'

'He actually had a wife and two daughters, correct?'

'Yes.'

'Was he between twenty-five and thirty-five years old?'

'No.'

'Actually, he was thirty-nine years old, correct?'

'Yes.'

'Did he have a minimal education?'

'No.'

'Actually, he had a master's degree in mechanical engineering, didn't he?'

'Then what was he doing there in that room?' Lloyd said angrily. 'Why was the makeup from the victims there? Why –'

'Answer the question asked of you, Lieutenant,' Judge Keyes interjected. 'Don't go asking questions. That isn't your job here.'

'Sorry, Your Honor,' Lloyd said. 'Yes, he had a master's degree. I'm not sure exactly what it was for.'

'You mentioned the makeup in your nonresponsive answer a moment ago,' Chandler said. 'What did you mean?'

'In the garage apartment where Church was killed. Makeup that belonged to nine of the victims was found in a cabinet in the bathroom. It tied him directly to those cases. Nine of eleven – it was convincing.'

'Who found the makeup in there?'

'Harry Bosch did.'

'When he went there alone and killed him.'

'Is that a question?'

'No, Lieutenant. I withdraw it.'

She paused to let the jury think about that while she flipped through her yellow pages.

'Lieutenant Lloyd, tell us about that night. What happened?'

Lloyd told the story as it had been described dozens of

64

times before. On TV, in newspapers, in Bremmer's book. It was midnight, squad B was going off shift when the task force hot line rang and Bosch took the call, the last of the night. A street prostitute named Dixie McQueen said she had just escaped from the Dollmaker. Bosch went alone because the others on squad B had gone home and he figured it might be another dead end. He picked the woman up at Hollywood and Western and followed her directions into Silverlake. On Hyperion she convinced Bosch she had escaped from the Dollmaker and pointed to the lighted windows of an apartment over a garage. Bosch went up alone. A few moments later Norman Church was dead.

'He kicked open the door?' Chandler asked.

'Yes. There was the thought that maybe he had gone and gotten somebody to take the prostitute's place.'

'Did he shout that he was police?'

'Yes.'

'How do you know?'

'He said so.'

'Any witnesses hear it?'

'No.'

'What about Miss McQueen, the prostitute?'

'No. Bosch had kept her in the car parked on the street in case there was trouble.'

'So what you're saying is we have Detective Bosch's word that he feared there might be another victim, that he identified himself and that Mr Church made a threatening move toward the pillow.'

'Yes,' Lloyd said reluctantly.

'I notice, Lieutenant Lloyd, that you wear a toupee yourself.'

There was some muffled laughter from the back. Bosch turned and saw that the media contingent was steadily growing. He saw Bremmer sitting in the gallery now.

'Yes,' Lloyd said. His face had turned red to match his nose.

'Have you ever put your toupee under your pillow? Is that the proper care for it?'

'No.'

'Nothing further, Your Honor.'

Judge Keyes looked at the clock at the wall and then at Belk.

'What do you think, Mr Belk? Break for lunch now so you won't be interrupted?'

'I only have one question.'

'Oh, then by all means, ask it.'

Belk took his pad to the lectern and leaned to the microphone.

'Lieutenant Lloyd, from all of your knowledge about this case, do you have any doubt whatsoever that Norman Church was the Dollmaker?'

'None at all. None . . . at . . . all.'

After the jury filed out, Bosch leaned to Belk's ear and urgently whispered, 'What was that? She tore him up and you asked only one question. What about all the other things that tied Church to the case?'

Belk held up his hand to calm Bosch and then spoke calmly.

'Because you are going to testify about all of that. This case is about you, Harry. We either win it or lose it with you.'

SIX

The Code Seven had closed its dining room during the recession and somebody put a salad and pizza bar in the space to serve the office workers from the civic center. The Seven's barroom was still open but the dining room had been the last place within walking distance of Parker Center that Bosch had liked to eat at. So during the lunch break he got his car out of the lot at Parker and drove over to the garment district to eat at Gorky's. The Russian restaurant served breakfast all day and he ordered the eggs, bacon and potatoes special and took it to a table where someone had left behind a copy of the *Times*.

The concrete blonde story had Bremmer's byline on it. It combined quotes from the opening arguments in the trial with the discovery of the body and its possible connection to the case. The story also reported that police sources revealed that Detective Harry Bosch had received a note from someone claiming to be the real Dollmaker.

There was obviously a leak in Hollywood Division but Bosch knew it would be impossible to trace the person down. The note had been found at the front desk and any number of uniform officers could have known about it and leaked the word to Bremmer. After all, Bremmer was a good friend to have. Bosch had even leaked information to him in the past and on occasion found Bremmer to be quite useful.

Citing the unnamed sources, the story said police investigators had not concluded whether the note was legitimate or if the discovery of the body was connected to the Dollmaker case which ended four years earlier.

The only other point of interest in the story for Bosch was the short history on the Bing's Billiards building. It had been burned on the second night of the riots, no arrests ever made. Arson investigators said the separations between the storage units were not bearing walls, meaning trying to stop the flames was like trying to hold water in a cup made of toilet paper. From ignition to full involvement of flames was only eighteen minutes. Most of the storage units were rented by movie industry people and some valuable studio props were either looted or lost in the fire. The building was a total loss. The investigators traced the origin to the billiard hall. A pool table had been set on fire and it went from there.

Bosch put the paper down and began thinking about Lloyd's testimony. He remembered what Belk had said, that the case rode on himself. Chandler must know this as well. She would be waiting for him, ready to make Lloyd's outing seem like a joy ride in comparison. He grudgingly had to admit to himself that he respected her skill, her toughness. It made him remember something and he got up to use the pay phone out front. He was surprised to find Edgar was at the homicide table and not out eating lunch.

'Any luck on the ID?' Bosch asked.

'No, man, the prints didn't check. No matches at all. She didn't have a record. We're still trying other sources, adult entertainment licenses, stuff like that.'

'Shit.'

'Well, we got something else cooking. Remember that CSUN anthropology professor I was telling you about? Well, he's been here all morning with a student, painting the plaster face and getting it ready. I got the press coming in at three to show it off. Rojas went out to buy a blonde wig we'll stick on it. If we get good play on the tube we might crack loose an ID.'

'Sounds like a plan.'

'Yeah. How's court? The shit hit the fan in the *Times* today. That guy Bremmer has some sources.'

'Court's fine. Let me ask you something. After you left the scene yesterday and went back to the station, where was Pounds?'

'Pounds? He was – we got back at the same time. Why?'

'When did he leave?'

'A little while later. Right before you got here.'

'Was he on the phone in his office?'

'I think he made a few calls. I wasn't really watching. What's going on, you think he's Bremmer's source?'

'One last question. Did he close the door when he was on the phone?'

Bosch knew Pounds was paranoid. He always kept the door to his office open and the blinds on the glass partitions up so he could see and hear what was happening in the squad room. If he ever closed either or both, the troops outside knew something was up.

'Well, now that you mention it, I think he did have the door closed a little while. What is it?'

'Bremmer I'm not worried about. But somebody was talking to Money Chandler. In court this morning she knew I had been called out to the scene yesterday. That wasn't in the *Times*. Somebody told her.'

Edgar was silent a moment before replying.

'Yeah, but why would Pounds talk to her?'

'I don't know.'

'Maybe Bremmer. He could have told her, even though it wasn't in his story.'

'The story says she couldn't be reached for comment. It's got to be somebody else. A leak. Probably the same person talked to Bremmer and Chandler. Somebody who wants to fuck me up.'

Edgar didn't say anything and Bosch let it go for now.

'I better head back to court.'

'Hey, how'd Lloyd do? I heard on KFWB he was the first wit.'

'He did about as expected.'

'Shit. Who's next?'

'I don't know. She has Irving and Locke, the shrink, on subpoena. My guess is, it will be Irving. He'll pick up where Lloyd left off.'

'Well, good luck. By the way, if you're looking for something to do. This press gig I'm holding will hit the TV news tonight. I'll be here waiting by the phones. If you want to answer a few, I could use the help.'

Bosch thought briefly about his plan for dinner with Sylvia. She'd understand.

'Yeah, I'll be there.'

The afternoon testimony was largely uneventful. Chandler's strategy, it seemed to Bosch, was to build a two-part question into the jury's eventual deliberation, giving her clients two shots at the prize. One would be the wrong-man theory, which held that Bosch had flat-out killed an innocent man. The second question would be the use of force. Even if the jury determined that Norman Church, family man, was the Dollmaker, serial killer, they would have to decide whether Bosch's actions were appropriate.

Chandler called her client, Deborah Church, to the witness stand right after lunch. She gave a tearful account of a wonderful life with a wonderful husband who fawned over everybody; his daughters, his wife, his mother and mother-in-law. No misogynistic aberrations here. No sign of childhood abuse. The widow held a box of Kleenex in her hand as she testified, going to a new tissue every other question.

She wore the traditional black dress of a widow. Bosch remembered how appealing Sylvia had been when he saw her at her husband's funeral dressed in black. Deborah Church looked downright scary. It was as if she reveled in her role here. The widow of the fallen innocent. The real victim. Chandler had coached her well.

It was a good show, but it was too good to be true and Chandler knew it. Rather than leave the bad things to be

70

drawn out on cross-examination, she finally got around to asking Deborah Church how, her marriage being so wonderful, her husband was in that garage apartment – which was rented under an alias – when Bosch kicked the door open.

'We had been having some difficulty.' She stopped to dab an eye with a tissue. 'Norman was going through a lot of stress – he had a lot of responsibility in the aircraft design department. He needed to expend it and so he took the apartment. He said it was to be alone. To think. I didn't know about this woman he brought there. I think it was probably his first time doing something like that. He was a naive man. I think she saw this. She took his money and then set him up by calling the police on him and giving the crazy story that he was the Dollmaker. There was a reward, you know.'

Bosch wrote a note on a pad he kept in front of him and slid it over to Belk, who read it and then jotted something down on his own pad.

'What about all of the makeup found there, Mrs Church?' Chandler asked. 'Can you explain that?'

'All I know is that I would have known if my husband was that monster. I would have known. If there was makeup found there, it was put there by somebody else. Maybe after he was already dead.'

Bosch believed he could feel the eyes of the courtroom burning into him as the widow accused him of planting evidence after murdering her husband.

After that, Chandler moved her questioning on to safer topics like Norman Church's relationship with his daughters and then ended her direct examination with a weeper.

'Did he love his daughters?'

'Very much so,' Mrs Church said as a new production of tears rolled down her cheeks. This time she did not wipe them away with a tissue. She let the jury watch them roll down her face into the folds of her double chin.

71

After giving her a few moments to compose herself, Belk got up and took his place at the lectern.

'Again, Your Honor, I will be brief. Mrs Church, I want to make this very clear to the jury. Did you say in your testimony that you knew about your husband's apartment but didn't know about any women he may or may not have brought there?'

'Yes, that is correct.'

Belk looked at his pad.

'Did you not tell detectives on the night of the shooting that you had never heard of any apartment? Didn't you emphatically deny that your husband even had such an apartment?'

Deborah Church didn't answer.

'I can arrange to have a tape of your first interview played in court if it will help refresh your –'

'Yes, I said that. I lied.'

'You lied? Why would you lie to the police?'

'Because a policeman had just killed my husband. I didn't – I couldn't deal with them.'

'The truth is you told the truth that night, correct, Mrs Church? You never knew about any apartment.'

'No, that's not true. I knew about it.'

'Had you and your husband talked about it?'

'Yes, we discussed it.'

'You approved of it?'

'Yes . . ., reluctantly. It was my hope he would stay at home and we could work this stress out together.'

'Okay, Mrs Church, then if you knew of the apartment, had discussed it and given your approval, reluctantly or not, why then did your husband rent it under a false name?'

She didn't answer. Belk had nailed her. Bosch thought he saw the widow glance in Chandler's direction. He looked at the lawyer but she made no move, no change in facial expression to help her client.

'I guess,' the widow finally said, 'that was one of the questions you could have asked him if Mr Bosch had not murdered him in cold blood.'

Without Belk's prompting, Judge Keyes said, 'The jury will disregard that last characterization. Mrs Church, you know better than that.'

'I'm sorry, Your Honor.'

'Nothing further,' Belk said as he left the lectern.

The judge called a ten-minute recess.

During the break, Bosch went out to the ash can. Money Chandler didn't come out but the homeless man made a pass. Bosch offered him a whole cigarette, which he took and put in his shirt pocket. He was unshaven again and the slight look of dementia was still in his eyes.

'Your name is Faraday,' Bosch said, as if speaking to a child.

'Yeah, what about it, Lieutenant?'

Bosch smiled. He had been made by a bum. All except for the rank.

'Nothing about it. I just heard that's what it was. I also heard you were a lawyer once.'

'I still am. I'm just not practicing.'

He turned and watched a jail bus go by on Spring, heading to the courthouse. It was full of angry faces looking out through the black wire windows. Somebody by one of the back windows made Bosch as a cop, too, and stuck his middle index finger up through the wire. Bosch smiled back at him.

'My name was Thomas Faraday. But now I prefer Tommy Faraway.'

'What happened to make you stop practicing law?'

Tommy looked back at him with milky eyes.

'Justice is what happened. Thanks for the smoke.'

He walked away then, cup in hand, and headed toward City Hall. Maybe that was his turf, too.

After the break, Chandler called a lab analyst from the coroner's office named Victor Amado. He was a very small and bookish-looking man with eyes that shifted from the judge to the jury as he walked to the witness chair. He was balding badly, though he seemed to be no more than twenty-eight. Bosch remembered that four years earlier he had all his hair and members of the task force referred to him as The Kid. He knew Belk was going to call Amado as a witness if Chandler didn't.

Belk leaned over and whispered that Chandler was following a good guy–bad guy pattern by alternating police witnesses with her sympathetic witnesses.

'She'll probably put one of the daughters up there after Amado,' he said. 'As a strategy, it is completely unoriginal.'

Bosch didn't mention that Belk's trust-us-we're-the-cops defense had been around as long as the civil suit.

Amado testified in painstaking detail about how he had been given all of the bottles and compacts containing makeup that were found in Church's Hyperion apartment and had then traced them to specific victims of the Dollmaker. He said he had come up with nine separate lots or groupings of makeup – mascara, blush, eyeliner, lipstick, etc. Each lot was connected through chemical analysis to samples taken from the faces of the victims. This was further corroborated by detectives who interviewed relatives and friends to determine what brands the victims were known to use. It all matched up, Amado said. And in one instance, he added, an eyelash found on a mascara brush in Church's bathroom cabinet was identified as having come from the second victim.

'What about the two victims no matching makeup was found for?' Chandler asked.

'That was a mystery. We never found their makeup.'

'In fact, with the exception of the eyelash that was allegedly found and matched to victim number two, you can't be one hundred percent sure that the makeup police did supposedly find in the apartment came from the victims, correct?'

'This stuff is mass produced and sold around the world. So there is a lot of it out there, but I would guess that the chances of nine different exact combinations of makeup being found like that by mere coincidence are astronomical.'

'I didn't ask you to guess, Mr Amado. Please answer the question I asked.'

After flinching at being dressed down, Amado said, 'The answer is we can't be one hundred percent sure, that is correct.'

'Okay, now tell the jury about the DNA testing you did that connected Norman Church to the eleven killings.'

'There wasn't any done. There –'

'Just answer the question, Mr Amado. What about serology tests, connecting Mr Church to the crimes?'

'There were none.'

'Then it was the makeup comparison that was the clincher – the linchpin in the determination that Mr Church was the Dollmaker?'

'Well, it was for me. I don't know about the detectives. My report said –'

'I'm sure for the detectives it was the bullet that killed him that was the clincher.'

'Objection,' Belk yelled angrily as he stood. 'Your Honor, she can't –'

'Ms Chandler,' Judge Keyes boomed. 'I have warned you both about exactly this sort of thing. Why would you go and say something you know full well is prejudicial and out of order?'

'I apologize, Your Honor.'

'Well, it's a little late for apologies. We'll discuss this matter after the jury goes home for the day.'

The judge then instructed the jurors to disregard her comment. But Bosch knew it had been a carefully thought out gambit by Chandler. The jurors would now see her even more as the underdog. Even the judge was against her – which he really wasn't. And they might be distracted, thinking about what just happened, when Belk stepped up to repair Amado's testimony.

'Nothing further, Your Honor,' Chandler said.

'Mr Belk,' the judge said.

Don't say just a few questions again, Bosch thought as his lawyer moved to the lectern.

'Just a few questions, Mr Amado,' Belk said. 'Plaintiff's counsel mentioned DNA and serology tests and you said they had not been done. Why is that?'

'Well, because there was nothing to test. No semen was ever recovered from any of the bodies. The killer had used a condom. Without samples to attempt to match to Mr Church's DNA or blood, there was not much point in running tests. We would have the victims' but nothing to compare it to.'

Belk drew a line with his pen through a question written on his pad.

'If there was no recovery of semen or sperm, how do you know these women were raped or even had engaged in consensual sexual activity?'

'The autopsies of all eleven of the victims showed vaginal bruising, much more than is considered usual or even possible from consensual sex. On two of the victims there was even tearing in the vaginal wall. The victims were brutally raped, in my estimation.'

'But these women came from walks of life where sexual activity was common and frequent, even "rough sex", if you will. Two of them performed in pornographic videos. How can you be sure they were sexually assaulted against their will?'

'The bruising was such that it would have been very painful, especially for the two with vaginal tears. Hemorrhaging was considered perimortem, meaning at the time of death. The deputy coroners who performed these autopsies unanimously concluded these women were raped.'

Belk drew another line on his pad, flipped the page and came up with a new question. He was doing well with Amado, Bosch thought. Better than Money had. It may have been a mistake for her to have called him as a witness.

'How do you know that the killer used a condom?' Belk asked. 'Couldn't these women have been raped with an object and that account for the lack of semen?'

'That could have happened and it could account for some of the damage. But there was clear evidence in five of the cases that they had had sex with a man wearing a condom.'

'And what was that?'

'We did rape kits. There was –'

'Hold it a second, Mr Amado. What is a rape kit?'

'It's a protocol for collecting evidence from bodies of people that may have been the victims of rape. In the case of a woman, we take vaginal and anal swabs, we comb the pubic area looking for foreign pubic hair, procedures such as that. We also take samples of blood and hair from the victim in case there is a call for comparison to evidence found on a suspect. It's collected together in an evidence kit.'

'Okay. Before I interrupted there, you were going to tell us about the evidence found in five of the victims that was indicative of sex with a man who wore a condom.'

'Yes, we did the rape kits each time we got a Dollmaker victim. And there was a foreign substance found in vaginal samplings in five of the victims. It was the same material in each of the women.'

'What was it, Mr Amado?'

'It was identified as a condom lubricant.'

'Was this material something that could be identified to a specific brand and style of condom?'

Looking at Belk, Bosch could see the heavy man was chomping at the bit. Amado was answering each question slowly and each time Bosch could see that Belk could barely wait for the answer before plowing ahead with a new question. Belk was on a roll.

'Yes,' Amado said. 'We identified the product. It was from a Trojan-Enz lubricated condom with special receptacle end.'

77

Looking at the court reporter, Amado said, 'That's spelled E-N-Z.'

'And that was the same for all five samples received from the five bodies?' Belk asked.

'Yes it was.'

'I am going to ask you a hypothetical question. Assuming that the attacker of eleven women used the same brand of lubricated condom, how could you account for lubrication being found in the vaginal sampling of only five victims?'

'I believe that a number of factors could be involved. Such as the intensity of the victim's struggle. But essentially it would be just a matter of how much of the lubricant came off the condom and stayed in the vagina.'

'When police officers brought you the various containers of makeup from the Hyperion apartment rented by Norman Church for analysis, did they bring anything else?'

'Yes they did.'

'What was that?'

'A box of Trojan-Enz lubricated condoms with special receptacle ends.'

'How many condoms did the box hold?'

'Twelve separately packaged condoms.'

'How many were still in the box when the police delivered it to you?'

'There were three left.'

'Nothing further.'

Belk returned to the defense table with a triumphant spring in his walk.

'A moment, Your Honor,' Chandler said.

Bosch watched her open a fat file full of police documents. She leafed through the pages and took out a short stack of documents held together with a paper clip. She read the top one quickly and then held it up to leaf through the rest. Bosch could see the top one was the protocol list from a rape kit. She was reading the protocols from all eleven victims.

Belk leaned over to him and whispered, 'She's about to

step into some deep shit. I was going to bring this up later, during your testimony.'

'Ms Chandler?' the judge intoned.

She jumped up.

'Yes, Your Honor, I'm ready. I have a quick redirect of Mr Amado.'

She brought the stack of protocols with her to the lectern, read the last two and then looked at the coroner's analyst.

'Mr Amado, you mentioned that part of the rape kit consisted of combing for foreign pubic hairs, do I have that right?'

'Yes.'

'Can you explain that procedure a little more?'

'Well, basically, the comb is passed through the pubic hair of the victim and it collects unattached hairs. Often-times, this unattached hair is from the victim's attacker, or possibly other sexual partners.'

'How's it get there?'

Amado's face flushed to a crimson hue.

'Well, uh, it – uh, during sex . . . there is I guess what you call friction between the bodies?'

'I am asking the questions, Mr Amado. You are answering.'

There was quiet tittering from the gallery seats. Bosch felt embarrassed for Amado and thought that his own face might be turning red.

'Yes, well, there is friction,' Amado said. 'And this causes some transference. Loose pubic hair from one person can be transferred to that of the other.'

'I see,' Chandler said. 'Now, you as coordinator of the Dollmaker evidence from the coroner's office were familiar with the rape kits of all eleven victims, correct?'

'Yes.'

'With how many of the victims did the findings include foreign pubic hair?'

Bosch understood what was happening now and realized that Belk was right. Chandler was walking into the buzz saw.

'All of them,' Amado answered.

Bosch saw Deborah Church raise her head and look sharply at Chandler at the lectern. Then she looked over at Bosch and their eyes met. She quickly looked away but Bosch knew. She, too, knew what was about to happen. Because she, too, knew her late husband the way Bosch had on that last night. She knew what he looked like naked.

'Ah, all of them,' Chandler said. 'Now, can you tell the jury how many of these pubic hairs found on these women were analyzed and identified as having been from the body of Norman Church?'

'None of them were from Norman Church.'

'Thank you.'

Belk was up and moving to the lectern before Chandler had time to remove her pad and the rape kit protocols. Bosch watched her sit down and saw the widow Church lean to her and desperately begin whispering. Bosch saw Chandler's eyes go dead. She held up her hand to tell the widow she had said enough and then leaned back and exhaled.

'Now, let's clear something up first,' Belk said. 'Mr Amado, you said you found pubic hairs on all of the eleven victims. Were these hairs all from the same man?'

'No. We found a multitude of samples. In most cases, what looked like hair from possibly two or three men on each victim.'

'What did you attribute this to?'

'Their lifestyle. We knew these were women with multiple sexual partners.'

'Did you analyze these samples to determine if there were common hairs? In other words, whether hair from one man was found on each of the victims.'

'No, we did not. There was a huge amount of evidence collected in these cases and manpower dictated that we focus on evidence that would help identify a killer. Because we had so many different samples, it was determined that this was evidence that would be held and then used to link or clear a suspect, once that suspect was in custody.'

'I see, well, then once Norman Church had been killed and was identified as the Dollmaker, did you then match any of the hairs from the victims to him?'

'We did not.'

'And why is that?'

'Because Mr. Church had shaved his body hair. There was no pubic hair to match.'

'Why would he have done that?'

Chandler objected on the grounds that Amado could not answer for Church and the judge sustained it. But Bosch knew it didn't matter. Everybody in the courtroom knew why Church had shaved himself – so he wouldn't leave pubic hairs behind as evidence.

Bosch looked at the jury and he saw two of the women writing in the notebooks the marshals had given them to help them keep track of important testimony. He wanted to buy Belk – and Amado – a beer.

SEVEN

It looked like a cake in a box, one of those novelty things custom-made to look like Marilyn Monroe or something. The anthropologist had painted on a beige skin tone and red lipstick to go with blue eyes. It looked like frosting to Bosch. A wavy blonde wig was added. He stood in the squad room looking down at the plaster image, wondering if it really looked like anybody at all.

'Five minutes till show time,' Edgar said.

He was sitting in his chair, which was turned toward the TV on the file cabinets. He was holding the channel changer. His blue suit coat was hung neatly on a hanger, which was hooked on the coatrack at the end of the table. Bosch took his jacket off and hung it on one of the coatrack pegs. He checked his slot in the message box and sat down at his spot at the homicide table. There had been a call from Sylvia, nothing else important. He dialed her number as the Channel 4 news began. He knew enough about the news priorities in this town to know the report on the concrete blonde wouldn't be a lead story.

'Harry, we're gonna need that line clear once they show it,' Edgar said.

'I'll only be a minute. They won't show it for a while. If they show it at all.'

'They'll show it. I made secret deals with all of them. They all think they'll be getting the exclusive if we get an ID. They all want to get a boo hoo story with the parents.'

'You're playing with fire, man. You make a promise like that and then they find out you fucked them around –'

Sylvia picked up the phone.

'Hey, it's me.'

'Hi, where are you?'

'The office. We have to watch the phones a while. They're putting the face of the victim from yesterday's case on TV tonight.'

'How was court?'

'It's the plaintiff's case at the moment. But I think we scored a couple punches.'

'I read the *Times* today at lunch.'

'Yeah, well, they got about half of it right.'

'Are you coming out? Like you said.'

'Well, eventually. Not right now. I've got to help answer phones on this and then it's depending on what we get. If we're skunked I'll be out early.'

He noticed he had lowered his voice so Edgar wouldn't hear his conversation.

'And if you get something good?'

'We'll see.'

An indrawn breath, then silence. Harry waited.

'You've been saying "we'll see" too much, Harry. We've talked about this. Sometimes –'

'I know that.'

' – I think that you just want to be left alone. Stay in your little house on the hill and keep the whole world out. Including me.'

'Not you. You know that.'

'Sometimes, I don't. I don't feel like I know it right now. You push me away just at the time when you need me – somebody – to be close.'

He had no answer. He thought of her there on the other end. She was probably sitting on the stool in the kitchen. She had probably already begun making a dinner for both of them. Or maybe she was getting used to his ways and had waited for the call.

'Look, I'm sorry,' he said. 'You know how it is. What are you doing about dinner?'

'Nothing, and I'm not going to do anything, either.'

Edgar made a low, quick whistle. Harry looked up at the TV and saw it was showing the painted face of the victim. The TV was on Channel 7 now. The camera showed a long close-up of the face. It looked all right on the tube. At least, it didn't look much like a cake. The screen flashed the detective bureau's two public numbers.

'They're showing it now,' Bosch said to Sylvia. 'I need to keep this line clear. Let me call you back later, when I know something.'

'Sure,' she said coldly and hung up.

Edgar had the TV on 4 now and they were showing the face. He then flipped to 2 and caught the last few seconds of their report on it. They had even interviewed the anthropologist.

'Slow news day,' Bosch said.

'Shit,' Edgar replied. 'We're banging on all cylinders now. All we –'

The phone rang and he grabbed it up.

'No, it just went out,' he said after listening for a few moments. 'Yeah, yeah, I will. Okay.'

He hung up and shook his head.

'Pounds?' Bosch asked.

'Yeah. Thinks we're going to have her name ten seconds after the broadcast went out. Christ, whadda nitwit.'

The next three calls were pranks, all testifying to the glaring lack of originality and the mental health of the TV viewing audience. All three callers said 'Your mother!' or words to that effect and hung up laughing. About twenty minutes later Edgar got a call and started taking notes. The phone rang again and Bosch took it.

'This is Detective Bosch, who am I speaking with?'

'Is this being taped?'

'No, it's not. Who is this?'

'Never mind, just thought you'd like to know the girl's name is Maggie. Maggie something or other. It's Latin. I seen her on videos.'

'What videos? MTV?'

'No, Sherlock. Adult videos. She fucked on film. She was good. She could put a rubber on a prick with her mouth.'

The line went dead. Bosch wrote a couple of notes down on the pad he had in front of him. Latin? He didn't think the way the face had been painted gave any indication that the victim was a Latina.

Edgar hung up then and said his caller had said her name was Becky, that she had lived in Studio City a few years back.

'What'd you get?'

'I got a Maggie. No last name. Possibly a Latin last name. He said she was in porno.'

'That would fit, except she don't look Mexican to me.'

'I know.'

The phone rang again. Edgar picked up and listened a few moments and then hung up.

'Another one that recognizes my mom.'

Bosch took the next one.

'I just wanted to tell you that the girl they were showing on TV was in porno,' the voice said.

'How do you know she was in porno?'

'I can tell by that thing they showed on TV. I rented a tape. Only once. She was in it.'

Only once, Bosch thought, but he remembered. Yeah, sure.

'You know her name?'

The other phone rang and Edgar picked it up.

'I don't know names, man,' Bosch's caller said. 'They all use fake ones anyway.'

'What was the name of the tape?'

'Can't remember. I was, uh, intoxicated when I saw it. Like I said, it was the only time.'

'Look, I'm not taking your confession. You got anything else?'

'No, smartass, I don't.'

'Who is this?'

'I don't have to say.'

'Look, we're trying to find a killer here. What was the name of the place you rented it?'

'I'm not telling you, you might be able to get my name from them. Doesn't matter, they have those tapes all over, every adult place.'

'How would you know if you only rented one once?'

The caller hung up.

Bosch stayed another hour. By the end they had five calls saying the painted face belonged to a porno starlet. Only one of the callers said her name was Maggie, the other four men saying they didn't pay much attention to names. There was one call naming her Becky of Studio City, and one saying she was a stripper who had worked for a while at the Booby Trap on La Brea. One man who called said the face belonged to his missing wife, but Bosch learned through further questioning that she had been missing only two months. The concrete blonde had been dead too long. The hope and desperation in the caller's voice seemed genuine to Bosch, and he didn't know whether he was telling the man good news by explaining that it could not be his wife or bad news because he was left in the void again.

There were three callers who gave vague descriptions of a woman they thought might be the concrete blonde, but after a few questions into each conversation Bosch and Edgar identified the callers as cop geeks, people who got a thrill from talking to the police.

The most unusual call was from a Beverly Hills psychic who mentioned that she had placed her hand on the TV screen while it showed the face and felt the dead woman's spirit cry out to her.

'What did it cry?' Bosch asked patiently.

'Praise.'

'Praise for what?'

'Jesus our savior, I would assume but I don't know. That was all I received. I might receive more if I could touch the actual plaster cast of the –'

'Well, did this spirit that was giving praise identify itself? See, that's what we're doing here. We're more interested in a name than cries of praise.'

'Someday you will believe but by then you will be lost.'

She hung up on him.

At seven-thirty Bosch told Edgar he was splitting.

'How 'bout you? You going to hang out for the eleven o'clock news?'

'Yeah, I'll be here but I can handle it. If I get a lot of calls I'll pull one of the dipshits off the desk.'

Stock that O.T., Bosch thought.

'What's next?' he asked.

'I don't know. What do you think?'

'Well, aside from all the calls saying it's your mother, this porno thing seems to be the way to go.'

'Leave my blessed mother out of it. How you think I can check the porno?'

'Administrative Vice. Guy over there, a detective-three, name of Ray Mora, he works porno. He's the best. He also was on the Dollmaker task force. Call him and see if he can come take a look at the face. He might've known her. Tell him we had one call saying her name was Maggie.'

'Will do. It fits with the Dollmaker, doesn't it? The porno, I mean.'

'Yeah, it fits.' He thought about this a moment, then added, 'Two of the other victims were in the business. The one that got away from him was, too.'

'The lucky one – she still in it?'

'Last I heard. But she might be dead now for all I know.'

'Still doesn't mean anything, Harry.'

'What?'

'The porno. Still doesn't mean it was the Dollmaker. The real one, I mean.'

Bosch just nodded. He had an idea about something to do on his way home. He went out to his Caprice and got the Polaroid camera out of the trunk. In the squad room, he took two shots of the face in the box and put them in his coat pocket after they developed.

Edgar watched this and asked, 'What're you going to do?'

'Might stop at that adult supermarket in the Valley on my way up to Sylvia's.'

'Don't get caught in one of those little rooms with your dick out.'

'Thanks for the tip. Let me know what Mora says.'

Bosch worked his way on surface streets up to the Hollywood Freeway. He went north and then exited on Lankershim, which took him into North Hollywood in the San Fernando Valley. He had all four windows down and the air was cool as it buffeted him from all directions. He smoked a cigarette, flicking the ashes into the wind. There was some techno-funk jazz on KAJZ so he turned the radio off and just drove.

The Valley was the city's bedroom community in more ways than the obvious. It was also home to the nation's pornography industry. The commercial-industrial districts of Van Nuys, Canoga Park, Northridge and Chatsworth housed hundreds of porno production outfits, distributors and warehouses. Modeling agencies in Sherman Oaks provided ninety percent of the women and men who performed in front of the cameras. And, consequently, the Valley was also one of the largest retail outlets for the material. It was made here, it was sold here – through video mail-order businesses also nestled in the warehouses with the production outfits, and places like X Marks the Spot on Lankershim Boulevard.

Bosch pulled into the lot in front of the huge store and appraised it for a few moments. It had formerly been a Pic N Pay supermarket, but the front plate-glass windows had been walled up. Under the red neon X Marks the Spot sign, the front wall was whitewashed and painted with black figures of naked and overly buxom female figures, like the metallic silhouettes Bosch saw all the time on the mudflaps of trucks on the freeway. The men who put those on their trucks were probably the same guys this place catered to, Bosch figured.

X Marks the Spot was owned by a man named Harold Barnes, who was a front for the Chicago Outfit. It grossed more than a million dollars a year – on the books. Probably another one under the counter. Bosch knew all of this from Mora of Ad-Vice, whom he had partnered with on some nights while they both were on the task force four years earlier.

Bosch watched a man of about twenty-five get out of his Toyota, walk quickly to the solid wood front door, and slip in like a secret agent. He followed. The front half of the former supermarket was dedicated to retail – the sale and rental of videos, magazines and other assorted adult-oriented and mostly rubber products. The rear was split between private 'encounter' rooms and private video booths. The entry to this area was through a curtained doorway. Bosch could hear heavy-metal rock music coming from back there mixed with the canned-sounding cries of phony passion coming from the video booths.

To his left was a glass counter with two men behind it. One was a big man, there to keep the peace; the other was smaller, older, there to take the money. Bosch knew by the way they looked at him and the skin stretched tight around their eyes that they had made him as soon as he had come in. He walked over and put one of the Polaroids on the counter.

'I am trying to ID her. Heard she worked in video, do you recognize her?'

The small guy leaned forward and looked while the other guy didn't move.

'Looks like a fucking cake, man,' the small guy said. 'I don't know any cakes. I eat cakes.'

He looked back at the big guy and they exchanged clever smiles.

'So you don't recognize her. What about you?'

'I say what he says,' the big guy said. 'I eat cakes, too.'

This time they laughed out loud and probably had to restrain themselves from exchanging a high five. The small guy's eyes sparkled behind rose-tinted glasses.

'Okay,' Bosch said. 'Then I'll just look around. Thanks.'

The big guy stepped forward and said, 'Just keep your gun covered, man, we don't want to excite the patrons.'

The big guy's eyes were dull and he set out a five-foot zone of body odor. A duster, Bosch thought. He wondered why the small guy didn't fire his ass.

'No more excited than they are,' Bosch said.

He turned from the counter to the two walls of shelves that were lined with hundreds of video boxes for sale or rent. There were a dozen men, including the secret agent, looking. Appraising the scene and the number of video boxes, Bosch somehow was reminded of how he once had read all the names on the Vietnam War Memorial wall while on a case. It had taken several hours.

The video wall proved to be less time consuming. Skipping the gay and black performer videos he scanned each box for a face like the concrete blonde's or the name Maggie. The videos were in alphabetical order and it took him nearly an hour to get to the T's. A face on the box of a video called *Tails from the Crypt* caught his eye. There was a nude woman lying in a coffin on the front. She was blonde and had an upturned nose like the plaster face in the box. He turned the box over and there was another photo of the actress, on her hands and knees with a man pressed up behind her. Her mouth was slightly open and her face was turned back toward her sex partner.

It was her, Bosch knew. He looked at the credits and saw that the name fit. He took the empty video box to the counter.

''Bout time,' said the small guy. 'We don't allow loitering here. The cops give us a hard time on that.'

'I want to rent this.'

'Can't, it's already rented. See, the box is empty.'

'She in anything else you know of?'

The small guy took the box and looked at the photographs.

'Magna Cum Loudly, yeah. I don't know. She was just getting started and then dropped out. Probably married a rich guy, lots of them do.'

The big guy stepped over to look at the box and Bosch stepped back, out of his odor zone.

'I'm sure they do,' he said. 'What else was she in?'

'Well,' the small guy said, 'she had just made her way out of the loops and then, pfffft, she's gone. *Tails* was her first top billing. She did a fabulous two-way in *Whore of the Roses* and that's what got her started. Before that it was just the loops.'

Bosch went back to the W's and found the box for *Whore of the Roses*. It also was empty and there were no photos of Magna Cum Loudly on it. Her name was last billing on the credits. He went back to the small guy and pointed to the Tails from the Crypt box.

'What about the box, then? I'll buy it.'

'We can't sell you just the box because then how do we display the video when it comes back? We don't sell many boxes here. Guys want stills, they buy magazines.'

'What's the price of the whole video? I'll buy it. When the renter brings it back you can hold it for me and I'll come pick it up. How much?'

'Well, *Tails* is popular. We're going with a $39.95 price tag but for you, Officer, I'll give our law enforcement discount. Fifty bucks.'

Bosch said nothing to that. He had the cash and paid it.

'I want a receipt.'

After the purchase was completed, the small guy put the video box in a brown paper bag.

'You know,' he said, 'Maggie Cum Loudly is still on a couple of our loops in the back. You might want to check it out.'

He smiled and pointed to a sign on the wall behind him.

'We have a no-exchange policy, by the way.'

Bosch smiled back.

'I'll check it out.'

'Hey, by the way, what name you want us to hold this video under when it comes back in?'

'Carlo Pinzi.'

It was the name of the Outfit's LA capo.

'Very fucking funny, Mr Pinzi, we'll do that.'

Bosch went through the curtain into the back rooms and was almost immediately met by a woman wearing high heels, a black G-string and an ice-cream man's coin changer on a belt, nothing else. Her large silicone-perfected breasts were dotted by unusually small nipples. Her dyed blonde hair was short and she had too much makeup around her glassy brown eyes. She looked like she was either nineteen or thirty-five.

'Do you want a private encounter or change for the video booths?' she asked.

Bosch took out his now thin fold of cash and gave her two dollars for quarters.

'Can I keep a dollar for myself? I don't get paid nothin', just tips.'

Bosch gave her another dollar and took his eight quarters to one of the small curtained booths where the occupied light wasn't on.

'Let me know if you need anything in there,' the woman in the G-string called after him.

She was either too stoned or too stupid or both not to have made him as a cop. Bosch waved her away and pulled the curtain shut behind him. The space he had was about the size of a phone booth. There was a glass viewing window through which he could see a video screen. Displayed on the screen was a directory of twelve different videos he could select from. It was all video now, though they were still called loops, after the 16mm film loops that ran over and over again in the first peep machines.

There was no chair but there was a small shelf with an ashtray and a Kleenex box on it. Used tissues were littered on the floor and the booth smelled like the industrial disinfectant they used in the coroner's vans. He put all eight quarters in the coin slot and the video picture came on.

It was two women on a bed kissing and massaging each other. It took Bosch only a few seconds to eliminate them as possibly being the girl on the video box. He began pushing the channel button and the picture jumped from coupling to coupling – heterosexual, homosexual, bisexual – his eyes lingering only long enough to determine whether the woman he was looking for was there.

She was on the ninth loop. He recognized her from the video box he had bought. Seeing her in motion also helped convince him that the woman who used the name Magna Cum Loudly was the concrete blonde. In the video she lay on a couch on her back, biting one of her fingers while a man knelt between her legs on the floor and rhythmically ground his hips into hers.

Knowing this woman was dead, had died violently, and standing there watching her submit to another kind of violence affected him in a way he was unsure he even understood. Guilt and sorrow welled up as he watched. Like most cops, he had spent a stint in vice. He had also seen some of the films of the two other adult film actresses who were killed by the Dollmaker. But this was the first time this uneasiness had hit him.

On the video, the actress took the finger out of her mouth and began to moan loudly, living up to her billing. Bosch fumbled with the sound knob and turned it down. But he could still hear her, her moans turned into shouts, from videos in other booths. Other men were watching the same show. It made Bosch feel creepy knowing the video had drawn the interest of different men for different reasons.

The curtain behind him rustled and he heard someone move behind him into the booth. At the same moment he felt a hand move up his thigh to his crotch. He reached into his jacket for his gun as he turned but then saw it was the coin changer.

'What can I do for you, darling?' she cooed.

He pushed her arm away from him.

'You can start by getting out of here.'

'C'mon, lover, why look at it on TV when you can be doing it? Twenty bucks. I can't go lower. I have to split it with the management.'

She was pressed against him now and Bosch couldn't tell if it was his breath or hers that was lousy with cigarettes. Her breasts were hard and she was pushing them against his chest. Then suddenly she froze. She had felt the gun. Their eyes held each other for a moment.

'That's right,' Bosch said. 'If you don't want to go for a ride to the cage, get out of here.'

'No problem, Officer,' she said.

She parted the curtain and was gone. Just then the screen went back to the directory. Bosch's two dollars were up.

As he walked out, he heard Magna Cum Loudly yelling in false joy from the other booths.

EIGHT

On the ride on the freeway to the next valley, he tried to imagine that life. He wondered what hope she might still have had and still nurtured and protected like a candle in the rain, even as she lay there on her back with distant eyes turned toward the stranger inside her. Hope must have been the only thing she had left. Bosch knew that hope was the lifeblood of the heart. Without it there was nothing, only darkness.

He wondered how the two lives – killer's and victim's – had crossed. Maybe the seed of lust and murderous desire had been planted by the same loop Bosch had just seen. Maybe the killer had rented the video Bosch had just paid fifty dollars for. Could it have been Church? Or was there another out there? The box, Bosch thought, and pulled off at the next exit, Van Nuys Boulevard in Pacoima.

He pulled to the curb and took the video box out of the brown paper bag the small guy had provided. He turned the light on in the car and studied every surface of the box, reading every word. But there was no copyright date that would have told him when the tape was made, whether it had been made before or after Church's death.

He got back on the Golden State, which took him north into the Santa Clarita Valley. After exiting on Bouquet Canyon Road he wound his way through a series of residential streets, past a seemingly endless line of California custom homes. On Del Prado, he pulled to the curb in front of the house with the Ritenbaugh Realty sign out front.

Sylvia had been trying to sell the house for more than a year, without luck. When he thought about it, Bosch was relieved. It kept him from facing a decision about what he and Sylvia would do next.

Sylvia opened the door before he reached it.

'Hey.'

'Hey.'

'What do you have?'

'Oh, it's something from work. I've gotta make a couple calls in a while. Did you eat?'

He bent down and kissed her and moved inside. She had on the gray T-shirt dress she liked to wear around the house after work. Her hair was loose and down to her shoulders, the blonde highlights catching the light from the living room.

'Had a salad. You?'

'Not yet. I'll fix a sandwich or something. I'm sorry about this. With the trial and now this new case, it's . . . well, you know.'

'It's okay. I just miss you. I'm sorry about how I acted on the phone.'

She kissed him and held him. He felt at home with her. That was the best thing. That feeling. He had never had it before and he would forget it at times when he was away from her. But as soon as he was back with her it was there.

She took him by the hand into the kitchen and told him to sit down while she made him a sandwich. He watched her put a pan on the stove and turn on the gas. Then she put four strips of bacon in the pan. While they cooked, she sliced a tomato and an avocado and laid out a bed of lettuce. He got up, took a beer from the fridge and kissed her on the back of the neck. He stepped back, annoyed that the memory of the woman grabbing him in the booth intruded on the moment. Why had that happened?

'What's the matter?'

'Nothing.'

She put two slices of sunflower bread into the toaster and

took the bacon out of the pan. A few minutes later she put the sandwich in front of him at the table and sat down.

'Who do you have to call?'

'Jerry Edgar, maybe a guy at Ad-Vice.'

'Ad-Vice? She was porno? This new victim?'

Sylvia had once been married to a cop and she made leaps of thought like a cop. Bosch liked that about her.

'Think so. I have a line on her. But I've got court, so I want to give it to them.'

She nodded. He never had to tell her not to ask too much. She always knew just when to stop.

'How was school today?'

'Fine. Eat your sandwich. I want you to hurry up and make your calls because I want us to forget about court and school and your investigation. I want us to open some wine, light some candles and get in bed.'

He smiled at her.

They had fallen into such a relaxed life together. The candles were always her signal, her way of initiating their lovemaking. Sitting there, Bosch realized he had no signals. She initiated it almost every time. He wondered what that meant about him. He worried that maybe theirs was a relationship solely founded on secrets and hidden faces. He hoped not.

'Are you sure nothing's wrong?' she asked. 'You're really spaced.'

'I'm fine. This is good. Thank you.'

'Penny called tonight. She's got two people interested, so she's going to have an open house on Sunday.'

He nodded, still eating.

'Maybe we could go somewhere for the day. I don't want to be here when she brings them through. We could even leave Saturday and go overnight somewhere. You could get away from all of this. Maybe Lone Pine would be good.'

'That sounds good. But let's see what happens.'

After she left the kitchen for the bedroom, Bosch called the bureau and Edgar picked up. Bosch deepened his voice and said, 'Yeah, you know that thing you showed on TV. The one that gots no name?'

'Yes, can you help us?'

'Sure can.'

Bosch covered his mouth with his hand to hold back the laughter. He realized he hadn't thought of a good punch line. His mind raced as he tried to decide what it should be.

'Well, who is it, sir?' Edgar said impatiently.

'It – it's – it's . . .'

'It's who?'

'It's Harve Pounds in drag!'

Bosch burst out laughing and Edgar easily guessed who it was. It was stupid, not even funny, but they both laughed.

'Bosch, what do you want?'

It took him some time to stop laughing. He finally said, 'Just checking in. Did you call Ray Mora?'

'Nah, I called over to Ad-Vice and they said he wasn't working tonight. I was going to talk to him tomorrow. How'd you do?'

'I think I've got a name. I'll give Mora a call at home so he can pull what they have on her first thing.'

He told Edgar the name and heard the other detective laugh.

'Well, at least it's original. How – what makes you think it's her?'

Bosch answered in a low voice in case his voice was carrying to the bedroom.

'I saw a loop and I have a box from a video with her picture on it. It looks like the plaster face you got. A little off on the wig. But I think it's her. I'll drop the box off on your desk on my way into court tomorrow.'

'Cool.'

'Maybe Mora can get an early start on getting her real name and prints over to you. She probably had an adult entertainment license. All right if I call him?'

'That's cool. You know him.'

They hung up. Bosch didn't have a home number for

Mora. He called Detective Services and gave his name and badge number and asked to be put through. It took about five minutes and then Mora answered after three rings. He seemed out of breath.

'It's Bosch, you gotta minute?'

'Bosch, yeah, Bosch, what's up, man?'

'How's business?'

'Still sucks.'

He laughed at what Bosch guessed was an insider's joke.

'Actually, it goes further down all the time – no pun intended. Video ruined it, Bosch. Made it too big. The industry got big, the quality got small. Nobody cares about quality anymore.'

Mora was talking more like a supporter of the porno industry than a watchdog.

'I miss the days when it was in those smoky theaters on Cahuenga and Highland. We had a better handle on things then. At least, I did. So how's court? I hear you guys caught another one that looks like the Dollmaker. What's going on with that? How could –'

'That's why I'm calling. I've got a name – I think she was from your side of the tracks. The victim.'

'Give it to me.'

'Magna Cum Loudly. Maybe known as Maggie, too.'

'Yeah, I've heard that one. She was around a while ago and then, you're right, she disappeared or dropped out.'

Bosch waited for more. He thought he heard a voice in the background – in person or on TV and Mora told him to hold on a minute. He couldn't make out what had been said or whether it was a man or a woman. It made him wonder what Mora had been doing when he called. There were rumors floating around the department about Mora having gotten too close to the subject he was expert in. It was a common cop malady. Still, he knew Mora had successfully fended off any attempts to transfer him in the early years of his assignment. Now, he had so much expertise, it would be ridiculous to move him. It would be like taking Orel

Hershiser off the Dodgers pitching staff and putting him in the outfield. He was good at what he did. He had to be left there.

'Um, Harry, I don't know. I think she was around a couple years ago. What I'm saying is, if it's her, then it couldn't have been Church. You know what I'm saying? I don't know how that plays with what you've got working on this.'

'Don't worry about it, Ray. If Church didn't do her, somebody else did. We still gotta get him.'

'Right. So I'll get on it. By the way, how'd you make her?'

Bosch told him about his visit to X Marks the Spot.

'Yeah, I know them guys. The big one, that's Carlo Pinzi the capo's nephew, Jimmie Pinzi. They call him Jimmie Pins. He may act big and dumb but he's really the little guy Pinkie's boss. Watches over the place for his uncle. The little one's called Pinkie on account of those glasses he wears. Pinkie and Pins. It's all an act. Anyway, they charged you about forty beans too many for that video.'

'That's what I guessed. Oh, and I was going to ask you, there's no copyright on the video box. Would that be on the video or is there any way I can figure out when this was made?'

'Usually they don't put the copyright on the box. Customers want fresh meat. So the players figure the customer sees a copyright on the box that's a couple years old, then they'll buy something else. It's a fast business. Perishable goods. So no dates. Sometimes they're not even on the video cartridge. Anyway, I've got catalogs at the office going back twelve years. I can find a date, no problem.'

'Thanks, Ray. I might not make it by. A guy from the homicide table, Jerry Edgar, might come by to see you. I got court.'

'That's fine, Harry.'

Bosch had nothing else to ask and was about to say goodbye when Mora spoke in the silence.

'You know, I think about it a lot.'

'What?'

'The task force. I wish I hadn't taken off early that night and I was there with you. Who knows, maybe we'd have gotten this guy alive.'

'Yeah.'

'Be no trial then – I mean, for you.'

Bosch was silent as he looked at the picture on the back of video box. The woman's face turned to the side, just like the plaster face. It was her. He felt sure of it.

'Ray, with only this name – Magna Cum Loudly – can you still get a real name, get prints?'

'Sure can. No matter what anybody thinks of the product, there is legit stuff and illegit stuff out there. This girl Maggie looks like she had graduated to the legit world. She was out of loops and that shit and was in mainstream adult video. That means she probably had an agent, had an adult entertainment license. They gotta get 'em to prove they're eighteen. So her license will have her real name on it. I can go through them and find her – they got their pictures on them. Might take me a couple hours but I can find her.'

'Okay, good, will you do that in the morning and, if Edgar doesn't come by, get the prints to him at Hollywood homicide?'

'Jerry Edgar. I'll do it.'

Neither spoke for a few moments as they thought about what they were doing.

'Hey, Harry?'

'Yeah.'

'The paper said that there was a new note, that true?'

'Yeah.'

'Is it legit? Did we fuck up?'

'I don't know yet, Ray, but I appreciate you saying "we". A lot of people just want to point at me.'

'Yeah, listen, I ought to tell you, I got subpoenaed today by that Money bitch.'

It didn't surprise Bosch, since Mora had been on the Dollmaker task force.

'Don't worry about it. She's probably papered everybody who was on the task force.'

'Okay.'

'But try to keep this new stuff under your hat if you can.'

'As long as I can.'

'She's got to know what to ask before she can ask it. I'm just looking for some time to work with this, see what it means.'

'No problem, man. You and I both know the right guy went down. No doubt about that, Harry.'

But saying it out loud like that put a doubt to it, Bosch knew. Mora was wondering the same things Bosch was.

'You need me to drop this video box off tomorrow so you know what she looks like before flipping through the files?'

'No, like I said, we've got all sorts of catalogs. I'll just look up *Tails from the Crypt* and get it from there. If that don't work I'll go through the agency books.'

They hung up and Bosch lit a cigarette, though Sylvia didn't like him doing it in the house. It wasn't that she had a problem with his smoking but she thought potential buyers might be turned off if they thought it had been a smoker's house. He sat there alone for several minutes, peeling the label off the empty beer bottle and thinking about how quickly things could change. Believe something for four years and then find out you might be wrong.

He brought a bottle of Buehler zinfandel and two glasses into the bedroom. Sylvia was in bed with the covers pulled up to her naked shoulders. She had a lamp on and was reading a book called *Never Let Them See You Cry*. Bosch walked to her side of the bed and sat down next to her. He poured out two glasses, they tapped them together and sipped.

'To victory in court,' she said.

'Sounds good to me.'

They kissed.

'Were you smoking out there again?'

'Sorry.'

'Was it bad news? The calls?'

'No. Just bullshit.'

'You want to talk?'

'Not now.'

He went into the bathroom with his glass and took a quick shower. The wine, which had been beautiful, tasted terrible after he brushed his teeth. When he came out, the reading light was out and the book put away. There were candles burning on both night tables and the bureau. They were in silver votive candle holders with crescent moons and stars cut out on the sides. The flickering flames threw blurry, moving patterns on the walls and curtains and in the mirror, like a silent cacophony.

She lay propped on three pillows, the covers off. He stood naked at the foot of the bed for a few moments and they smiled at each other. She was beautiful to him, her body tan and almost girlish. She was thin, with small breasts and a small, flat stomach. Her chest was freckled from too many summer days at the beach while growing up.

He was eight years older and knew he looked it, but he was not ashamed of his physical appearance. At forty-three, he still had a flat stomach and his body was still ropey with muscles – muscles not created on machines but by lifting the day-to-day weight of his life, his mission. His body hair was curiously going to gray at a much faster pace than the hair on his head. Sylvia often would kid him about this, accusing him of having dyed his hair, of having a vanity they both knew he did not have.

When he climbed onto the bed next to her she ran her fingers over his Vietnam tattoo and the scars a bullet had left on his right shoulder a few years earlier. She traced the surgery zipper the way she did every time they were together here.

'I love you, Harry,' she said.

He rolled onto her and kissed her deeply, letting her taste

of red wine and the feel of her warm skin take him away from worry and the images of violent ends. He was in the temple of home, he thought but did not say. I love you, he thought but did not say.

NINE

For everything that had gone well for Bosch on Tuesday, the following morning provided a fresh undoing. The first disaster occurred in Judge Keyes's chambers, where he convened lawyers and clients after studying the note from the alleged Dollmaker in private for a half hour. His private reading had come after Belk had argued for an hour against the inclusion of the note in the trial.

'I have read the note and considered the arguments,' he said. 'I cannot see how this letter, note, poem, whatever, can possibly be withheld from this jury. It is so on point to the thrust of Ms Chandler's case that it is the point. I'm not making any judgment on whether it's for real or from some crackpot, that will be for the jury to figure out. If they càn. But because the investigation is still underway is no reason to withhold this. I am granting the subpoena and, Ms Chandler, you can introduce this at the appropriate time, provided you've put down the proper foundation. No pun intended. Mr Belk, your exception to this ruling will be noted for the record.'

'Your Honor?' Belk tried.

'No, we'll have no more argument on it. Let's move on out to court.'

'Your Honor! We don't know who wrote this. How can you allow it into evidence when we don't have the slightest idea where it came from or who sent it?'

'I know the ruling is a disappointment, so I'm allowing you some leeway as far as not coming down on you for that showing of your apparent disrespect for the wishes of this court. I said no more argument, Mr Belk, so I'll go over this only one time. The fact that this note of unknown origin led directly to the discovery of a body bearing all the similarities of a Dollmaker victim is in itself a verification of some authenticity. This is no prank, Mr Belk. No joke. There is something here. And the jury is going to see it. Let's go. Everybody out.'

Court had no sooner been called into session than the next debacle occurred. Belk, perhaps dazed by his defeat in chambers, waltzed into a trap Chandler had deftly set for him.

Her first witness of the day was a man named Wieczorek, who testified that he knew Norman Church quite well and was sure he had not committed the eleven murders attributed to him. Wieczorek and Church had worked together for twelve years in the design lab, he said. Wieczorek was in his fifties, with white hair trimmed so short his pink scalp showed through.

'What makes you so confident in your belief that Norman was not a killer?' Chandler asked.

'Well, for one thing, I know for a fact he didn't kill one of those girls, the eleventh, because he was with me the whole time she was getting . . . whatever. He was with me. Then the police kill him and pin eleven murders on him. Well, I figure, if I know he didn't kill one of those girls, then they are probably lying about the rest. The whole thing is a cover-up for them killing –'

'Thank you, Mr Wieczorek,' Chandler said.

'Just saying what I think.'

Belk stood and objected anyway, going to the lectern and whining that the entire answer was speculation. The judge agreed but the damage was done. Belk strode back to his chair and Bosch watched him leaf through a thick transcript of a deposition taken of Wieczorek a few months earlier.

Chandler asked a few more questions about where the witness and Church were on the night the eleventh victim was murdered and Wieczorek answered that they were at his own apartment with seven other men holding a bachelor party for a fellow employee from the lab.

'How long was Norman Church at your apartment?'

'The whole time of the party. I'd say from nine o'clock on. We finished up after two in the morning. The police said that girl, the eleventh one, went to some hotel at one and got herself killed. Norman was with me at one o'clock in the morning.'

'Could he have slipped away for an hour or so without you realizing it?'

'No way. You're in a room with eight guys and you know if one mysteriously disappears for a half hour.'

Chandler thanked him and sat down. Belk leaned to Bosch and whispered, 'I wonder what he's going to do with the new asshole I'm going to tear him.'

He got up armed with the deposition transcript and lumbered to the lectern as if he were lugging an elephant rifle. Wieczorek, who wore thick glasses that magnified his eyes, watched him suspiciously.

'Mr Wieczorek, do you remember me? Remember the deposition I took of you a few months back?'

Belk held the transcript up, as a reminder.

'I remember you,' Wieczorek said.

'Ninety-five pages, Mr Wieczorek. Nowhere in this transcript is there any mention of any bachelor party. Why is that?'

'I guess because you didn't ask.'

'But you didn't bring it up, did you? The police are saying your best buddy murdered eleven women, you supposedly know that's a lie, but you don't say a thing, is that right?'

'Yeah, that's right.'

'Care to tell us why?'

'Far as I was concerned, you were part of it. I only answered what I was asked. I wasn't volunteering shi – uh, nothing.'

'Let me ask you, did you ever tell the police this? Back

then, back when Church was killed and all the headlines said he killed eleven women? Ever pick up the phone one time and tell them they got the wrong guy?'

'No. At the time I didn't know. It was only when I read a book that came out on the case a couple years ago and there were details in there about when that last girl got killed. Then I knew he was with me during that whole time. I called the police and asked for the task force and they said it was disbanded long ago. I left a message for that fellow the book said was in charge, Lloyd, I think it was, and he never called me.'

Belk exhaled into the lectern's microphone, creating a loud sigh that indicated his weariness in dealing with this moron.

'So, if I can recap, you are telling this jury that two years after the murders, when this book came out, you read it and immediately realized you had an ironclad alibi for your dead friend. Am I missing anything, Mr Wieczorek?'

'Uh, just the part about suddenly realizing. It wasn't sudden.'

'Then what was it?'

'Well, when I read the date – September 28 – it set me to thinking and I just remembered that the bachelor party was on September 28 that year and Norman was there at my house all that time. So then I verified it and called Norman's wife to tell her he wasn't what they said he was.'

'You verified it? With the others at the party?'

'No, didn't have to.'

'Then how, Mr Wieczorek?' Belk asked in an exasperated tone.

'I looked at the video I had of that night. It had the date and time down in the corner of the frame.'

Bosch saw Belk's face turn a lighter shade of pale. The lawyer looked at the judge, then down at his pad, then back up at the judge. Bosch felt his heart sink. Belk had broken the same cardinal rule Chandler had broken the day before. He had asked a question for which he didn't already know the answer.

It didn't take a lawyer to know that since it was Belk who had drawn out mention of the videotape, Chandler was now free to explore it, to move to introduce the videotape as evidence. It had been a clever trap. Because it was new evidence from Wieczorek, not contained in his deposition, Chandler would have had to inform Belk earlier if she planned to draw it out on direct examination. Instead, she had skillfully allowed Belk to blunder in and draw it out. He now stood there defenseless, hearing it for the first time along with the jurors.

'Nothing further,' Belk said and returned to his seat with his head down. He immediately pulled one of the law books on the table onto his lap and began paging through it.

Chandler went to the lectern for redirect.

'Mr Wieczorek, this tape you mentioned to Mr Belk, do you still have it?'

'Sure, brought it with me.'

Chandler then moved to have the tape shown to the jury. Judge Keyes looked at Belk, who lumbered slowly to the lectern.

'Your Honor,' Belk managed to say, 'can defense have a ten-minute recess to research case law?'

The judge glanced at the clock.

'It's a little early, isn't it, Mr Belk? We just started.'

'Your Honor,' Chandler said. 'The plaintiff has no objection. I'll need time to set up the video equipment.'

'Very well,' the judge said. 'Ten minutes for counsel. The jury can take a fifteen-minute break and then report back to the assembly room.'

While they stood for the jury, Belk was flipping pages in the heavy law book. And when it was time to sit down, Bosch pulled his chair close to his lawyer's.

'Not now,' Belk said. 'I've got ten minutes.'

'You fucked up.'

'No, we fucked up. We are a team. Remember that.'

Bosch left his teammate there while he went out to smoke a cigarette. When he got to the statue, Chandler was already there. He lit a smoke anyway and kept his distance. She looked at him and smirked. Bosch spoke.

'You tricked him, didn't you?'

'Tricked him with the truth.'

'Is it?'

'Oh, yeah.'

She put a half-smoked cigarette in the sand of the ash can and said, 'I better get back in there and get the equipment set up.'

She smirked again. Bosch wondered if she was that good or it was Belk who was that bad.

Belk lost his half-hour argument to keep the tape from being introduced. He said that since it was not brought up during deposition, it was new evidence which the plaintiff could not submit at so late a date. Judge Keyes denied his claim, pointing out what everyone knew, that it had been Belk who had brought the tape to light.

After the jury was brought back in, Chandler asked Wieczorek several questions about the tape and where it had been for the last four years. After Judge Keyes dismissed one more objection from Belk, she rolled a TV/VCR combination to a position in front of the jury box and put in the tape, which Wieczorek had retrieved from a friend sitting in the gallery. Bosch and Belk had to stand up and move into the gallery seats to get a view of the TV screen.

As he made the move, Harry saw Bremmer from the *Times* sitting in one of the back rows. He gave a small nod to Bosch. Harry wondered if he was there to cover the trial or because he was subpoenaed.

The tape was long and boring but was not continuous. It was stopped and started during the evening of the bachelor party but the digital readout in the lower right corner kept the time and date. If it was correct, it was true that Church had an alibi for the last killing attributed to him.

It was dizzying for Bosch to watch. There was Church, no toupee, bald as a baby, drinking beer and laughing with his friends. The man Bosch had killed, toasting a friend's marriage, looking like the All American nerd that Bosch knew he had not been.

The tape lasted ninety minutes, climaxing with a visit from a telegram stripper who sang a song to the groom-to-be, dropping lingerie on his head as she removed each piece. In the video, Church seemed embarrassed to be seeing this, his eye more on the groom than on the woman.

Bosch pulled his eyes from the screen to watch the jury and he could see the tape was devastating to his defense. He looked away.

After the tape was finished, Chandler had a few more questions for Wieczorek. They were questions Belk would have asked but she was beating him to the punch.

'How is the date and time set on the video frame?'

'Well, when you buy it, you set it. Then the battery keeps it going. Never had to fiddle with it after I bought it.'

'But if you wanted to, you could put in any date you wanted, anytime you wanted, correct?'

'I s'pose.'

'So, say you were going to take a video of a friend to be used later as an alibi, could you set the date back, say a year, and then take the video?'

'Sure.'

'Could you put a date on an already existing video?'

'No. You can't superimpose a date over an existing video. Doesn't work that way.'

'So, in this case, how could you do it? How could you make a phony alibi for Norman Church?'

Belk stood up and objected on the grounds that Wieczorek's answer would be speculation, but Judge Keyes overruled him, saying the witness had expertise with his own camera.

'Well, you couldn't do that now 'cause Norman's dead,' Wieczorek said.

'So what you are saying is that in order to make a phony

tape you would have to have conspired with Mr Church to make it before he was killed by Mr. Bosch, correct?'

'Yes. We'd have to have known that somewhere down the line he'd need this tape and he'd have to've told me what date to set it on and so on and so forth. It's all pretty farfetched, especially because you can pull the newspapers from that year and find the wedding announcement that says my friend got married September thirtieth. That'll show you that his bachelor party had to have been the twenty-eighth or thereabouts. It's not a phony.'

Judge Keyes agreed with Belk's objection to the last sentence as being nonresponsive to the question and told the jury to disregard it. Bosch knew they didn't need to have heard it. They all knew the tape wasn't a phony. He did, too. He felt clammy and sick. Something had gone wrong but he didn't know what. He wanted to get up and walk out but he knew that to do so would be an admission of guilt so loud the walls would shake as if during an earthquake.

'One last question,' Chandler said. Her face had become flushed as she rode this one to victory. 'Did you ever know Norman Church to wear a hairpiece of any kind?'

'Never. I knew him a lot of years and I never saw or heard of such a thing.'

Judge Keyes turned the witness back over to Belk, who lumbered to the lectern without his yellow pad. He was apparently too flustered by this turnabout to remember to say, 'Just a few questions.' Instead he got right to his meager damage-control effort.

'You say you read a book about the Dollmaker case and then discovered this tape's date matched one of the killings, is that right?'

'That's right.'

'Did you look into finding alibis for the other ten murders?'

'No, I didn't.'

'So. Mr Wieczorek, you have nothing to offer in terms

of defending your longtime friend against these other cases
a task force of numerous officers connected to him?'

'The tape put the lie to all of 'em. Your task –'

'You're not answering the question.'

'Yes I am, you show the lie on one of the cases, it puts a lie
to the whole shooting match, you ask me.'

'We're not asking you, Mr. Wieczorek. Now, uh, you
said you never saw Norman Church wear a hairpiece,
correct?'

'That's what I said, yes.'

'Did you know he kept that apartment, using a false
name?'

'No, I did not.'

'There was a lot you didn't know about your friend,
wasn't there?'

'I suppose.'

'Do you suppose it is possible that just as he had that
apartment without you knowing, that he occasionally wore
a hairpiece without you knowing?'

'I suppose.'

'Now, if Mr. Church was the killer police claim him to
be, and used disguises as police said the killer did, wouldn't
it be –'

'Objection,' Chandler said.

' – expected that there would be something such –'

'Objection!'

' – as a toupee in the apartment?'

Judge Keyes sustained Chandler's objection to Belk's
question as seeking a speculative answer, and chastised Belk
for continuing the question after the objection was lodged.
Belk took the berating and said he had no further questions.
He sat down, sweat lines gliding out of his hairline and
running down his temples.

'Best you could do,' Bosch whispered.

Belk ignored it, took out a handkerchief and wiped his
face.

After accepting the videotape as evidence, the judge

broke for lunch. After the jury was out of the courtroom a handful of reporters quickly moved up to Chandler. Bosch watched this and knew it was the final arbiter of how things were going. The media always gravitated to the winners, the perceived winners, the eventual winners. It's always easier to ask them questions.

'Better start thinking of something, Bosch,' Belk said. 'We could have settled this six months ago for fifty grand. Way things are going, that would have been nothing.'

Bosch turned and looked at him. They were at the railing behind the defense table.

'You believe it, don't you? The whole thing. I killed him, then we planted everything that connected him to it.'

'Doesn't matter what I believe, Bosch.'

'Fuck you, Belk.'

'Like I said, you better start thinking of something.'

He pushed his wide girth through the gate and headed out of the courtroom. Bremmer and another reporter approached him but he waved them away. Bosch followed him out a few moments later and also brushed the reporters off. But Bremmer kept stride with him as he took the hallway to the escalator.

'Listen, man, my ass is on the line here, too. I wrote a book about the guy and if it was the wrong guy, I want to know.'

Bosch stopped and Bremmer almost bumped into him. He looked closely at the reporter. He was about thirty-five, overweight, with brown, thinning hair. Like many men, he made up for this by growing a thick beard, which only served to make him look older. Bosch noticed that the reporter's sweat had stained the underarms of his shirt. But body odor wasn't his problem; cigarette breath was.

'Look, you think it's the wrong guy, then write another book and get another hundred thousand advance. What do you care if it's the wrong guy or not?'

'I have a reputation in this town, Harry.'

'So did I. What are you going to write tomorrow?'

'I have to write what's going down in there.'

'And you're also testifying? Is that ethical, Bremmer?'

'I'm not testifying. She released me from the subpoena yesterday. I just had to sign a stipulation.'

'To what?'

'That said that to the best of my knowledge the book I wrote contained true and accurate information. The source of that information was almost wholly from police sources and police and other public records.'

'Speaking of sources, who told you about the note for yesterday's story?'

'Harry, I can't reveal that. Look at how many times I've kept you confidential as a source. You know I can never reveal sources.'

'Yeah, I know that. I also know somebody is setting me up.'

Bosch stepped onto the escalator and went down.

TEN

Administrative Vice is located on the third floor of the
Central Division station in downtown. Bosch got there in
ten minutes and found Ray Mora behind his desk in the
squad room, with the telephone held to his ear. Open on his
desk was a magazine with color photographs of a couple
engaged in sex. The girl in the photos looked very young.
Mora was glancing at the photos and turning the pages
while listening to the caller. He nodded to Bosch and
pointed to a seat in front of his desk.

'Well, that was all I was checking,' Mora said into the
phone. 'Just trying to put a line in the water. Ask around
and let me know what you come up with.'

Then there was more listening. Bosch looked at the vice
cop. He was about Harry's size, with deep bronze skin and
brown eyes. His straight brown hair was trimmed short and
he had no facial hair. Like most vice cops, he affected a
casual appearance. Blue jeans and black polo shirt, open at
the neck. If Bosch could see under the desk he knew he'd
find cowboy boots. Bosch could see a gold medallion
hanging high on his chest. Imprinted on it was a dove, its
wings open, the symbol of the Holy Spirit.

'You think you can get me the shoot location?'

Silence. Mora finished with the magazine, wrote something on the front cover and picked up another and began
paging through it.

Bosch noticed the Adult Film Performers Guild calendar
taped to the side of a vertical file on his desk. There was a
photo of a porn star named Delta Bush lounging nude above

116

the days of the week. She had become well known in recent years because she was linked romantically in the gossip tabs to a mainline movie star. On the desk below the calendar was a religious statue Bosch identified as the Infant of Prague.

He knew this because one of his foster mothers had given him a similar statue when he was a boy and was being sent back to McClaren. He hadn't been what the fosters had in mind. Giving him the statue and saying good-bye, the woman had explained to him that the infant was known as the Little King, the saint who took special care to hear the prayers of children. Bosch wondered if Mora knew that story, or if the statue was there as some kind of joke.

'All I'm saying is try,' Mora said into the phone. 'Get me the shoot. Then you'll be in line for the snitch fund . . . Yeah, yeah. Later.'

He hung up.

'Hey, Harry, whereyat?'

'Edgar's been here, huh?'

'Just left a little while ago. He talk to you?'

'No.'

Mora noticed Bosch looking at the spread on the page he had the magazine open to. It was two women kneeling in front of a man. He put a yellow Post-it on the page and closed it.

'Lord, I gotta look through all this shit. Got a tip that this publisher is using underage models. You know how I check?'

Bosch shook his head.

'It's not the face or the tits. It's ankles, Harry.'

'Ankles.'

'Yeah, ankles. Something about them. They are just smoother on younger chicks. I can usually tell, over or under eighteen, by the ankles. Then, of course, I go out and confirm with birth certificates, DLs, etc. It's crazy but it works.'

'Good for you. What did you tell Edgar?'

The phone rang. Mora picked up, said his name and listened a few moments.

'I can't talk now. I have to get back to you. Whereyat?'

He hung up after making a note.

'Sorry. I gave Edgar the ID. Maggie Cum Loudly. I had prints, photos, the whole thing. I got some stills of her in action, if you want to see.'

He pushed his chair back toward a file cabinet but Bosch told him never mind with the stills.

'Whatever. Anyway, Edgar has it all. Took prints to the coroner's I think, to confirm the ID. Chick's name was Rebecca Kaminski. Becky Kaminski. Be twenty-three if she were alive today. Formerly of Chicago before she came on out to sin city for fame and fortune. What a waste, huh? She was a fine young piece, God bless her.'

Bosch felt uncomfortable with Mora. But this was not new. When they had worked the task force together, Harry had never had the feeling that the killings meant much to the vice detective. Didn't make much of a dent. Mora was just putting in his time, lending his help where it was needed. He definitely was good in his area of expertise, but it didn't seem to matter to him whether the Dollmaker was stopped or not.

Mora had a strange way of mingling gutter talk and Jesus talk. At first Bosch had thought he was simply playing the born-again line that was popular in the department a few years earlier, but he was never sure. He once saw Mora cross himself and say a silent prayer at one of the Dollmaker murder scenes. Because of the uneasiness Bosch felt, he had had little contact with Mora since the Norman Church shooting and the breakup of the task force. Mora went back to Ad-Vice and Bosch was shipped to Hollywood. Occasionally the two would see each other in the courthouse or at the Seven or the Red Wind. But even at the bars, they were usually with different groups and sat apart, taking turns sending beers back and forth.

'Harry, she was definitely among the living until at least

two years ago. That flick you came across, *Tails from the Crypt*, it was made two years ago. Means Church definitely didn't do her . . . Probably whoever sent the note did. I don't know if that is good or bad news for you.'

'I don't either.'

Church had a rock-solid alibi for the Kaminski killing; he was dead. With that added to the apparent alibi Wieczorek's video-tape provided Church for the eleventh killing, Bosch's sense of paranoia was turning to panic. For four years there had been no doubt for him about what he had done.

'So how's the trial going, anyway?' Mora asked.

'Don't ask. Can I use your phone?'

Bosch dialed Edgar's pager number and then punched in Mora's phone number. After he hung up to wait for the call back, he didn't know what else to say.

'The trial's a trial. You still supposed to testify?'

'I guess. I'm on for tomorrow. I don't know what she wants from me. I wasn't even there the night you took that bastard down.'

'Well, you were on the task force with me. That's good enough to drag you into it.'

'Well, we'll –'

The phone rang and Mora picked it up. He then passed it to Bosch.

'Whereyat, Harry?'

'I'm here with Mora. He filled me in. Anything on the prints?'

'Not yet. I missed my man at SID. Musta gone to lunch. So I left the prints there. Should have a confirmation later today. But I'm not waiting on it.'

'Where are you now?'

'Missing Persons. Trying to see if this girl ever got reported missing, now that I have a name to go with the body.'

'You gonna be there a while?'

'Just started. We're looking through hard copies. They only went to computer eighteen months ago.'

'I'll be over.'

'You got your trial, man.'

'I have some time.'

Bosch felt that he had to keep moving, to keep thinking. It was the only way to keep from examining the horror building in his mind, the possibility he had taken down the wrong man. He drove back to Parker Center and took the stairs down to the first subterranean level. Missing Persons was a small office inside the Fugitives section. Edgar was sitting on a desk, looking through a stack of white forms. Bosch recognized these as cases that were not even investigated after the reports had been made. They would have been in files if there had been any follow-up.

'Nothing so far, Harry,' Edgar said. He then introduced Bosch to Detective Morgan Randolph, who was sitting at a nearby desk. Randolph gave Bosch a stack of reports and he spent the next fifteen minutes looking through the pages, each one an individual story of someone's pain that had fallen on the deaf ears of the department.

'Harry, on the description, look for a tattoo above the ass,' Edgar said.

'How do you know?'

'Mora had some photos of Magna Cum Loudly. In action, as Mora says. And there's a tattoo – it's Yosemite Sam, you know, the cartoon? – to the left of the dimple over the left side of her ass.'

'Well, did you find that on the body?'

'Didn't notice it 'cause of the severe skin discoloration. But I didn't really look at the backside, either.'

'What's going on with that? I thought you said the cut was going to be done yesterday.'

'Yeah, that's what they said, but I called over and they're still backed up from the weekend. They haven't even prepped it yet. I called Sakai a little while ago and he's going to take a look in the freezer after lunch. Check on the tattoo.'

Bosch looked back at his stack. The recurrent theme was

the young ages of the missing people. LA was a drain which drew a steady stream of the nation's runaways. But there were many who disappeared from here as well.

Bosch finished his stack without seeing the name Rebecca Kaminski, her alias, or anyone that matched her description. He looked at his watch and knew he had to get back to court. He took another stack off Randolph's desk anyway and began to wade through it. As he searched, he listened to the banter between Edgar and Randolph. It was clear that they had known each other before this day's meeting. Edgar called him Morg. Bosch figured they might've known each other from the Black Peace Officers Association.

He found nothing in the second stack.

'I gotta go. I'm gonna be late.'

'Okay, man. I'll let you know what we find.'

'And the prints, too, okay?'

'You got it.'

Court was already in session when Bosch got to courtroom 4. He quietly opened the gate, went through and took his seat next to Belk. The judge eyed him disdainfully but said nothing. Bosch looked up to see Assistant Chief Irvin Irving in the witness seat. Money Chandler was at the lectern.

'Good going,' Belk whispered to him. 'Late for your own trial.'

Bosch ignored him and watched as Chandler began asking Irving general questions about his background and years on the force. They were preliminary questions; Bosch knew he couldn't have missed much.

'Look,' Belk whispered next. 'If you don't care about this, at least pretend you do for the jury's sake. I know we are only talking about taxpayers' money here, but act like it's going to be your own money they will be deciding to give.'

'I got tied up. It won't happen again. You know, I'm trying to figure out this case. Maybe that doesn't matter to you, since you've already decided.'

He leaned back in his chair to get away from Belk. He was reminded that he had not eaten lunch by a sharp signal of resentment from his stomach. He tried to concentrate on the testimony.

'As assistant chief, what does your command include?' Chandler asked Irving.

'I am presently the commanding officer of all detective services.'

'At the time of the Dollmaker investigation, you were one rank below. A deputy chief, correct?'

'Yes.'

'As such you were in charge of the Internal Affairs Division, correct?'

'Yes. IAD and Operations Bureau, which basically means I was in charge of managing and allocating the department's personnel.'

'What is the mission of the IAD, as it is known?'

'To police the police. We investigate all citizen complaints, all interior complaints of misconduct.'

'Do you investigate police shootings?'

'Not per se. There is an Officer Involved Shooting team that handles the initial investigation. After that, if there is an allegation of misconduct or any impropriety, it is forwarded to IAD for follow-up.'

'Yes, and what do you recall of the IAD investigation of the shooting of Norman Church by Detective Harry Bosch?'

'I recall all of it.'

'Why was it referred to IAD?'

'The shooting team determined that Detective Bosch had not followed procedures. The shooting itself was within departmental policy but some of his actions prior to the gunfire were not.'

'Can you be more specific?'

'Yes. Basically, he went there alone. He went to this man's apartment without backup, placing himself in danger. It ended in the shooting.'

'It's called cowboying it, isn't it?'

'I've heard the phrase. I don't use it.'

'But does it fit?'

'I wouldn't know.'

'You wouldn't know. Chief, would you know if Mr Church would be alive today if Detective Bosch had not created this situation by playing cow –'

'Objection!' Belk shrieked.

But before he could walk to the lectern to argue, Judge Keyes sustained the objection and told Chandler to avoid speculative questions.

'Yes, Your Honor,' she said pleasantly. 'Chief, basically what you have testified to is that Detective Bosch set in motion a series of events that ultimately ended with an unarmed man being killed, am I right?'

'That is incorrect. The investigation found no substantive indication or evidence that Detective Bosch deliberately set this scenario in motion. It was spur of the moment. He was checking out a lead. When it looked good, he should have called for backup. But he didn't. He went in. He identified himself and Mr Church made the furtive move. And here we are. That is not to say that the outcome would have been different had there been a backup. I mean, anybody who would disobey an order from a police officer holding a gun would probably do it with two officers holding guns.'

Chandler successfully had the last sentence of the answer struck from the record.

'To come to the conclusion that Detective Bosch did not intentionally set the situation into motion, did your investigators study all facets of the shooting?'

'Yes, indeed.'

'How about Detective Bosch, was he studied?'

'Unquestionably. He was rigorously questioned about his actions.'

'And about his motives?'

'His motives?'

'Chief, did you or any of your investigators know that Detective Bosch's mother was slain in Hollywood about thirty years ago by a killer who was never arrested? That prior to that, she had a record for multiple arrests for loitering?'

Bosch felt his skin go hot, as if klieg lights had been turned on him, and that everyone in the courtroom was staring at him. He was sure they were. But he looked only at Irving, who stared silently ahead, a palsied look on his face, the capillaries on either side of his nose flaring. When Irving didn't answer, Chandler prompted him.

'Did you know, Chief? It is referenced in Detective Bosch's personnel file. When he applied to the force, he had to say if he had ever been the victim of a crime. He lost his mother, he wrote.'

Finally, Irving said, 'No, I did not know.'

'I believe that loitering was a euphemism for prostitution in the 1950s, when Los Angeles was engaged in a denial of crime problems such as rampant prostitution on Hollywood Boulevard, is that correct?'

'I don't recall that.'

Chandler asked to approach the witness and handed Irving a thin stack of papers. She gave him nearly a minute to read through them. He furrowed his brow as he read and Bosch could not see his eyes. The muscles of his cheeks bunched together below his temples.

'What is that, Chief Irving?' Chandler asked.

'It is what we call a due diligence report detailing the investigation of a homicide. It is dated November 3, 1962.'

'What is a due diligence report?'

'Every unsolved case is looked at annually – we call it due diligence – until such time that we feel the prognosis for bringing the case to a successful conclusion is hopeless.'

'What is the victim's name and circumstances of her death?'

'Marjorie Phillips Lowe. She was raped and strangled, October 31, 1961. Her body was found in an alley behind Hollywood Boulevard between Vista and Gower.'

'What is the investigator's conclusion, Chief Irving?'

'It says that at this time, which was a year after the crime, there are no workable leads and prognosis for successful conclusion of the case is deemed hopeless.'

'Thank you. Now, one more thing, is there a box on the cover form listing next of kin?'

'Yes, it identifies the next of kin as Hieronymus Bosch. Next to that in brackets it says "Harry". A box marked "son" has been checked off.'

Chandler referred to her yellow pad for a few moments to let this information soak into the jury. It was so quiet Bosch could actually hear Chandler's pen scratching on the pad as she made a notation.

'Now,' she said, 'Chief Irving, would knowing about Detective Bosch's mother have caused you to take a closer look at this shooting?'

After a long moment of silence, he said, 'I can't say.'

'He shot a man suspected of doing almost the exact same thing that had happened to his mother – his mother's slaying being unsolved. Are you saying you don't know if that would have been germane to your investigation?'

'I, yes . . . I don't know at this time.'

Bosch wanted to put his head down on the table. He had noticed that even Belk had stopped scribbling notes and was just watching the interchange between Irving and Chandler. Bosch tried to shake off the anger he felt and concentrate on how Chandler had obtained the information. He realized she had probably gotten the P-file in a discovery motion. But the details of the crime and his mother's background would not be in it. She had most likely procured the due diligence report from the archives warehouse on a Freedom of Information petition.

He realized he had missed several questions to Irving. He began watching and listening again. He wished he had a lawyer like Money Chandler.

'Chief, did you or any IAD detectives go to the scene of the shooting?'

'No, we did not.'

'So your information about what happened came from members of the shooting team, who in turn got their information from the shooter, Detective Bosch, correct?'

'Essentially, yes.'

'You have no personal knowledge of the evidentiary layout: the toupee under the pillow, the cosmetics beneath the sink in the bathroom?'

'Correct. I was not there.'

'Do you believe all of that was there as I just stated?'

'Yes, I do.'

'Why?'

'It was all there in the reports – reports from several different officers.'

'But all originating with the information from Detective Bosch, correct?'

'To a degree. There were investigators swarming that place. Bosch didn't tell them what to write.'

'Before, as you say, they swarmed the place, how long was Bosch there alone?'

'I don't know.'

'Is that piece of information on any report that you know of?'

'I'm not sure.'

'Isn't it true, Chief, that you wanted to fire Bosch and refer this shooting to the district attorney's office for the filing of criminal charges against him?'

'No, that is wrong. The DA looked at it and passed. It's routine. They said it was within policy, too.'

Well, score one for me, Bosch thought. It was the first misstep he had seen her take with Irving.

'What happened to the woman who gave Bosch this tip? Her name was McQueen. I believe she was a prostitute.'

'She died about a year later. Hepatitis.'

'At the time of her death was she part of an ongoing investigation of Detective Bosch and this shooting?'

'Not that I am aware of and I was in charge of IAD at the time.'

'What about the two IAD detectives who investigated the shooting? Lewis and Clarke, I believe their names were. Didn't they continue their investigation of Bosch long after the shooting had been determined officially to be within policy?'

Irving took a while to answer. He was probably leery of being led to slaughter again.

'If they conducted such an ongoing investigation it was without my knowledge or approval.'

'Where are those detectives now?'

'They are also dead. Both killed in the line of duty a couple years ago.'

'As the commander of IAD wasn't it your practice to initiate covert investigations of problem officers that you had marked for dismissal? Wasn't Detective Bosch one of those officers?'

'The answer to both questions is no. Unequivocally, no.'

'And what happened to Detective Bosch for his violation of procedures during the shooting of the unarmed Norman Church?'

'He was suspended for one deployment period and transferred within detective services to Hollywood Division.'

'In English, that means he was suspended for a month and demoted from the elite Robbery-Homicide squad to the Hollywood Division, correct?'

'You could say it that way.'

Chandler flipped a page up on her pad.

'Chief, if there were no cosmetics in the bathroom and no evidence that Norman Church was anything other than a lonely man who had taken a prostitute to his apartment, would Harry Bosch still be on the force? Would he have been prosecuted for killing this man?'

'I'm not sure I understand the question.'

'I'm asking, sir, did the alleged evidence tying Mr

Church to the killings that was allegedly found in his apartment save Detective Bosch? Did it not only save his job but save him from criminal prosecution?'

Belk stood up and objected, then walked to the lectern.

'She is asking him to speculate again, Your Honor. He can't tell what would have happened given an elaborate set of circumstances that didn't exist.'

Judge Keyes clasped his hands together in front of him and leaned back thinking. Then he abruptly leaned forward to the microphone.

'Ms Chandler is laying the groundwork to make a case that the evidence in the apartment was fabricated. I'm not saying whether she has adequately done this or not, but since that is her mission I think the question is answerable. I'm going to allow it.'

After some thought, Irving finally said, 'I can't answer that. I don't know what would have happened.'

ELEVEN

Bosch was able to smoke two cigarettes during the ten-minute recess that followed the end of Irving's testimony. On redirect Belk had asked only a few questions, trying to rebuild a fallen house with a hammer but no nails. The damage was done.

Chandler had so far used the day to skillfully plant the seeds of doubt about both Church and Bosch. The alibi for the eleventh killing opened the door to Church's possible innocence. And now she had subscribed a motive to Bosch's action: revenge for a murder more than thirty years old. By the end of the trial the seeds would be in full bloom.

He thought about what Chandler had said about his mother. Could she have been right? Bosch had never consciously considered it. It was always there – the idea of revenge – flickering in some part of his mind with the distant memories of his mother. But he had never taken it out and examined it. Why had he gone out there alone that night? Why hadn't he called one of the others back in – Mora or any of the investigators in his command?

Bosch had always told himself and others it was because he doubted the whore's story. But now, he knew, it was his own story he was beginning to doubt.

Bosch was so deep in these thoughts that he did not notice Chandler had come through the door until the flare of her lighter caught his eye. He turned and stared at her.

'I won't stay long,' she said. 'Just a half.'

'I don't care.'

He was almost done with the second cigarette.

'Who's next?'

'Locke.'

The USC psychologist. Bosch nodded, though he immediately saw this as a break from her good guy-bad guy pattern. Unless she counted Locke as a good guy.

'Well, you're doing good,' Bosch said. 'But I guess you don't need me to tell you that.'

'No, I don't.'

'You may even win – you probably will win, but ultimately you're wrong about me.'

'Am I? . . . Do you even know?'

'Yeah, I know. I know.'

'I have to go.'

She stubbed the cigarette out. It was less than half smoked. It would be a prize for Tommy Faraway.

Dr John Locke was a gray-bearded, bald and bespectacled man who looked as though he could have used a pipe to complete the picture of university professor and researcher of sexual behavior. He testified that he had offered his expertise to the Dollmaker task force after reading about the killings in the newspapers. He helped an LAPD psychiatrist draw up the first profiles of the suspect.

'Tell the jury about your expertise,' Chandler asked.

'Well, I am the director of the Psychohormonal Research Laboratory at USC. I am founder of that unit as well. I have conducted wide-ranging studies of sexual practice, paraphilia and psychosexual dynamics.'

'What is a paraphilia, doctor? In language we will all understand, please.'

'Well, in layman's terms, paraphilia are what are commonly referred to by the general public as sexual perversions – sexual behavior generally considered unacceptable by society.'

'Such as strangling your sex partner?'

'Yes, that would be one of them, big time.'

There was a polite murmur of humor in the courtroom

and Locke smiled. He seemed very at ease on the witness stand, Bosch thought.

'Have you written scholarly articles or books about these subjects you mentioned?'

'Yes, I have contributed numerous articles to research publications. I've written seven books on various subjects, sexual development of children, prepubescent paraphilia, studies of sadomasochism – the whole bondage thing, pornography, prostitution. My last book was on childhood development histories of deviant murderers.'

'So you've been around the block.'

'Only as a researcher.'

Locke smiled again and Bosch could see the jury warming to him. All twenty-four eyes were on the sex doctor.

'Your last book, the one on the murderers, what was it called?'

'*Black Hearts: Cracking the Erotic Mold of Murder.*'

Chandler took a moment to look at her notes.

'What do you mean by "erotic mold"?'

'Well, Ms Chandler, if I could digress a moment, I think I should fill in some background.'

She nodded her go-ahead.

'There are generally two fields, or two schools of thought, when it comes to the study of sexual paraphilia. I am what you call a psychoanalyst, and psychoanalysts believe that the root of paraphilia in an individual comes from hostilities nurtured in childhood. In other words, sexual perversions – in fact, even normal erotic interests – are formed in early childhood and then manifest in expressions as the individual becomes an adult.

'On the other hand, behaviorists view paraphilia as learned behaviors. An example being, molestation in the home of a child may trigger similar behavior by him as an adult. The two schools, for lack of a better word, are not that divergent. They are actually quite closer than psychoanalysts and behaviorists usually like to admit.'

He nodded and folded his hands together, seeming to have forgotten the original question.

'You were going to tell us about erotic molds,' Chandler prompted.

'Oh yes, I'm sorry, I lost the train there. Uh, the erotic mold is the description I use to cover the whole shebang of psychosexual desires that go into an individual's ideal erotic scene. You see, everybody has an ideal erotic scene. This could include the ideal physical attributes of a lover, the location, the type of sex act, the smell, taste, touch, music, whatever. Everything, all the ingredients that go into this individual achieving the ultimate erotic scene. A leading authority on this, out of Johns Hopkins University, calls it a "lovemap". It is sort of a guide to the ultimate scene.'

'Okay, now in your book, you applied it to sexual murderers.'

'Yes, with five subjects – all convicted of murder involving a sexual motivation or practice – I attempted to trace each man's erotic mold. To crack it open and trace the parts back to development in childhood. These men had damaged molds, so to speak. I wanted to find where the damage took place.'

'How did you pick your subjects?'

Belk stood up and made an objection and moved to the lectern.

'Your Honor, as fascinating as all of this is, I don't believe it is on point to this case. I will stipulate Dr Locke's expertise in this field. I don't think we have to go through the history of five other murderers. We are here in trial on a case about a murderer who is not even mentioned in Dr Locke's book. I am familiar with the book. Norman Church is not in it.'

'Ms Chandler?' Judge Keyes said.

'Your Honor, Mr Belk is correct about the book. It's about sadistic sex killers. Norman Church is not in it. But its significance to this case will be clear in the next set of questions. I think Mr Belk realizes this and that is the reason for his objection.'

'Well, Mr Belk, I think the time for an objection was probably about ten minutes ago. We are well into this line of questioning and I think we need to see it through now. Besides, you are correct about it being rather fascinating. Go on, Ms Chandler. The objection is overruled.'

Belk dropped back into his chair and whispered to Bosch, 'He's gotta be banging her.' It was said just loud enough that Chandler might have heard him, but not the judge. If she did, she showed nothing.

'Thank you, Your Honor,' she said. 'Dr Locke, Mr Belk and I were correct when we said that Norman Church was not one of the subjects of your study, were we not?'

'Yes, that is correct.'

'When did the book come out?'

'Just last year.'

'That would be three years after the end of the Dollmaker case?'

'Yes.'

'Well, having been part of the Dollmaker task force and obviously becoming familiar with the crimes, why didn't you include Norman Church in your study? It would seem to be an obvious choice.'

'It would seem that way but it wasn't. First of all, Norman Church was dead. I wanted subjects that were alive and cooperative. But incarcerated, of course. I wanted people that I could interview.'

'But of the five subjects you wrote about, only four are alive. What about the fifth, a man named Alan Karps, who was executed in Texas before you even began your book? Why not Norman Church?'

'Because, Ms Chandler, Karps had spent much of his adult life in institutions. There were voluminous public records on his treatment and psychiatric study. With Church there was nothing. He had never been in trouble before. He was an anomaly.'

Chandler looked down at her yellow pad and flipped a page, letting the point she just scored hang in the quiet courtroom like a cloud of cigarette smoke.

'But you did at least make preliminary inquiries about Church, didn't you?'

Locke hesitated before answering.

'Yes, I made a very preliminary inquiry. It amounted to contacting his family and asking his wife if she would grant me an interview. She turned me down. Since the man himself was dead and there were no records about him – other than the actual details of the murders, which I was already familiar with – I didn't pursue it. I went with Karps in Texas.'

Bosch watched Chandler cross several questions off on her legal pad and then flip several pages to a new set. He guessed that she was changing tack.

She said, 'While you were working with the task force you drew up a psychological profile of the killer, correct?'

'Yes,' Locke said slowly. He adjusted himself in the chair, straightening up for what he knew was coming.

'What was that based on?'

'An analysis of the crime scenes and method of homicide filtered through what little we know about the deviant mind. I came up with common attributes that I thought might be part of our suspect's makeup – no pun intended.'

No one in the courtroom laughed. Bosch looked around and saw that the spectator rows were becoming crowded. This must be the best show in the building, he thought. Maybe all of downtown.

'You were not very successful, were you? If Norman Church was the Dollmaker, that is.'

'No, not very successful. But that happens. It's a lot of guesswork. Rather than a testimonial to my failure, it is more a testimonial to how little we know about people. This man's behavior did not make so much as a blip on anybody's radar screen – not counting, of course, the women he killed – until the night he was shot.'

'You speak as if it is a given that Norman Church was the killer, the Dollmaker. Do you know that to be true based on indisputable facts?'

'Well, I know it to be true because it is what the police told me.'

'If you take it backwards, doctor. If you start with what you know about Norman Church now and leave out what the police have told you about the supposed evidence, would you ever believe him capable of what he has been accused of?'

Belk was about to stand up to object but Bosch strongly put his hand on his arm and held him down. Belk turned and looked angrily at him but by then Locke was answering.

'I wouldn't be able to count him in or out as a suspect. We don't know enough about him. We don't know enough about the human mind in general. All I know is, anybody is capable of anything. I could be a sexual killer. Even you, Ms Chandler. We all have an erotic mold and for most of us, it is quite normal. For some it may be a bit unusual but still only playful. For the others, on the extreme, who find they can only reach erotic excitement and fulfillment through administering pain, even killing their partners, it is buried deep and dark.'

Chandler was looking down at her pad and writing when he finished. When she didn't ask another question immediately, he continued unbidden.

'Unfortunately, the black heart is not worn on the sleeve. The victims who see it usually don't live to talk about it.'

'Thank you, Doctor,' Chandler said. 'I have nothing further.'

Belk plowed in without any preliminary soft-ball questions, a look of concentration on his wide florid face that Bosch had not seen previously.

'Doctor, these men with these so-called paraphilia, what do they look like?'

'Like anybody. There is no look that gives them away.'

'Yes, and are they always on the prowl? You know,

looking to indulge their aberrant fantasies by acting them out?'

'No, actually, studies have shown that these people obviously know they have aberrant tastes and they work to keep them in check. Those brave enough to come forward with their problems often lead completely normal lives with the aid of chemical and psychological therapy. Those that don't are periodically overcome by the compulsion to act out, and they may follow these urges and commit a crime.

'Psychosexually motivated serial killers often exhibit patterns that are quite repetitive, so that police tracking them can almost predict within a few days or a week when they will strike. This is because the buildup of stress, the compulsion to act, will follow a pattern. Often, what you have are decreasing intervals – the overpowering urge comes back sooner and sooner each time.'

Belk was leaning over the lectern, his weight firmly against it.

'I see, but between these moments of compulsion when the acts take place, does this man seem to have a normal life or, you know, is he standing in the corner, slobbering? Or whatever?'

'No, nothing like that – at least, until the intervals become so short that they literally don't exist. Then you might have someone out there always on the prowl, as you said. But between the intervals there is normalcy. The aberrant sexual act – rape, strangulation, voyeurism, anything – will provide the subject with the memory to construct fantasy. He will be able to use the act to fantasize and stimulate arousal during masturbation or normal sex.'

'Do you mean that he will sort of replay the murder in his mind so that he can become sexually aroused for having normal sexual intercourse with, say, his wife?'

Chandler objected and Belk had to rephrase the question so it was not leading Locke.

'Yes, he will replay the aberrant act in his mind so that he can accomplish the act that is socially acceptable.'

'So in doing so, a wife, for example, might not even know of her husband's real desires, correct?'

'That is correct. It has happened often.'

'And a person such as this could carry on at work and with friends and not reveal this side of himself, correct?'

'Again, that is correct. There is ample evidence of this in the case histories of sexual sadists who kill. Ted Bundy led a well-documented double life. Randy Kraft, killer of dozens of hitchhikers here in Southern California. I could name many, many more. You see, this is the very reason they kill so many victims before being caught, and then it is usually only because of a small mistake.'

'Like with Norman Church?'

'Yes.'

'As you testified earlier, you could not find or gather enough information about Norman Church's early development and behavior to include him in your book. Does that fact dissuade you from belief that he was the killer police claim him to be?'

'Not in the least. As I said, these desires can be easily cloaked in normal behavior. These people know they have desires that are not accepted by society. Believe me, they take pains to hide them. Mr Church was not the only subject I considered for the book and then discarded for lack of valuable information. I did preliminary studies of at least three other serial killers who were either dead or uncooperative and dropped them as well because of the lack of public record or background on them.'

'You mentioned earlier that the roots of these problems are planted in childhood. How?'

'I should have said "may", the roots may be planted in childhood. It is a difficult science and nothing is known for sure. Getting to your question, if I had a definite answer I guess I wouldn't have a job. But what psychoanalysts such as myself believe is that the paraphilia can come through emotional or physical trauma or both. It basically is a synthesis of these, possibly some biological determinants and social learning. It is hard to pinpoint, but we believe it happens very early, generally five to eight years of age. One of the fellows in my book was molested by an uncle at age three. My thesis, or belief or whatever you want to call it, is that this trauma set him on the trail toward becoming a murderer of homosexuals. In most of these killings he emasculated his victims.'

The courtroom had become so quiet during Locke's testimony that Bosch heard the slight bump of one of the rear doors opening. He glanced back and saw Jerry Edgar taking a seat in the rear row. Edgar nodded at Harry, who looked up at the clock. It was 4:15; the trial would be recessed for the day in fifteen minutes. Bosch figured Edgar was on his way back from the autopsy.

'Would the childhood trauma that's at the root of a person's criminal activities as an adult need to be so overt? In other words, as traumatic as molestation?'

'Not necessarily. It could be rooted in more traditional emotional stress placed on a child. The awesome pressure to succeed in a parent's eyes, coupled with other things. It is hard to discuss this in a hypothetical context because there are so many dimensions of human sexuality.'

Belk followed up with a few more general questions about Locke's studies before ending. Chandler asked a couple more questions on redirect but Bosch had lost interest. He knew that Edgar would not have come to the courtroom unless he had something important. Twice he glanced back at the clock on the wall and twice he looked at his watch. Finally, when Belk said he had nothing further on cross, Judge Keyes called it a day.

Bosch watched Locke step down and head out through the gate and toward the door. A couple of the reporters followed him. Then the jury stood and filed out.

Belk turned to Bosch as they watched and said, 'Better be ready tomorrow. My guess is that it's going to be your turn in the sun.'

*

'What've you got, Jerry?' Bosch asked when he caught up with Edgar in the hallway leading to the escalator.

'Your car over at Parker Center?'

'Yeah.'

'I'm there, too. Let's walk that way.'

They got on the escalator but didn't talk because it was crowded with spectators from the courtroom. Out on the sidewalk, when they were alone, Edgar pulled a folded white form out of his coat pocket and handed it to Bosch.

'All right, we got it confirmed. The prints Mora dug up on Rebecca Kaminski match the hand mold we made on the concrete blonde. I also just came from the autopsy and the tattoo is there, above the ass. Yosemite Sam.'

Bosch unfolded the paper. It was a photocopy of a standard missing person report.

'That's a copy of the report on Rebecca Kaminski, also known as Magna Cum Loudly. Missing twenty-two months and three days.'

Bosch was looking at the report.

'Doesn't look like any doubt to me,' he said.

'Nope, no doubt. It was her. The autopsy also confirms manual strangulation as the cause. The knot pulled tight on the right side. Most likely a lefty.'

They walked without talking for half a block. Bosch was surprised by how warm it was for so late in the day. Finally, Edgar spoke.

'So, obviously, we've got it confirmed; this may look like one of Church's dolls but there's no way in the world he did it unless he came back from the dead . . .

'So I did some checking at the bookstore over by Union Station. Bremmer's book, *The Dollmaker,* with all the details a copycat would need, was published in hardback seventeen months after you put Church in the dirt. Becky Kaminski goes missing about four months after the book came out. So our killer could've bought the book and then used it as a sort of blueprint on what to do to make it look like that Dollmaker.'

Edgar looked over at him and smiled.

'You're in the clear, Harry.'

Bosch nodded, but didn't smile. Edgar didn't know about the videotape.

They walked down Temple to Los Angeles Street. Bosch didn't notice the people around him, the homeless shaking their cups on the corners. He almost crossed Los Angeles in front of traffic until Edgar put a hand on his arm. While waiting for the walk sign, he looked down and scanned the report again. It was bare bones. Rebecca Kaminski had simply gone out on a 'date' and not returned. She was meeting the unnamed man at the Hyatt on Sunset. That was it. No follow-up, no additional information. The report had been made by a man named Tom Cerrone, who was identified in the report as Kaminski's roommate in Studio City. The light changed and they walked across Los Angeles Street and then right toward Parker Center.

'You going to talk to this Cerrone guy, the roommate?' he asked Edgar.

'I don't know. Probably get around to it. I'm more interested in what you think about all of this, Harry. Where do we go from here? Bremmer's book was a fuckin' bestseller. Anybody who read it is a suspect.'

Bosch said nothing until they got to the parking lot and stopped near the entrance booth before separating. Bosch looked down at the report in his hands and then up at Edgar.

'Can I keep this? I might take a run by the guy.'

'Be my guest . . . Another thing you should know, Harry.'

Edgar reached in his inside coat pocket and pulled out another piece of paper. This one was yellow and Bosch knew it was a subpoena.

'I got served at the coroner's office. I don't know how she knew I was there.'

'When d'you have to be in court?'

'Tomorrow at ten. I had nothing to do with the Dollmaker task force so we both know what she's going to ask about. The concrete blonde.'

TWELVE

Bosch threw his cigarette into the fountain that was part of the memorial to officers killed in the line of duty and walked through the glass doors into Parker Center. He badged one of the cops behind the front desk and walked around to the elevators. There was a red line painted on the black tile floor. That was the route visitors were told to take if they were going to the Police Commission hearing room. There was also a yellow line for Internal Affairs and a blue for applicants who wanted to become cops. It was a tradition for cops standing around waiting for elevators to stand on the yellow line, thereby making any citizens who were going to IAD – usually to file complaints – walk around them. This maneuver was usually accompanied by a baleful stare from cop to citizen.

Every time Bosch waited for an elevator he remembered the prank he had been partially responsible for while still in the academy. He and another cadet had come into Parker Center at four one morning, drunk and hiding paint brushes and cans of black and yellow paint in their windbreakers. In a quick and daring operation, his partner had used the black paint to obliterate the yellow line on the tile floor while Bosch painted a new yellow line which went past the elevators, down the hall, into a men's room and right to a urinal. The prank had given them near legendary status in their class, even among the instructors.

He got off the elevator on the third floor and walked back to the Robbery-Homicide Division. The place was empty. Most RHD cops worked a strict seven-to-three shift. That way the job didn't get in the way of all the moonlighting gigs they had lined up. RHD dicks were the cream of the department. They got all the best gigs. Chauffeuring visiting Saudi princes, security work for studio bosses, body-guarding Vegas high rollers – LVPD did not allow its people to moonlight, so the high-paying jobs fell to LAPD.

When Bosch had first been promoted to RHD there were still a few detective-threes around who had worked body-guard duty for Howard Hughes. They had spoken of the experience as if that was what the RHD job was all about, a means to an end, a way to get a job working for some deranged billionaire who didn't need any bodyguards because he never went anywhere.

Bosch walked to the rear of the room and turned on one of the computers. He lit a cigarette while the tube warmed up and took the report Edgar had given him out of his coat pocket. The report was nothing. It had never been looked at, acted on, cared about.

He noticed it was a walk-in – Tom Cerrone had come into the North Hollywood Division station and made the report at the front desk. That meant it had probably been written up by a probationary rookie or a burned-out vet who didn't give a shit. In either case, it was not taken for what it was: a cover-your-ass report.

Cerrone said he was Kaminski's roommate. According to the brief summary, two days before the report was made she had told Cerrone she was going on a blind date, meeting an unnamed man at the Hyatt on the Sunset Strip and that she hoped the guy wasn't a creep. She never came back. Cerrone got worried and went to the cops. The report was taken, passed through North Hollywood detectives where it didn't make a blip on anyone's screen and then sent to Missing Persons in downtown where four detectives are charged with finding the sixty people reported missing on average each week in the city.

In reality, the report was put in a stack of others like it and was not looked at again until Edgar and his pal, Morg, found it. None of this bothered Bosch, though anyone who spent two minutes reading the report should have known that Cerrone wasn't what he said he was. But Bosch figured Kaminski was dead and in the concrete long before the report was made. So there was nothing anyone could have done anyway.

He punched the name Thomas Cerrone into the computer and ran a search on the California Department of Justice information network. As he expected, he got a hit. The computer file on Cerrone, who was forty years old, showed he had been popped nine times in as many years for soliciting for prostitution and twice for pandering.

He was a pimp, Bosch knew. Kaminski's pimp. Harry noticed that Cerrone was on thirty-six months' probation for his last conviction. He got out his black telephone book and rolled his chair over to a desk with a phone. He dialed the after-hours number for the county probation department and gave the clerk who answered Cerrone's name and DOJ number. She gave back Cerrone's current address. The pimp had come down in the world, from Studio City to Van Nuys, since Kaminski had gone to the Hyatt and not come back.

After hanging up, he thought of calling Sylvia and wondered if he should tell her it was likely he would be called by Chandler to testify the next day. He was unsure if he wanted her to be there, to see him cornered on the witness stand by Money Chandler. He decided not to call.

Cerrone's home address was an apartment on Sepulveda Boulevard in an area where prostitutes were not too discreet about how they got their customers. It was still daylight and Bosch counted four young women spread apart over a two-block stretch. They wore halter tops and short shorts. They held their thumb out like hitchhikers when cars went by. But it was clear they were only interested in a ride around the corner to a parking lot where they could take care of business.

Bosch parked at the curb across from the Van-Aire Apartments, where Cerrone had told his probation officer he was living. A couple of the numbers from the address had fallen off the front wall but it was readable because the smog had left the rest of the wall a dingy beige. The place needed new paint, new screens, some plastering to fill in the cracks in the facade and probably new tenants.

Actually, it needed to be knocked down. Start over, Bosch thought as he crossed the street. Cerrone's name was on the residents list next to the front security door but no one answered the buzzer at apartment six. Bosch lit a cigarette and decided to hang around for a while. He counted twenty-four units on the residents list. It was six o'clock. People would be coming home for dinner. Someone would come along.

He walked away from the door and back out to the curb. There was graffiti on the sidewalk, all of it in black paint. The monikers of the local homeboys. There was also a scrip painted in block letters that asked, R U THE NEX RODDY KING? He wondered how someone could misspell a name that had been heard and printed so many times.

A woman and two young children came to the steel-grated door from the other side. Bosch timed his approach so that he was at the door just as she opened it.

'Have you seen Tommy Cerrone around?' he asked as he passed her.

She was too busy with the children to answer. Bosch walked into the courtyard to get his bearings and to look for a door with a six on it – Cerrone's apartment. There was graffiti on the concrete floor of the courtyard, a gang insignia Bosch couldn't make out. He found number six on the first floor toward the back. There was a rusted-out hibachi grill on the ground next to the door. There was also a child's bike with training wheels parked under the front window.

The bike didn't fit. Bosch tried to look in but the curtains were drawn, leaving only a three-inch band of darkness he could not see beyond. He knocked on the door and as was his practice, stepped to the side. A Mexican woman with what looked like an eight-month pregnancy beneath her faded pink bathrobe answered the door. Behind the small woman Bosch could see a young boy sitting on the living room floor in front of a black-and-white TV tuned to a Spanish language channel.

'Hola,' Bosch said. 'Señor Tom Cerrone aqui?'

The woman stared at him with frightened eyes. She seemed to close in on herself, as if to get smaller before him. Her arms moved up from her side and closed over her swollen belly.

'No migra,' Bosch said. 'Policia. Tomás Cerrone. Aqui?'

She shook her head no and began to close the door. Bosch put his hand out to stop it. Struggling with his Spanish he asked if she knew Cerrone and where he was. She said he only came once a week to collect the mail and the rent. She moved back a step and gestured to the card table where there was a small stack of mail. Bosch could see an American Express bill on top. Gold Card.

'Teléfono? Necesidad urgente?'

She looked down from his eyes and her hesitation told him she had a number.

'Por favor?'

She told him to wait and she left the doorway. While she was gone the boy sitting ten feet inside the door turned from the TV – Bosch could see it was some kind of game show – and looked at him. Bosch felt uncomfortable. He looked away, into the courtyard. When he looked back the boy was smiling. He had his hand up and was pointing a finger at Bosch. He made a shooting sound and giggled. Then the mother was back at the door with a piece of paper. There was a local phone number on it, that was all.

Bosch copied it down in a small notebook he carried and then told her he would take the mail. The woman turned and looked at the card table as if the answer to what she should do was sitting on it with the mail. Bosch told her it would be okay and she finally lifted the stack and handed it to him. The frightened look was in her eyes again.

He stepped back and was going to walk away when he stopped and looked back at her. He asked how much the rent was and she told him it was one hundred dollars a week. Bosch nodded and walked away.

Out on the street he walked down to a pay phone that was in front of the next apartment complex. He called the downtown communications center, gave the operator the phone number he had just gotten and said he needed an address. While he waited he thought about the pregnant woman and wondered why she stayed. Could things be worse back in the Mexican town she came from? For some, he knew, the journey here was so difficult that returning was out of the question.

As he was flipping through Cerrone's mail, one of the hitchhikers walked up to him. She wore an orange tank top over her surgically augmented breasts. Her cutoff jeans were cut so high above the thighs that the white pockets hung out below. In one of the pockets he could see the distinctive shape of a condom package. She had the gaunt, tired look of a strawberry – a woman who would do anything, anytime, anywhere to keep crack in her pipe. Factoring in her deteriorated appearance, he put her age at no more than twenty. To Bosch's surprise, she said, 'Hey, darling, looking for a date?'

He smiled and said, 'You're going to have to be more careful than that, you want to stay out of the cage.'

'Oh, shit,' she said and turned to walk away.

'Wait a minute. Wait a minute. Don't I know you? Yeah, I know you. It's . . . what's your name, girl?'

'Look, man, I'm not talking to you and I'm not blowing you, so I gotta go.'

'Wait. Wait. I don't want anything. I just thought, you know, that we'd met. Aren't you one of Tommy Cerrone's girls? Yeah, that's where I met you.'

The name put a slight stutter in her step. Bosch let the phone dangle by its cord and caught up to her. She stopped.

'Look, I'm not with Tommy anymore, okay? I gotta go to work.'

She turned from him and put her thumb out as a wave of southbound traffic started by.

'Wait a minute, just tell me something. Tell me where Tommy is these days. I need to get with him on something.'

'On what? I don't know where he is.'

'A girl. You remember Becky? Couple years ago. Blonde, liked red lipstick, had a set like yours. She mighta used the name Maggie. I want to find her and she was working for Tom. You remember her?'

'I wasn't even around then. And I haven't seen Tommy in four months. And you are full of shit.'

She walked off and Bosch called after her, 'Twenty bucks.'

She stopped and came back.

'For what?'

'An address. I'm not bullshitting. I want to talk to him.'

'Well, give it.'

He took the money out of his wallet and gave it to her. It occurred to him that Van Nuys Vice might be watching him from somewhere around here and wondering why he was giving a hooker a twenty.

'Try the Grandview,' she said. 'I don't know the number or anything but it's on the top floor. You can't tell'm I sent ya. He'll fuck me up.'

She walked away putting the money in one of the flapping pockets. He didn't have to ask her where the Grandview was. He watched her cut in between two apartment buildings and disappear, probably going to get a rock. He wondered if she had told the truth and why he could find it in himself to give her money but not the woman in apartment six. The police operator had hung up by the time he got back to the pay phone.

Bosch redialed and asked for her and she gave him the

147

address that went with the phone number he'd gotten. Suite P-1, the Grandview Apartments, on Sepulveda in Sherman Oaks. He had just wasted twenty bucks on crack cocaine. He hung up.

In the car, he finished looking through the mail. Half of it was junk mail, the rest credit card bills and mailers from Republican candidates. There was also a post card invitation to an Adult Film Performers Guild awards banquet in Reseda the following week.

Bosch opened the American Express bill. The illegality of this did not concern him in the least. Cerrone was a criminal who was lying to his probation officer. There would be no complaint from him. The pimp owed American Express $1855.05 this month. The bill was two pages, and Bosch noticed two billings for airline flights to Las Vegas and three billings from Victoria's Secret. Bosch was familiar with Victoria's Secret, having studied the mail-order lingerie catalog at Sylvia's on occasion. In one month, Cerrone had ordered nearly $400 in lingerie by mail. The money paid by the poor woman who rented the apartment Cerrone was using as a front for a probation address was basically subsidizing the lingerie bills of Cerrone's whores. It angered Bosch, but it gave him an idea.

The Grandview Apartments were the ultimate California ideal. Built alongside a shopping mall, the building afforded its tenants the ability to walk directly from their apartment into the mall, thereby cutting out the heretofore required middle ground for all Southern California culture and interaction: the car. Bosch parked in the mall's garage and entered the outer lobby through the rear entrance. It was an Italian marble affair with a grand piano in its center that was playing by itself. Bosch recognized the song as a Cab Calloway standard, 'Everybody That Comes to My Place Has to Eat.'

There was a directory and a phone on the wall by the

security door that led to the elevators. The name next to P-1 was Kuntz. Bosch took it to be an inside joke. He lifted the phone and pushed the button. A woman answered and he said, 'UPS. Gotta package.'

'Uh,' she said. 'From who?'

'Um, it says, I can't read the writing – looks like Victor's secretary or something.'

'Oh,' she said and he heard her giggle. 'Do I have to sign?'

'Yes, ma'am, I need a signature.'

Rather than buzz him in, she said she would come down. Bosch stood at the glass door for two minutes waiting before he realized the scam wouldn't work. He was standing there in a suit and had no package in his hand. He turned his back to the elevator just as the polished chrome doors began to part.

He took a step toward the piano and looked down as if he was fascinated by it and didn't notice the elevator's arrival. From behind him he heard the security door start to open and he turned around.

'Are you UPS?'

She was blonde and stunning even in her blue jeans and pale blue Oxford shirt. Their eyes met and right away Bosch knew she knew it was a scam. She immediately tried to close the door but Bosch got there in time and pushed his way through.

'What are you doing? I –'

Bosch clamped a hand over her mouth because he thought she was about to scream. Covering half her face accentuated the fright in her eyes. She didn't seem as stunning to Bosch anymore.

'It's okay. I'm not going to hurt you, I just want to talk to Tommy. Let's go up.'

He slowly pulled his hand back and she didn't scream.

'Tommy's not there,' she said in a whisper, as if to signal her cooperation.

'Then we can wait.'

He gently pushed her toward the elevator and punched the button.

She was right. Cerrone wasn't there. But Bosch didn't have to wait long. He had barely had time to check on the opulent furnishings of the two-bedroom, two-bath and loft apartment with private roof garden when the man arrived.

Cerrone stepped through the front door, *Racing Forum* in hand, just as Bosch stepped into the living room from the balcony that overlooked Sepulveda and the crowded Ventura Freeway.

Cerrone initially smiled at Bosch but then the face became blank. This often happened to Bosch with crooks. He believed it was because the crooks often thought they recognized him. And it was true they probably did. Bosch's picture had been in the paper and on TV several times in the last few years, including once this week. Harry believed that most crooks who read the papers or watched the news looked closely at the pictures of the cops. They probably thought it gave them an added advantage, someone to look out for. But instead it bred familiarity. Cerrone had smiled as though Bosch was a long-lost friend, then he realized it was probably the enemy, a cop.

'That's right,' Bosch said.

'Tommy, he made me bring him up,' the girl said. 'He called on the –'

'Shut up,' Cerrone barked. Then, to Bosch, he said, 'If you had a warrant, you wouldn't be here alone. No warrant, get the fuck out.'

'Very observant,' Bosch said. 'Sit down. I have questions.'

'Fuck you and the questions you rode in on. Get out.'

Bosch sat down on a black leather couch and took out his cigarettes.

'Tom, if I go, it's to go see your PO and see about getting you revoked for this address scam you're playing. The probation department frowns on cons telling them they live one place when they actually live somewhere else. Especially when one's a dump and one's the Grandview.'

Cerrone threw the *Forum* across the room at the girl.

'See?' he said. 'See the shit you got me in?'

She seemed to know better than to say anything. Cerrone folded his arms and stood in the living room but he wasn't going to sit down. He was a well-built guy gone to fat. Too many afternoons at Hollywood or Del Mar, sipping cocktails and watching the ponies.

'Look, what do you want?'

'I want to know about Becky Kaminski.'

Cerrone looked puzzled.

'You remember, Maggie Cum Loudly, the blonde with the tits you probably had her enlarge. You were bringing her up through the video business, doin' some outcall work on the side, and then she disappeared on you.'

'What about her? That was a long time ago.'

'Twenty-two months and three days, I am told.'

'So what? She turned up and is saying some shit about me, it don't matter. Take it to court, man. We'll see –'

Bosch jumped up off the couch and slapped him hard across the face, then pushed him over a black leather chair onto the floor. Cerrone's eyes immediately went to the girl's, which told Bosch that he had complete control of the situation. The power of humiliation sometimes was more awesome than a gun held to the head. Cerrone's face was a bright red all over.

Bosch's hand stung. He bent over the fallen man and said, 'She didn't turn up and you know it. She's dead and you knew it when you made the missing person report. You were just covering your ass. I want to know how you knew.'

'Look, man, I didn't have any –'

'But you knew she wasn't coming back. How?'

'I just had a hunch. She didn't turn up for a couple days.'

'Guys like you don't go to the police on hunches. Guys like you, they get their place broken into, they don't even call the cops. Like I said, you were just covering your ass. You didn't want to get blamed 'cause you knew she wasn't coming back alive.'

'Awright, awright, it was more than a hunch. Okay? It was the guy. I never saw him but his voice and some of the things he said. It was familiar, you know? Then after I sent her and she didn't come back, it dawned on me. I remembered him. I had sent him somebody else once and she ended up dead.'

'Who?'

'Holly Lere. I can't remember her real name.'

Bosch could. Holly Lere was the porno name of Nicole Knapp. The seventh victim of the Dollmaker. He sat back down on the couch and put a cigarette in his mouth.

'Tommy,' the girl said, 'he's smoking.'

'Shut the fuck up,' he said to her.

'Well, you said no smoking in here except on the bal –'

'Shut the fuck up!'

'Nicole Knapp,' Bosch said.

'Yeah, that's it.'

'You knew the cops said the Dollmaker got her?'

'Yeah, and I always thought that until Becky disappeared and I remembered this guy and what he said.'

'But you didn't tell anybody. You didn't call the cops.'

'It's like you said, man, guys like me, we don't call.'

Bosch nodded.

'What did he say? The caller, what was it he said?'

'He said, "I have a special need tonight." Both times. Just like that. He said the same thing both times. And his voice was weird. It was like he was talking through clenched teeth or something.'

'And you sent her to that.'

'I didn't put it together until after she didn't come back. Look, man, I made a report. I told the cops the hotel she went to and they never did nothing. I'm not the only one to blame. Shit, the cops said that guy was caught, that he was dead. I thought it was safe.'

'Safe for you, or the girls you put out on the street?'

'Look, you think I would've sent her if I knew? I had a lot invested in her, man.'

'I'm sure you did.'

Bosch looked over at the blonde and wondered how long it would be before she looked like the one he had given the twenty to on the street. His guess was that Cerrone's girls all ended up used up and on the street with their thumb out, or they ended up dead. He looked back at Cerrone.

'Did Rebecca smoke?'

'What?'

'Smoke. Did she smoke? You lived with her, you should know.'

'No, she didn't smoke. It's a disgusting habit.'

Cerrone looked over at the blonde and glared. Bosch dropped his cigarette on the white rug and ground it out as he stood up. He headed toward the door but stopped after he opened it.

'Cerrone, the woman in that dump your mail goes to?'

'What about her?'

'She doesn't pay rent anymore.'

'What are you talking about?'

He climbed up from the floor, regaining a measure of his pride.

'I'm talking about her not paying you rent anymore. I'm going to check on her from time to time. If she's paying rent, your PO gets a call and your scam gets blown. Probation gets revoked and you do your time. It's tough to run an outcall business from county lockup. Only two phones on each floor and the brothers control who uses them and for how long. I guess you'd have to cut them in.'

Cerrone just stared at him, anger thumping in his temples.

'And she better still be there when I check,' Bosch said. 'If I hear she went back to Mexico, I blame you and make the call. If I hear she bought a fucking condo, I make the call. She just better be there.'

'That's extortion,' Cerrone said.

'No, asshole, that's justice.'

He left the door open. Out in the hallway waiting for the elevator, he once again heard Cerrone yell, 'Shut the fuck up!'

THIRTEEN

The last vestiges of the evening rush hour made it a slow run up to Sylvia's. She was sitting at the dining room table in faded blue jeans and a Grant High T-shirt, reading book reports, when he came in. One of the eleventh-grade English classes she taught down in the Valley at Grant was called Los Angeles in Literature. She had told him she developed the class so the students might come to know their city better. Most of them came from other places, other countries. She had once told him that the students in one of her classes accounted for eleven different native languages.

He put his hand on the back of her neck and bent down to kiss her. He noticed the reports were on Nathanael West's *Day of the Locust*.

'Ever read it?' she asked.

'Long time ago. Some English teacher in high school made us read it. She was crazy.'

She elbowed him in the thigh.

'All right, wise guy. I try to rotate the tough ones with the easy ones. I assigned them *The Big Sleep*.'

'That's probably what they thought this one should've been called.'

'Aren't you the life of the party today. Something good happen?'

'Actually, no. Everything is turning to shit out there. But in here . . . it's different.'

She got up and they embraced. He ran his hand up and down her back the way he knew she liked.

'What's happening on the case?'

'Nothing. Everything. I might be going into the mud puddle. Wonder if I can get a job after this as a private eye. Like Marlowe.'

She pushed away.

'What are you talking about?'

'I'm not sure. Something. I have to work on it tonight. I'll take the kitchen table. You can stay out here with the locusts.'

'It's your turn to cook.'

'Then, I'm going to hire the colonel.'

'Shit.'

'Hey, that's not a good thing for an English teacher to say. What's the matter with the colonel?'

'He's been dead for years. Never mind. It's okay.'

She smiled at him. This ritual occurred often. When it was his turn to cook he usually took her out. He could see she was disappointed by the prospect of fried chicken to go. But there was too much going on, too much to think about.

She had a face that made him want to confess everything bad he had ever done. Yet he knew he could not. She knew it, too.

'I humiliated a man today.'

'What? Why?'

'Because he humiliates women.'

'All men do that, Harry. What did you do to him?'

'Knocked him down in front of his woman.'

'He probably needed it.'

'I don't want you to come to court tomorrow. I'm probably going to be called by Chandler to testify but I don't want you there. It's going to be bad.'

She was silent for a moment.

'Why do you do this, Harry? Tell me all these things that you do but keep the rest a secret? In some ways we are so intimate and in others . . . You tell me about the men you knock down but not about you. What do I know about you, your past? I want us to get to that, Harry. We have to or

155

we'll end up humiliating each other. That's how it ended for me before.'

Bosch nodded and looked down. He didn't know what to say. He was too burdened by other thoughts to get into this now.

'You want the extra crispy?' he finally asked.

'Fine.'

She went back to her book reports and he went out to get dinner.

After they were done eating and she went back to the dining room table, he opened his briefcase on the kitchen table and took out the blue murder books. He had a bottle of Henry Weinhard's on the table but no cigarette. He wouldn't smoke inside. At least not while she was awake.

He unsnapped the first binder and laid out the sections on each of the eleven victims across the table. He stood up with the bottle so he could look down and take them all in at once. Each section was fronted by a photograph of the victim's remains, as they were found. There were eleven of these photos in front of him. He did some thinking on the cases and then went into the bedroom and checked the suit he had worn the day before. The Polaroid of the concrete blonde was still in the pocket.

He brought it back to the kitchen and laid it on the table with the others. Number twelve. It was a horrible gallery of broken, abused bodies, their garish makeup showing false smiles below dead eyes. Their bodies were naked, exposed to the harsh light of the police photographer.

Bosch drained the bottle and kept staring. Reading the names and the dates of the deaths. Looking at the faces. All of them lost angels in the city of night. He didn't notice Sylvia come in until it was too late.

'My God,' she said in a whisper as she saw the photos. She took a step backward. She was holding one of her students' papers in her hand. Her other hand had come up to her mouth.

'I'm sorry, Sylvia,' Bosch said. 'I should've warned you not to come in.'

'Those are the women?'

He nodded.

'What are you doing?'

'I'm not sure. Trying to make something happen, I guess. I thought if I looked at them all again I might get an idea, figure out what's happening.'

'But how can you look at those? You were just standing there looking.'

'Because I have to.'

She looked down at the paper in her hand.

'What is it?' he asked.

'Nothing. Uh, one of my students wrote something. I was going to read it to you.'

'Go ahead.'

He stepped over to the wall and turned off the light that hung over the table. The photos and Bosch became shrouded in darkness. Sylvia stood in the light cast from the dining room through the kitchen entrance.

'Go ahead.'

She held up the paper and said, 'It's a girl. She wrote, "West foreshadowed the end of Los Angeles's halcyon moment. He saw the city of angels becoming a city of despair, a place where hopes get crushed under the weight of the mad crowd. His book was the warning." '

She looked up.

'She goes on but that was the part I wanted to read. She's only a tenth-grader taking advanced classes but she seemed to grasp something so strong there.'

He admired her lack of cynicism. Bosch's first thought was that the kid had plagiarized – where'd she get a word like halcyon? But Sylvia saw past that. She saw the beauty in things. He saw the darkness.

'It's good,' he said.

'She's African-American. She comes up on the bus. She's one of the smartest I have and I worry about her on the bus. She said the trip is seventy-five minutes each way and that is the time when she reads the assignments I give. But I worry about her. She seems so sensitive. Maybe too much so.'

'Give her time and she'll grow a callous on her heart. Everybody does.'

'No, not everybody, Harry. That's what I worry about with her.'

She looked at him there in the darkness for a long moment.

'I'm sorry I intruded.'

'You never intrude on me, Sylvia. I am sorry I brought this home. I can leave if you want, take it to my place.'

'No, Harry, I want you here. You want me to put on some coffee?'

'No, I'm fine.'

She went back to the living room and he turned the light back on. He looked over the gallery again. Though they looked the same in death because of the makeup applied by each one's killer, the women fell into numerous physical categories according to race, size, coloring, and so on.

Locke had told the task force that this meant that the killer was simply an opportunistic predator. Not concerned with body type, only the acquisition of a victim which he could then place into his erotic program. He did not care if they were black or white as long as he could snatch them with as little notice as possible. He was a bottom feeder. He moved on a level where the women he encountered were victims long before he got to them. They were women who had already given up their bodies to the unloving hands and eyes of strangers. They were out there waiting for him. The question, Bosch now knew, was whether the Dollmaker was still out there, too.

He sat down and from the pocket of the binder he pulled a map of West LA. Its creases cracked and split in some sections as he unfolded it and put it down on top of the photos. The round black stickers that represented locations where bodies had been found were still in place. The victim's name and date of discovery were written next to each black dot. Geographically, the task force had found no significance until after Church was dead. The bodies were found in locations stretching from Silverlake to Malibu. The Dollmaker littered the entire Westside. Still, for the most part, the bodies were clustered in Silverlake and Hollywood, with only one found in Malibu and one in West Hollywood.

The concrete blonde was found farther south in Hollywood than any of the previous bodies. She was also the only one that had been buried. Locke had said location of disposal was probably a choice of convenience. After Church was dead this seemed true. Four of the bodies had been dumped within a mile of his Silverlake apartment. Another four were in eastern Hollywood, not a long drive, either.

The dates had done nothing for the investigation. No pattern. Initially there was a decreasing-interval pattern between discoveries of victims, then it began to vary widely. The Dollmaker would go five weeks between strikes, then two weeks, then three. Nothing to make of this; the detectives on the task force simply let it go.

Bosch moved on. He began reading the background packets that had been drawn up on each victim. Most of these were short – two to three pages about their sad lives. One of the women who worked Hollywood Boulevard at night was going to beautician school by day. Another had been sending money to Chihuahua, Mexico, where her parents believed she had a good job as a tour guide at the famous Disneyland. There were odd matches between some of the victims, but nothing that ever amounted to anything.

Three of the Boulevard whores went to the same doctor for weekly clap shots. Members of the task force put him under surveillance for three weeks. But one night while they were watching him, the real Dollmaker picked up a prostitute on Sunset and her body was found in Silverlake the next morning.

Two of the other women also shared a doctor. The same Beverly Hills plastic surgeon had performed breast-implant surgery on them. The task force had rallied on this discovery, for a plastic surgeon remakes images, similarly after a fashion to the way the Dollmaker used makeup. The plastic man, as he was called by the cops, was also placed under surveillance. But he never made a suspicious move and seemed to be the picture of domestic bliss with a wife whose physical features he had sculpted to his own liking. They were still watching him when Bosch took the telephone tip that led to the shooting of Norman Church.

As far as Bosch knew, neither doctor ever knew he had been watched. In the book Bremmer wrote, they were identified by pseudonyms.

Nearly two-thirds through the background packets, as he read about Nicole Knapp, the seventh victim, Bosch saw the pattern within the pattern. He had somehow missed it before. All of them had. The task force, Locke, the media. They had put all the victims into the same classification. A whore is a whore is a whore. But there were differences. Some were streetwalkers, some were higher up the scale as escorts. Within these two groups, some were also dancers; one was a telegram stripper. And two made livings in the pornography trade – as had the latest victim, Becky Kaminski – while taking outcall hooking assignments on the side.

Bosch took the packets and photos of Nicole Knapp, the seventh victim, and Shirleen Kemp, the eleventh victim, off the table. These were the two porn actresses, known on video as Holly Lere and Heather Cumhither, respectively.

He then paged through one of the binders until he found the package on the lone survivor, the woman who had gotten away. She, too, was a porn actress who took outcall sex jobs. Her name was Georgia Stern. Her video name was Velvet Box. She had gone to the Hollywood Star Motel to meet a date arranged through the outcall service she advertised in the local sex tabloids. After she arrived, her client asked her to undress. She turned her back to do this, offering a show of modesty in case that was a turn-on for the client. She then saw the leather strap of her purse come over her head and he began choking her from behind. She fought, as probably all the victims had, but she was able to get free by driving an elbow into her attacker's ribs, then turning and delivering a kick to his genitals.

She ran naked from the room, all thought of modesty long gone. By the time police went back in, the attacker was gone. It was three days before the reports on the incident filtered their way to the task force. By then the hotel room had been used dozens of times – the Hollywood Star offered hourly rates – and it was useless as far as gathering physical evidence went.

Reading the reports on it now, Bosch realized why the composite drawing that Georgia Stern had helped a police artist sketch was so different from the appearance of Norman Church.

It had been a different man.

An hour later, he turned one of the binders to the last page, where he had kept a listing of phone numbers and addresses of the principals involved in the investigation. He went to the wall phone and dialed the home of Dr John Locke. He hoped the psychologist had not changed his number in four years.

Locke picked up after five rings.

'Sorry, Dr Locke, I know it's getting late. It's Harry Bosch.'

'Harry, how are you? I am sorry we didn't get to talk today. It was not the best circumstance for you, I'm sure, but I –'

'Yes, Doctor, listen, something's come up. It's related to the Dollmaker. I have some things I want to show you and talk about. Would it be possible for me to come there?'

There was a lengthy silence before Locke answered.

'Would that be about this new case I've read about in the paper?'

'Yes, that and some other things.'

'Well, let's see, it's nearly ten o'clock. Are you sure this can't wait until tomorrow morning?'

'I am in court tomorrow morning, Doctor. All day. It's important. I'd really appreciate your time. I'll be there before eleven and be out before twelve.'

When Locke didn't say anything, Harry wondered if the soft-spoken doctor was afraid of him or just didn't want a killer cop in his home.

'Besides,' Bosch said into the silence, 'I think you'll find it interesting.'

'Very well,' Locke said.

After getting the address, Harry packed all the paperwork back into the two binders. Sylvia came into the kitchen after hesitating at the doorway until she was sure the photos were packed away.

'I heard you talking. Are you going to his place tonight?'

'Yeah, right now. In Laurel Canyon.'

'What's going on?'

He stopped his hurried movement. He had both binders stacked under his right arm.

'I . . . well, we missed something. The task force. We messed up. I think all along there were two, but I didn't see it until now.'

'Two killers?'

'I think so. I want to ask Locke about it.'

'Are you coming back tonight?'

'I don't know. It will be late. I was thinking about just going to my place. Check my messages, get some fresh clothes.'

'This weekend is not looking good, is it?'

'What – oh, yeah, Lone Pine, yeah. Well, uh, I –'

'Don't worry about it. But I may want to hang out at your place while they have the open house here.'

'Sure.'

She walked him to the door and opened it. She told him to be careful and to call her the next day. He said he would. At the threshold he hesitated. He said, 'You know, you were right.'

'About what?'

'What you said about men.'

FOURTEEN

Laurel Canyon is a winding cut through the Santa Monica Mountains that connects Studio City with Hollywood and the Sunset Strip. On the south side, where the road drops below Mulholland Drive and the fast four lanes thin to two crumbling invitations to a head-on collision, the canyon becomes funky LA, where forty-year-old Hollywood bungalows sit next to multilevel glass contemporaries that sit next to gingerbread houses. Harry Houdini built a castle in here among the steep hillsides. Jim Morrison lived in a clapboard house near the little market that still serves as the canyon's only commercial outpost.

The canyon was a place where the new rich – rock stars, writers, film actors and drug dealers – came to live. They braved the mudslides and the monumental traffic tie-ups just to call Laurel Canyon home. Locke lived on Lookout Mountain Drive, a steep upward grade off Laurel Canyon Boulevard that made Bosch's department-issue Caprice work extra hard. The address he was looking for could not be missed because it blinked in blue neon from the front wall of Locke's house. Harry pulled to the curb behind a multicolor Volkswagen van that was at least twenty-five years old. Laurel Canyon was like that, a time warp.

Bosch got out, dropped his cigarette in the street and stepped on it. It was very quiet and dark. He heard the Caprice's engine ticking away its heat, the smell of burning oil wafting from the undercarriage. He reached in through the open window and grabbed the two binders.

It had taken most of an hour to get to Locke's and during

that time Bosch had been able to refine his thoughts on the discovery of the pattern within a pattern. He also realized along the way that there was a key way of attempting to confirm it.

Locke answered with a glass of red wine in his hand. He was barefoot and wearing blue jeans and a surgeon's green shirt. Hanging from a leather thong around his neck was a large pink crystal.

'Good evening, Detective Bosch. Please come in.'

He led the way through an entry hall to a large living room/dining room area with a wall of French doors that opened onto a brick patio surrounding a lighted blue pool. Bosch noticed the pinkish carpet was dirty and worn but otherwise the place was not bad for a college sex professor and author. He noticed the water of the pool was choppy, as if someone had been swimming recently. He thought he smelled a trace of stale marijuana smoke.

'Beautiful place,' Bosch said. 'You know we're almost neighbors. I live on the other side of the hill. On Woodrow Wilson.'

'Oh, really? How come it took you so long to get here?'

'Well, actually, I didn't come from home. I was at a friend's place up in Bouquet Canyon.'

'Ah, a girlfriend, that explains the forty-five-minute wait.'

'Sorry to hold you up, Doctor. Why don't we get on with this so I don't keep you any longer than necessary.'

'Yes, please.'

He signaled Bosch to put the binders down on the dining room table. He didn't ask if Harry wanted a glass of wine, an ashtray or even a pair of swimming trunks.

'I'm sorry to intrude,' Harry offered. 'I'll be quick.'

'Yes, you said that. I'm sorry this came up now myself. Testifying put me back a day on my research and writing schedule and I was trying to recoup tonight.'

Bosch noticed his hair wasn't wet. Maybe he had been working while someone else had been in the pool.

Locke took a seat at the dining room table and Bosch told the story of the concrete blonde investigation in exact chronological order after starting by showing him the copy of the new note left at the station on Monday.

While telling the details of the latest death, Bosch saw Locke's eyes brighten with interest. When he was done, the psychologist folded his arms and closed his eyes and said, 'Let me think about this before we go on.'

He sat perfectly still. Bosch wasn't sure what to make of it. After twenty seconds went by, he finally said, 'If you're going to think, I'm going to borrow your phone.'

'In the kitchen,' Locke said without opening his eyes.

Bosch got Amado's phone number from the task force list in the binder and called him. He could tell he had awakened the coroner's analyst.

After identifying himself, Bosch said, 'Sorry to wake you. But things are happening very quickly on this new Dollmaker case. Did you read about it in the paper?'

'Yeah. But they said it wasn't known for sure if it was the Dollmaker.'

'Right. That's what I'm working on. I have a question.'

'Go ahead.'

'You testified yesterday about the rape kits taken from each victim. Where are they now? The evidence, I mean.'

There was a long silence before Amado said, 'They're probably still in evidence storage. The coroner's policy is to keep evidence seven years after resolution of a case. You know, in case of appeals or something. Now, since your perp is dead, there would be no reason to keep the stuff even that long. But it takes an order from the medical examiner to clear out an evidence locker. The chances are the ME at the time would not have thought or remembered to do this after you, uh, killed Church. It's too big of a bureaucracy to run that well. My guess is the kits would still be there. The evidence custodian would only request a disposal order after seven years.'

'Okay,' Bosch said, excitement evident in his voice.

'What about the condition? Would it still be usable as evidence? And for analysis?'

'Should be no deterioration, I would think.'

'How full's your plate?'

'It's always full. But you've got me hooked here. What's up?'

'I need someone to pull the kits from victims seven and eleven. That's Nicole Knapp and Shirleen Kemp. Got it? Seven and eleven, like the store.'

'I got it. Seven eleven. Then what?'

'Cross-reference the pubic combs. Look for the same foreign hair in both places, on both women. How long will it take?'

'Three, four days. We have to send that to the DOJ lab. I can put a rush on it, maybe get it sooner. Can I ask you something? Why are we doing this?'

'I think there was someone else besides Church. A copycat. He did seven, eleven and the one this week. And I'm thinking he might not have been smart enough to shave himself like Church. If you find similar hair in the combs, I think that will clinch it.'

'Well, I can tell you something right off that is interesting about those two. Seven and eleven.'

Bosch waited.

'I reviewed everything before I testified, so it's still fresh, you know? Remember I testified that two of the victims had extreme damage, vaginal tears? Well, it was those two, seven and eleven.'

Bosch thought about this for a few moments. From out in the dining room he heard Locke say, 'Harry?'

'Be right there,' he called out. To Amado, he said, 'That's interesting.'

'It means this second guy, whoever he is, he's rougher trade than Church. Those two women were hurt the most.'

Something came together in Bosch's mind then. Something that had not seemed right about Amado's testimony the day before. Now it was clear.

'The condoms,' he said.

'What about them?'

'You testified that it was a box of twelve, only three left.'

'That's right! Nine used. You subtract victims seven and eleven from the list and you have nine victims. It fits, Harry. Okay, first thing tomorrow, I'm on this. Give me three days, max.'

They hung up and Bosch wondered if Amado would get any sleep tonight.

Locke had replenished his wineglass but still did not ask Bosch if he wanted a glass when he returned to the dining room. Bosch sat down across the table from him.

'I'm ready to go on,' Locke said.

'Let's do it.'

'You're saying that the body found this week exhibited every known detail ascribed to the Dollmaker?'

'Right.'

'Except now we have a new method of disposal. A private disposal as opposed to the public challenge of the others. It's all very interesting. What else?'

'Well, from trial testimony I think we can eliminate Church as the perp in the eleventh killing. A wit produced a tape in –'

'A wit?'

'A witness. In court. He was a friend of Church's. He came in with a video that showed Church at a party at the time number eleven got abducted. The tape is convincing.'

Locke nodded his head and was silent. At least he didn't close his eyes, Bosch thought. The psychologist thoughtfully rubbed the graying whiskers on his chin, which made Bosch do the same thing.

'Then there is number seven,' Bosch said.

He told Locke about the information he got from Cerrone, about the voice the pimp had recognized.

'Voice identification wouldn't pass as evidence but say for the sake of argument he is right. That connects the concrete blonde to our seventh victim. The videotape eliminates

Church from the eleventh case. Amado, the guy from the coroner's office, I don't know if you remember him, he says numbers seven and eleven had similar injuries, injuries that stood out if compared with those of the others.

'Another thing I just remembered is the makeup. After Church was dead they found the makeup in the Hyperion apartment, remember? They matched it to nine of the victims. The two victims there was no makeup for were –'

'Seven and eleven.'

'Right. So what we have are multiple ties between these two cases – seven and eleven. Then you have a tangential connection to number twelve, this week's victim, based on the pimp recognizing the customer's voice. The connection gets stronger if you look at the lifestyles of the three women. All were in porno, all worked outcall.'

'I see the pattern within the pattern,' Locke said.

'Gets better. Now, we add in our lone survivor, she was also in porno and did outcall work.'

'And she described an attacker who looked nothing like Church.'

'Exactly. That's because I don't think it was Church. I think the three, plus the survivor, make up one set of victims of one killer. The remaining nine are another set with another killer. Church.'

Locke got up and began pacing back and forth on one side of the dining room table. He kept his hand to his chin.

'Anything else?'

Bosch opened one of the binders and took out the map and a folded piece of paper on which he had earlier written a series of dates. He carefully unfolded the map and spread it on the table. He leaned in and over it.

'Okay, look. Let's call the nine Group A and the three Group B. On the map I have circled the locations where Group A victims were found. You see, if you take the Group B victims out of the picture, you have a nice geographic concentration. Group B vics were found in Malibu, West Hollywood, South Hollywood. But the A list was concentrated here in eastern Hollywood and Silverlake.'

Bosch ran his finger in a circle on the map, showing the dumping zone Church had used.

'And here in almost the center of this zone is Hyperion Street – Church's killing pad.'

He straightened up and dropped the folded paper on the map.

'Now here is a list of dates of the eleven killings originally attributed to Church. You see there is an interval pattern at the start – thirty days, thirty-two days, twenty-eight, thirty-one, thirty-one. But then the pattern goes to hell. Remember that? How it confused us back then?

'Yes, I do.'

'We have twelve days, then sixteen, then twenty-seven, thirty and eleven. The pattern disintegrates into no pattern. But now separate the dates of Group A and Group B.'

Bosch unfolded the paper. There were two columns of dates. Locke leaned over the table into the light to study the columns. Bosch could see a thin line, a scar, on the top of his bald and freckled crown.

'On Group A we now have a pattern,' Bosch continued. 'A clearly discernable pattern of intervals. We have thirty days, thirty-two, twenty-eight, thirty-one, thirty-one, twenty-eight, twenty-seven and thirty. On Group B we have eighty-four days between the two killings.'

'Better stress management.'

'What?'

'The intervals between the acting out of these fantasies is dictated by the buildup of stress. I testified about this. The better the actor handles it, the longer the interval between killings. The second killer has better stress management. Or, at least, had it back then.'

Bosch watched him pace the room. He took out a cigarette and lit it. Locke said nothing.

'What I want to know is, is this possible?' Bosch asked. 'I mean, is there any precedent for this that you know of?'

'Of course, it's possible. The black heart does not beat alone. You don't even have to look outside the boundaries of your own jurisdiction to find ample evidence it is possible. Look at the Hillside Stranglers. There was even a book written about them called *Two of a Kind*.

'Look at the similarities in the method of operation employed by the Nightstalker and the Sunset Strip Strangler in the early eighties. The short answer is, yes, it's possible.'

'I know about those cases but this is different. I worked some of those and I know this is different. The Hillside Stranglers worked together. They were cousins. The other two were similar but there were major differences. Here, someone came along and copied the other exactly. So closely that we missed it and he got away.'

'Two killers working independently of each other but using exactly the same methodology.'

'Right.'

'Again, I say anything is possible. Another example: remember in the eighties there was the Freeway Killer in Orange and LA counties?'

Bosch nodded. He had never worked those cases so he knew little about them.

'Well, one day they got lucky and caught a Vietnam vet named William Bonin. They tied him to a handful of the cases and believed he was good for the rest. He went to death row but the killings kept happening. They kept right on happening until a highway patrol officer pulled over a guy named Randy Kraft who was driving down the freeway with a body in his car. Kraft and Bonin didn't know each other but for a while they secretly shared the nom de plume "The Freeway Killer". Each working independently of the other, out there killing. And being mistaken for the same person.'

That sounded close to the theory Bosch was working with. Locke continued talking, no longer bothered by the late-night intrusion.

'Do you know, there is a guard on death row at San Quentin whom I know from doing research up there. He told me there are four serial killers, including Kraft and Bonin, waiting for the gas. And, well, the four of them play cards every day. Bridge. Among them, they've got fifty-nine convictions for murder. And they play bridge. Anyway, the point is, he says Kraft and Bonin think so much alike that as a team they are almost never beaten.'

Bosch started refolding the map. Without looking up, he said, 'Kraft and Bonin, did they kill their victims the same way? The exact same way?'

'Not exactly. But my point is that there could be two. But the follower in this case is smarter. He knew exactly what to do to have all the police go the other way, to put it on Church. Then, when Church was dead and no longer available for use as camouflage, the follower went under-ground, so to speak.'

Bosch looked up at him and a thought suddenly struck him that spun everything he knew into a new light. It was like the cue ball hitting a rack of eight, colors shooting off in all directions. But he didn't say anything. This new thought was too dangerous to bring up. Instead he asked Locke a question.

'But even when this follower went underground, he kept the same program as the Dollmaker,' Bosch said. 'Why do it, if no one was going to see it? Remember, with the Dollmaker we believed his leaving of the bodies in public locations, their faces painted, was part of the erotic program. Part of his turn-on. But why did the second killer do it – follow the same program – if the body was never intended to be found?'

Locke put both hands on the table to brace his weight and thought a moment. Bosch thought he heard a sound from the patio. He looked through the open French doors and saw only the darkness of the steep hillside rising above the illuminated pool. Its kidney-shaped surface was calm now. He looked at his watch. It was midnight.

'It's a good question,' Locke said. 'I don't know the

answer. Maybe the acolyte knew that eventually the body would be revealed, that he himself might want to reveal it. You see, we probably have to assume now that it was the follower who sent the notes to you and the newspaper four years ago. It shows the exhibitionistic portion of his program. Church apparently didn't find the same need to torment his hunters.'

'The follower got off on tweaking us.'

'Exactly. What he was doing was having his fun, taunting his trackers and all the while the blame for the murders he committed went to the real Dollmaker. Follow?'

'Yes.'

'Okay, so what happened? The real Dollmaker, Mr Church, is killed by you. The follower no longer has a cover. So what he does is, he continues his work – his killing – but now he buries the victim, hides her under concrete.'

'You're saying he still follows the whole erotic program with the makeup and everything but then buries her so no one will see her?'

'So no one will know. Yes, he follows the program because that is what turned him on in the first place. But he can no longer afford to discard the bodies publicly because that would reveal his secret.'

'So then, why the note? Why send a note to the police this week that opens him to exposure?'

Locke paced around the dining room table thinking.

'Confidence,' he finally said. 'The follower has become strong over the past four years. He thinks he is invincible. It is a common trait in the disassembling phase of a psychopath. A state of confidence and invulnerability rises as, in actuality, the psychopath is making more and more mistakes. Disassembling. Becoming vulnerable to discovery.'

'So because he has gotten away with his actions for four years, he thinks he is clear and is so untouchable that he sends another note to tweak us?'

'Exactly, but that is only one factor. Another is pride, authorship. This big trial on the Dollmaker has begun and he wants to steal some of the attention. You must understand, he craves attention for his acts. After all, it was the follower, not Church who sent the letters earlier. So being prideful and feeling above the reach of the police – I guess, godlike is the way to describe his sense of himself – he writes the note this week.'

'Catch me if you can.'

'Yes, one of the oldest games around. . . . And lastly, he might have sent the note because he is still angry with you.'

'Me?'

Bosch was surprised. He had never considered this.

'Yes, you took Church away. You ruined his perfect cover. I don't imagine the note and its mention in the press has helped your court case any, has it?'

'No. It might sink me.'

'Yes, so maybe this is the follower's way of repaying you. His revenge.'

Bosch thought about all of this for a moment. He could almost feel the adrenaline surging through his body. It was after midnight but he wasn't the least bit tired. He had a focus now. He was no longer lost in the void.

'You think there are more out there, don't you?' he asked.

'You mean women in concrete, or similar confinement? Yes, unfortunately, I do. Four years is a long time. Many others are out there, I'm afraid.'

'How do I find him?'

'I'm not sure. My work has usually come at the end. After they're caught. After they're dead.'

Bosch nodded, closed the binders and put them under his arm.

'There is one thing, though,' Locke said. 'Look at his pool of victims. Who are they? How does he get to them? The three who are dead and the survivor, they all were in the porno industry, you said.'

Bosch put the binders back down on the table. He lit another cigarette.

'Yes, they all did outcall work, too,' he said.

'Yes. So while Church was the opportunistic killer,

174

taking victims of any size, age or race, the follower was more specific in his tastes.'

Bosch recalled the porno victims quickly.

'Right, the follower's victims were white, young, blonde and large-breasted.'

'That is a clear pattern. Did these women advertise their outcall services in the adult-related media?'

'I know two of them did, and the survivor. The latest victim did outcall but I'm not sure how she advertised.'

'Did the three who did advertise include photographs of themselves in the copy?'

Bosch could specifically remember only Holly Lere's ad, and it did not include her photo. Just her stage name, a phone drop and a guarantee of lewd pleasure.

'I don't think so. The one I remember didn't. But her porno name was in the ad. So anyone familiar with her work in video would know her physical appearance and attributes.'

'Very good. We are already creating a profile of the follower. He is someone who uses adult videos to choose the women for his erotic program. He then contacts them through ads in the adult media by seeing either their names or photos in the advertisements. Have I helped you, Detective Bosch?'

'Absolutely. Thanks for the time. And keep this under your hat. I'm not sure we want to go public with this yet.'

Bosch picked up the binders again and headed toward the door but Locke stopped him.

'We haven't finished, you know.'

Bosch turned around.

'How do you mean?' he asked, though he knew.

'You haven't spoken about the aspect of this that is most troubling. The question of how our follower learned the killer's routine. The task force did not divulge every detail of the Dollmaker's program to the media. Not back then. Details were held back so the loonies who confessed would not know exactly what to confess to. It was a safeguard. The task force could quickly eliminate the bogus confessions.'

'So?'

'So the question is, how did the follower know?'

'I don't –'

'Yes, you do. The book Mr Bremmer wrote made those details available to the world. That, of course, could account for the concrete blonde. . . . But not, as I am sure you have realized, for victims seven and eleven.'

Locke was right. It was what Bosch had realized earlier. He avoided thinking about it because he dreaded the implications.

Locke said, 'The answer is that the follower was somehow privy to the details. The details are what triggered his action. You have to remember that what we are dealing with here is someone who very likely was already in the midst of some great internal struggle when he stumbled onto an erotic program that matched his own needs. This man already had problems, whether they had manifested in his committing crimes or not. He was a sick puppy, Harry, and he saw the Dollmaker's erotic mold and realized, That's me. That's what I want, what I need for fulfillment. He then adopted the Dollmaker's program and acted on it, to the very last detail. The question is, how did he stumble onto it? And the answer is, he was given access.'

For a moment they just looked at each other, then Bosch spoke.

'You're talking about a cop. Someone on the task force. That can't be. I was there. We all wanted this guy to go down. Nobody was . . . getting off on this, man.'

'Possibly a member of the task force, Harry, only possibly. But remember, the circle of those who knew about the program was much larger than just the task force. You have medical examiners, investigators, beat cops, photographers, reporters, paramedics, the passersby who found the bodies – many people who had access to details the follower obviously knew about.'

Bosch tried to pull together a quick profile in his mind. Locke read him.

'It would have to be someone in or around the investigation, Harry. Not necessarily a vital part or a continuous part. But someone who intersected with the investigation at a point that would allow him to gain knowledge of the full program. More than what was publicly known at the time.'

Bosch said nothing until Locke prompted him.

'What else, Harry? Narrow it down.'

'Left-handed.'

'Possibly but not necessarily. Church was left-handed. The follower may only have used the left hand to make the perfect copy of Church's crimes.'

'That's right but then there are the notes. Suspicious docs said they believed it was a left-handed writer. They weren't one hundred percent. They never are.'

'Okay, then, possibly left-handed. What else?'

Bosch thought for a moment.

'Maybe a smoker. There was a package found in the concrete. Kaminski, the victim, didn't smoke.'

'Okay, that's good. These are the things you need to think about to narrow it down. It's in the details, Harry, I'm sure of it.'

A cool wind came down the hillside and in through the French doors and chilled Bosch. It was time to go, to be alone with this.

'Thanks again,' he said as he started once more for the door.

'What will you do?' Locke called after him.

'I don't know yet.'

'Harry?'

Bosch stopped at the threshold and looked back at Locke, the pool glowing eerily in the darkness behind him.

'The follower, he may be the smartest to come along in a long time.'

'Because he's a cop?'

'Because he probably knows everything about the case that you know.'

*

It was cold in the Caprice. At night the canyons always carried a dark chill. Bosch turned the car around and it floated quietly down Lookout Mountain to Laurel Canyon. He took a right and drove to the canyon market, where he bought a six-pack of Anchor Steam. Then he took his beer and his questions back up the hill to Mulholland.

He drove to Woodrow Wilson Drive and then down to his small house that stood on cantilevers and looked out across the Cahuenga Pass. He had left no lights on inside because with Sylvia in his life he never knew how long he would go without being here.

He opened the first beer as soon as the Caprice was parked at the curb in front. A car slowly went by and left him in the dark. He watched one of the beams from the spotlights at Universal City cut across the clouds over the house. Another one chased after it a few seconds later. The beer felt and tasted good going down his throat. But it felt heavy in his stomach and Bosch stopped drinking. He put the bottle back in its carton.

But it wasn't the beer, he knew, that was really bothering him. It was Ray Mora. Of all the people who were close enough to the case to know the details of the program, Mora was the one who jabbed at Bosch's gut. The follower's three victims were porno actresses. And that was Mora's gig. He probably knew them all. The question that was now beginning to push its way into Bosch's mind was, did he kill them all? It bothered him to even think about it, but he knew he had to. Mora was a logical starting point when Bosch considered Locke's advice. The vice cop stood out in Bosch's mind as someone who easily intersected both worlds: the porn trade and the Dollmaker's. Was it just coincidence or enough to classify Mora as an actual suspect? Bosch wasn't sure. He knew he had to proceed as cautiously with an innocent man as he would with a guilty man.

Inside, the place smelled musty. He went directly to the rear sliding door and opened it. He stood there for a moment listening to the hissing sound of traffic coming up from the freeway at the bottom of the pass. The sound never died. No matter what time, what day, there was always traffic down there, blood coursing through the veins of the city.

The light on the answering machine was blinking the number three. Bosch hit rewind and lit a cigarette. The first voice was Sylvia's: 'I just want to say good-night, sweetheart. I love you and be careful.'

Jerry Edgar was next: 'Harry, it's Edgar. Wanted to let you know, I'm off it. Irving called me at home and told me to turn everything I've got over to RHD in the morning. To a Lieutenant Rollenberger. Take care, buddy. And watch six.'

Watch six, Bosch thought. Watch your back. He hadn't heard that one since Vietnam. And he knew Edgar had never been there.

'It's Ray,' the last voice on the tape said. 'I've been thinking about this concrete blonde job and have a few ideas you might be interested in. Call me in the morning and we'll talk.'

FIFTEEN

'I want a continuance.'

'What?'

'You have to get the trial delayed. Tell the judge.'

'What the fuck are you talking about, Bosch?'

Bosch and Belk were sitting at the defense table, waiting for the Thursday morning court session to begin. They were speaking in loud whispers and Bosch thought that when Belk cursed, it came off as sounding too contrived as if he were a sixth-grader trying to fit in with the eighth-graders.

'I am talking about that witness yesterday, Wieczorek, he was right.'

'About what?'

'The alibi, Belk. The alibi on the eleventh victim. It's legit. Church didn't –'

'Wait a minute,' Belk yelped. Then in a low whisper he said, 'If you are about to confess to me that you killed the wrong guy, I don't want to hear it, Bosch. Not now. It's too late.'

He turned back to his legal tablet.

'Belk, listen goddammit, I'm not confessing anything. I got the right guy. But we missed something. Another guy. There were two killers. Church is good for nine – the nine we tied up on the makeup comparisons. The other two, and the one we found in the concrete this week, were done by somebody else. You have to stop this thing until we figure out what exactly is going on. If it comes out in court it will tip the second killer, the follower, to how close we are to him.'

Belk threw his pen down on the pad and it bounced off the table. He didn't get up to get it.

'I'm going to tell you what's going on, Bosch. We are not stopping anything. Even if I wanted to, I probably couldn't – the judge is in her pants. All she needs to do is object and no sale, no delay. So I'm not even going to bring it up. You have to understand something, Bosch, this is a trial. This is the controlling factor of your universe right now. You don't control it. You can't expect the trial to recess every time you need to change your story . . .'

'You finished?'

'Yes, I'm finished.'

'Belk, I understand everything you just said. But we have to protect the investigation. There is another guy out there killing people. And if Chandler puts me or Edgar up there and starts asking questions, the killer is going to read about it and know everything we've got. We'll never get him then. You want that?'

'Bosch, my duty is to win this case. If in doing that, it compromises your –'

'Yeah, but don't you want to know the truth, Belk? I think we're close. Delay it until next week and by then we'll have it together. We'll be able to come in here and blow Money Chandler out of the water.'

Bosch leaned back, away from him. He was tired of fighting him.

'Bosch, how long you been a cop?' Belk asked without looking at him. 'Twenty years?'

That was close. But Bosch didn't answer. He knew what was coming.

'And you're going to sit there and talk to me about truth? When was the last time you saw a truthful police report? When was the last time that you put down the un-adulterated truth in a search warrant application? Don't tell me about truth. You want truth, go see a priest or something. I don't know where to go, but don't come in here. After twenty on the job you should know, the truth has got nothing to do with what goes on in here. Neither does justice. Just words in a law book I read in my previous life.'

Belk turned away and took another pen out of his shirt pocket.

'Okay, Belk, you're the man. But I'm going to tell you how it's going to look when it comes out. It's going to come out in bits and pieces and it will look bad. That's Chandler's specialty. It will look like I hit the wrong guy.'

Belk was ignoring him, writing on his yellow pad.

'You fool, she is going to stick it into us so deep it's going to come out the other side. You keep writing her off as having the judge's hand on her ass, but we both know that's how you deal with the fact that you couldn't carry her lunch. For the last time, get a delay.'

Belk stood up and walked around the table to pick up the fallen pen. After straightening up, he adjusted his tie and his cuffs and sat back down. He leaned over his pad and without looking at Bosch said, 'You're just afraid of her, aren't you, Bosch? Don't want to be on the stand with the cunt asking questions. Questions that might expose you for what you are: a cop who likes killing people.'

Now he turned and looked at Bosch.

'Well, it's too late. Your time has come and there is no backing away. No delays. Show time.'

Harry stood up and bent over the fat man.

'Fuck you, Belk. I'm going outside.'

'That's nice,' Belk said. 'You know, you guys are all the same. You blow some guy away and then come in here and think that just because you wear that badge that you have some kind of a divine right to do whatever you want. That badge is the biggest power trip going.'

Bosch went out to the bank of phones and called Edgar. He picked up on the homicide table after one ring.

'I got your message last night.'

'Yeah, well, that's all there is. I'm gone. RHD came up this morning and took my file. Saw them snoopin' around your spot, too, but they didn't take anything.'

'Who came?'

'Sheehan and Opelt. You know 'em?'

'Yeah, they're okay. You coming over here on the subpoena?'

'Yeah, I gotta be there by ten.'

Bosch saw the door to courtroom 4 open and the deputy marshal leaned out and signaled to him.

'I gotta go.'

Back in the courtroom, Chandler was at the lectern and the judge was speaking. The jury was not in the box yet.

'What about the other subpoenas?' the judge asked.

'Your Honor, my office is in the process of notifying those people this morning, releasing them.'

'Very well, then. Mr Belk, ready to proceed?'

As Bosch came through the gate Belk passed him on the way to the lectern without even looking at him.

'Your Honor, since this is unexpected, I would ask for a half-hour recess so I can consult with my client. We would be ready to proceed after that.'

'Very well, we're going to do exactly that. Recess for a half hour. I'll see all parties back here then. And Mr Bosch? I expect you to be in your place there, the next time I come out ready to begin. I don't like sending marshals up and down the halls when the defendant knows where he ought to be and when he ought to be there.'

Bosch said nothing.

'Sorry, Your Honor,' Belk said for him.

They stood as the judge left the bench and Belk said, 'Let's go down the hall to one of the lawyer-client conference rooms.'

'What happened?'

'Let's go down the hall.'

As he was going through the courtroom door, Bremmer was coming in, holding his notebook and pen.

'Hey, what's happening?'

'I don't know,' Bosch said. 'Half-hour recess.'

'Harry, I have to talk to you.'

'Later.'

'It's important.'

At the end of the hall near the lavatories there were several small attorney conference rooms, all about the size of the interrogation rooms at the Hollywood station. Bosch and Belk went into one and took chairs on either side of a gray table.

'What happened?' Bosch asked.

'Your heroine rested.'

'Chandler rested without calling me?'

This seemed to make no sense to Bosch.

'What's she doing?' he asked.

'She's being extremely shrewd. It's a very smart move.'

'Why?'

'Look at the case. She is in very good shape. If it ended today and went to the jury, who would win? She would. See, she knows you have to get on the stand and defend what you did. Like I told you the other day, we win or lose with you. You either take the ball and ram it down her throat or you fumble it. She knows that and if she was to call you, she would ask the questions first, then I would come in with the fungoes – the easy ones that you'd hit out of the park.

'Now she's reversing that. My choice is to not call you and lose the case, or to call you and essentially give her the best shot at you. Very shrewd.'

'So what are we going to do?'

'Call you.'

'What about the delay?'

'What delay?'

Bosch nodded. There was no changing it. There would be no delay. He realized he had handled it badly. He had approached Belk the wrong way. He should have tried to make Belk believe it had been his own idea to go for a delay. Then it would have worked. Instead, Bosch was beginning to feel the jitters – that uneasy feeling that came with approaching the unknown. He felt the way he did before he

184

climbed down into a VC tunnel for the first time in Vietnam. It was fear, he knew, blossoming like a black rose in the pit of his chest.

'We've got twenty-five minutes,' Belk said. 'Let's forget about delays and try to work out how we want your testimony to go. I am going to lead you down the path. The jury will follow. But remember, you have to take it slow or you will lose them. Okay?'

'We got twenty minutes,' Bosch corrected him. 'I need to go out for a smoke before I sit up there on the stand.'

Belk pressed on as if he hadn't heard.

'Remember, Bosch, there could be millions of dollars at stake here. It may not be your money but it may be your career.'

'What career?'

Bremmer was hanging around the door to the conference room when Bosch came out twenty minutes later.

'Get it all?' Harry asked.

He walked by him and headed toward the escalator. Bremmer followed.

'No, man, I wasn't listening. I'm just waiting for you. Listen, what's going on with the new case? Edgar won't tell me shit. Did you get an ID or what?'

'Yeah, we ID'd her.'

'Who was it?'

'Not my case, man. I can't give it out. Besides, I give it to you and you'll run to Money Chandler with it, right?'

Bremmer stopped walking beside him.

'What? What are you talking about?'

Then he scurried up to Bosch's side and whispered.

'Listen, Harry, you're one of my main sources. I wouldn't screw you like that. If she's getting inside shit, look for somebody else.'

Bosch felt bad about accusing the reporter. He'd had no evidence.

'You sure? I'm mistaken about this, right?'

'Absolutely. You're too valuable to me. I wouldn't do it.'

'Okay, then.'

That was as close as he'd come to an apology.

'So what can you tell me about the ID?'

'Nothing. It's still not my case. Try RHD.'

'RHD has it? They took it from Edgar?'

Bosch got on the escalator and looked back at him. He nodded as he went down. Bremmer didn't follow.

Money Chandler was already on the steps smoking when Bosch came out. He lit a cigarette and looked back at her.

'Surprise, surprise,' he said.

'What?'

'Resting.'

'Only a surprise to Bulk,' she said. 'Any other lawyer would have seen it coming. I almost feel sorry for you, Bosch. Almost, but not quite. In a civil rights case, the chances of a win are always a long shot. But going up against the city attorney's office always kind of levels the playing field. These guys like Bulk, they couldn't make it on the outside. . . . If he had to win in order to eat, your lawyer would be a thin man. He needs that steady paycheck from the city coming in, win or lose.'

What she said, of course, was correct. But it was old news. Bosch smiled. He didn't know how to act. A part of himself liked her. She was wrong about him, but somehow he liked her. Maybe it was her tenacity, because her anger – though misdirected – was so pure.

Maybe it was because she wasn't afraid to talk to him outside of court. He had seen how Belk studiously avoided coming in contact with Church's family. Before getting up during recesses, he would sit at the defendant's table until he was sure they were all safely down the hall and on the escalator. But Chandler didn't play that kind of game. She was an up-front player.

Bosch guessed that this was what it was like when two

boxers touched gloves before the bell. He changed the subject.

'I talked to Tommy Faraday out here the other day. He's Tommy Faraway now. I asked him what happened but he didn't say. He just said justice happened, whatever that means.'

She blew a long stream of blue smoke out but didn't say anything for a while. Bosch looked at his watch. They had three minutes.

'You remember the Galton case?' she said. 'It was a civil rights case, an excessive force.'

Bosch thought about it. The name was familiar but it was difficult to place in the blend of excessive force cases he had heard or known about over the years.

'It was a dog case, right?'

'Yes. André Galton. This was before Rodney King, back when the wide majority of people in this city did not believe that their police engaged in horrible abuses as a matter of routine. Galton was black and driving with an expired tag through the hills of Studio City when a cop decided to pull him over.

'He had done nothing wrong, wasn't wanted, just had the tag one month overdue. But he ran. Great mystery of life, he ran. He got all the way up to Mulholland and ditched the car at one of those pull-offs where people look out at the view. Then he jumped out and climbed down the incline. There was nowhere to go down there but he wouldn't come back up and the cops wouldn't go down – too dangerous, they claimed at the trial.'

Bosch remembered the story now but he let her tell it. Her indignation was so pure and stripped of lawyerly pose that he just wanted to hear her tell it.

'So they sent a dog down,' she said. 'Galton lost both testicles and had permanent nerve damage to the right leg. He could walk but he had to kind of drag it behind him. . . .'

'Enter Tommy Faraday,' Bosch prompted.

'Yeah, he took the case. It was dead bang. Galton had done nothing wrong but to run. The response of the police certainly did not meet the offense. Any jury would see this. And the city attorney's office knew this. In fact, I think it was Bulk's case. They offered half a million to settle and Faraday passed. He thought he'd get a minimum three times that in trial, so he passed.

'And like I said, this was in the old days. Civil rights lawyers call it BK, that's short for Before King. A jury listened to four days of evidence and found for the cops in thirty minutes. Galton got nothing but a dead leg and a dead dick out of the whole thing. He came out here afterward and went to that hedge right there. He had hidden a gun – wrapped it in plastic and buried it there. He came over to the statue here and put the gun in his mouth. Faraday was coming through the door just then and saw it happen. Blood all over the statue, everywhere.'

Bosch didn't say anything. He remembered the case very clearly now. He looked up at the City Hall tower and watched the gulls circling above it. He always wondered what drew them there. It was miles from the ocean but there were always seabirds on top of City Hall. Chandler kept talking.

'Two things I've always been curious about,' she said. 'One, why did Galton run? And, two, why did he hide the gun? And I think the answers are both the same. He had no faith in justice, in the system. No hope. He had done nothing wrong but he ran because he was a black man in a white neighborhood and he had heard the stories all his life about what white cops do to black men in that position. His lawyer told him he had a dead-bang case, but he brought a gun to the courthouse because he had heard all his life about what jurors decide when it's a black man's word against the cops.'

Bosch looked at his watch. It was time to go in but he did not want to walk away from her.

'So that's why Tommy said justice happened,' she said.

'That was justice for André Galton. Faraday referred all his cases to other lawyers after that. I took a few. And he never set foot in a courtroom again.'

She stubbed out what was left of her cigarette.

'End of story,' she said.

'I'm sure the civil rights lawyers tell that one a lot,' Bosch said. 'And now you put me and Church into that, is that it? I'm like the guy who sent the dog down the hill after Galton?'

'There are degrees, Detective Bosch. Even if Church was the monster you claim, he didn't have to die. If the system turns away from the abuses inflicted on the guilty, then who can be next but the innocents? You see, that's why I have to do what I'm going to do to you in there. For the innocents.'

'Well, good luck,' he said.

He put his own cigarette out.

'I won't need it,' she said.

Bosch followed her gaze to the statue above the spot where Galton had killed himself. Chandler looked at it as if the blood were still there.

'That's justice,' she said, nodding at the statue. 'She doesn't hear you. She doesn't see. She can't feel you and won't speak to you. Justice, Detective Bosch, is just a concrete blonde.'

SIXTEEN

The courtroom seemed as silent as a dead man's heart while Bosch walked behind the plaintiff and defendant tables and in front of the jury box to get to the witness stand. After taking the oath he gave his full name and the clerk asked him to spell it.

'H-I-E-R-O-N-Y-M-U-S B-O-S-C-H.'

Then the judge turned it over to Belk.

'Tell us a little bit about yourself, Detective Bosch, about your career.'

'I've been a police officer nearly twenty years. I currently am assigned to the homicide table at Hollywood Division. Before that –'

'Why do they call it a table?'

Jesus, Bosch thought.

'Because it's like a table. It is six small desks pushed together to make a long table, three detectives on each side. It's always called a table.'

'Okay, go on.'

'Before this assignment I spent eight years in Robbery-Homicide Division's Homicide Special squad. Before that I was a detective on the homicide table in North Hollywood and robbery and burglary tables in Van Nuys. I was on patrol about five years, mostly in the Hollywood and Wilshire divisions.'

Belk slowly led him through his career up until the time he was on the Dollmaker task force. The questioning was slow and boring – even to Bosch, and it was his life. Every now and then he would look at the jurors when he answered a question and only a few seemed to be looking at him or paying attention. Bosch felt nervous and his palms were damp. He had testified in court at least a hundred times. But never like this, in his own defense. He felt hot though he knew the courtroom was overly cool.

'Now where was the task force physically located?'

'We used a second-floor storage room at the Hollywood station. It was an evidence and file storage room. We temporarily moved that stuff out into a rented trailer and used the room. We also had a room at Parker Center. The night shift, which I was on, generally worked out of Hollywood.'

'You were closer to the source, correct?'

'We thought so, yes. Most of the victims were taken from Hollywood streets. Many were later found in the area.'

'So you wanted to be able to act quickly on tips and leads and being right there in the center of things helped you do that, correct?'

'Correct.'

'On the night you got the call from the woman named Dixie McQueen, how did you get that call?'

'She called in on nine one one and when the dispatcher realized what she was talking about, the call was transferred out to the task force in Hollywood.'

'Who answered it?'

'I did.'

'Why is that? I thought you testified you were the supervisor of the night shift. Didn't they have people answering phones?'

'Yes, we had people, but this call came in late. Everybody had left for the night. I was only there because I was bringing the Chronological Investigation Record up to date – we had to turn it in at the end of each week. I was the only one there. I answered.'

'When you went to meet this woman, why didn't you call for a backup?'

'She hadn't told me enough over the phone to convince

me there was anything to it. We were getting dozens of calls a day. None of them amounted to anything. I have to admit I went to take her report not believing it would amount to anything.'

'Well, if you thought that, Detective, why did you go to her? Why not just take her information over the phone?'

'The main reason was that she said she didn't know the address she had been to with this man, but could show me the place if I drove her down Hyperion. Also, there seemed to be something genuine about her complaint, you know? It seemed that something had definitely scared her. I was about to head home so I thought I would just check it out on the way.'

'Tell us what happened after you got to Hyperion.'

'When we got there we could see lights on in the apartment over the garage. We even saw a shadow pass across one of the windows. So we knew the guy was still there. That's when Miss McQueen told me about the makeup she saw in the cabinet under the sink.'

'What did that mean to you?'

'A lot. It immediately got my attention because we had never said in the press that the killer was keeping the victims' makeup. It had leaked that he was painting their faces but not that he also kept their makeup. So when she told me she had seen this collection of makeup, it all clicked. It gave what she said some immediate legitimacy.'

Bosch drank some water from a paper cup the marshal had filled for him earlier.

'Okay, what did you do next?' Belk said.

'It occurred to me that in the time it had taken her to call me and for me to pick her up and get back to Hyperion, he could have gone out and gotten another victim. So I knew there was a good chance there was another woman up there in danger. I went up. I ran up.'

'Why didn't you call for backup?'

'First of all, I did not believe there was time to wait even five minutes for backup. If he had another woman in there, five minutes could mean her life. Secondly, I did not have a rover with me. I couldn't make the call even if I wanted to –'

'A rover?'

'A portable radio. Detectives usually take them on assignment. Problem is, there are not enough of them to go around. And since I was going home I didn't want to take one because I wasn't coming back until the next evening shift. That would mean one less rover available during the next day.'

'So you couldn't radio for backup. What about a phone?'

'It was a residential neighborhood. I could drive out and find a pay phone or knock on somebody's door. It was about one A.M. and I didn't think people would open their doors quickly to a single man claiming to be a police officer. Everything was a question of time. I didn't believe I had any. I had to go up by myself.'

'What happened?'

'Believing someone was in imminent danger, I went through the door without knocking. I was holding my gun out.'

'Kicked it open?'

'Yes.'

'What did you see?'

'First of all, I announced myself. I yelled, "Police". I moved a few steps into the room – it was a studio apartment – and I saw the man later identified as Church standing next to the bed. It was a foldout bed from a couch.'

'What was he doing?'

'He was standing there naked, next to the bed.'

'Did you see anyone else?'

'No.'

'What next?'

'I yelled something along the lines of "Freeze" or "Don't move" and took another step into the room. At first he didn't move. Then he suddenly reached down to the bed and his hand swept under the pillow. I yelled, "No," but he continued the movement. I could see his arm move as if his hand had grasped something and he started bringing the hand out. I fired one time. It killed him.'

'How far away from him would you say you were?'

'I was twenty feet away. It was one big room. We were at opposite sides of it.'

'And did he die instantly?'

'Very quickly. He dropped across the bed. The autopsy later showed the bullet entered under the right arm – the one he was reaching under the pillow with – and crossed through the chest. It hit his heart and both lungs.'

'After he was down, what did you do?'

'I went to the bed and checked to see if he was alive. He was still alive at that point, so I handcuffed him. He died a few moments later. I lifted the pillow. There was no gun.'

'What was there?'

Looking directly at Chandler, Bosch said, 'Great mystery of life, he had been reaching for a toupee.'

Chandler had her head down and was busy writing but she stopped and looked up at him and their eyes locked momentarily until she said, 'Objection, Your Honor.'

The judge agreed to strike Bosch's comment about the mystery of life. Belk asked a few more questions about the shooting scene and then moved on to the investigation of Church.

'You were no longer part of that, correct?'

'No, as is routine I was assigned desk duty while my actions in the shooting were investigated.'

'Well, were you made aware of the results of the task force's investigation into Church's background?'

'Generally. Because I had a stake in the outcome, I was kept informed.'

'What did you learn?'

'That the makeup found in the bathroom cabinet was tied to nine of the victims.'

'Did you ever have any doubts yourself or hear of any doubts from other investigators as to whether Norman Church was responsible for the deaths of those women?'

'For those nine? No, no doubts at all. Ever.'

'Well, Detective Bosch, you heard Mr Wieczorek testify about being with Mr Church on the night the eleventh victim, Shirleen Kemp, was killed. You saw the videotape presented as evidence. Didn't that raise any doubts?'

'It does about that case. But Shirleen Kemp was not among the nine whose makeup was found in Church's apartment. There is no doubt in my mind or in anybody's on the task force that Church killed those nine women.'

Chandler objected to Bosch speaking for the rest of the task force and the judge sustained it. Belk changed the subject, not wanting to venture any further into the area of victims seven and eleven. His strategy was to avoid any reference to a second killer, leaving that to Chandler to take a swing at on cross-examination, if she wanted to.

'You were disciplined for not going in with backup. Do you feel the department handled the matter correctly?'

'No.'

'How so?'

'As I explained, I did not believe I had a choice in what I did. If I had to do it again – even knowing I would be transferred as a result – I would do the same thing. I would have to. If there had been another woman in there, another victim, and I had saved her, I probably would have been promoted.'

When Belk didn't immediately ask a follow-up question, Bosch continued.

'I believe the transfer was a political necessity. The bottom line was, I shot an unarmed man. It did not matter that the man I shot was a serial killer, a monster. Besides, I was carrying baggage from –'

'That will be fine –'

'Run-ins with –'

'Detective Bosch.'

Bosch stopped. He had made his point.

'So what you are saying is you don't have any regrets about what happened in the apartment, correct?'

'No, that's not correct.'

This apparently surprised Belk. He looked down at his notes. He had asked a question he expected a different reply to. But he realized he had to follow through.

'What do you regret?'

'That Church made that move. He drew the fire. There was nothing I could do but respond. I wanted to stop the killings. I didn't want to kill him to do that. But that's the way it turned out. It was his play.'

Belk showed his relief by breathing heavily into the microphone before saying he had no further questions.

Judge Keyes said there would be a ten-minute break before cross-examination began. Bosch returned to the defense table, where Belk whispered that he thought they had done well. Bosch didn't respond.

'I think everything is going to ride on her cross. If you can get through it without heavy damage I think we've got it.'

'What about when she brings up the follower, introduces the note?'

'I don't see how she can. If she does, she'll be flying blind.'

'No, she won't. She's got a source in the department. Someone fed her stuff about the note.'

'I'll ask for a sidebar conference if it gets to that point.'

That wasn't very encouraging. Bosch looked at the clock, trying to gauge whether he had time for a smoke. He didn't think so and got up and went back to the witness stand. He passed behind Chandler, who was writing on a legal pad.

'Great mystery of life,' she said without looking up.

'Yeah,' Bosch said without looking back at her.

As he sat and waited, he saw Bremmer come in, followed by the guy from the *Daily News* and a couple of wire service reporters. Somebody had put out the word that the top act was about to begin. Cameras were not allowed in federal court, so one of the stations had sent a sketch artist over.

From the witness seat, Bosch watched Chandler working. He guessed she was writing out questions for him.

196

Deborah Church sat next to her with her hands folded on the table, her eyes averted from Bosch. A minute later the door to the jury room opened and the jurors filed into the box. Then the judge came out. Bosch took a deep breath and got ready as Chandler walked to the lectern with her yellow pad.

'Mr Bosch,' she began, 'how many people have you killed?'

Belk immediately objected and asked for a sidebar. The attorneys and the court reporter moved to the side of the bench and whispered for five minutes. Bosch only heard bits and pieces, most of it from Belk, who was loudest. At one point he argued that one shooting only was in dispute – the Church slaying – and all others were irrelevant. He heard Chandler say that the information was relevant because it illustrated the mind-set of the defendant. Bosch couldn't hear the judge's response but after the attorneys and reporter were back in place, the judge said, 'The defendant will answer the question.'

'I can't,' Bosch replied.

'Detective Bosch, the court is ordering you to answer.'

'I can't answer it, Judge. I don't know how many people I've killed.'

'You served in combat in Vietnam?' Chandler asked.

'Yes.'

'What were your duties?'

'Tunnel rat. I went into the enemy's tunnels. Sometimes this resulted in direct confrontation. Sometimes I used explosives to destroy tunnel complexes. It's impossible for me to know how many people were in them.'

'Okay, Detective, since you finished your duties with the armed services and became a police officer, how many people have you killed?'

'Three, including Norman Church.'

'Can you tell us about the two incidents not involving Mr Church? In general.'

'Yes, one was before Church, the other after. The first

time I killed someone it was during a murder investigation. I went to question a man I thought was a witness. Turned out he was the killer. When I knocked on the door, he fired a shot through it. Missed me. I kicked the door open and went in. I heard him running toward the rear of the house. I followed him to the yard, where he was climbing over a fence. As he was about to go over, he twisted around to take another shot at me. I fired first and he went down.

'The second time, this was after Church, I was involved in a murder and robbery investigation with the FBI. There was a shoot-out between two suspects and myself and my partner at the time, an FBI agent. I killed one of the suspects.'

'So in those two cases, the men you killed were armed?'

'That is correct.'

'Three shootings involving deaths, that is quite a lot, even for a twenty-year veteran, isn't it?'

Bosch waited a beat for Belk to make an objection but the fat man was too busy writing on his tablet. He had missed it.

'Um, I know twenty-year cops who have never even had to draw their guns, and I know some that have been involved in as many as seven deaths. It's a matter of what kind of cases you draw, it's a matter of luck.'

'Good luck or bad luck?'

This time Belk objected and the judge sustained it. Chandler quickly went on.

'After you killed Mr Church while he was unarmed, did you feel badly about it?'

'Not really. Not until I got sued and heard you were the lawyer.'

There was laughter in the courtroom and even Honey Chandler smiled. After he had quieted the room with a sharp rebuke from his gavel, the judge instructed Bosch to keep his answers on point and to refrain from personal asides.

'No bad feelings,' Bosch said. 'Like I said before, I would rather have taken Church alive than dead. But I wanted to take him off the street, either way.'

'But you set the whole thing up, tactically, so that it had to end in his permanent removal, didn't you?'

'No, I didn't. Nothing was set up. Things just happened.'

Bosch knew better than to show any anger toward her. Rather than make angry denouncements, the rule of thumb was to answer each question as if he was dealing with a person who was simply mistaken.

'You were, however, satisfied that Mr Church had been killed while unarmed, nude, totally defenseless?'

'Satisfaction doesn't enter into it.'

'Your Honor,' Chandler said. 'May I approach the witness with an exhibit? It's marked plaintiff's 3A.'

She handed copies of a piece of paper to Belk and the judge's clerk, who handed it over the bench to the judge. While the judge was reading it, Belk went to the lectern and objected.

'Your Honor, if this is offered as impeachment, I don't see how it is valid. These are the words of a psychiatrist, not my client.'

Chandler moved to the microphone and said, 'Judge, if you look in the section marked Summary, the last paragraph is what I would like to be read by the witness. You will also notice that the defendant signed the statement at the bottom.'

Judge Keyes read some more, wiped his mouth with the back of his hand and said, 'I'll accept it. You may show it to the witness.'

Chandler brought another copy up to Bosch and placed it in front of him without looking at him. Then she walked back to the lectern.

'Can you tell us what that is, Detective Bosch?'

'It's a confidential psychological release form. Supposedly confidential, I guess I should say.'

'Yes, and what does it relate to?'

'My release allowing me to return to duty after the Church shooting. It is routine to be interviewed by the department's psychiatrist after being involved in a shooting. Then he clears you to return to duty.'

'You must know him well.'

'Excuse me?'

'Ms Chandler, that's not necessary,' Judge Keyes said before Belk got up.

'No, Your Honor. Strike that. You were cleared to return to duty – to your new assignment in Hollywood – after the interview, correct?'

'Correct.'

'Isn't it true that this is really nothing more than a rubber-stamp process? The psychiatrist never holds an officer back from returning on psychiatric grounds?'

'No on the first question. I don't know on the second.'

'Well, let me turn it around. Have you ever heard of an officer being held back by the psychiatric interview?'

'No, I haven't. They're supposed to be confidential so I doubt I would hear anything anyway.'

'Will you please read the last paragraph of the summary section on the report in front of you?'

'Yes.'

He picked up the paper and began reading. Silently.

'Out loud, Detective Bosch,' she said in an exasperated tone. 'I thought that was implicit in the question.'

'Sorry. It says: "Through his war and police experiences, most notably including the aforementioned shooting resulting in fatality, the subject has to a high degree become desensitized to violence. He speaks in terms of violence or the aspect of violence being an accepted part of his day-to-day life, for all of his life. Therefore, it is unlikely that what transpired previously will act as a psychological deterrent should he again be placed in circumstances where he must act with deadly force in order to protect himself or others. I believe he will be able to act without delay. He will be able to pull the trigger. In fact, his conversation reveals no ill effects at all from the shooting, unless his sense of satisfaction with the outcome of the incident – the suspect's death – should be deemed inappropriate." '

Bosch put the paper down. He noticed the entire jury was looking at him now. He had no idea whether the report was highly damaging or helpful to his cause.

'The subject of that report is you, correct?' Chandler asked.

'Yes, it's me.'

'You just testified that there was no satisfaction, but the report by the psychiatrist said you did feel a sense of satisfaction with the outcome of the incident. Which is right?'

'Those are his words on the report, not mine. I don't think I would have said that.'

'What would you have said?'

'I don't know. Not that.'

'Then why did you sign the release form?'

'I signed it because I wanted to get back to work. If I was going to argue with him about what words he used, I was never going to get back to work.'

'Tell me, Detective, did the psychiatrist who examined you and made that report know about your mother?'

Bosch hesitated.

'I don't know,' he finally answered. 'I didn't tell him. I don't know if he would have had the information previously.'

He could hardly concentrate on his words, for his mind was scrambling.

'What happened to your mother?'

He looked directly at Chandler for a long moment before answering. She didn't look away.

'As was testified to earlier, she was killed. I was eleven. It happened in Hollywood.'

'And no one was ever arrested, correct?'

'That is correct. Can we go on to something else? This has already been testified about.'

Bosch looked over at Belk who got the point and stood up and objected to Chandler's repetitive line of questioning.

'Detective Bosch, do you want a break?' Judge Keyes asked. 'To sort of calm down a little?'

'No, Judge, I'm fine.'

'Well, I'm sorry. I can't restrict proper cross-examination. The objection is overruled.'

The judge nodded to Chandler.

'I'm sorry to ask such personal questions, but, after she was gone, did your father raise you?'

'You're not sorry. You –'

'Detective Bosch!' the judge boomed. 'We cannot have this. You must answer the questions asked of you. Say nothing else. Just answer the questions.'

'No. I never knew my father. I was put in the youth hall and then foster homes.'

'Any brothers or sisters?'

'No.'

'So the man who strangled your mother not only took the one closest to you, he destroyed much of your life at that point?'

'I'd say so.'

'Did the crime have something to do with your becoming a policeman?'

Bosch found he could no longer look at the jury. He knew his face had turned red. And he felt as if he were dying under a magnifying glass.

'I don't know. I never really analyzed myself to that extent.'

'Did it have something to do with the satisfaction you felt in killing Mr Church?'

'As I said before, if there was any satisfaction – you keep using that word – it was that I was satisfied with closing the case. To use your word, the man was a monster. He was a killer. I was satisfied we stopped him, wouldn't you be?'

'You're answering the questions, Detective Bosch,'

Chandler said. 'The question I now have is, did you stop the killings? All of them?'

Belk jumped up and asked for a sidebar conference. The judge said to the jurors, 'We're going to take that break now after all. We'll call you back when we're ready.'

SEVENTEEN

Belk asked for a discussion of his objection to Chandler's question out of earshot of the press, so the judge convened a hearing in his chambers. The hearing included the judge, Chandler, Belk, Bosch, the court reporter and the court clerk. They had to drag a couple of chairs in from the courtroom, then they all took places around the judge's huge desk. It was dark mahogany and looked like a box a small foreign car could have come in.

The first thing the judge did was light a cigarette. When Bosch saw Chandler follow suit, he did the same. The judge pushed the ashtray on his desk to the corner so they all could get at it.

'So, Mr Belk, it's your party,' the judge said.

'Your Honor, I am concerned with the direction Miss Chandler is taking this.'

'Call her Ms Chandler, Mr Belk. You know she prefers it. As far as which way she's going, how can you tell from one question?'

It was obvious to Bosch that Belk may have objected too soon. It was unclear how much information Chandler had, aside from the note. But Bosch thought Belk's tap-dancing around the problem was a waste of time.

'Judge,' he said. 'If I answer that last question it will compromise an ongoing investigation.'

The judge leaned back in his padded leather chair.

'How so?' he asked.

'We believe there is another killer,' Bosch said. 'The body found this week was identified yesterday and it has been determined that she could not have been killed by Church. She was alive up until two years ago. The –'

'The method used by the killer was identical to that of the real Dollmaker,' Belk interjected. 'The police believe there is a follower, someone who knew how Church killed and followed the same pattern. There is evidence to suggest the follower was responsible for the seventh and eleventh victims previously attributed to Church.'

Bosch said, 'The follower would have to be someone close to the original investigation, someone who knew the details.'

Belk said, 'If you allow her to open this line of questioning, it will be reported by the media and it will tip off the follower. He will know how close he is to being revealed.'

The judge was silent as he considered all of this for a moment.

'That all sounds real interesting and I wish you all the best of luck catching this follower, as you call him,' he finally said. 'But the problem you have, Mr Belk, is that you haven't given me any legal reason to stop your client from answering the question Ms Chandler put to him. No one wants to compromise an investigation. But you put your client on the stand.'

'That's if there is a second killer,' Chandler said. 'It's obvious there was only one killer and it wasn't Church. They've come up with this elaborate –'

'Ms Chandler,' the judge interrupted. 'That's for the jury to decide. Save your argument for them. Mr Belk, the problem is this is your witness. You called him and you've left him open to this line of questioning. I don't know what to tell you. I'm certainly not going to clear the media out of there. Off the record here, Miss Penny.'

The judge watched the court reporter lift her fingers from the keys.

'Mr Belk, you're fucked – 'scuse the language, ladies. He's gonna answer the question and the one after that and the one after that. Okay, we're back on.'

The reporter put her fingers back on the keys.

'Your Honor, this can't –'

'I've made my ruling, Mr Belk. Anything else?'

Belk then surprised Bosch.

'We would like a continuance.'

'What?'

'Your Honor, plaintiff opposes,' Chandler said.

'I know you do,' the judge said. 'What are you talking about, Mr Belk?'

'Your Honor, you have to put the trial on hiatus. Until at least next week. It will give the investigation time to possibly come to some fruition.'

'Some fruition? Forget it, Belk. You're in the middle of a trial, my friend.'

Belk stood and leaned across the great wide desk.

'Your Honor, I request an emergency stay of these proceedings while we take the matter on appeal to the ninth district.'

'You can appeal anything you like, Mr Belk, but there is no stay. We're in trial here.'

There was silence as everyone looked at Belk.

'What if I refuse to answer?' Bosch asked.

Judge Keyes looked at him a long moment and said, 'Then I'll hold you in contempt. Then I'll ask you to answer again and if you refuse again I will put you in jail. Then when your attorney here asks for bail while he appeals, I will say no bail. All of this will take place out there in front of the jury and the media folks. And I will place no restrictions on what Ms Chandler does or doesn't say to the reporters in the hallway. So, what I am saying is, you can try to be some kind of hero and not answer, but the story will get to the media anyway. It's like I said a few minutes ago to Mr Belk when we were off the rec –'

'You can't do this,' Belk suddenly erupted. 'It, it – it's not right. You have to protect this investigation. You –'

'Son, don't you ever tell me what I have to do,' the judge said very slowly and sternly. He seemed to grow in stature while Belk shrank back away from him. 'Only thing I have to do is ensure there is a fair trial on this matter. You are asking me to sit on information that could be vital to the plaintiff's case. You are also trying to intimidate me and that is one thing I don't take to. I'm no county judge that needs your nod every time an election comes 'round. I'm appointed for life. We're off here.'

Miss Penny stopped typing. Bosch almost didn't want to see Belk's slaughter. The deputy city attorney's head was bowed and he had assumed the posture of the doomed. The back of his neck was turned up and ready to receive the axe.

'So my advice here is that you get your fat ass out there and start working on how the hell you're going to salvage this on redirect. Because in five minutes Detective Bosch is going to answer that question or he's going to be handing his gun and his badge and his belt and shoelaces over to a marshal at the federal lockup. We're back on. Hearing adjourned.'

Judge Keyes brought his arm down and ground his cigarette into the ashtray. He never took his eyes off Belk.

As the procession made its way back into the courtroom, Bosch moved up closely behind Chandler. He glanced back to make sure the judge had turned to go to the bench and then said in a low voice, 'If you're getting your information from inside the department, I'm going to burn your source down when I find him.'

She didn't miss a stride. She didn't even turn back when she said, 'You mean, if you're not already ashes.'

Bosch took his place at the witness stand and the jury was brought back in. The judge told Chandler to continue.

'Rather than have the reporter find the last question, let me just rephrase it. After you killed Mr Church, did the so-called Dollmaker killings stop?'

Bosch hesitated, thinking. He looked out into the spectator section and saw that there were more reporters now – or at least people he thought were reporters. They all sat together.

He also saw Sylvia, sitting in the back row by herself. She offered a small smile to him which he did not return. He wondered how long she had been out there.

'Detective Bosch?' the judge prompted.

'I can't answer the question without compromising an ongoing investigation,' Bosch finally said.

'Detective Bosch, we just went over this,' the judge said angrily. 'Answer the question.'

Bosch knew that his refusal and jailing would not stop the story from getting out. Chandler would tell all the reporters as the judge had given her the okay to do. So putting himself in jail, he knew, only stopped him from chasing the follower. He decided to answer. He carefully composed a statement while stalling by taking a long, slow drink of water from the paper cup.

'Norman Church obviously stopped killing people after he was dead. But there was somebody – there is somebody else still out there. A killer who uses the same methods as Norman Church.'

'Thank you, Mr Bosch. And when did you come to that conclusion?'

'This week, when another body was found.'

'Who was that victim?'

'A woman named Rebecca Kaminski. She had been missing two years.'

'The details of her death matched the murders of the other Dollmaker victims?'

'Exactly, except for one thing.'

'And that was what?'

'She had been entombed in concrete. Hidden. Norman Church always discarded his victims in public places.'

'No other differences?'

'Not that I know of at the moment.'

'Yet, because she died two years after Norman Church was killed by you, there is no way possible that he is responsible.'

'Correct.'

'Because he was dead he has the perfect alibi, doesn't he?'

'Correct.'

'How was the body found?'

'As I said, it had been buried in concrete.'

'And what led police to the spot where it was buried?'

'We received a note with directions.'

Chandler then offered a copy of the note as plaintiff's exhibit 4A and Judge Keyes accepted it after overruling an objection by Belk. Chandler then handed a copy to Bosch to identify and read.

'Out loud this time,' she said before he could start. 'For the jury.'

Bosch felt eerie reading the words of the follower out loud in the quiet courtroom. After a beat of silence when he was done, Chandler began again.

' "I'm still in the game," he writes. What does that mean?'

'It means he is trying to take credit for all of the killings. He wants attention.'

'Could that be because he committed all of the murders?'

'No, because Norman Church committed nine of them. The evidence found in Church's apartment irrefutably links him to those nine. There is no doubt.'

'Who found this evidence?'

Bosch said, 'Me.'

'So, then, isn't there a lot of doubt, Detective Bosch? Isn't this idea of a second killer who uses the exact same method preposterous?'

'No, it's not preposterous. It is happening. I did not kill the wrong man.'

'Isn't it the truth that this talk of a copycat killer, a follower, is all an elaborate charade for covering up the fact that you did exactly that, killed the wrong man? An innocent, unarmed man who had done nothing worse than hire a prostitute with his wife's tacit approval?'

'No, it's not. Norman Church killed –'

'Thank you, Mr Bosch.'

'– a lot of women. He was a monster.'

'Like the one who killed your mother?'

He unconsciously looked out into the audience, saw Sylvia and then looked away. He tried to compose himself, slow his breathing. He was not going to let Chandler tear him open.

'I would say yes. They were probably similar. Both monsters.'

'That's why you killed him, wasn't it? The toupee wasn't under the pillow. You killed him in cold blood because you saw your mother's killer.'

'No. You are wrong. Don't you think if I was going to make up a story I could come up with something better than a toupee? There was a kitchenette, knives in the drawer. Why would I plant –'

'Hold it, hold it, hold it,' Judge Keyes barked. 'Now, we've gone off the tracks here. Ms Chandler, you started making statements instead of asking questions and, Detective Bosch, you did the same thing instead of answering. Let's start over.'

'Yes, Your Honor,' Chandler said. 'Isn't it true, Detective Bosch, that the whole thing – this pinning all the murders on Norman Church – was an elaborate cover-up that is now unraveling with the discovery of the woman in the concrete this week?'

'No, it is not true. Nothing is unraveling. Church was a killer and he deserved what he got.'

Bosch mentally flinched and closed his eyes as soon as the words were out of his mouth. She had done it. He opened his eyes and looked at Chandler. Her eyes seemed flat and blank, emotionless.

Softly, she said, 'You say he deserved what he got. When were you appointed judge, jury and executioner?'

Bosch drank more water from the cup.

'What I meant was that it was his play. Whatever happened to him, he was ultimately responsible. You put something in play like that and you have to accept the consequences.'

'Like Rodney King deserved what he got?'

'Objection!' Belk shouted.

'Like André Galton deserved what he got?'

'Objection!'

'Sustained, sustained,' the judge said. 'All right now, Ms Chandler, you –'

'They're not the same.'

'Detective Bosch, I sustained the objections. That means don't answer.'

'No further questions at this time, Your Honor,' Chandler said.

Bosch watched her walk to the plaintiff's table and drop her tablet onto the wooden surface. The loose strand of hair was there at the back of her neck. He was sure now that even that detail was part of her carefully planned and orchestrated performance during the trial. After she sat down, Deborah Church reached over and squeezed her arm. Chandler didn't smile or make any gesture in return.

Belk did what he could to repair the damage on redirect examination, asking more details about the heinous nature of the crimes, and the shooting and investigation of Church. But it seemed as if no one was listening. The courtroom had been sucked into a vacuum created by Chandler's cross-examination.

Belk was apparently so ineffective that Chandler didn't bother to ask anything on recross and Bosch was excused from the witness seat. He felt as if the walk back to the defense table covered at least a mile.

'Next witness, Mr Belk?' the judge asked.

'Your Honor, can I have a few minutes?'

'Surely.'

Belk turned to Bosch and whispered, 'We're going to rest, you have a problem with that?'

'I don't know.'

'There is no one else to call, unless you want to get other members of the task force over here. They'll say the same thing you did and get the same treatment from Chandler. I'd rather leave that alone.'

'What about bringing Locke back? He'll back me up on everything I said about the follower.'

'Too risky. He is a psychologist, for everything we get him to say is a possibility, she'll also get him to concede it is possibly not. He hasn't been deposed on this matter and we won't know for sure what he would say. Besides, I think we need to stay off the second killer. It's confusing the jury and we –'

'Mr Belk,' the judge said. 'We're waiting.'

Belk stood up and said, 'Your Honor, the defense rests.'

The judge stared a long moment at Belk before turning to the jury and telling them they were excused for the day because the lawyers would need the afternoon to prepare closing arguments and he would need time to prepare jury instructions.

After the jury filed out, Chandler went to the lectern. She asked for a directed verdict in favor of the plaintiff, which the judge denied. Belk did the same thing, asking for a verdict in favor of the defendant. In a seemingly sarcastic tone, the judge told him to sit down.

Bosch met Sylvia in the hallway outside after the crowded courtroom took several minutes to empty. There was a large gathering of reporters around the two lawyers and Bosch took her arm and moved her down the hall.

'I told you not to come here, Sylvia.'

'I know, but I felt I had to come. I wanted you to know that I support you no matter what. Harry, I know things about you the jury will never know. No matter how she tries to portray you, I know you. Don't forget that.'

She was wearing a black dress with a silvery-white pattern that Bosch liked. She looked very beautiful.

'I, uh, I – how long were you here?'

'For most of it. I'm glad I came. I know it was rough, but I saw the goodness of what you are come through all the harshness of what you sometimes have to do.'

He just looked at her a moment.

'Be optimistic, Harry.'

'The stuff about my mother . . .'

'Yes, I heard it. It hurt me that this is where I learned about it. Harry, where are we if there are those kinds of secrets between us? How many times do I have to tell you that it is endangering what we have?'

'Look,' he said, 'I can't do this right now. Deal with this and you, us – it's too much for right now. It's not the right place. Let's talk about it later. You're right, Sylvia, but I, uh, I just can't . . . talk. I –'

She reached up and straightened his tie and then smoothed it on his chest.

'It's okay,' she said. 'What will you do now?'

'Follow the case. Whether officially or not, I have to follow this. I have to find the second man, the second killer.'

She just looked at him for a few moments and he knew she had probably hoped for a different answer.

'I'm sorry. It's not something I can put off. Things are happening.'

'I'm going to go in to school then. So I don't lose the whole day. Will you be up to the house tonight?'

'I'll try.'

'Okay, see you, Harry. Be optimistic.'

He smiled and she leaned into him and kissed him on the cheek. Then she walked off toward the escalator.

Bosch was watching her go when Bremmer came up.

'You want to talk about this? That was some interesting testimony in there.'

'I said all I'm saying on the stand.'

'Nothing else?'

'Nope.'

'What about what she says? That the second killer is really the first and that Church didn't kill anybody.'

'What do you expect her to say? It's bullshit. Just remember, what I said in the courtroom was under oath.

213

What she says out here isn't. It's bullshit, Bremmer. Don't fall for it.'

'Look, Harry, I have to write this. You know? It's my job. You going to understand that? No hard feelings?'

'No hard feelings, Bremmer. Everybody has got their job to do. Now I'm going to go do mine, okay?'

He walked off toward the escalator. Outside at the statue, he lit a cigarette and gave one to Tommy Faraway, who had been sifting through the ash can.

'What's happening, Lieutenant?' the homeless man asked.

'Justice is happening.'

EIGHTEEN

Bosch drove over to Central Division and found an open parking space at the front curb. For a while, he sat in his car looking at two trustees from the lockup washing the painted enamel mural that stretched along the front wall of the bunkerlike station. It was a depiction of a nirvana where black and white and brown children played together and smiled at friendly police officers. It was a depiction of a place where the children still had hope. In angry black spray paint along the bottom of the mural someone had written, 'This is a damnable lie!'

Bosch wondered whether someone from the neighborhood or a cop had done it. He smoked two cigarettes and tried to clear his mind of what had happened in the courtroom. He felt strangely at peace with the idea that some of his secrets had been revealed. But he held little hope for the outcome of the trial. He had moved into a feeling of resignation, an acceptance that the jury would find against him, that the twisted delivery of evidence in the case would convince them that he had acted, if not like the monster Chandler had described, then at least in an undesirable and reckless manner. They would never know what it was like to have to make such decisions as he had made in so fleeting a moment.

It was the same old story that every cop knew. The citizens want their police to protect them, to keep the plague from their eyes, from their doors. But those same John Q.'s are the first to stare wide-eyed and point the finger of outrage when they see close up exactly what the job they've given the cops entails. Bosch wasn't a hardliner. He didn't condone the actions taken by police in the André Galton cases and the Rodney King cases. But he understood those actions and knew that his own actions ultimately shared a common root.

Through political opportunism and ineptitude, the city had allowed the department to languish for years as an understaffed and underequipped paramilitary organization. Infected with political bacteria itself, the department was top-heavy with managers while the ranks below were so thin that the dog soldiers on the street rarely had the time or inclination to step out of their protective machines, their cars, to meet the people they served. They only ventured out to deal with the dirtbags and, consequently, Bosch knew, it had created a police culture in which everybody not in blue was seen as a dirtbag and was treated as such. Everybody. You ended up with your André Galtons and your Rodney Kings. You ended up with a riot the dog soldiers couldn't control. You ended up with a mural on a station house wall that was a damnable lie.

He badged his way past the front desk and took the stairs up to the Administrative Vice offices. At the door to the squad room he stood for a half minute and watched Ray Mora sitting at his desk on the other side of the room. It looked as if Mora was writing a report, rather than typing it. That probably meant it was a Daily Activity Report, which required little attention – just a few lines – and wasn't worth the time it took to get up and find a working typewriter.

Bosch noticed that Mora wrote with his right hand. But he knew this did not eliminate the vice cop as possibly being the follower. The follower knew the details and would have known about pulling the ligature around his victim's neck from the left side, thereby emulating the Dollmaker. Just as he knew about painting the white cross on the toe.

Mora looked up and saw him.

'What're you doing over there, Harry?'

'Didn't want to interrupt.'

Bosch walked over.

'What, interrupt a day report? Are you kidding?'

'Thought it might be something important.'

'It's important for me to get my paycheck. That's about it.'

Bosch dragged a chair away from an empty desk and pulled it up and sat down. He noticed the statue of the Infant of Prague had been moved. Turned, actually. Its face was no longer looking at the nakedness of the actress on the porn calendar. Bosch looked at Mora and realized he was not sure how to proceed here.

'You left a message last night.'

'Yeah, I was thinking . . .'

'About what?'

'Well, we know Church didn't kill Maggie Cum Loudly because of the timing, right? He was already dead when she got her ass dropped in the concrete.'

'That's right.'

'So, we've gotta copycat.'

'Right again.'

'So I was thinking: what if the copycat who did her started earlier?'

Bosch felt his throat start to tighten. He tried not to show Mora anything. Just gave him the deadpan look.

'Earlier?'

'Yeah. What if the two other porno chicks who were killed were actually done by the copycat? Who says he had to start after Church was dead?'

Bosch felt the full chill now. If Mora was the follower, was he so confident that he would risk laying the whole pattern out for Bosch? Or could his hunch – after all, that's all it was, a guess – be completely out of line? Regardless, it felt creepy sitting with Mora, his desk covered by magazines with sex acts depicted on the covers, the calendar girl leering from the vertical file. The statue's clay face turned away. Bosch realized that Delta Bush, the actress on the calendar Mora had displayed, was blonde-haired and buxom. She fit the pattern. Was that why Mora had put up the calendar?

'You know, Ray,' he said, after composing his voice into a monotone, 'I've been thinking the same thing. It fits better that way, all the evidence, I mean, if the follower did all three of them . . . What made you think of it?'

Mora put the report he was working on away in a desk drawer and leaned onto his desk. Subconsciously he brought his left hand up and pulled the Holy Spirit medal from his open collar. He rubbed it between his thumb and forefinger as he leaned back in his seat again, elbows on the arm rests.

He dropped the medal and said, 'Well, I remembered something is what I did. It was a tip that I got right before you nailed Church. See, I dropped it when you dropped Church.'

'You're talking about four years ago.'

'Yeah. We all thought that was it, end of case, when you got Church.'

'Get to it, Ray, what'd you remember?'

'Yeah, right, well, I remember a couple days, maybe a week before you got Church, I was given one of the call-in tips. It was given to me 'cause I was the resident expert on porno and it was a porno chick who called it in. She used the name Gallery. That's it, just Gallery. She was in the bottom-line stuff. Loops, live shows, peep booths, nine hundred phone call stuff. And she was just beginning to move up, get her name on some video boxes.

'Anyway, she called the task force – this was right before you nailed Church – and said there was a Tom that'd been making the rounds of the sets up in the Valley. You know, watching the action, hanging out with the producers, but he wasn't like the other Toms.'

'I don't know what you mean. Toms?'

'That's short for Peeping Tom. That's what the girls call these guys who hang out on the sets. Usually they're friendly with the producer or they've kicked in part of the budget. They throw a grand to the producer and he lets the guy hang around and watch 'em shoot. It's pretty common. These shoots draw a lot of people for whom seeing it on video isn't enough. They want to be right up there and see it live.'

'All right, so what about this guy?'

'Well, Harry, look, there's really only one reason these people hang around the sets. They're hitting on the chicks between takes. I mean, these guys wanna get laid. Or they want to make flicks themselves. They want to break in. And that was the thing with this guy. He wasn't hitting on anybody. He was just hanging around. She – this is Gallery – said she never saw this dude make the move on anybody. He talked to some of the girls but never left with any of them.'

'And that's what made him weird? He didn't want to get laid?'

Mora raised his hands and shrugged like he knew it sounded weak.

'Yeah, basically. But listen, Gallery worked shoots with both Heather Cumhither and Holly Lere, the two Doll-maker victims, and she said it was on those shoots that she saw this Tom. That's why she called.'

Now the story had Bosch's attention. But he didn't know what to make of it. Mora could be simply trying to deflect attention, to send Bosch down the wrong trail.

'She didn't have a name on the guy?'

'No, that was the problem. That was why I didn't jump all over it. I had a backlog of tips I was assigned and she calls in with this one without a name. I would have gotten to it eventually, but a few days later you put Church's dick in the dirt and that was that.'

'You let it go.'

'Yeah, dropped it like a bag of shit.'

Bosch waited. He knew Mora would go on. He had more to say. There had to be more.

'So the thing is, when I looked up the card on Magna Cum Loudly for you yesterday, I recognized some of her early titles. She worked with Gallery in some of her early work. That's what made me remember the tip. So just stringing along on a hunch, I try to look Gallery up, ask around with some people in the business I know, and it turns out Gallery dropped out of the scene three years ago. Just like that. I mean, I know a top producer with the Adult Film Association and he told me she dropped out right in the middle of one of his shoots. Never said a word to anyone. And no one ever heard from her again. The producer, he remembered it pretty clearly 'cause it cost him a lot of money to reshoot the flick. There would've been no continuity if he just dumped in another actress to take her place.'

Bosch was surprised that continuity was even a factor in such films. He and Mora were both silent a moment, thinking about the story, before Bosch finally spoke.

'So, you're thinking she might be in the ground somewhere? Gallery, I'm talking about. In concrete like the one we found this week.'

'Yeah, that's exactly what I'm thinking. People in the industry – I mean, they are not your mainstream people, so there are plenty of disappearing acts. I remember this one broad, she dropped out, next thing I know I see her in *People* magazine. One of those stories about some celebrity fund-raiser and she's on the arm of what's his name, guy has his own TV show about the guy in charge of a kennel. Noah's Bark. I can't think of –'

'Ray, I don't give –'

'Okay, okay, anyway the point is, these chicks drop in and out of the biz all the time. Not unusual. They aren't the smartest people in the first place. They just get it in their mind to do something else. Maybe they meet a guy who they think is going to keep them in cocaine and caviar, be their sugar daddy, like that Noah's Bark asshole, and they never show up for work again – until they find out they were wrong. As a group, they don't look much past the next line of blow.

'Y'ask me, what they're all looking for is Daddy. They all got knocked around when they were a kid and this is some fucked-up way of showing they're worth something to Daddy. Least I read that somewhere. Prob'ly bullshit like everything else.'

Bosch didn't need the psychology lesson.

'C'mon Ray, I'm in court and I'm trying to run down this case. Get to the point. What about Gallery?'

'What I'm saying is that with Gallery the situation's unusual 'cause it's been almost three years and she never came back. See, they always come back. Even if they've fucked over a producer so bad he had to do reshoots, they always come back. They start at the bottom – loops, fluffing – and work their way back up.'

'Fluffing?'

'A fluff is off-camera talent, you could say. Girls who keep the acts up and ready to perform while they're getting cameras ready, moving lights, changing angles. Things like that, if you know what I mean.'

'Yeah, I know what you mean.'

Bosch was depressed after hearing about the business for ten minutes. He looked at Mora, who had been in Ad-Vice for as long as Bosch could remember.

'What about the survivor? You ever check with her on this tip?'

'Never got around to it. Like I said, I dropped it when you dropped Church. Thought we were done with the whole thing.'

'Yeah, so did I.'

Bosch took out a small pocket notebook and wrote down a few notes from the conversation.

'Did you save any notes from this? From back then?'

'Nope, they're gone. The original tip sheet is probably in the main task force files. But it won't say more than I just told you.'

Bosch nodded. Mora was probably right.

'What did this Gallery look like?'

'Blonde, nice set – definitely Beverly Hills plastic. I think I got a picture here.'

He rolled his chair to the file cabinets behind him and dug through one of the drawers, then rolled back with a file. From it he pulled an 8 × 10 color publicity shot. It was a blonde woman posed at the edge of the ocean. She was nude. She had shaved her pubic area. Bosch handed the photo back to Mora and felt embarrassed, as if they were two boys in the schoolyard telling secrets about one of the girls. He thought he saw a slight smile on Mora's face and wondered if the vice cop found humor in his discomfort or it was something else.

'Hell of a job you've got.'

'Yeah, well, somebody's gotta do it.'

Bosch studied him a moment. He decided to take a chance, to try to figure out what made Mora hang on to the job.

'Yeah, but why you, Ray? You've been doing this a long time.'

'I guess I'm a watchdog, Bosch. The Supreme Court says this stuff is legal to a point. That makes me one of the pointmen. It's gotta be monitored. It's gotta be kept clean, no joke intended. That means these people've gotta be licensed, of legal age, and nobody's forced to do something they don't want to do. I spend a lot of days looking through this trash, looking for the stuff even the Supreme Court couldn't take. Trouble is, community standards. LA doesn't have any, Bosch. Hasn't been a successful obscenity prosecution here in years. I've made some underage cases. But I'm still looking for my first obscenity jacket.'

He stopped a moment before saying, 'Most cops do a year in Ad-Vice and then transfer out. That's all they can take. This is my seventh year, man. I can't tell you why. I guess because there's no shortage of surprises.'

'Yeah, but year after year of this shit. How can you take it?'

Mora's eyes dropped to the statue on the desk.

'I'm provided for. Don't worry about me.' He waited another beat and said, 'I've got no family. No wife anymore. Who's going to complain about what I do, anyway?'

Bosch knew from their work on the task force that Mora had volunteered for the B squad, to work nights, because his wife had just left him. He had told Bosch that he found it hardest to get through the nights. Bosch now wondered if Mora's ex-wife was blonde and, if she was, what it would mean.

'Look, Ray, I've been thinking the same things, about this follower. And she fits, you know? Gallery. The three vics and the survivor were all blondes. Church wasn't choosey but the follower apparently is.'

'Hey, you're right,' Mora said, looking at the photo of Gallery. 'I hadn't thought about that.'

'Anyway, this four-year-old tip is as good a place to start as any. There also might be other women, other victims. What've you got going?'

Mora smiled and said, 'Harry, doesn't matter what I got going. It's dogshit compared to this. I gotta vacation next week but I don't leave till Monday. Till then, I'm on it.'

'You mentioned the adult association. Is that –'

'Adult Film Association, yeah. It's run out of a lawyer's office in Sherman Oaks.'

'Yeah, you tight with anybody there?'

'I know the chief counsel. He's interested in keeping the biz clean, so he's a cooperative individual.'

'Can you talk to him, ask around, try to find out if anybody else dropped out like Gallery? They'd have to be blonde and built.'

'You want to know how many other victims we might have.'

'That's right.'

'I'll get on it.'

'What about the agents and the performers guild?'

Bosch nodded at the calendar with Delta Bush on it.

'I'll hit them, too. Two agents handle ninety percent of the casting in this business. They'd be the place to start.'

'What about outcall? Do all of the women do it?'

'Not the top ranks of performers. But the ones below that, yeah, they pretty much go the outcall route. See, the top performers, they spend ten percent of the time making movies and the rest out on the road dancing. They go from strip club to strip club, make a lot of money. They can make a hundred grand a year dancing. Most people think they're getting a bundle to do the nasty on video. That's wrong. It's the dancing. Then if you go below that level, to the performers either going up or coming down, they're the ones you find doing outcall work in addition to the movies and the dancing. A lot of money there, too. These chicks will pull down a grand a night for outcall work.'

'Do they work with pimps, what?'

'Yeah, some got management but it's not a requirement. It's not like the street, where a girl needs her pimp to protect her from the bad johns and other whores. In outcall, all you need is an answering service. Chick puts her ad and her picture in the X press and the calls come in. Most have rules. They won't go to anybody's house, strictly hotel work. They can control the class of clientele they keep by the expense of the hotel. Good way to keep the riff-raff out.'

Bosch thought about Rebecca Kaminski and how she had gone to the Hyatt on Sunset. A nice place, but the riff-raff got in.

Apparently thinking the same thing, Mora said, 'It doesn't always work, though.'

'Obviously.'

'So, I'll see what I can come up with, okay? But off the top of my head, I don't think there will be many. If there was a bunch of women doing the sudden and permanent disappearing act like Gallery did, I think I would've gotten wind of it.'

'You got my beeper number?'

Mora wrote it down and Bosch headed out of the office.

He was heading across the lobby past the front desk when the pager on his belt sounded. He checked the number and saw it was a 485 exchange. He assumed Mora had forgotten to tell him something. He took the stairs back up to the second floor and ducked back into the Ad-Vice squad room.

Mora was there, holding the photo of Gallery and staring at it in a contemplative manner. He looked up then and saw Bosch.

'Did you just beep me?'

'Me? No.'

'Oh, I just thought you were trying to catch me before I left. I'm gonna use one of the phones.'

'You're welcome to 'em, Harry.'

Bosch walked to an empty desk and dialed the number from the pager. He saw Mora slide the photo into the file. He put the file into a briefcase that was on the floor next to his chair.

A male voice answered the call after two rings.

'Chief Irvin Irving's office, this is Lieutenant Felder, how can I help you?'

NINETEEN

As with all three of the department's assistant chiefs, Irving had his own private conference room at Parker Center. It was furnished with a large, round, Formica-topped table and six chairs, a potted plant and a counter that ran along the rear wall. There were no windows. The room could be entered through a door from Irving's adjutant's office or from the sixth floor's main hallway. Bosch was the last one to arrive at the summit meeting called by Irving, taking the last chair. In the others sat the assistant chief, followed counterclockwise by Edgar and three men from Robbery-Homicide Division. Two of them Bosch knew, detectives Frankie Sheehan and Mike Opelt. They had also been attached to the Dollmaker task force four years earlier.

The third man from RHD Bosch knew by name and reputation only. Lieutenant Hans Rollenberger. He had been promoted to RHD sometime after Bosch had been demoted out of it. But friends like Sheehan kept Bosch informed. They told him Rollenberger was another cookie-cutter bureaucrat who avoided controversial and career-threatening decisions the way people avoid pan-handlers on the sidewalk, pretending not to see or hear them. He was a climber and, therefore, he couldn't be trusted. In RHD, the troops already referred to him as 'Hans Off', because that was the kind of commander he was. Morale in RHD, the unit every detective in the police department aspired to, was probably the lowest since the day the Rodney King video hit the TV.

'Sit down, Detective Bosch,' Irving said cordially. 'I think you know everybody.'

Before Bosch could answer, Rollenberger sprang from his chair and offered his hand.

'Lieutenant Hans Rollenberger.'

Bosch shook it, then they both sat down. Bosch noticed a large stack of files at the center of the table and immediately recognized them as the Dollmaker task force case files. The murder books Bosch had were his own personal files. What was piled on the table was the entire main file, probably pulled out of the archives warehouse.

'We're sitting down to see what we can do about this problem that's come up with the Dollmaker case,' Irving said. 'I have – as Detective Edgar has probably told you, I am swinging this case over to RHD. I am prepared to have Lieutenant Rollenberger put as many people on it as needed. I have also arranged for the loan of Detective Edgar to the case and you, as soon as you are free from the trial. I want results quickly. This is already turning into a public relations nightmare with what I understand was revealed during testimony today in your trial.'

'Yeah, well, sorry about that. I was under oath.'

'I understand that. The problem was you were testifying to things only you knew about. I had my adjutant sit in and he informed us of your, uh, theory on what has happened with this new case. Last night, I made the decision to have RHD handle the matter. After hearing the sense of your testimony today, I want to task-force this and get it going.

'Now, I want you to bring us up to speed on exactly what is going on, what you think, what you know. Then, we will plan from there.'

They all looked at Bosch for a moment and he was unsure where to begin. Sheehan stepped in with a question. It was a signal that he believed Irving was playing on the level on this one, that Bosch could feel safe.

'Edgar says it's a copycat. That there is no problem with Church?'

'That's right,' Bosch answered. 'Church was the man. But he was good for nine of the victims, not eleven. He spawned a follower halfway through his run and we didn't see it.'

'Tell it,' Irving said.

He did. It took Bosch forty-five minutes to tell it. Sheehan and Opelt asked several questions as he went. The only thing or person he did not mention was Mora.

At the end, Irving said, 'When you ran this follower theory by Locke, did he say it's possible?'

'Yes. With him I think he thinks anything is possible. But he was useful. He made it pretty clear for me. I want to keep him informed. He's good to bounce stuff off of.'

'I understand there's a leak. Could it be Locke?'

Shaking his head, Bosch said, 'I didn't go to him until last night and Chandler has known things from the start. She knew I was out at the scene the first day. Today she seemed to know the direction we are going, that there is a follower. She's got a good source keeping her informed. And Bremmer over at the *Times,* who knows. He's got a lot of sources.'

'Okay,' Irving said. 'Well, aside from Dr Locke being the exception, nothing in this room leaves this room. No one talks to anyone. You two' – he looked at Bosch and Edgar – 'don't even tell your supervisors at Hollywood what you're doing.'

Without naming Pounds, Irving was postulating his suspicion that Pounds could be a leak. Edgar and Bosch nodded in agreement.

'Now' – Irving looked at Bosch – 'where do we go from here?'

Without hesitation, Bosch said, 'We have to retrace the investigation. Like I told you, Locke said it was someone who had intimate access to the case. Who knew every detail and then copied them. It was a perfect cover. For a while, at least.'

'You're talking about a cop,' Rollenberger said, his first words since the briefing began.

'Maybe. But there are other possibilities. The suspect pool is actually pretty large. You got the cops, people who found the bodies, the coroner's staff, passersby at the crime scenes, reporters, lot of people.'

'Shit,' Opelt said. 'We're going to need more people.'

'Don't worry about that,' Irving said. 'I'll get more. How do we narrow it down?'

Bosch said, 'When we look at the victims we learn things about the killer. The victims and the survivor generally fall into the same archetype. Blonde, well built, worked in porno and did outcall work on the side. Locke thinks that is how the follower picked his victims. He saw them in videos, then found the means of contacting them in the outcall ads in the local adult newspapers.'

'It's like he went shopping for victims,' Sheehan said.

'Yeah.'

'What else?' Irving said.

'Not a lot. Locke said the follower is very smart, much more so than Church was. But that he could be disassembling, as he calls it. Coming apart. That's why he sent the note. Nobody would've ever known but then he sent the note. He's moved into a phase where he wants the attention that the Dollmaker had. He got jealous that this trial threw attention on Church.'

'What about other victims?' Sheehan asked. 'Ones we don't know about yet? It's been four years.'

'Yeah, I'm working on that. Locke says there's gotta be others.'

'Shit,' Opelt said. 'We need more people.'

Everyone was quiet while they thought about this.

'What about the FBI, shouldn't we contact their behavioral science people?' Rollenberger asked.

Everyone looked at Hans Off as if he were the kid who came to the sandlot football game wearing white pants.

'Fuck them,' Sheehan said.

'We seem to have a handle on this – initially, at least,' Irving said.

'What else do we know about the follower?' Rollenberger said, hoping to immediately deflect attention from his miscue. 'Do we have any physical evidence that can give us any insight into him?'

'Well, we need to track down the survivor,' Bosch said. 'She gave a composite drawing that everyone dismissed after I nailed Church. But now we know her drawing was probably of the follower. We need to find her and see if there is anything else that she has, that she can still remember, that will help.'

As he said this Sheehan dug through the stack of files on the table and found the composite. It was very generic and didn't look like anyone Bosch recognized, least of all Mora.

'We have to assume he wore disguises, same as Church, so the composite might not help. But she might remember something else, something about the suspect's manners that might let us know if it was a cop.

'Also, I'm having Amado at the coroner's office compare the rape kits between the two victims we now attribute to the follower. There's a good chance the follower may have made a mistake here.'

'Explain,' Irving said.

'The follower did everything the Dollmaker did, right?'

'Right,' Rollenberger said.

'Wrong. He only did what was known at the time about the Dollmaker. What we knew. What we didn't know was that Church had been smart. He had shaved his body so he would not leave trace hair evidence behind. We didn't know that until after he was dead, so neither did the follower. And by then he had already done two of the victims.'

'So there is a chance those two rape kits hold physical evidence to our guy,' Irving said.

'Right. I'm having Amado cross-check between the two kits. He should know something by Monday.'

'That's very good, Detective Bosch.'

Irving looked at Bosch and their eyes met. It was as if the

assistant chief was sending him a message and taking one at the same time.

'We'll see,' Bosch said.

'Other than that, that's all we've got, right?' Rollenberger said.

'Right.'

'No.'

It was Edgar, who up until now had been silent. Everyone looked at him.

'In the concrete we found – actually, Harry found it – a cigarette pack. It went in when the concrete was wet. So there's a good chance they were the follower's. Marlboro regulars. Soft pack.'

'They also could have been the vic's, right?' Rollenberger asked.

'No,' Bosch said. 'I talked to her manager last night. He said she didn't smoke. The smokes were in all likelihood the follower's.'

Sheehan smiled at Bosch and Bosch smiled back. Sheehan held his hands together as if waiting for handcuffs.

'Here I am boys,' he said. 'That's my brand.'

'Mine, too,' Bosch said. 'But I've got you beat. I'm left-handed, too. I better get an alibi working.'

The men at the table smiled. Bosch dropped his smile when he suddenly thought of something but knew he could not say anything yet. He looked at the files stacked at the center of the table.

'Shit, every cop smokes Marlboros or Camels,' Opelt said.

'It's a dirty habit,' Irving said.

'I agree,' said Rollenberger, a little too quickly.

It brought silence back to the table.

'Who's your suspect?'

It was Irving who asked it. He was looking at Bosch again with those eyes Harry couldn't decipher. The question shocked Bosch. Irving knew. Somehow he knew. Harry didn't answer.

'Detective, it is clear you've had a handle on what's going on for a day. You've also been on this case from the start. I think you've got someone in mind. Tell us. We need to start somewhere.'

Bosch hesitated again but finally said, 'I'm not sure . . . and I don't want . . .'

'To ruin someone's career if you're wrong? To set the dogs on a possibly innocent man? That's understood. But we can't have you pursuing this on your own. Haven't you learned anything from this trial? I believe "cowboying" was the term Money Chandler used to describe it.'

They were all looking at him. He was thinking of Mora. The vice cop was strange but was he that strange? Over the years Bosch had often been investigated by the department and did not want to bring that kind of weight down on the wrong person.

'Detective?' Irving prompted. 'Even if all you have is a hunch, then you must tell us. Investigations start with hunches. You want to protect one person but what are we going to do? We are about to go out and investigate cops. What difference is it if we start with this person or come to him in time? Either way we will get to him. Give us the name.'

Bosch thought about everything Irving had said. He wondered what his own motive was. Was he protecting Mora or simply keeping him for himself? He thought a few more moments and finally said, 'Give me five minutes alone in here with the files. If there is something there that I think is there, then I'll tell you.'

'Gentlemen,' Irving said, 'let's go get some coffee.'

After the room was cleared, Bosch looked at the files for nearly a minute without moving. He felt confused. He wasn't sure whether he wanted to find something that would convince him Mora was the follower or convince him he was not. He thought about what Chandler had said to the jury about monsters and the black abyss where they dwell.

Whoever fights monsters, he thought, should not think too hard about it.

He lit a cigarette and pulled the stack close to him and began looking for two files. The chronologies file was near the top. It was thin. It was basically a quick guide to important dates in the investigation. He found the task force personnel file at the bottom of the stack. It was thicker than the first he pulled out because it contained the weekly shifts schedule for the detectives assigned to the task force and the overtime approval forms. As the detective-three in charge of the B squad, Bosch had been in charge of keeping the personnel file up to date.

From the chronologies file, Bosch quickly looked up the times and dates that the first two porno actresses were murdered and other pertinent information about the way they were lured to their death. Then he looked up the same information about the lone survivor. He wrote it all down in order on a page of his pocket notebook.

- June 17, 11 P.M.
  Georgia Stern aka Velvet Box
  survivor

- July 6, 11:30 P.M.
  Nicole Knapp aka Holly Lere
  W. Hollywood

- Sept 28, 4 A.M.
  Shirleen Kemp aka Heather Cumhither
  Malibu

Bosch opened the personnel file and pulled the shift schedules for the weeks the women were attacked or murdered. June seventeenth, the night Georgia Stern was attacked, was a Sunday, which was the B squad's night off. Mora could've done it, but so could anyone else who was on the squad.

233

On the Knapp case, Bosch got a hit and his fingers trembled a little as he held the schedule for the week of July 1. His adrenaline was moving faster now. July sixth, the day Knapp was sent on an outcall request at 9 P.M., and was found dead on the sidewalk on Sweetzer in West Hollywood at 11:30 P.M., was a Friday. Mora was on the schedule to be working the three-to-midnight shift with the B squad, but there next to his name in Bosch's own writing was the word 'sick'.

Bosch quickly pulled out the schedule for the week of September twenty-second. The nude body of Shirleen Kemp had been found at the side of the Pacific Coast Highway in Malibu at four in the morning on Friday, September twenty-eighth. He realized that wasn't enough information and looked for the file that contained the investigation of her death.

He quickly read through the file and learned that Kemp had a phone service that had logged a call for her services at the Malibu Inn at 12:55 A.M. When detectives went there they learned from phone records that at 12:55 A.M. a call had been placed by the occupant of room 311. The front desk staff could not provide a good description of the man in 311 and the identification he gave proved to be false. He had paid in cash. The one thing the desk people could say with absolute accuracy was that he checked in at 12:35 A.M. Each registration card was punched with the time. The man had called for Heather Cumhither twenty minutes after he checked in.

Bosch referred back to the work schedule. On the Thursday night before Kemp was murdered, Mora had worked. But he had apparently come in and left early. He had signed in at 2:40 P.M. and out at 11:45 P.M.

That gave him fifty minutes to get from the Hollywood station to the Malibu Inn and checked into room 311 at 12:35 A.M., Friday. Bosch knew that it could be done. Traffic would be light on the PCH that late at night.

It could be Mora.

He noticed that the cigarette he had set on the edge of the table had burned down to the butt and it had discolored the Formica edge. He quickly dropped the cigarette into a pot containing a ficus plant in the corner of the room and turned the table around so the burn mark was positioned at the spot where Rollenberger had been sitting. He waved one of the files in the air to disperse the smoke and then opened the door to Irving's office.

'Raymond Mora.'

Irving had said the name out loud apparently to see how it sounded. He said nothing else when Bosch was finished telling what he knew. Bosch watched him and waited for more but the assistant chief only sniffed at the air, identified the cigarette smoke and frowned.

'Another thing,' Bosch said. 'Locke wasn't the only one I talked to about the follower. Mora knows just about everything I just told you. He was on the task force and we went to him this week for help on the ID of the concrete blonde. I was over at Ad-Vice when you paged me. He had called me last night.'

'What did he want?' Irving asked.

'He wanted to let me know that he thought the follower might've done the two porno queens from the original eleven. He said it had just come to him, that maybe the follower had started way back then.'

'Shit,' Sheehan said, 'this guy is playing with us. If he –'

'What did you tell him?' Irving interrupted.

'I told him I was thinking that, too. And I asked him to check with his sources to see if he could find out if there were other women who disappeared or dropped out of the business like Becky Kaminski did.'

'You asked him to go to work on this?' Rollenberger said, his eyebrows arched in astonishment and outrage.

'I had to. It was the obvious thing for me to ask him. If I didn't, he'd know I was suspicious.'

'He's right,' Irving said.

Rollenberger's chest seemed to deflate a little bit. He couldn't get anything right.

'Yes, now I see,' he dutifully responded. 'Good work.'

'We're going to need more people,' Opelt said, since everybody was being so agreeable.

'I want to begin surveillance on him by tomorrow morning,' Irving said. 'We're going to need at least three teams. Sheehan and Opelt will be one. Bosch, you're involved in court and Edgar, I want you working on tracking down the survivor, so you two are out. Lieutenant Rollenberger, who else can you spare?'

'Well, Yde is sitting around since Buchert is on vacation. And Mayfield and Rutherford are in court on the same case. I can shake one of them loose to pair with Yde. That's all I've got, unless you want to pull back on some ongoing –'

'No, I don't want that. Get Yde and Mayfield in on this. I'll go to Lieutenant Hilliard and see what she can spare from the Valley. She's had three teams on the catering truck case for a month and they're at the wall. I'll take a team off of that.'

'Very good, sir,' Rollenberger said.

Sheehan looked at Harry and made a face like he was going to puke with this guy in charge. Bosch held back his smile. There was always this giddiness that detectives felt when they received their marching orders and were about to go out into the hunt.

'Opelt, Sheehan, I want you on Mora tomorrow morning at eight,' Irving said. 'Lieutenant, I want you to set up a meeting with the new people tomorrow morning. Bring them up to date on what we have and have one team take over surveillance from Opelt and Sheehan at four P.M. They stay with Mora until lights out. If overtime is needed, I'm authorizing it. The other pair will take the surveillance at eight A.M. Saturday and Opelt and Sheehan will take it back at four. Rotate like that. The night-shift watchers have to stay with him until they are sure he is in his home in bed for the night. I want no mistakes. If this guy pulls off something while we're watching him, we can all kiss our careers good-bye.'

'Chief?'

'Yes, Bosch.'

'There is no guarantee that he is going to do something. Locke said he thinks the follower has a lot of control. He doesn't think he is out there hunting every night. He thinks he controls the urge and lives pretty normally, then strikes at irregular intervals.'

'There is no guarantee that we'll even be watching the right man, Detective Bosch, but I want to watch him anyway. I am sitting here hoping we are dreadfully wrong about Detective Mora. But the things you have said here are convincing in a circumstantial way. Nothing near being usable in court. So we watch him and hope if it's him we'll see the sign before he hurts anybody else. My –'

'I agree, sir,' Rollenberger said.

'Don't interrupt me, Lieutenant. My forte is neither detective work nor psychoanalysis, but something tells me that whoever the follower is, he's feeling the pressure. Sure, he brought it on himself with that note. And he may think this is a cat-and-mouse game he can master. Nevertheless, he is feeling the pressure. And one thing I know, just from being a cop, when the pressure is on these people, the edge-dwellers I call them, then they react. Sometimes they crack, sometimes they act out. So what I am saying is, knowing what I know about this case, I want Mora covered if he even walks outside to get the mail.'

They sat there in silence. Even Rollenberger, who seemed cowed by his misstep in interrupting Irving.

'Okay, then, we have our assignments. Sheehan, Opelt, surveillance. Bosch, you are freelancing until you get done with the trial. Edgar, you have the survivor and when you have the time do some checking on Mora. Nothing that will get back to him.'

'He's divorced,' Bosch offered. 'Got divorced right before the Dollmaker task force was put together.'

'All right, there's your start. Go to court, pull his divorce. Who knows, we might get lucky. Maybe his wife dropped him because he liked making her up like a doll. Things have been hard enough on this case, we could use a break like that.'

Irving looked around the table at each man's face.

'The potential for embarrassment to the department on this case is huge. But I don't want anybody holding back. Let the stones fall where they will. . . . Okay, then, everybody has their assignments. Go to it. Everyone is excused with the exception of Detective Bosch.'

As the others filed out of the room, Bosch thought Rollenberger's face showed his disappointment at not getting a chance for a private ass-kissing conference with Irving.

After the door closed, Irving was quiet for a few moments as he composed what he wanted to say. Throughout most of Bosch's career as a detective, Irving had been a nemesis of sorts, always trying to control him and bring him into the fold. Bosch had always resisted. Nothing personal, it just wasn't Bosch's gig.

But now Bosch sensed a softening in Irving. In the way he had treated Bosch during the meeting, in the way he testified earlier in the week. He could have hung Bosch out to dry but didn't. Yet, it wasn't something Bosch could or would acknowledge. So he sat there silently and waited.

'Good work on this, Detective. Especially with the trial and everything going on.'

Bosch nodded but knew that wasn't what this was about.

'Uh, that's why I held you here. The trial. I wanted to – let's see, how do I say this . . . I wanted to tell you, and excuse the language, but I don't give a flying fuck what that jury decides or how much money they give those people. That jury has no idea what it's like to be out there on the edge. To have to make the decisions that may cost or save lives. You can't take a week to accurately examine and judge the decision you had to make in a second.'

Bosch was trying to think of something to say and the silence seemed to drag on too long.

'Anyway,' Irving finally said, 'I guess it's taken me four years to come to that conclusion. But better late than never.'

'Hey, I could use you for closing arguments tomorrow.'

Irving's face cringed, the muscular jaws flexing as if he had just taken a mouthful of cold sauerkraut.

'Don't get me started on that, either. I mean, what is this city doing? The city attorney's office is nothing but a school. A law school for trial lawyers. And the taxpayers pay the tuition. We get these greenhorn, uh, uh, preppies, who don't know the first thing about trial law. They learn from the mistakes they make in court when it counts – for us. And when they finally get good and know what the hell they're doing, they quit and then they're the lawyers suing us!'

Bosch had never seen Irving so animated. It was as if he had taken off the starched public persona he always wore like a uniform. Harry was entranced.

'Sorry about that,' Irving said. 'I get carried away. Anyway, good luck with this jury but don't let it worry you.'

Bosch said nothing.

'You know, Bosch, it only takes a half-hour meeting with Lieutenant Rollenberger in the room for me to want to take a good look at myself and this department and where it's headed. He's not the LAPD I joined or you joined. He's a good manager, yes, and so am I, at least I think so. But we can't forget we're cops . . .'

Bosch didn't know what to say, or if he should say anything. It seemed that Irving was almost rambling now. As if there was something he wanted to say, but was looking for anything else to say instead.

'Hans Rollenberger. What a name, huh? I can guess, the detectives in his crew must call him "Hans Off", am I right?'

'Sometimes.'

'Yes, well, I guess that's expected. He – uh, you know, Harry, I've got thirty-eight years in the department.'

Bosch just nodded. This was getting weird. Irving had never even called him by his first name before.

'And, uh, I worked Hollywood patrol for a lot of years right out of the academy. . . . That question Money Chandler asked me about your mother. That really came out of the blue and I'm sorry about that, Harry, sorry for your loss.'

'It was a long time ago.' Bosch waited a beat. Irving was looking down at his hands, which were clasped on the table. 'If that's it, I think I'll –'

'Yes, that's basically it, but, you know, what I wanted to tell you is that I was there that day.'

'What day?'

'That day that your mother – I was the RO.'

'The reporting officer?'

'Yes, I was the one that found her. I was walking a foot beat on the Boulevard and I ducked into that alley off of Gower. I usually hit it once a day and, uh, I found her. . . . When Chandler showed me those reports I recognized the case right away. She didn't know my badge number – it was there on the report – or she would've known I was the one who found her. Chandler would've had some kind of a field day with that, I guess . . .'

This was hard for Bosch to sit through. Now he was glad Irving wasn't looking at him. He knew, or thought he knew, what it was that Irving wasn't saying. If he had worked the Boulevard foot beat, then he had known Bosch's mother before she was dead.

Irving glanced up at him and then looked away, toward the corner of the room. His eyes fell on the ficus plant.

'Somebody put a cigarette butt in my pot,' he said. 'That yours, Harry?'

TWENTY

Bosch was lighting a cigarette as he used his shoulder to push through one of the glass doors at the entrance to Parker Center. Irving had jolted him with his small-world story. Bosch had always figured he'd run into somebody in the department who knew her or knew the case. Never did Irving fit into that scenario.

As he walked through the south lot to the Caprice he noticed Jerry Edgar standing at the corner of Los Angeles and First waiting for the cross light. Bosch looked at his watch and saw it was 5:10, quitting time. He thought Edgar was probably walking up to the Code Seven or the Red Wind for a draft before fighting the freeway. He thought that wasn't a bad idea. Sheehan and Opelt were probably already sitting on stools at one of the bars.

By the time Bosch got to the corner, Edgar had a block and a half lead on him and was walking up First toward the Seven. Bosch picked up the pace. For the first time in a long time, he felt the actual mental craving for alcohol. For just a while he wanted to forget Church and Mora and Chandler and his own secrets and what Irving had told him in the conference room.

But then Edgar walked right on by the billy club that served as the door handle at the Seven without even giving it a glance. He crossed Spring and walked alongside the *Times* building toward Broadway. Then it's the Red Wind, Bosch thought.

The Wind was okay as far as a watering hole went. They had Weinhard's by the bottle instead of on draft, so the place lost points there. Another minus was that the yuppies from the *Times* newsroom favored the place and it often was more crowded with reporters than cops. The big plus, however, was that on Thursdays and Fridays they had a quartet come in and play sets from six to ten. They were mostly retired club men who weren't too tight, but it was as good a way as any to miss the rush hour.

He watched Edgar cross Broadway and stay on First instead of taking a left to go down to the Wind. Bosch slowed his pace a bit so Edgar could renew his block-and-a-half lead. He lit another cigarette and felt uneasy about the prospect of following the other detective but did it anyway. There was a bad feeling beginning to nag at him.

Edgar turned left on Hill and ducked into the first door on the east side, across from the new subway entrance. The door he went through was to the Hung Jury, a bar that was off the lobby of the Fuentes Legal Center, an eight-story office building solely occupied by attorney offices. Mostly, the tenants were defense and litigation attorneys who had chosen the nondescript if not ugly building because of its main selling point; it was only a half block from the county courts building, a block from the criminal courts building and a block and a half from the federal building.

Bosch knew all of this because Belk had told him all about it on the day the two of them had come to the Fuentes Legal Center to find Honey Chandler's office. Bosch had been subpoenaed to give a deposition in the Norman Church case.

The uneasy feeling turned into a hollow in his gut as he passed the door to the Hung Jury and went into the main lobby of the Fuentes Center. He knew the layout of the bar, having dropped in for a beer and a shot after the deposition with Chandler, and he knew there was an entrance off the building's lobby. He pushed through the lobby entrance door now and stepped into an alcove where there were two pay phones and the doors to the restrooms. He moved up to the corner and carefully looked into the bar area.

A juke box Bosch couldn't see was playing Sinatra's 'Summer Wind', a barmaid with a puffy wig and bills wrapped through her fingers – tens, fives, ones – was delivering a batch of martinis to a four top of lawyers sitting near the front entrance and the bartender was leaning over the dimly lit bar smoking a cigarette and reading the *Hollywood Reporter*. Probably an actor or a screenwriter when he wasn't tending bar, Bosch thought. Maybe a talent scout. Who in this town wasn't?

When the bartender leaned forward to stub out his smoke in an ashtray, Bosch saw Edgar sitting at the far end of the bar with a draft beer in front of him. A match flared in the darkness next to him and Bosch watched Honey Chandler light a smoke and then drop her match into an ashtray next to what looked like a Bloody Mary.

Bosch moved back into the alcove, out of sight.

He waited next to an old plywood shack that was built on the sidewalk at Hill and First and served as a news and magazine stand. It had been closed and boarded for the night. As it grew dark and the streetlights came on, Bosch spent his time fending off panhandlers and passing prostitutes looking for one last businessman's special before heading from downtown into Hollywood for the evening – and the rougher – tratle.

By the time he saw Edgar come out of the Hung Jury, Bosch had a nice little pile of cigarette butts on the sidewalk at his feet. He flicked the one he had going into the street and stepped back alongside the news stand so Edgar wouldn't notice him. Bosch saw no sign of Chandler and assumed that she had left the bar through the other door and gone down to the garage and her car. Edgar probably had wisely declined a ride over to the Parker Center lot.

As Edgar passed the stand Bosch stepped out behind him.

'Jerry, whereyat?'

Edgar jumped as if an ice cube had been pressed against his neck and whipped around.

'Harry? What're you – hey, you wanna grab a drink? That's what I was looking to do.'

Bosch let him stand there and squirm for a few seconds before saying, 'You already had your drink.'

'What do you mean?'

Bosch took a step toward him. Edgar looked genuinely scared.

'You know what I mean. A beer for you, right? Bloody Mary for the lady.'

'Listen, Harry, look, I –'

'Don't call me that. Don't ever call me Harry again. Understand? You want to talk to me, call me Bosch. That's what the people who aren't my friends call me, the people I don't trust. Just call me that.'

'Can I explain? Har – uh, I'd like the chance to explain.'

'What's to explain? You fucked me over. Nothing to explain about that. What'd you tell her tonight? You just run down everything we just talked about in Irving's office? I don't think she needs it, pal. The damage is already done.'

'No. She left a long time ago. I was in there most of the time alone thinking about how to get out of this. I didn't tell her shit about today's meeting. Harry, I didn't –'

Bosch took one more step and in a quick motion brought his hand up, palm out, and hit Edgar in the chest, knocking him backward.

'I said don't call me that!' he yelled. 'You fuck! You – we worked together, man. I taught you . . . I'm in that courtroom getting fucked in the ass and I find out you're the guy, you're the goddamn leak.'

'I'm sorry. I –'

'What about Bremmer? You the one who told him about the note? Is that where you're going for a drink now? Going to meet Bremmer? Well, don't let me stop you.'

'No, man, I haven't talked to Bremmer. Look, I made a mistake, okay? I'm sorry. She screwed me, too. It was like blackmail. I couldn't – I tried to get out of it but she had me by the shorthairs. You gotta believe me, man.'

Bosch looked at him for a long moment. It was fully dark now but he thought he saw that Edgar's eyes were shiny in the glow of the streetlights. Maybe he was holding back tears. But what were they tears for, Bosch wondered. For the loss of the relationship they had? Or were they tears of fear? Bosch felt the surge of his power over Edgar. And Edgar knew he had it.

In a low and very even voice Bosch said, 'I want to know everything. You are going to tell me what you did.'

The quartet at the Wind was on a break. They sat at a table in the back. It was a dark, wood-paneled room like hundreds of others in the city. A red leatherette pad ran along the edge of the cigarette-scarred bar and the barmaids wore black uniforms and white aprons and they all had too much red lipstick on their thin lips. Bosch ordered a double shot of Jack Black straight up and a bottle of Weinhard's. He also gave the barmaid money for a pack of cigarettes. Edgar, who now wore the face of a man whose life had run out on him, ordered Jack Black, water back.

'It's the damn recession,' Edgar began before Bosch asked a question. 'Real estate is in the toilet. I had to drop that gig and we had the mortgage and, you know how it is, man, Brenda had gotten used to a cert –'

'Fuck that. You think I want to hear about how you sell me out because your wife has to drive a Chevy instead of a BMW? Fuck you. You –'

'It's not like that. I –'

'Shut up. I'm talking. You're going to –'

They both shut up while the barmaid put the drinks and cigarettes down. Bosch put a twenty on her tray. He never took his dark, angry eyes off Edgar.

'Now, skip the bullshit and tell me what you did.'

Edgar threw back his shot and washed it down with water before starting.

'Uh, you see, uh, it was late Monday afternoon, this was after we'd been out to the scene at Bing's and I was back at the office. And I got a call at the office and it was Chandler. She knew something was up. I don't know how but she knew, but she knew about the note we got and the body being found. She musta gotten tipped by Bremmer or something. She started asking questions, you know, "Was it confirmed as the Dollmaker?" Things like that. I put her off. No comment . . .'

'And then?'

'Then, well, she offered me something. I'm two back on the mortgage and Brenda doesn't even know.'

'What'd I tell you? I don't want to hear your sad story, Edgar. I'm telling you, I don't have any sympathy for that. You tell it and it will only make me madder.'

'All right, all right. She offered me money. I said I'd think about it. She said if I wanted to deal to meet her at the Hung Jury that night. . . . You won't let me say why, but I had reasons and so I went. Yeah, I went.'

'Yeah, and you fucked yourself up,' Bosch said, hoping to knock down the defiant tone that had crept into Edgar's voice.

He had finished the last of his Jack Black and signaled the barmaid but she didn't see him. The musicians were taking their places behind their instruments. The front man was a saxophone player and Bosch wished he was here under other circumstances.

'What did you give her?'

'Just what we knew that day. But she already had just about everything already. I told her you said it looked like the Dollmaker. It wasn't a lot, Ha – and most of it was in the paper the next day, anyway. And I wasn't Bremmer's source on that. You have to believe me.'

'You told her I came out there? To the scene?'

'Yeah, I told her. What was the big secret about that?'

Bosch thought about all of this for a few minutes. He watched the band start up with a Billy Strayhorn number called 'Lush Life'. Their table was far enough away from the quartet that it wasn't too loud. Harry's eyes scanned the rest of the bar to see if anyone else was into it and he saw Bremmer sitting at the bar nursing a beer. He was with a group of what looked like reporter types. One of the other men even had one of those long, skinny notebooks that reporters always carry sticking out of his back pocket.

'Speaking of Bremmer, there he is. Maybe he wants to check a detail or two with you after we're done.'

'Harry, it's not me.'

Bosch let him get away with the Harry that time. He was getting tired and depressed with this scene. He wanted to get it over with and get out of there, go see Sylvia.

'How many times did you talk to her?'

'Every night.'

'She turned it on you, didn't she? You had to go see her.'

'I was stupid. I needed the money. Once I met her the first night she had me by the balls. She said she wanted updates on the investigation or she'd tell you I was the leak, she'd inform IAD. Fuck, she never even paid me.'

'What happened tonight to make her split early?'

'She said the case was over, going to closing arguments tomorrow, so it didn't matter what was happening in the case. She cut me loose.'

'But it won't end there. You know that, don't you? Whenever she needs a plate run, an address from DMV, a witness's unlisted number, she's going to call you. She's got you, man.'

'I know. I'll have to deal with it.'

'All for what? What was the price, that first night?'

'I wanted one goddamn mortgage payment. . . . Can't sell the fuckin' house, can't make the mortgage, I don't know what I'm going to do.'

'What about me? Aren't you worried about what I'm going to do?'

'Yes. Yes, I am.'

Bosch looked back at the quartet. They were staying with

247

a Strayhorn set and were on to 'Blood Count'. There was a journeyman quality to the sax man's work. He stayed on point and his phrasing was clean.

'What are you going to do?' Edgar asked.

Bosch didn't have to think, he already knew. He didn't take his eyes from the sax man as he spoke.

'Nothing.'

'Nothing?'

'It's what you are going to do. I can't work with you anymore, man. I know we got this thing with Irving but that's it, that's the end. After this is over you go to Pounds and tell him you want to transfer out of Hollywood.'

'But there aren't openings in homicide anywhere else. I looked at the board, you know how rarely they come.'

'I didn't say anything about homicide. I just said you're going to ask for a transfer. You ask for the first thing open, understand? I don't care if you end up on autos in the Seventy-seventh, you take the first thing you can get.'

Now he looked at Edgar, whose mouth was slightly open, and said, 'That's the price you pay.'

'But homicide is what I do, you know that. It's where it's at.'

'And you're not where it's at anymore. This isn't negotiable. Unless you want to take your chances with IAD. But either you go to Pounds or I go to them. I can't work with you anymore. That's it.'

He looked back at the band. Edgar was silent and after a few moments Bosch told him to leave.

'You go first. I can't walk with you back to Parker.'

Edgar stood up and hovered near the table for a few moments before saying, 'Someday, you're going to need all the friends you can get. That's the day you'll remember doing this to me.'

Without looking at him, Bosch said, 'I know.'

After Edgar had gone Bosch got the barmaid's attention and ordered another round. The quartet played 'Rain Check' with some improvisational riffs that Bosch liked. The whiskey was beginning to warm his gut and he sat back and smoked and listened, trying not to think about anything to do with cops and killers.

But soon he felt a presence nearby and turned to see Bremmer standing there with his bottle of beer in hand.

'I take it by the look on Edgar's face when he left that he won't be coming back. Can I join you?'

'No, he won't be back and you can do whatever you want, but I'm off duty, off the record and off the road.'

'In other words, you ain't saying shit.'

'You got it.'

The reporter sat down and lit a cigarette. His small but sharp green eyes squinted through the smoke.

'It's okay, 'cause I'm not working either.'

'Bremmer, you're always working. Even now, I say the wrong word and you aren't going to forget about it.'

'I suppose. But you forget the times we worked together. The stories that helped you, Harry. I write one story that doesn't go the way you want and all of that is forgotten. Now I'm just "that damn reporter" who –'

'I haven't forgotten shit. You're sitting here, right? I remember what you did for me and I'll remember what you did against me. It all evens out in the end.'

They sat in silence for a while and listened to the music. The set ended just as the barmaid was putting Bosch's third double Jack Black on the table.

'I'm not saying I would ever reveal it,' Bremmer said, 'but how come my source on the note story was so important?'

'It's not that important anymore. At the time I just wanted to know who was trying to nail me.'

'You said that before. That someone was setting you up. You really think that?'

'It doesn't matter. What kind of story did you write for tomorrow?'

The reporter straightened up and and his eyes brightened.

'You'll see it. Pretty much a straight court story. Your testimony about someone else continuing the killings. It's going out front. It's a big story. That why I'm here. I always come in for a pop after I hit the front page.'

'Party time, huh? What about my mother? Did you put that stuff in?'

'Harry, if that's what you are worried about, forget it. I didn't even mention that in the story. To be honest, it's of course vitally interesting to you, but as far as a newspaper story goes, I thought it was too much inside baseball. I left it out.'

'Inside baseball?'

'Too arcane, like the stats those sports guys on TV throw around. You know, like how many fastballs Lefty So and So threw during the third inning of the fifth game of the 1956 World Series. I thought the stuff with your mother – Chandler's attempt to use it as your motivation for dropping this guy – was going too far inside.'

Bosch just nodded. He was glad that part of his life would not be in the hands of a million newspaper buyers tomorrow, but he acted nonchalant about it.

'But,' Bremmer said, 'I gotta tell you, if we get a verdict back on this that goes against you and the jurors start saying they thought you did it to avenge your mother's death, then that is usable and I won't have a choice.'

Bosch nodded again. It seemed fair enough. He looked at his watch and saw it was nearly ten. He knew he should call Sylvia and he knew he should get out of there before the next set started and he became entranced by the music again.

He finished his drink and said, 'I'm gonna hit it.'

'Yeah, me, too,' Bremmer said. 'I'll walk out with you.'

Outside, the chilled night air cut through Bosch's whiskey daze. He said good-bye to Bremmer and put his hands in his pockets as he started down the sidewalk.

'Harry, you walking all the way back to Parker Center? Hop in. My car is right here.'

Bosch watched Bremmer unlock the passenger door to his Le Sabre, which was parked right at the curb in front of the Wind. Bosch got in without a word of thanks and leaned over and unlocked the other side. When he was drunk he went through a stage where he said almost nothing, just vegetated in his own juices and listened.

Bremmer started the conversation during the four blocks to Parker Center.

'That Money Chandler is something else, isn't she? She really knows how to play a jury.'

'You think she's got it, don't you?'

'It's going to be close, Harry. I think. But even if it's one of those statement verdicts that are popular these days against the LAPD, she'll get rich.'

'Whaddaya mean?'

'You haven't been in federal court before have you?'

'No. I try not to make it a habit.'

'Well, in a civil rights case, if the plaintiff wins – in this case, Chandler – then the defendant – in this case the city is paying your tab – has to pay the lawyer's fees. I guarantee you, Harry, that in her closing argument tomorrow Money will tell those jurors that all they need to do is make a statement that you acted wrongly. And even damages of a dollar make that statement. The jury will see that as the easy way out. They can say you were wrong and only give a dollar in damages. They won't know, because Belk is not allowed to tell them, that even if the plaintiff wins a dollar, Chandler bills the city. And that won't be a dollar. More like a couple hundred thousand of them. It's a scam.'

'Shit.'

'Yeah, that's the justice system.'

Bremmer pulled into the lot and Bosch pointed out his Caprice in one of the front rows.

'You going to be all right to drive?' Bremmer asked.

'No problem.'

Bosch was about to close the door when Bremmer stopped him.

'Hey, Harry, we both know I can't reveal my source. But I can tell you who it isn't. And I'll tell you it is not someone you'd expect. You know? Edgar and Pounds, if that's who you think it is, forget it. You'd never guess who it was, so don't bother. Okay?'

Bosch just nodded and shut the door.

TWENTY-ONE

After fumbling to find the right one, Bosch put the key in the ignition but didn't turn it. He briefly considered whether he should try to drive or whether he should go get coffee from the cafeteria first. He looked up through the windshield at the gray monolith that was Parker Center. Most of the lights were on but he knew the offices had emptied. The lights of the squad rooms were always left on to give the appearance that the fight against crime never sleeps. It was a lie.

He thought of the couch that was kept in one of the RHD interrogation rooms. That was also an alternative to driving. Unless, of course, it was already taken. But then he thought of Sylvia and how she had come to court despite what he had said about not wanting her there. He wanted to get home to her. Yes, he thought, home.

He put his hand on the key but then dropped it away again. He rubbed his eyes. They were tired and there were so many thoughts swimming in the whiskey. There was the sound of the tenor sax floating there, too. His own improvisational riff.

He tried to think of what Bremmer had just said, that Bosch would never guess who the source was. Why had he said it that way? He found that more tantalizing than wondering who his source actually was.

It didn't matter, he told himself. All would be over soon. He leaned his head against the side window, thinking about the trial and his testimony. He wondered how he had looked up there, all eyes on him. He never wanted to be in that position again. Ever. To have Honey Chandler cornering him with words.

Whoever fights monsters, he thought. What had she told the jury? About the abyss? Yes, where monsters dwell. Is that where I dwell? In the black place? The black heart, he remembered then. Locke had called it that. The black heart does not beat alone. In his mind he replayed the vision of Norman Church being knocked upright by the bullet and then flopping helplessly naked on the bed. The look in the dying man's eyes stayed with him. Four years later and the vision was as clear as yesterday. Why was that, he wanted to know. Why did he remember Norman Church's face and not his own mother's? Do I have the black heart, Bosch asked himself. Do I?

The darkness came up on him then like a wave and pulled him down. He was there with the monsters.

There was a sharp rap on the glass. Bosch abruptly opened his eyes and saw the patrolman next to the car holding his baton and flashlight. Harry quickly looked around and grabbed the wheel and put his foot on the brake. He didn't think he had been driving that badly, then he realized he hadn't been driving at all. He was still in the Parker Center lot. He reached over and rolled the window down.

The kid in the uniform was the lot cop. The lowest-rated cadet in each academy class was first assigned to watch the Parker Center lot during P.M. watch. It was a tradition but it also served a purpose. If the cops couldn't prevent car break-ins and other crime in the parking lot of their own headquarters, then it begged the question, where could they stop crime?

'Detective, are you all right?' he said as he slid his baton back into the ring on his belt. 'I saw you get dropped off and get in your car. Then when you didn't leave I wanted to check.'

'Yes,' Bosch managed to say. 'I'm, uh, fine. Thanks. I musta dozed off there. Been a long day.'

'Yes, they all are. Be careful now.'

'Yes.'

'Are you okay driving?'

'Fine. Thank you.'

'You sure?'

'I'm sure.'

He waited until the cop walked away before starting the car. Bosch looked at his watch and figured he had slept for no more than thirty minutes. But the nap, and the sudden waking, had refreshed him. He lit a cigarette and pulled the car out onto Los Angeles Street and took it to the Hollywood Freeway entrance.

As he drove north on the freeway he rolled the window down so the cool air would keep him alert. It was a clear night. Ahead of him, the lights of the Hollywood Hills ascended into the sky where spotlights from two different locations behind the mountains cut through the darkness. He thought it was a beautiful scene, yet it made him feel melancholy.

Los Angeles had changed in the last few years, but then there was nothing new about that. It was always changing and that was why he loved it. But riot and recession had left a particularly harsh mark on the landscape, the landscape of memory. Bosch believed he would never forget the pall of smoke that hung over the city like some kind of supersmog that could not be lifted by the evening winds. The TV pictures of burning buildings and looters unchecked by the police. It had been the department's darkest hour and it still had not recovered.

And neither had the city. Many of the ills that led to such volcanic rage were still left untended. The city offered so much beauty and yet it offered so much danger and hate. It was a city of shaken confidence, living solely on its stores of hope. In Bosch's mind he saw the polarization of the haves and have-nots as a scene in which a ferry was leaving the dock. An overloaded ferry leaving an overloaded dock, with some people with a foot on the boat and a foot on the dock.

The boat was pulling further away and it would only be so long before those in the middle would fall in. Meanwhile, the ferry was still too crowded and it would capsize at the first wave. Those left on the dock would certainly cheer this. They prayed for the wave.

He thought of Edgar and what he had done. He was one of those about to fall in. Nothing could be done about it. He and his wife, whom Edgar could not bring himself to tell about their precarious position. Bosch wondered if he had done the right thing. Edgar had spoken of the time that would come when Bosch would need every friend he could get. Would it have been wiser to bank this one, to let Edgar go, no harm no foul? He didn't know, but there was still time. He would have to decide.

As he drove through the Cahuenga Pass he rolled the window back up. It was getting cold. He looked up into the hills to the west and tried to spot the unlighted area where his dark house sat. He felt glad that he wasn't going up there tonight, that he was going to Sylvia.

He got there at 11:30 and used his own key to get in. There was a light on in the kitchen but the rest of the place was dark. Sylvia was asleep. It was too late for the news and the late-night talk shows never held his interest. He took his shoes off in the living room so as to not make any noise and went down the hall to her bedroom.

He stood still in the complete darkness, letting his eyes adjust.

'Hi,' she said from the bed, though he could not yet see her.

' 'Lo.'

'Where have you been, Harry?'

She said it sweetly and with sleep still in her voice. It was not a challenge or a demand.

'I had to do a few things, then I had a few drinks.'

'Hear any good music?'

'Yeah, they had a quartet. Not bad. Played a lot of Billy Strayhorn.'

'Do you want me to fix you something?'

'Nah, go to sleep. You have school tomorrow. I'm not that hungry anyway and I can get something if I want it.'

'C'mere.'

He made his way to the bed and crawled across the down quilt. Her hand came up and around his neck and she pulled him down into a kiss.

'Yes, you did have a few drinks.'

He laughed and then so did she.

'Let me go brush my teeth.'

'Wait a minute.'

She pulled him down again and he kissed her mouth and neck. She had a milky sweet smell of sleep and perfume about her that he liked. He noticed that she was not wearing a nightgown, though she usually did. He put his hand under the covers and traced the flatness of her stomach. He brought it up and caressed her breasts and then her neck. He kissed her again and then pushed his face into her hair and neck.

'Sylvia, thank you,' he whispered.

'For what?'

'For coming today and being there. I know what I said before but it meant something to see you when I looked out there. It meant a lot.'

That was all he could say about it. He got up then and went into the bathroom. He stripped off his clothes and carefully hung them on hooks on the back of the door. He would have to wear them again in the morning.

He took a quick shower, then shaved and brushed his teeth with the second set of toiletries he kept in her bathroom. He looked in the mirror as he brushed his damp hair back with his hands. And he smiled. It might have been the residue of the whiskey and beer, he knew. But he doubted it. It was because he felt lucky. He felt that he was neither on the ferry with the mad crowd nor left behind on the dock with the angry crowd. He was in his own boat. With just Sylvia.

257

*

They made love the way lonely people do, silently, with each trying too hard in the dark to please the other until they were almost clumsy about it. Still, there was a healing sense about it for Bosch. Afterward, she lay next to him, her finger tracing the outline of his tattoo.

'What are you thinking about?' she asked.

'Nothing. Just stuff.'

'Tell me.'

He waited a few moments before answering.

'Tonight I found out somebody betrayed me. Somebody close. And, well, I was just thinking that maybe I'd had it wrong. That it really wasn't me who was betrayed. It was himself. He had betrayed himself. And maybe living with that is punishment enough. I don't think I need to add to it.'

He thought about what he had said to Edgar at the Red Wind and decided he would have to stop him from going to Pounds for the transfer.

'Betrayed how?'

'Uh, consorting with the enemy, I guess you'd call it.'

'Honey Chandler?'

'Yeah.'

'How bad is it?'

'Not too bad, I guess. It's just that he did it that matters. It hurts, I guess.'

'Is there anything you can do? Not to him, I mean. I mean to limit the damage.'

'No. Whatever damage there is, it's already done. I only figured out it was him tonight. It was by accident, otherwise I probably would have never even thought of him. Anyway, don't worry about it.'

She caressed his chest with the tips of her fingernails.

'If you're not worried, I'm not.'

He loved her knowing the boundaries of how much she could ask him, and that she didn't even think to ask him who it was he was talking about. He felt totally comfortable with her. No worries, no anxieties. It was home to him.

He was just beginning to fall off when she spoke again.

'Harry?'

'Uh huh.'

'Are you worried about the trial, how the closing arguments will go?'

'Not really. I don't like being in the fishbowl, sitting at that table while everybody gets their chance to explain why they think I did what I did. But I'm not worried about the outcome, if that's what you mean. It doesn't mean anything. I just want it to be over and I don't really care anymore what they do. No jury can sanction what I did or didn't do. No jury can tell me I was right or wrong. You know? This trial could last a year and it wouldn't tell them everything about that night.'

'What about the department? Will they care?'

He told her what Irving had told him that afternoon about what effect the trial's outcome would have. He didn't say anything about what the assistant chief had said about knowing his mother. But Irving's story crossed through his mind and for the first time since he had been in bed he felt the need for a cigarette.

But he didn't get up. He put the urge out of his mind and they lay quietly for a while after that. Bosch kept his eyes open in the dark. His thoughts were now about Edgar and then they segued to Mora. He wondered what the vice cop was doing at the same moment. Was he alone in the dark? Was he out looking?

'I meant what I said earlier today, Harry,' Sylvia said.

'What's that?'

'That I want to know all about you, your past, the good and the bad. And I want you to know about me. . . . Don't ignore this. It could hurt us.'

Her voice had lost some of its sleepy sweetness. He was silent and closed his eyes. He knew this one thing was more important to her than anything. She had been the loser in a past relationship where the stories of the past were not used as the building blocks of the future. He brought his hand up and rubbed his thumb along the back of her neck. She always smelled powdery after sex, he thought, yet she had not even gotten up to go into the bathroom. This was a mystery to him. It took him a while to answer her.

'You have to take me without a past. . . . I've let it go and don't want to go back to examine it, to tell it, to even think about it. I've spent my whole life getting away from my past. You understand? Just because a lawyer can throw it at me in a courtroom doesn't mean I have to . . .'

'What, tell me?'

He didn't answer. He turned his body into her and kissed and embraced her. He just wanted to hold her, to pull back away from this cliff.

'I love you,' she said.

'I love you,' he said.

She pulled herself closer to him and put her face in the crook of his neck. Her arms held him tightly, as if maybe she was scared.

It was the first time he had said it to her. It was the first time he had said it to anyone as far back as he could remember. Maybe he had never said it. It felt good to him, almost like a palpable presence, a warm flower of deep red opening in his chest. And he realized he was the one who was a little bit scared. As if by simply saying the words he had taken on a great responsibility. It was scary yet exciting. He thought of himself in the mirror, smiling.

She held herself pressed against him and he could feel her breath against his neck. In a short while her breathing became more measured as she fell asleep.

Lying awake, Bosch held her like that until well into the night. Now sleep would not come to him and with the insomnia came realities that robbed him of the good feelings he had only minutes before. He had thought about what she had said about betrayal and trust. And he knew that the pledges they spoke to each other this night would founder if built on deception. He knew what she had said was true. He would have to tell her who he was, what he was, if the words he had spoken were ever to be more than words. He thought about what Judge Keyes had said about words being beautiful and ugly on their own. Bosch had spoken the word love. He knew now that he must make it either ugly or beautiful.

The bedroom's windows were on the east side of the house and the light of dawn was just beginning to cling to the edges of the blinds when Bosch finally closed his eyes and slept.

TWENTY-TWO

Bosch looked rumpled and worn-out when he entered the courtroom Friday morning. Belk was already there, scribbling on his yellow pad. He looked up and appraised him as Bosch sat down.

'You look like shit and smell like an ashtray. And the jury will know that's the same suit and tie you wore yesterday.'

'A clear sign I'm guilty.'

'Don't be such a smartass. You never know what may turn a juror one way or the other.'

'I don't really care. Besides, you're the one who has to look good today, right, Belk?'

This was not an encouraging thing to say to a man at least eighty pounds overweight who broke out in flop sweat every time the judge looked at him.

'What the hell do you mean you don't care? Everything is on the line today and you waltz in looking like you slept in your car and say you don't care.'

'I'm relaxed, Belk. I call it Zen and the art of not giving a shit.'

'Why now, Bosch, when I could have settled this for five figures two weeks ago?'

'Because I realize now that there are things more important than what twelve of my so-called peers think. Even if, as peers, they wouldn't give me the time of day on the street.'

Belk looked at his watch and said, 'Leave me alone, Bosch. We start in ten minutes and I want to be ready. I'm still working on my argument. I'm going to go shorter than even Keyes demanded.'

Earlier in the trial, the judge had determined that closing arguments would be no longer than a half hour for each side. This was to be divided, with the plaintiff – in the person of Chandler – arguing for twenty minutes followed by the defendant's lawyer – Belk – delivering his entire thirty-minute argument. The plaintiff would then be allowed the last ten minutes. Chandler would have first and last word, another sign, Bosch believed, that the system was stacked against him.

Bosch looked over at the plaintiff's table and saw Deborah Church sitting there by herself, eyes focused straight ahead. The two daughters were in the first row of the gallery behind her. Chandler was not there but there were files and yellow pads laid out on the table. She was around.

'You work on your speech,' he said to Belk. 'I'll leave you alone.'

'Don't be late coming back. Not again, please.'

As he had hoped, Chandler was outside smoking by the statue. She gave him a cold glance, said nothing and then took a few steps away from the ash can in order to ignore him. She had on her blue suit – it was probably her lucky suit – and the one tress of blonde hair was loose from the braid at the back of her neck.

'Rehearsing?' Bosch asked.

'I don't need to rehearse. This is the easy part.'

'I suppose.'

'What's that mean?'

'I don't know. I suppose you're freer from the constraints of law during the arguments. Not as many rules of what you can and can't say. I think that's when you'd be in your element.'

'Very perceptive.'

That was all she said. There was no indication that she knew her arrangement with Edgar had been discovered. Bosch had been counting on that when he rehearsed what he was going to say to her. After waking from his brief sleep, he had looked at the events of the night before with a fresh mind and eyes and had seen something that was missed before. It was now his intention to play her. He had thrown her the soft pitch. Now he had a curve.

'When this is over,' he said, 'I'd like the note.'

'What note?'

'The note the follower sent you.'

A look of shock hit her face but was then quickly erased with the indifferent look she normally gave him. But she had not been quick enough. He had seen the look in her eyes, she sensed danger. He knew then he had her.

'It's evidence,' he said.

'I don't know what you're talking about, Detective Bosch. I need to get back inside.'

She stubbed a half-smoked cigarette with a lipstick print on the butt into the ash can, then took two steps toward the door.

'I know about Edgar. I saw you with him last night.'

That stopped her. She turned around and looked at him.

'The Hung Jury. A Bloody Mary at the bar.'

She weighed her response and then said, 'Whatever he told you, I'm sure it was designed to place him in the best light. I would be careful if you are planning to go public with it.'

'I'm not going public with anything . . . unless you don't give me the note. Withholding evidence of a crime is a crime in itself. But I don't need to tell you that.'

'Whatever Edgar told you about a note is a lie. I told him noth –'

'And he told me nothing about a note. He didn't need to. I figured it out. You called him Monday after the body was found because you already knew about it and knew it was connected to the Dollmaker. I wondered how, and then it was clear. We got a note but that was secret until the next day. The only one who found out was Bremmer but his story said you couldn't be reached for comment. That was because you were out meeting Edgar. He said you called that afternoon asking about the body. You asked if we got a note. That was because you got a note, Counselor. And I need to see it. If it is different from the one we got, it could be helpful.'

She looked at her watch and quickly lit another cigarette.

'I can get a warrant,' he said.

She laughed a fake sort of laugh.

'I'd like to see you get a warrant. I'd like to see the judge in this town who would sign a warrant allowing the LAPD to search my house with this case in the papers every day. Judges are political animals, Detective, nobody's going to sign a warrant and then possibly come out on the wrong end of this.'

'I was thinking more along the lines of your office. But thanks for at least telling me where it is.'

The look came back into her face for a split second. She had slipped and maybe that was as big a shock to her as anything he had said. She put the cigarette into the sand after two puffs. Tommy Faraway would cherish it when he found it later.

'We convene in one minute. Detective, I don't know anything about a note. Understand? Nothing at all. There is no note. If you try to make any trouble over this, I will make even more for you.'

'I haven't told Belk and I'm not going to. I just want the note. It's got nothing to do with the case at trial.'

'That's easy for . . .'

'For me to say because I haven't read it? You're slipping, Counselor. Better be more careful than that.'

She ignored that and went on to other business.

'Another thing, if you think my . . . uh, arrangement with Edgar is grounds for a mistrial motion or a misconduct complaint, you will find that you are dead wrong. Edgar agreed to our relationship without any provocation. He suggested it, in fact. If you make any complaint I will sue you for slander and send out press releases when I do it.'

He doubted anything that happened was at Edgar's suggestion but let it go. She gave him her best dead-eyed, killer look, then opened the door and disappeared through it.

Bosch finished his smoke, hoping his play might at least knock her off speed a little bit during her closing argument. But most of all he was pleased that he had gotten tacit confirmation of his theory. The follower had sent her a note.

The silence that descended over the courtroom as Chandler walked to the lectern was the kind of tension-filled quiet that accompanies the moment before a verdict is read. Bosch felt that this was because the verdict was a foregone conclusion in many of the minds in the courtroom and Chandler's words here would serve as his coup de grâce. The final, deadly blow.

She began with the perfunctory thank-yous to the jury for their patience and close attention to the case. She said she was fully confident that they would fairly deliberate a verdict.

In the trials Bosch had attended as an investigator, this was always stated by both lawyers to the jury, and he always thought it was a crock. Most juries have members who are there simply to avoid going to work at the factory or office. But once there, the issues are either too complicated or scary or boring and they spend their days in the box just trying to stay awake between the breaks, when they can fortify themselves with sugar, caffeine and nicotine.

After that opening salutation, Chandler quickly got to the heart of the matter. She said, 'You will recall that on Monday I stood before you and gave you the road map. I told you what I would set out to prove, what I needed to prove and now it is your job to decide if I have done that. I think when you consider the week's testimony, you will have no doubt that I have.

'And speaking of doubt, the judge will instruct you but I

266

would like to take a moment to explain to you once again that this is a civil matter. It is not a criminal case. It is not like Perry Mason or like anything else you have seen on TV or at the movies. In a civil trial, in order for you to find for the plaintiff, it requires only that a preponderance of the evidence be in favor of the plaintiff's case. A preponderance, what does that mean? It means the evidence for the plaintiff's case outweighs the evidence against it. A majority. It can be a simple majority, just fifty percent, plus one.'

She spent a lot of time on this subject because this would be where the case was won or lost. She had to take twelve legally inept people – this was guaranteed by the juror selection process – and relieve them of media-conditioned beliefs or perceptions that cases were decided by reasonable doubts or beyond the shadow of doubt. That was for criminal cases. This was civil. In civil, the defendant lost the edge he got in criminal.

'Think of it as a set of scales. The scales of justice. And each piece of evidence or testimony introduced has a certain weight, depending on the validity you give it. One side of the scales is the plaintiff's case and the other, the defendant's. I think that when you have gone into the jury room to deliberate and have properly weighed the evidence of the case, there will be no doubt that the scales are tipped in the plaintiff's favor. If you find that is indeed the case, then you must find for Mrs Church.'

With the preliminaries out of the way, Bosch knew that she now had to finesse the rest, because the plaintiff was essentially presenting a two-part case, hoping to win at least one of them. One being that maybe Norman Church was the Dollmaker, a monstrous serial killer, but even if so, Bosch's actions behind the badge were equally heinous and should not be forgiven. The second part, the one that would surely bring untold riches if the jury bought it, was that Norman Church was an innocent and that Bosch had cut him down in cold blood, depriving his family of a loving husband and father.

'The evidence presented this week points to two possible findings by you,' Chandler told the jury. 'And this will be the most difficult task you have, to determine the level of Detective Bosch's culpability. Without a doubt it is clear that he acted rashly, recklessly and with wanton disregard for life and safety on the night Norman Church was killed. His actions were inexcusable and a man paid for it with his life. A family paid for it with its husband and father.

'But you must look beyond that at the man who was killed. The evidence – from the videotape that is a clear alibi for one killing attributed to Norman Church, if not all of them, to the testimony of loved ones – should convince you that the police had the wrong man. If not, then Detective Bosch's own acknowledgments on the witness stand make it clear that the killings did not stop, that he killed the wrong man.'

Bosch saw that Belk was scribbling on his pad. Hopefully, he was making note of all the things about Bosch's testimony and others that Chandler was conveniently leaving out of her argument.

'Lastly,' she was saying, 'you must look beyond the man who was killed and look at the killer.'

Killer, Bosch thought. It sounded so awful when applied to him. He said the word over and over in his mind. Yes, he had killed. He had killed before and after Church, yet being called simply a killer without the explanations attached somehow seemed horrible. In that moment he realized that he did care after all. Despite what he had said earlier to Belk, he wanted the jury to sanction what he had done. He needed to be told he had done the right thing.

'You have a man,' she said, 'who has repeatedly shown the taste for blood. A cowboy who killed before and since the episode with the unarmed Mr Church. A man who shoots first and looks for evidence later. You have a man with a deep-seated motive for killing a man who he thought might be a serial killer of women, of women from the street . . . like his own mother.'

268

She let that float out there for a while as she pretended to be checking a point or two in the notes on her pad.

'When you go back into that room, you will have to decide if this is the kind of police officer you want in your city. The police force is supposed to mirror the society it protects. Its officers should exemplify the best in us. Ask yourself while you deliberate, who does Harry Bosch exemplify? What segment of our society does he present the mirror image of? If the answers to those questions don't trouble you, then return with a verdict in the defendant's favor. If they do trouble you, if you think our society deserves better than the cold-blooded killing of a potential suspect, then you have no choice but to return a verdict finding for the plaintiff.'

Chandler paused here to go to the plaintiff's table and pour a glass of water. Belk leaned close to Bosch and whispered, 'Not bad but I've seen her do better. . . . I've also seen her do worse.'

'The time she did worse,' Bosch whispered back, 'did she win?'

Belk looked down at his pad, making the answer clear. As Chandler was returning to the lectern he leaned back to Bosch.

'This is her routine. Now she'll talk about money. After getting the water, Money always talks about money.'

Chandler cleared her throat and began again.

'You twelve people are in a rare position. You have the ability to make societal change. Not many people ever get that chance. If you feel Detective Bosch was wrong, to whatever degree, and find for the plaintiff, you will be making change because you will be sending a clear signal, a message to every police officer in this city. From the chief and the administrators inside Parker Center two blocks from here to every rookie patrol officer on the street, the message will be that we do not want you to act this way. We will not accept it. Now, if you return such a verdict you must also set monetary damages. This is not a complicated task. The complicated part is the first part, deciding whether Detective Bosch was right or wrong. The damages can be anything, from one dollar to one million dollars or more. It doesn't matter. What is important is the message. For with the message, you will bring justice for Norman Church. You will bring justice to his family.'

Bosch looked around behind himself and saw Bremmer in the gallery with the other reporters. Bremmer smiled slyly and Bosch turned back around. The reporter had been right on the money about Money.

Chandler walked back to the plaintiff's table, picked up a book and took it back to the lectern. It was old and without a dust jacket, its green cloth binding cracking. Bosch thought he could see a mark, probably a library stamp, on the top edge of its pages.

'In closing now,' she said, 'I would like to address a concern you might have. I know it is one I might have if I were in your place. And that is, how is it that we have come to have men like Detective Bosch as our police? Well, I don't think we can hope to answer that and it is not at point in this case. But if you recall, I quoted to you the philosopher Nietzsche at the beginning of the week. I read his words about the black place he called the abyss. To paraphrase him, he said we must take care that whoever fights monsters for us does not also become a monster. In today's society it is not hard to accept that there are monsters out there, many of them. And so it is not hard, then, to believe that a police officer could become a monster himself.

'After we finished here yesterday, I spent the evening at the library.'

She glanced over at Bosch as she said this, flaunting the lie. He stared back at her and refused the impulse to look away.

'And I'd like to finish by reading something I found that Nathaniel Hawthorne wrote about the same subject we are dealing with today. That chasm of darkness where it can be easy for a person to cross over to the wrong side. In his book *The Marble Faun,* Hawthorne wrote, "The chasm was merely one of the orifices of that pit of blackness that lies beneath us . . . everywhere."

'Ladies and gentlemen, be careful in your deliberations and be true to yourselves. Thank you.'

It was so quiet that Bosch could hear her heels on the rug as she walked back to her seat.

'Folks,' Judge Keyes said, 'we're gonna take a fifteen-minute break and then Mr Belk gets his turn.'

As they were standing for the jury, Belk whispered, 'I can't believe she used the word orifice in her closing argument.'

Bosch looked at him. Belk seemed gleeful but Bosch recognized that he was just latching on to something, anything, so that he could pump himself up and get ready for his own turn behind the lectern. For Bosch knew that whatever words Chandler had used, she had been awfully good. Appraising the sweating fat man next to him, he felt not one bit of confidence.

Bosch went out to the justice statue and smoked two cigarettes during the break but Honey Chandler never came out. Tommy Faraway swung by, however, and clicked his tongue approvingly when he found the nearly whole cigarette she had put in the ash can before. He moved on without saying anything else. It occurred to Bosch that he had never seen Tommy Faraway smoke one of the stubs he culled from the sand.

Belk surprised Bosch with his closing. It wasn't half bad. It was just that he wasn't in the same league as Chandler. His closing was more a reaction to Chandler's than a stand-alone treatise on Bosch's innocence and the unfairness of the accusations against him. He said things like, 'In all of Ms Chandler's talk about the two possible findings you can come up with, she completely forgot about a third, that being that Detective Bosch acted properly and wisely. Correctly.'

It scored points for the defense but it was also a backhanded confirmation by the defense that there were two possible findings for the plaintiff. Belk did not see this but Bosch did. The assistant city attorney was giving the jury three choices now, instead of two, and still only one choice absolved Bosch. At times he wanted to pull Belk back to the table and rewrite his script. But he couldn't. He had to hunker down as he had in the tunnels of Vietnam when the bombs would be hitting above ground, and hope that there were no cave-ins.

The middle of Belk's argument was largely centered on the evidence linking Church to the nine murders. He repeatedly hammered home that Church was the monster in this story, not Bosch, and the evidence clearly backed that up. He warned the jurors that the fact that similar murders apparently continued was unrelated to what Church had done and how Bosch reacted in the apartment on Hyperion.

He finally hit what Bosch figured to be his stride near the end. An inflection of true anger entered his voice when he criticized Chandler's description of Bosch as having acted recklessly and with wanton disregard for life.

'The truth is that life was all Detective Bosch had on his mind when he went through that door. His actions were predicated on the belief that another woman, another victim, was there. Detective Bosch had only one choice. That was to go through that door, secure the situation and deal with the consequences. Norman Church was killed when he refused repeated orders from a police officer and made the move to the pillow. It was a hand he dealt, not Bosch, and he paid the ultimate price.

'But think of Bosch in that situation. Can you imagine being there? Alone? Afraid? It is a unique individual who faces that kind of situation without flinching. It is what our society calls a hero. I think when you return to the jury room and carefully weigh the facts, not the accusations, of this case you will come to that same conclusion. Thank you very much.'

Bosch couldn't believe Belk had used the word hero in a closing argument but decided not to bring that up with the portly lawyer as he returned to the defense table.

Instead, he whispered, 'You did good. Thanks.'

Chandler went to the lectern for her last shot and promised to be brief. She was.

'You can easily see the disparity of the beliefs the lawyers have in this case. The same disparity between the meanings of the words hero and monster. I suspect, as we all probably do, that the truth of this case and Detective Bosch is somewhere in between.

'Two last things before you begin deliberations. First, I want you to remember that both sides had the opportunity here to present full and complete cases. In Norman Church's behalf, we had a wife, a coworker, a friend, stand up and testify to his character, to what kind of man he was. Yet, the defense chose to have only one witness testify before you. Detective Bosch. No one else stood up for Detective –'

'Objection!' Belk yelled.

'– Bosch.'

'Hold it right there, Ms Chandler,' Judge Keyes boomed.

The judge's face became very red as he thought about how to proceed.

'I should clear the jury out of here to do what I am going to do but I think if you're going to play with fire you have to accept the burns. Ms Chandler, I'm holding you in contempt of this court for that grievous display of poor judgment. We'll talk about sanctions at a later date. But I guarantee that it won't be a pleasant date to look forward to.'

The judge then swiveled in his chair toward the jury and leaned forward.

'Folks, this lady should never have said that. You see, the defense is not obligated to put anybody up as a witness and whether they do or don't, that cannot be seen as a reflection on their guilt or innocence on the matter before you. Ms Chandler darn well knew this. She's an experienced trial lawyer and you better believe she knew this. The fact that she went and said it anyway, knowing Mr Belk over there and myself would practically hit the ceiling, I think shows a cunning on her behalf that I find very distasteful and troubling in a court of law. I'm going to complain about that to the state law board but –'

'Your Honor,' Chandler cut in. 'I object to you tell –'

'Don't interrupt, Counselor. You stand there and keep quiet until I am through.'

'Yes, Your Honor.'

'I said keep quiet.' He turned back to the jury. 'As I was saying, what happens to Ms Chandler is not for you to worry about. See, she's taking a gamble that no matter what I say to you now, you will still think about what she said about Detective Bosch not bringing any supporters to testify. I tell you now with the sternest admonition I can offer, do not think about that. What she said means nothing. In fact, I suspect that if he wanted to, Detective Bosch and Mr Belk could muster a line of police officers ready to testify that would stretch out that door all the way to Parker Center if they thought they wanted it. But they don't. That's the strategy they chose and it is not your duty to question it in any way. Any way at all. Any questions?'

No one in the jury box even moved. The judge turned his chair back and looked at Belk.

'Anything you want to say, Mr Belk?'

'One moment, Your Honor.'

Belk turned to Bosch and whispered, 'What do you think? He's primed to grant a mistrial. I've never seen him so mad. We'd get a new trial, maybe by then this copycat thing will be wrapped up.'

Bosch thought a moment. He wanted this over and did not like the prospect of going through another trial with Chandler.

'Mr Belk?' the judge said.

'I think we go with what we've got,' Bosch whispered. 'What do you think?'

Belk nodded and said, 'I think he might have just given us the verdict.'

Then he stood in his place and said, 'Nothing at this time, Your Honor.'

'You sure now?'

'Yes, Your Honor.'

'Okay, Ms Chandler, like I said, we'll deal with this at a later time but we will deal with it. You can proceed now, but be very careful.'

'Your Honor, thank you. I want to say before going on that I apologize for my line of argument. I meant no disrespect to you. I, uh, was speaking extemporaneously and got carried away.'

'You did. Apology accepted, but we will still deal with the contempt order later. Let's proceed. I want the jury to begin their work right after lunch.'

Chandler adjusted her position at the lectern so that she was looking at the jury.

'Ladies and gentlemen, you heard Detective Bosch on the stand yourself. I ask you, lastly, to remember what he said. He said Norman Church got what he deserved. Think about that statement coming from a police officer and what it means. "Norman Church got what he deserved." We have seen in this courtroom how the justice system works. The checks and balances. The judge to referee, the jury to decide. By his own admission, Detective Bosch decided that was not necessary. He decided there was no need for a judge. No need for a jury. He robbed Norman Church of his chance for justice. And so, ultimately, he robbed you. Think about that.'

She picked her yellow pad up off the lectern and sat down.

TWENTY-THREE

The jury began its deliberations at 11:15 and Judge Keyes ordered the federal marshals to arrange for lunch to be sent in. He said the twelve would not be interrupted until 4:30, unless they came up with a verdict first.

After the jury had filed out, the judge ordered that all parties be able to appear for a reading of the verdict within fifteen minutes of notification by the clerk. That meant Chandler and Belk could go back to their respective offices to wait. Norman Church's family was from Burbank so the wife and two daughters opted to go to Chandler's office. For Bosch, the Hollywood station would have been more than a fifteen-minute commute, but Parker Center was a five-minute walk. He gave the clerk his pager number and told her he'd be there.

The last piece of business the judge brought up was the contempt order against Chandler. He set a hearing for it to be discussed for two weeks later and then banged his gavel down.

Before leaving the courtroom, Belk took Bosch aside and said, 'I think we're in pretty good shape but I'm nervous. You want to spin the dice?'

'What are you talking about?'

'I could try to low-ball Chandler one last time.'

'Offer to settle?'

'Yeah. I have carte blanche from the office for anything up to fifty. After that, I'd have to get approval. But I could throw the fifty at her and see if they'd take it to walk away now.'

'What about legal fees?'

'On a settlement, she'd have to take the cut from the fifty. Someone like her, she's probably going forty percent. That'd be twenty grand for a week in trial and a week picking a jury. Not bad.'

'You think we're going to lose?'

'I don't know. I'm just thinking of all the angles. You never know what a jury will do. Fifty grand would be a cheap way out. She might take it, the way the judge came down on her there at the end. She's the one who's probably scared of losing now.'

Belk didn't get it, Bosch knew. Maybe it had been too subtle for him. The whole contempt thing had been Chandler's last scam. She had purposely committed the infraction so the jury would see her being slapped down by the judge. She was showing them the justice system at work: a bad deed met with stern enforcement and punishment. She was saying to them, do you see? This is what Bosch escaped. This is what Norman Church faced, but Bosch decided to take the judge and jury's role instead.

It was clever, maybe too clever. The more Bosch thought about it, the more he wondered how much the judge had been a willing and knowing player in it. He looked at Belk and saw the young assistant city attorney apparently suspected none of this. Instead, he thought of it as a stroke on his side of the page. Probably in two weeks, when Keyes lets her go with a hundred-dollar fine and a lecture during the contempt hearing, he'll get it.

'You can do whatever you want,' he told Belk. 'But she isn't going to take it. She's in on this one until the end.'

At Parker Center Bosch went into Irving's conference room through the door that opened directly off the hallway. Irving had decided the day before that the now-called Follower Task Force would work out of the conference room so the assistant chief could be kept up on developments to the minute. What wasn't said about the move but was known was that keeping the group out of one of the squad rooms improved the chance that word of what was happening would remain secure – for at least a few days.

When Bosch walked in only Rollenberger and Edgar were in the room. Bosch noticed that four phones had been installed and were on the round meeting table. There were also six rovers – Motorola two-way radios – and a main communications console on the table, ready to be used as needed. When Edgar looked up and saw Bosch he immediately looked away and picked up a phone to make a call.

'Bosch,' Rollenberger said. 'Welcome to our operations center. Are you free from the trial? No smoking in here, by the way.'

'I'm free until a verdict but I've got a fifteen-minute leash on me. Anything going on? What's Mora doing?'

'Not much is happening. Been quiet. Mora spent the morning in the Valley. Went to an attorney's office in Sherman Oaks and then to a couple of casting agencies, also in Sherman Oaks.'

Rollenberger was looking at a logbook in front of him on the table.

'After that he went to a couple houses in Studio City. There were vans outside of these houses and Sheehan and Opelt said they thought they might be making movies at these locations. He didn't stay long at either place. Anyway, he's back over at Ad-Vice now. Sheehan called in a couple minutes ago.'

'Did we get the extra people?'

'Yeah, Mayfield and Yde will take the watch at four from the first team. Then we've got two other teams after that.'

'Two?'

'Chief Irving changed his mind and wants an around-the-clock watch. So we'll be on him through the night, even if he just stays at home and sleeps. Personally, I think it's a good idea that we go 'round the clock.'

Yeah, especially since Irving decided to do it, Bosch thought but didn't say. He looked at the radios on the table.

'What's our freek?'

'Uh, we're on . . . frequency, frequency – oh, yeah, we're on five. Symplex five. It's a DWP communications freek that they only use during a public emergency. Earthquake, flooding, stuff like that. Chief thought it be best to keep off our own freeks. If Mora is our man, then he might be keeping an ear to the radio.'

Bosch thought Rollenberger probably thought it was a good idea, but didn't ask him.

'I think it's a good idea to play it safe this way,' the lieutenant said.

'Right. Anything else I should know?' He looked at Edgar, who was still on the phone. 'What's Edgar got?'

'Still trying to locate the survivor from four years ago. He already pulled a copy of Mora's divorce file. It was uncontested.'

Edgar hung up, finished writing something in a notebook and then stood up without looking at Bosch. He said, 'I'm going down to get a cup.'

'Okay,' Rollenberger said. 'We should have our own coffeemaker in here by this afternoon. I talked it over with the chief and he was going to requisition one.'

Bosch said, 'Good idea. I think I'm going down with Edgar.'

Edgar walked quickly down the hallway so that he could stay ahead of Bosch. At the elevator he pushed the button but then without breaking stride walked past the elevator and into the stairwell to go down. Bosch followed and after they had gone down one floor, Edgar stopped and whipped around.

'What are you following me for?'

'Coffee.'

'Oh, bullshit.'

'Did –'

'No, I didn't talk to Pounds yet. I've been busy, remember?'

'Good, then don't.'

'What are you talking about?'

'If you haven't talked to Pounds about it, then don't. Forget about it.'

'Serious?'

'Yeah.'

He stood there looking at Bosch, still skeptical.

'Learn from it. So will I. I already have. Okay?'

'Thanks, Harry.'

'No, don't "Thanks, Harry" me. Just say "okay".'

'Okay.'

They walked down to the next floor and to the cafeteria. Rather than sit in front of Rollenberger and talk, Bosch suggested they take their coffee to one of the tables.

'Hans Off, what a trip, man,' Edgar said. 'I keep picturing this cuckoo clock, only it's him that comes out and says, "Great idea, Chief! Great idea, Chief!" '

Bosch smiled and Edgar laughed. Harry could tell a great burden had been lifted off the man and so he was heartened by what he had done. He felt good about it.

'So, nothing on the survivor yet?' he said.

'She's out there somewhere. But the four years since she escaped from the Follower have not been good to Georgia Stern.'

'What happened?'

'Well, by reading her sheet and talking to some guys in street vice, it looks like she got on the needle. After that, she probably got too skaggy-looking to make movies. I mean, who wants to watch a film like that and the girl's got track marks up her arms or her thighs or her neck. That's the problem with the porno business if you're a hype. You're naked, man, you can't hide that shit.

'Anyway, I talked to Mora, just to make a routine contact and to tell him I was looking for her. He kinda gave me that rundown on how needle marks are the quickest way out of the business. But he had nothing else. You think that was cool, talking to him?'

Bosch considered it a few moments and then said, 'Yeah,

I do. Best way to keep him from being suspicious is to act like he knows as much as we do. If you hadn't asked him and then he heard from a source or somebody else in vice that you were looking for her, then he'd probably tumble to us.'

'Yeah, that's the way I figured it, so I called him this morning and asked a few questions and then went on. Far as he knows, you and me are the only ones working this new case. He doesn't know anything about our task force. So far.'

'Only problem with asking him about the survivor is that if he knows you're looking, he may go looking for her. We'll have to be careful about that. Let the surveillance teams know.'

'Yeah, I will. Maybe Hans Off can tell 'em. You ought to hear this guy on the rovers, sounds like a fuckin' Eagle Scout.'

Bosch smiled. He imagined Hans Off cut no slack in the use of radio code designations.

'Anyway, so that's why she isn't in the porno biz anymore,' Edgar said, getting back to the survivor. 'In the last three years, we got check charges, a couple of possessions, a couple prostitution rousts and many, many under-the-influence beefs. She's been in and out. Always time served, never anything serious. Two, three days at a time. Not enough to help her kick, either.'

'So where's she work?'

'The Valley. I've been on the phone with Valley Vice all morning. They say she usually works the Sepulveda corridor with the other street pros.'

Bosch remembered the young women he had seen the other afternoon while tracing down Cerrone, Rebecca Kaminski's manager/pimp. He wondered if he had seen or even talked to Georgia Stern and not known it.

'What is it?'

'Nothing. I was out there the other day and was wondering if I'd seen her. You know, not knowing who she was. Did the vice guys say whether she had protection?'

'Nah, no pimp that they know of. I got the idea she's bottom drawer stuff. Most pimps have better ponies.'

'So, is Vice up there looking for her?'

'Not yet,' Edgar said. 'They have training today, but they'll be out on Sepulveda tomorrow night.'

'Any recent photos?'

'Yeah.'

Edgar reached into his sport coat and pulled out a stack of photos. They were copies of a booking photo. Georgia Stern certainly looked used up. Her bleached-blonde hair showed at least an inch of dark roots. There were circles under her eyes so deep they looked as though they had been cut into her face with a knife. Her cheeks were gaunt and she was glassy-eyed. Lucky for her she had fixed before she was busted. It meant less time in the cage hurting, waiting and craving the next fix.

'This is three months old. Under the influence. She did two in Sybil and out.'

Sybil Brand Institute was the county's holding jail for women. Half of it was equipped to handle narcotics addicts.

'Get this,' Edgar said. 'I forgot about this. This guy Dean up in Valley Vice says he was the one who made this bust on her and when he was booking her he found a bottle of powder and was just about ready to run her ticket up to possession when he realized the bottle was a legit scrip. He said the powder was AZT. You know, for AIDS. She's got the virus, man, and she's out there on the street. On Sepulveda. He asked her if she makes 'em use rubbers and her answer was, "Not if they don't want to."'

Bosch just nodded. The story was not unusual. It had been Bosch's experience that most prostitutes despised the men they waved down and serviced for money. Those who became sick got it either from their customers or from dirty needles, which also sometimes came from customers. Either way, he believed it was part of the psychology to not care about passing it on to the population that may have given it to you. It was the belief that what goes around comes around.

'Not if they don't want to,' Edgar said again, shaking his head. 'I mean, man, that's cold.'

Bosch finished his coffee and pushed his chair back. There was no smoking in the cafeteria so he wanted to go down to the lobby and out by the fallen-officers memorial to smoke. As long as Rollenberger was camped out in the conference room, smoking there was out.

'So –'

Bosch's pager went off and he visibly flinched. He had always subscribed to the theory that a quick verdict was a bad verdict was a stupid verdict. Hadn't they given the evidence careful consideration? He pulled it off his belt and looked at the number on the display. He breathed easier. It was an LAPD exchange.

'I think Mora is calling me.'

'Better be careful. What were you going to say?'

'Uh, oh, yeah, I was just wondering if Stern will be any good to us if we find her. It's been four years. She's on the spike and sick. I wonder if she'll even remember the Follower.'

'Yeah, I was thinking that, too. But my only alternatives are to go back to Hollywood and report to Pounds or volunteer for one of the surveillance shifts on Mora. I'm sticking on this. I'm going up there to Sepulveda tonight.'

Bosch nodded.

'Hans Off said you pulled the divorce. Nothing there?'

'Not really. She filed but then Mora didn't contest it. File's about ten pages, that's it. Only one thing of note in it, and I don't know if it means anything or not.'

'What?'

'She filed on the usual grounds. Irreconcilable differences, mental cruelty. But in the records, she also mentions the loss of consortium. You know what that is?'

'No sex.'

'Yeah. What do you think that means?'

Bosch thought for a few moments and said, 'I don't know. They split just before the Dollmaker stuff. Maybe he was into some strange stuff, building up to the killings. I can ask Locke.'

'Yeah, that's what I was thinking. Anyway, I had DMV run the wife and she's still alive. But I was thinking we shouldn't approach her. Too dangerous. She might tip him.'

'Yeah, don't go near her. Did DMV fax her DL?'

'Yeah. She's blonde. Five-foot-four, hundred and ten. It was only a face shot on the driver's license but I'd say she fits.'

Bosch nodded and stood up.

After taking one of the rovers from the conference room, Bosch drove over to Central Division and parked in the back lot. He was still within the fifteen-minute radius of the federal courthouse. He left the rover in the car and walked out to the sidewalk and around front to the public entrance. He did this so he could see if he could spot Sheehan and Opelt. He assumed they would have to be parked within sight of the lot's exit so they would see Mora leaving, but he did not see them or any car that looked suspicious.

A pair of headlights briefly flashed from a parking lot behind an old gas station that was now a taco stand, featuring a sign that said HOME OF THE KOSHER BURRITO – PASTRAMI! He saw two figures in the car, which was a gray Eldorado, and just looked away.

Mora was at his desk eating a burrito that looked disgusting to Bosch because he could see it was filled with pastrami. It looked unnatural.

'Harry,' he said with his mouth full.

'How is it?'

'It's okay. I'll go back to plain beef after this. I just tried it 'cause I saw a couple guys from RHD over across the street. One of 'em said they come all the way over from Parker to get these kosher things there. Thought I'd give it a try.'

'Yeah, I think I've heard of that place.'

'Well, you ask me, it ain't worth coming over from Parker Center for.'

He wrapped what was left in the oil-stained paper it came in and then got up and walked out of the squad room. Bosch heard the package hit the bottom of a trash can in the hallway and then Mora was back.

'Don't want it to stink up my trash can.'

'So, you buzzed?'

'Yeah, that was me. How's the trial?'

'Waiting on a verdict.'

'Shit, that's scary.'

Bosch knew from experience that if Mora wanted to tell you something, he would tell you in his own time. It would do him no good to keep asking the vice cop why he beeped him.

Back in his chair, Mora swiveled around to the filing cabinets behind him and began opening drawers. Over his shoulder, he said, 'Hang on, Harry. I gotta get some stuff together for you here.'

It took him two minutes during which Bosch saw him open several different files, take out photos and create a short stack. Then he turned back around.

'Four,' he said. 'I've come up with four more actresses that dropped out under what might be termed suspicious circumstances.'

'Only four.'

'Yeah. Actually, there were more than four chicks that people mentioned. But only four fit that profile we talked about. Blonde and built. There is also Gallery, who we already knew about, and your concrete blonde. So we've got six all together. Here are the new ones.'

He handed the group of photos across the desk to Bosch. Harry slowly looked through them. They were color publicity glossies with each woman's name printed in the white border at the bottom of the photo. Two of the women were naked and posing indoors on chairs, their legs apart.

The other two were photographed at the beach and were wearing bikinis that would probably be illegal on most public beaches. To Bosch, the women in the photos almost looked interchangeable. Their bodies were similar. Their faces had the same fake pouts that were intended to show mystery and sexual abandonment at the same time. Each of the women had hair so blonde it was nearly white.

'All Snow Whites,' Mora said, an unneeded commentary that made Bosch look up from the photos to look at him. The vice cop just stared back and said, 'You know, the hair. That's what a producer calls them when he's casting movies. He says he wants a Snow White for this part 'cause he already has a red or whatever. Snow White. It's like the model name. These chicks are all interchangeable.'

Bosch looked back down at the photos, not trusting that his eyes would not give his suspicions away.

He realized, though, that much of what Mora had just said was true. The main physical differences between the women in the photos were the tattoos and their locations on each body. Each woman had a small tattoo of a heart or a rose or a cartoon character. Candi Cummings had a heart just to the left of her carefully trimmed triangle of pubic hair. Mood Indigo had some kind of cartoon just above her left ankle but Bosch couldn't make it out because of the angle the photograph had been taken from. Dee Anne Dozit had a heart wrapped in a vine of barbed wire about six inches above the left nipple, which was pierced with a gold ring. And TeXXXas Rose had a red rose on the soft part of her right hand between the thumb and first finger.

Bosch realized they might all be dead now.

'No one's heard from them?'

'No one in the biz, at least.'

'You're right. Physically, they fit.'

'Yeah.'

'They did outcall?'

'I assume they did, but I'm not sure yet. The people I talked to dealt with them in the film biz so they didn't know what these girls did when the cameras stopped rolling, so to speak. Or, so they said. My next step was to get some back issues of the sex rags and look for ads.'

'Any dates? You know, when they disappeared, stuff like that?'

'Just generally speaking. These people, the agents and the moviemakers, they don't have minds for dates. We're dealing with memories, so I've only got a general picture. If I find out they ran outcall ads, I'll narrow it down pretty close to exact dates when I find out when they last ran. Anyway, let me give you what I got. You got your notebook?'

Mora told him what he had. No specific dates, just months and years. Adding in the approximate dates when Rebecca Kaminski, the concrete blonde, Constance Calvin, who became Gallery on film, and the seventh and eleventh victims originally attributed to Church had disappeared, there was a rough pattern of disappearances of the porno starlets about every six to seven months. The last disappearance was Mood Indigo, eight months earlier.

'See the pattern? He's due. He's out there hunting.'

Bosch nodded and looked up from his notebook at Mora and thought he saw a gleam in his dark eyes. He thought he could see through them into a black emptiness inside. In that one chilling moment Bosch thought he saw the confirmation of evil in the other man. It was as if Mora was challenging him to come farther into the dark with him.

TWENTY-FOUR

Bosch knew he was stretching his leash by going down to USC, but it was two o'clock and his choice was to hang around the conference room with Rollenberger and wait for a verdict or do something useful with his time. He decided on the latter and got on the Harbor Freeway going south. Depending on how northbound traffic on the freeway was, he could conceivably get back to downtown in fifteen minutes if a verdict came in. Getting a parking space at Parker Center and walking over to the courthouse would be another matter.

The University of Southern California was located in the tough neighborhoods that surround the Coliseum. But once through the gate and into the general campus, it seemed as bucolic as Catalina, though Bosch knew this peace had been interrupted with a quickening frequency in recent years, to the point that even Trojan football practice could be dangerous. A couple of seasons back a stray bullet from one of the daily drive-by shootings in the nearby neighborhoods had struck a gifted freshman linebacker while he stood with teammates on the practice field. It was incidents like that that had administrators complaining on a routine basis to the LAPD and students longingly thinking about UCLA, which was cheaper and located in the relatively crime-free suburban milieu of Westwood.

Bosch easily found the psychology building with a map given to him at the entry gate, but once he was inside the four-story brick building there was no directory to help him find Dr John Locke or the psychohormonal studies lab. He walked down one lengthy hallway and then took stairs to the second floor. The first female student he asked for directions to the lab laughed, apparently believing his question was a come-on, and walked away without answering. He finally was directed to the basement of the building.

He read the signs on the doors as he walked along the dimly lit corridor and finally found the lab at the second-to-last doorway at the end of the hall. A blonde student sat behind a desk in the entry. She was reading a thick textbook. She looked up and smiled and Bosch asked for Locke.

'I'll call. Does he expect you?'

'You never know with a shrink.'

He smiled but she didn't get it, then he wondered if it was even a joke.

'No, I didn't say I was coming.'

'Well, Dr Locke has student labs running all day. I shouldn't disturb him if –'

She finally looked up and saw the badge he was holding.

'I'll call right away.'

'Just tell him it's Bosch and I need a few minutes if he can spare them.'

She spoke briefly on the phone to someone, reiterating what Bosch had just said. She then waited silently for a few moments, said 'Okay' and hung up.

'The grad assistant said Dr Locke said he will come get you. It should only be a few minutes.'

He thanked her and sat in one of the chairs by the door. He looked around the entry room. There was a bulletin board with handprinted announcements pinned to the cork. Mostly they were the roommate-wanted type of posting. There was an announcement of a party for psych undergrads this coming Saturday.

There was one other desk in the room in addition to the one the student occupied. But this one was empty at the moment.

'This part of the curriculum?' he asked. 'You have to put in time here as the receptionist?'

She looked up·from the textbook.

'No, it's just a job. I'm in child psych but jobs in the lab there are hard to come by. Nobody likes working down here in the basement. So this was open.'

'How come?'

'All the creepy psychology is down here. Psychohormonal at this end. There is –'

The door opened on the other side of the room and Locke stepped through. He was wearing blue jeans and a tie-dyed T-shirt. He stuck his hand out to Bosch and Harry noticed the leather thong tied around his wrist.

'Harry, how goes it?'

'Fine. I'm fine. How're you? I'm sorry to barge in on you like this but I was wondering if you have a few minutes. I have some new information on that thing I bothered you with the other night.'

'No bother at all. Believe me, it's great to get my fingers on a real case. Student labs can be boring.'

He told Bosch to follow him and they went back through the door, down a hallway and into a suite of offices. Locke led him to the room in the back which was his office. Rows of textbooks and what Bosch guessed were collected theses lined shelves on the wall behind his desk. Locke dropped into a padded chair and put a foot up on the desk. A green banker's light on the table was lit, and the only other light came from a small casement window set high on the wall to the right. Every now and then the light from the window would flicker as someone up on the ground level walked by and briefly blocked its path, a human eclipse.

Looking up at the window, Locke said, 'Sometimes I feel like I'm working in a dungeon down here.'

'I think the student out front thinks so, too.'

'Melissa? Well, what do you expect? She's chosen child psychology as her major and I can't seem to convince her to cross to my side of the road. Anyway, I doubt you·came to campus to hear stories about pretty young students, though I don't suppose it could hurt.'

'Maybe some other time.'

Bosch could smell that someone had smoked in the room, though he saw no ashtray. He took his cigarettes out without asking.

'You know, Harry, I could hypnotize you and alleviate that problem for you.'

'No thanks, Doc, I hypnotized myself once and it didn't work.'

'Really, are you one of the last of the dying breed of LAPD hypnotists? I heard about that experiment. Courts shot it down, right?'

'Yeah, wouldn't accept hypnotized witnesses in court. I'm the last one they taught who's still in the department. I think.'

'Interesting.'

'Anyway, there've been some developments since we last talked and I thought it would be good to touch base with you, see what you think. I think you steered us right with that porno angle and maybe you'll come up with something now.'

'What have you got?'

'We have –'

'First off, do you want some coffee?'

'Are you having any?'

'Never touch it.'

'Then I'm fine. We've come up with a suspect.'

'Really?'

He dropped his foot off the desk and leaned forward. He seemed genuinely interested.

'And he had a foot in both camps, like you said. He was on the task force and his beat, uh, his area of expertise is the pornography business. I don't think I should identify him at this time because –'

'Of course not. I understand. He's a suspect, hasn't been charged with anything. Detective, don't worry, this entire conversation is off the record. Speak freely.'

Bosch used a trash can next to Locke's desk as an ashtray.

'I appreciate it. So, we are watching him, seeing what he is doing. But it gets tricky here. See, because he is probably the department's top man on the porno industry, it is natural we go to him for advice and information.'

'Naturally, if you didn't, he would most assuredly become suspicious of the fact that you are suspicious of him. Oh what a wonderful web we weave, Harry.'

'Tangled.'

'What?'

'Nothing.'

Locke got up and started pacing around the room. He put his hands in his pockets and then took them out. He was staring at nothing, just thinking the whole time.

'Go on, this is great. What'd I tell you? Two independent actors playing the same role. The black heart does not beat alone. Go on.'

'Well, like I said, it was natural to go to him and we did. We suspected that, with the discovery of the body this week and what you said, that there might be others. Other women who disappeared who were in that business.'

'So you asked him to check it out? Excellent.'

'Yes, I asked him yesterday. And today he gave me four more names. We already had the name of the concrete blonde found this week and one other that the suspect provided the other day. So you add the first two – Dollmaker victims seven and eleven – and now we have a total of eight. The suspect was under surveillance all day so we know he did the legwork needed to come up with these new names. He didn't just give me four names. He went through the motions.'

'Of course he would do that. He would keep up the appearance of normal routine life whether he knew he was being followed or not. He would already know these names, you understand, but he would still go out and get them by doing the routine legwork. It's one of the signs of how smart he –'

He stopped, put his hands in his pocket and frowned while seemingly staring at the floor between his feet.

'You said six new names plus the first two?'

'Right.'

'Eight kills in almost five years. Any chance there are others?'

'I was going to ask you that. This information comes from the suspect. Would he lie? Would he tell us less, give us fewer names than there actually were to screw with us, to mess up the investigation?'

'Ah.' He continued pacing but didn't continue speaking for a half minute. 'My gut instinct is to say no. No, he would not screw with you, as you say. He would do his job in earnest. I think if all he has given you are five new names, then that's all there are. You have to remember that this man thinks he is superior to you, the police, in every aspect. It would not be unusual for him to be perfectly honest with you about some aspects of the case.'

'We have a rough idea of the times. The times of the killings. What it looks like is that he slowed his pace after the Dollmaker was killed. When he started hiding them, burying them, because he couldn't blend in any longer with the Dollmaker, the intervals lengthened. It looks like he went from less than two months between kills during the Dollmaker period to seven months. Maybe even longer. The last disappearance was almost eight months ago.'

Locke looked up from the floor at Bosch.

'And all this recent activity,' he said. 'The trial in the papers. His sending the note. His involvement as a detective in the case. The high activity will speed the end of the cycle. Don't lose him, Harry. It could be time.'

He turned and looked at the calendar that hung on the wall next to the door. There was some kind of maze-like design above the chart of the month's days. Locke started laughing. Bosch didn't get it.

'What?' he asked.

'Jeez, this weekend is a full moon, too.' He spun around to look at Bosch. 'Can you take me on the surveillance?'

'What?'

'Take me along. It would be the rarest of opportunities in the field of psychosexual studies. To observe the stalking pattern of a sexual sadist as it is actually taking place. Unbelievable. Harry, this could get me a grant from Hopkins. It could . . . it could' – his eyes lit up as he looked at the casement window – 'get me out of this fucking dungeon!'

Bosch stood up. He was thinking he had made a mistake. Locke's vision of his own future was obscuring everything else. He had come for help, not to make Locke shrink of the year.

'Look, we're talking about a killer here. Real people. Real blood. I'm not going to do anything that might compromise the investigation. A surveillance is a delicate operation. When you add that it is a cop we are watching, then it makes it even harder. I can't bring you along. Don't even ask. I can tell you things here and fill you in whenever I can but there is no way I or my commander on this would approve bringing a civilian along for the ride.'

Locke's eyes dropped and he looked like a chastised boy. He took a quick glance at the window again and walked around behind the desk. He sat down and his shoulders dropped.

'Yes, of course,' he said quietly. 'I completely understand, Harry. I got carried away there. The important thing is that we stop this man. We'll worry about studying him later. Now, a seven-month cycle. Wow, that's impressive.'

Bosch flicked his ashes and sat back down.

'Well, we don't know for sure, considering the source. There still could be others.'

'I doubt it.'

Locke pinched the bridge of his nose and leaned back in his chair. He closed his eyes. He did not move for several seconds.

'Harry, I'm not sleeping. Just concentrating. Just thinking.'

Bosch watched him for a few moments. It was weird. He then noticed that lined on a shelf just above Locke's head were the books the psychologist had written. There were several, all with his name on the spine. There were several duplicates, too. Maybe, Bosch thought, so he could give them away. He saw five copies of *Black Hearts,* the book Locke had mentioned during his testimony, and three copies of a book called, *The Private Sex Life of the Public Porn Princess.*

'You wrote about the porno business?'

He opened his eyes.

'Why, yes. That was the book I did before *Black Hearts.* Did you read it?'

'Uh, no.'

He closed his eyes again.

'Of course not. Despite the sexy title it really is a textbook. Used at the university level. Last I checked with my publisher, it was being sold in the bookstores at a hundred and forty-six universities, including Hopkins. It's been out two years, fourth printing, still haven't seen a royalty check. Would you like to read it?'

'I would.'

'Well, if you go by the student union on your way out of here, they sell it there. It's steep, I should warn you. Thirty bucks. But I'm sure you can expense it. I should also warn you, it's quite explicit.'

Bosch was annoyed that Locke didn't give him one of the extra copies on the shelf. Perhaps, it was Locke's childlike way of getting back at him for nixing the surveillance ride-along. He wondered what Melissa, the child-psych major, would make of such behavior.

'There is something else about this suspect. I don't know what it means.'

Locke opened his eyes but didn't move.

'He was divorced about a year before the Dollmaker

killings began. In the divorce record there's mention by the wife that there was a loss of consortium. Would that still fit?'

'They stopped doing it, huh?'

'I guess. It was in the court file.'

'It could fit. But to be honest, we shrinks could find a way to make any activity fit into any prognosis we make. That's the field for you. But it could be a case where your suspect simply became impotent with his wife. He was moving toward the erotic mold, and she had no part in it. In effect, he was leaving her behind.'

'So it is not seen by you to be a cause for rethinking our suspicions of this man?'

'On the contrary. My view is that it is more evidence that he has gone through major psychological changes. His sexual persona is evolving.'

Bosch gave this some thought while trying to envision Mora. The vice cop spent every day in the tawdry milieu of pornography. After a while, he couldn't get it up for his own wife.

'Is there anything else you can tell me? Anything about this suspect that might help us? We don't have anything on him. No probable cause. We can't arrest him. All we can do is watch. And that gets dangerous. If we lose him –'

'He could kill.'

'Right.'

'And then you are still left with no probable cause, no evidence.'

'What about trophies? What do I look for?'

'Where?'

'In his home.'

'Ah, I see. You plan to continue your professional interaction with him, to visit him at home. On a ruse, perhaps. But you won't be able to move about freely.'

'I might be able to, if someone else keeps him occupied. I'll go with somebody else.'

Locke leaned forward in his chair, his eyes wide. It was starting again, his excitement.

'What if you kept him busy and I had a look around? I am the expert on this, Harry. You would be better at keeping him busy. You could talk detective talk, I'd ask to use the bathroom. I would have a better grasp of –'

'Forget it, Dr Locke. Listen to me, there is no way it's going to happen that way. Okay? It's too dangerous. Now, do you want to help me here or not?'

'Okay, okay. Again, I'm sorry. The reason I am so exited by the prospect of being inside this man's house and mind is that I think that this man, who is on a killing cycle of seven months plus, would almost certainly have trophies that would help him feed into his fantasy and recreate his kills; thereby dulling urges to physically act out.'

'I understand.'

'You've got a man with an unusually long cycle. Believe me, during those seven months the impulses to act out, to go out and kill, do not lie dormant. They are there. They are always there. Remember, the erotic mold? I testified about it?'

'I remember.'

'Okay, well, he is going to need to satisfy that erotic mold. To fulfill it. How does he do it? How does he last six or seven or eight months? The answer is, he has trophies. These are reminders of past conquests. By conquests I mean kills. He has things that remind him and help bring the fantasy alive. It's not the real thing by a long shot but he can still use the reminders to widen the cycle, to stave off the impulse to act. He knows the less he kills, the less chance there is that he will be caught.

'If you're right about him, he is now nearly eight months into a cycle. It means he is pushing the edge of the envelope, all the while trying to maintain his control. Yet at the same time we have this note and his strange compulsion to not be overlooked. To stand up and say, I'm better than the Dollmaker. I go on! And if you don't believe me, check out what I left in the concrete at such and such a place. The note shows severe disassembling at the same time he is locked in this tremendous battle to control the impulses. He has gone seven months plus!'

Bosch pressed his cigarette against the side of the trash can and dropped it in. He took out his notebook. He said, 'The clothing of the victims, both the Dollmaker's and the Follower's, was never found. These could be the trophies he uses?'

'They could be, but put the notebook away, Harry. It's easier than that. Remember, what you have here is a man who chose his victims after seeing them in videos? So what better way to keep his fantasies alive than through videos. If you get free of him in the house, look for videos, Harry. And a camera.'

'He videotaped the killings,' Bosch said.

It wasn't a question. He was just repeating Locke, preparing himself for what was ahead with Mora.

'Of course, we can't say for sure,' Locke said. 'Who knows? But I'd put my money on it. You remember Westley Dodd?'

Bosch shook his head no.

'He was the one they executed a couple of years ago in Washington. Hanged him – a perfect example of what goes around comes around. He was a child-killer. Liked to hang kids in his closet, on coat hangers. And he also had a Polaroid camera he liked to use. After his arrest the police found a carefully kept photo album, complete with Polaroids of the little boys he killed – hanging in the closet. He had taken the time to carefully label each picture with a caption. Very sick stuff. But as sick as it was, I guarantee you that that photo album saved the lives of other little boys. Absolutely. Because he could use it to indulge his fantasy and not act it out.'

Bosch nodded his understanding. Somewhere in Mora's house he would find a video or maybe a photographic gallery that would turn most people's stomachs. But for Mora it was what kept him out of the black place for as long as eight months at a time.

'What about Jeffrey Dahmer?' Locke said. 'Remember him, in Milwaukee? He was a cameraman, too. Liked taking pictures of corpses, parts of corpses. Helped him go undetected by the police for years and years. Then he started keeping the corpses. That was his mistake.'

They were silent for a few moments after that. Bosch's head filled with horrible images of the dead he had seen. He rubbed his eyes as if that might erase them.

'What's that they say about photos?' Locke asked then. 'On the TV commercials? Something like "the gift that keeps on giving". Then what's that make videotape to a serial killer?'

Before leaving campus, Bosch dropped by the student union and went into the bookstore. He found a stack of copies of Locke's book on the porno business in the section on psychology and social studies. The top one on the stack was well worn around the edges from being thumbed through. Bosch took the one below it.

When the girl at the register opened the book to get the price it flopped open to a black-and-white photo of a woman performing fellatio on a man. The girl's face turned red but not as scarlet as Bosch's.

'Sorry,' was all he could think to say.

'That's okay, I've seen it before. The book, I mean.'

'Yeah.'

'Are you teaching a class with it next semester?'

Bosch realized that since he was too old to look like a student, seemingly the only valid reason for him to be buying the book was if he was a teacher. He thought that explaining that his interest was as a police officer would sound phony and get him more attention than he wanted.

'Yes,' he lied.

'Really, what's it called? Maybe I'll take it.'

'Uh, well, I haven't decided yet. I'm still formulating a –'

'Well, what's your name? I'll look for it in the catalog.'

'Uh . . . Locke. Dr John Locke, psychology.'

'Oh, you wrote the book. Yeah, I've heard of you. I'll look the class up. Thanks and have a good day.'

She gave him his change. He thanked him and left with the book in a bag.

TWENTY-FIVE

Bosch was back in the federal courthouse shortly after four. While they waited for Judge Keyes to come out and dismiss the jury for the weekend, Belk whispered that he had called Chandler's office during the afternoon and offered the plaintiff fifty grand to walk away from the case.

'She told you to shove it.'

'She wasn't that polite, actually.'

Bosch smiled and looked over at Chandler. She was whispering something to Church's wife but must have felt Bosch's stare. She stopped speaking and looked over at him. For nearly half a minute they engaged in an adolescent stare-down contest, with neither backing down until the door to the judge's chambers opened and Judge Keyes bounded out and up to his place on the bench.

He had the clerk buzz in the jury. He asked if there was anything anybody needed to talk about and, when there wasn't, he instructed the jurors to avoid reading newspaper accounts of the case or watching the local TV news. He then ordered the jurors and all other parties to the case to be back by 9:30 A.M., Monday, when deliberations would begin again.

Bosch stepped on the escalator to go down to the lobby exit right behind Chandler. She was standing about two steps up from Deborah Church.

'Counselor?' he said in a low voice so the widow would not hear. Chandler turned around on the step, grabbing the handrail for balance.

'The jury is out, there is nothing that can change the case

now,' he said. 'Norman Church himself could be waiting for us in the lobby and we wouldn't be able to tell the jury. So, why don't you give me the note? This case might be over, but there is still an investigation.'

Chandler said nothing the rest of the way down. But in the lobby she told Deborah Church to go on out to the sidewalk and she'd be along soon. Then she turned to Bosch.

'Again, I deny there is a note, okay?'

Bosch smiled.

'We're already past that, remember? You slipped up yesterday. You said –'

'I don't care what I said or you said. Look, if the guy sent me a note, it would've just been a copy of what you already got. He wouldn't waste his time writing a new one.'

'I appreciate you at least telling me that, but even a copy could be helpful. There could be fingerprints. The copy paper might be traceable.'

'Detective Bosch, how many times did you pull prints from the other letters he sent?'

Bosch didn't answer.

'That's what I figured,' she said. 'Have a good weekend.'

She turned and pushed her way through the exit door. Bosch waited a few seconds, put a cigarette in his mouth and went out himself.

Sheehan and Opelt were in the conference room filling in Rollenberger on their surveillance shift. Edgar was also sitting at the round table listening. Bosch saw he had a photo of Mora on the table in front of him. It was a face shot, like the one the department takes of every cop every year when they reissue ID cards.

'If it happens, it's not going to happen during the day anyway,' Sheehan was saying. 'So maybe tonight they'll have good luck.'

'All right,' Rollenberger said. 'Just type something up for the chron log and you guys can call it a day. I'll need it because I have a briefing with Chief Irving at five. But remember, you're both on call tonight. It's going to be all hands. If Mora starts acting hinky I want you to get back out there with Mayfield and Yde.'

'Right,' Opelt said.

While Opelt sat down at the lone typewriter Rollenberger had requisitioned, Sheehan poured them cups of coffee from the Mr Coffee that had appeared on the counter behind the round table sometime during the afternoon. Hans Off wasn't much of a cop but he could sure set up an Ops Center, Bosch thought. He poured himself a cup and joined Sheehan and Edgar at the table.

'I missed most of that,' he said to Sheehan. 'Sounds like nothing happened.'

'Right. After you dropped by, he went back out to the Valley in the afternoon and stopped by a bunch of different offices and warehouses in Canoga Park and Northridge. We've got the addresses if you want 'em. They were all porno distributors. Never stayed more than a half hour at any of them but we don't know what he was doing. Then he came back, did a little office work and went home.'

Bosch assumed Mora was checking with other producers, trying to hunt down more victims, maybe asking about the mystery man Gallery had described four years ago. He asked Sheehan where Mora lived and wrote down the Sierra Bonita Avenue address in his notebook. He wanted to warn Sheehan about how close he had come to blowing the operation at the taco stand but didn't want to do so in front of Rollenberger. He'd mention it later.

'Anything new?' he asked Edgar.

'Nothing on the survivor, yet,' Edgar answered. 'I'm leaving in five minutes to go up to Sepulveda. The girls do a lot of rush-hour work up there, maybe I'll see her, pick her up.'

Having gotten the updates from everyone else, Bosch told the detectives in the room about the information he had gotten from Mora and what Locke thought of it. At the end,

Rollenberger whistled at the information as if it were a beautiful woman.

'Man, the chief should know this pronto. He might want to double up on the surveillance.'

'Mora's a cop,' Bosch said. 'The more bodies you put on the watch, the better chance he has of making them. If he knows we're watching him, you can forget the whole thing.'

Rollenberger thought about this and nodded, but said, 'Well, we still have to let the man know what's developing. Tell you what, nobody go anywhere for a few minutes. I'll see if I can get with him a little early and we'll see where we go from there.'

He stood up with some papers in his hand and knocked on the door leading to Irving's office. He then opened it and disappeared through.

'Dipshit,' Sheehan said after the door was closed. 'Goin' in for a little mouth-to-ass resuscitation.'

Everybody laughed.

'Hey, you two,' Bosch said to Sheehan and Opelt. 'Mora mentioned your little meeting at the taco stand.'

'Shit!' Opelt exclaimed.

'I think he bought the kosher burrito line,' Bosch said and started laughing. 'Until he tasted one! He couldn't get why you guys'd come all the way over from Parker for one of those shitty things. He threw half of his out. So if he sees you again out there, he'll put it together. Watch your ass.'

'We will,' Sheehan said. 'That was Opelt's idea, that kosher burrito shit. He –'

'What? What'd you want me to say? The guy we're watching suddenly walks up to the car and says, "What's happening, boys?" I had to think of –'

The door opened and Rollenberger came back in. He went to his place but didn't sit down. Instead, he put both hands on the table and sternly leaned forward as if he had just been given orders from God.

'I've brought the chief up to date. He's very pleased with everything we've come up with in just twenty-four hours.

He is concerned about losing Mora, especially with the shrink saying we are at the end of the cycle, but he doesn't want to change the surveillance. Adding another team doubles the chance Mora will see something. I think he's right. It's a very good idea to maintain status quo. We –'

Edgar tried to hold back a laugh but couldn't. It sounded more like a sneeze.

'Detective Edgar, something funny?'

'No, I think I'm getting a cold or something. Go on, please.'

'Well, that's it. Proceed as planned. I will inform the other surveillance teams of what Bosch has come up with. We have Rector and Heikes taking the midnight shift, then the presidents tomorrow morning at eight.'

The presidents were a pair of RHD partners named Johnson and Nixon. They didn't like being called the presidents, especially Nixon.

'Sheehan, Opelt, you are back on tomorrow at four. You've got Saturday night, so be bright. Bosch, Edgar, still freelancing. See what you can come up with. Keep your pagers on and the rovers handy. We might need to pull everybody together on short notice.'

'OT approved?' Edgar asked.

'All weekend. But if you're on the clock, I want to see the work. Only humps on this job, no freeloading. All right, that's it.'

Rollenberger sat down then and pulled his chair close to the table. Bosch figured it was to cover up an erection, he seemed to get off so much on being the taskmaster here. All of them but Hans Off pushed into the hallway then and headed to the elevator.

'Who's drinking tonight?' Sheehan asked.

'More like, who isn't,' Opelt answered.

Bosch got to his house by seven, after having only one beer at the Code Seven and finding that the alcohol was a turn-off after the overindulgence of the night before. He called

Sylvia and told her there was no verdict yet. He said he was going to shower and change clothes and he would be up to see her by eight.

His hair was still damp when she opened her door. She grabbed him as soon as he stepped in and they held each other and kissed in the entry of her house for a long time. It was only when she stepped back that he saw she was wearing a black dress with a neckline that cut deeply between her breasts and a hemline about four inches over her knees.

'How'd it go today, the closing arguments and all?'

'Fine. What are you all dressed up for?'

'Because I am taking you out to dinner. I made reservations.'

She leaned into him and kissed him on the mouth.

'Harry, last night was the best night we've ever had together. It was the best night I can remember with anyone. And not because of the sex. Actually, you and I have done better.'

'Always room for improvement. How 'bout a little practice before dinner?'

She smiled and told him there was no time.

They drove down through the Valley and into Malibu Canyon to the Saddle Peak Lodge. It was an old hunting lodge and the menu featured a vegetarian's nightmare. It was all meat, from venison to buffalo. They each had a steak and Sylvia ordered a bottle of Merlot. Bosch sipped his slowly. He thought the meal and the evening were wonderful. They talked little about the case or anything else. They did a lot of looking at each other.

When they returned to her house, Sylvia turned down the air-conditioner thermostat and built a fire in the living room fireplace. He just watched her; he had never been good at building fires that lasted. Even with the AC on sixty it got very warm. They made love on a blanket she spread out in front of the fireplace. They were perfectly relaxed and moved smoothly together.

Afterward, he watched the fire reflect on the light sheen of sweat on her chest. He kissed her there and put his head down to listen to her heart. The rhythm was strong and it beat counterpoint to his own. He closed his eyes and started thinking of ways to guard against ever losing this woman.

The fire was nothing but a few glowing embers when he woke up in the darkness. There was a shrill sound and he was very cold.

'Your beeper,' Sylvia said.

He crawled to the pile of clothes near the couch, traced the sound and cut it off.

'God, what time is it?' she said.

'I don't know.'

'That's scary. I remember when –'

She stopped herself. Bosch knew it was a story about her husband that she was about to tell. She must have decided not to let his memory intrude here. But it was too late. Bosch found himself wondering if Sylvia and her husband had ever turned down the thermostat on a summer night and made love in front of the fireplace on that same blanket.

'Aren't you going to call?'

'Huh? Oh. Yeah. I'm, uh, just trying to wake up.'

He pulled his pants on and went into the kitchen. He slid the door closed so the light would not bother her. After flicking the switch he looked at the clock on the wall. It was a plate and where the numbers should be were different vegetables. It was half past the carrot, meaning one-thirty. He realized he and Sylvia had been asleep only about an hour. It had seemed like days.

The number had an 818 area code and he didn't recognize it. Jerry Edgar picked up after a half ring.

'Harry?'

'Yeah.'

'Sorry to bother you, man, especially since you're not home.'

'It's okay. What's up?'

'I'm on Sepulveda just south of Roscoe. I got her, man.'

Bosch knew he was talking about the survivor.

'What'd she say? She look at Mora's picture?'

'No. No, man, I don't really have her. I'm watching her. She's on the stroll here.'

'Well, why don't you pick her up?'

'Because I'm alone. I think I could use some backup. I try to take her alone she might bite or something. You know, she's got AIDS.'

Bosch was silent. Through the phone he could hear cars passing Edgar.

'Hey, man, I'm sorry. I shouldn't've called. I thought you might want to get in on this. I'll call the Van Nuys watch commander and get a couple uniforms out here. Have a good –'

'Forget it, I'll be there. Give me half an hour. You been out there all night?'

'Yeah. Went home for dinner. I've been looking all over. Didn't see her till now.'

Bosch hung up wondering if Edgar had really missed her until now or if he was just filling his overtime envelope. He walked back into the living room. The light was on and Sylvia was not on the blanket.

She was in her bed, under the covers.

'I gotta go out,' he said.

'I thought that's what it sounded like, so I decided to come in here. Nothing romantic about sleeping on the floor in front of a dead fireplace by yourself.'

'Are you mad?'

'Of course not, Harry.'

He leaned over the bed and kissed her and she put her hand on the back of his neck.

'I'll try to get back.'

'Okay. Can you turn the thermostat back up on your way out? I forgot.'

Edgar was parked in front of a Winchell's Donuts store,

308

apparently not realizing the comic implications of this.
Bosch parked behind him and then got in his car.

'Whereyat, Harry?'

'Where's she at?'

Edgar pointed across the street and up a block and a half.
At the intersection of Roscoe and Sepulveda there was a bus
bench with two women sitting on it and three standing
nearby.

'She's the one in red shorts.'

'You sure?'

'Yeah, I drove up to the light and eyeballed her. It's her.
Problem is, we might have a cat fight if we go over there and
try to take her. All them girls are working. The Sepulveda
bus line stops running at one.'

Bosch saw the one in the red shorts and tank top lift her
shirt as a car drove by on Sepulveda. The car braked but
then, after a moment of driver hesitation, went on.

'She had any business?'

'A few hours ago she had one guy. Walked him into that
alley behind the mini-mall, did him there. Other than that
it's been dry. She's too skaggy for your discerning john.'

Edgar laughed. Bosch thought about how Edgar had just
slipped up by saying he had been watching her for a few
hours. Well, he thought, at least he didn't beep me while
the fire was going.

'So if you don't want a cat fight, what's the plan?'

'I was thinking you'd drive up to Roscoe and take a left.
Then come into the alley from the back way. You wait there
and get down low. I'll walk over and tell her I want the nasty
and she'll walk me back. Then we take her. But watch her
mouth. She might be a spitter, too.'

'Okay, let's get it over with.'

Ten minutes later Bosch was slouched behind the wheel
and parked in the alley, when Edgar came walking in from
the street. Alone.

'What?'

'She made me.'

'Well, shit, why didn't you just take her? If she made you there's nothing else we can do, she'll know I'm a cop if I try her again five minutes later.'

'All right, she didn't make me.'

'What's going on?'

'She wouldn't go with me. She asked if I had some brown sugar to trade and when I said no, no drugs, she said she doesn't do colored dick. You believe that shit? I haven't been called colored since I grew up in Chicago.'

'Don't worry about it. Wait here and I'll go.'

'Goddam whore.'

Bosch got out of the car and over the roof said, 'Edgar, cool it. She's a whore and a hype, for Chrissake. You care about that?'

'Harry, you have no idea what it's like. You see the way Rollenberger looks at me? I bet he counts the rovers every time I walk out of the room. German fuck.'

'Hey, you're right, I don't know what it's like.'

He took his jacket off and threw it in the car. Then he unbuttoned the top three buttons of his shirt and walked off toward the street.

'Be right back. You better hide. If she sees a colored guy she might not come into the alley with me.'

They borrowed an interview room in the Van Nuys detective bureau. Bosch knew his way around the place because he had worked on the robbery table here after first getting his detective's badge.

What became immediately clear from the start was that the man Edgar had seen Georgia Stern go into the alley with earlier was not a john. He was a dealer and she had probably fixed in the alley. She might have paid for the shot with sex, but that still didn't make the dealer a john.

Regardless of who he was and what she did, she was on the nod when Bosch and Edgar brought her in and, therefore, was almost totally useless. Her eyes were droopy and dilated and would become fixed on objects in the distance. Even in the ten-by-ten interview room she looked as though she was staring at something a mile away.

Her hair was rumpled and the black roots were longer than in the photo Edgar had. She had a sore on the skin below her left ear, the kind of sore addicts get from nervously rubbing the same spot over and over. Her upper arms were as thin as the legs of the chair she sat on. Her deteriorated state was heightened by the T-shirt, which was several sizes too big. The neckline drooped to expose her upper chest and Bosch could see that she used the veins in her neck when she was banging heroin from a needle. Bosch could also see that despite her emaciated condition, she still had large, full breasts. Implants, he guessed, and for a moment a vision of the concrete blonde's desiccated body flashed to him.

'Miss Stern?' Bosch began. 'Georgia? Do you know why you're here? Do you remember what I told you in the car?'

'I mem'er.'

'Now, do you remember the night the man tried to kill you? More than four years ago? A night like this? June seventeenth. Remember?'

She nodded dreamily and Bosch wondered if she knew what he was talking about.

'The Dollmaker, remember?'

'He's dead.'

'That's right, but we need to ask you some questions about the man anyway. You helped us draw this picture, remember?'

Bosch unfolded the composite drawing he had taken from the Dollmaker files. The drawing looked like neither Church nor Mora, but the Dollmaker was known to wear disguises so it was reasonable to believe the Follower did as well. Even so, there was always the chance a physical feature, like maybe Mora's penetrating eyes, would poke through the memory.

She looked at the composite for a long time.

'He was killed by the cops,' she said. 'He deserved it.'

Even coming from her, it felt reassuring to Bosch to hear someone say the Dollmaker got what he deserved. But he knew what she didn't, that they weren't dealing with the Dollmaker here.

'We're going to show you some pictures. You got the six-pack, Jerry?'

She looked up abruptly and Bosch realized his mistake. She thought he was referring to beer, but a six-pack in cop terminology was a package of six mugshots which are shown to victims and witnesses. They usually contain photos of five cops and one suspect with the hope that the wit will point to the suspect and say that's the one. This time the six-pack contained photos of six cops. Mora's was the second one.

Bosch lined them up on the table in front of her and she looked for a long time. She laughed.

'What?' Bosch asked.

She pointed to the fourth photo.

'I think I fucked him once. But I thought he was a cop.'

Bosch saw Edgar shake his head. The photo she had pointed to was of an undercover Hollywood Division narcotics officer named Arb Danforth. If her memory was correct, then Danforth was probably venturing off his beat into the Valley to extort sex from prostitutes. Bosch guessed that he was probably paying them with heroin stolen from evidence envelopes or suspects. What she had just said should be forwarded in a report to Internal Affairs, but both Edgar and Bosch knew without saying a word that neither of them would do that. It would be like committing suicide in the department. No street cop would ever trust them again. Still, Bosch knew Danforth was married and that the prostitute carried the AIDS virus. He decided he would drop Danforth an anonymous note telling him to get a blood test.

'What about the others, Georgia?' Bosch said. 'Look at their eyes. Eyes don't change when somebody's in a disguise. Look at the eyes.'

While she bent down to look closer at the pictures Bosch looked at Edgar, who shook his head. This was going nowhere, he was saying, and Bosch nodded that he knew. After a minute or so, her head jerked as she stopped herself from nodding off.

'Okay, Georgia, nothing there, right?'

'No.'

'You don't see him?'

'No. He's dead.'

'Okay, he's dead. You stay here. We're going out into the hall to talk for a minute. We'll be right back.'

Outside, they decided it might be worth booking her on an under-the-influence charge into Sybil Brand and trying her again when she came off the high. Bosch noted that Edgar was eager to do this and volunteered to drive her downtown to Sybil. Bosch knew this was because it would make Edgar's OT envelope thicker, not because he wanted to get the woman into the narco unit at Sybil and get her straightened out for a while. Compassion had nothing to do with it.

TWENTY-SIX

Sylvia had pulled the bedroom's heavy curtains across the blinds and the room stayed dark until well after the sun was up on Saturday morning. When Bosch awoke alone in her bed, he pulled his watch off the nightstand and saw it was already eleven. He had dreamed but when he woke the dream receded into the darkness and he couldn't reach back to grasp it. He lay there for nearly fifteen minutes trying to bring it back, but it was gone.

Every few minutes he would hear Sylvia make some kind of household noise. Sweeping the kitchen floor, emptying the dishwasher. He could tell she was trying to be quiet but he heard it anyway. There was the back door being opened and the splashing of water in the potted plants that lined the porch. It hadn't rained in at least seven weeks.

At 11:20 the phone rang and Sylvia got to it after one ring. But Bosch knew it was for him. His muscles tensed as he waited for the bedroom door to open and for her to summon him to the call. He had given Sylvia's phone number to Edgar when they were leaving the Van Nuys Division seven hours earlier.

But Sylvia never came and when he relaxed again he could hear parts of her conversation on the phone. It sounded like maybe she was counseling a student. After a while it sounded like she was crying.

Bosch got up, pulled on his clothes and walked out of the bedroom while trying to smooth his hair. She was at the table in the kitchen, holding the cordless phone to her ear.

She was drawing circles on the tabletop with her finger and he had been right, she was crying.

'What?' he whispered.

She held her hand up, signaling him not to interrupt. He didn't. He just watched her on the phone.

'I'll be there, Mrs Fontenot, just call me with the time and address . . . yes . . . yes, I will. Once again, I am so very sorry. Beatrice was such a fine young woman and student. I was very proud of her. Oh, my gosh . . .'

A strong gush of tears came as she hung up. Bosch came to her and put his hand on her neck.

'A student?'

'Beatrice Fontenot.'

'What happened?'

'She's dead.'

He leaned down and held her. She cried.

'This city. . . ,' she began but didn't finish. 'She's the one who wrote what I read to you the other night about *Day of the Locust*.'

Bosch remembered. Sylvia had said she worried about the girl. He wanted to say something but he knew there was nothing to say. This city. It seemed to say it all.

They spent the day around the house, doing odd jobs, cleaning up. Bosch cleared the charred logs out of the fireplace and then joined Sylvia in the backyard, where she was working in the garden, pulling weeds and cutting flowers for a bouquet she was going to take to Mrs Fontenot.

They worked side by side but Sylvia spoke very little. Every now and then she would offer a sentence. She said it had been a drive-by shooting on Normandie. She said it happened the night before and that the girl was taken to Martin Luther King, Jr, Hospital, where she was determined to be brain-dead. They turned the machine off in the morning and harvested the organs for donating.

'That's weird, that they call it harvesting,' she said.

'Sounds like a farm or people growing on trees or something.'

In the midafternoon she went into the kitchen and made an egg salad sandwich and a tuna fish sandwich. She cut them in half and they each had a half of both sandwiches. He made iced tea with slices of orange in the glass. She said that after the huge steaks they'd eaten the night before, she never wanted beef again. It was the day's only attempt at humor, but nobody smiled. She put the dishes in the sink afterward but didn't bother to rinse them. She turned and leaned on the counter and stared down at the floor.

'Mrs Fontenot said the funeral would be sometime next week, probably Wednesday. I think I'm going to bring the class down. Get a bus.'

'I think that'd be nice. Her family would appreciate it.'

'Her two older brothers are dealers. She told me they sell crack.'

He didn't say anything. He knew that was probably the reason the girl was dead. Since the Bloods-Crips gang truce, the street dealing in South Central had lost its command structure. There was a lot of infringement of turfs. A lot of drive-bys, a lot of innocents left dead.

'I think I'll ask her mother if I could read her book report. At the service. Or after. Maybe they'd know then what a loss this was.'

'They probably know already.'

'Yes.'

'You want to take a nap, try to sleep?'

'Yes, I think I will. What are you going to do?'

'I have some stuff to do. Make some calls. Sylvia, I'm going to have to go out tonight. Hopefully, not for long. I'll get back as soon as I can.'

'I'll be all right, Harry.'

'Good.'

Bosch looked in on her at about four and she was sleeping

soundly. He could see where the pillow was wet from her crying.

He went down the hall to a bedroom that was used as a study. There was a desk with a phone on it. He closed the door so as not to disturb her.

The first call he made was to Seventy-seventh Street Division detectives. He asked for the homicide table and got a detective named Hanks. He didn't give a first name and Bosch didn't know him. Bosch identified himself and asked about the Fontenot case.

'What's your angle, Bosch? Hollywood, you said?'

'Yeah, Hollywood, but there's no angle. It's private. Mrs Fontenot called the girl's teacher this morning. The teacher's a friend of mine. She's upset and I was, you know, just trying to find out what happened.'

'Look, I don't have time to be holding people's hands. I'm working a case.'

'In other words, you've got nothing.'

'You've never worked the seven-seven, have you?'

'No. This the part where you tell me how tough it is?'

'Hey, fuck you, Bosch. What I'm gonna tell you is that there is no such thing as a witness south of Pico. Only way we clear a case is we get lucky and pull some prints, or we get luckier and the dude walks in and says, "I's sorry, I did it." You wanna guess how many times that happens?'

Bosch didn't say anything.

'Look, the teacher ain't the only one upset, okay? This is a bad one. They're all bad but some are bad on bad. This is one of those. Sixteen-year-old girl home reading a book, babysittin' her younger brother.'

'Drive-by?'

'Yeah, you got it. Twelve holes in the walls. It was an AK. Twelve holes in the walls and one round in the back of her head.'

'She never knew, did she?'

'No, she never knew what hit her. She must've caught the first one. She never ducked.'

'It was a round meant for one of the older brothers, right?'

Hanks was quiet for a couple of seconds. Bosch could hear a radio squawking in the background of the squad room.

'How you know that, the teacher?'

'The girl told her the brothers sell crack.'

'Yeah? They were walking around MLK this morning boo-hooing like they was altar boys. I'll check it out, Bosch. Anything else I can do you for?'

'Yeah. The book. What was she reading?'

'The book?'

'Yeah.'

'It was called *The Big Sleep*. And that's what she got, man.'

'You can do me a favor, Hanks.'

'What's that?'

'If you talk to any reporters about this, leave the part about the book out.'

'What do you mean?'

'Just leave it out.'

Bosch hung up. He sat at the desk and felt ashamed that when Sylvia had first talked of the girl, he had been suspicious of her fine school work.

After a few minutes thinking about that, he picked the phone up again and called Irving's office. The phone was picked up on half a ring.

'Hello, this is Los Angeles Police Department Assistant Chief Irvin Irving's office, Lieutenant Hans Rollenberger speaking, how can I help you?'

Bosch figured Hans Off must be expecting Irving himself to call in and therefore trotted out the full-count official telephone greeting that was in the officer's manual but was roundly ignored by most of the people who answered phones in the department.

Bosch hung up without saying anything and redialed so the lieutenant could go through the whole spiel again.

'It's Bosch. I'm just checking in.'

'Bosch, did you just call a few moments ago?'

'No, why?'

'Nothing. I'm here with Nixon and Johnson. They just came in and Sheehan and Opelt are with Mora now.'

Bosch noticed how Rollenberger didn't dare call them the presidents when they were in the same room with him.

'Anything happen today?'

'No. The subject spent the morning at home, then a little while ago he went up to the Valley, visited a few more warehouses. Nothing suspicious.'

'Where is he now?'

'At home.'

'What about Edgar?' ·

'Edgar was here. He went over to Sybil to interview the survivor. He found her last night but she apparently was too dopey to talk to. He's giving it another try, now.'

Then in a lower voice, he said, 'If she confirms an ID of Mora, do we move?'

'I don't think it would be a good idea. It's not enough. And we'd tip our hand.'

'My thoughts exactly,' he said louder now, so the presidents would know he was clearly in command here. 'We stick to him like glue and we'll be there when he makes his move.'

'Hopefully. How're you working this with the surveillance teams? They giving you blow by blow?'

'Absolutely. They're on rovers and I'm listening here. I know every move the subject makes. I'm staying on late tonight. I have a feeling.'

'About what?'

'I think t'night's the night, Bosch.'

Bosch woke Sylvia at five but then sat on the bed and rubbed her back and neck for a half hour. After that, she got up and took a shower. Her eyes still looked sleepy when she came out to the living room. She wore her gray cotton

T-shirt dress. Her blonde hair was tied in a tail behind her head.

'When do you have to go?'

'A little while.'

She didn't ask where he was going or what for. He didn't offer to tell her.

'You want me to make you some soup or something?' he asked.

'No, I'm fine. I don't think I'm going to be hungry tonight.'

The phone rang and Harry answered it in the kitchen. It was a reporter from the *Times* who had gotten the number from Mrs Fontenot. The reporter wanted to speak with Sylvia about Beatrice.

'About what?' Bosch asked.

'Well, Mrs Fontenot said Mrs Moore said several nice things about her daughter. We are doing a major story on this because Beatrice was such a good kid. I thought Mrs Moore would want to say something.'

Bosch told her to hold on and went to find Sylvia. He told her about the reporter and Sylvia quickly said she wanted to talk about the girl.

She stayed on the phone fifteen minutes. While she was talking, Bosch went out to his car, turned on the rover and switched it to Symplex five, the DWP frequency. He heard nothing.

He pressed the transmit button and said, 'Team One?'

A few seconds passed and he was about to try again when Sheehan's voice came back on the rover.

'Who's that?'

'Bosch.'

'What it be?'

'How's our subject?'

The next voice was Rollenberger's coming in over Sheehan.

'This is Team Leader, please use your code designations when on the air.'

Bosch smirked. The guy was an ass.

'Leader of the team, what's my designation?'

'You are Team Six, this is Team Leader, out.'

'Rrrrrogaaahhhh that, dream leader.'

'Say again?'

'Say again?'

'Your last transmission, Team Five, what was that?'

Rollenberger's voice had a frustrated quality to it. Bosch was smiling. He could hear a clicking sound over the radio and he knew it was Sheehan punching his transmit button, showing his approval.

'I asked who was on my team.'

'Team Six, you are solo at this time.'

'Then should I have another code, Team Leader? Perhaps, Solo Six?'

'Bo – uh, Team Six, please keep off the air unless you need or are giving information.'

'Rrrogaahhh!'

Bosch put the radio down for a moment and laughed. He had tears in his eyes and he realized he was laughing too hard at something that was mildly humorous at best. He figured it was the release of some of the tension of the day. He picked up the radio again and called Sheehan back.

'Team One, is the subject moving?'

'That's affirmative, Solo – I mean, Team Six.'

'Where is he?'

'He is code seven at the Ling's Wings at Hollywood and Cherokee.'

Mora was eating at a fast-food restaurant. Bosch knew that would not give him enough time to do what he planned, especially since he was a half hour's drive from Hollywood.

'Team One, how's he look? Is he staying out tonight?'

'Looking good. Looks like he is going cruising.'

'Talk to you later.'

'Rrrrrogah!'

He could tell Sylvia had been crying again when he came

inside but her spirits seemed improved. Maybe it was past her, he thought, the initial pain and anger. She was sitting in the kitchen drinking a cup of hot tea.

'Do you want a cup, Harry?'

'No, I'm fine. I'm going to have to go.'

'Okay.'

'What'd you tell her, the reporter?'

'I told her everything I could think of. I hope she does a good story.'

'They usually do.'

It appeared that Hanks hadn't told the reporter about the book the girl had been reading. If he had, the reporter would definitely have told Sylvia to get her reaction. He realized that Sylvia's returning strength was due to her having talked about the girl. He had always marveled about how women wanted to talk, to maybe set the record straight about someone they knew or loved who had died. It had happened to him countless times while making next-of-kin notifications. The women were hurt, yes, but they wanted to talk. Standing in Sylvia's kitchen, he realized that the first time he had met her was on such a mission. He had told her about her husband's death and they had stood in the same room they were in now, and she had talked. Almost from the start, Bosch had been hooked deeply in the heart by her.

'You going to be all right while I'm gone?'

'I'll be fine, Harry. I'm feeling better.'

'I'll try to get back as soon as I can, but I can't be sure when that will be. Get something to eat.'

'Okay.'

At the door, they hugged and kissed and Bosch had an overwhelming urge not to go, to stay with her and hold her. He finally broke away.

'You are a good woman, Sylvia. Better than I deserve.'

She reached up and put her hand on his mouth.

'Don't say that, Harry.'

TWENTY-SEVEN

Mora's house was on Sierra Linda, near Sunset. Bosch pulled to the curb a half block away and watched the house as it grew dark outside. The street was mostly lined with Craftsman bungalows with full porches and dormer windows projecting from the sloping roofs. Bosch guessed it had been at least a decade since the street was as pretty as its name sounded. Many of the houses on the block were in disrepair. The one next to Mora's was abandoned and boarded. On other properties it was clear the owners had opted for chain-link fences instead of paint the last time they had the money to make a choice. Almost all had bars over their windows, even the dormers up top. There was a car sitting on cinderblocks in one of the driveways. It was the kind of neighborhood where you could find at least one yard sale every weekend.

Bosch had the rover on low on the seat next to him. The last report he had heard was that Mora was in a bar near the Boulevard called the Bullet. Bosch had been there before and pictured it in his mind, with Mora sitting at the bar. It was a dark place with a couple of neon beer signs, two pool tables and a TV bolted to the ceiling over the bar. It wasn't a place to go for a quick one. There was no such thing as one drink at the Bullet. Bosch figured Mora was digging in for the evening.

As the sky turned deep purple, he watched the windows of Mora's house but no light came on behind any of them. Bosch knew Mora was divorced but he didn't know if he now had a roommate. Looking at the dark place from the Caprice, he doubted it.

'Team One?' Bosch said into the rover.

'Team One.'

'This is Six, how's our boy?'

'Still bending the elbow. What are you up to tonight, Six?'

'Just hanging around the house. Let me know if you need anything, or if he starts to move.'

'Will do.'

He wondered if Sheehan and Opelt understood what he was saying and he hoped Rollenberger did not. He leaned over to the glove compartment and got his bag of picks out. He reached inside his blue plastic raid jacket and put them in the left pocket. Then he turned the rover's volume control knob to its lowest setting and put it inside the windbreaker in the other pocket. Because it said LAPD in bright yellow letters across the back of the jacket, he wore it inside out.

He got out, locked the car and was ready to cross the street when he heard a transmission from the radio. He got his keys back out, unlocked the car and got back in. He turned the radio up.

'What's that, One? I missed it.'

'Subject is moving. Westbound on Hollywood.'

'On foot?'

'Negative.'

Shit, Bosch thought. He sat in the car for another forty-five minutes while Sheehan radioed reports of Mora's seemingly aimless cruising up and down Hollywood Boulevard. He wondered what Mora was doing. The cruising was not part of the profile of the second killer. The Follower, as far as they knew, worked exclusively out of hotels. That's where he lured his victims. The cruising didn't fit.

The radio was quiet for ten minutes and then Sheehan came up on the air again.

'He's dropping down to the strip.'

The Sunset Strip was another problem altogether. The

strip was in LA but directly south of it was West Hollywood, sheriff's department jurisdiction. If Mora dropped down south and started to make some kind of move, it could result in jurisdictional problems. A guy like Hans Off was completely frightened of jurisdictional problems.

'He's down to Santa Monica Boulevard now.'

That was West Hollywood. Bosch expected Rollenberger to come up soon on the radio. He wasn't wrong.

'Team One, this is Team Leader. What is the subject doing?'

'If I didn't know what this guy was into, I'd say he was cruising Boystown.'

'All right, Team One, keep an eye on him but we don't want any contact. We're out of bounds here. I'll contact the sheriff's watch office and inform.'

'We're not planning any contact.'

Five minutes passed. Bosch watched a man walking his guard dog down Sierra Linda. He stopped to let the animal relieve itself on the burned-out lawn in front of the abandoned house.

'We're cool,' Sheehan's voice said. 'We're back in the country.'

Meaning back inside the boundaries of Los Angeles.

'One, what's your twenty?' Bosch asked.

'Still Santa Monica, going east. Past La Brea – no, he's northbound now on La Brea. He might be going home.'

Bosch slid low in his seat in case Mora came down the street. He listened as Sheehan reported that the vice cop was now eastbound on Sunset.

'Just passed Sierra Linda.'

Mora was staying out. Bosch sat back up. He listened to five minutes of silence.

'He's going to the Dome,' Sheehan finally said.

'The Dome?' Bosch responded.

'Movie theater on Sunset just past Wilcox. He's parked. He's paying for a ticket and is going in. Musta just been driving around till showtime.'

Bosch tried to picture the area in his mind. The huge geodesic dome was one of Hollywood's landmark theaters.

'Team One, this is Team Leader. I want to split you up here. One of you goes in with the subject, one stays on the car, out.'

'Roger that. Team One, out.'

The Dome was ten minutes away from Sierra Linda. Bosch figured that meant that at maximum he had an hour and a half inside the house unless Mora left the movie early.

He quickly got out of the car again, crossed the street and moved up the block to Mora's house. The wide porch completely cloaked the front door in shadows. Bosch knocked on it and while he waited he turned to look at the house across the street. There were lights on downstairs and he could see the bluish glow of a TV on the curtains behind one of the upstairs rooms.

Nobody answered. He stepped back and appraised the front windows. He saw no warnings about security systems, no alarm tape on the glass. He looked between the bars and through the glass into what he believed was the living room. He looked up into the corners of the ceiling, searching for the dull glow of a motion detector. As he expected, there was nothing. Every cop knew the best defense was a good lock or a mean dog. Or both.

He went back to the door, opened the pouch and took out the penlight. There was black electrical tape over the end so that when he switched it on only a narrow beam of light was emitted. He knelt down and looked at the locks on the door. Mora had a dead bolt and a common key-entry knob. Bosch put the penlight in his mouth and aimed the beam at the dead bolt. With two picks, a tension wrench and a hook, he began working. It was a good lock with twelve teeth, not a Medeco but a cheaper knockoff. It took Bosch ten minutes to turn it. By then sweat had come down out of his hair and was stinging his eyes.

He pulled his shirt out of his pants and wiped his face. He also wiped the picks, which had become slippery with sweat, and took a quick look at the house across the street. Nothing seemed changed, nothing seemed amiss. The TV was still on upstairs. He turned back and put the beam on the knob. Then he heard a car coming. He cut the light and crawled behind the porch riser until it had passed.

Back at the door he palmed the knob and was working the hook in when he realized there was no pressure on the knob. He turned it and the door opened. The knob hadn't been locked. It made sense, Bosch knew. The dead bolt was the deterrent. If a burglar got by that, the knob lock was a gimme. Why bother locking it?

He stood in the darkness of the entrance without moving, letting his eyes adjust. When he was in Vietnam he could drop into one of Charlie's tunnels and he would have night eyes in fifteen seconds. Now it took him longer. Out of practice, he guessed. Or getting old. He stood in the entry for nearly a minute. When the shapes and shadows filled in, he called out, 'Hey, Ray? You here? You left your door unlocked. Hello?'

There was no answer. He knew Mora wouldn't have a dog, not living alone and working a cop's hours.

Bosch took a few steps farther into the house and looked at the dark shapes of the furniture in the living room. He had creeped places before, even a cop's house, but the feeling always seemed new, that feeling of exhilaration, jagged fear and panic, all in one. It felt as though his center of gravity had dropped into his balls. He felt a strange power that he knew he could never describe to anyone.

For a brief moment the panic rose and threatened the delicate balance of his thoughts and feelings. The headline flashed in his mind – COP ON TRIAL CAUGHT IN BREAK-IN – but he quickly dismissed it. To think about failure was to invite failure. He saw the stairs and immediately moved toward them. His thought was that Mora would keep his trophies either in his bedroom or near a TV, which also could mean both. Rather than work his way toward the bedroom, he would start there.

327

The second floor was divided into two bedrooms with a bathroom in between them. The bedroom to the right had been converted to a carpeted gym. There was an assortment of chrome-plated equipment, a rowing machine, a stationary bike and a contraption Bosch didn't recognize. There was a rack of free weights and a bench press with a chest bar across it. On one wall of the room was a floor-to-ceiling mirror. It was spidered by a shatter point about face high in the center. For a moment Bosch looked at himself and studied his shattered reflection. He thought of Mora studying his own face there.

Bosch looked at his watch. It had already been thirty minutes since Mora had gone into the theater. He took out the radio.

'One, how's he doin'?'

'He's still inside. How're you doing?'

'Just hanging around. Call if you need me.'

'Anything interesting on TV?'

'Not yet.'

Then Rollenberger's voice came up.

'Teams One and Six, let's drop the banter and use the radio for pertinent transmissions only. Team Leader, out.'

Neither Bosch nor Sheehan acknowledged him.

Bosch moved across the hallway into the other bedroom. This was where Mora slept. The bed was unmade and clothing was draped over a chair by the window. Bosch peeled some of the tape off his light to give him a wider swath of vision.

On the wall over the bed he saw a portrait of Jesus, his eyes cast downward, his sacred heart visible in his chest. Bosch moved to the bed table and held the light briefly on a framed photo that stood next to the alarm clock. It was a young blonde woman and Mora. His ex-wife, he assumed. Her hair was bleached and Bosch recognized that she fit into the physical archetype of the victims. Was Mora killing his ex-wife over and over? he wondered again. That would be one for Locke and the other headshrinkers to decide. On the table behind the photo was a religious holy card. Bosch picked it up and put the light on it. It was a picture of the Infant of Prague, a golden halo shooting up from behind the little king's head.

The night table's drawer contained mostly innocuous junk: playing cards, aspirin bottles, reading glasses, condoms – not the brand favored by the Dollmaker – and a small telephone book. Bosch sat on the bed and leafed through the phone book. There were several women listed by first names but he was not surprised to find none of the names of the women associated with the Follower or Dollmaker cases listed.

He closed the drawer and put the light on the shelf beneath it. There he found a foot-high stack of explicit pornography magazines. Bosch guessed there were more than fifty, their covers featuring glossy photos of couplings of all equations: male-female, male-male, female-female, male-female-male, and so on. He flipped through a handful of them and saw a check mark made with a Magic Marker on the top right corner of each cover, as he had seen Mora do with the magazines at his office. Mora was taking his work home. Or had he brought the magazines here for another reason?

Looking at the magazines, Bosch felt a tightening in his crotch and some strange feeling of guilt descended on him. What about me? he wondered. Am I doing more than my job here? Am I the voyeur? He put the stack back in place. He knew there were too many magazines for him to go through to try to find victims of the Follower. And if he found any, what would that prove?

There was a tall oak armoire against the wall opposite the bed. Bosch opened its doors and found a television and videocassette recorder inside. There were three videotape cassettes stacked on top of the TV. They were 120-minute tapes. He opened the two drawers in the cabinet and found one more cassette in the top drawer. The bottom drawer contained a collection of store-bought porno tapes. He slid a couple of these tapes out, but again there were too many of them and not enough time. His attention was drawn to the four tapes used for home recording.

He turned on the TV and VCR and checked to see if there was another tape already inserted. There wasn't. He put in one of the tapes that had been stacked on top of the TV. It only showed static. He hit the fast-forward play button and watched as the static continued until the end of the tape. It took him fifteen minutes to run through the three tapes that had been on top of the television. Each was blank.

A curious thing, Bosch thought. He had to assume that the tapes had been used at one time because they were no longer in the cardboard jackets and plastic wrap they came from in the store in. Though he did not own a VCR, he was familiar with them and it occurred to him that people usually did not erase their home tapes. They just taped new programs over the old ones. Why had Mora taken the time to erase what had been on these tapes? He was tempted to take one of the blank tapes to have it analyzed but decided it would be too risky. It would probably be missed by Mora.

The last home tape, the one from the top drawer, wasn't blank. It contained scenes of an interior of a house. A child was playing with a stuffed animal on the floor. Through the window behind the girl Bosch could see a snow-covered yard. Then a man entered the video frame and hugged the girl. At first Bosch thought it was Mora. Then the man said, 'Gabrielle, show Uncle Ray how much you like the horsie.'

The girl hugged the stuffed horse and yelled, 'Fankoo Uggle Way.'

Bosch turned the tape off, returned it to the armoire's top drawer once again and then pulled both drawers out and looked below them. Nothing else. He stepped up onto the bed so he could see on top of the armoire and there was nothing there, either. He turned the equipment off and returned the armoire to the condition it was in when he opened it. He looked at his watch. Nearly an hour had gone by now.

The walk-in closet was neatly lined on both sides with clothes on hangers. The floor had eight pairs of shoes parked toe-in against the back wall. He found nothing else of interest and retreated into the bedroom. He took a quick look under the bed and through the drawers of the bureau but found nothing of interest. He moved back down the stairs and quickly looked into the living room but there was no TV. There was none in the kitchen or dining room either.

Bosch followed a hallway off the kitchen into the back of the house. There were three doors off the hallway and this area appeared to be either a converted garage or an addition that was constructed in recent years. There were air-conditioning vents in the ceiling of the hallway and the white pine flooring was much newer than the scarred and browned oak floors throughout the rest of the first floor.

The first door opened into a laundry room. Bosch quickly opened the cabinets above the washer and dryer and found nothing of interest. The next door was to a bathroom with newer fixtures than those he had seen in the bathroom upstairs.

The last door opened into a bedroom with a four-poster bed as its centerpiece. The coverlet was pink and it had the feel of a woman's room. It was the perfume, Bosch realized. But, still, the room did not have a lived-in feeling. It seemed more like a room waiting for its occupant's return. Bosch wondered if Mora might have a daughter away at college, or was this the room his ex-wife used before she finally ended the marriage and left?

There was a TV and VCR on a cart in the corner. He went to it and opened the video storage drawer below the VCR but it was empty except for a round metal object the size of a hockey puck. Bosch picked it up and looked at it but could not tell what it was. He thought it might be from the weight set upstairs. He put it back and closed the drawer.

He opened the drawers of the white dresser but found nothing but women's underwear in the top drawer. The

331

second drawer held a box containing a palette of varying colors of eye makeup and several brushes. There was also a round plastic container of beige facial powder. The makeup containers were for home use, too large to carry in a purse and therefore could not have come from any of the Follower's victims. They belonged to whoever used this room.

There was nothing at all in the bottom three drawers. He looked at himself in the mirror above the bureau and saw he was sweating again. He knew he was using too much time. He looked at his watch; sixty minutes had gone by now.

Bosch opened the closet door and immediately launched himself backward as a jolt of fear punched into his chest. He took cover to the side of the door while drawing his gun.

'Ray! That you?'

No one answered. He realized he was leaning against the light switch for the deep, walk-in closet. He flicked it on and swung into the doorway in a low crouch, his gun pointing at the man he had seen when he opened the door.

He quickly reached outside the door and killed the light. On the shelf above the clothes bar was a round Styrofoam ball on which sat a wig of long black hair. Bosch caught his breath and stepped all the way into the closet. He studied the wig without touching it. How does this fit? he wondered. He turned to his right and found more pieces of women's sheer lingerie and a few thin silk dresses on hangers. On the floor beneath them, parked toe-in to the wall, was a pair of red shoes with stiletto heels.

On the other side of the closet, behind some clothes in dry-cleaner bags, stood a camera tripod. Bosch's adrenaline began flowing again at a quicker pace. He quickly raised his eyes and began looking among the boxes on the shelves above the clothing bar. One box was marked with Japanese writing and he carefully pulled it down, finding it surprisingly heavy. Opening it, he found a video camera and cassette recorder.

The camera was large and he recognized that it was not a

department store-bought piece of equipment. It was more like the kind of camera Bosch had seen used by TV news crews. It had a detachable industrial battery and a strobe. It was connected by an eight-foot coaxial cable to the recorder. The recorder had a playback screen and editing controls.

He thought that Mora's having such obviously expensive equipment was curious but he did not know what to make of it. He wondered if the vice cop had seized it from a porno producer and never turned it in to the evidence lockup. He pressed a button that opened the cassette housing on the recorder but it was empty. He repacked the equipment in the box and replaced it on the shelf, all the while wondering why a man with such a camera would have only blank tapes. He realized, as he took another quick look around the closet, that the tapes he had found so far might have recently been erased. He knew if that was the case, Mora might have tumbled to the surveillance.

He looked at his watch. Seventy minutes. He was pushing the envelope.

As he closed the closet door and turned around, he caught his own image in the mirror over the bureau. He quickly turned to the door to go. That was when he saw the rack of lights on a track running high on the wall above the bedroom door. There were five lights and he did not need to turn them on to be able to tell they focused on the bed.

He focused on the bed himself for a moment as he began to put it together. He took another glance at his watch, though he already knew it was time to go, and headed for the door.

As he crossed the room he looked at the TV and VCR again and realized that he had forgotten something. He quickly dropped to his knees in front of the machines and turned the VCR on. He hit the eject button and a videocassette popped out. He pushed it back in and hit the rewind button. He turned the TV on and pulled out the rover.

'One, how we doing?'

'Movie's getting out now. I'm watching for him.'

That wasn't right, Bosch knew. No general release movie was that short. And he knew the Dome was a single theater. One movie shown at a time. So Mora had gone into the theater after the movie had started. If he had really gone in. An adrenaline-charged alert swept over him.

'You sure it's over, One? He's barely been in there an hour.'

'We're going in!'

There was panic in Sheehan's voice. Then Bosch understood. We're going in. Opelt had not followed Mora into the theater. They had clicked off on Rollenberger's order to split up but they hadn't followed the order. They couldn't. Mora had seen Sheehan and Opelt the day before at the burrito stand by Central Division. There was no way one of them could go into a dark theater looking for Mora and risk being seen by the vice cop first. If that happened, Mora would instantly tumble to the setup. He would know. Sheehan had rogered the order from Rollenberger because the alternative was to tell the lieutenant that they had fucked up the day before.

The VCR rewind clicked off. Bosch sat there motionless, his finger poised in front of the VCR. He knew they had been made. Mora was a cop. He had made the tail. The theater stop had been a scam.

He hit the play button.

This tape had not been erased. The quality of the image on it was better than Bosch had seen in the video booth at X Marks the Spot four nights earlier. The tape had all the production values of a feature-length porno tape. Framed in the TV picture was the four-poster bed on which two men were engaged in sex with a woman. Bosch watched for a moment and hit the fast forward button while the picture was still on the screen. The players in the video began a quick jerking motion that was almost comedic. Bosch watched as they changed couplings over and over. Every conceivable coupling in fast speed. Finally, he returned it to normal speed and studied the players.

The woman did not fit the Follower's mold. She wore the black wig. She was also rail-thin and young. In fact, she wasn't a woman – legally, at least. Bosch doubted she was more than sixteen years old. One of her partners was young, too, perhaps he was her age or less. Bosch couldn't be sure. He was sure, however, that the third participant was Ray Mora. His face was turned away from the camera but Bosch could tell. And he could see the gold medal, the Holy Spirit, bouncing on his chest. He turned the tape off.

'I forgot about that tape, didn't I?'

Still on his knees in front of the television, Bosch turned. Ray Mora was standing there with a gun pointed at his face.

'Hey, Ray.'

'Thanks for reminding me.'

'Don't worry about it. Look, Ray, why don't you put –'

'Don't look at me.'

'What?'

'I don't want you to look at me! Turn around, look at the screen.'

Bosch obediently looked at the blank screen.

'You're a leftie, right? With your right hand take out your gun and slide it across the floor this way.'

Bosch carefully followed the orders. He thought he heard Mora pick the gun up off the floor.

'You fucks think I'm the Follower.'

'Look, I'm not going to lie to you, Ray, we were checking you out, that's all. . . . I know now, I know we're wrong. You –'

'The kosher burrito boys. Somebody ought to teach them how to follow a fucking suspect. They don't know shit . . . took me a while but I figured something was going down after I saw them.'

'So we're wrong about you, right, Ray?'

'You have to ask, Bosch? After what you just saw? The

answer is, yeah, you got your head up your ass. Whose idea was it to check me out? Eyman? Leiby?'

Eyman and Leiby were the co-commanders of Administrative Vice.

'No. It came from me. It was my call.'

A long moment of silence followed this confession.

'Then maybe I ought to just blow your head off right here. Be within my rights, wouldn't it?'

'Look, Ray –'

'Don't!'

Bosch stopped from turning all the way and looked back at the television.

'You do that, Ray, and your life unalterably changes. You know that.'

'It did that as soon as you broke in, Bosch. Why shouldn't I just take it to the logical conclusion? Cap you and just disappear.'

' 'Cause you're a cop, Ray.'

'Am I? Am I still going to be a cop if I let you go? You going to kneel there and tell me you'll make it right for me?'

'Ray, I don't know what to tell you. Those kids on the video are underage. But I only know that because of an illegal search. You end this now and put away the gun, we can work something out.'

'Yeah, Harry? Can everything go back to the way it was? The badge is all I've got. I can't give –'

'Ray. I –'

'Shut up! Just shut up! I'm trying to think.'

Bosch felt the anger hitting him in the back like rain.

'You know my secret, Bosch. How the fuck does that make you feel?'

Bosch had no answer. His mind was tumbling, trying to come up with the next move, the next sentence, when he flinched at the sound of Sheehan's voice coming over the rover in his pocket.

'We lost him. He's not in the theater.'

There was a sharp degree of urgency in Sheehan's voice.

Bosch and Mora were silent, listening.

'What do you mean, Team One?' Rollenberger's voice said.

'Who's that?' Mora asked.

'Rollenberger, RHD,' Bosch answered.

Sheehan's voice said, 'The movie got out ten minutes ago. People came out but he didn't. I went in, he's gone. His car is still here but he's gone.'

'I thought one of you went in?' Rollenberger barked, his own voice tightening with panic.

'We did, but we lost him,' Sheehan said.

'Liar,' Mora said. A long moment of silence followed before he said, 'Now, they'll probably start hitting the hotels, looking for me. Because to them, I'm the Follower.'

'Yes,' Bosch said. 'But they know I'm here, Ray. I should call in.'

As if on cue, Sheehan's voice came from the rover.

'Team Six?'

'That's Sheehan, Ray. I'm Six.'

'Call him. Be careful, Harry.'

Bosch slowly took the radio out of his pocket with his right hand and held it up to his mouth. He pressed the transmitter.

'One, did you find him?'

'Negative. In the wind. What's on TV?'

'Nothing. There's nothing on tonight.'

'Then you ought to leave the house and help us out.'

'Already on the way,' Bosch said quickly. 'Where are you at?'

'Bo – uh, Team Six, this is Team Leader, we need you to come in. We're bringing in the task force to help locate the suspect. All units will meet at the Dome parking lot.'

'Be there in ten. Out.'

He dropped his arm back to his side.

'A whole task force, huh?' Mora asked.

Bosch looked down and nodded.

'Look, Ray, that was all code. They know I went to your

337

house. If I don't show up at the Dome in ten minutes they'll come looking for me here. What do you want to do?'

'I don't know . . . but I guess that gives me at least fifteen minutes to decide, doesn't it?'

'Sure, Ray. Take your time. Don't make a mistake.'

'Too late for that,' he said, almost wistfully. Then he added, 'Tell you what. Take out the tape.'

Bosch ejected the tape and held it up over his left shoulder to Mora.

'No, no, I want you to do this for me, Harry. Open the bottom drawer and take out the magnet.'

That's what the hockey puck was. Bosch put the tape on top of the stand next to the TV and reached down for the magnet. Feeling its heaviness as he lifted it, he wondered if he'd have a chance, if he could maybe turn and hurl it at Mora before the vice cop got off a shot.

'You'd be dead before you tried,' Mora said, knowing his thoughts. 'You know what to do with it.'

Bosch ran the magnet over the top side of the tape.

'Let's put it in and see how we did,' Mora instructed.

'Okay, Ray. Whatever you say.'

Bosch put the tape into the VCR and pushed the play button. The screen filled with the static of a dead channel. It cast a grayish shroud of dull light over Bosch. He hit the fast forward button and the static continued. The tape had been wiped clean.

'Good,' Mora said. 'That ought to do it. That was the last tape.'

'No evidence, Ray. You're in the clear.'

'But you'll always know. And you'll tell them, won't you, Harry? You'll tell IAD. You'll tell the world. I'll never be clear, so don't fuckin' say I'll be clear. Everyone will know.'

Bosch didn't answer. After a moment, he thought he heard the creaking of the wood floor. When Mora spoke, he was very close behind.

'Let me give you a tip, Harry. . . . Nobody in this world is who they say they are. Nobody. Not when they're in their own room with the door shut and locked. And nobody knows anybody, no matter what they think. . . . The best you can hope for is to know yourself. And sometimes when you do, when you see your true self, you have to turn away.'

Bosch heard nothing for several seconds. He kept his eyes on the television screen and thought he could see ghosts forming and disintegrating in the static. He felt the grayish-blue glow burning behind his eyes and the start of a headache. He hoped he was going to live long enough to get it.

'You were always a good guy to me, Harry. I –'

There was a sound from the hallway, then a shout.

'Mora!'

It was Sheehan's voice. Immediately it was followed by light that flooded the room. Bosch heard the pounding of several feet on the wood floor, then there was a shout from Mora and the sound of impact as he was tackled. Bosch took his thumb off the rover's transmit button and began to throw himself to the right, out of harm's way. And in that moment, a gunshot cracked across the room, echoing, it seemed, as loudly as anything he had ever heard.

·

TWENTY-EIGHT

Once Bosch had cleared the rover channel, Rollenberger came up almost immediately.

'Bosch! Sheehan – Team One! What is happening there. What is – report immediately.'

After a long moment went by, Bosch answered calmly.

'This is Six. Team Leader, be advised you should proceed to the subject's twenty.'

'His home? What – did we have shots fired?'

'Team Leader, be advised to keep the channel open. And all task force units, disregard the call out. All units are ten-seven until further notice. Unit Five, are you up?'

'Five,' Edgar responded.

'Five, could you meet me at our subject's twenty?'

'On my way.'

'Six out.'

Bosch turned off the rover before Rollenberger could get back on the channel.

It took the lieutenant a half hour to get from the Parker Center operations post to the house on Sierra Linda. By the time he arrived, Edgar was already there and a plan was in place. Bosch opened the front door just as Rollenberger reached it. The lieutenant strode through the entrance with a face turned red with equal parts of anger and befuddlement.

'Okay, Bosch, what the hell is going on here? You had no authority to cancel the call out, to countermand my order.'

'I thought the less people that know, the better,

Lieutenant. I called out Edgar. I thought that would be enough to handle it and that way not too many would –'

'Know what, Bosch? Handle what? What is going on here?'

Bosch looked at him a moment before answering, then in an even voice said, 'One of the men in your command conducted an illegal search of the suspect's residence. He was caught in the act when the suspect eluded the surveillance you were supervising. That's what happened.'

Rollenberger reacted as if he had been slapped.

'Are you crazy, Bosch? Where's the phone? I want –'

'You call Chief Irving and you can forget about ever running a task force again. You can forget about a lot of things.'

'Bullshit! I had nothing to do with this. You went freelancing on your own and got your fingers caught in the jar. Where's Mora?'

'He's upstairs in the room to the right, handcuffed to the Nautilus machine.'

Rollenberger looked around at the others standing in the living room. Sheehan, Opelt, Edgar. They all gave him deadpan looks. Bosch said, 'If you knew nothing about it, *Lieutenant,* you'll have to prove that. Everything said on Symplex five tonight is on the reel-to-reel down at the city com center. I said I was in the house, you were listening. You even spoke to me a few times.'

'Bosch, you were talking in codes, I didn't – I knew nuh –'

Rollenberger suddenly sprang wildly at Bosch, his hands up and going for his neck. Bosch was ready and reacted more aggressively. He pounded both palms into the other man's chest and slammed him back against a hallway wall. A picture two feet to his side slid off the wall and clattered to the floor.

'Bosch, you fool, the bust is ruined now,' he said while slumped against the wall. 'It was all il –'

'There's no bust. He's the wrong man. I think. But we

341

have to be sure. You want to help us search the place and think about how to contain this, or do you want to call out the chief and explain how badly you handled your command?'

Bosch stepped away, adding, 'The phone's in the kitchen.'

The search of the house took more than four hours. The five of them, working methodically and silently, searched every room, every drawer, every cabinet. What little evidence they gathered of Detective Ray Mora's secret life they put on the dining room table. All the while, their host remained in the upstairs gym room, cuffed to one of the chrome bars of the weight machine. He was accorded fewer rights than a murderer would have received had he been arrested in his home. No phone call. No lawyer. No rights. This was always the case when cops investigated cops. Every cop knew the most flagrant abuses of police power occurred when cops turned on their own.

Occasionally, as they began the initial work, they would hear Mora call out. He called for Bosch most often, sometimes Rollenberger. But no one came to him until finally Sheehan and Opelt – concerned that the neighbors would hear and maybe call the police – went into the room and gagged him with a bathroom towel and black electrical tape.

The silence of the searchers was not in deference to the neighbors, however. The detectives worked quietly because of the tensions among them. Though Rollenberger was visibly angry with Bosch, most of the tension was derived from Sheehan and Opelt having blown the surveillance, which directly led to Mora's discovery of Bosch inside his house. No one except Rollenberger was upset by Bosch's illegal entry of the house. Bosch's own home had been similarly violated at least twice that he knew about during times when he had been the focus of internal investigations. Just like the badge, it came with the job.

When they completed the search the dining room table was stacked with the porno magazines and store-bought tapes, the video equipment, the wig, the women's clothing and Mora's personal phone book. The television that had been hit by Mora's stray shot was also there. By then Rollenberger had cooled somewhat, having apparently used the hours to consider his situation as well as to search.

'All right,' he said as the other four convened around the table and surveyed its contents. 'What have we got? Number one, are we confident Mora is not our man?'

Rollenberger looked around the room and his eyes stopped on Bosch.

'What do you think, Bosch?'

'You heard my story. He denied it and what was on the last tape before he made me erase it doesn't fit with the Follower.' Looked completely consensual, though the boy and girl with him were obviously underage. He isn't the Follower.

'Then what is he?'

'Somebody with problems. I think he got bent by staying too long in vice and started making his own flicks.'

'Was he selling them?'

'I don't know. I doubt it. No evidence of that here. He didn't go very far in hiding himself in the tape I saw. I think it was just his own stuff. He wasn't in it for money. It was something deeper.'

No one said anything, so Bosch continued.

'My guess is that he made our tail sometime after we set up on him and began getting rid of the evidence. Tonight he was probably playing around with the tail, trying to figure what we were on him for. He got rid of most of the evidence, but if you put somebody on that phone book, my bet is you'll put it together. Some of those listings with only a first name. You track them and you'll probably find some of the kids he used in his videos.'

Sheehan made a move to pick up the phone book.

'Leave it,' Rollenberger said. 'If anybody continues this it will be Internal Affairs.'

'How they going to do that?' Bosch asked.

'What do you mean?'

'It's all fruit of the poison tree. The search, everything. All of it's illegal. We can't move against Mora.'

'And we can't let him carry a badge, either,' Rollenberger said testily. 'The man should be in jail.'

The following silence was broken by the sound of Mora's hoarse but loud voice from upstairs. He had somehow slipped the gag.

'Bosch! Bosch! I wanna deal, Bosch. I'll give –' he began coughing ' – I'll give him to you, Bosch. You hear me! You hear me!'

Sheehan headed toward the stairs, which began in the alcove outside the dining room. He said, 'This time I'll make it so tight the fuck will strangle.'

'Wait a minute,' Rollenberger ordered.

Sheehan stopped at the archway leading to the alcove.

'What's he saying?' Rollenberger said. 'Who will he give?'

He looked at Bosch, who shrugged his shoulders. They waited, Rollenberger looking up at the ceiling, but Mora was silent.

Bosch stepped over to the table and picked up the phone book. He said, 'I think I've got an idea.'

The odor of Mora's sweat filled the room. He sat on the floor, his hands cuffed behind him and to the work-out machine. The towel that had been wrapped around his mouth and taped had slipped down to his neck so that it looked like a cervical collar. The front of it was damp with spittle and Bosch guessed that Mora had loosened it by working his jaw up and down.

'Bosch, unhook me.'

'Not yet.'

Rollenberger stepped forward.

'Detective Mora, you have problems. You've –'

'You've got problems. You're the one. All of this is

344

illegal. How you going to explain this? Know what I'm going to do? I'm going to hire that bitch Money Chandler and sue the department for a million dollars. Yeah, I'll –'

'Can't spend a million dollars in jail, Ray,' Bosch said.

He held up Mora's phone book so that the vice cop could see it.

'This gets dropped off at Internal Affairs and they'll make a case. All those names and numbers, there's gotta be somebody that would talk about you. Somebody underage probably. Think we're giving you a hard time? Wait until IAD takes over. They'll make a case, Ray. And they'll make it without tonight's search. That will just be your word against ours.'

Bosch saw a quick movement in Mora's eyes and he knew he had struck bone. Mora was afraid of the names in the book.

'So,' Bosch said, 'what deal did you have in mind, Ray?'

Mora looked away from the book, first to Rollenberger and then to Bosch and then back to Rollenberger.

'You can make a deal?'

'I have to hear it first,' Rollenberger said.

'Okay, this is the deal. I walk and I give you the Follower. I know who it is.'

Bosch was immediately skeptical but said nothing. Rollenberger looked at him and Bosch shook his head once.

'I know,' Mora said. 'The Peeping Tom I told you about. That was no bullshit. I got the ID today. It fits. I know who it is.'

Now Bosch took him more seriously. He folded his arms in front of his body, threw a quick glance at Rollenberger.

'Who?' Rollenberger said.

'What's the deal first?'

Rollenberger stepped to the window and parted the curtains. He was turning it over to Bosch, who took a step forward and squatted like a baseball catcher in front of Mora.

'This is the deal. It is offered only this one time. Take it or let the chips fall where they may. You give the name to me and your badge to Lieutenant Rollenberger. You resign immediately from the department. You agree not to sue the department or any of us individually. In exchange, you walk.'

'How do I know you'll –'

'You don't. And how do we know that you'll keep your end? I hang on to the phone book, Ray. You try to fuck us and it goes to IAD. Do we have a deal?'

Mora stared at him without speaking a long moment. Finally, Bosch got up and turned to the door. Rollenberger headed that way, too, and said, 'Unhook him, Bosch. Take him to Parker and book him on assault on a police officer, unlawful sex with a minor, pandering, anything you can think –'

'We gotta deal,' Mora blurted. 'But I've got no insurance.'

Bosch turned back to look at him.

'That's right, you don't. The name?'

Mora looked from Bosch to Rollenberger.

'Unhook me.'

'The name, Mora,' Rollenberger said. 'This is it.'

'It's Locke. The fucking shrink. You assholes, you put the finger on me and the whole time he's the one pushing the buttons.'

Bosch was jolted but in that same moment he began immediately to see how it could be. Locke knew the Dollmaker's program, he fit the Follower's profile.

'He was the Tom?'

'Yeah, it was him. Got'm ID'd by a producer today. He went around saying he was writin' a book so he could get close to the girls. Then he killed them, Bosch. The whole time he's been playing doctor with you, Bosch, he's been out there . . . killing.'

Rollenberger turned to Bosch and said, 'What do you think?'

Bosch left the room without answering. He went down

346

the stairs and trotted out the door to his car. Locke's book was on the back seat where Bosch had left it the day he bought it. As he headed back into the house with it he noticed that the first etchings of dawn's light were in the sky.

On Mora's dining room table, Bosch opened the book and began leafing through it until he came to a page marked Author's Note. In the second paragraph, Locke wrote, 'The material for this book was gathered over the course of three years from interviews with countless adult film performers, many of whom requested that they remain anonymous or be identified only by their stage names. The author wishes to thank them and the film producers who granted him access to the sets and production offices at which these interviews were conducted.'

The mystery man. Bosch realized Mora could be right that Locke was the man whom the video performer Gallery had reported as a suspect when she called the original task force tip number four years earlier. Bosch next flipped to the index of the book and ran his fingers down the names. Velvet Box was listed. So were Holly Lere and Magna Cum Loudly.

Bosch quickly reviewed in his mind Locke's involvement in the case. He would definitely fit as a suspect for the same reasons Mora had fit. He had had a foot in both camps, as Locke himself had described it. He had access to all information about the Dollmaker deaths and, at the same time, was conducting research for a book on the psychology of female performers in the pornography industry.

Bosch became excited, but more so he was angry. Mora had been right. Locke had punched his buttons, to the point that he had helped set the cops on the path to the wrong man. If Locke was the Follower, he had played Bosch perfectly.

Rollenberger dispatched Sheehan and Opelt to Locke's house to put him under immediate surveillance. 'This time don't fuck it up,' he said as he recovered some of his command presence.

Next he announced there would be a meeting of the task force at noon Sunday, little more than six hours away. He said they would then discuss seeking a search warrant for Locke's home and office and decide what moves to make. As he headed to the door, Rollenberger looked at Bosch and said, 'Go cut him loose. Then, Bosch, you better go get some sleep. You're going to need it.'

'What about you? How're you going to handle Irving on this?'

Rollenberger was looking down at the gold detective's shield he held in his hand. It was Mora's. He closed his hand over it and put it in his sport coat pocket. Then he looked at Bosch.

'That's my business, isn't it, Bosch? Don't worry about it.'

After the others had left, Bosch and Edgar went up the stairs to the gym room. Mora was silent and refused to look at them as they removed the handcuffs. They said nothing and left him there, the towel still around his neck like a noose, staring at his fractured image in the wall mirror.

Bosch lit a cigarette and looked at his watch when he got to his car. It was 6:20 and he was too wired to go home to sleep. He got in the car and pulled the rover from his pocket.

'Frankie, you up?'

'Yo,' Sheehan responded.

'Anything?'

'Just got here. No life showing. Don't know whether he's here or not. Garage door is down.'

'Okay, then.'

Bosch thought of an idea. He picked up Locke's book and took the cover off it. He folded it and put it in his pocket, then he started the car.

After stopping for coffee at a Winchell's, Bosch got to the

Sybil Brand Institute by seven. Because of the early hour, he had to get the watch commander's approval to interview Georgia Stern.

He could see she was sick as soon as she was brought into the interview room. She sat hunched over with her arms folded in front of her, as if she were carrying a bag of groceries that had broken and was guarding against losing anything.

'Remember me?' he asked.

'Man, you gotta get me out.'

'Can't do that. But I can get them to take you into the clinic. You can get methadone in your orange juice.'

'I wanna get out.'

'I'll get you in the clinic.'

She dropped her head in defeat. She started a slight rocking motion, back and forth. She seemed pitiful to Bosch. But he knew he had to let it go. There were more important things, and she couldn't be saved.

'You remember me?' he asked again. 'From the other night?'

She nodded.

'We showed you pictures? I've got another.'

He put the dust jacket from the book on the table. She looked at Locke's photo for a long while.

'Well?'

'What? I seen him. He talked to me once.'

'About what?'

'Making movies. He was – I think he's an interviewer.'

'Interviewer?'

'I mean like a writer. He said it was for a book. I told him don't use any of my names but I never checked.'

'Georgia, think back. Hard. This is very important. Could he also be the one who attacked you?'

'You mean the Dollmaker? The Dollmaker's dead.'

'I know that. I think it was someone else who attacked you. Look at the photo. Was it him?'

She looked at the photo and shook her head.

349

'I don't know. They told me it was the Dollmaker, so I forgot what he looked like after he was killed.'

Bosch leaned back in his chair. It was useless.

'You still going to get me in the clinic?' she asked timidly after seeing his change in mood.

'Yeah. You want for me to tell them you've got the virus?'

'What virus?'

'AIDS.'

'What for?'

'To get you whatever medicine you need.'

'I don't have AIDS.'

'Look, I know the last time Van Nuys Vice put the bust on you you had AZT in your purse.'

'That's for protection. I got that from a friend-a-mine who's sick. He gave me the bottle and I put cornstarch in it.'

'Protection?'

'I don't want to work for no pimp. Some asshole comes up and says he's now your man, I show 'em the shit and say I got the virus, you know, and he splits. They don't want girls with AIDS. Bad for their business.'

She smiled slyly and Bosch changed his mind about her. She might be saved after all. She had the instincts of a survivor.

The Hollywood Station detective bureau was completely deserted, which was not unusual for nine on a Sunday morning. After stealing a cup of coffee from the watch office while the sergeant was busy at the wall map, Bosch went to the homicide table and called Sylvia but got no answer. He wondered if she was gardening out back and hadn't heard the phone or had gone out, maybe to get the Sunday paper to read the story about Beatrice Fontenot.

Bosch leaned back in his chair. He didn't know what his next move was. He used the rover to check with Sheehan and once again was told that there had been no movement at Locke's house.

'Think we should go up and knock?' Sheehan asked.

He wasn't expecting an answer and Bosch didn't give one. But he started thinking about it. It gave him another idea. He decided he would go to Locke's house to finesse him. To run the story about Mora by him and see how Locke reacted and if he would say the vice cop was probably the Follower.

He threw the empty coffee cup in the trash can and looked over at his slot in the memo and mail box on the wall. He saw he had something in there. He got up and took three pink phone message forms and a white envelope back to his desk. He looked at the messages and one by one dismissed them as unimportant and put them on his message spike to be considered later. Two were from TV reporters and one was from a prosecutor asking about evidence in one of his other cases. All the calls had come in Friday.

Then he looked at the envelope and felt a chill, like a cold steel ball rolling down the back of his neck. It had only his name on the outside but the distinctive printing style could mean it was from nobody else. He dropped the envelope on the table, opened his drawer and dug around in the notebooks, pens and paper clips until he found a pair of rubber gloves. Then he carefully opened the Follower's message.

> *Long aft' the body stops stinking*
> *Of me you'll be thinking*
> *For taking your precious blonde*
> *Oft' your bloody hands*
>
> *I'll make her my dolly*
> *Aft' I've had my sweet jolly*
> *And maybe to leave then*
> *For other soft lands*
>
> *No air for her to swallow*
> *Aft' me dare you not follow*
> *Her last word, my gosh!*
> *A sound like Boschhhhhh*

As he left the station, he ran through the watch commander's office, almost knocked down the startled duty sergeant and yelled: 'Get hold of Detective Jerry Edgar! Tell'm to come up on the rover. He'll know what I mean.'

TWENTY-NINE

Getting to the freeway was so frustrating that Bosch believed he could actually feel his blood pressure rising. His skin began to feel tight around his eyes, his face grew warm. There was some kind of Sunday morning performance at the Hollywood Bowl and traffic on Highland was backed up to Fountain. Bosch tried taking some side streets but so were many of the people going to the Bowl. He was deep into this quagmire before he cursed himself for not remembering that he had the bubble and siren. Working homicide, it had been so long since he had to race to get anywhere that he had forgotten.

After he slid the bubble onto the roof and hit the siren, the cars began to part in front of him and he remembered how easy it could be. He had just gotten onto the Hollywood Freeway and was speeding north through the Cahuenga Pass when Jerry Edgar's voice came up on the rover on the seat next to him.

'Harry Bosch?'

'Yeah, Edgar, listen. I want you to call the sheriff's department, Valencia station, and tell them to get a car to Sylvia's house code three. Tell them to make sure she's okay.'

Code three meant lights and siren, an emergency. He gave Edgar her address.

'Make the call now and then come back up.'

'Okay, Harry. What's going on?'

'Make the call now!'

Three minutes later Edgar was back on the radio.

'They're on the way. What've you got?'

'I'm on my way, too. What I want you to do is go in to the division. I left a note on my desk. It's from the Follower. Secure it and then call Rollenberger and Irving and tell 'em what's happening.'

'What is happening?'

Bosch had to swerve into the median to avoid hitting a car that pulled into the lane in front of him. The driver hadn't seen Bosch coming and Bosch knew he was going too fast – a steady ninety-three – for the siren to give much of a warning to the cars ahead of him.

'The note's another poem. He says he is going to take the blonde off my hands. Sylvia. There's no answer at her house but there still may be time. I don't think I was supposed to find the note until Monday, when I came in for work.'

'On my way. Be careful, buddy. Stay cool.'

Stay cool, Bosch thought. Right. He thought of what Locke had told him about the Follower being angry, wanting to get back at him for putting down the Dollmaker. Not Sylvia, he hoped. He wouldn't be able to live with it.

He picked the radio back up.

'Team One?'

'Yo,' Sheehan replied.

'Go get him. If he's there, bring him in.'

'You sure?'

'Bring him in.'

There was a lone sheriff's car in front of Sylvia's house. When Bosch pulled to a stop, he saw a uniform deputy standing on the front step, back to the door. It looked as if he was guarding the place. As if he was protecting a crime scene.

As he started to get out, Bosch felt a sharp stabbing pain on the left side of his chest. He held still for a moment and it eased. He ran around the car and across the lawn, working his badge out of his pocket as he went.

'LAPD, what've you got?'

'It's locked. I walked around, all windows and doors secured. No answer. Looks like nobody's –'

Bosch pushed past him and used his key to open the door. He ran from room to room, making a quick search for obvious signs of foul play. There were none. The deputy had been right. Nobody was home. Bosch looked in the garage and Sylvia's Cherokee was not there.

Still, Bosch made a second sweep of the house, opening closets, looking under beds, looking for any indication that something was amiss. The deputy was standing in the living room when Bosch finally came out of the bedroom wing.

'Can I go now? I was pulled off a call that seems a little more important than this.'

Bosch noted the annoyance in the deputy's voice and nodded for him to go. He followed him out and got the rover out of the Caprice.

'Edgar, you up?'

'What do you have there, Harry?'

There was the sound of genuine dread in his voice.

'Nothing here. No sign of her or anything else.'

'I'm at the station, you want me to put a BOLO out?'

Bosch described Sylvia and her Cherokee for the Be On Look Out dispatch that would go out to all patrol cars.

'I'll put it out. We got the task force coming in. Irving, too. We'll be meeting here. There's nothing else to do but wait.'

'I'm going to wait here a while. Keep me posted. . . . Team One, you up?'

'Team One,' Sheehan said. 'We went up to the door. Nobody home. We're standing by. If he shows, we'll bring him in.'

Bosch sat in the living room, his arms folded in front of him, for more than an hour. He now knew why Georgia Stern had held herself this way at Sybil Brand. There was comfort in it. Still, the silence of the house was nerve-racking. He

355

was staring at the portable phone he had put on the coffee table, waiting for it to ring, when he heard a key hit the lock on the front door. He jumped up and was moving toward the entry when the door opened and a man stepped in. It wasn't Locke. It wasn't anyone Bosch knew, but he had a key.

Without hesitating Bosch moved into the entrance and slammed the man up against the door as he turned to close it.

'Where is she?' he shouted.

'What? What?' the man cried out.

'Where is she?'

'She couldn't come. I'm going to watch it for her. She's got another open in Newhall. Please!'

Bosch realized what was happening just as the pager on his belt sounded its shrill tone. He stepped away from the man.

'You're the realtor?'

'I work for her. What are you doing? Nobody's supposed to be here.'

Bosch pulled the pager off his belt and saw the readout was his home phone number.

'I have to make a call.'

He went back to the living room. Over his shoulder he heard the real estate man say, 'Yeah, you do that! What the hell is going on here?'

Bosch punched the number into the phone and Sylvia picked up after one ring.

'Are you okay?'

'Yes, Harry, where are you?'

'At your place. Where have you been?'

'I picked up a pie at Marie Callendar's and took it and the flowers I cut to the Fontenots. I just felt like doing –'

'Sylvia, listen to me. Is the door locked?'

'What? I don't know.'

'Put the phone down and go make sure. Make sure the sliding door to the porch is locked, too. And the door to the carport. I'll wait.'

'Harry, what is –'

'Go do it now!'

She was back in a minute. Her voice sounded very timid.

'Okay, everything's locked.'

'Okay, good. Now listen, I'm coming there right now and it will only take me half an hour. In the meantime, no matter who comes to the door, don't answer it and don't make any sound. Understand?'

'You're scaring me, Harry.'

'I know that. Do you understand what I said?'

'Yes.'

'Good.'

Bosch thought for a moment. What else could he tell her?

'Sylvia, after we are done here. I want you to go to the closet near the front door. On the shelf there is a white box. Take it down and take out the gun. There are bullets in the red box in the cabinet over the sink. The red box, not the blue. Load the gun.'

'I can't do – what are you telling me?'

'Yes, you can, Sylvia. Load the gun. Then wait for me. If anybody comes through the door and it's not me, protect yourself.'

She didn't say anything.

'I'm on my way. I love you.'

While Bosch was on the freeway going south, Edgar came up on the radio and told him Sheehan and Opelt still had made no sighting of Locke. The presidents had been dispatched to USC but Locke was not at his office, either.

'They're going to sit on both locations. I'm working on a warrant for the house now. But I don't think the PC is there.'

Bosch knew he was probably right. Mora's identification of Locke as the man hanging around porno sets and the names of three of the victims in his book were not probable cause to search his house.

He told Edgar that he had located Sylvia and was headed

357

to her now. After signing off, he realized that her trip to the Fontenot house might have saved her life. He saw a symbiotic grace in that. A life taken, a life saved.

Before opening the door to his house he loudly announced he was there, then turned the key and walked into Sylvia's trembling arms. He held her to his chest and said into the radio, 'We're all safe here,' then turned it off.

They sat down on the couch and Bosch told her everything that had happened since they had last been together. He could tell by her eyes that it scared her more knowing what was going on than not.

She, in turn, explained that she had to get out of the house because the realtor was holding an open house. That was why she had gone to Bosch's house after visiting the Fontenots. He explained that he had forgotten about the open house.

'You might need to get a new realtor after today,' he said.

They laughed together to let some of the tension go.

'I'm sorry,' he said. 'This should never have involved you.'

They sat in silence for a while after that. She leaned against him as if she was weary of everything.

'Why do you do this, Harry? You deal with so much – the most awful people and the things they do. Why do you keep going?'

He thought about that but knew there was no real answer and that she wasn't expecting one.

'I don't want to stay here,' he said after a while.

'We can go back to my house at four.'

'No, let's just get out of here.'

The two-room suite at the Loews Hotel in Santa Monica gave them a sweeping view of the ocean across a wide beach. It was the kind of room that came with two full-length terrycloth robes and gold foil-wrapped chocolates left on the pillow. The suite's front door was off the fourth

358

landing of a five-story atrium with a wall of glass that faced the ocean and would capture the entire arc of the sunset.

There was a porch with two chaise lounges and a table and they had lunch delivered by room service there. Bosch had brought the rover in with him but it was turned off. He would keep in touch as the search for Locke went on, but he was out of it for the day.

He had called in and talked to Edgar and then Irving. He told them he would stay with Sylvia, though it seemed unlikely that the Follower would make a move now. He was not needed anyway because the task force was in a holding pattern, waiting for Locke to turn up or something else to break.

Irving had said the presidents had contacted the dean of the psychology department at USC who, in turn, contacted one of Locke's graduate assistants. She reported that Locke had mentioned on Friday that he would be in Las Vegas for the weekend, staying at the Stardust. He taught no classes on Mondays, so he would not be back at the school until Tuesday.

'But we checked the Stardust,' Irving said. 'Locke had a reservation but never checked in.'

'What about the warrant?'

'We've had three turn-downs from three judges. You know it's pretty weak when a judge won't rubber-stamp a search warrant for us. We're going to have to let that jell for a while. In the meantime, we'll be watching his house and his office. I'd like to leave it that way until he surfaces and we can talk to him.'

Bosch heard the doubt in Irving's voice. He wondered how Rollenberger had explained the leap in the investigation from Mora to Locke as the suspect.

'You think we're wrong?'

He realized there was a quiver of doubt in his own voice.

'I don't know. We traced the note. Partially. It was left at the front desk sometime Saturday night. The deskman went back for coffee about nine, got sidetracked by the

359

watch commander and when he came back out it was there on the counter. He had an Explorer put it in your slot. The only thing it means for sure is that we were wrong about Mora. Anyway, the point is, we could be wrong again. Right now all we have are hunches. Good hunches, mind you, but that's all. I want to proceed a little more carefully this time.'

The translation was, you screwed us up with your hunch on Mora. We are going to be more skeptical this time. Bosch understood this.

'What if the Vegas trip was a cover? The note says something about moving on. Maybe Locke's running.'

'Maybe.'

'Should we put out a BOLO, get an arrest warrant?'

'I think we're going to wait until at least Tuesday, Detective. Give him a chance to come back. Just two more days.'

It was clear Irving wanted to sit tight. He was going to wait for events to control what he would do next.

'Okay, I'll check in later.'

They napped in the king-size bed until it was dark and then Bosch turned on the news to see if any of what had happened in the last twenty-four hours had leaked.

It hadn't, but midway through the newscast on 2, Bosch stopped flipping through the channels with the selector. The story that stopped him was an update on the Beatrice Fontenot killing. A photo of the girl, her hair in cornrows, appeared on the right side of the screen.

The blonde anchor said, 'Police announced today that they have identified a suspected gunman in the death of sixteen-year-old Beatrice Fontenot. The man they are looking for is an alleged drug dealer who was a rival of Beatrice's older brothers, Detective Stanley Hanks said. He said the shots fired at the Fontenot house were in all probability meant for the brothers. Instead, a bullet struck Beatrice, an honor student at Grant High in the Valley, in the head. Her funeral is scheduled for later this week.'

Bosch turned off the television and looked back at Sylvia, who was propped up on two pillows against the wall. They didn't say anything.

After a room service dinner, which they ate with almost no conversation in the front room of the suite, they took turns in the shower. Bosch went second and as the coarse water stung his scalp, he decided that it was time for him to lose all his baggage, to come clean. He trusted his faith in her, in her desire to know all of him. And he knew that if he did nothing, he was risking what they had each day he kept the secrets of his life inside. Somehow, he knew facing her was facing himself. He had to accept what he was, where he had come from and what he had become if he was to be accepted by her.

They were in their bleached white bathrobes, she in the chair by the sliding door, he standing near the bed. Beyond her through the door, he could see the full moon casting a shifting reflection on the Pacific. He didn't know how to start.

She had been leafing through a hotel magazine filled with suggestions for tourists on what to do in the city. None of them were things that people who lived here ever did. She closed it and put it on the table. She looked at him and then looked away. She started before he could say a word.

'Harry, I want you to go home.'

He sat on the edge of the bed, put his elbows on his knees and ran his hands through his hair. He had no idea what was going on.

'What do you mean?'

'Too much death.'

'Sylvia?'

'Harry, I've done so much thinking this weekend that I can't think anymore. But I know this, we have to be apart for a while. I have to sort things out. Your life, it's . . .'

'Two days ago you said our problem was that I held things back from you. Now you're saying you don't want to know about me. Your –'

'I'm not talking about you. I'm talking about what you do.'

He shook his head.

'Same thing, Sylvia. You should know that.'

'Look, it's been a rough couple of days. I just need some time to decide if this is right for me. For us. Believe me, I'm thinking about you, too. I'm not sure I'm the right one for you.'

'I am, Sylvia.'

'Please don't say that. Don't make it any more difficult. I –'

'I don't want to go back to being without you, Sylvia. That's all I know right now. I don't want to be alone.'

'Harry, I don't want to hurt you and I would never ever ask you to change for me. I know you and I don't think you could change even if you wanted to. So . . . what I have to decide is whether I can live with that and live with you. . . . I do love you, Harry, but I need some time . . .'

She was crying now. Bosch could see it in the mirror. He wanted to get up to hold her but he knew it was the wrong move. He was the cause of her tears. There was a long silence, both of them sitting in private pain. She was looking down into her lap where her hands held each other. He looked out at the ocean and saw a drift-fishing boat cut across the reflected path of the moon on its way toward the Channel Islands.

'Say something to me,' she finally said.

'I'll do whatever you want,' he said. 'You know that.'

'I'll go into the bathroom until you get dressed and leave.'

'Sylvia, I want to know that you are safe. I would like to ask you to let me sleep in the other room. In the morning, we'll figure something out. I'll leave then.'

'No. We both know nothing will happen. That man, Locke, he's probably far away, running from you, Harry. I'll be safe. I'll take a taxi to school tomorrow and I'll be safe. Just give me some time.'

'Time to decide.'

'Yes. To decide.'

She got up and walked quickly by him to the bathroom. He put his arm out but she brushed by it. After the door closed he could hear her pull tissues from the dispenser. Then he could hear her crying.

'Please leave, Harry,' she said after a while. 'Please.'

He heard her turn the water on, so she wouldn't hear him if he said anything. Bosch felt like a fool to be sitting there in his luxury bathrobe. It ripped when he pulled it off.

That night he took a blanket from the trunk of the Caprice and made a bed on the sand about a hundred yards from the hotel. But he didn't sleep. He sat with his back to the ocean and his eyes on the curtained sliding door on the fourth floor balcony next to the atrium. Through the glass wall of the atrium he could also see her front door and would know if anyone approached. It was cold on the beach but he didn't need the sea wind's chill to stay awake.

THIRTY

Bosch was ten minutes late coming into the courtroom Monday morning. He had waited to make sure Sylvia got a cab and was safely off to school before going home and changing into the same suit he had worn Friday. But as he hurried in, he saw that Judge Keyes wasn't on the bench and Chandler wasn't at the plaintiff's table. Church's widow sat alone, looking straight forward in a prayerful pose.

Harry sat down next to Belk and said, 'What's up?'

'We were waiting for you and Chandler. Now we're just waiting for her. The judge was not happy about it.'

Bosch saw the judge's clerk get up from her desk and knock on the chambers door. She then poked her head in and he could hear her say, 'Detective Bosch is here. Ms Chandler's secretary still hasn't located her.'

The constricting feeling in his chest began then. Bosch felt himself immediately begin to sweat. How could he have missed it? He leaned forward and put his face into his hands.

'I gotta make a call,' he said and stood up.

Belk turned, probably to tell him not to go anywhere, but was silenced by the opening of the chambers door. Judge Keyes strode out and said, 'Remain seated.'

He took his place on the bench and told the clerk to buzz the jury in. Bosch sat down.

'We're going to go ahead and get them started again without Ms Chandler being here. We'll deal with her tardiness at a later date.'

The jury filed in and the judge asked them if anybody had anything they wanted to bring up, a scheduling problem or anything else. No one said a word.

'All right then, we're going to send you back in to continue deliberations. The marshal will come speak to you later about lunch. By the way, Ms Chandler had a scheduling conflict this morning and that's why you don't see her there at the plaintiff's table. You are to pay no mind to that. Thank you very much.'

They filed back out. The judge instructed the parties who were present to stay within fifteen minutes of the courtroom again, then told the clerk to keep trying to find Chandler. With that, he stood up and walked back to his chambers.

Bosch was up quickly and out the door of the courtroom. He went to the pay phones and dialed the communications center. After giving his name and badge number, he asked the phone clerk to run a code-three DMV search on the name Honey Chandler. He said he needed the address and would hold.

The rover would not work until he was out of the courthouse underground garage. Once he was out on Los Angeles Street he tried again and got hold of Edgar, who had his rover on. He gave him the Carmelina Street address in Brentwood he had gotten for Chandler.

'Meet me there.'

'On my way.'

He drove down to Third and took it up through the tunnel and onto the Harbor Freeway. He was just hitting the Santa Monica Freeway when his pager sounded. He looked at the number while driving and didn't recognize it. He exited the freeway and pulled over at a Korea Town grocery store with a phone on the wall out front.

'Courtroom four,' said the woman who answered his call.

'It's Detective Bosch, did someone beep me?'

'Yes, we did. We have a verdict. You need to get back here right away.'

'What do you mean? I was just there. How'd they –'

'It's not unusual, Detective Bosch. They probably came to an agreement Friday and decided to take the weekend to see if they wanted to change their minds. Look, it gets them out of another day of work.'

Back in the car, he picked up the rover again.

'Edgar, you there?'

'Uh, not quite. You?'

'I gotta turn around. Got a verdict. Can you check this out?'

'No problem. What am I checking out?'

'It's Chandler's house. She's blonde. She didn't show up in court today.'

'I get the picture.'

Bosch had never thought he would hope to see Honey Chandler in court at the table opposite his but he did. She wasn't there, though. A man Harry didn't recognize was sitting with the plaintiff.

As he walked to the defense table, Bosch saw that a couple of reporters, including Bremmer, were already in the courtroom.

'Who's that?' he asked Belk about the man next to the widow.

'Dan Daly. Keyes grabbed him out of the hallway to sit with the woman during the verdict. Chandler is apparently incommunicado. They can't find her.'

'Anybody go to her house?'

'I don't know. I assume they called. What do you care? You should be worried about this verdict.'

Judge Keyes came out then and took his place. He nodded to the clerk, who buzzed the jury. As the twelve filed in, none of them looked at Bosch but almost all of them eyed the man sitting next to Deborah Church.

'Again, folks,' the judge began, 'a scheduling conflict has

prevented Ms Chandler from being here. Mr Daly, a fine lawyer, has agreed to sit in her stead. I understand from the marshal that you have reached a verdict.'

Several of the twelve heads nodded. Bosch finally saw one man look at him. But then he looked away. Bosch could feel his heart pounding and he was unsure if it was because of the impending verdict or the disappearance of Honey Chandler. Or both.

'Can I have the verdict forms, please?'

The jury foreman handed a thin stack of papers to the marshal who handed them to the clerk who handed them to the judge. It was excruciating to watch. The judge had to put on a pair of reading glasses and then took his time studying the papers. Finally, he handed the papers back to the clerk and said, 'Publish the verdict.'

The clerk did a rehearsal reading in her head first and then began.

'In the above entitled matter on the question of whether defendant Hieronymus Bosch did deprive Norman Church of his civil rights to protection against unlawful search and seizure, we find for the plaintiff.'

Bosch didn't move. He looked across the room and saw that now all the jurors were looking at him. His eyes turned to Deborah Church and he saw her grab the arm of the man next to her, even though she didn't know him, and smile. She was turning that smile triumphantly toward Bosch when Belk grabbed his arm.

'Don't worry,' he whispered. 'It's the damages that count.'

The clerk continued.

'The jury hereby awards to the plaintiff in compensatory damages the amount of one dollar.'

Bosch heard Belk whisper a gleeful 'Yes!' under his breath.

'In the matter of punitive damages, the jury awards the plaintiff the amount of one dollar.'

Belk whispered it again, only this time loud enough to be

heard in the gallery. Bosch looked at Deborah Church just as the triumph dropped out of her smile and her eyes turned dead. It all seemed surrealistic to Bosch, as if he were observing a play but was actually on the stage with the actors. The verdict meant nothing to him. He just watched everybody.

Judge Keyes began his thank-you speech to the jury, telling them how they had performed their Constitutional duties and should be proud to have served and to be Americans. Bosch tuned it out and just sat there. Sylvia came to mind and he wished he could tell her.

The judge banged down the gavel and the jury filed out for the last time. Then he left the bench and Bosch thought he might have had an annoyed look on his face.

'Harry,' Belk said. 'It's a damn good verdict.'

'Is it? I don't know.'

'Well, it's a mixed verdict. But essentially the jury found what we already admitted to. We said you made mistakes going in like you did but you already had been reprimanded by your department for that. The jury found as a matter of law that you should not have kicked down the door like that. But in awarding only two dollars they were saying they believed you. Church made the furtive move. And Church was the Dollmaker.'

He patted Bosch's back. He was probably waiting for Harry to thank him but it didn't come.

'What about Chandler?'

'Well, there's the rub, so to speak. The jury found for the plaintiff so we are going to have to pick up her tab. She'll probably ask for about one-eighty, maybe two hundred. We'll probably settle it for ninety. It's not bad, Harry. Not at all.'

'I gotta go.'

Bosch stood up and waded through a clot of people and reporters to get out of the courtroom. He moved quickly to the escalator and once on started fumbling to get the last cigarette out of his pack. Bremmer jumped on the step behind him, his notebook out and ready.

'Congrats, Harry,' he said.

Bosch looked at him. The reporter seemed sincere.

'For what? They said I'm some kind of a Constitutional goon.'

'Yeah, but you walk away two bucks light. That ain't bad.'

'Yeah, well . . .'

'Well, any comment on the record? I take it "Constitutional goon" was off, right?'

'Yeah, I'd appreciate that. Uh, tell you what, let me think for a while. I've gotta go but I'll call you later. Why don't you go back up and talk to Belk. He needs to see his name in the paper.'

Outside he lit the cigarette and pulled the rover out of his pocket.

'Edgar, you up?'

'Here.'

'How is it?'

'Better come on out, Harry. Everybody's rolling on it.'

Bosch threw the cigarette in the ash can.

They had done a bad job of keeping it contained. By the time Bosch got to the house on Carmelina, there was already one news copter circling overhead and two other channels were there on the ground. It would not be long until it was a circus. The case would have two big draws: the Follower and Honey Chandler.

Bosch had to park two houses away because of the glut of official cars and vans lining both sides of the street. Parking control officers were just beginning to put down flares and close the street to traffic.

The property had been preserved by yellow plastic police lines. Bosch signed an attendance log held by a uniform officer at the tape and slipped underneath. It was a two-story Bauhaus-style home set on a hillside. Standing outside, Bosch knew the floor-to-ceiling windows of the upstairs rooms would offer sweeping views of the flats below. He counted two chimneys. It was a nice house in a nice neighborhood filled with nice lawyers and UCLA professors. Not anymore, he thought. He wished he had a cigarette as he headed in.

Edgar was standing just inside the door in a tiled entryway. He was talking on a mobile phone and it sounded as if he was telling the media relations unit to send people out to handle this. He saw Bosch and pointed up the stairs.

The staircase was right off the entry and Bosch went up. There was a wide hallway that passed four doorways upstairs. A group of detectives milled about outside the farthest door and occasionally they looked inside at something. Bosch walked over.

In a way, Bosch knew, he had trained his mind to be almost like that of a psychopath. He practiced the psychology of objectification when at a death scene. Dead people weren't people, they were objects. He had to look at bodies as corpses, as evidence. It was the only way to deal with it and get the job done. It was the only way to survive. But this, of course, was always easier said or thought about than done. Often Bosch stumbled.

As a member of the original Dollmaker task force, he had seen the last six of the victims attributed to the serial killer. He saw them 'in situ', as it was called – in the situation in which they were found. None of them was easy. There was something that seemed so helpless about these victims that it overwhelmed his best efforts at objectification. And knowing that they came from street backgrounds had made it all the worse. It was as if the torture visited upon each one by her killer was only the last in a life of indignities.

Now he looked down at the naked and tortured body of Honey Chandler and no manner of mental tricks or deception could prevent the horror he saw from burning into his soul. For the first time in his years as a homicide investigator, he wanted to close his eyes and just go away.

But he didn't. Instead, he stood with the other men who looked down with dead eyes and nonchalant poses. Like a gathering of serial killers. Something made him think of the bridge game at San Quentin that Locke had mentioned. A foursome of psychopaths sitting around the table, more killings to their credit than cards on the table.

Chandler was faceup, her arms outstretched at her sides. Her face was garishly painted with makeup. It hid much of the purplish discoloration which spread from her neck up. A leather strap, cut from a purse which lay spilled on the floor, was tied tightly around her neck, knotted on the right side as if pulled closed with a left hand. In keeping with the prior cases, whatever restraints and gag the killer used had been taken away with him.

But there was something outside of the program. Bosch saw that the Follower was improvising, now that he was no longer operating under the camouflage of the Dollmaker. Chandler's body was riddled with cigarette burns and bite marks. Some of them had bled and some were purplish with bruising, meaning the torture had taken place while she was still alive.

Rollenberger was in the room and was giving orders, even telling the photographer what angles he wanted. Nixon and Johnson were also in the room. Bosch realized, as probably Chandler had, that the final indignity was that her uncovered body would be left on display for hours in view of men who had despised her in life. Nixon looked up and saw Bosch in the hallway and stepped out of the room.

'Harry, what made you tumble to her?'

'She didn't show up for court today. Thought it was worth checking out. Guess she was the blonde. Too bad I didn't see it right away.'

'Yeah.'

'Got a TOD yet?'

'Yeah, an estimate. Coroner's tech says time of death was at least forty-eight hours ago.'

Bosch nodded. It meant she was dead before he even found the note. It made it a little easier.

'Hear anything on Locke?'

'Nada.'

'You and Johnson on point on this one?'

'Yeah, Hans Off put us on it. Edgar discovered it but he's primary on last week's case. I know it was your tumble but I guess Hans Off figured with court and –'

'Don't worry about it. What do you need me to do?'

'You tell me. What do you want to do?'

'I want to stay out of there. I didn't like her but I liked her, you know what I mean?'

'I think so. Yeah, this one's bad. You notice he's changing? He's biting now. Burning.'

'Yeah, I noticed. Anything else new?'

'Not that we can tell.'

'I'm going to have a look around the rest of the house. Is it clean?'

'We haven't had time to dust. Just a quick look through. Use gloves and let me know what you find.'

Bosch went to one of the equipment boxes lined along the wall in the hallway and pulled a pair of plastic gloves from a dispenser that looked like a Kleenex box.

Irving passed by him wordlessly on the staircase, their eyes barely holding each other's for a second. When he got down to the entry, he saw two deputy chiefs standing out on the front steps. They weren't doing anything, just standing where they would be sure to be seen on the TV footage looking serious and concerned. Bosch could see that a growing number of reporters and cameramen were gathering at the plastic line.

He looked around and found Chandler's home office in a small room off the living room. Two of the walls contained built-in shelves that were lined with books. The room had one window that looked out onto the commotion just beyond the front lawn. He pulled on the gloves and began looking through the drawers of the desk. He didn't find what he was looking for but he could tell the desk had been rifled by someone else. Things were scattered in the drawers, papers from files were outside of files. It wasn't as neat as Chandler had kept her things on the plaintiff's table.

He checked underneath the blotter. The note from the Follower wasn't there. There were two books on the desk, *Black's Law Dictionary* and the *California Penal Code*. He fanned the pages of both but there was no note. He leaned back in the leather desk chair and looked up at the two walls of books.

He figured it would take two hours to go through all the books and he still might not find the note. Then he noticed the cracked green spine of a book on the second-to-the-top shelf nearest the window. He recognized the book. It was the one Chandler had read from during closing arguments. *The Marble Faun.* He got up and pulled the book out of its slot.

The note was there, folded into the center of the book. So was the envelope it came in. And Bosch quickly learned he had guessed correctly about her. The note was a photocopy of the page dropped at the police station last Monday, the day of opening statements. What was different about this one was the envelope. It hadn't been dropped off. It had been mailed. The envelope was stamped and then canceled in Van Nuys on the Saturday before opening statements.

Bosch looked at the postmark and knew it would be impossible to try any kind of trace on it. There would also be numerous prints on it from the many postal employees who handled it. He decided the note would be of little evidentiary value.

He left the office, carrying the note and envelope by the corners with his gloved hands. He had to go upstairs to find a tech with plastic evidence bags to place them in. He looked through the doorway into the bedroom and saw the coroner's tech and two body movers spreading open a plastic bag on a gurney. The public display of Honey Chandler was about to end. Bosch stepped back so he did not have to watch. Edgar walked over after reading the note, which the tech was labeling.

'He sent the same note to her? How come?'

'Guess he wanted to make sure we didn't sit on the one he dropped off for us. If we did, he could count on her bringing it up.'

'If she had the note all along, how come she wanted to subpoena ours? She could've just taken this one into court.'

'I think maybe she thought she'd get more mileage out of ours. Making the police turn it over gave it more legitimacy in the eyes of the jury. If she had just presented her own, my lawyer could've gotten it shot down. I don't know. It's just a guess.'

Edgar nodded.

'By the way,' Bosch said, 'how'd you get in when you got here?'

'Front door was unlocked. No scratches on the lock or other signs of break-in.'

'The Follower came here and was let in. . . . She wasn't lured to him. Something's going on. He's changing. He's biting and burning. He's making mistakes. He's letting something get to him. Why'd he go for her, rather than stick to his pattern of ordering victims from the sex tabs?'

'Too bad Locke's the fucking suspect. It'd be nice to ask him what all this means.'

'Detective Harry Bosch!' a voice called from downstairs. 'Harry Bosch!'

Bosch walked to the top of the stairs and looked down. A young patrolman, the one who was keeping the scene attendance log at the tape, stood in the entry area looking up.

'Guy at the tape wants to come in. Said he's a shrink who's been working with you.'

Bosch looked over at Edgar. Their eyes locked. He looked back down at the patrolman.

'What's his name?'

The patrolman looked down at his clipboard and read off, 'John Locke, from USC.'

'Send him in.'

Bosch started down the stairs and beckoned to Edgar with his hand. He said, 'I'm taking him into her office. Tell Hans Off and then come down.'

Bosch told Locke to sit in the chair behind the desk while he chose to stay standing. Through the window behind the psychologist, Bosch saw the press gathering into a tight group in preparation for a briefing by someone from media relations.

'Don't touch anything,' Bosch said. 'What're you doing here?'

'I came as soon as I heard,' Locke said. 'But I thought you said you had the suspect under surveillance.'

'We did. It was the wrong guy. How did you hear?'

'It's all over the radio. I heard it while I was driving in and came right here. They didn't put out the exact address but once I got to Carmelina this wasn't hard to find. Just follow the helicopters.'

Edgar slipped into the room then and closed the door.

'Detective Jerry Edgar, meet Dr John Locke.'

Edgar nodded but made no move to shake his hand. He stayed back, leaning against the door.

'Where've you been? We've been trying to find you since yesterday.'

'Vegas.'

'Vegas? Why'd you go to Vegas?'

'Why else, to gamble. I'm also thinking about a book project on the legal prostitutes that work in the towns north of – look, aren't we wasting time here? I'd like to view the body in situ. Then I could give you a read on it.'

'Body's already moved, Doc,' Edgar said.

'It is? Shit. Maybe I could survey the scene and –'

'We've already got too many people up there right now,' Bosch said. 'Maybe later. What do you make of bite marks? Cigarette burns?'

'Are you saying that's what you've found this time?'

'Plus, it wasn't a bimbo from the sex tabs,' Edgar added. 'He came here, she didn't come to him.'

'He is changing quickly. It appears to be complete disassembling. Or some unknown force or reason compelling his actions.'

'Such as?' Bosch asked.

'I don't know.'

'We tried to call you in Vegas. You never checked in.'

'Oh, the Stardust? Well, coming in I saw the new MGM had just opened and decided to see if they had a room. They did. I was there.'

'Anyone with you?' Bosch asked.

'The whole time?' Edgar added.

A puzzled look came over Locke's face.

'What is going –'

He understood now. He shook his head.

'Harry, are you kidding?'

'No. Are you, coming here like this?'

'I think you –'

'No, don't answer that. Tell you what, it would probably be best for all of us if you know your rights before we go any further. Jerry, you got a card?'

Edgar pulled out his wallet and from it took a white plastic card with the Miranda warning printed on it. He started reading it to Locke. Both Bosch and Edgar knew the warning by heart but a departmental memo that was distributed with the plastic card said it was best practice to read directly from a card. This made it difficult for a defense attorney to later attack in court how the police administered the rights warning to a client.

As Edgar read the card, Bosch looked out the window at the huge clot of reporters standing around one of the deputy chiefs. He saw that Bremmer was there now. But the deputy chief's words must not have meant much; the reporter was not writing anything down. He was just standing to the side of the pack and smoking. He was probably waiting for the real info from the real guns, Irving and Rollenberger.

'Am I under arrest?' Locke asked when Edgar was done.

'Not yet,' said Edgar.

'We just need to clear some things up,' Bosch said.

'I resent the hell out of this.'

'I understand. Now, do you want to clear this trip to Vegas up? Was there anyone with you?'

'From six o'clock Friday until I got out of my car down the block ten minutes ago, there has been a person with me every minute of every day except when I was in the bathroom. This is ridic –'

'And that is who, this person?'

'It's a friend of mine. Her name is Melissa Mencken.'

Bosch remembered the young woman named Melissa who was in Locke's front office.

'The child-psych major? From your office? The blonde?'

'That's right,' Locke answered reluctantly.

'And she will tell us you were together the whole time? Same room, same hotel, same everything, right?'

'Yes. She'll confirm it all. We were just coming back when we heard about this on the radio. KFWB. She's out there waiting for me in the car. Go talk to her.'

'What kind of car?'

'It's the blue Jag. Look, Harry, you go talk to her and clear this up. If you don't make noise about me being with a student, I won't make a sound about this . . . this interrogation.'

'This is no interrogation, Doctor. Believe me, if we interrogate you, you'll know it.'

He nodded to Edgar, who slipped out the door to go find the Jag. When they were alone, Bosch pulled a high-backed chair away from the wall and sat down in front of the desk to wait.

'What happened to the suspect you were following, Harry?'

'We did.'

'What's that supposed to –'

'Never mind.'

377

They sat in silence for nearly five minutes until Edgar stuck his head in the door and signaled Bosch to come out.

'Checks out, Harry. I talked to the girl and her story is the same. There also were credit card receipts in the car. They checked into the MGM Saturday at three. There was a gas receipt in Victorville, had the time on it. Nine o'clock in the morning Saturday. Victorville's what, an hour away. Looks like they were on the road when Chandler got it. Besides, the girl says they also spent Friday night together at his house in the hills. We can do some more checking but I think he's being legit with us.'

'Well. . . ,' Bosch said, not completing the thought. 'Why don't you go up and spread the word that he looks clear. I want to take him up to look around, if he still wants to.'

'Will do.'

Bosch went back into the study. He sat in the chair that was in front of the desk. Locke studied him.

'Well?'

'She's too scared, Locke. She isn't going along. She's telling us the truth.'

'What the fuck are you talking about?' Locke yelled.

Now Bosch studied him. The surprise on his face, the utter fright, was too genuine. Bosch was sure now. He was sorry, yet felt some perverse feeling of power, having run Locke through the scam.

'You're clear, Dr Locke. Just had to be sure. I guess the criminal only comes back to the scene of the crime in movies.'

Locke took a deep breath and looked down into his lap. Bosch thought he looked like a driver who had just pulled to the side of the road to collect himself after missing a head-on collision with a truck by a matter of inches.

'Goddammit, Bosch, for a minute there, I had bad dreams, you know?'

Bosch nodded. He knew about bad dreams.

'Edgar's going up to smooth the way. He's going to ask

the lieutenant if you can go up and give a read on the scene. If you still want to.'

'Excellent,' he said, but there wasn't much excitement left in him.

They sat in silence after that. Bosch took out his cigarettes and found the pack empty. But he put the pack back in his pocket so as not to leave false evidence in the trash can.

He didn't feel like talking to Locke anymore. Instead, he looked past him and out the window at the activity on the street. The media pack had dispersed after the briefing. Now some of the TV reporters were taping their reports with the 'death house' behind them. Bosch could see Bremmer interviewing the neighbors across the street and writing feverishly in his notebook.

Edgar came in then and said, 'We're ready for him upstairs.'

Staring out the window, Bosch said, 'Jerry, can you take him up? I just thought of something I need to do.'

Locke stood up and looked at the two detectives.

'Fuck you,' he said. 'Both of you. Fuck you. . . . There, I just had to say that. Now, let's forget about it and go to work.'

He crossed the room to Edgar. Bosch stopped him at the door.

'Dr Locke?'

He turned back to Bosch.

'When we catch this guy, he'll want to gloat, won't he?'

Locke thought for a while and said, 'Yes, he'll be very pleased with himself, his accomplishments. That might be the hardest part for him, keeping quiet when he knows he should. He'll want to gloat.'

They left then and Bosch looked out the window for a few more minutes before getting up.

Some of the reporters who knew who he was pressed against the yellow tape and began shouting questions as he came out. He ducked under the tape and said he could make no comment and that Chief Irving was coming out soon. That seemed to mollify them temporarily and he started walking down the street to his car.

He knew Bremmer was the master of the anti-pack. He always let the pack move in and do their thing, then he came in after, by himself, to get what he wanted. Bosch wasn't mistaken. Bremmer showed up at the car.

'Pullin' out already, Harry?'

'No, I just need to get something.'

'Pretty bad in there?'

'Is this on or off the record?'

'Whatever you like.'

Bosch opened the car door.

'Off the record, yes, it's pretty bad in there. On the record, no comment.'

He leaned in and made a show of looking in the glove compartment and not finding what he wanted.

'What are you guys calling this one? I mean, you know, since the Dollmaker was already taken.'

Bosch got back out.

'The Follower. That's off the record, too. Ask Irving.'

'Catchy.'

'Yeah, I thought you reporters would like that.'

Bosch pulled the empty cigarette pack out of his pocket, crumpled it and threw it into the car and closed the door.

'Give me a smoke, will you?'

'Sure.'

Bremmer pulled a soft pack of Marlboros out of his sport coat and shook one out for Bosch. Then he lit it for him with a Zippo. With his left hand.

'Hell of a city we live in, Harry, isn't it.'

'Yeah. This city . . .'

THIRTY-ONE

At 7:30 that night, Bosch was sitting in the Caprice in the back parking lot of St Vibiana's in downtown. From his angle, he could look a half block up Second Street to the corner at Spring. But he couldn't see the *Times* building. That didn't matter, though. He knew that every *Times* employee without parking privileges in the executive garage would have to cross the corner of Spring and Second to get to one of the employee garages a half block down Spring. He was waiting for Bremmer.

After leaving the scene at Honey Chandler's house, Bosh had gone home and slept for two hours. The he had paced in his house on the hill, thinking about Bremmer and seeing how perfectly he fit the mold. He called Locke and asked a few more general questions about the psychology of the Follower. But he did not tell Locke about Bremmer. He told no one about this, thinking three strikes and you're out. He came up with a plan, then dropped by Hollywood Division to gas up the Caprice and get the equipment he would need.

And now he waited. He watched a steady procession of homeless people walking down Second. As if heeding a siren's call, they were heading toward the Los Angeles Mission a few blocks away for a meal and a bed. Many carried with them or pushed in shopping carts their life's belongings.

Bosch never took his eyes off the corner but his mind drifted far from there. He thought of Sylvia and wondered what she was doing at that moment and what she was thinking. He hoped she didn't take too long to decide, because he knew his mind's instinctual protective devices and responses had begun to react. He was already looking at the positives that would come if she didn't come back. He told himself she made him weak. Hadn't he thought of her immediately when he found the note from the Follower? Yes, she had made him vulnerable. He told himself she might not be good for his life's mission, let her go.

His heartbeat jacked up a notch when he saw Bremmer step onto the corner and then walk in the direction of the parking garages. A building blocked Bosch's view after that. He quickly started the car and pulled out onto Second and up to Spring.

Down the block Bremmer entered the newer garage with a card key and Bosch watched the auto door and waited. In five minutes a blue Toyota Celica came out of the garage and slowed while the driver checked for traffic on Spring. Bosch could see clearly it was Bremmer. The Celica pulled onto Spring and so did Bosch.

Bremmer headed west on Beverly and into Hollywood. He made one stop at a Vons and came out fifteen minutes later with a single bag of groceries. He then proceeded to a neighborhood of single-family homes just north of the Paramount studio. He drove down the side of a small stuccoed house and parked in the detached garage in the back. Bosch pulled to the curb one house away and waited.

All the houses in the neighborhood were one of three basic designs. It was one of the cookie-cutter victory neighborhoods that had sprung up after World War II in the city, with affordable homes for returning servicemen. Now you'd probably need to be making a general's pay to buy in. The '80s did that. The occupation army of yuppies had the place now.

Each lawn had a little tin sign planted in it. They were from three or four different home-security companies but they all said the same thing. ARMED RESPONSE. It was the epitaph of the city. Sometimes Bosch thought the Hollywood sign should be taken down off the hill and replaced with those two words.

Bosch waited for Bremmer to either come around to the front to check his mail or to put lights on inside the house. When neither happened after five minutes, he got out and approached the driveway, his hand unconsciously tapping his sport coat on the side, making sure he had his Smith & Wesson. It was there, but he kept it holstered.

The driveway was unlit and in the recessed darkness of the open garage Bosch could only see the faint reflection of the red lenses of the taillights of Bremmer's car. But there was no sign of Bremmer.

A six-foot wooden-plank fence ran along the right side of the drive, separating Bremmer's property from his neighbor's. Branches of bougainvillea in bloom hung over and Bosch could hear faint television sounds from the house next door.

As he walked between the fence and Bremmer's house toward the garage, Bosch knew he was completely vulnerable. But he also knew that drawing his weapon couldn't help him here. Favoring the side of the drive nearest the house, he walked to the garage and stopped before its darkness. Standing beneath an old basketball goal with a bent rim, he said, 'Bremmer?'

There was no sound save for the ticking of the engine of the car in the garage. Then, from behind, Bosch heard the light scraping of a shoe on concrete. He turned. Bremmer stood there, grocery bag in hand.

'What are you doing?' Bosch asked.

'That's what I should ask.'

Bosch watched his hands as he spoke.

'You never called. So I came by.'

'Called about what?'

'You wanted a comment about the verdict.'

'You were supposed to call me. Remember? Doesn't matter, the story's been put to bed now. Besides, the verdict kind of took a back seat to the other developments of the day, if you know what I mean. The story on the Follower – and Irving did use that name on the record – is going out front.'

Bosch took a few steps toward him.

'Then how come you're not at the Red Wind? I thought you said you always go for a pop when you hit the front page.'

Holding the bag in his right arm, Bremmer reached into the pocket of his coat but Bosch heard the sound of keys.

'I didn't feel like it tonight. I kind've liked Honey Chandler, you know? What are you really doing here, Harry? I saw you following me.'

'You going to ask me in? Maybe we can have that beer, toast your front-page story. One-A is what you reporters call it, right?'

'Yeah. This one's going above the fold.'

'Above the fold, I like that.'

They stared at each other in the darkness.

'Whaddaya say? About the beer.'

'Sure,' Bremmer said. He turned and went to the house's back door and unlocked it. He reached in and hit switches that turned on lights over the door and in the kitchen beyond. Then he stepped back and held out his arm for Bosch to go in first.

'After you. Go into the living room and have a seat. I'll get a couple bottles and be right there.'

Bosch walked through the kitchen and down a short hall to the living room and dining room. He didn't sit down but rather stood near the curtain drawn across one of the front windows. He parted it and looked into the street and at the houses across. There was no one. No one had seen him come here. He wondered if he had made a mistake.

He looked down at the old-style radiator beneath the window, touched it with his hand. It was cold. Its iron coils had been painted black.

He stood there for a few more moments and then turned

and looked around at the rest of the room. It was nicely furnished with blacks and grays. Bosch sat on a black leather couch. He knew if he arrested Bremmer in the house, he would be able to make a quick cursory search of the premises. If he found anything of an incriminating nature all he had to do was come back with a warrant. Bremmer, being a police and courts reporter, would know that, too. Why'd he let me in? Bosch wondered. Have I made a mistake? He began to lose confidence in his plan.

Bremmer brought out two bottles, no glasses, and sat in a matching chair to Bosch's right. Bosch studied his bottle for a long moment. There was a bubble pushing up from the top. It burst and he held the bottle up and said, 'Above the fold.'

'Above the fold,' Bremmer toasted back. He didn't smile. He took a pull from his bottle and put it down on the coffee table.

Bosch took a large gulp from his bottle and held it in his mouth. It was ice cold and hurt some of his teeth. There was no known history of the Dollmaker or the Follower using drugs on their victims. He looked at Bremmer, their eyes locked for a moment, and he swallowed. It felt good going down.

Leaning forward, elbows on his knees, he held the bottle in his right hand and looked at Bremmer looking back at him. He knew from talking with Locke that the Follower would not be driven by conscience to admit anything. He had no conscience. The only way was trickery, to play on the killer's pride. He felt his confidence coming back. He stared at Bremmer with a glare that burned right through him.

'What is it?' the reporter asked quietly.

'Tell me you did it for the stories, or the book. To get above the fold, to have a bestseller, whatever. But don't tell me you're the sick fuck the shrink says you are.'

'What are you talking about?'

'Skip the bullshit, Bremmer. It's you and you know I know it's you. Why else would I waste my time being here?'

'The Dol – the Follower? You're saying I'm the Follower? Are you crazy?'

'Are you? That's what I want to know.'

Bremmer was silent for a long time. He seemed to retreat into himself, like a computer running a long equation, the Please Wait sign flashing. The answer finally registered and his eyes focused again on Bosch.

'I think you should go, Harry.' He stood up. 'It's very plain to see you've been under a lot of pressure with this case and I think –'

'You're the one coming apart, Bremmer. You've made mistakes. A lot of them.'

Bremmer suddenly dove into Bosch, rolling so that his left shoulder slammed into Bosch's chest, pinning him to the couch. Bosch felt air burst from his lungs and sat helplessly as Bremmer worked his hands under Harry's sport coat and got to the gun. Bremmer then pulled away, switching off the safety and pointing the weapon at Bosch's face.

After nearly a minute of silence during which both men simply stared at each other, Bremmer said, 'I admit only one thing: You have me intrigued, Harry. But before we go any further with this discussion, there is something I have to do.'

A sense of relief and anticipation flooded Bosch's body. He tried not to show it. Instead he tried to put a look of terror on his face. He stared wide-eyed at the gun. Bremmer bent over him and ran his heavy hand down Bosch's chest and into his crotch, then around his sides. He found no wire.

'Sorry to get so personal,' he said. 'But you don't trust me and I don't trust you, right?'

Bremmer straightened and stepped back and sat down.

'Now, I don't need to remind you, but I will. I have the advantage here. So answer my questions. What mistakes? What mistakes have I made? Tell me what I did wrong, Harry, or I'll kneecap you with the first bullet.'

Bosch tantalized him with silence for a few moments as he thought about how to proceed.

'Well,' he finally began. 'Let's go back to the basics first. Four years ago you were all over the Dollmaker case. As a reporter. From the start. It was your stories about the early cases that made the department form the task force. As a reporter you had access to the suspect intelligence, you probably had the autopsy reports. You also had sources like me and probably half the dicks on the task force and in the coroner's office. What I am saying is you knew what the Dollmaker did. Right down to the cross on the toenail, you knew. Later, after the Dollmaker was dead, you used it in your book.'

'Yeah, I knew. It means nothing, Bosch. A lot of people knew.'

'Oh, it's Bosch now. No more Harry? Have I suddenly become contemptible in your eyes? Or does the gun give you that sense that we are no longer equals?'

'Fuck you, Bosch. You're stupid. You've got nothing. What else you got? You know, this is great. It will definitely be worth a chapter in the book I do on the Follower.'

'What else've I got? I've got the concrete blonde. And I've got the concrete. Did you know you dropped your cigarettes when you were pouring the concrete? Remember that? You were driving home, wanted a smoke and you reached into your pocket and there was nothing there.

'See, just like Becky Kaminski, they were in there waiting for us. Marlboro soft pack. That's your brand, Bremmer. That's mistake number one.'

'A lot of people smoke them. Good luck taking this to the DA.'

'A lot of people are left-handed, too, like you and the Follower. And me. But there's more. You want to hear it?'

Bremmer looked away from him, toward the window, and said nothing. Maybe it was a trick, Bosch thought, that he wanted Bosch to go for the gun.

'Hey, Bremmer!' he almost yelled. 'There's more.'

Bremmer's face snapped back into a stare at Bosch.

'Today after the verdict you said I should be happy because the verdict would leave the city only two bucks light. But when we had a drink the other night, remember, you gave me the big rundown on how Chandler would be able to charge the city a hundred grand or so if she won even a dollar judgment from the jury. Remember? So it makes me think that when you told me this morning the verdict was only going to cost two dollars, you knew it was only going to cost two dollars because you knew Chandler was dead and couldn't collect. You knew that because you killed her. Mistake number two.'

Bremmer shook his head as if he were dealing with a child. His aim with the gun drooped to Bosch's midsection.

'Look, man, I was trying to make you feel good when I said that today, okay? I didn't know if she was alive or dead. No jury is going to make that leap of faith.'

Bosch smiled brilliantly at him.

'So now at least you have me past the DA's office and to a jury. I guess my story is improving, isn't it?'

Bremmer coldly smiled back, raised the gun.

'Is that it, Bosch? Is that all you have?'

'I saved the best stuff for last.'

He lit a cigarette, never taking his eyes off Bremmer.

'You remember before you killed Chandler, how you tortured her? You must remember that. You bit her. And burned her. Well, everyone was standing around in that house today wondering why the Follower was changing, doing all this new stuff – changing the mold. Locke, the shrink, he was the most puzzled of all. You really fucked with his mind, man. I kinda like that about you, Bremmer. But, you see, he didn't know what I knew.'

He let that sit out there for a while. He knew Bremmer would bite.

'And what did you know, Sherlock?'

Bosch smiled. He was in complete control now.

'I knew why you did that to her. It was simple. You

wanted your note back, didn't you? But she wouldn't tell you where it was. See, she knew she was dead whether she gave it to you or not, so she took it – everything you did to her, she took – and she didn't tell you. That woman had a lot of guts and in the end she beat you, Bremmer. She's the one who got you. Not me.'

'What note?' Bremmer said weakly after a long moment.

'The one you fucked up with. You missed it. It's a big house to search, especially when you've got a dead woman lying in the bed. That'd be hard to explain if somebody happened to drop by. But don't worry, I found it. I've got it. Too bad you don't read Hawthorne. It was sitting there in his book. Too bad. But like I said, she beat you. Maybe there is justice sometimes.'

Bremmer had no snappy comeback. Bosch looked at him and thought that he was doing well. He was almost there.

'She kept the envelope, too, in case you were wondering. I found that, too. And so I started wondering, why would he torture her for this note when it was the same one he dropped off for me? It was just a photocopy. Then I figured it out. You didn't want the note. You wanted the envelope.'

Bremmer looked down at his hands.

'How am I doing? Am I losing you?'

'I have no idea,' Bremmer said, looking back up. 'You're fucking delirious as far as I'm concerned.'

'Well, I only have to worry about making sense to the DA, don't I? And what I'm going to explain to him is that the poem on the note was in response to the story you wrote that appeared in the paper on Monday, the day the trial started. But the postmark on the envelope was the Saturday before. See, there's the puzzle. How would the Follower know to write a poem making reference to the newspaper article two days before it was in the newspaper? The answer is, of course, that he, the Follower, had prior knowledge of the article. He wrote that article. That also explains how you knew about the note in the next day's story. You were your own source, Bremmer. And that is mistake number three. Three strikes and you're out.'

The silence that followed was so complete that Bosch could hear the low hiss coming from Bremmer's bottle of beer.

'You're forgetting something, Bosch,' Bremmer finally said. 'I'm holding the gun. Now, who else have you told this crazy story to?'

'Just to finish the housekeeping,' Bosch said, 'the new poem you dropped off for me this past weekend was just a front. You wanted the shrink and everybody else to make it look like you killed Chandler as a favor to me or some psycho bullshit, right?'

Bremmer said nothing.

'That way nobody would see the true reason you went after her. To get the note and the envelope back. . . . Shit, you being a reporter she was familiar with, she probably invited you in when you knocked on her door. Kind of like you inviting me in here. Familiarity breeds danger, Bremmer.'

Bremmer said nothing.

'Answer a question for me, Bremmer. I'm curious why you dropped one note off and mailed the other. I know, being a reporter, you could blend in at the station, drop it on the desk and nobody would remember. But why mail it to her? Obviously, it was a mistake – that's why you went back and killed her. But why'd you make it?'

The reporter looked at Bosch for a long moment. Then he glanced down at the gun as if to reassure himself that he was in control and would get out of this. The gun was powerful bait. Bosch knew he had him.

'The story was supposed to run that Saturday, that's what it was scheduled for. But some dumb-ass editor held it, ran it Monday. I had mailed the letter before I looked at the paper that Saturday. That was my only mistake. But you're the one who made the big mistake.'

'Oh, yeah? What's that?'

'Coming here alone . . .'

Now it was Bosch who was silent.

'Why come here alone, Bosch? Is this how you did it with the Dollmaker? You went alone so you could kill him in cold blood?'

Bosch thought a moment.

'That's a good question.'

'Well, that was your second mistake. Thinking I was as unworthy an opponent as him. He was nothing. You killed him and therefore he deserved to die. But now it is you who deserve to die.'

'Give me the gun, Bremmer.'

He laughed as if Bosch had asked a crazy question.

'You think –'

'How many were there? How many women are buried out there?'

Bremmer's eyes lit with pride.

'Enough. Enough to fulfill my special needs.'

'How many? Where are they?'

'You'll never know, Bosch. That will be your pain, your last pain. Never knowing. And losing.'

Bremmer raised the gun so that its muzzle pointed to Bosch's heart. He pulled the trigger.

Bosch watched his eyes as the metallic click sounded. Bremmer pulled the trigger again and again. The same result, the growing terror in his eyes.

Bosch reached into his sock and pulled the extra clip, the one that was loaded with fifteen XTP bullets. He wrapped his fist around the cartridge and in one swift motion came off the couch and swung his fist into Bremmer's jaw. The impact of the blow knocked the reporter backward in his chair. His weight made the chair crash backward and he spilled to the floor. He dropped the Smith and Bosch quickly gathered it up, ejected the empty clip and put in the live ammunition.

'Get up! Get the fuck up!'

Bremmer did as he was told.

'Are you going to kill me now? Is that it, another kill for the gunslinger?'

'That's up to you, Bremmer.'

'What are you talking about?'

'I'm talking about how I want to blow your head off, but for me to do that you have to make the first move, Bremmer. Just like with the Dollmaker. It was his play. Now it's yours.'

'Look, Bosch, I don't want to die. Everything I said – I was just playing a game. You're making a mistake here. I just want to get it cleared up. Please, just take me to county and it will all get cleared up. Please.'

'Did they plead like that when you had the strap around their necks? Did they? Did you make them plead for their lives, or for their deaths? What about Chandler? At the end, did she beg you to kill her?'

'Take me to county. Arrest me and take me to county.'

'Then get against that wall, you fat fuck and put your hands behind your back.'

Bremmer obeyed. Bosch dropped his cigarette into an ashtray on the table and followed Bremmer to the wall. When he closed the handcuffs over the reporter's wrists, Bremmer's shoulders dropped as he apparently felt safe. He started squirming his arms, chafing his wrists on the cuffs.

'See that?' he said. 'You see that, Bosch? I'm making marks on my wrists. You kill me now, they'll see the marks and know it was an execution. I'm not some dumb fuck like Church that you can slaughter like an animal.'

'No, that's right, you know all the angles, don't you?'

'All of them. Now take me down to county. I'll be out before you wake up tomorrow. Know what all this is, what you've got? Just the wild speculation of a rogue cop. Even a federal jury agreed you go too far, Bosch. This won't work. You've got no evidence.'

Bosch turned him away from the wall so that their faces were no more than two feet apart, their beer breath mixing.

'You did it, didn't you? And you think you're going to walk, don't you?'

Bremmer stared at him and Bosch saw the gleam of pride in his eyes again. Locke had been right about him. He was gloating. And he couldn't shut up even though he knew his life might depend on it.

'Yes,' he said in a low, strange voice. 'I did it. I'm the man. And, yes, I will walk. You wait and see. And when I'm out there you'll think of me every night for the rest of your life.'

Bosch nodded.

'But I never said that, Bosch. It will be your word against mine. A rogue cop – it will never get to court. They couldn't afford to put you on the stand against me.'

Bosch leaned closer to him and smiled.

'Then I suppose it's a good thing I taped it.'

Bosch walked over to the radiator and pulled the microrecorder from between two of the iron coils. He held it up on his palm for Bremmer to see. Bremmer's eyes became enraged. He had been tricked. He had been cheated.

'Bosch, that tape is inadmissible. That's entrapment. I have not been advised. I have not been advised!'

'I'm advising you of your rights now. You weren't under arrest until now. I wasn't going to advise you until I arrested you. You know police procedure.'

Bosch was smiling at him, digging it in.

'Let's go, Bremmer,' he said when he got tired of the victory.

393

THIRTY-TWO

It was an irony that Bosch savored Tuesday morning when he read Bremmer's above-the-fold story on the killing of Honey Chandler. He had booked the reporter into county jail on a no-bail hold shortly before midnight and had not alerted media relations. The word had not gotten out by the last deadline and now the paper had a front-page story about a murder that was written by the murderer. Bosch liked that. He smiled as he read it.

The one person Bosch had told was Irving. He had the com center patch him through on a phone line and in a half-hour-long conversation he told the assistant chief every step he had taken and described every building block of evidence that led to the arrest. Irving said nothing congratulatory, nor did he chastise Bosch for making the arrest alone. Either or both would come later, after it was seen whether the arrest would stick. Both men knew this.

At 9 A.M. Bosch was seated in front of a filing deputy's desk at the district attorney's office in the downtown criminal courts building. For the second time in eight hours he carefully went over the details of what happened and then played the tape of his conversation with Bremmer. The deputy DA, whose name was Chap Newell, made notations on a yellow pad while listening to the tape. He often furrowed his brow or shook his head because the sound was not good. The voices in Bremmer's living room had bounced through the iron radiator coils and had a tinny echo on the tape. Still, the words that were most important were audible.

Bosch just watched without saying a word. Newell looked as if he could be no more than three years out of law school. Because the arrest had not made a splash in the papers or on TV yet, it had not received the attention of one of the senior attorneys in the filings division. It had gone to Newell on the routine rotation.

When the tape was done, Newell made a few more notes to look as if he knew what he was doing and then looked up at Bosch.

'You haven't said anything about what was in his house.'

'I didn't find anything on the quick search I made last night. There are others there now, with a warrant, doing a more thorough job.'

'Well, I hope they find something.'

'Why, you've got the case right there.'

'And it is a good case, Bosch. Really good work.'

'Coming from you, that means a lot.'

Newell looked at him and narrowed his eyes. He wasn't sure what to make of that.

'But, uh . . .'

'But what?'

'Well, there's no question we can file with this. There is a lot here.'

'But what?'

'I'm looking at it from a defense lawyer's perspective. What really do we have here? A lot of coincidences. He's left-handed, he smokes, he knew details about the Doll-maker. But those things are not hard evidence. They can apply to a lot of people.'

Bosch started lighting a cigarette.

'Please don't do –'

He exhaled and blew the smoke across the desk.

'– never mind.'

'What about the note and the postmark?'

'That's good but it is complicated and difficult to grasp. A good lawyer could make a jury see it as just another coincidence. He could confuse the issue, is what I'm trying to say.'

'What about the tape, Newell? We have him confessing on tape. What more do you –'

'But during the confession he disavows the confession.'

'Not at the end.'

'Look, I'm not planning on using the tape.'

'What are you talking about?'

'You know what I'm talking about. He confessed before you advised him. It brings up the specter of entrapment.'

'There is no entrapment. He knew I was a cop and he knew his rights whether I advised him or not. He had a fucking gun on *me*. He freely made those statements. When he was formally arrested, I advised him.'

'But he searched you for a wire. That is a clear indication of his desire not to be taped. Plus, he dropped the bomb – his most damaging statement – after you cuffed him but before you advised him. That could be dicey.'

'You're going to use the tape.'

Newell looked at him a long time. A red blotchiness appeared on his young cheeks.

'You are not in a position to tell me what I'm going to use, Bosch. Besides, if that's all we go with it will probably be up to the state court of appeals if we use it, because if Bremmer has any kind of a lawyer at all that's where he'll take it. We'll win the question here in superior because half the judges on those benches worked in the DA's office at one time or another. But when it gets up to appeals or to the state supreme court in San Francisco, it's anybody's guess. Is that what you want? To wait a couple years and have it blown out then? Or do you want to get it done correctly right from the get go?'

Bosch leaned forward and looked angrily at the young lawyer.

'Look, we're still working other angles. We're not done. There will be more evidence accumulated. But we have to charge this guy or let him go. We've got forty-eight hours from last night to file. But if we don't file right now with no bail, he'll grab a lawyer and get a bail hearing. The judge won't honor the no-bail arrest if you haven't even filed a single charge yet. So file on him now. We'll get all the evidence you need to back it up.'

Newell nodded as if he agreed but said, 'Thing is, I like to have the whole package, everything we can get, when I file a case. That way we know how we are going to work the prosecution, right from the start. We know if we are going to go with a plea bargain or go balls to the wall.'

Bosch got up and walked to the office's open door. He stepped into the hall and looked at the plastic name plate affixed to the wall outside. Then he came back in.

'Bosch, what are you doing?'

'It's funny. I thought you were a filing deputy. I didn't know you were a trial deputy, too.'

Newell dropped his pencil on his pad. His face got redder, the blotches spreading to his forehead.

'Look, I am a filing deputy. But it is part of my responsibility to make sure we have the best case possible from the get go. Every case that comes through that door I could file on, but that's not the point. The point is to have good, credible evidence and a lot of it. Cases that don't backfire. So I push, Bosch. I –'

'How old are you?'

'What?'

'How old?'

'Twenty-six. What's that got to –'

'Listen to me, you little prick. Don't you ever call me by my last name again. I was making cases like this before you cracked your first law book and I'll be making them long after you move your convertible Saab and your self-centered white-bread show to Century City. You can call me Detective or Detective Bosch, you can even call me Harry. But don't you ever call me just Bosch again, understand?'

Newell's mouth had dropped open.

397

'Do you understand?'

'Sure.'

'Another thing, we're going to get more evidence and we're going to get it as soon as we can. But, in the meantime, you're going to file one charge of first-degree murder on Bremmer with a no-bail hold because we are going to make sure – from the get go, Mr Newell – that this scumbag never sees the light of day again.

'Then, when we have more evidence, if you are still attached to this case, you will file multiple counts under theories of linkage between the deaths. At no time will you worry about the so-called package you will hand off to the trial attorney. The trial attorney will make those decisions. Because we both know that you are really just a clerk, a clerk who files what is brought to him. If you knew enough to even sit in court next to a trial attorney you would not be here. Do you have any questions?'

'No,' he said quickly.

'No, what?'

'No ques – No, Detective Bosch.'

Bosch went back to Irving's conference room and used the rest of the morning to work up an application for a search warrant to collect hair, blood and saliva specimens along with a dental mold from Bremmer.

Before taking it to the courthouse, he attended a brief meeting of the task force where they all reported on their respective assignments.

Edgar said he had been to Sybil Brand and had shown Georgia Stern, who was still being held there, a photo of Bremmer but she could not identify him as her attacker. She could not rule him out, either.

Sheehan said he and Opelt had shown the mug shot of Bremmer to the manager of the storage facility at Bing's and the man said Bremmer might have been one of the renters of the storage rooms two years earlier but he couldn't be sure.

He said it was too long ago to remember well enough to send a man to the gas chamber.

'The guy's a wimp,' Sheehan said. 'My feeling was he recognized Bremmer but was too scared to stick it in all the way. We're going to hit him again tomorrow.'

Rollenberger called the presidents up on the rover and they reported from Bremmer's house that there was nothing yet. No tapes, no bodies, nothing.

'I say we go for a warrant to dig up the yard, under the foundation,' Nixon said.

'We might go to that,' Rollenberger radioed back. 'Meantime, keep at it.'

Lastly, Yde reported by rover that he and Mayfield were getting the runaround from the *Times* lawyers and had not yet been able to so much as approach Bremmer's desk in the newsroom.

Rollenberger reported that Heikes and Rector were out of pocket, running down background on Bremmer. After that, he said that Irving had scheduled a five o'clock press conference to discuss the case with the media. If anything new was discovered, let Rollenberger know before then.

'That's it,' Rollenberger said.

Bosch got up to head out.

The medical clinic on the high-power floor of the county jail reminded Bosch of Frankenstein's laboratory. There were chains on every bed and rings bolted to the tile walls to tether patients to. The pull-down lights over each bed were caged in steel so patients couldn't get to the light bulbs and use them as weapons. The tile was supposed to be white but over the years had surrendered to a depressing off-yellow.

Bosch and Edgar stood in the doorway to one of the bays where there were six beds and watched as Bremmer, who was lying in the sixth bed, was given a shot of sodium pentothal to make him more cooperative, more malleable. He had refused to give the court-ordered dental mold and samples of blood, saliva and hair.

After the drug began to take effect, the doctor pulled open the reporter's mouth, put two clamps in to hold it open and pushed a little square block of clay over the front upper teeth. He then followed the same procedure with the lower front teeth. When he was done, he relaxed the clamps and Bremmer appeared to be asleep.

'If we asked him something now, he'd tell the truth, right?' Edgar asked. 'That's truth serum they're givin' him, right?'

'Supposedly,' Bosch said. 'But it'd prob'ly get the case thrown out of court.'

The little gray blocks with teeth indentations were slid into plastic cases. The doctor closed them and handed them to Edgar. He then drew blood, wiped a cotton swab in Bremmer's mouth and cut snippets of hair from the suspect's head, chest and pubic area. He put these in envelopes which went into a small cardboard box like the kind chicken nuggets come in at fast-food restaurants.

Bosch took the box and they left then, Bosch going to the coroner's office to see Amado, the analyst, and Edgar going to Cal State Northridge to see the forensic archaeologist who had helped with the concrete blonde reconstruction.

By quarter to five, everyone was back in the conference room but Edgar. They were all milling about, waiting to watch Irving's press conference. There had been no other progress since noon.

'Where do you think he stashed everything, Harry?' Nixon asked as he was pouring coffee.

'I don't know. Probably has a storage locker somewhere. If he has tapes, I doubt he'd part with them. He probably has a drop somewhere. We'll find them.'

'What about the other women?'

'They're out there somewhere, under the city. Only way they'll come up is by luck.'

'Or if Bremmer talks,' Irving said. He had just come in.

There was a good feeling in the room. Despite the day's

slow progress, everyone to a man had no doubt they finally had the right man. And that certainty validated what they were about. So they wanted to drink coffee and hang out. Even Irving.

At five minutes before five, when Irving was going over some of the reports typed during the day for the last time before facing the media, Edgar came up on the rover. Rollenberger quickly picked up a radio and answered back.

'What do you have, Team Five?'

'Is Harry there?'

'Yes, Team Five, Team Six is present. What have you got?'

'I've got the package. Definite match between the suspect's teeth and the impressions on the victim.'

'Roger that, Team Five.'

There was a whoop in the conference room and a lot of backslapping and high fives. 'He is going down,' Nixon exclaimed.

Irving picked up his papers and headed for the hallway door. He wanted to be on time. At the doorway he passed close to Bosch.

'We're gold, Bosch. Thanks.'

Bosch just nodded.

A few hours later Bosch was back at the county jail. It was after lock-down so the deputies wouldn't bring Bremmer out to see him. Instead, he had to go into the high-power module, the deputies watching him on remote cameras. He walked along the row of cells to 6-36 and looked through the wired one-foot-square window in the single-piece steel door.

Bremmer was on 'keep away' status, so he was in there alone. He didn't notice Bosch watching. He lay on the bottom bunk on his back, his hands laced behind his head. His eyes were open and staring straight up. Bosch recognized the withdrawal state he had seen for a moment the night before. It was as if he wasn't there. Bosch leaned his mouth to the screen.

401

'Bremmer, you play bridge?'

Bremmer looked over at him, only moving his eyes.

'What?'

'I said, do you play bridge? You know, the card game?'

'What the fuck do you want, Bosch?'

'I just dropped by to tell you a little while ago they added three more to the one this morning. Linkage. You just got the concrete blonde and the two from before, the ones we first gave to the Dollmaker. You also got an attempted murder on the survivor.'

'Oh, well, what's the difference? You got one, you got 'em all. All I need to do is beat the Chandler case and the others fall like dominoes.'

'Except that isn't going to happen. We got your teeth, Bremmer, just as good as fingerprints. And we got the rest. I just came from the coroner's. They matched your pubic hair to samples found on victims seven and eleven – the ones we gave the Dollmaker credit for. You ought to think about dealing, Bremmer. Tell where the others are and they'll probably let you live. That's why I asked about bridge.'

'What about it?'

'Well, I hear there's some guys up at Q play a good bridge game. They're always looking for new blood. You'll probably like 'em, have a lot in common.'

'Why don't you leave me alone, Bosch?'

'I will. I will. But just so you know it, man, they're on death row. But don't worry about that, when you get there you'll get a lot of card playing in. What's the average lead time? Eight, ten years before they gas somebody? That's not bad. Unless, of course, you talk a deal.'

'There is no deal, Bosch. Get out of here.'

'I'm going. Believe me, it's nice to be able to walk out of this place. I'll see you then, okay? You know, in eight or ten years. I'm going to be there, Bremmer. When they strap you in. I'm going to be watching through the glass when the gas comes up. And then I'll come out and tell the reporters how you died. I'll tell them you went screaming, that you weren't much of a man.'

'Fuck you, Bosch.'

'Yeah, fuck me. See you then, Bremmer.'

THIRTY-THREE

After Bremmer's arraignment Tuesday morning, Bosch got permission to take the rest of the week off in lieu of receiving all of the overtime he had built up on the case.

He spent the time hanging around the house, doing odd jobs and taking it easy. He replaced the wood railing on the back porch with new lengths of weather-treated oak. And while he was at Home Depot getting the wood, he also picked up new cushions for the chairs and the chaise lounge on the porch.

He began reading the *Times* sports pages again, noting the statistical changes in team ranks and player performances.

And, occasionally, he'd read one of the many stories the *Times* ran in the Metro section about what was becoming known nationwide as the Follower case. But it didn't really hold his fascination. He knew too much about the case already. The one interest he had in the stories was in the details about Bremmer that were coming out. The *Times* had sent a staffer to Texas, where Bremmer had been raised in an Austin suburb, and the reporter had returned with a story culled from old children's-court files and neighborhood gossip. He'd been raised by his mother in a single-parent home; his father, an itinerant blues musician, he saw once or twice a year at the most. The mother was described by former neighbors as a disciplinarian and plain mean-spirited when it came to her son.

The worst thing that the reporter came up with on Bremmer was that he was suspected but never charged in the arson of a neighbor's toolshed when he was thirteen. It was said by neighbors that his mother punished him as if he had committed the crime anyway, not allowing him to leave their tiny house the rest of the summer. The neighbors said that around the same time the neighborhood began to experience a problem with pets disappearing but this was never attributed to young Bremmer. At least until now. Now the neighbors seemed engaged in blaming Bremmer for any malady that beset their street that year.

A year after the fire Bremmer's mother died of alcoholism and the boy was raised after that on a state boys' farm, where the young charges wore white shirts and blue ties and blazers to classes, even when the thermometer went off the chart. The story said he worked as a reporter on one of the farm's student newspapers, thus beginning a journalism career that would eventually take him to Los Angeles.

His history was all grist for people like Locke to consider, to use as fuel for speculation on how the child Bremmer made the adult Bremmer do the things he did. It just made Bosch feel sad. He couldn't help, however, but stare for a long time at the photo of the mother the *Times* had dug up somewhere. In the picture she stood in front of the door to a sun-burned ranch-style house with her hand on a young Bremmer's shoulder. She had bleached-blonde hair and a provocative figure and large chest. She wore too much makeup, Bosch thought as he stared at the picture.

Aside from the Bremmer articles, the story he read and reread several times was in the Metro section of Thursday's paper. It was about the burial of Beatrice Fontenot. Sylvia was quoted in the article and it described how the Grant High teacher had read some of the girl's schoolwork at the memorial service. There was a photo from the service but Sylvia wasn't in it. It was of Beatrice's mother's stoic, tear-lined face at the funeral. Bosch kept the Metro page on the table next to the chaise lounge and read the story again every time he sat down there.

*

When he grew restless around the house he would drive. Down out of the hills, he'd head across the Valley with no place in particular to go. He'd drive forty minutes to have a hamburger at an In 'N' Out stand. Having grown up in the city, he liked to drive it, to know every one of its streets and corners. Once on Thursday and again on Friday morning his drives took him past Grant High but he never saw Sylvia through the windows of the classrooms as he went by. He felt sick at heart when he thought of her but he knew the closest he could come to her was to drive by the school. It was her move and he must wait for her to make it.

On Friday afternoon, when he came back from his drive, he saw the message light flashing on his phone machine and his hopes rushed into his throat. He thought maybe she had seen his car and was calling because she knew how his heart hurt. But when he played the message it was just Edgar asking him to call.

Eventually, he did.

'Harry, you're missing everything?'

'Yeah, what?'

'Well, we had *People* magazine in here yesterday.'

'I'll watch for you on the cover.'

'Just kidding. Actually, we've got big developments.'

'Yeah, what?'

'All this publicity was bound to do us good. Some lady over in Culver City called up and said she recognized Bremmer, that he had a storage locker at her place, but under the name Woodward. We got a warrant and popped it first thing this morning.'

'Yeah.'

'Locke was right. He videotaped. We found the tapes. His trophies.'

'Jesus.'

'Yeah. If there was ever a doubt there ain't now. Got seven tapes and the camera. He must not have taped the first two, the ones we thought were the Dollmaker's. But we got tapes of seven others including Chandler and Maggie Cum Loudly. Bastard taped everything. Just horrible stuff. They're working up formal IDs on the other five victims on the tapes, but it looks like it's going to be the ones on the list Mora came up with. Gallery and the other four porno chicks.'

'What else was in the locker?'

'Everything. We've got everything. We've got cuffs, belts, gags, a knife and a Glock nine. His whole killing kit. He must've used the gun to control them. That's why there was no sign of a struggle at Chandler's. He used the gun. We figure he'd hold it on them until he could cuff 'em and gag 'em. From the tapes, it looks like all the kills took place in Bremmer's house, the rear bedroom. Except Chandler, of course. She got it at home. . . . Those tapes, Harry, I couldn't watch.'

Bosch could imagine. He envisioned the scenes and felt an unexpected flutter in his heart, as if it had torn loose inside of him and was banging against his ribs like a bird trying to break out of its cage.

'Anyway, the DA's got it and the big development is Bremmer's going to talk.'

'He is?'

'Yeah, he heard we had the tapes and everything else. I guess he told his lawyer to deal. He's going to get life without the possibility of parole in exchange for leading us to the bodies and letting the shrinks have at him, study what makes him tick. My vote is they squash him like a fly, but I guess they are considering the families and science.'

Bosch was silent. Bremmer would live. At first he didn't know what to think. Then he realized he could live with the deal. It had bothered him that those women might never be found. That was why he had visited Bremmer at the jail the day charges were first filed. Whether the victims had families who cared or not, he didn't want to leave them down there in the black chasm of the unknown.

It wasn't a bad deal, Bosch decided. Bremmer would be

alive, but he wouldn't be living. It might even be worse for him than the gas chamber. And that would be justice, he thought.

'Anyway,' Edgar said, 'thought you'd want to know.'

'Yeah.'

'It's a weird fuckin' thing, you know? It being Bremmer. It's weirder than if it was Mora, man. A reporter! And, man, I knew the guy, too.'

'Yeah, well, a lot of us did. I guess nobody knows anybody like they think.'

'Yeah. Seeya, Harry.'

Late that afternoon, he stood on the back deck, leaning forward on his new oak railing, looking out into the pass and thinking about the black heart. Its rhythm was so strong it could set the beat of a whole city. He knew it would always be the background beat, the cadence, of his own life. Bremmer would be banished now, hidden away forever, but he knew there would be another after him. And another after him. The black heart does not beat alone.

He lit a cigarette and thought about Honey Chandler, crowding his last view of her from his mind with the vision of her holding forth in court. That would always be her place in his mind. There had been something so pure and distilled about her fury – like the blue flame on a match before it burns out on its own. Even directed at him he could appreciate it.

His mind wandered to the statue at the courthouse steps. He still couldn't think of her name. A concrete blonde, Chandler had called her. Bosch wondered what Chandler had thought about justice at the end. At her end. He knew there was no justice without hope. Did she still have any hope left at the end? He believed that she did. Like the pure blue flame dimming to nothing, it was still there. Still hot. It was what allowed her to beat Bremmer.

He did not hear Sylvia until she stepped out onto the porch.

He looked up and saw her there and wanted to go to her immediately, but held back. She was wearing blue jeans and a dark blue denim shirt. He'd bought the shirt for her birthday and he took that as a good sign. He guessed she had probably come from school, it having recessed for the weekend only an hour earlier.

'I called your office and they told me you were off. I thought I would come by to see how you were. I've been reading all about the case.'

'I'm okay, Sylvia. How are you?'

'I'm fine.'

'How are we?'

She smiled a little at that.

'Sounds like one of those bumper stickers you see. "How'm I driving?" . . . Harry, I don't know how we are. I guess that's why I'm here.'

There was an uneasy silence as she looked around the porch and out into the pass. Bosch crushed his cigarette out and dropped it in an old coffee can he kept by the door.

'Hey, new cushions.'

'Yeah.'

'Harry, you have to understand why I needed some time. It's –'

'I do.'

'Let me finish. I rehearsed this enough times, I'd like to get a chance to actually say it to you. I just wanted to say that it is going to be very hard for me, for us, if we go on. It is going to be hard to deal with our pasts, our secrets, and most of all what you do, what you bring home with you . . .'

Bosch waited for her to continue. He knew she wasn't done.

'I know I don't have to remind you, but I've been through it before with a man I loved. And I saw it all go bad and – you know how it ended. There was a lot of pain for both of us. So you have to understand why I needed to take a step back and take a look at this. At us.'

He nodded but she wasn't looking at him. Her not looking concerned him more than her words. He couldn't bring himself to speak, though. He didn't know what he could say.

'You live a very hard struggle, Harry. Your life, I mean. A cop. Yet with all your baggage I see and know there are still very noble things about you.'

Now she looked at him.

'I do love you, Harry. I want to try to keep that alive because it's one of the best things about my life. One of the best things I know. I know it will be hard. But that might make it all the better. Who knows?'

He went to her then.

'Who knows?' he said.

And they held each other for a long time, his face next to hers, smelling her hair and skin. He held the back of her neck as though it was as fragile as a porcelain vase.

After a while they broke apart but only long enough to get on the chaise lounge together. They sat silently, just holding each other, for the longest time – until the sky started to dim and turn red and purple over the San Gabriels. Bosch knew there were still the secrets he carried, but they would keep for now. And he would avoid that black place of loneliness for just a while longer.

'Do you want to go away this weekend?' he asked. 'Get away from the city? We could take that trip up to Lone Pine. Stay in a cabin tomorrow night.'

'That would be wonderful. I could – We could use it.'

A few minutes later she added, 'We might not be able to get a cabin, Harry. There's so few of them and they're usually booked by Friday.'

'I already have one on reserve.'

She turned around so she could face him. She smiled slyly and said, 'Oh, so you knew all the time. You were just hanging around waiting for me to come back. No sleepless nights, no surprise.'

He didn't smile. He shook his head and for a few

moments he looked out at the dying light reflected on the west wall of the San Gabriels.

'I didn't know, Sylvia,' he said. 'I hoped.'

The Last
Coyote

Michael
Connelly

This is for Marcus Grupa

✧ ✧ ✧ ✧ ✧ ✧ ✧

'A ny thoughts that you'd like to start with?'
'Thoughts on what?'
'Well, on anything. On the incident.'
'On the incident? Yes, I have some thoughts.'
She waited but he didn't continue. He had decided before he even got to Chinatown that this would be the way he would be. He'd make her have to pull every single word out of him.

'Could you share them with me, Detective Bosch?' she finally asked. 'That is the purpose of –'

'My thoughts are that this is bullshit. Total bullshit. That's the purpose. That's all.'

'No, wait. How do you mean, bullshit?'

'I mean, okay, I pushed the guy. I guess I hit him. I'm not sure exactly what happened but I'm not denying anything. So, fine, suspend me, transfer me, take it to a Board of Rights, whatever. But going this way is bullshit. ISL is bullshit. I mean, why do I have to come here three times a week to talk to you like I'm some kind of – you don't even know me, you don't know anything about me. Why do I have to talk to you? Why do you have to sign off on this?'

'Well, the technical answer is right there in your own statement. Rather than discipline you the department wants to treat you. You've been placed on involuntary stress leave, which means –'

I

'I know what it means and that's what's bullshit. Somebody arbitrarily decides I'm under stress and that gives the department the power to keep me off the job indefinitely, or at least until I jump through enough hoops for you.'

'Nothing about this was arbitrary. It was predicated on your actions, which I think clearly show –'

'What happened had nothing to do with stress. What it was about was ... never mind. Like I said, it's bullshit. So why don't we just cut through it and get to the point. What do I have to do to get back to my job?'

He could see the anger flare behind her eyes. His total disavowal of her science and skill cut to her pride. Quickly the anger was gone, though. Dealing with cops all the time, she had to be used to it.

'Can't you see that all of this is for your own welfare? I have to assume the top managers of this department clearly see you as a valued asset or you wouldn't be here. They'd have put you on a disciplinary track and you'd be on your way out. Instead, they are doing what they can to preserve your career and its incumbent value to the department.'

'Valued asset? I'm a cop, not an asset. And when you're out there on the street nobody's thinking about incumbent value. What does that mean, anyway? Am I going to have to listen to words like that in here?'

She cleared her throat before speaking sternly.

'You have a problem, Detective Bosch. And it goes far beyond the incident that resulted in your being placed on leave. That's what these sessions are going to be all about. Do you understand? This incident is not unique. You have had problems before. What I am trying to do, what I have to do before I can sign off on your return to duty in any capacity, is get you to take a look at yourself. What are you doing? What are you about? Why do these problems happen to you? I want these sessions to be an open

2

dialogue where I ask a few questions and you speak your mind, but with a purpose. Not to harass me and my profession or the leadership of the department. But to talk about you. This is about you in here, no one else.'

Harry Bosch just looked at her silently. He wanted a cigarette but would never ask her if he could smoke. He would never acknowledge in front of her that he had the habit. If he did, she might start talking about oral fixations or nicotine crutches. He took a deep breath instead and looked at the woman on the other side of the desk. Carmen Hinojos was a small woman with a friendly face and manner. Bosch knew she wasn't a bad person. He'd actually heard good things about her from others who had been sent to Chinatown. She was just doing her job here and his anger was not really directed at her. He knew she was probably smart enough to know that, too.

'Look, I'm sorry,' she said. 'I should not have started with that kind of open question. I know that this is an emotional subject with you. Let's try to start again. By the way, you can smoke if you'd like.'

'Is that in the file, too?'

'It's not in the file. It didn't need to be. It's your hand, the way you keep bringing it up to your mouth. Have you been trying to quit?'

'No. But it's a city office. You know the rules.'

It was a thin excuse. He violated that law every day at the Hollywood Station.

'That's not the rule in here. I don't want you to think of this as being part of Parker Center or part of the city. That's the chief reason these offices are away from that. There are no rules like that here.'

'Doesn't matter where we are. You're still working for the LAPD.'

'Try to believe that you are away from the Los Angeles Police Department. When you are in here, try to believe

3

that you're just coming to see a friend. To talk. You can say anything here.'

But he knew she could not be seen as a friend. Never. There was too much at stake here. Just the same, he nodded once to please her.

'That's not very convincing.'

He hiked his shoulders as if to say it was the best he could do, and it was.

'By the way, if you want I could hypnotize you, get rid of your dependency on nicotine.'

'If I wanted to quit, I could do it. People are either smokers or they're not. I am.'

'Yes. It's perhaps the most obvious symptom of a self-destructive nature.'

'Excuse me, am I on leave because I smoke? Is that what this is about?'

'I think you know what it's about.'

He said nothing else, remembering his decision to say as little as possible.

'Well, let's continue then,' she said. 'You've been on leave ... let's see, Tuesday a week?'

'Right.'

'What have you been doing with your time?'

'Filling out FEMA forms mostly.'

'FEMA?'

'My house was red-tagged.'

'The earthquake was three months ago. Why have you waited?'

'I've been busy. I've been working.'

'I see. Did you have insurance?'

'Don't say "I see," because you don't. You couldn't possibly see things the way I do. The answer is no, no insurance. Like most everybody else, I was living in denial. Isn't that what you people call it? I bet you had insurance.'

'Yes. How bad was your house hit?'

4

'Depends on who you ask. The city inspectors say it's totaled and I can't even go inside. I think it's fine. Just needs some work. They know me by name at Home Depot now. And I've had contractors do some of it. It'll be done soon and I'll appeal the red tag. I've got a lawyer.'

'You're living there still?'

He nodded.

'Now that's denial, Detective Bosch. I don't think you should be doing that.'

'I don't think you have any say about what I do outside my job with the department.'

She raised her hands in a hands-off manner.

'Well, while I don't condone it, I suppose it serves its purpose. I think it's good that you have something to keep you occupied. Though I'd much rather it be a sport or a hobby or maybe plans for a trip out of town, I think it's important to keep busy, to keep your mind off the incident.'

Bosch smirked.

'What?'

'I don't know. Everybody keeps calling it the incident. It kind've reminds me of how people called it the Vietnam conflict, not the war.'

'Then what would you call what happened?'

'I don't know. But incident … it sounds like … I don't know. Antiseptic. Listen, Doctor, let's go back a minute. I don't want to take a trip out of town, okay? My job is in homicide. It's what I do. And I'd really like to get back to it. I might be able to do some good, you know.'

'If the department lets you.'

'If you do. You know it's going to be up to you.'

'Perhaps. Do you notice that you speak of your job as if it's a mission of some sort?'

'That's about right. Like the Holy Grail.'

He said it with sarcasm. This was getting intolerable and it was only the first session.

'Is it? Do you believe your mission in life is to solve murders, to put bad people in jail?'

He used the shoulder hike to say he didn't know. He stood up and walked to the window and looked down on Hill Street. The sidewalks were crowded with pedestrians. Every time he had been down here they were crowded. He noticed a couple of Caucasian women walking along. They stood out in the sea of Asian faces like raisins in rice. They passed the window of a Chinese butcher shop and Bosch saw a row of smoked ducks hanging whole, by their necks.

Farther up the road he saw the Hollywood Freeway overpass, the dark windows of the old sheriff's jail and the Criminal Courts building behind it. To the left of that he could see the City Hall tower. Black construction tarps hung around the top floors. It looked like some kind of mourning gesture but he knew the tarps were to hold debris from falling while earthquake repairs were made. Looking past City Hall, Bosch could see the Glass House. Parker Center, police headquarters.

'Tell me what your mission is,' Hinojos said quietly from behind him. 'I'd like to hear you put it in words.'

He sat back down and tried to think of a way to explain himself but finally just shook his head.

'I can't.'

'Well, I want you to think about that. Your mission. What is it really? Think about that.'

'What's your mission, Doctor?'

'That's not our concern here.'

'Of course it is.'

'Look, Detective, this is the only personal question I will answer. These dialogues are not to be about me. They are about you. My mission, I believe, is to help the men

6

and women of this department. That's the narrow focus. And by doing that, on a grander scale I help the community, I help the people of this city. The better the cops are that we have out on the street, the better we all are. The safer we all are. Okay?'

'That's fine. When I think about my mission, do you want me to shorten it to a couple sentences like that and rehearse it to the point that it sounds like I'm reading out of the dictionary?'

'Mr – uh, Detective Bosch, if you want to be cute and contentious the whole time, we are not going to get anywhere, which means you are not going to get back to your job anytime soon. Is that what you're looking for here?'

He raised his hands in surrender. She looked down at the yellow legal pad on the desk. With her eyes off him, he was able to study her. Carmen Hinojos had tiny brown hands she kept on the desk in front of her. No rings on either hand. She held an expensive-looking pen in her right hand. Bosch always thought expensive pens were used by people overly concerned with image. But maybe he was wrong about her. She wore her dark brown hair tied back. She wore glasses with thin tortoiseshell frames. She should have had braces when she was a kid but didn't. She looked up from the pad and their eyes locked.

'I am told this inci – this … situation coincided with or was close to the time of the dissolving of a romantic relationship.'

'Told by who?'

'It's in the background material given to me. The sources of this material are not important.'

'Well, they are important because you've got bad sources. It had nothing to do with what happened. The dissolving, as you call it, was almost three months ago.'

'The pain of these things can last much longer than that.

7

I know this is personal and may be difficult but I think we should talk about this. The reason is that it will help give me a basis for your emotional state at the time the assault took place. Is that a problem?'

Bosch waved her on with his hand.

'How long did this relationship last?'

'About a year.'

'Marriage?'

'No.'

'Was it talked about?'

'No, not really. Never out in the open.'

'Did you live together?'

'Sometimes. We both kept our places.'

'Is the separation final?'

'I think so.'

Saying it out loud seemed to be the first time Bosch acknowledged that Sylvia Moore was gone from his life for good.

'Was this separation by mutual agreement?'

He cleared his throat. He didn't want to talk about this but he wanted it over with.

'I guess you could say it was mutual agreement, but I didn't know about it until she was packed. You know, three months ago we were holding each other in bed while the house was shaking apart on the pad. You could say she was gone before the aftershocks ended.'

'They still haven't.'

'Just a figure of speech.'

'Are you saying the earthquake was the cause of the breakup of this relationship?'

'No, I'm not saying that. All I'm saying is that's when it happened. Right after. She's a teacher up in the Valley and her school got wrecked. The kids were moved to other schools and the district didn't need as many teachers. They offered sabbaticals and she took one. She left town.'

'Was she scared of another earthquake or was she scared of you?'

She looked pointedly at him.

'Why would she be scared of me?'

He knew he sounded a little too defensive.

'I don't know. I'm just asking questions. Did you give her a reason to be scared?'

Bosch hesitated. It was a question he had never really touched on in his private thoughts about the breakup.

'If you mean in a physical way, no, she wasn't scared and I gave her no reason to be.'

Hinojos nodded and wrote something on her pad. It bothered Bosch that she would make a note about this.

'Look, it's got nothing to do with what happened at the station last week.'

'Why did she leave? What was the real reason?'

He looked away. He was angry. This was how it was going to be. She would ask whatever she wanted. Invade him wherever there was an opening.

'I don't know.'

'That answer is not acceptable in here. I think you do know, or at least have your own beliefs as to why she would leave. You must.'

'She found out who I was.'

'She found out who you were, what does that mean?'

'You'd have to ask her. She said it. But she's in Venice. The one in Italy.'

'Well, then what do you think she meant by it?'

'It doesn't matter what I think. She's the one who said it and she's the one who left.'

'Don't fight me, Detective Bosch. Please. There is nothing I want more than for you to get back to your job. As I said, that's my mission. To get you back there if you can go. But you make it difficult by being difficult.'

'Maybe that's what she found out. Maybe that's who I am.'

'I doubt the reason is as simplistic as that.'

'Sometimes I don't.'

She looked at her watch and leaned forward, dissatisfaction with the session showing on her face.

'Okay, Detective, I understand how uncomfortable you are. We're going to move on, but I suspect we will have to come back to this issue. I want you to give it some thought. Try to put your feelings into words.'

She waited for him to say something but he didn't.

'Let's try talking about what happened last week again. I understand it stemmed from a case involving the murder of a prostitute.'

'Yes.'

'It was brutal?'

'That's just a word. Means different things to different people.'

'True, but taking its meaning to you, was it a brutal homicide?'

'Yes, it was brutal. I think almost all of them are. Somebody dies, it's brutal. For them.'

'And you took the suspect into custody?'

'Yes, my partner and I. I mean, no. He came in voluntarily to answer questions.'

'Did this case affect you more than, say, other cases have in the past?'

'Maybe, I don't know.'

'Why would that be?'

'You mean why did I care about a prostitute? I didn't. Not more than any other victim. But in homicide there is one rule that I have when it comes to the cases I get.'

'What is that rule?'

'Everybody counts or nobody counts.'

'Explain it.'

'Just what I said. Everybody counts or nobody counts. That's it. It means I bust my ass to make a case whether it's a prostitute or the mayor's wife. That's my rule.'

'I understand. Now, let's go to this specific case. I'm interested in hearing your description of what happened after the arrest and the reasons you may have for your violent actions at the Hollywood Division.'

'Is this being taped?'

'No, Detective, whatever you tell me is protected. At the end of these sessions I will simply make a recommendation to Assistant Chief Irving. The details of the sessions will never be divulged. The recommendations I make are usually less than half a page and contain no details from the dialogues.'

'You wield a lot of power with that half page.'

She didn't respond. Bosch thought for a moment while looking at her. He thought he might be able to trust her but his natural instinct and experience was that he should trust no one. She seemed to know his dilemma and waited him out.

'You want to hear my side of it?'

'Yes, I do.'

'Okay, I'll tell you what happened.'

❖ ❖ ❖ ❖ ❖ ❖ ❖

Bosch smoked along the way home but realized that what he really wanted was not a cigarette, but a drink to deaden his nerves. He looked at his watch and decided it was too early to stop at a bar. He settled for another cigarette and home.

After negotiating the drive up Woodrow Wilson, he parked at the curb a half block from the house and walked back. He could hear gentle piano music, something classical, coming from the home of one of his neighbors but he couldn't tell which house. He didn't really know any of his neighbors or which one might have a piano player in the family. He ducked under the yellow tape strung in front of the property and entered through the door in the carport.

This was his routine, to park down the street and hide the fact that he lived in his own house. The house had been red-tagged as uninhabitable after the earthquake and ordered demolished by a city inspector. But Bosch had ignored both orders, cut the lock on the electric box, and had been living in it for three months.

It was a small house with redwood siding that stood on steel pylons anchored in the sedimentary bedrock folded and formed as the Santa Monica Mountains rose out of the desert during the Mesozoic and Cenozoic eras. The pylons had held true in their moorings during the quake, but the overlying house had shifted atop them, breaking partially free of the pylons and seismic bolts. It slid. All of about two inches. Still, it was enough. Though short on distance the slide was long on damage. Inside, the woodframe house flexed and window and door frames lost their square. The glass shattered, the front door became terminally closed, frozen in a frame that had canted to the north with the rest of the house. If Bosch wanted to open that door, he would probably need to borrow the police tank with the battering ram. As it was, he'd had to use a crowbar to open the carport door. Now that door served as the main entrance to his home.

Bosch had paid a contractor five thousand dollars to jack the house up and then over the two inches it had moved. It was then put down in its proper space and rebolted to the pylons. After that, Bosch was content to work as time allowed on reframing windows and interior doors himself. The glass came first and in the months after that he reframed and rehung the interior doors. He worked from books on carpentry and often had to do individual projects two and three times until he had them reasonably correct. But he found the work enjoyable and even therapeutic. Working with his hands became a respite from his job in homicide. He left the front door as it was, thinking that somehow it was fitting, that it was a salute to the power of nature. And he was content to use the side door.

All of his efforts did not save the house from the city's list of condemned structures. Gowdy, the building inspector who had been assigned to this section of the hills, kept it red-tagged as condemned, despite Bosch's work, and so began the hiding game in which Bosch made his entrances and exits as surreptitiously as a spy's to a foreign embassy. He tacked black plastic tarps over the inside of the front windows so they would emit no telltale light. And he always watched for Gowdy. Gowdy was his nemesis.

13

In the meantime, Bosch hired a lawyer to appeal the inspector's edict.

The carport door granted entry directly into the kitchen. After he came in, Bosch opened the refrigerator and retrieved a can of Coca-Cola, then stood in the doorway of the aging appliance letting its breath cool him while he studied its contents for something suitable for dinner. He knew exactly what was on the shelves and in the drawers but still he looked. It was as if he hoped for the surprise appearance of a forgotten steak or chicken breast. He followed this routine with the refrigerator often. It was the ritual of a man who was alone. He knew this also.

On the back deck Bosch drank the soda and ate a sandwich consisting of five-day-old bread and slices of meat from plastic packages. He wished he had potato chips to go with it because he would undoubtedly be hungry later after having only the sandwich for dinner.

He stood at the railing looking down at the Hollywood Freeway, near capacity now with the Monday-evening commute. He had gotten out of downtown just before the crest of the rush-hour wave had broken. He would have to guard against going overtime on the sessions with the police psychologist. They were scheduled for 3:30 P.M. on Mondays, Wednesdays and Fridays. Did Carmen Hinojos ever let a session go over? he wondered. Or was hers a nine-to-five mission?

From his vantage on the mountain, he could see almost all northbound lanes of the freeway as it cut through the Cahuenga Pass to the San Fernando Valley. He was reviewing what had been said during the session, trying to decide whether it was a good or bad session, but his focus drifted and he began to watch the point where the freeway came into view as it crested the pass. Absentmindedly, he would choose two cars that came over about even with each other and follow them through the mile-long segment of the freeway that was visible from the deck. He'd pick one or the other and follow the race, unknown to its drivers, until the finish line, which was the Lankershim Boulevard exit.

After a few minutes of this he realized what he was doing and spun around, away from the freeway.

'Jesus,' he said out loud.

He knew then that keeping his hands busy would not be enough while he was away from his job. He went back inside and got a bottle of Henry's from the refrigerator. Right after he opened the beer the phone rang. It was his partner, Jerry Edgar, and the call was a welcome distraction from the silence.

'Harry, how's things in Chinatown?'

Because every cop secretly feared that he or she might one day crack from the pressures of the job and become a candidate for therapy sessions at the department's Behavioral Sciences Section, the unit was rarely spoken of by its formal name. Going to BSS sessions was more often referred to as 'going to Chinatown' because of the unit's location there on Hill Street, several blocks from Parker Center. If it became known about a cop that he was going there, the word would spread that he had the Hill Street blues. The six-story bank building where the BSS was located was known as the 'Fifty-One-Fifty' building. This was not its address. It was the police radio code number for describing a crazy person. Codes like this were part of the protective structure used to belittle and, therefore, more easily contain their own fears.

'Chinatown was great,' Bosch said sarcastically. 'You ought to try it some day. It's got me sitting here counting cars on the freeway.'

'Well, at least you won't run out.'

'Yeah. What's going on with you?'

'Pounds finally did it.'

'Did what?'

'Stuck me with somebody new.'

Bosch was silent a moment. The news gave him a sense of finality. The thought that maybe he would never get his job back began to creep into his mind.

'He did?'

'Yeah, he finally did. I caught a case this morning. So he stuck one of his suckups with me. Burns.'

'Burns? From autos? He's never worked homicide. Has he ever even worked CAPs?'

Detectives usually followed one of two paths in the department. One was property crimes and the other was crimes against persons. The latter included specializing in homicide, rape, assault and robbery. CAPs detectives had the higher-profile cases and usually viewed property crime investigators as paper pushers. There were so many property crimes in the city that the investigators spent most of their time taking reports and processing the occasional arrest. They actually did little detective work. There was no time to.

'He's been a paper guy all the way,' Edgar said. 'But with Pounds that doesn't matter. All he cares about is having somebody on the homicide table who isn't going to give his shit back to him. And Burns is just the guy. He probably started lobbying for the job the minute the word went out about you.'

'Well, fuck him. I'm gonna get back to the table and then he goes back to autos.'

Edgar took his time before answering. It was as if Bosch had said something that made no sense to him.

'You really think that, Harry? Pounds ain't going to stand for you coming back. Not after what you did. I told him when he told me I was with Burns that, you know, no offense but I'd wait until Harry Bosch came back and he said if I wanted to handle it that way, then I'd be waitin' until I was an old man.'

'He said that? Well, fuck him, too. I still got a friend or two in the department.'

'Irving still owes you, doesn't he?'

'I guess maybe I'll find out.'

He didn't go further with it. He wanted to change the subject. Edgar was his partner but they had never gotten to the point where they completely confided in each other. Bosch played the mentor role in the relationship and he trusted Edgar with his life. But that was a bond that held fast on the street. Inside the department was another matter. Bosch had never trusted anyone, never relied on anyone. He wasn't going to start now.

'So, what's the case?' he asked, to divert the conversation.

'Oh, yeah, I wanted to tell you about it. This was weird, man. First the killing's weird, then what happened after. The call out was to a house on Sierra Bonita. This is about five in the A.M. The citizen reports he heard a sound like a gunshot, only muffled-like. He grabs his deer rifle out of the closet and goes outside to take a look. This is a neighborhood that's been picked clean lately by the hypes, you know? Four B and Es on his block alone this month. So, he was ready with the rifle. Anyway, he goes down his driveway with the gun – the garage is in the back – and he sees a pair of legs hanging out of the open door of his car. It was parked in front of the garage.'

'He shoots him?'

'No, that's the crazy thing. He goes up with his gun but the guy in his car is already dead. Stabbed in the chest with a screwdriver.'

Bosch didn't get it. He didn't have enough of the facts. But he said nothing.

'The air bag killed him, Harry.'

'What do you mean, the air bag killed him?'

'The air bag. This goddamn hype was stealing the air bag out of the steering wheel and somehow the thing went off. It inflated instantly, like it was supposed to, and drove the screwdriver right into his heart, man. I've never seen anything like it. He must've been holding the screwdriver backwards or he was using the butt-end to bang on the wheel. We haven't exactly figured out that part yet. We talked to a guy at Chrysler. He says that you take the protective cover off, like this dude had, and even static electricity can set the thing off. Our dead guy was wearing a sweater. I don't know, could've been it. Burns says it's the first death by static cling.'

While Edgar chuckled at his new partner's humor, Bosch thought about the scenario. He remembered a department info bulletin going out on air bag thefts the year before. They had become a hot commodity in the underground market, with thieves getting as much as three hundred dollars apiece for air bags from unscrupulous body shops. The body shops would buy them for three hundred and turn around and charge a customer nine hundred to install one. That was double the profit derived when ordering from the manufacturer.

'So it goes down as accidental?' Bosch asked.

'Yeah, accidental death. But the story ain't over. Both doors of the car were open.'

'The dead guy had a partner.'

'That's what we figure. And so if we find the fucker we can charge him. Under the felony homicide law. So we had SID laser the inside of the car and pull all the prints they could. I took 'em down to Latents and talked one of the techs into scanning them and running them on the AFIS. And bingo.'

'You got the partner?'

'Dead bang. That AFIS computer has got a long reach,

Harry. One of the nets is the US Military Identification Center in St Louis. We got a match on our guy outta there. He was in the Army ten years ago. We got his ID from that, then got an address from the DMV and picked him up today. He copped on the ride in. He's gonna go away for a while.'

'Sounds like a good day, then.'

'Didn't end there, though. I haven't told you the weird part yet.'

'Then tell me.'

'Remember I said we lasered the car and took all the prints?'

'Right.'

'Well, we got another match, too. This one on the crime indexes. A case outta Mississippi. Man, all days should be like this one was.'

'What was the match?' Bosch asked. He was growing impatient with the way Edgar was parceling out the story.

'We matched prints put on the net seven years ago by something called the Southern States Criminal Identification Base. It's like five states that don't add up in population to half of LA. Anyway, one of the prints we put through today matched the doer on a double homicide in Biloxi all the way back in 'seventy-six. Some guy the papers there called the Bicentennial Butcher on account he killed two women on the Fourth of July.'

'The car's owner? The guy with the rifle?'

'Damn right. His fingerprints were on the cleaver left in one girl's skull. He was a bit surprised when we came back to his house this afternoon. We said, "Hey, we caught the partner of the guy who died in your car. And by the way, you're under arrest for a two-bagger, motherfucker." I think it blew his mind, Harry. You shoulda been there.'

Edgar laughed loudly into the phone and Bosch knew,

after only one week of being grounded, how much he missed the job.

'Did he cop?'

'No, he kept quiet. You can't be that stupid and get away with a double murder for almost twenty years. That's a nice run.'

'Yeah, what's he been doing?'

'Looks like he's just been laying low. Owns a hardware on Santa Monica. Married and has a kid and a dog. A total reform case. But he's going back to Biloxi. I hope he likes southern cooking 'cause he won't be coming back here anytime soon.'

Edgar laughed again. Bosch said nothing. The story was depressing because it was a reminder of what he was no longer doing. It also reminded him about what Hinojos had asked about defining his mission.

'Got a couple of Mississippi state troopers comin' out tomorrow,' Edgar said. 'Talked to them a little while ago and they are happy campers.'

Bosch didn't say anything for a while.

'Harry, you still there?'

'Yeah, I was just thinking about something … Well, it sounds like a hell of a day of crime fighting. How's the fearless leader taking it?'

'Pounds? Jesus, he's got a hard-on over this the size of a Louisville slugger. You know what he's doing? He's trying to figure out a way to take credit for all three clearances. He's trying to put the Biloxi cases on our rate.'

It didn't surprise Bosch. It was a widespread practice among department managers and statisticians to add positive credit to crime clearance levels whenever and wherever possible. In the air bag case, there was no actual murder. It was an accident. But because the death occurred during the commission of a crime, California law held that an accomplice to the crime could be charged

20

with his partner's death. Bosch knew that based on the partner's arrest for murder, Pounds intended to add a case to the murder clearance chart. He would not balance this by adding a case to the murder occurrence chart because the death by air bag was an accident. This little statistical two-step would result in a nice little boost for the Hollywood Division's overall homicide clearance rate, which in recent years had continually threatened to dip below fifty percent.

But unsatisfied with the modest jump this accounting deception would provide, Pounds intended to boldly add the two Biloxi murders to the clearance chart as well. After all, it could be argued, his homicide squad did clear two more cases. Adding a total of three cleared cases to one side of the chart without adding any to the other would likely give a tremendous boost to the overall clearance rate – as well as to the image of Pounds as a detective bureau commander. Bosch knew that Pounds was probably delighted with himself and the accomplishments of the day.

'He said our rate would jump six points,' Edgar was saying. 'He was a very pleased man, Harry. And my new partner was very pleased he had pleased his man.'

'I don't want to hear any more.'

'I didn't think so. So what are you doing to keep busy, besides counting cars on the freeway? You must be bored stiff, Harry.'

'Not really,' Bosch lied. 'Last week I finished fixing the deck. This week I'll –'

'Harry, I'm telling you, you're wasting your time and money. The inspectors are going to find you in there and kick you out on your ass. Then they'll tear the place down themselves and hand you the bill. Your deck and the whole house will be in the back of a dump truck then.'

'I hired a lawyer to work on it.'

'What's he gonna do?'

'I don't know. I want to appeal the red tag. He's a land use guy. He said he can work it out.'

'I hope so. I still think you ought to tear it down and start over.'

'I didn't win the lotto yet.'

'The feds've got disaster loans. You could get one and –'

'I've applied, Jerry, but I like my house the way it is.'

'Okay, Harry. I hope your lawyer works it out. Anyway, I gotta go. Burns wants to have a beer over at the Short Stop. He's there waiting.'

The last time Bosch had been at the Short Stop, a hole-in-the-wall cop bar near the academy and Dodger Stadium, it had still had I SUPPORT CHIEF GATES bumper stickers on the wall. For most cops, Gates was a dying ember of the past, but the Short Stop was a place where old-liners went to drink and remember a department that no longer existed.

'Yeah, have fun over there, Jerry.'

'Take care, man.'

Bosch leaned against a counter and drank his beer. He came to the conclusion that Edgar's call had been a cleverly disguised way of telling Bosch that he was choosing sides and cutting him loose. That was okay, Bosch thought. Edgar's first allegiance was to himself, to surviving in a place that could be treacherous. Bosch couldn't hold that against him.

Bosch looked at his reflection in the glass of the oven door. The image was dark but he could see his eyes in the shadow and the line of his jaw. He was forty-four years old and in some ways looked older. He still had a full head of curly brown hair but both the hair and the mustache were going to gray. His black-brown eyes seemed to him tired and used up. His skin had the pallor of a night watchman's. Bosch was still leanly built but sometimes his clothes hung on him as if they had been issued at one of the downtown missions or he had recently been through a bad illness.

He broke away from his reflection and grabbed another beer out of the refrigerator. Outside on the deck, he saw the sky was now brightly lit with the pastels of dusk. It would be dark soon, but the freeway below was a bright river of moving lights, its current never ebbing for a moment.

Looking down on the Monday night commute, he saw the place as an anthill with the workers moving along in lines. Someone or some force would soon come along and kick the hill again. Then the freeways would fall, the houses would collapse and the ants would just rebuild and get in line again.

He was bothered by something but was not quite sure what it was. His thoughts swirled and mixed. He began to see what Edgar had told him about his case in the context of his dialogue with Hinojos. There was some connection there, some bridge, but he couldn't get to it.

He finished his beer and decided that two would be enough. He went to one of the lounge chairs and sat down with his feet up. What he wanted to do was give everything a rest. Mind and body. He looked up and saw the clouds had now been painted orange by the setting sun. They looked like molten lava moving slowly across the sky.

Just before he dozed off a thought pushed through the lava. Everybody counts or nobody counts. And then, in the last moment of clarity before sleep, he knew what the connecting ribbon that had run through his thoughts had been. And he knew what his mission was.

❖ ❖ ❖ ❖ ❖ ❖ ❖

In the morning Bosch dressed without showering so he could immediately begin work on the house and blank out the lingering thoughts from the night before with sweat and concentration.

But clearing the thoughts away was not easy. As he dressed in old lacquer-stained jeans, he caught a glimpse of himself in the cracked mirror over the bureau and saw that his T-shirt was on backward. Printed across his chest on the white shirt was the homicide squad's motto.

OUR DAY BEGINS WHEN YOUR DAY ENDS

It was supposed to be on the back of the shirt. He pulled it off, turned it and put it back on. Now in the mirror he saw what he was supposed to see. A replica of a detective's badge on the left breast of the shirt and the smaller printing that said LAPD HOMICIDE.

He brewed a pot of coffee and took it and a mug out to the deck. Next he lugged out his toolbox and the new door he had bought at Home Depot for the bedroom. When he was finally ready and had the mug filled with steaming black coffee, he sat on the footrest of one of the lounge chairs and placed the door on its side in front of him.

The original door had splintered at the hinges during the quake. He had tried to hang the replacement a few days earlier but it was too large to fit the door jamb. He

24

figured he needed to shave no more than an eighth of an inch off the opening side to make the fit. He set to work with the plane, moving the instrument slowly back and forth along the edge as the wood peels fell away in paper-thin curls. Occasionally he would stop and study his progress and run his hand along the area of his work. He liked being able to see the progress he was making. Few other tasks in life seemed that way to him.

But still, he could not concentrate for long. His focus on the door was interrupted by the same intrusive thought that had haunted him the night before. Everybody counts or nobody counts. It was what he had told Hinojos. It was what he had told her he believed. But did he? What did it mean to him? Was it merely a slogan like the one on the back of his shirt or was it something he lived by? These questions mingled with the echoes of the conversation he'd had the night before with Edgar. And with a deeper thought that he knew he had always had.

He took the plane off the door edge and ran his hand along the smooth wood again. He thought he had it right and carried it inside. Over a drop cloth in an area of the living room he had reserved for woodworking, he ran a sheet of small-grain sandpaper over the door edge until it was perfectly smooth to his touch.

Holding the door vertically and balancing it on a block of wood, he eased it into the hinges and then dropped the pins in. He tapped them home with a hammer and they went in easily. He had oiled the pins and hinges earlier and so the bedroom door opened and closed almost silently. Most important, though, was that it closed evenly in the jamb. He opened and closed it several more times, just staring at it, pleased with his accomplishment.

The glow of his success was short-lived, for having completed the project left his mind open to wander. Back out on the deck the other thoughts came back as he swept the wood shavings into a small pile.

Hinojos had told him to stay busy. Now he knew how he would do it. And in that moment he realized that no matter how many projects he found to take his time, there was one job he still had to do. He leaned the broom against the wall and went inside to get ready.

❖ ❖ ❖ ❖ ❖ ❖ ❖

The LAPD storage facility and aerosquad headquarters known as Piper Tech was on Ramirez Street in downtown, not far from Parker Center. Bosch, in a suit and tie, arrived shortly before eleven at the gate. He held his LAPD identification card out the window and was quickly waved in. The card was all he had. The card, along with his gold badge and gun, had been taken from him when he was placed on leave the week before. But it was later returned so that he could gain entry to the BSS offices for the stress therapy sessions with Carmen Hinojos.

After parking, he walked to the beige-painted storage warehouse that housed the city's history of violence. The quarter-acre building contained the files of all LAPD cases, solved or unsolved. This was where the case files came when nobody cared anymore.

At the front counter a civilian clerk was loading files onto a cart so that they could be wheeled back into the expanse of shelves and forgotten. By the way she studied Bosch, he knew it was rare that anyone ever showed up here in person. It was all done by telephones and city couriers.

'If you're looking for city council minutes, that's building A, across the lot. The one with brown trim.'

Bosch held up his ID card.

'No, I want to pull a case.'

He reached into his coat pocket while she walked up to

27

the counter and bent forward to read his card. She was a small black woman with graying hair and glasses. The name tag affixed to her blouse said her name was Geneva Beaupre.

'Hollywood,' she said. 'Why didn't you just ask for it to be sent out in dispatch? There ain't no hurry on these cases.'

'I was downtown, over at Parker … I wanted to see it as soon as I could, anyway.'

'Well, you got a number?'

From his pocket he pulled a piece of notebook paper with the number 61–743 written on it. She bent to study it and then her head jerked up.

'Nineteen sixty-one? You want a case from – I don't know where nineteen sixty-one is.'

'It's here. I've looked at the file before. I guess there was someone else clerking here back then, but it was here.'

'Well, I'll look. You're going to wait?'

'Yeah, I'll wait.'

This seemed to disappoint her but Bosch smiled at her in the most friendly way he could muster. She took the paper with her and disappeared into the stacks. Bosch walked around the small waiting area by the counter for a few minutes and then stepped outside to smoke a cigarette. He was nervous for a reason he could not exactly place. He kept moving, pacing.

'Harry Bosch!'

He turned and saw a man approaching him from the helicopter hangar. He recognized him but couldn't immediately place him. Then it hit him: Captain Dan Washington, a former Hollywood patrol skipper who was now commander of the aerosquadron. They shook hands cordially and Bosch immediately hoped Washington did not know of his ISL situation.

'Howzit going in the 'wood?'

'Same old same old, Captain.'

'You know, I miss that place.'

'You're not missing much. How is it with you?'

'Can't complain. I like the detail but it's more like being an airport manager than a cop, I guess. It's as good a place to lay low as any other.'

Bosch recalled that Washington had gotten into a political scrap with the department weight and taken the transfer as a means of survival. The department had dozens of out-of-the-way jobs like Washington's, where you could lay up and wait for your political fortunes to change.

'What're you doing over here?'

There it was. If Washington knew Bosch was on leave, then admitting he was pulling an old case file would be admitting he was violating the leave order. Still, as his position in the aerosquad attested, Washington was not a straight-line company man. Bosch decided to run the risk.

'I'm just pulling an old case. I got some free time and thought I'd check a few things.'

Washington narrowed his eyes and Bosch knew that he knew.

'Yeah ... well, listen, I gotta run, but hang in there, man. Don't let the book men get you down.'

He winked at Bosch and moved on.

'I won't, Captain. You either.'

Bosch felt reasonably sure Washington wouldn't mention their meeting to anybody. He stepped on his cigarette and went back inside to the counter, privately chastising himself anyway for having gone outside and advertised that he was there. Five minutes later he started hearing a squeaking sound coming from one of the aisles between the stacks. In a moment Geneva Beaupre appeared pushing a cart with a blue three-ring binder on it.

It was a murder book. It was at least two inches thick,

29

dusty, and with a rubber band around it. The band held an old green checkout card to the binder.

'Found it.'

There was a note of triumph in her voice. It would be the major accomplishment of her day, Bosch guessed.

'Great.'

She dropped the heavy binder on the counter.

'Marjorie Lowe. Homicide, 1961. Now ...' She took the card off the binder and looked at it. 'Yes, you were the last to take this out. Let's see, that was five years ago. You were with Robbery-Homicide then ...'

'Yes. And now I'm in Hollywood. You want me to sign for it again?'

She put the card down in front of him.

'Yes. Put your ID number there, too, please.'

He quickly did as he was told and he could tell she was studying him as he wrote.

'A lefty.'

'Yeah.'

He slid the card back across the counter to her.

'Thanks, Geneva.'

He looked at her, wanting to say something else, but decided it might be a mistake. She looked back at him and a grandmotherly smile formed on her face.

'I don't know what you're doing, Detective Bosch, but I wish you good luck. I can tell it's important, you coming back to this after five years.'

'It's been longer than that, Geneva. A lot longer.'

❖ ❖ ❖ ❖ ❖ ❖ ❖

Bosch cleared all the old mail and carpentry books off the dining room table and placed the binder and his own notebook on top of it. He went to the stereo and loaded a compact disc, 'Clifford Brown with Strings.' He went to the kitchen and got an ashtray, then he sat down in front of the blue murder book and looked at it for a long time without moving. The last time he'd had the file, he had barely looked at it as he skimmed through its many pages. He hadn't been ready then and had returned it to the archives.

This time, he wanted to be sure he was ready before he opened it, so he sat there a long time just studying the cracked plastic cover as if it held some clue to his preparedness. A memory crowded into his mind. A boy of eleven in a swimming pool clinging to the steel ladder at the side, out of breath and crying, the tears disguised by the water that dripped out of his wet hair. The boy felt scared. Alone. He felt as if the pool were an ocean that he must cross.

Brownie was working through 'Willow Weep for Me,' his trumpet as gentle as a portrait painter's brush. Bosch reached for the rubber band he had put around the binder five years earlier and it broke at his touch. He hesitated only another moment before opening the binder and blowing off the dust.

The binder contained the case file on the October 28, 1961, homicide of Marjorie Phillips Lowe. His mother.

The pages of the binder were brownish yellow and stiff with age. As he looked at them and read them, Bosch was initially surprised at how little things had changed in nearly thirty-five years. Many of the investigative forms in the binder were still currently in use. The Preliminary Report and the Investigating Officer's Chronological Record were the same as those presently used, save for word changes made to accommodate court rulings and political correctness. Description Boxes marked NEGRO had sometime along the line been changed to BLACK and then AFRICAN-AMERICAN. The list of motivations on the Preliminary Case Screening chart did not include DOMESTIC VIOLENCE or HATRED/PREJUDICE classifications as they did now. Interview summary sheets did not include boxes to be checked after Miranda warnings had been given.

But aside from those kinds of changes, the reports were the same and Bosch decided that homicide investigation was largely the same now as back then. Of course, there had been incredible technological advances in the past thirty-five years but he believed there were some things that were always the same and always would remain the same. The legwork, the art of interviewing and listening, knowing when to trust an instinct or a hunch. Those were things that didn't change, that couldn't.

The case had been assigned to two investigators on the Hollywood homicide table. Claude Eno and Jake McKittrick. The reports they filed were in chronological order in the binder. On their preliminary reports the victim was referred to by name, indicating she had immediately been identified. A narrative on these pages said the victim was found in an alley behind the north side of Hollywood Boulevard between Vista and Gower. Her skirt and undergarments had been ripped open by her attacker. It was presumed that she had been sexually assaulted and strangled. Her body had been dropped into an open trash bin located next to the rear door of a Hollywood souvenir store called Startime Gifts & Gags. The body was discovered at 7:35 A.M. by a foot patrol officer who walked a beat on the Boulevard and usually checked the back alleys at the beginning of each shift. The victim's purse was not found with her but she was quickly identified because she was known to the beat officer. On the continuation sheet it was made clear why she was known to him.

> Victim had a previous history of loitering arrests in the Hollywood. (See AR 55–002, 55–913, 56–111, 59–056, 60–815 and 60–1121) Vice Detective Gilchrist and Stano described victim as a prostitute who periodically worked in the Hollywood area and had been repeatedly warned off. Victim lived at El Rio Efficiency Apts located two blocks northerly of crime scene. It was believed that the victim had been currently involved in call girl prostitution activities. R/O 1906 was able to make identification of the victim because of familiarity of having seen victim in the area in previous years.

Bosch looked at the reporting officer's serial number. He knew that 1906 belonged to a patrolman then who was now one of the most powerful men in the department. Assistant Chief Irvin S. Irving. Once Irving had confided to Bosch that he had known Marjorie Lowe and had been the one who found her.

Bosch lit a cigarette and read on. The reports were sloppily written, perfunctory, and filled with careless misspellings. In reading them, it was clear to Bosch that Eno and McKittrick did not invest much time in the case. A prostitute was dead. It was a risk that came with her job. They had other fish to fry.

33

He noticed on the Death Investigation Report a box for listing the next of kin. It said;

Hieronymus Bosch (Harry), son, age 11, McClaren Youth Hall. Notification made 10/28–1500 hrs. Custody of Department of Public Social Services since 7/60 – UM. (See victim's arrest reports 60–815 and 60–1121) Father unknown. Son remains in custody pending foster placement.

Looking at the report, Bosch could easily decipher all of the abbreviations and translate what was written. UM stood for unfit mother. The irony was not lost on him even after so many years. The boy had been taken from a presumably unfit mother and placed in an equally unfit system of child protection. What he remembered most was the noise of the place. Always loud. Like a prison.

Bosch remembered McKittrick had been the one who came to tell him. It was during the swimming period. The indoor pool was frothing with waves as a hundred boys swam and splashed and yelled. After being pulled from the water, Harry wore a white towel that had been washed and bleached so many times that it felt like cardboard over his shoulders. McKittrick told him the news and he returned to the pool, his screams silenced beneath the waves.

Quickly leafing through the supplemental reports on the victim's prior arrests, Bosch came to the autopsy report. He skipped most of it, not needing the details, and settled on the summary page, where there were a couple of surprises. The time of death was placed at seven to nine hours before discovery. Near midnight. The surprise was in the official cause of death. It was listed as blunt-force trauma to the head. The report described a deep contusion over the right ear with swelling but no laceration that caused fatal bleeding in the brain. The report said the killer might have believed he strangled the victim after knocking her unconscious but it was the coroner's conclusion that she was already dead when the killer wrapped Marjorie Lowe's own belt around her neck and tied it off. The report stated further that while semen was recovered from the vagina there were no other injuries commonly associated with rape.

Rereading the summary with an investigator's eyes, Bosch could see the autopsy conclusions only muddied the waters for the original two detectives. The initial assumption based on the appearance of the body was that Marjorie Lowe was the victim of a sex crime. That raised the specter of a random encounter – as random as the couplings of her profession – leading to her death. But the fact that strangulation occurred after death and that there was no convincing physical evidence of rape raised another possibility as well. They were factors from which it could also be speculated that the victim had been murdered by someone who then attempted to disguise his involvement and motivation in the randomness of a sex crime. Bosch could think of only one reason for such misdirection, if that had been the case. The killer knew the victim. As he moved on, he wondered if McKittrick and Eno had made any of the same conclusions he had made.

There was an eight-by-ten envelope next in the file which was marked as containing crime scene and autopsy photos. Bosch thought about it a long moment and then put the envelope aside. As with the last time he had pulled the murder book out of the archives, he couldn't look.

Next was another envelope with an evidence inventory list stapled to it. It was almost blank.

EVIDENCE RECOVERED
Case 61–743
Latent fingerprints taken from leather belt with silver sea shells.

SID report no. 1114 11/06/61
Murder weapon recovered – black leather belt with
sea shells attached. Property of victim.
Victims clothing, property. Filed w/ evidence
custodian – Locker 73B LAPDHQ
  1 blouse, white – blood stain
  1 black skirt – torn at seam
  1 pair black high heel shoes
  1 pair black sheer stockings, torn
  1 pair undergarments, torn
  1 pair gold colored earrings
  1 gold colored hoop bracelet
  1 gold chain necklace w/cross

That was it. Bosch studied the list for a long time before
jotting the particulars down in his notebook. Something
about it bothered him but he couldn't draw it out. Not
yet. He was taking in too much information and he would
have to let it settle some before the anomalies floated to
the surface.

He dropped it for the moment and opened the evidence
envelope, breaking the seal of a red tape that had cracked
with age. Inside was a yellowed print card on which two
complete fingerprints, from a thumb and an index finger,
and several partials had been taped after being lifted with
black powder from the belt. Also in the envelope was a
pink check card for the victim's clothes, which had been
placed in an evidence locker. The clothes had never been
retrieved because a case had never been made. Bosch put
both items aside, wondering what would have happened
to the clothing. In the mid-sixties Parker Center had
been built and the department moved out of the old head
quarters. It was long gone now, falling to the wrecking
ball. What happened to the evidence from unsolved
cases?

Next in the file was a group of summary reports on interviews conducted during the first days of the investigation. Most of these were of people with peripheral knowledge of the victim or the crime. People like other residents in the El Rio Apartments and other women in the same profession as the victim. There was one short summary that caught Bosch's eye. It was from an interview conducted three days after the murder with a woman named Meredith Roman. She was described in the report as an associate and sometime roommate of the victim. At the time of the report she also lived in the El Rio, one floor up from the victim. The report had been typed up by Eno, who seemed to be the clear-cut winner in illiteracy when comparing the reports of the two investigators assigned to the case.

Meredith Roman (10–9–30) was interviewed at length this date at her apartment in the El Rio Efficiencies where she lived one floor above the victim's apartment. Miss Roman was able to provide this detective with very little useful information in relation to the activities of Marjorie Lowe during the period of the last week of live.

Miss Roman acknowledged that she has engaged in prostitutional acts while in the company of the victim on numrus occassion in the previous eight years but she has no booking record to date. (later confirmed) She told the undersigned detective that such engagements were skeduled by a man named Johnny Fox, (2–2–33) who resides at 1110 Ivar in Hollywood. Fox, age 28, has no records of arrests but vice intelligence confirms he has been a suspect previously in cases of pandering, malicious assault and sales of heroin.

Miss Roman states that the last time she saw the victim was at a party on second floor of the

Roosevelt Hotl on 10/21. Miss Roman did not attend party with victim but saw her there momentarily for a short conversation.

Miss Roman states that she now has plans to retire from the business of prostitution and leave Los Angeles. She stated that she will provide detectives with a forwarding adress and telephone number so that she can be contacted if necessary. Her demenor was corperative with the undersigned.

Bosch immediately looked through the summaries again for the report on Johnny Fox. There was none there. He flipped to the front of the binder to the Chronological Record and looked for an entry that would indicate whether they had even talked to Fox. The CR was just a log of one-line entries with references to other reports. On the second page he found a single notation.

11–3 800–2000 Watched Fox apt. No show.

There was no other mention of Fox in the record. But as Bosch read through the CR to the end, another entry caught his eye.

11–5 940 A. Conklin called to skedule meeting.

Bosch knew the name. Arno Conklin had been a Los Angeles district attorney in the 1960s. As Bosch remembered it, 1961 was too early for Conklin to have been DA, but he would still have been one of the office's top prosecutors. His interest in a prostitute's murder seemed curious to Bosch. But there was nothing in the binder that held an answer. There was no summary report of a meeting with Conklin. Nothing.

He noted that the misspelling of the word *schedule* in the CR entry had been made earlier in the summary of the Roman interview typed by Eno. Bosch concluded from this that Conklin had called Eno to set the meeting.

However, the significance of this, if any, he didn't know. He wrote Conklin's name down at the top of a page in his notebook.

Getting back to Fox, Bosch could not understand why he was not located and interviewed by Eno and McKittrick. It seemed that he was a natural suspect – the victim's pimp. Or, if Fox had been interviewed, Bosch could not understand why there was no report in the murder book on such a key part of the investigation.

Bosch sat back and lit a cigarette. Already, he was tense with the suspicion that things were amiss with the case. He felt the stirring of what he knew was outrage. The more he read the more he believed the case had been mishandled from the start.

He leaned back over the table and continued flipping through the pages of the binder while he smoked. There were more meaningless interview summaries and reports. It was all just filler. Any homicide cop worth his badge could churn out reports like these by the dozens if he wanted to fill a binder and make it look like he'd done a thorough investigation. It appeared that McKittrick and Eno were as skilled at it as the best. But any homicide cop worth his badge could also tell filler when he saw it. And that's what Bosch saw here. The hollow feeling in his stomach grew more pronounced.

Finally, he came to the first Follow-Up Homicide Investigation Report. It was dated one week after the murder and written by McKittrick.

Homicide of Marjorie Phillips Lowe remains open at this time, no suspects identified.

Investigation at this time has determined that victim was engaged in prostitution in the Hollywood area and may have fallen victim to a customer who committed the homicide.

Preliminary suspect John Fox denied involvement

in the incident and has been cleared at this time through fingerprint comparison and confirmation of alibi through witnesses.

No suspects at this time have been identified. John Fox states that on Friday, 11/30 at approximately 2100 hours the victim left her residence at the El Rio Apts to go to an unknown location for the purposes of prostitution. Fox states the arrangement was made by victim and he was not made privy to it. Fox siad it was not unusual practice for victim to make arrangements for liaissons without his knowledge.

Victim's undergarment was found with body in ripped condition. Noted, however, a pair of stockings also belonging to the victim showed no tears and were believed to possibly have been removed voluntarily.

Experience and instinct of investigators leads to the conclusion that the victim met with foul play at the unknown location after voluntarily arriving and possibly removing some clothing. The body was then transported to the trash bin in the alleyway between Vista and Gower, where it was discovered the following morning.

Witness Meredith Roman was reinterviewed this date and asked to amend her earlier statement. Roman informed this investigator that it was her belief that the victim had gone to a party in Hancock Park the night previous to the discovery of her body. She could provide no address or name of party at the location. Miss Roman said her plan was to attend with victim but on the previous evening she was assaulted by John Fox in a dispute over money. She could not attend the party because she believed a bruise on her face made her unpresentable. (Fox readily acknowledged striking Roman in subsequent telephone interview. Roman refused charges.)

Investigation is termed at standstill as no further leads have been provided at this time. Investigators are currently seeking the aid of vice section officers in regard to knowledge of similar incidents and/or possible suspects.

Bosch read the page again and tried to interpret what was really being said about the case. One thing that was clear from it was that regardless of whether there was an interview summary report in the binder, Johnny Fox had obviously been interviewed by Eno and McKittrick. He had been cleared. The question Bosch now had was, why did they not type up a summary report, or had it been typed up and later removed from the murder book? And if so, who removed it and why?

Lastly, Bosch was curious about the lack of any mention of Arno Conklin in the summary or any other report save for the investigative chronology. Maybe, Bosch thought, more than just the Fox interview summary had been lifted from the binder.

Bosch got up and went to his briefcase, which he kept on the counter near the kitchen door. From it he took his personal phone book. He didn't have a number for LAPD archives so he called the regular records number and was transferred. A woman answered after nine rings.

'Uh, Mrs Beaupre? Geneva?'

'Yes?'

'Hello, this is Harry Bosch. I was there earlier today to pick up a file.'

'Yes, from Hollywood. The old case.'

'Yes. Could you tell me, do you still have the checkout card there at the counter?'

'Hold the line. I already filed it.'

A moment later she was back.

'Yes, I have it here.'

'Could you tell me, who else has checked this binder out in the past?'

'Why would you need to know that?'

'There are pages missing from the file, Mrs Beaupre. I'd like to know who might have them.'

'Well, you checked it out last. I mentioned that be –'

'Yes, I know. About five years ago. Is there any listing of it being taken out before that or since then? I didn't notice when I signed the card today.'

'Well, hold the line and let me see.' He waited and she was back quickly. 'Okay, I've got it. According to this card, the only other time that file was ever taken out was in 1972. You're talking way back.'

'Who checked it out back then?'

'It's scribbled here. I can't – it looks like maybe Jack … uh, Jack McKillick.'

'Jake McKittrick.'

'Could be.'

Bosch didn't know what to think. McKittrick had the file last but that was more than ten years after the murder. What did it mean? Bosch felt confusion ambush him. He didn't know what he had been expecting but he'd hoped there would have been something other than a name scribbled more than twenty years ago.

'Okay, Mrs Beaupre, thanks very much.'

'Well, if you've got missing pages I'm going to have to make a report and give it to Mr Aguilar.'

'I don't think that will be necessary, ma'am. I may be wrong about the missing pages. I mean, how could there be missing pages if nobody's looked at it since the last time I had it?'

He thanked her again and hung up, hoping his attempt at good humor would persuade her to do nothing about his call. He opened the refrigerator and looked inside while he thought about the case, then closed it and went back out to the table.

The last pages in the murder book were a due diligence report dated November 3, 1962. The department's homicide procedures called for all unsolved cases to be reviewed after a year by a new set of detectives with an eye toward looking for something that the first set of investigators might have missed. But, in practice, it was a rubber stamp process. Detectives didn't relish the idea of finding the mistakes of their colleagues. Additionally, they had their own case loads to worry about. When assigned DDs, as they were called, they usually did little more than read through the file, make a few calls to witnesses and then send the binder to archives.

In this case, the DD report by the new detectives, named Roberts and Jordan, drew the same conclusions as the reports by Eno and McKittrick. After two pages detailing the same evidence and interviews already conducted by the original investigators, the DD report concluded that there were no workable leads and the prognosis for 'successful conclusion' of the case was hopeless. So much for due diligence.

Bosch closed the murder book. He knew that after Roberts and Jordan had filed their report, the binder had been shipped to archives as a dead case. It had gathered dust there until, according to the checkout card, McKittrick pulled it out for unknown reasons in 1972. Bosch wrote McKittrick's name under Conklin's on the page in the notebook. Then he wrote the names of others he thought it would be useful to interview. If they were still alive and could be found.

Bosch leaned back in his chair, realizing that the music had stopped and he hadn't even noticed. He checked his watch. It was two-thirty. He still had most of the afternoon but he wasn't sure what to do with it.

He went to the bedroom closet and took the shoebox off the shelf. It was his correspondence box, filled with letters and cards and photos he had wished to keep over the course of his life. It contained objects dated as far back as his time in Vietnam. He rarely looked in the box but his mind kept an almost perfect inventory of what was in it. Each piece had a reason for being saved.

On top was the latest addition to the box. A postcard from Venice. From Sylvia. It depicted a painting she had seen in the Palace of the Doges. Hieronymus Bosch's 'The Blessed and the Damned.' It showed an angel escorting one of the blessed through a tunnel to the light of heaven. They both floated skyward. The card was the last he had heard from her. He read the back.

Harry, thought you'd be interested in this piece of your namesake's work. I saw it in the Palace. It's beautiful. By the way, I love Venice! I think I could stay forever! S.

But you don't love me, Bosch thought as he put the card aside and began to dig through the other pieces in the box. He wasn't distracted again. About halfway through the box he found what he was looking for.

✦ ✦ ✦ ✦ ✦ ✦ ✦

The midday drive out to Santa Monica was long. Bosch had to take the long way, the 101 to the 405 and then down, because the 10 was still a week away from being reopened. By the time he got into Sunset Park it was after three. The house he was looking for was on Pier Street. It was a small Craftsman bungalow set on the crest of a hill. It had a full porch with red bougainvillea running along the railing. He checked the address painted on the mailbox against the envelope that contained the old Christmas card on the seat next to him. He parked at the curb and looked at the card once more. It had been addressed to him five years earlier, care of the LAPD. He had never responded to it. Not until now.

As he got out he could smell the sea and guessed that there might be a limited ocean view from the house's western windows. It was about ten degrees cooler than it had been at his home and so he reached back into his car for the sport coat. He walked to the front porch while putting it on.

The woman who answered the white door after one knock was in her mid-sixties and looked it. She was thin, with dark hair, but the gray roots were beginning to show and she was ready for another dye job. She wore thick red lipstick, a white silk blouse with blue seahorses on it over navy blue slacks. She readily smiled a greeting and Bosch recognized her, but he could see that his own image was completely alien to her. It had been almost thirty-five years since she had seen him. He smiled back anyway.

'Meredith Roman?'

She lost her smile as quickly as she had found it before.

'That's not my name,' she said in a clipped tone. 'You have the wrong place.'

She moved to close the door but Bosch put his hand on it to stop her. He tried to be as unthreatening about it as he could. But he could see panic starting in her eyes.

'It's Harry Bosch?' he said quickly.

She froze and looked Bosch in the eyes. He saw the panic go away. Recognition and memories flooded her eyes like tears. The smile came back.

'Harry? Little Harry?'

He nodded.

'Oh, darling, c'mere.' She drew him into a tight hug and talked in his ear. 'Oh, so good to see you after — let me look at you.'

She pushed him back and held her hands wide as if appraising a roomful of paintings at once. Her eyes were animated and sincere. It made Bosch feel good and sad at the same time. He shouldn't have waited so long. He should have visited for reasons other than the one that brought him here now.

'Oh, come in, Harry. Come in.'

Bosch entered a nicely furnished living room. The floor was red oak and the stucco walls were clean and white. The furniture was mostly matching white rattan. The place was light and bright but Bosch knew he was there to bring darkness.

'Meredith is no longer your name?'

'No, Harry, not for a long time.'

'What do I call you?'

'My name is Katherine. With a K. Katherine Register. Spelled like the cash register but you pronounce it *ree* as in

46

reefer. That's what my husband used to say. Boy, he was so straight. Outside of me the closest that man ever came to something illegal was to say the word.'

'He *used* to say that?'

'Have a seat, Harry, for crying out loud. Yes, used to. He passed away five years ago last Thanksgiving.'

Bosch sat down on the couch and she took the chair across the glass coffee table.

'I'm sorry.'

'It's okay, you didn't know. You never even knew him and I've been a different person for a long time. Can I get you something? Some coffee or maybe something stronger?'

It occurred to him that she had sent him the card on the Christmas soon after her husband's death. He was hit with another wave of guilt for not having responded.

'Harry?'

'Oh, uh, no, I'm fine. I … do you want me to call you by your new name?'

She started laughing at the ridiculousness of the situation and he joined in.

'Call me any damn thing you want.' She laughed girlishly, a laugh he remembered from a long time before. 'It's great to see you. You know, to see how, uh …'

'I turned out?'

She laughed again.

'I guess so. You know, I knew you were with the police because I had read your name in some of the news stories.'

'I know you knew. I got the Christmas card you sent to the station. That must have been right after your husband died. I, uh, I'm sorry I never wrote back or visited. I should have.'

'That's okay, Harry, I know you're busy with the job and a career and all … I'm glad you got my card. Do you have a family?'

'Uh, no. How about you? Any children?'

'Oh, no. No children. You have a wife, don't you, a handsome man like you?'

'No, I'm alone right now.'

She nodded, seeming to sense that he wasn't here to reveal his personal history to her anyway. For a long moment they just both looked at each other and Bosch wondered what she really thought of his being a cop. The initial delight in seeing each other was descending into the uneasiness that comes when old secrets come close to the surface.

'I guess ...'

He didn't finish the thought. He was grappling for a way into the conversation. His interviewing skills had deserted him.

'You know, if it's not too much trouble, I'd take a glass of water.'

It was all he could think of.

'Be right back.'

She got up quickly and went to the kitchen. He heard her getting ice out of a tray. It gave him time to think. It had taken him an hour to drive to her house but he hadn't given one thought to what this would be like or how he would get to what he wanted to say and ask. She came back in a few minutes with a glass of ice water. She handed it to him and put a round coaster made of cork on the glass-topped coffee table in front of him.

'If you're hungry, I can bring out some crackers and cheese. I just didn't know how much time you –'

'No, I'm fine. This is great, thanks.'

He saluted her with the glass and drank half of it, then put it down on the table.

'Harry, use the coaster. Getting rings out of the glass is murder.'

Bosch looked down at what he had done.

'Oh, sorry.'

He corrected the placement of his glass.

'You're a detective.'

'Yes. I work in Hollywood now ... Uh, but I'm not really working right now. I'm on sort of a vacation.'

'Oh, that must be nice.'

Her spirits seemed to lift, as if she knew there was a chance he was not here on business. Bosch knew it was time to get to the point.

'Uh, Mer – uh, Katherine, I need to ask you about something.'

'What is it, Harry?'

'I look around here and I see you have a very nice home, a different name, a different life. You're no longer Meredith Roman and I know you don't need me to tell you that. You've got ... I think what I'm saying is the past may be a difficult thing to talk about. I know it is for me. And, believe me, I don't want to hurt you in any way.'

'You're here to talk about your mother.'

He nodded and looked down at the glass on the cork coaster.

'Your mother and I were best friends. Sometimes I think I had almost as much a hand in raising you as she did. Until they took you away from her. From us.'

He looked back up at her. Her eyes were looking hard at distant memories.

'I don't think a day goes by that I don't think about her. We were just kids. Having a good time, you know. We never thought either of us could get hurt.'

She suddenly stood up.

'Harry, come here. I want to show you something.'

He followed her down a carpeted hallway and into a bedroom. There was a four-poster bed with light blue coverings, an oak bureau and matching bedside tables. Katherine Register pointed to the bureau. There were several photos in ornate stand-up frames on top. Most of them were of Katherine and a man who seemed much older than she was in the photos. Her husband, Bosch guessed. But she pointed to one that was to the right side of the grouping. The photo was old, its color faded. It was a picture of two young women with a tiny boy of three or four.

'I've always had that there, Harry. Even when my husband was alive. He knew my past. I told him. It didn't matter. We had twenty-three great years together. You see, the past is what you make of it. You can use it to hurt yourself or others or you can use it to make yourself strong. I'm strong, Harry. Now, tell me why you came to visit me today.'

Bosch reached for the framed photo and picked it up.

'I want ...' He looked up from the photo to her. 'I'm going to find out who killed her.'

An undecipherable look froze on her face for a moment and then she wordlessly took the frame out of his hands and put it back on the bureau. Then she pulled him into another deep embrace, her head against his chest. He could see himself holding her in the mirror over the bureau. When she pulled back and looked up at him he saw the tears were already down her cheeks. There was a slight tremor in her lower lip.

'Let's go sit down,' he said.

She pulled two tissues out of a box on the bureau and he led her back to the living room and to her chair.

'Do you want me to get you some water?'

'No, I'm fine. I'll stop crying, I'm sorry.'

She wiped at her eyes with the tissues. He sat back down on the couch.

'We used to say we were the two musketeers, both for one and one for both. It was stupid, but it was because we were so young and so close.'

'I'm starting from scratch with it, Katherine. I pulled the old files on the investigation. It –'

She made a dismissing sound and shook her head.

'There was no investigation. It was a joke.'

'That's my sense of it, too, but I don't understand why.'

'Look, Harry, you know what your mother was.' He nodded and she continued. 'She was a party girl. We both were. I'm sure you know that's the polite way of saying it. And the cops really didn't care that one of us ended up dead. They just wrote the whole damn thing off. I know you're a policeman now, but that's the way it was then. They just didn't care about her.'

'I understand. Things probably are not too much different now, believe it or not. But there has to have been more to it than that.'

'Harry, I don't know how much you want to know about your mother.'

He looked at her.

'The past made me strong, too. I can handle it.'

'I'm sure it did … I remember that place where they put you. McEvoy or something like –'

'McClaren.'

'That's it, McClaren. What a depressing place. Your mother would come home from visiting you and just sit down and cry her eyes out.'

'Don't change the subject, Katherine. What is it I should know about her?'

She nodded but hesitated for a moment before continuing.

'Mar knew some policemen. You understand?'

He nodded.

'We both did. It was the way it worked. You had to get along to go along. That's what we called it anyway. And when you have that situation and she ends up dead, it's usually best for the cops to just sweep it under the rug. Let sleeping dogs lie, as they say. You pick the cliché. They just didn't want anyone embarrassed.'

'Are you saying you think it was a cop?'

'No. I'm not saying that at all. I have no idea who did it, Harry. I'm sorry. I wish I did. But what I'm saying is, I think those two detectives that were assigned to investigate this knew where it could lead. And they weren't going to go that way because they knew what was good for them in the department. They weren't stupid in that way and like I said, she was a party girl. They didn't care. Nobody did. She got killed and that was that.'

Bosch looked around the room, not sure what to ask next.

'Do you know who the policemen she knew were?'

'It was a long time ago.'

'You knew some of the same policemen, didn't you?'

'Yes. I had to. That was the way it worked. You used your contacts to keep you out of jail. Everybody was for sale. Back then, at least. Different people wanted different forms of payment. Some of them, money. Some of them, other things.'

'It said in the mur – the file that you never had a record.'

'Yes, I was lucky. I was picked up a few times but never booked once. They always turned me loose once I could make a call. I kept a clean record because I knew a lot of policemen, honey. You understand?'

'Yes, I understand.'

She didn't look away when she said it. All these years in the straight life and she still had a whore's pride. She could talk about the low points of her life without flinching or batting an eye. It was because she had made it through and there was dignity in that. Enough to last the rest of her life.

'Do you mind if I smoke, Harry?'

'No, not if I can.'

They took out cigarettes and Bosch got up to light them.

'You can use that ashtray on the side table. Try not to get ashes on the rug.'

She pointed to a small glass bowl on the table at the other end of the couch. Bosch reached over for it and then held it with one hand while he smoked with the other. He looked down into it as he spoke.

'The policemen you knew,' he said, 'and who she probably knew, you don't remember any names?'

'I said it was a long time ago. And I doubt they had anything to do with this, with what happened to your mother.'

'Irvin S. Irving. Do you remember that name?'

She hesitated a moment as the name rolled around in her mind.

'I knew him. I think she did, too. He was on the beat on the Boulevard. I think it would have been hard for her not to know him ... but I don't know. I could be wrong.'

Bosch nodded.

'He was the one who found her.'

She hiked her shoulders in a what's-that-prove gesture.

'Well, somebody had to find her. She was left out there in the open like that.'

'What about a couple of vice guys, Gilchrist and Stano?'

She hesitated before answering.

'Yes, I knew them ... they were mean men.'

'Would my mother have known them? In that way?'

She nodded.

'What do you mean that they were mean? In what way?'

'They just ... they just didn't care about us. If they wanted something, whether it was a little piece of information you might have picked up on a date or something more … personal, they just came and took it. They could be rough. I hated them.'

'Did they –'

'But could they have been killers? My feeling at the time, and now, is no. They weren't killers, Harry. They were cops. True, they were bought and paid for, but it seemed everybody was. But it wasn't like it is today where you read the paper and you see some cop on trial for killing or beating or whatever. It's – sorry.'

'It's okay. Anybody else you can think of?'

'No.'

'No names?'

'I put that all out of my mind a long time ago.'

'Okay.'

Bosch wanted to take out his notebook but he didn't want to make this seem like an interview. He tried to remember what else he had read in the murder book that he could ask about.

'What about this guy Johnny Fox?'

'Yes, I told those detectives about him. They got all excited but then nothing ever happened. He was never arrested.'

'I think he was. But then he was let go. His fingerprints didn't match the killer's.'

She raised her eyebrows.

'Well, that's news to me. They never told me anything about any fingerprints.'

'On your second interview – with McKittrick, you remember him?'

'Not really. I just remember that there were police, you know? Two detectives. One was smarter than the other, that's what I remember. But I don't remember which one was which. It seemed like the dumber one was in charge and that was par for the course in those days.'

'Well, anyway, McKittrick talked to you the second

54

time. In his report he said you changed your story and you told about this party in Hancock Park.'

'Yes, the party. I didn't go because that … Johnny Fox hit me the night before and I had a bruise on my cheek. It was gorgeous. I played around with makeup but I couldn't do anything about the swelling. Believe me there wasn't much business in Hancock Park for a party girl with a knot on her face.'

'Who was having the party?'

'I don't remember. I don't know if I even knew whose party it was.'

Something about the way she answered bothered Bosch. Her tone had changed and it came across as almost a rehearsed answer.

'Are you sure you don't remember?'

'Of course, I'm sure.' Katherine stood up. 'I think I'm going to get some water now.'

She took his glass to refill and left the room again. Bosch realized that his familiarity with the woman, his emotion in seeing her again after so long, had blocked most of his investigative instincts. He had no feel for the truth. He could not tell whether there was more to what she was telling him or not. He decided he had to somehow steer the conversation back to the party. He thought she knew more than she had said all those years ago.

She came back with two glasses filled with ice water and placed his back down on the cork coaster. Something about the way she was so careful about putting the glass down gave him a knowledge about her that had not come through in her spoken words. It was simply that she had worked hard to attain the level she was at in life. That position and the material things it brought with it – like glass coffee tables and plush carpets – meant a lot to her and were to be taken care of.

She took a long drink from her glass after sitting down.

'Let me tell you something, Harry,' she said. 'I didn't tell them everything. I didn't lie, but I didn't tell them everything. I was afraid.'

'Afraid of what?'

'I became afraid on the day they found her. You see, I'd gotten a call that morning. Before I even knew what had happened to her. It was a man, but a voice I didn't recognize. He told me if I said anything I would be next. I remember, he said, "My advice to you, little lady, is to get the hell out of Dodge." Then, of course, I heard the police were in the building and had gone to her apartment. Then I heard she was dead. So I did what I was told. I left. I waited about a week until the police said they were done with me, then I moved to Long Beach. I changed my name, changed my life. I met my husband down there and then years later we moved here. ... You know, I've never been back to Hollywood, not even to drive through. It's an awful place.'

'What was it that you didn't tell Eno and McKittrick?'

Katherine looked down at her hands as she spoke.

'I was afraid, you see, so I didn't tell everything ... but I knew who she was going to see there, at the party. We were like sisters. Lived in the same building, shared clothes, secrets, everything. We talked every morning, had our coffee together. We had no secrets between us. And we were going to go to the party together. Of course, after that ... after Johnny hit me, she had to go alone.'

'Who was she going to meet there, Katherine?' Bosch prompted.

'You see that is the right question but the detectives never asked that. They only wanted to know whose party it was and where it was. That didn't matter. What was important was who was she going to meet there and they never asked that.'

'Who was it?'

She looked away from her hands and to the fireplace. She stared at the cold, blackened logs left from an old fire the way some people stare mesmerized by a burning fire.

'It was a man named Arno Conklin. He was a very important man in the –'

'I know who he was.'

'You do?'

'His name came up in the records. But not that way. How could you not tell the cops this?'

She turned and looked at him sharply.

'Don't you look at me that way. I told you I was scared. I'd been threatened. And they wouldn't have done anything with it anyway. They were bought and paid for by Conklin. They wouldn't go near him on just the word of a … call girl who didn't see anything but knew a name. I had to think of myself. Your mother was dead, Harry. There was nothing I could do about it.'

He could see the sharp edges of anger in her eyes. He knew it was directed at him but more toward herself. She could list all her reasons out loud but inside Bosch thought she paid a price every day for not having done the right thing.

'You think Conklin did it?'

'I don't know. All I know is that she'd been with him before and there was never anything violent. I don't know the answer to that.'

'Any idea now who called you?'

'No, none.'

'Conklin?'

'I don't know. I didn't know his voice anyway.'

'Did you ever see them together, my mother and him?'

'Once, at a dance at the Masonic. I think it was the night they met. Johnny Fox introduced them. I don't think Arno knew … anything about her. At least, then.'

'Could it have been Fox who called you?'

'No. I would've recognized his voice.'

Bosch thought a moment.

'Did you ever see Fox again after that morning?'

'No. I avoided him for a week. It was easy because I think he was hiding from the cops. But after that I was gone. Whoever called me, he put the fear of God in me. I left town for Long Beach the day the cops said they were done with me. Packed one suitcase and took the bus ... I remember, your mother had some of my clothes in her apartment. Things that she had borrowed. I didn't even bother to try to get them. I just took what I had and left.'

Bosch was silent. He had nothing else to ask.

'I think about those days a lot, you know,' Katherine said. 'We were in the gutter, your mother and I, but we were good friends and we had fun in spite of it all.'

'You know, all my memories ... you're in a lot of them. You were always there with her.'

'We had a lot of laughs in spite of everything,' she said wistfully. 'And you, you were the highlight of it all. You know, when they took you away from her, it nearly killed her right then ... She never stopped trying to get you back, Harry. I hope you know that. She loved you. I loved you.'

'Yes, I know that.'

'But after you were gone, she wasn't the same. Sometimes I think what happened to her was sort of inevitable. Sometimes I think it was like she had been heading toward that alley for a long time beforehand.'

Bosch stood up, looking at the sorrow in her eyes.

'I better go. I'll let you know what happens.'

'I'd like that. I'd like to stay in touch.'

'I'd like that, too.'

He headed toward the door knowing that they wouldn't stay in touch. Time had eroded the bond between them. They were strangers who shared the same story. On the outside step he turned and looked back at her.

'The Christmas card you sent. You wanted me to look into this back then, didn't you?'

She brought out the faraway smile again.

'I don't know. My husband had just died and I was taking stock, you know? I thought about her. And you. I'm proud of how I turned out, Little Harry. So I think about what there could have been for her and you. I'm still mad. Whoever did this should ...'

She didn't finish but Bosch nodded.

'Good-bye, Harry.'

'You know, my mother, she had a good friend.'

'I hope so.'

❖ ❖ ❖ ❖ ❖ ❖ ❖ ❖

Back in his car Bosch took his notebook out and looked at the list.

> Conklin
> McKittrick & Eno
> Meredith Roman
> Johnny Fox

He drew a line through Meredith Roman's name and studied those left on it. He knew that the way he had ordered the names was not the same order in which he would attempt to interview them. He knew that before he could approach Conklin, or even McKittrick and Eno, he needed more information.

He took his phone book out of his coat pocket and his portable from his briefcase. He dialed the Department of Motor Vehicles law enforcement line in Sacramento and identified himself to the clerk as Lieutenant Harvey Pounds. He gave Pounds's serial number and asked for a license check on Johnny Fox. After checking his notebook, he gave the appropriate date of birth. As he did this he ran the numbers and figured that Fox was now sixty-one years old.

As he continued to wait he smiled because Pounds would have some explaining to do in about a month. The department had recently begun to audit use of the DMV trace service. Because the *Daily News* had reported that cops all over the department were secretly doing the traces for friendly reporters and private detectives with liberal expense accounts, the new chief had cracked down by requiring all calls and computer link-ups to DMV to be documented on the newly implemented DMVT form, which required attribution of traces to a specific case or purpose. The forms were sent to Parker Center and then audited against the list of traces provided each month by the DMV. When the lieutenant's name showed up on the DMV list in the next audit and there was no corresponding DMVT form, he'd get a call from the auditors.

Bosch had gotten the lieutenant's serial number off his ID card one day when Pounds had left it clipped to his jacket on the coatrack outside his office. He'd written it down in his phone book on a hunch that one day it would come in handy.

The DMV clerk finally came back on the line and said there was no driver's license presently issued to a Johnny Fox with the birth date Bosch had provided.

'Anything close?'

'No, honey.'

'That's Lieutenant, miss,' Bosch said sternly. 'Lieutenant Pounds.'

'That's Ms, Lieutenant. Ms Sharp.'

'And I bet you are. Tell me, Ms Sharp, how far back does that computer run go?'

'Seven years. Anything else?'

'How do I check the years before that?'

'You don't. If you want a hand records search you drop us a letter, Loo-ten-ANT. It will take ten to fourteen days. In your case, count on the fourteen. Anything else?'

'No, but I don't like your demeanor.'

'That makes us even. Good-bye.'

Bosch laughed out loud after flipping the phone closed. He was sure now that trace wouldn't get lost in the process. Ms. Sharp would see to that. The name Pounds would probably be on the top of the list when it came in to Parker Center. He dialed Edgar's number on the homicide table next and caught him before he had left the bureau for the day.

'Harry, what's up?'

'You busy?'

'No. Nothing new.'

'Can you run a name for me? I already did DMV but I need somebody to do the computer.'

'Uh …'

'Look, can you or can't you? If you're worried about Pounds, then –'

'Hey, Harry, cool it. What's wrong with you, man? I didn't say I couldn't do it. Just give me the name.'

Bosch couldn't understand why Edgar's attitude enraged him. He took a breath and tried to calm down.

'The name's John Fox. Johnny Fox.'

'Shit, there's going to be a hundred John Foxes. You got a DOB?'

'Yeah, I got a DOB.'

Bosch checked his notebook again and gave it to him.

'What'd he do to you? Say, how you doing?'

'Funny. I'll tell you later. You going to run it?'

'Yes, I said I'll do it.'

'Okay, you got my portable number. If you can't get through, leave me a message at home.'

'When I can get to it, Harry.'

'What, you said nothing's happening.'

'Nothing is, but I'm working, man. I can't be running around doing shit for you all the time.'

Bosch was stunned into a short moment of silence.

'Hey, Jerry, fuck you, I'll do it myself.'

'Look, Harry, I'm not saying I'm –'

62

'No, I mean it. Never mind. I don't want to compromise you with your new partner or your fearless leader. I mean after all, that's what it's about, isn't it? So don't give me this shit about working. You're not working. You're about to go out the door for home and you know it. Or wait a minute, maybe it's drinks with Burnsie again tonight.'

'Harry –'

'Take care, man.'

Bosch flipped the phone closed and sat there letting the anger work out of him like heat from the grill of a radiator. The phone rang while it was still in his hand and he immediately felt better. He flipped it open.

'Look, I'm sorry, okay?' he said. 'Forget it.'

There was a long silence.

'Hello?'

It was a woman's voice. Bosch felt immediately embarrassed.

'Yes?'

'Detective Bosch?'

'Yes, I'm sorry, I thought it was someone else.'

'Like who?'

'Who is this?'

'It's Dr Hinojos.'

'Oh.' Bosch closed his eyes and the anger came back. 'What can I do for you?'

'I was just calling to remind you that we have a session tomorrow. Three-thirty. You will be there?'

'I don't have a choice, remember? And you don't have to call to remind me about our sessions. Believe it or not, I have an appointment calendar, a watch, an alarm clock, all of that stuff now.'

He immediately thought he had gone over the top with the sarcasm.

'Sounds like I caught you at a bad time. I'll let –'

'You did.'

'– you go. See you tomorrow, Detective Bosch.'

'Good-bye.'

He snapped the phone closed again and dropped it on the seat. He started the car. He took Ocean Park out to Bundy and then up toward the 10. As he approached the freeway overpass he saw the eastbound cars on top weren't moving and the on ramp was jammed with cars waiting to wait.

'Fuck it,' he said out loud.

He went by the freeway ramp without turning and then under the overpass. He took Bundy up to Wilshire and then headed west into downtown Santa Monica. It took him fifteen minutes to find street parking near the Third Street Promenade. He had been avoiding multilevel parking garages since the quake and didn't want to start using them now.

What a walking contradiction, Bosch thought as he prowled for a parking spot along the curb. You live in a condemned house the inspectors claim is ready to slide down the hill but you won't go into a parking garage. He finally found a spot across from the porno theater about a block from the Promenade.

Bosch spent the rush hours walking up and down the three-block stretch of outdoor restaurants, movie theaters and shops. He went into the King George on Santa Monica, which he knew was a hangout for some of the detectives out of West LA Division, but didn't see anybody he knew. After that, he ate pizza from a to-go joint and people-watched. He saw a street performer juggling five butcher knives at once. And he thought he might know something about how the man felt.

He sat on a bench and watched the droves of people pass him by. The only ones who stopped and paid attention to him were the homeless, and soon he had no change or dollar bills left to give them. Bosch felt alone. He thought about Katherine Register and what she had said about the past. She had said she was strong but he knew that comfort and strength could come from sadness. That was what she had.

He thought about what she had done five years ago. Her husband dead, she had taken stock of her life and found the hole in her memories. The pain. She had sent him the card in hopes he might do something then. And it had almost worked. He had pulled the murder book from the archives but hadn't had the strength, or maybe it was the weakness, to look at it.

After it got dark he walked down Broadway to Mr B's, found a stool at the bar and ordered a draft with a Jack Daniels depth charge. There was a quintet playing on the small stage in the back, the lead on tenor saxophone. They were finishing up 'Do Nothing Till You Hear from Me' and Bosch got the idea he had come in at the end of a long set. The sax was draggy. It wasn't a clean sound.

Disappointed, he looked away from the group and took a large swallow of beer. He checked his watch and knew he'd have clear driving if he left now. But he stayed. He picked the shot up and dropped it into the mug and drank deeply from the brutal mix. The group moved into 'What a Wonderful World.' No one in the band stepped up to sing the words but, of course, nobody could touch Louis Armstrong's vocals if they tried. It was okay, though. Bosch knew the words.

> I see trees of green
> Red roses, too
> I see them bloom
> For me and you
> And I think to myself
> What a wonderful world

The song made him feel lonely and sad but that was okay. Loneliness had been the trash can fire he huddled around for most of his life. He was just getting used to it again. It had been that way for him before Sylvia and it could be that way again. It would just take time and the pain of letting her go.

In the three months since she had left, there had been the one postcard and nothing else. Her absence had fractured the sense of continuity in his life. Before her, his job had always been the iron rails, as dependable as the sunset over the Pacific. But with her he had attempted to switch tracks, the bravest jump he had ever made. But somehow he had failed. It wasn't enough to keep her and she was gone. And now he felt he had run clear off the tracks. Inside, he felt as fragmented as his city. Broken, it seemed at times, at every level.

He heard a female voice from nearby singing the words of the song. He turned to see a young woman a few stools away, her eyes closed as she sang very softly. She sang only to herself but Bosch could hear.

> I see skies of blue
> And clouds of white
> The bright blessed day
> The dark sacred night
> And I think to myself
> What a wonderful world

She wore a short white skirt, a T-shirt and a brightly colored vest. Bosch guessed she wasn't older than twenty-five and he liked the idea that she even knew the song. She sat straight, her legs crossed. Her back swayed with the music of the saxophone. Her face was framed by brown hair and was turned upward, her lips slightly apart, almost angelic. Bosch thought she was quite beautiful, so totally lost in the majesty of the music. Clean or not, the sound took her away and he admired her for letting it. He knew that what he saw in her face was what a man would see if he made love to her. She had what other cops called a getaway face. So beautiful it would always be a shield. No matter what she did or what was done to her, her face would be her ticket. It would open doors in front of her, close them behind her. It would let her get away.

The song ended and she opened her eyes and clapped. No one else had applauded until she began. Then everyone in the bar, Bosch included, joined in. Such was the power of the getaway face. Bosch turned and flagged the bartender for another shot and beer. When it was down in front of him he took a glance over at the woman, but she was gone. He turned and checked the bar's door and saw it closing. He'd missed her.

❖ ❖ ❖ ❖ ❖ ❖ ❖

On the way home he worked his way up to Sunset and took that all the way into the city. Traffic was sparse. He had stayed out later than he had planned. He smoked and listened to the all-news channel on the radio. There was a report about Grant High finally reopening in the Valley. It was where Sylvia had taught. Before going to Venice.

Bosch was tired and guessed that he probably wouldn't pass a breath test if stopped. He dropped his speed to below the limit as Sunset cut through Beverly Hills. He knew the cops in BH wouldn't cut him a break and that would be all he'd need on top of the involuntary stress leave.

He turned left at Laurel Canyon and took the winding road up the hill. At Mulholland he was about to turn right on red when he checked the traffic from the left and froze. He saw a coyote step out of the brush of the arroyo to the left of the roadway and take a tentative look around the intersection. There were no other cars. Only Bosch saw this.

The animal was thin and ragged, worn by the struggle to sustain itself in the urban hills. The mist rising from the arroyo caught the reflection of the street lights and cast the coyote in almost a dim blue light. And it seemed to study Bosch's car for a moment, its eyes catching the reflection of the stoplight and glowing. For just a moment Bosch believed that the coyote might be looking directly at him. Then the animal turned and moved back into the blue mist.

A car came up behind him and honked. Bosch had the green light. He waved and made the turn onto Mulholland. But then he pulled to the side. He put the car in park and got out.

It was a cool evening and he felt a chill as he walked across the intersection to the spot where he had seen the blue coyote. He wasn't sure what he was doing but he wasn't afraid. He just wanted to see the animal again. He stopped at the edge of the drop-off and looked down into the darkness below. The blue mist was all around him now. A car passed behind him and when the noise receded he listened and looked intently. But there was nothing. The coyote was gone. He walked back to his car and drove on Mulholland to Woodrow Wilson Drive to home.

Later, as he lay in his bed after more drinks and with the light still on, he smoked the last cigarette of the night and stared up at the ceiling. He'd left the light on but his thoughts were of the dark, sacred night. And the blue coyote. And the woman with the getaway face. Soon all of those thoughts disappeared with him into the dark.

❖ ❖ ❖ ❖ ❖ ❖ ❖

Bosch got little sleep and was up before the sun. The last cigarette of the night before had nearly been his last for all time. He had fallen asleep with it between his fingers, only to be jolted awake by the searing pain of the burn. He dressed the wounds on two fingers and tried to return to sleep, but it wouldn't take him. His fingers throbbed and all he could think of was how many times he had investigated the deaths of hapless drunks who had fallen asleep and self-immolated. All he could think of was what Carmen Hinojos would have to say about such a stunt. How was that for a symptom of self-destruction?

Finally, as dawn's light began to leak into the room he gave up on sleep and got up. While coffee brewed in the kitchen he went into the bathroom and rebandaged the burns on his fingers. As he taped the fresh gauze on, he glanced at himself in the mirror and saw the deep lines under his eyes.

'Shit,' he said to himself. 'What's going on?'

He had black coffee on the back deck while watching the silent city come awake. There was a crisp chill in the air and the earthy smell of eucalyptus was rising from the tall trees down in the pass. The marine fog layer had filled the pass and the hills were just mysterious silhouettes in the mist. He watched the morning begin for nearly an hour, fascinated by the show he had from his deck.

It wasn't until he went back inside for a second cup that

he noticed the red light flashing on his phone machine. He had two messages that had probably been left the day before and that he hadn't noticed after coming in last night. He pressed the play button.

'Bosch, this is Lieutenant Pounds calling on Tuesday at three thirty-five. I have to inform you that while you are on leave and until your, uh, status with the department is decided, you will be required to return your vehicle to the Hollywood Division garage. I have here that it is a four-year-old Chevrolet Caprice, tag number one-adam-adam-three-four-zero-two. Please make arrangements immediately to have the car turned in and checked out. This order is per *Standard Practices Manual* citation three dash thirteen. Violation could result in suspension and/or dismissal. Again, this is an order from Lieutenant Pounds, now three thirty-six on Tuesday. If there is any part of this message that you do not understand, feel free to contact me at the office.'

The machine reported the message had actually been left at 4 P.M. Tuesday, probably right before Pounds had gone home for the day. Fuck him, Bosch thought. The car's a piece of shit anyway. He can have it.

The second message was from Edgar.

'Harry, you there? It's Edgar ... Okay, listen, let's forget about today, okay? I mean it. Let's just say I was a prick and you were a prick and we're both pricks and forget it. Whether it turns out you are my partner or you were my partner, I owe you a lot, man. And if I ever act like I forgot that, hit me alongside the head like you did today. Now, to the bad news. I checked everything on this Johnny Fox. I got exactly nothing, man. That's from the NCIC, DOJ, DPP, Corrections, National Warrants, everything. I ran the works on him. Looks like this guy is clean, if he's alive. You say he doesn't even have a DL so that makes me think maybe you got a phony name there or maybe this guy ain't among the living. So, that's that. I don't know what you're up to but if you want anything else, give a call … Oh, and hang in there, buddy. I'm ten-seven after this so you can reach me at home if –'

The message cut off. Edgar had run out of time. Bosch rewound the tape and poured his coffee. Back on the deck he mulled over the whereabouts of Johnny Fox. When he had gotten nothing on the DMV trace, Bosch had assumed Fox might be in prison, where driver's licenses weren't issued or needed. But Edgar had not found him there nor had he found his name on any national computer that tracks criminals. Now Bosch guessed that Johnny Fox had either gone straight or, as Edgar had suggested, was dead. If Bosch was betting, he'd take the latter. Men like Johnny Fox didn't go straight.

Bosch's alternative was to go down to the Los Angeles County Hall of Records and look for a death certificate but without a date of death it would be a needle in the haystack search. It might take him days. Before he'd do that, he decided, he'd try an easier way, the *LA Times*.

He went back inside to the phone and dialed a reporter named Keisha Russell. She was new on the cop beat and still struggling to find her way. She had made a subtle attempt to recruit Bosch as a source a few months earlier. The way reporters usually did that was to write an inordinate number of stories on a crime that did not merit such intense attention. But the process put them in constant contact with the detectives on the case and that allowed them the chance to ingratiate themselves and hopefully procure the investigators as future sources.

Russell had written five stories in a week about one of Bosch's cases. It was a domestic violence case in which a husband had disregarded a temporary restraining order and gone to his separated wife's new apartment on Franklin. He carried her to the fifth-floor balcony and threw her off.

He went over next. Russell had talked to Bosch repeatedly during the stretch of stories. The resultant dispatches were thorough and complete. It was good work and she began to earn Bosch's respect. Still, he knew that she hoped that the stories and her attention would be the building blocks of a long reporter/investigator relationship. Since then not a week had gone by that she didn't call Bosch once or twice to bullshit, pass along departmental gossip she had picked up from other sources, and ask the one question all reporters live and die by: 'Anything going on?'

She answered on the first ring and Bosch was a little surprised she was in so early. He was planning on leaving a message on her voice mail.

'Keisha, it's Bosch.'

'Hey, Bosch, how you doing?'

'Okay, I guess. I guess you heard about me.'

'Not everything, but I heard you went on temporary leave. But nobody would tell me why. You want to talk about it?'

'No, not really. I mean, not now. I have a favor to ask. If it works out, I'll give you the story. That's the deal I've made in the past with other reporters.'

'What do I have to do?'

'Just walk over to the morgue.'

She groaned.

'I mean the newspaper morgue, right there at the Times.'

'Oh, that's better. What do you need?'

'I've got a name. It's old. I know the guy was a dirtbag in the fifties and at least the early sixties. But I've lost track of him after that. Thing is, my hunch is that he's dead.'

'You want an obit?'

'Well, I don't know if this is the type of guy the Times would write an obituary on. He was strictly small time, near as I can tell. I was thinking that there might be a story, you know, if his death was sort of untimely.'

'You mean like if he got his shit blown away.'

'You got it.'

'Okay, I'll take a look.'

She seemed eager, Bosch sensed. He knew that she thought that by doing this favor she would be cementing their relationship in place and it would only pay dividends in the future. He said nothing that would dissuade her of this.

'What's the name?'

'His name is John Fox. He went by Johnny. Last I have a trace on him is 1961. He was a pimp, general piece of trash.'

'White, black, yellow or brown?'

'General piece of white trash, you could say.'

'You have a birth date? It will help narrow it down if there's more than one Johnny Fox in the clips.'

He gave it to her.

'Okay, where you going to be?'

Bosch gave her his portable phone number. He knew that would set the hook. The number would go right onto the source list she kept in her computer like gold earrings in a jewelry box. Having the number where he could be reached at almost any time was worth the search in the morgue.

'Okay, listen, I've got a meeting with my editor – that's the only reason I'm in this early. But after, I'll go take a look. I'll call you as soon as I have something.'

'If there is something.'

'Right.'

After Bosch hung up he ate some Frosted Flakes from a box he took out of the refrigerator and turned on the news radio. He had discontinued the newspaper after the

74

earthquake in case Gowdy, the building inspector, happened by early and saw it out front, a clue that someone was inhabiting the uninhabitable. There was nothing much in the top of the news summary that interested him. No homicides in Hollywood, at least. He wasn't missing out on anything.

There was one story after the traffic report that caught his attention. An octopus on display at a city aquarium in San Pedro had apparently killed itself by pulling a water circulation tube out of its tank fitting with one of its tentacles. The tank emptied and the octopus died. Environmental groups were calling it suicide, a desperate protest by the octopus against its captivity. Only in LA, Bosch thought as he turned the radio off. A place so desperate even the marine life was killing itself.

He took a long shower, closing his eyes and holding his head directly under the spray. As he was shaving in front of the mirror after, he couldn't help but study the circles under his eyes again. They seemed even more pronounced than earlier and fit nicely with the eyes cracked with red from his drinking the night before.

He put the razor down on the edge of the sink and leaned closer to the mirror. His skin was as pale as a recycled paper plate. As he appraised himself, the thought he had was that he had once been considered a handsome man. Not anymore. He looked beaten. It seemed that age was gripping him, beating him down. He thought that he resembled some of the old men he'd seen after they were found dead in their beds. The ones in the rooming houses. The ones living in refrigerator boxes. He reminded himself more of the dead than the living.

He opened the medicine cabinet so the reflection would go away. He looked among the various items on the glass shelves and chose a squeeze bottle of Murine. He put in a heavy dose of the eye drops, wiped the excess spill off his face with a towel and left the bathroom without closing the cabinet and having to look at himself again.

He put on his best clean suit, a gray two-piece, and a white button-down shirt. He added his maroon tie with gladiator helmets on it. It was his favorite tie. And his oldest. One edge of it was fraying but he wore it two or three times a week. He'd bought it ten years earlier when he was first assigned to homicide. He pegged it in place on his shirt with a gold tie tack that formed the number 187 – the California penal code for homicide. As he did this, he felt a measure of control come back to him. He began to feel good and whole again, and to feel angry. He was ready to go out into the world, whether or not it was ready for him.

❖ ❖ ❖ ❖ ❖ ❖ ❖

osch pulled the knot of his tie tight against his throat
before pulling open the back door of the station. He
took the hallway to the rear of the detective bureau
and then the aisle between the tables toward the front,
where Pounds sat in his office behind the glass windows
that separated him from the detectives he commanded.
Heads at the burglary table bobbed up as he was noticed,
then at the robbery and homicide tables. Bosch did not
acknowledge anyone, though he almost lost a step when
he saw someone sitting in his seat at the homicide table.
Burns. Edgar was there at his own spot, but his back was to
Bosch's path and he didn't see Harry coming through the
room.

But Pounds did. Through the glass wall he saw Bosch's
approach to his office and he stood up behind his desk.

The first thing Bosch noticed as he got closer was that
the glass panel that he had broken just a week before in the
office had already been replaced. He thought it was strange
that this could happen so quickly in a department where
more vital repairs – such as replacing the bullet-riddled
windshield of a patrol car – normally took a month of red
tape and paper pushing. But those were the priorities of
this department.

'Henry!' Pounds barked. 'Come in here.'

An old man who sat at the front counter and took calls
on the public line and gave general directions jumped up

and doddered into the glass office. He was a civilian volunteer, one of several who worked in the station, mainly retirees that most cops referred to collectively as members of the Nod Squad.

Bosch followed the old man in and put his briefcase down on the floor.

'Bosch!' Pounds yelped. 'There's a witness here.'

He pointed to old Henry, then out through the glass. 'Witnesses out there as well.'

Bosch could see that Pounds still had deep purple remnants of broken capillaries under each eye. The swelling was gone, though. Bosch walked up to the desk and reached into the pocket of his coat.

'Witnesses to what?'

'To whatever you're doing here.'

Bosch turned to look at Henry.

'Henry, you can leave now. I'm just going to talk to the lieutenant.'

'Henry, you stay,' Pounds commanded. 'I want you to hear this.'

'How do you know he'll remember it, Pounds? He can't even transfer a call to the right table.'

Bosch looked back at Henry again and fixed him with a stare that left no doubt who was in charge in the glass room.

'Close the door on your way out.'

Henry made a timid glance back at Pounds but then quickly headed out the door, closing it as instructed. Bosch turned back to Pounds.

The lieutenant slowly, like a cat sneaking past a dog, lowered himself into his seat, perhaps thinking or knowing from experience that there might be more safety in not being at a face-to-face level with Bosch. Harry looked down and saw that there was a book open on the desk. He reached down and turned the cover to see what it was.

'Studying for the captain's exam, Lieutenant?'

Pounds shrank back from Bosch's reach. Bosch saw it was not the captain's exam manual but a book on creating and honing motivational skills in employees. It had been written by a professional basketball coach. Bosch had to laugh and shake his head.

'Pounds, you know, you're really something. I mean, at least you're entertaining. I gotta give you that.'

Pounds grabbed the book back and shoved it in a drawer.

'What do you want, Bosch? You know you're not supposed to be in here. You're on leave.'

'But you called me in, remember?'

'I did not.'

'The car. You said you wanted the car.'

'I said turn it in at the garage. I didn't say come in here. Now get out!'

Bosch could see the rosy spread of anger on the other man's face. Bosch remained cool and took that as a sign of a declining level of stress. He brought his hand out of his pocket with the car keys in them. He dropped them on the desk in front of Pounds.

'It's parked out by the drunk tank door. You want it back, you can have it. But you take it through the checkout at the garage. That's not a cop's job. That's a job for a bureaucrat.'

Bosch turned to leave and picked up his briefcase. He then opened the door to the office with such force that it swung around and banged against one of the glass panels of the office. The whole office shook but nothing broke. He walked around the counter, saying, 'Sorry about that, Henry,' without looking at the old man, and then headed down the front hall.

A few minutes later he was standing on the curb on Wilcox, in front of the station, waiting for the cab he had called with his portable. A gray Caprice, almost a duplicate of the car he had just turned in, pulled up in front of him and he bent down to look in. It was Edgar. He was smiling. The window glided down.

'You need a ride, tough guy?'

Bosch got in.

'There's a Hertz on La Brea near the Boulevard.'

'Yeah, I know it.'

They drove in silence for a few minutes, then Edgar laughed and shook his head.

'What?'

'Nothing ... Burns, man. I think he was about to shit his pants when you were in there with Pounds. He thought you were gonna come outta there and throw his ass outta your chair at the table. He was pitiful.'

'Shit. I should've. I didn't think of it.'

Silence came back again. They were on Sunset coming up to La Brea.

'Harry, you just can't help yourself, can you?'

'I guess not.'

'What happened to your hand?'

Bosch held it up and studied the bandage.

'Ah, I hit it last week when I was working on the deck. Hurt like a son of a bitch.'

'Yeah, you better be careful or Pounds is going to be on you like a son of a bitch.'

'He already is.'

'Man, he's nothing but a bean counter, a punk. Why can't you just leave it alone? You know you're just –'

'You know, you're beginning to sound like the shrink they're sending me to. Maybe I should just sit with you for an hour today, what you say?'

'Maybe she's talking some sense to you.'

'Maybe I should've taken the cab.'

'I think you should figure out who your friends are and listen to them for once.'

'Here it is.'

Edgar slowed in front of the rental car agency. Bosch got out before the car was even stopped.

'Harry, wait a minute.'

Bosch looked back in at him.

'What's going on with this Fox thing? Who is the guy?'

'I can't tell you now, Jerry. It's just better this way.'

'You sure?'

Bosch heard the phone in his briefcase start to ring. He looked down at it and then back at Edgar.

'Thanks for the ride.'

He closed the car door.

❖ ❖ ❖ ❖ ❖ ❖ ❖

The call was from Keisha Russell at the *Times*. She said she'd found one small story in the morgue under Fox's name but she wanted to meet with Bosch to give it to him. He knew it was part of the game, part of making the pact. He looked at his watch. He could wait to see what the story said. He told her he'd buy her lunch at the Pantry in downtown.

Forty minutes later she was already in a booth near the cashier's cage when he got there. He slipped into the opposite side of the booth.

'You're late,' she said.

'Sorry, I was renting a car.'

'They took your car, huh? Must be serious.'

'We're not going to talk about that.'

'I know. You know who owns this place?'

'Yeah, the mayor. Doesn't make the food bad.'

She curled her lip and looked around as if the place were crawling with ants. The mayor was a Republican. The *Times* had gone with the Democrat. What was worse, for her, at least, was that the mayor was a supporter of the Police Department. Reporters didn't like that. That was boring. They wanted City Hall infighting, controversy, scandal. It made things more interesting.

'Sorry,' he said. 'I guess I could've suggested Gorky's or some more liberal establishment.'

'Don't worry about it, Bosch. I'm just funnin' with ya.'

She wasn't more than twenty-five, he guessed. She was a dark-complected black woman who had a beautiful grace about her. Bosch had no idea where she was from but he didn't think it was LA. She had the touch of an accent, a Caribbean lilt, that maybe she had worked on smoothing out. It was still there, though. He liked the way she said his name. In her mouth, it sounded exotic, like a wave breaking. He didn't mind that she was little more than half his age and addressed him only by his last name.

'Where you from, Keisha?'

'Why?'

'Why? Because I'm interested is all. You're on the beat. I wanna know who I'm dealing with.'

'I'm from right here, Bosch. I came from Jamaica when I was five years old. I went to USC. Where are you from?'

'Right here. Been here all my life.'

He decided not to mention the fifteen months he spent fighting in the tunnels in Vietnam and the nine in North Carolina training for it.

'What happened to your hand?'

'Cut it working on my house. Been doing odd jobs while I'm off. So, what's it been like taking Bremmer's place on the cop beat? He'd been there a long time.'

'Yeah, I know. It's been difficult. But I'm making my way. Slowly. I'm making friends. I hope you'll be one of my friends, Bosch.'

'I'll be your friend. When I can. Let's see what you got.'

She brought a manila file up onto the table but the waiter, an old bald man with a waxed mustache, arrived before she could open it. She ordered an egg salad sandwich. He ordered a well-done hamburger and fries. She frowned and he guessed why.

'You're vegetarian, right?'

'Yes.'

'Sorry. Next time you pick the place.'

83

'I will.'

She opened the file and he noticed she had several bracelets on her left wrist. They were made of braided thread in many bright colors. He looked in the file and saw a photocopy of a small newspaper clipping. Bosch could tell by the size of the clip that it was one of the stories that gets buried in the back of the paper. She passed it over to him.

'I think this is your Johnny Fox. The age is right but it does not describe him like you did. White trash, you said.'

Bosch read the story. It was dated September 30, 1962.

CAMPAIGN WORKER VICTIM OF HIT AND RUN
By Monte Kim, *Times* Staff Writer

A 29-year-old campaign worker for a candidate for the district attorney's office was killed Saturday when he was struck by a speeding car in Hollywood, the Los Angeles police reported.

The victim was identified as Johnny Fox, who lived in an apartment on Ivar Street in Hollywood. Police said Fox had been distributing campaign literature supporting district attorney hopeful Arno Conklin at the corner of Hollywood Boulevard and La Brea Avenue when he was cut down by the speeding car as he crossed the street.

Fox was crossing the southbound lanes of La Brea about 2 P.M. when the car struck him. Police said it appeared Fox was killed on impact and his body was dragged for several yards by the car.

The car that hit Fox slowed momentarily after the collision but then sped away, police said. Witnesses told investigators the car proceeded south on La Brea at a high rate of speed. Police have not located the vehicle and witnesses could not provide a clear description of the make and model year. Police said an investigation is continuing.

Conklin campaign manager Gordon Mittel said Fox had

joined the campaign only a week ago.

Reached at the district attorney's office, where he is in charge of the special investigation branch under retiring DA John Charles Stock, Conklin said he had not yet met Fox but regretted the death of the man working for his election. The candidate declined further comment.

Bosch studied the clip for a long moment after reading it. 'This Monte Kim, is he still at the paper?'

'Are you kidding? That's like a millennium ago. Back then the newsroom was a bunch of white guys sitting around in white shirts and ties.'

Bosch looked down at his own shirt, then at her.

'Sorry,' she said. 'Anyway, he's not around. And I don't know about Conklin. A little before my time. Did he win?'

'Yeah. I think he had two terms, then I think he ran for attorney general or something and got his ass handed to him. Something like that. I wasn't here then.'

'I thought you said you've been here all your life.'

'I went away for a while.'

'Vietnam, right?'

'Right.'

'Yeah, a lot of cops your age were there. Must've been a trip. Is that why you all became cops? So you could keep carrying guns?'

'Something like that.'

'Anyway, if Conklin's still alive, he's probably an old man. But Mittel's still around. Obviously, you know that. He's probably in one of these booths eating with the mayor.'

She smiled and he ignored it.

'Yeah, he's a big shot. What's the story on him?'

'Mittel? I don't know. First name on a big downtown

law firm, friend of governors and senators and other powerful people. Last I heard, he's running the financing behind Robert Shepherd.'

'Robert Shepherd? You mean that computer guy?'

'More like computer magnate. Yeah, don't you read the paper? Shepherd wants to run but doesn't want to use up his own money. Mittel is doing the fund-raising for an exploratory campaign.'

'Run for what?'

'Jesus, Bosch, you don't read the paper or watch TV.'

'I've been busy. Run for what?'

'Well, like any egomaniac I guess he wants to run for president. But for now he's looking at the Senate. Shepherd wants to be a third-party candidate. Says the Republicans are too far right and the Democrats too left. He's right down the middle. And from what I hear, if anybody can get the money together for him to do the third-candidate dance, it's Mittel.'

'So Mittel wants to make himself a president.'

'I guess. But what are you asking me about him for anyway? I'm a cop reporter. You're a cop. What's this have to do with Gordon Mittel?'

She pointed to the photocopy. Bosch became aware that he might have asked too many questions.

'I'm just trying to catch up,' he said. 'Like you said, I don't read the papers.'

'That's *paper,* not papers,' she said smiling. 'I better not catch you reading or talking to the *Daily Snews.*'

'Hell hath no fury like a reporter scorned, right?'

'Something like that.'

He felt assured that he had deflected her suspicions. He held up the photocopy.

'There was no follow-up to this? They never caught anybody?'

'I guess not or there would be a story.'

'Can I keep this?'

'Sure.'

'You feel like taking another walk back to the morgue?'

'For what?'

'Stories about Conklin.'

'There will be hundreds, Bosch. You said he was DA for two terms.'

'I only want stories from before he was elected. And if you have the time, throw in stories on Mittel, too.'

'You know, you're asking a lot. I could get in trouble if they knew I was doing clip searches for a cop.'

She put on a fake pout and he ignored that, too. He knew what she was driving at.

'You want to tell me what this is about, Bosch?'

He still didn't say anything.

'I didn't think so. Well, look, I've got two interviews to do this afternoon. I'm going to be gone. What I can do is get an intern to get the clips together and leave it all for you with the guard in the globe lobby. It will be in an envelope so nobody will know what it is. Would that be okay?'

He nodded. He'd been to Times Square before on a handful of occasions, usually meetings with reporters. It was a block-sized building with two lobbies. The center-piece of the lobby at the First and Spring entrance was a huge globe that never stopped rotating, just as the news never stopped happening.

'You'll just leave it under my name? Won't that get you in trouble? You know, like you said, being too friendly with a cop. That's got to be against the rules over there.'

She smiled at his sarcasm.

'Don't worry. If an editor or somebody asks, I'll just say it's an investment in the future. You better remember that, Bosch. Friendship is a two-way street.'

'Don't worry. I never forget that.'

He leaned forward across the table so he was up close to her face.

'I want you to remember something, too. One of the reasons I'm not telling you why I need this stuff is because I'm not sure what it means. If anything. But don't you get too curious. Don't you go making any calls. You do that, and you might mess things up. I might get hurt. You might get hurt. Got it?'

'Got it.'

The man with the waxed mustache appeared at the side of the table with their plates.

✧ ✧ ✧ ✧ ✧ ✧ ✧

'I noticed you arrived early today. Am I to take that as a sign that you want to be here?'

'Not especially. I was downtown having lunch with a friend, so I just came over.'

'Well, it's good to hear you were out with a friend. I think that is good.'

Carmen Hinojos was behind her desk. The notebook was out and open but she sat with her hands clasped together in front of her. It was as if she was going out of her way to make no move that could be construed as threatening to the dialogue.

'What happened to your hand?'

Bosch held it up and looked at the bandages on his fingers.

'I hit it with a hammer. I was working on my house.'

'That's too bad. I hope it's okay.'

'I'll live.'

'Why are you so dressed up? I hope you don't feel you have to do that for these sessions.'

'No. I … I just like following my routine. Even if I'm not going to work, I got dressed like I was.'

'I understand.'

After she made an offer of coffee or water and Bosch declined, she got the session going.

'Tell me, what would you like to talk about today?'

'I don't care. You're the boss.'

89

'I'd rather that you not look at the relationship in that way. I'm not your boss, Detective Bosch. I'm just a facilitator, someone to help you talk about whatever you want, whatever you want to get off your chest.'

Bosch was silent. He couldn't think of anything to volunteer. Carmen Hinojos drummed her pencil on her yellow tablet for a few moments before taking up the slack.

'Nothing at all, huh?'

'Nothing comes to mind.'

'Then why don't we talk about yesterday. When I called you, to remind you of our session today, you obviously seemed upset about something. Was that when you hit your hand?'

'No, that wasn't it.'

He stopped but she said nothing and he decided to give in a little bit. He had to admit to himself that there was something about her that he liked. She was not threatening and he believed she was telling the truth when she said she was there only to help him.

'What happened when you called was that I had found out earlier that my partner, you know, my partner before all of this, had been paired up with a new man. I've been replaced already.'

'And how'd that make you feel?'

'You heard how I was. I was mad about it. I think anybody would be. Then I called my partner up later and he treated me like yesterday's news. I taught that guy a lot and ...'

'And what?'

'I don't know. It hurt, I guess.'

'I see.'

'No, I don't think you do. You'd have to be me to see it the way I did.'

'I guess that's true. But I can sympathize. Let's leave it at that. Let me ask you this. Shouldn't you have expected your partner to be paired up again? After all, isn't it a department rule that detectives work in pairs? You are on leave for a so-far-unknown period of time. Wasn't it a given that he'd get a new partner, whether permanent or otherwise?'

'I suppose.'

'Isn't it safer to work in pairs?'

'I suppose.'

'What is your own experience? Did you feel safer the times you were with a partner on the job as opposed to those times when you were alone?'

'Yes, I felt safer.'

'So what happened was inevitable and inarguable, yet still it made you angry.'

'It wasn't that it happened that brought it on. I don't know, it was the way he told me and then the way he acted when I called. I really felt left out. I asked him for a favor and he … I don't know.'

'He what?'

'He hesitated. Partners don't do that. Not with each other. They're supposed be there for each other. It's supposedly a lot like a marriage, but I've never been married.'

She paused to write some notes, which made Bosch wonder what had just been said that was so important.

'You seem,' she said while still writing, 'to have a low threshold for the toleration of frustrations.'

Her statement immediately made him angry but he knew that if he showed it then he would be confirming her statement. He thought maybe it was a trick designed to elicit such a response. He tried to calm himself.

'Doesn't everybody?' he said in a controlled voice.

'I suppose, to a degree. When I reviewed your records I saw that you were in the Army during the Vietnam War. Did you see any combat?'

'Did I *see* any combat? Yes, I saw combat. I was in the middle of combat, too. I was even under it. Why do people always ask, did you *see* combat, like it was a goddamn movie they took you to over there?'

She was quiet for a long time, holding the pen but doing no writing. It seemed like she was simply waiting for the sails of his anger to lose the wind. He waved his hand in a gesture he hoped told her that he was sorry, that it was behind him, that they should move on.

'Sorry,' he said, just to make sure.

She still didn't say anything and her stare was beginning to weigh on him. He looked away from her to the bookshelves along one wall of the office. They were filled with heavy, leather-bound psychiatry texts.

'I am sorry to intrude on such an emotionally sensitive area,' she finally said. 'The reason –'

'But that's what this is all about, right? What you have is a license to intrude and I can't do anything about it.'

'So, then, accept it,' she said sternly. 'We've been over this before. To help you we have to talk about you. Accept it and maybe we can move on. Now, as I was saying, the reason I mentioned the war was that I wanted to ask you if you are familiar with post-traumatic stress syndrome. Have you ever heard of it?'

He looked back at her. He knew what was coming.

'Yes, of course. I've heard of it.'

'Well, Detective, in the past it's primarily been associated with servicemen returning from the war but it's not just a war or post-war problem. It can happen in any kind of stressful environment. Any kind. And I have to say I think that you are a walking, talking example of this disorder's symptoms.'

'Jesus … ,' he said, shaking his head. He turned in his seat so he wasn't looking at her or her bookcase. He stared at the sky through the window. It was cloudless. 'You people sit up here in these offices and have no idea …'

He didn't finish. He just shook his head. He reached to his neck and loosened his tie. It was like he couldn't get enough air into his chest.

'Hear me out, Detective, okay? Just look at the facts here. Can you think of anything more stressful to be in this city during the last few years than a police officer? Between Rodney King and the scrutiny and villainy that brought, the riots, fires, floods and earthquakes, each officer on this force has had to write the book on stress management and, of course, mismanagement.'

'You left out killer bees.'

'I'm being serious.'

'So am I. It was on the news.'

'With all that's happened and gone on in this city, with every one of these calamities, who is in the middle every time? The police officers. The ones who have to respond. The ones who can't stay at home, duck down and wait until it's over. So let's go from that generalization to the individual. You, Detective. You have been a front-line contender with all of these crises. At the same time you've had your real job to contend with. Homicide. It's one of the highest-stress jobs in the department. Tell me, how many murders have you investigated in the last three years?'

'Look, I'm not looking for an excuse. I told you before that I did what I did because I wanted to. It had nothing to do with riots or –'

'How many dead bodies have you looked at? Just answer my question, please. How many dead bodies? How many widows did you break the news to? How many mothers did you tell about their dead children?'

He brought his hands up and rubbed his face. All he knew was that he wanted to hide from her.

'A lot,' he finally whispered.

'More than a lot ...'

He exhaled loudly.

'Thank you for answering. I'm not trying to corner you. The point of my questions and the treatise on the social, cultural and even geologic fragmentation of this city is that what I'm saying here is that you've been through more than most, okay? And this doesn't even include the baggage you might still have from Vietnam or the loss of the romantic relationship. But whatever the reasons, the symptoms of stress are showing. They are there, plain as day. Your intolerance, your inability to sublimate frustrations, most of all your assault on your commanding officer.'

She paused but Bosch didn't say anything. He had a feeling she wasn't finished. She wasn't.

'There are other signs as well,' she continued. 'Your refusal to leave your damaged home can be perceived as a form of denial of what is happening around you. There are physical symptoms. Have you looked at yourself in the mirror lately? I don't think I need to ask to know that you're drinking too much. And your hand. You didn't hurt yourself with a hammer. You fell asleep with a cigarette in your hand. That is a burn and I'd bet my state license on it.'

She opened a drawer and took out two plastic cups and a bottle of water. She filled the cups and pushed one across the desk to him. A peace offering. He watched her silently. He felt exhausted, unrepairable. He also couldn't help but be amazed by her at the same time she was so expertly cutting him open. After she took a sip of water she continued.

'These things are all indicative of a diagnosis of post-traumatic stress syndrome. However, we have one problem with that. The word *post* when used in such a diagnosis indicates the time of stress has passed. That's not the case here. Not in LA. Not with your job. Harry, you are in a nonstop pressure cooker. You owe yourself some breathing room. That's what this leave is all about. Breathing room. Time to recoup and recover. So don't fight it. Grab it. That's the best advice I can give you. Grab it and use it. To save yourself.'

Bosch breathed out heavily and held up his bandaged hand.

'You can keep your state license.'

'Thank you.'

They rested a moment until she continued in a voice meant to soothe him.

'You also have to know you are not alone. This is nothing to be embarrassed about. There has been a sharp increase in incidents of officer stress in the last three years. Behavioral Sciences Services just made a request to the City Council for five more psychologists. Our caseload went from eighteen hundred counseling sessions in 1990 to more than double that last year. We've even got a name for what's going on here. The blue angst. And you have it, Harry.'

Bosch smiled and shook his head, still clinging to what denial he had left.

'The blue angst. Sounds like the name of a Wambaugh novel, doesn't it?'

She didn't answer.

'So what you're saying is that I'm not going to get my job back.'

'No, I'm not saying that at all. All I am saying is that we have a lot of work ahead of us.'

'I feel like I've been broken down by the world champ. You mind if I call you sometime when I'm trying to get a confession out of a hump who won't talk to me?'

'Believe me, just saying that is a start.'

'What do you want me to do?'

'I want you to want to come here. That's all. Don't look at it as a punishment. I want you to work with me, not against me. When we talk I want you to talk about everything and nothing. Anything that comes to mind. Hold back nothing. And one other thing. I'm not telling you to completely cut it out, but you have to cut back on the drinking. You have to have a clear mind. As you obviously know, the effects of alcohol stay with an individual long after the night they were consumed.'

'I'll try. All of it. I'll try.'

'That's all I ask. And since you suddenly seem so willing, I have another thought. I have a cancelation of a session tomorrow at three. Can you make it?'

Bosch hesitated, didn't say anything.

'We seem to finally be working well and I think it will help. The sooner we get through with our work, the sooner you should be able to get back to your work. What do you say?'

'Three?'

'Yes.'

'Okay, I'll be here.'

'Good. Let's get back to our dialogue. Why don't you start? Whatever you want to talk about.'

He leaned forward and reached for the cup of water. He looked at her as he drank from it, then put the cup back on the desk.

'Just say anything?'

'Anything. Whatever is happening in your life or mind that you want to talk about.'

He thought for a long moment.

'I saw a coyote last night. Near my house. I … I was drunk, I guess, but I know I saw him.'

'Why was that significant to you?'

He tried to compose the proper answer.

'I'm not sure … I guess there's not too many left in the hills in the city – least near where I live. So whenever I see one, I get this feeling that it might be the last one left out there. You know? The last coyote. And I guess that would bother me if it ever turned out to be true, if I never saw one again.'

She nodded as if he had scored some point in a game he wasn't sure how to play.

'There used to be one that lived in the canyon below my house. I'd see him down there and –'

'How do you know it was a he? And I think you called the one you saw last night a he. How are you sure?'

'I'm not sure. I guess I don't even know. It's just a guess.'

'Okay. Go on.'

'Um, he – it – lived down there below my house and I used to see him from time to time. After the earthquake it was gone. I don't know what happened to it. Then I saw this one last night. Something about the mist and the light out there … it looked like its coat was blue. He looked hungry. There is something … they're kind of sad and threatening at the same time. You know?'

'Yes, I do.'

'Anyway, I thought about him when I got in bed after I got home. That was when I burned my hand. I fell asleep with the cigarette. But before I woke up I had this dream. I mean, I think it was a dream. Maybe like a daydream, like I was still kind of awake. And in it, whatever it was, the coyote was there again. But it was with me. And we were in the canyon or on a hill or something and I wasn't really sure.'

He held up his hand.

'And then I felt the fire.'

She nodded but didn't say anything.

'So what do you think?' he asked.

'Well, interpretation of dreams is not something I do often. Frankly, I'm not sure of its value. The real value I think I see in what you just told me was the willingness to tell me. It shows me a one-eighty-degree turn in your approach to these sessions. For what it's worth, I think it's clear you identify with the coyote. Perhaps, there are not many policemen like you left and you feel the same threat to your existence or your mission. I don't really know. But look at your own words. You called them sad and threatening at the same time. Could that be you also?'

He drank from his cup before answering.

'I've been sad before. But I've found comfort in it.'

They sat in silence for a while, digesting what had been said. She looked at her watch.

'We still have some time. Is there anything else you want to talk about? Maybe something related to this story?'

He contemplated the question for a while and took out a cigarette.

'How much time do we have?'

'As long as you want. Don't worry about the time. I want to do this.'

'You've talked about my mission. You told me to think about my mission. And you said the word again just a minute ago.'

'Yes.'

He hesitated.

'What I say here is protected, right?'

She furrowed her brow.

'I'm not talking about anything illegal. What I mean is, whatever I tell you in here, you're not going to tell people, right? It won't get back to Irving.'

'No. What you tell me stays right here. That's an absolute. I told you, I make a single, narrowly focused recommendation for or against return to duty that I give to Assistant Chief Irving. That's it.'

He nodded, hesitated again and then made his decision. He would tell her.

'Well, you were talking about my mission and your mission and so on and, well, I think I've had a mission for a long time. Only I didn't know it, or I mean … I didn't accept it. I didn't acknowledge it. I don't know how to explain it right. Maybe I was afraid or something. I put it off. For a lot of years. Anyway, what I'm telling you is that I've accepted it now.'

'I'm not sure I'm following you. Harry, you have to come out and tell me what you're talking about.'

He looked down at the gray rug in front of him. He spoke to it because he didn't know how to say it to her face.

'I'm an orphan … I never knew my father and my mother was murdered in Hollywood when I was a kid. Nobody … there never was any arrest made.'

'You're looking for her killer, aren't you?'

He looked up at her and nodded.

'That's my mission right now.'

She showed no shock on her face, which in turn surprised him. It was as if she expected him to say what he had just said.

'Tell me about it.'

❖ ❖ ❖ ❖ ❖ ❖ ❖

Bosch sat at his dining room table with his notebook out and the newspaper clips that Keisha Russell had had a *Times* intern gather for him sitting in front of him in two separate stacks. One stack for Conklin stories and one for Mittel stories. There was a bottle of Henry's on the table and through the evening he had been nursing it like cough syrup. The one beer was all he would allow himself. The ashtray, however, was loaded and there was a pall of blue smoke around the table. He had placed no limit on cigarettes. Hinojos had said nothing about smoking.

She'd had plenty to say about his mission, though. She'd flatly counseled him to stop until he was better emotionally prepared to face what he might find. He told her that he was too far down the road to stop. Then she said something that he kept thinking about as he drove home and it intruded even now.

'You better think about this and make sure it's what you want,' she said. 'Subconsciously or not, you may have been working toward this all your life. It could be the reason you are who you are. A policeman, a homicide investigator. Resolving your mother's death could also resolve your need to be a policeman. It could take your drive, your mission, away from you. You have to be prepared for that or you should turn back.'

Bosch considered what she had said to be true. He

knew that all his life it had been there. What had happened to his mother had helped define everything he did after. And it was always there in the dark recesses of his mind. A promise to find out. A promise to avenge. It was never anything that had been spoken aloud or even thought about with much focus. For to have done that was to plan and this was no part of a grand agenda. Still, he was crowded with the feeling that what he was doing was inevitable, something scheduled by an unseen hand a long time ago.

His mind put Hinojos aside and focused on a memory. He was under the surface of the water, eyes open and looking up toward the light above the pool. Then, the light was eclipsed by a figure standing above, the image murky, a dark angel hovering above. Bosch kicked off the bottom and moved toward the figure.

Bosch picked up the bottle of beer and finished it in one pull. He tried to concentrate again on the newspaper clips in front of him.

He had initially been surprised at how many stories there were about Arno Conklin prior to his ascendance to the throne of the district attorney's office. But as he started to read through them he saw most of the stories were mundane dispatches from trials in which Conklin was the prosecuting attorney. Still, Bosch got somewhat of a feel for the man through the cases he tried and his style as a prosecutor. It was clear that his star rose both in the office and the public's eyes with a series of highly publicized cases.

The stories were in chronological order and the first dealt with the successful prosecution in 1953 of a woman who poisoned both her parents and then stored their bodies in trunks in the garage until neighbors complained about the smell to the police a month later. Conklin was quoted at length in several articles on the case. One time he was described as the 'dashing deputy district attorney.' The case was one of the early forerunners of the insanity defense. The woman claimed diminished capacity. But judging by the number of articles, there was a public furor over the case and the jury only took a half hour to convict. The defendant received the death penalty and Conklin's place in the public arena as a champion of public safety, a seeker of justice, was secured. There was a photo of him talking to the reporters after the verdict. The paper's earlier description of him had him down perfectly. He was a dashing man. He wore a dark three-piece suit, had short blond hair and was cleanshaven. He was lean and tall and had the ruddy, All-American look that actors pay surgeons thousands for. Arno was a star in his own right.

There were more stories about more murder cases in the clips after that first one. Conklin won every one of them. And he always asked for – and got – the death penalty. Bosch noticed that in the stories from the later fifties, he had been elevated in title to senior deputy district attorney and then by the end of the decade to assistant, one of the top jobs in the office. It was a meteoric rise to have taken place in only a decade.

There was one report on a press conference in which DA John Charles Stock announced he was placing Conklin in charge of the Special Investigations Unit and charging him with cleaning up the myriad vice problems that threatened the social fabric of Los Angeles County.

'I've always gone to Arno Conklin with the toughest jobs,' the DA said. 'And I go to him again. The people of the Los Angeles community want a clean community and, by God, we will have it. To those who know we are coming for you, my advice is, move out. San Francisco will have you. San Diego will have you. But the City of Angels won't have you!'

Following that there were several stories spread over a

couple of years with splashy headlines about crackdowns on gambling parlors, pipe dens, whorehouses and the street prostitution trade. Conklin worked with a task force of forty cops comprised of loaners from all departments in the county. Hollywood was the main target of 'Conklin's Commandos,' as the *Times* dubbed the squad, but the scourge of the law came down on wrongdoers all over the county. From Long Beach to the desert, all those who labored for the wages of sin were running scared – at least according to the newspaper articles. Bosch had no doubt that the vice lords Conklin's Commandos were targeting operated business as usual and that it was only the bottom feeders, the replaceable employees, that were getting the hook.

The last Conklin story in the stack was on his February 1, 1962, announcement that he would run for the top spot in the district attorney's office on a campaign of renewed emphasis on ridding the county of the vices that threatened any great society. Bosch noted that part of the stately speech he delivered on the steps of the old downtown courthouse was a well-known police philosophy that Conklin, or his speechwriter, had apparently appropriated as original thought.

People sometimes say to me, 'What's the big deal, Arno? These are victimless crimes. If a man wants to place a bet or sleep with a woman for money, what's wrong with that? Where's the victim?' Well, my friends, I'll tell you what's wrong with that and who the victim is. We're the victim. All of us. When we allow this kind of activity to occur, when we simply look the other way, then it weakens us all. Every one of us.

I look at it this way. These so-called little crimes are each like a broken window in an abandoned house. Doesn't seem like a big problem, right?

Wrong. If nobody fixes that window, pretty soon kids come along and think nobody cares. So they throw a few rocks and break a few more windows. Next, the burglar drives down the street and sees the house and thinks nobody around there cares. So he sets up shop and starts breaking into houses while the owners are at work.

Next thing you know, another miscreant comes along and steals cars right off the street. And so on and so on. The residents start to see their own neighborhood with different eyes then. They think, Nobody cares anymore, so why should I? They wait an extra month before cutting the grass. They don't tell the boys hanging on the corner to put the cigarettes out and go back to school. It's gradual decay, my friends. It happens all across this great country of ours. It sneaks in like weeds in our yard. Well, when I'm district attorney the weeds are coming out by the roots.

The story ended by reporting that Conklin had chosen a young 'firebrand' from his office to manage his campaign. He said that Gordon Mittel would resign from the DA's office and begin work immediately. Bosch reread the story and immediately became transfixed by something that hadn't registered during his first read. It was in the second paragraph.

For the well-known and not-press-shy Conklin, it will be his first run for public office. The 35-year-old bachelor and Hancock Park resident said he has planned the run for a long time and has the backing of retiring DA John Charles Stock, who also appeared at the press conference.

Bosch turned the pages of his notebook back to the list of names he had written before and wrote 'Hancock Park' after Conklin's name. It wasn't much but it was a little piece of verification of Katherine Register's story. And it was enough to get Bosch's juices going. It made him feel that at least he had a line in the water.

'Fucking hypocrite,' he whispered to himself.

He drew a circle around Conklin's name in the notebook. He absentmindedly kept circling it as he tried to decide what he should do next.

Marjorie Lowe's last known destination was a party in Hancock Park. According to Katherine Register, she was more specifically going to meet Conklin. After she was dead, Conklin had called the detectives on the case to make an appointment but any record of the interview, if any occurred, was missing. Bosch knew it was all a general correlation of facts but it served to deepen and solidify the suspicion he had felt from the night he had first looked through the murder book. Something was not right about the case. Something didn't fit. And the more he thought about it, the more he believed Conklin was the wrong piece.

He reached into his jacket, which was on the chairback behind him, and took out his small phone book. He took it into the kitchen, where he dialed the home line of Deputy District Attorney Roger Goff.

Goff was a friend who shared Bosch's affection for the tenor saxophone. They'd spent many days in court sitting side by side during trials and many nights in jazz bars side by side on stools. Goff was an old-line prosecutor who had been with the office nearly thirty years. He had no political aspirations inside or outside of the office. He just liked his job. He was a rarity because he never tired of it. A thousand deputies had come in, burned out, and gone on to corporate America during Goff's watch, but he stayed. He now labored in the criminal courts building with prosecutors and public defenders twenty years his junior.

But he was still good at it and, more important, still had the fire in his voice when he stood before a jury and called down the outrage of God and society against those in the defendant's chair. His mixture of tenacity and plain fairness had made him a legend in downtown legal and law enforcement circles. And he was one of the few prosecutors Bosch had unconditional respect for.

'Roger, Harry Bosch.'

'Hey, goddamnit, how you doing?'

'I'm fine. What are you up to?'

'Watching the tube like everybody else. What're you doing?'

'Nothing. I was just thinking, you remember Gloria Jeffries?'

'Glo – shit, of course I do. Let's see. She's … yeah, she's the one with the husband got quaded in the motorcycle accident, right?'

Recalling the case, it sounded as if he were reading it off one of his yellow tablets.

'She got tired of caring for him. So one morning he's in bed and she sits on his face until she smothers him. It was about to go by as a natural but a suspicious detective named Harry Bosch wouldn't let it go. He came up with a witness who Gloria had told everything to. The clincher, the thing that got the jury, was that she told the wit that when she smothered him, it was the first orgasm the poor devil had ever been able to give her. How is that for a memory?'

'Damn, you're good.'

'So what about her?'

'She's raising up at Frontera. Getting ready to. I was wondering if you'd have time to write a letter.'

'Fuck, already? What was that, three, four years ago?'

'Almost five. I hear she's got the book now and goes to

the board next month. I'll write a letter but it'd be good if there was one from the prosecutor, too.'

'Don't worry about it, I got a standard in my computer. All I do is change the name and the crime, throw in a few of the gruesome details. The basic line is that the crime was too heinous for parole to be considered at this time. It's a good letter. I'll send it out tomorrow. It usually works charms.'

'Good. Thanks.'

'You know, they gotta stop giving the book to those women. They all get religion when they're coming up. You ever go to one of those hearings?'

'A couple.'

'Yeah, sit through a half a day of them if you have the time and aren't feeling particularly suicidal sometime. They sent me out to Frontera once when one of the Manson girls was up. See, with the big ones like that they send a body out instead of a letter. So, I went out and I sat through about ten of these things waiting for my girl to come up. And let me tell you, everybody's quoting Corinthians, they're quoting Revelations, Matthew, Paul, John three-sixteen, John this, John that. And it works! It goddamn works. These old guys on the board eat that shit up. Plus I guess they're all sitting up there getting thick in their pants having all these women groveling in front of them. Anyway, you got me started, Harry. It's your fault, not mine.'

'Sorry about that.'

'It's okay. So what else is new? Haven't seen you in the building. You got anything coming my way?'

It was the question Bosch had been waiting for Goff to get to so he could nonchalantly steer the conversation toward Arno Conklin.

'Ah, nothing much. It's been slow. But, hey, let me ask you, did you know Arno Conklin?'

'Arno Conklin? Sure, I knew him. He hired me. What are you asking about him for?'

'Nothing. I was going through some old files, making room in one of the cabinets, and I came across some old newspapers. They were pushed into the back. There were some stories about him and I thought of you, thought it was about when you started.'

'Yeah, Arno, tried to be a good man. A little high and mighty for my taste, but I think he was a decent man overall. Especially considering he was both a politician and a lawyer.'

Goff laughed at his own line but Bosch was silent. Goff had used the past tense. Bosch felt a heavy presence push into his chest and he only realized then how strong the desire to avenge could be.

'He's dead?'

He closed his eyes. He hoped Goff wouldn't detect the urgency he had let slip into his voice.

'Oh, no, he's not dead. I meant, you know, when I knew him. He was a good man then.'

'He's still practicing law somewhere?'

'Oh, no. He's an old man. Retired. Once a year they wheel him out at the annual prosecutors banquet. He personally hands out the Arno Conklin Award.'

'What's that?'

'Some piece of wood with a brass plate on it that goes to the administrative prosecutor of the year, if you can believe that. That's the guy's legacy, an annual award to a so-called prosecutor who doesn't set foot inside a court-room all year. It always goes to one of the division heads. I don't know how they decide which one. Prob'ly whoever got his or her nose farthest up the DA's ass that year.'

Bosch laughed. The line wasn't that funny but he was also feeling the relief of learning that Conklin was still alive.

'It's not funny, Bosch. It's fucking sad. Administrative prosecutor, whoever heard of such a thing? An oxymoron. Like Andrew and his screenplays. He deals with these studio people called, get this, creative executives. There's your classic contradiction. Well, there you go, Bosch, you got me going again.'

Bosch knew Andrew was Goff's roommate but he had never met him.

'Sorry, Roger. Anyway, what do you mean, they wheel him out?'

'Arno? Well, I mean they wheel him out. He's in a chair. I told you, he's an old man. Last I heard he was in some full-care retirement home. One of the classy ones in Park La Brea. I keep saying I'm going to see him one day, thank him for hiring me way back when. Who knows, maybe I could put in a word for that award or something.'

'Funny guy. You know, I heard that Gordon Mittel used to be his frontman.'

'Oh, yeah, he was the bulldog outside the door. Ran his campaigns. That's how Mittel got started. Now that's one mean – I'm glad he got out of criminal law and into politics, he'd be a motherfucker to come up against in court.'

'Yeah, I've heard,' Bosch said.

'Whatever you've heard, you can double it.'

'You know him?'

'Not now and not then. I just knew to keep clear. He was already out of the office by the time I came in. But there were stories. Supposedly in those early days, when Arno was the heir apparent and everybody knew it, there was a lot of maneuvering. You know, to get next to him. There was one guy, Sinclair I think his name was, that was set to run Arno's campaign. Then one night the cleaning lady found some porno shots under his blotter. There was an internal investigation and the photos proved to be stolen from another prosecutor's case files. Sinclair was dumped. He always claimed he was set up by Mittel.'

'Think he was?'

'Yes. It was Mittel's style … But who knows.'

Bosch sensed that he had said and asked enough to pass it off as conversation and gossip. Anything further and Goff might get suspicious about the call.

'So what's the deal?' he asked. 'You zipped up for the night or you want to go by the Catalina? I heard Redman's in town to do Leno. I'd bet you the cover charge that he and Branford drop by to sit in on the late set.'

'Sounds tempting, Harry, but Andrew's making a late dinner now and I think we're just going to stay at home tonight. He's counting on it. You mind?'

'Not at all. Anyway, I'm trying not to bend the elbow so much lately. I need to give it a rest.'

'Now that, sir, is quite admirable. I think you deserve a piece of wood with a brass plate on it.'

'Or a shot of whiskey.'

After hanging up Bosch sat back down at the desk and wrote notes on the highlights of the conversation with Goff into his notebook. Next he pulled the stack of clips on Mittel in front of him. These were more recent clips than those on Conklin because Mittel had not made a name for himself until much later. Conklin had been his first step up the ladder.

Most of the stories were just mentions of Mittel as being in attendance at various galas in Beverly Hills or as host of various campaign or charity dinners. From the start he was a money man, a man politicians and charities went to when they wanted to cast their nets into the rich enclaves of the Westside. He worked both sides, Republican, Democrat, it didn't seem to matter. His profile grew, though, when he started working for candidates on a larger scale. The current governor was a client. So, too, were a handful of congressman and senators from other western states.

A profile written several years earlier – and apparently without his cooperation – ran under the headline THE PRESIDENT'S MAIN MONEY MAN. It said Mittel had been tapped to round up California contributors for the president's reelection war chest. It said the state was one of the cornerstones of the national campaign's funding plan.

The story also noted the irony that Mittel was a recluse in the high-profile world of politics. He was a backstage man who abhorred the spotlight. So much so that he had repeatedly turned down patronage jobs from those he'd helped elect.

Instead, Mittel elected to stay in Los Angeles, where he was the founding partner of a powerful financial district law firm, Mittel, Anderson, Jennings & Rountree. Still, it seemed to Bosch that what this Yale-educated lawyer did had little to do with law as Bosch knew it. He doubted Mittel had been inside a courtroom in years. That made Harry think of the Conklin award and he smiled. Too bad Mittel had quit the DA's office. He might've been in line for it someday.

There was a photo that ran with the profile. It showed Mittel at the bottom of the steps of Air Force One greeting the then president at LAX. Though the article had been published years earlier, Bosch was nevertheless startled by how young Mittel was in the photo. He looked at the story again and checked the man's age. Doing the arithmetic, he realized that currently Mittel was barely sixty years old.

Bosch pushed the newspaper clips aside and got up. For a long time he stood at the sliding glass door to the deck and stared at the lights across the pass. He began to consider what he knew about circumstances thirty-three years old. Conklin, according to Katherine Register, knew

Marjorie Lowe. It was clear from the murder book that he had somehow reached into the investigation of her death for reasons unknown. His reach was then apparently covered up for reasons unknown. This had occurred only three months before he announced his candidacy for district attorney and less than a year before a key figure in the investigation, Johnny Fox, died while in his political employ.

Bosch thought that it was obvious that Fox would have been known to Mittel, the campaign manager. Therefore, he further concluded, whatever it was that Conklin did or knew, it was likely that Mittel, his frontman and the architect of his political run, had knowledge of it as well.

Bosch went back to the table and turned to the list of names in his notebook. Now he picked up the pen and circled Mittel's name as well. He felt like having another beer but he settled for a cigarette.

✦ ✦ ✦ ✦ ✦ ✦ ✦

In the morning Bosch called the LAPD personnel office and asked them to check whether Eno and McKittrick were still current. He doubted they were still around but knew he had to make the check. It would be embarrassing if he went through a search for them only to find one or both still on the payroll. The clerk checked the roll and told him no such officers were currently on the force.

He decided he would have to put on his Harvey Pounds pose after that. He dialed the DMV in Sacramento, gave the lieutenant's name and asked for Ms Sharp again. By the tone she inflected in the single word 'Hello' after picking up the phone, Bosch had no doubt that she remembered him.

'Is this Ms Sharp?'

'That's who you asked for, isn't it?'

'I did, indeed.'

'Then it's Ms Sharp. What can I do for you?'

'Well, I wanted to mend our fences, so to speak. I have a few more names I need driver's license addresses for and I thought that directly working with you would expedite the matter and perhaps repair our working relationship.'

'Honey, we don't have a working relationship. Hold the line, please.'

She punched the button before he could say anything. The line was dead for so long that he began to believe his

113

scam to burn Pounds wasn't worth it. Finally, a different clerk picked up and said Ms Sharp had instructed her to help. Bosch gave her Pounds's serial number and then the names Gordon Mittel, Arno Conklin, Claude Eno and Jake McKittrick. He said he needed the home addresses on their licenses.

He was put on hold again. During the time he waited he held the phone to his ear with his shoulder and fried an egg over easy in a pan on the stove. He made a sandwich out of it with two slices of white toast and cold salsa from a jar he kept in the refrigerator. He ate the dripping sandwich while leaning over the sink. He had just wiped his mouth and poured himself a second cup of coffee when the clerk finally picked back up.

'Sorry it took so long.'

'No problem.'

He then remembered he was Pounds and wished he hadn't said that.

The clerk explained that she had no addresses or license information on Eno or McKittrick, then gave him addresses for Conklin and Mittel. Goff had been right. Conklin lived in Park La Brea. Mittel lived above Hollywood on Hercules Drive in a development called Mount Olympus.

Bosch was too preoccupied at that point to continue the Pounds charade. He thanked the clerk without further confrontation and hung up. He thought about what his next move should be. Eno and McKittrick were either dead or out of state. He knew he could get their addresses through the department's personnel office but that might take all day. He picked up the phone again and called Robbery-Homicide, asking for Detective Leroy Ruben. Ruben had put nearly forty years in on the department, half of it in RHD. He might know something about Eno and McKittrick. He might also know Bosch was on stress leave.

'Ruben, can I help you?'

'Leroy, it's Harry Bosch. What do you know?'

'Not much, Harry. Enjoying the good life?'

Right away he was telling Bosch he knew of his situation. Bosch knew now that his only alternative was to be straight with him. To a point.

'It ain't bad. But I'm not sleeping late every day.'

'No? What're you getting up for?'

'I'm kind've freelancing on an old case, Leroy. That's why I called. I want to try to track down a couple of old dicks. Thought maybe you'd know of them. They were out of Hollywood.'

'Who are they?'

'Claude Eno and Jake McKittrick. Remember them?'

'Eno and McKittrick. No … I mean, yeah, I think I remember McKittrick. He checked out … it must've been ten, fifteen years ago. He went back to Florida, I think. Yeah, Florida. He was here in RHD for a year or so. At the end there. The other one, Eno, I don't remember any Eno.'

'Well, it was worth a try. I'll see what I can find in Florida. Thanks, Leroy.'

'Hey, Harry, what gives anyway?'

'It's just an old case I had in my desk. It's giving me something to do while I see what happens.'

'Any word?'

'Not yet. They got me talking to the shrink. If I can talk my way past her, I'll get back to the table. We'll see.'

'Okay, well, good luck. You know, me and some of the boys here, when we heard that story we laughed our asses off. We heard about that guy Pounds. He's an asshole. You done good, kid.'

'Well, let's hope I didn't do so good that I lost my job.'

'Ah, you'll be all right. They send you to Chinatown a few times, brush you off and send you back into the ring. You'll be okay.'

'Thanks, Leroy.'

After hanging up, Bosch got dressed for the day, putting on a fresh shirt and the same suit as the day before.

He headed downtown in his rented Mustang and spent the next two hours in a bureaucratic maze. He first went to the Personnel Office at Parker Center, told a clerk what he wanted and then waited half an hour for a supervisor to tell him all over again. The supervisor told him he had wasted his time and that the information he sought was at City Hall.

He walked across the street to the City Hall annex, took the stairs up and then crossed on the tramway over Main Street into the white obelisk of City Hall. He took the elevator up to the Finance Department, on nine, showed his ID card to another counter clerk and told her that, in the interest of streamlining the process, maybe he should talk to a supervisor first.

He waited on a plastic chair in a hallway for twenty minutes before he was ushered into a small office cramped with two desks, four file cabinets and several boxes on the floor. An obese woman with pale skin and black hair, sideburns and the slight hint of a mustache sat behind one of the desks. On her calendar blotter Bosch noticed a food stain from some prior mishap. There was also a reusable plastic quart soda container with a screw-on top and straw on her desk. A plastic name plate on the desk said Mona Tozzi.

'I'm Carla's supervisor. She said you are a police officer?'

'Detective.'

He pulled the chair away from the empty desk and sat down in front of the fat woman.

'Excuse me, but Cassidy is probably going to need her chair when she gets back. That's her desk.'

'When's she coming back?'

'Anytime. She went up for coffee.'

'Well, maybe if we hurry we'll be done by then and I'll be out of here.'

She gave a short who-do-you-think-you-are laugh that sounded more like a snort. She said nothing.

'I've spent the last hour and a half trying to get just a couple addresses from the city and all I get are a bunch of people who want to send me to someone else or make me wait out in the hall. And what's funny about that is that I work for the city myself and I'm trying to do a job for the city and the city isn't giving me the time of day. And, you know, my shrink tells me I've got this post-traumatic stress stuff and should take life easier. But, Mona, I gotta tell you, I'm getting pretty fucking frustrated with this.'

She stared at him a moment, probably wondering if she could possibly make it out the door if he decided to go nuts on her. She then pursed her lips, which served to change her mustache from a hint to an announcement, and took a hard pull on the straw of her soda container. Bosch saw a liquid the color of blood go up through the straw into her mouth. She cleared her throat before talking in a comforting tone.

'Tell you what, Detective, why don't you tell me what it is you are trying to find?'

Bosch put on his hopeful face.

'Great. I knew there was somebody who cared. I need to get the addresses where pension checks for two different retired officers are sent each month.'

Her eyebrows mated as she frowned.

'I'm sorry, but those addresses are strictly confidential. Even within the city. I couldn't give –'

'Mona, let me explain something. I'm a homicide

investigator. Like you, I work for the city. I have leads on an old unsolved murder that I am following up on. I need to confer with the original case detectives. We're talking about a case more than thirty years old. A woman was killed, Mona. I can't find the two detectives that originally worked the case and the police personnel people sent me over here. I need the pension addresses. Are you going to help me?'

'Detective – is it Borsch?'

'Bosch.'

'Detective Bosch, let me explain something to you. Just because you work for the city does not give you access to confidential files. I work for the city but I don't go over to Parker Center and say let me see this or let me see that. People have a right to privacy. Now, this is what I can do. And it is all I can do. If you give me the two names, I will send a letter to each person asking them to call you. That way, you get your information, I protect the files. Would that work for you? They'll go out in the mail today. I promise.'

She smiled but it was the phoniest smile Bosch had seen in days.

'No, that wouldn't work at all, Mona. You know, I'm really disappointed.'

'I can't help that.'

'But you can, don't you see?'

'I have work to do, Detective. If you want me to send the letter, give me the names. If not, that's your decision.'

He nodded that he understood and brought his briefcase up from the floor to his lap. He saw her jump when he angrily unsnapped the locks. He opened it and took out his phone. He flipped it open and dialed his home number, then waited for the machine to pick up.

Mona looked annoyed.

'What are you doing?'

He held his hand up for silence.

'Yes, can you transfer me to Whitey Springer?' he said to his tape.

He watched her reaction while acting like he wasn't. He could tell, she knew the name. Springer was the City Hall columnist for the *Times*. His specialty was writing about the small bureaucratic nightmares, the little guy against the system. Bureaucrats could largely create these nightmares with impunity, thanks to civil service protections, but politicians read Springer's column and they wielded tremendous power when it came to patronage jobs, transfers and demotions at City Hall. A bureaucrat vilified in print by Springer might be safe in his or her job but there likely would never be advancement, and there was nothing stopping a city council member from calling for an audit on an office or a council observer to sit in the corner. The word to the wise was to stay out of Springer's column. Everybody knew that, including Mona.

'Yeah, I can hold,' Bosch said into the phone. Then to Mona, he said, 'He's gonna love this one. He's got a guy trying to solve a murder, the victim's family waiting for thirty-three years to know who killed her, and some bureaucrat sitting in her office sucking on a quart of fruit punch isn't giving him the addresses he needs just to talk to the other cops who worked the case. I'm not a newspaper man but I think that's a column. He'll love it. What do you think?'

He smiled and watched her face flush almost as red as her fruit punch. He knew it was going to work.

'Okay, hang up the phone,' she said.

'What? Why?'

'HANG UP! Hang up and I'll get the information.'

Bosch flipped the phone closed.

'Give me the names.'

He gave her the names and she got up angrily and

silently to leave the room. She could barely fit around the desk but made the maneuver like a ballerina, the pattern instilled in her body's memory by repeated practice.

'How long will this take?' he asked.

'As long as it takes,' she answered, regaining some of her bureaucratic bluster at the door.

'No, Mona, you got ten minutes. That's all. After that, you better not come back 'cause Whitey's gonna be sitting here waiting for you.'

She stopped and looked at him. He winked.

After she left he got up and went around the side of the desk. He pushed it about two inches closer to the opposite wall, narrowing her path back to her chair.

She was back in seven minutes, carrying a piece of paper. But Bosch could see it was trouble. She had a triumphant look on her face. He thought of that woman who had been tried a while back for cutting off her husband's penis. Maybe it was the same face she had when she ran out the door with it.

'Well, Detective Borsch, you've got a little problem.'

'What is it?'

She started around the desk and immediately rammed her thick thigh into its Formica-topped corner. It looked more embarrassing than painful. She had to flail her arms for balance and the impact of the collision shook the desk and knocked her container over. The red liquid began leaking out of the straw onto the blotter.

'Shit!'

She quickly moved the rest of the way around the desk and righted the container. Before sitting down she looked at the desk, suspicious that it had been moved.

'Are you all right?' Bosch asked. 'What is the problem with the addresses?'

She ignored his first question, forgot her embarrassment and looked at Bosch and smiled. She sat down. She spoke

120

as she opened a desk drawer and took out a wad of napkins stolen from the cafeteria.

'Well, the problem is you won't be talking to former detective Claude Eno anytime soon. At least, I don't think you will.'

'He's dead.'

She started wiping up the spill.

'Yes. The checks go to his widow.'

'What about McKittrick?'

'Now McKittrick is a possibility. I have his address here. He's over in Venice.'

'Venice? So what's the problem with that?'

'That's Venice, Florida.'

She smiled, delighted with herself.

'Florida,' Bosch repeated.

He had no idea there was a Venice in Florida.

'It's a state, over on the other side of the country.'

'I know where it is.'

'Oh, and one other thing. The address I have is only a P.O. box. Sorry about that.'

'Yeah, I bet. What about a phone?'

She tossed the wet napkins into a trash can in the corner of the room.

'We have no phone number. Try information.'

'I will. Does it say there when he retired?'

'You didn't ask me to get that.'

'Then give me what you've got.'

Bosch knew he could get more, that they'd have to have a phone number somewhere, but he was handicapped because this was an unauthorized investigation. If he pushed things too far, then he'd only succeed in having his activities discovered and then halted.

She floated the paper across the desk to him. He looked at it. It had two addresses on it, the P.O. box for

McKittrick and the street address in Las Vegas for Eno's widow. Her name was Olive.

Bosch thought of something.

'When do the checks go out?'

'Funny you should ask.'

'Why?'

'Because today's the last day of the month. They always go out the last day of the month.'

That was a break and he felt like he deserved it, that he had worked for it. He picked up the paper she had given him and slipped it into his briefcase, then he stood up.

'Always a pleasure to do work with the public servants of the city.'

'Likewise. And, uh, Detective? Could you return the chair to the place you found it? As I said, Cassidy will need it.'

'Of course, Mona. Pardon my forgetfulness.'

❖ ❖ ❖ ❖ ❖ ❖ ❖

After the bout with bureaucratic claustrophobia, Bosch decided he needed some air to recover. He took the elevator down to the lobby and out the main doors to Spring Street. As he walked out, he was directed by a security officer to walk down the right side of the wide-staired entrance to the great building because there was a film location shoot taking place on the left side. Bosch watched what they were doing as he stepped down the stairs and then decided to take a break and have a smoke.

He sat down on one of the concrete sidings along the stairs and lit a cigarette. The film shoot involved a group of actors posing as reporters who rushed down the stairs of City Hall to meet and question two men getting out of a car at the curb. They rehearsed it twice and then shot it twice while Bosch sat there and smoked two cigarettes. Each time, the reporters all yelled the same thing at the two men.

'Mr Barrs, Mr Barrs, did you do it? Did you do it?'

The two men refused to answer and pushed through the pack and up the stairs with the reporters backtracking. On one of the takes one of the reporters stumbled as he moved backwards, fell on his back on the stairs and was partially trampled by the others. The director kept the scene going, perhaps thinking that the fall added a touch of realism to the scene.

Bosch figured that the filmmakers were using the steps

and front facade of City Hall as a courthouse setting. The men coming from the car were the defendant and his high-priced lawyer. He knew that City Hall was frequently used for such shots because it actually looked more like a courthouse than any real courthouse in the city.

Bosch was bored after the second take, though he guessed there would be many more. He got up and walked down to First and then over to Los Angeles Street. He took that back to Parker Center. Along the way he was asked for spare change only four times, which he thought was a low count for downtown and possibly a sign of improving economic times. In the lobby of the police building he passed the bank of pay phones and on a whim stopped, picked one of the phones off the hook and dialed 305–555–1212. He had dealt with Metro-Dade Police in Miami several times over the years and 305 was the only Florida area code that readily came to mind. When the operator came on he asked for Venice and she informed him that 813 was the proper area code.

He then redialed and got information in Venice. First he asked the operator what the nearest large city to Venice was. She told him that was Sarasota and he asked what the nearest large city was to that. When she said St Petersburg, he finally started getting his bearings. He knew where St Petersburg was on a map – the west coast of Florida – because he knew the Dodgers occasionally played spring training games there and he had looked it up once.

He finally gave the operator McKittrick's name and promptly got a tape recording saying the number was unlisted at the customer's request. He wondered if any of the detectives he had dealt with by phone at Metro-Dade could get the number for him. He still had no idea exactly where Venice was or how far it was from Miami. Then he decided to leave it alone. McKittrick had taken steps to make it difficult to be contacted. He used a P.O. box and had an unlisted phone. Bosch didn't know why a retired cop would take such steps in a state three thousand miles away from where he had worked but he felt sure that the best approach to McKittrick was going to have to be in person. A telephone call, even if Bosch got the number, was easy to avoid. Someone standing right at your door was different. Besides, Bosch had caught a break; he knew McKittrick's pension check was in the mail to his P.O. box. He was sure he could use it to find the old cop.

He clipped his ID card to his suit and went up to the Scientific Investigation Division. He told the woman behind the counter that he had to talk to someone in Latent Prints and pushed through the half door and down the hall to the print lab like he always did, without waiting for her go-ahead.

The lab was a large room with two rows of work tables with overhead fluorescent lights. At the end of the room were two desks with AFIS computer terminals on them. Behind them was a glass-walled room with the mainframes inside. There was condensation on the glass because the mainframe room was kept cooler than the rest of the lab.

Because it was lunch time there was only one technician in the lab and Bosch didn't know him. He was tempted to turn around and come back later when someone else might be there, but the tech looked up from one of the computer terminals and saw him. He was a tall, skinny man with glasses and a face that had been ravaged by acne when he was younger. The damage gave him a permanently sullen expression.

'Yes?'

'Yeah, hi, howya doin'?'

'I'm doing fine. What can I do for you?'

'Harry Bosch, Hollywood Division.'

He put out his hand and the other man hesitated, then shook it tentatively.

'Brad Hirsch.'

'Yeah, I think I've heard your name. We've never worked together but that probably won't last. I work homicide so it seems I basically get around to working with everybody in here eventually.'

'Probably.'

Bosch sat down on a chair to the side of the computer module and pulled his briefcase onto his lap. He noticed that Hirsch was looking into his blue computer screen. He seemed more comfortable looking there than at Bosch.

'Reason I'm here is, at the moment, it's kind of slow out in Tinseltown. And so I've been going through some old cases. I came across this one from nineteen sixty-one.'

'Nineteen sixty-one?'

'Yeah, it's old. A female ... cause of death blunt force trauma, then he made it look like a strangulation, a sex crime. Anyway, nobody was ever popped for it. It never went anywhere. In fact, I don't think anyone's really looked at it since the due diligence in sixty-two. A long time. Anyway, the thing is, the reason I'm here, is that back then the cops on this pulled a decent set of prints at the crime scene. They got a bunch of partials and some full rounds. And I've got them here.'

Bosch took the yellowed print card out of the briefcase and held it out to the man. Hirsch looked at it but didn't take it. He looked back at the computer screen and Bosch placed the print card down on the keyboard in front of him.

'And, well, as you know, that was before we had these fancy computers and all of this technology you got here. All they did with this back then was use it to compare these to a suspect's prints. They got no match, they let the guy go and then they just shoved these in an envelope. They've been sitting in the case file ever since. So what I was thinking was, we could –'

'You want to run them through AFIS.'

126

'Yeah, right. You know, take a shot at it. Spin the dice, maybe we get lucky and pick up a hitchhiker on the information highway. It's happened before. Edgar and Burns out on the Hollywood table nailed an old one this week with an AFIS run. I was talking to Edgar and he said one of you guys down here – I think it was Donovan – said the computer has access to millions of prints from all across the country.'

Hirsch nodded unenthusiastically.

'And that's not just criminal print files, right?' Bosch asked. 'You've got military, law enforcement, civil service, everything. That right?'

'Yes, that's right. But, look, Detective Bosch, we –'

'Harry.'

'Okay, Harry. This is a great tool that's getting better all the time. You're correct about that but there still are human and time elements here. The comparison prints have to be scanned and coded and then those codes have to be entered into the computer. And right now we have a backup that's running twelve days.'

He pointed to the wall above the computer. There was a sign with changeable numbers on it. Like the signs in the union office that said X number of days since the last death in the line of duty.

AUTOMATED FINGERPRINT IDENTIFICATION SYSTEM
Search Requests Will Take 12 Days To Process
No Exception!

'So, you see, we can't take everybody who walks in here and put them at the front of the pack, okay? Now if you want to fill out a search request form, I can –'

'Look, I know there are exceptions. Especially in homicide cases. Somebody made that run for Burns and Edgar the other day. They didn't wait twelve days. They were put through right away and they cleared three homicides just like that.'

Bosch snapped his fingers. Hirsch looked at him and then back to the computer.

'Yes, there are exceptions. But that comes from on high. If you want to talk to Captain LeValley, maybe she'll approve it. If you –'

'Burns and Edgar didn't talk to her. Somebody just did it for them.'

'Well, then that was against the rules. They must have known somebody who did it for them.'

'Well, I know you, Hirsch.'

'Why don't you just fill out a request and I'll see what –'

'I mean, what's it take, ten minutes?'

'No. In your case much longer. This print card you have is an antique. It's obsolete. I'd have to run it through the Livescan machine, which would then assign codes to the prints. Then I'd have to hand-enter the codes it gives me. Then depending on the restrictions on the run you want, it could take –'

'I don't want any restrictions. I want it compared to all data bases.'

'Then the computer time can run as long as thirty, forty minutes.'

With a finger Hirsch punched his glasses back up his nose as if punctuating his resolve not to break the rules.

'Well, Brad,' Bosch said, 'the problem is I don't know how much time I've got on this. Certainly not twelve days. No way. I'm working on it now because I have the time, but the next time I get a fresh call that will be it, I'll be off it. That's the nature of homicide, you know? So, are you sure there isn't something we can do right now?'

Hirsch didn't move. He just stared at the blue screen. It reminded Bosch of the youth hall, when kids would literally shut down like a computer on standby when the bullies taunted them.

'What are you doing now, Hirsch? We could do it right now.'

Hirsch looked at him for a long moment before talking.

'I'm busy. And look, Bosch, I know who you are, okay? That's an interesting story about pulling old cases but I know it's a lie. I know you're on a stress leave. The story's getting around. And you shouldn't even be here and I shouldn't be talking to you. So, could you please leave me alone? I don't want to get into trouble. I don't want people to get the wrong idea, you know?'

Bosch looked at him but Hirsch's eyes had moved back onto the computer screen.

'Okay, Hirsch, let me tell you a real story. One –'

'I really don't want any more stories, Bosch. Why don't you just –'

'I'm going to tell you this story, then I'm leaving, okay? Just this one story.'

'Okay, Bosch, okay. You tell the story.'

Bosch looked at him silently and waited for Hirsch to make eye contact but the latent print technician's eyes remained on the computer screen as if it were his security blanket. Bosch told the story anyway.

'One time, a long time ago, I was almost twelve and I'm swimming in this pool, you see, and I'm under the water but I've got my eyes open. And I look up and I see up through the water up to the edge of the pool. I see this dark figure. You know, it was hard to figure out what it was, all wavy and all. But I could tell it was a man and there wasn't supposed to be a man up there. So I came up for air at the side of the pool and I was right. It was a man. He was wearing this dark suit. And he reached down and grabbed me by the wrist. I was just a scrawny little runt. It was easy for him to do. He pulled me out and he gave me this towel to put on my shoulders and he led me over to a chair and he told me … he told me that my mother was dead. Murdered. He said they didn't know who did it, but whoever he was, he left his fingerprints. He said, "Don't worry, son, we got the fingerprints and they're as good as gold. We'll get him." I remember those words exactly. "We'll get him." Only they never did. And now I'm going to. That's my story, Hirsch.'

Hirsch's eyes dropped down to the yellowed print card on the keyboard.

'Look, man, it's a bad story, but I can't be doing this. I'm sorry.'

Bosch stared at him a moment and then slowly stood up.

'Don't forget the card,' Hirsch said.

He picked it up and held it up to Bosch.

'I'll leave it here. You're going to do the right thing, Hirsch. I can tell.'

'No, don't. I can't do –'

'*I'm leaving it here!*'

The power of his voice shocked even Bosch and it seemed to have scared Hirsch. The print tech replaced the card on the keyboard. After a few seconds of silence Bosch leaned down and spoke quietly.

'Everybody wants the chance to do the right thing, Hirsch. It makes them feel good inside. Even if doing it doesn't exactly fit inside the rules, sometimes you have to rely on the voice inside that tells you what to do.'

Bosch stood back up and took out his wallet and a pen. He pulled out a business card and wrote some numbers on it. He put it down on the keyboard next to the print card.

'That's got my portable and my home on it. Don't bother calling the office, you know I won't be there. I'll be waiting to hear from you, Hirsch.'

He walked slowly out of the lab.

❖ ❖ ❖ ❖ ❖ ❖ ❖

W aiting for the elevator, Bosch guessed that his effort to persuade Hirsch had fallen on deaf ears. Hirsch was the type of guy whose exterior scars masked deeper interior wounds. There were a lot in the department like him. Hirsch had grown up intimidated by his own face. He'd probably be the last person to dare go outside the bounds of his job or the rules. Another department automaton. For him, doing the right thing was ignoring Bosch. Or turning him in.

He punched at the elevator button with his finger again and contemplated what else he could do. The AFIS search was a long shot but he still wanted it done. It was a loose end and any thorough investigation took care of loose ends. He decided he would give Hirsch a day and then he'd make another run at him. If that didn't work, he'd try another tech. He'd try them all until he got the killer's prints into that machine.

The elevator finally opened and he squeezed on. That was one of the only things you could rely on inside Parker Center. Cops would come and go, chiefs, even political power structures, but the elevators would always move slowly and always be crowded when they got to you. Bosch pushed the unlighted button marked B as the doors slowly closed and the square room started to descend. While everyone stood and stared blankly at the lighted numbers over the door, Bosch looked down at his briefcase. No one in the small space spoke. Until, as the car slowed to its next stop, Bosch heard his first name spoken from behind. He turned his head slightly, not sure if it had been someone speaking to him or the name had been directed toward someone else.

His eyes fell on Assistant Chief Irvin S. Irving standing in the rear of the elevator. They exchanged nods just as the doors opened on the first floor. Bosch wondered if Irving had seen him push the button for the basement. There was no reason for a man on involuntary stress leave to be going to the basement.

Bosch decided the car was too crowded for Irving to have seen what button he had pushed. He stepped off the elevator into the alcove off the main lobby and Irving followed him out and caught up with him.

'Chief.'

'What brings you all the way in, Harry?'

It was said casually but the question signaled that there was more than passing interest from Irving. They started walking toward the exit, Bosch quickly putting a story together.

'I have to go over to Chinatown anyway, so I dropped by to go to payroll. I wanted to see about them sending my check to my house instead of out to Hollywood, since I'm not sure when I'll be back.'

Irving nodded and Bosch was pretty sure he had bought it. He was about Bosch's size but had the stand-out feature of a completely shaved head. That feature and his reputation for intolerance for corrupt cops got him the nickname within the department of Mr Clean.

'You're in Chinatown today? I thought you were Monday, Wednesday, Friday. That was the schedule I approved.'

'Yes, that's the schedule. But she had an opening come up today and wanted me to come in.'

'Well, I'm glad to hear you being so cooperative. What happened to your hand?'

'Oh, this?' Bosch held up his hand as if it were someone else's that he had just noticed at the end of his arm. 'I've been using some of my free time to do some work around the house and I cut it on a piece of broken glass. I'm still doing clean-up from the quake.'

'I see.'

Bosch guessed that he didn't buy that one. But he didn't really care.

'I'm getting a quick lunch in the federal plaza,' Irving said. 'You want to come along?'

'Thanks just the same, Chief. I already ate.'

'Okay, well, take care of yourself. I mean that.'

'I will. Thanks.'

Irving started off and then stopped.

'You know, we're handling this situation with you a little differently because I hope to get you back in there at Hollywood homicide without any change in grade or position. I'm waiting to hear from Dr Hinojos but I understand it will be a few more weeks, at least.'

'That's what she tells me.'

'You know, if you're willing to do it, an apology in the form of a letter to Lieutenant Pounds could be beneficial. When push comes to shove, I'm going to have to sell him on letting you back in there. That will be the hard part. I think getting you a clean bill from the doctor won't be a problem. I can simply issue the order and Lieutenant Pounds will have to accept it, but that won't ease the pressure there. I would rather work it that he accepts your return and everybody's happy.'

'Well, I heard he already's got a replacement for me.'

'Pounds?'

'He paired my partner with somebody off autos.

133

Doesn't sound to me like he's expecting or planning on me coming back, Chief.'

'Well, that's news to me. I'll talk to him about that. What do you think about this letter? It could go a long way toward helping your situation.'

Bosch hesitated before answering. He knew Irving wanted to help him. The two of them shared an unspoken bond. Once they had been complete enemies in the department. But contempt had eroded into a truce which now was more a line of wary mutual respect.

'I'll think about the letter, Chief,' Bosch finally said. 'I'll let you know.'

'Very well. You know, Harry, pride gets in the way of a lot of the right decisions. Don't let that happen to you.'

'I'll think about it.'

Bosch watched him bound off around the fountain memorial to officers killed in the line of duty. He watched until Irving got to Temple and started to cross Los Angeles Street to the federal plaza, where there was an array of fast-food emporiums. Then Bosch figured it was safe and turned to go back inside.

He skipped waiting for the elevator again and went down the stairs to the basement.

Most of the underground floor of Parker Center was taken up by the Evidence Storage Division. There were a few other offices, like the Fugitives Division, but it was generally a quiet floor. Bosch found no pedestrian traffic on the long yellow linoleum hallway and was able to get to the steel double doors of ESD without running into anyone else he knew.

The police department held physical evidence on investigations that had not yet gone to the district attorney or city attorney for filing. Once that happened, the evidence usually stayed with the prosecutor's office.

Essentially, that made ESD the city's temple of failure.

What was behind the steel doors Bosch opened was the physical evidence from thousands of unsolved crimes. Crimes that had never resulted in prosecution. It even smelled of failure. Because it was in the basement of the building, there was a damp odor here that Bosch always believed was the rank stink of neglect and decay. Of hopelessness.

Bosch stepped into a small room that was essentially a wire-mesh cage. There was another door on the other side but there was a sign on it that said ESD STAFF ONLY. There were two windows cut in the mesh. One was closed and a uniform officer sat behind the other working on a crossword puzzle. Between the two windows was another sign that said DO NOT STORE LOADED FIREARMS. Bosch walked up to the open window and leaned on the counter. The officer looked up after filling in a word on the puzzle. Bosch saw the name tag on his uniform said Nelson. Nelson read Bosch's ID card so Bosch didn't have to bother to introduce himself, either. It worked out nicely.

'Her ... on – how you say that?'

'Hieronymus. Rhymes with anonymous.'

'Hieronymus. Isn't there a rock and roll band named that?'

'Maybe.'

'What can I do for you, Hieronymus from Hollywood?'

'I got a question.'

'Shoot.'

Bosch put the pink evidence check slip on the counter.

'I want to pull the box on this case. It's pretty old. Would it still be around anywhere?'

The cop took the slip, looked at it and whistled when he saw the year. While writing the case number down on a request log, he said, 'Should be here. Don't see why not. Nothing gets tossed, you know. You want to look at the

Black Dahlia case, we got that. That's what, fifty-something years old. We got 'em going back even further. If it ain't solved, it's here.'

He looked up at Bosch and winked.

'Be right back. Why don't you fill out the form.'

Nelson pointed with his pen out the window to a counter on the back wall where the standard request forms were. He got up and disappeared from the window. Bosch heard him yell to someone else in the back.

'Charlie! Hey, Char-LEE!'

A voice from somewhere in the back yelled a response that was unintelligible.

'Take the window,' Nelson called back. 'I'm taking the time machine.'

Bosch had heard about the time machine. It was a golf cart they used to get back to the deep recesses of the storage facility. The older the case, the farther back in time it went, the farther away it was from the front windows. The time machine got the window cops back there.

Bosch walked over to the counter and filled out a request form, then reached in the window and put it on the crossword puzzle. While he was waiting, he looked around and noticed another sign on the back wall. NARCOTICS EVIDENCE NOT RELEASED WITHOUT 492 FORM. Bosch had no idea what that form was. Somebody came through the steel doors then carrying a murder book. A detective, but Bosch didn't recognize him. He opened it on the counter, got a case number and then filled out a form. He then went to the window. There was no sign of Charlie. After a few minutes, the detective turned to Bosch.

'Anybody working back there?'

'Yeah, one guy went to get me a box. He told another guy to watch. I don't know where he is.'

'Shit.'

He rapped sharply with his knuckles on the counter. In a few minutes another uniform cop came to the window. He was an old horse, with white hair and a pear shape. Bosch guessed he'd been working in the basement for years. His skin was as white as a vampire's. He took the other detective's evidence request slip and was gone. Then both Bosch and the other detective were left waiting. Bosch could tell the other man had started looking at him but was acting like he wasn't.

'You're Bosch, right?' he finally asked. 'From Hollywood?'

Bosch nodded. The other man put out his hand and smiled.

'Tom North, Pacific. We've never met.'

'No.'

Bosch shook his hand but didn't act enthusiastic about the introduction.

'We never met but listen, I worked Devonshire burglary for six years before I got my homicide gig in Pacific. Know who my CO was up there back then?'

Bosch shook his head. He didn't know and he didn't care but North didn't seem to realize that.

'Pounds. Lieutenant Harvey "Ninety-eight" Pounds. The fuck. He was my CO. So, anyway, I heard through the network, you know, what you did to his ass. Put his face right through the fuckin' window. That's great, man, fuckin' great. More power to you. I laughed my ass off when I heard that.'

'Well, I'm glad it entertained you.'

'No, really, I know you're getting piped for it. I heard about that, too. But I just wanted to let you know you made my day and a lot of people are with you, man.'

'Thanks.'

'So what are you doing down here? I heard they had you on the Fifty-One-Fifty list.'

It annoyed Bosch to realize that there were those in the department whom he didn't even know who knew what had happened to him and what his situation was. He tried to keep calm.

'Listen, I –'

'Bosch! You gotta box!'

It was the time traveler, Nelson. He was at the window, pushing a light blue box through the opening. It was about the size of a boot box and was held closed with red tape that was cracking with age. It looked like the box was powdered with dust. Bosch didn't bother finishing his sentence. He waved off North and went to the box.

'Sign here,' Nelson said.

He put a yellow slip down on top of the box. It kicked up a small dust cloud, which he waved away with his hand. Bosch signed the paper and took the box in two hands. He turned and saw North looking at him. North just nodded once. He seemed to know it wasn't the right time to ask questions. Bosch nodded back and headed to the door.

'Uh, Bosch?' North said. 'I didn't mean anything about what I said. About the list. No offense, okay?'

Bosch stared at him as he pushed through the door with his back. But he didn't say anything. He then proceeded down the hall carrying the box with two hands, as if it contained something precious.

✦ ✦ ✦ ✦ ✦ ✦ ✦

C armen Hinojos was in her waiting room when
Bosch got there a few minutes late. She ushered
him in and waved off his apology for lateness as if it
was unnecessary. She wore a dark blue suit and as he
passed her in the doorway he smelled a light soapy
fragrance. He took the seat on the right side of the desk
near the window again.

Hinojos smiled and Bosch wondered why. There were
two chairs on the other side of the desk from her. So far, in
three meetings, he had taken the same one each time. The
one closest to the window. He wondered if she had taken
note of this and what, if anything, it meant.

'Are you tired?' she asked. 'You don't look like you got
much sleep last night.'

'I guess I didn't. But I'm fine.'

'Have you changed your mind about anything we
discussed yesterday?'

'No, not really.'

'You are continuing this private investigation?'

'For now.'

She nodded in a way that told him she expected his
reply.

'I want to talk about your mother today.'

'Why? It's got nothing to do with why I'm here, why
I'm on leave.'

'I think it's important. I think it will help us get to what

139

is happening with you, what has made you take on this private investigation of yours. It might explain a lot about your recent actions.'

'I doubt it. What do you want to know?'

'When you spoke yesterday, you made several references to her lifestyle, but you never really came out and said what she did, what she was. Thinking about it after the session, I was wondering if you have trouble accepting what she was. To the point of not being able to say she –'

'Was a prostitute? There, I said it. She was a prostitute. I'm a grown man, Doctor. I accept the truth. I accept the truth in anything as long as it's the truth. I think you're going far afield here.'

'Perhaps. What do you feel about her now?'

'What do you mean?'

'Anger? Hatred? Love?'

'I don't think about it. Certainly not hate. I loved her at the time. After she was gone that didn't change.'

'What about abandonment?'

'I'm too old for that.'

'What about back then? Back when it happened.'

Bosch thought a moment.

'I'm sure there was some of that. Her lifestyle, her line of work, got her killed. And I was left behind the fence. I guess I was mad about that and felt abandoned. I was also hurt. The hurt was the worst part. She loved me.'

'What do you mean, left behind the fence?'

'I told you yesterday. I was in McClaren, the youth hall.'

'Right. So her death prevented you from leaving there, correct?'

'For a while.'

'How long?'

'I was there on and off until I was sixteen. I lived a few months two different times with some fosters but I always got sent back. Then, when I was sixteen, another couple took me. I was with them until I was seventeen. I found out later that they kept getting the DPSS checks for a year after I'd split.'

'DPSS?'

'Department of Public Social Services. Now they call it the Division of Youth Services. Anyway, when you took a kid into your home as foster parents, you got a monthly support payment. A lot of people took kids in just for those checks. I'm not saying these people did, but they never told DPSS I wasn't in their home anymore after I left.'

'I understand. Where were you?'

'Vietnam.'

'Wait a minute, let's go back. You said that two different times before this you lived with foster parents but were then sent back. What happened? Why were you sent back?'

'I don't know. They didn't like me. They said it wasn't working out. I went back into the dorms behind the fence and waited. I think getting rid of a teenage boy was about as easy as selling a car with no wheels. The fosters always wanted the younger ones.'

'Did you ever run away from the hall?'

'A couple times. I always got caught in Hollywood.'

'If placing teenagers was so difficult, how did it happen to you the third time, when you were even older, sixteen?'

Bosch laughed falsely and shook his head.

'You'll get a kick out of this. I was chosen by this guy and his wife because I was left-handed.'

'Left-handed? I don't follow.'

'I was a lefty and I could throw a pretty good fastball.'

'What do you mean?'

'Ah, Jesus, it was – see, Sandy Koufax was with the Dodgers then. He was a lefty and I guess they were paying him about a zillion bucks a year to pitch. This guy, the foster, his name was Earl Morse, he had played semipro baseball or something and never really made it. So, he wanted to *create* a left-handed major league prospect. Good left-handers were pretty rare back then, I guess. Or he thought that. Anyway, they were the hot commodity. Earl thought he'd grab some kid with some potential, slap him into shape and then be his manager or agent or something when it came to contract time. He saw it as his way back into the game. It was crazy. But I guess he'd seen his own big league dream crash and burn. So he came out to McClaren and took a bunch of us into the field for a catch. We had a team, we played other halls, sometimes the schools in the Valley let us play them. Anyway, Earl took us out to throw the ball around and it was a tryout but none of us knew it at the time. It didn't even enter my mind what was going on until later. Anyway, he glommed on to me when he saw I was a lefty and could throw. He forgot the others like they were last season's program.'

Bosch shook his head again at the memory.

'What happened? You went with him?'

'Yeah. I went with him. There was a wife, too. She never said much to me or him. He used to make me throw a hundred balls a day at a tire hanging in the backyard. Then every night he'd have these coaching sessions. I put up with it for about a year and then I split.'

'You ran away?'

'Sort of. I joined the Army. I had to get Earl to sign for me, though. At first he wouldn't do it. He had major league plans for me. But then I told him I was never going to pick up another baseball as long as I lived. He signed. Then he and the wife kept cashing those DPSS checks while I was overseas. I guess the extra money helped make up for losing the prospect.'

She was quiet for a long time. It looked to Bosch like

she was reading her notes but he had not seen her write anything during this session.

'You know,' he said into the silence, 'about ten years later, when I was still in patrol, I pulled over a drunk driver coming off the Hollywood Freeway onto Sunset. He was all over the place. When I finally got him over and got up there to the window, I bent over to look in and it was Earl. It was a Sunday. He was coming home from the Dodgers. I saw the program on the seat.'

She looked at him but didn't say anything. He was looking at the memory still.

'I guess he'd never found that lefty he was looking for ... Anyway, he was so drunk he didn't recognize me.'

'What did you do?'

'Took his keys and called his wife ... I guess it was the only break I ever gave the guy.'

She looked back down at the pad while asking her next question.

'What about your real father?'

'What about him?'

'Did you ever know who he was? Did you have any relationship at all?'

'I met him once. I was never curious about it until I came back from overseas. Then I traced it down. Turned out he was my mother's lawyer. He had a family and all of that. He was dying when I met him, looked like a skeleton ... So I never really knew him.'

'His name was Bosch?'

'No. My name was just something she came up with. The painter, you know. She thought LA was a lot like his paintings. All the paranoia, the fear. Once she gave me a book that had his paintings in it.'

More silence followed as she thought about this one, too.

'These stories, Harry,' she finally said, 'these stories that you tell are heartbreaking in their own way. It makes me see the boy who became the man. It makes me see the depth of the hole left by your mother's death. You know, you would have a lot to blame her for and no one would blame you for doing it.'

He looked at her pointedly while composing a response.

'I don't blame her for anything. I blame the man who took her from me. See, these are stories about me. Not her. You can't get the feel for her. You can't know her like I did. All I know is that she did all she could to get me out of there. She never stopped telling me that. She never stopped trying. She just ran out of time.'

She nodded, accepting his answer. A few moments passed.

'Did there come a time when she told you what she did … for a living?'

'Not really.'

'How did you know?'

'I can't remember. I think I really didn't know for sure what she did until she was gone and I was older. I was ten when they took me away. I didn't really know why.'

'Did she have men stay with her while you were together?'

'No, that never happened.'

'But you must have had some idea about this life she was leading, that you both were leading.'

'She told me she was a waitress. She worked nights. She used to leave me with a lady who had a room at the hotel. Mrs DeTorre. She watched four or five kids whose mothers were doing the same thing. None of us knew.'

He finished there but she didn't say anything and he knew he was expected to continue.

'One night I snuck out when the old lady fell asleep and I walked down to the Boulevard to the coffee shop where she said she worked. She wasn't in there. I asked and they didn't know what I was talking about ...'

'Did you ask your mother about it?'

'No ... The next night I followed her. She left in her waitress uniform and I followed her. She went to her best friend's place upstairs. Meredith Roman. When they came out, they were both wearing dresses, makeup, the whole thing. Then they both left in a cab and I couldn't follow them.'

'But you knew.'

'I knew something. But I was like nine or something. How much could I know?'

'What about the charade she followed, dressing every night like a waitress, did that anger you?'

'No. The opposite. I thought that was ... I don't know, there was something noble about her doing that for me. She was protecting me, in a way.'

Hinojos nodded that she saw his point.

'Close your eyes.'

'Close my eyes?'

'Yes, I want you to close your eyes and think back to when you were a boy. Go ahead.'

'What is this?'

'Indulge me. Please.'

Bosch shook his head as if annoyed but did as she asked. He felt stupid.

'Okay.'

'Okay, I want you to tell me a story about your mother. Whatever image or episode with her that you have the clearest in your mind, I want you to tell it to me.'

He thought hard. Images of her passed through and disappeared. Finally, he came to one that stayed.

'Okay.'

'Okay, tell it.'

'It was at McClaren. She had come to visit and we were out at the fence at the ballfield.'

'Why do you remember this story?'

'I don't know. Because she was there and that always made me feel good, even though we always ended up crying. You should have seen that place on visiting day. Everybody crying … And I remember it, too, because it was near the end. It wasn't too long after that she was gone. Maybe a few months.'

'Do you remember what you talked about?'

'A lot of stuff. Baseball, she was a Dodgers fan. I remember one of the older kids had taken my new sneakers that she had given me for my birthday. She noticed I didn't have 'em on and she got pretty mad about it.'

'Why did the older boy take your sneakers?'

'She asked the same thing.'

'What did you tell her?'

'I told her the kid took my shoes because he could. You see, they could call that place whatever they wanted but basically it was a prison for kids and it had the same societies as a prison has. Your dominant cliques, your submissives, everything.'

'What were you?'

'I don't know. I pretty much kept to myself. But when some older, bigger kid took my shoes, I was a submissive. It was a way of surviving.'

'Your mother was unhappy about this?'

'Well, yeah, but she didn't know the score. She wanted to go complain or something. She didn't know that if she did that it would only make it worse for me there. Then she suddenly did realize what the deal was. She started crying.'

Bosch was silent, picturing the scene perfectly in his

mind. He remembered the dampness in the air and the smell of the orange blossoms from the nearby groves.

Hinojos cleared her throat before breaking into his memory.

'What did you do when she started crying?'

'I probably started crying, too. I usually did. I didn't want her to feel bad but there was a comfort in knowing she knew what was happening to me. Only mothers can do that, you know? Make you feel good when you're sad ...'

Bosch still had his eyes closed and was seeing only the memory.

'What did she tell you?'

'She ... she just told me she was going to get me out. She said that her lawyer was going to go to court soon to appeal the custody ruling and the unfit mother finding. She said there were other things she could do, too. The point was, she was getting me out.'

'That lawyer was your father?'

'Yes, but I didn't know it ... Anyway, what I'm saying is that the courts were wrong about her. That's the thing that bothers me. She was good to me and they didn't see that ... anyway, I remember she promised me that she would do what she had to do, but she would get me out.'

'But she never did.'

'No. Like I said, she ran out of time.'

'I'm sorry.'

Bosch opened his eyes and looked at her.

'So am I.'

✦ ✦ ✦ ✦ ✦ ✦ ✦

osch had parked in a public lot off Hill Street. It cost
him twelve dollars for his car. He then got onto the
101 and headed north toward the hills. As he drove,
he occasionally looked over at the blue box on the seat
next to him. But he didn't open it. He knew that he had to
but he would wait for home.

He turned the radio on and listened as the DJ
introduced a song by Abbey Lincoln. Bosch had never
heard it before but he immediately liked the words and the
woman's smoky voice.

> Bird alone, flying high
> Flying through a clouded sky
> Sending mournful, soulful sounds
> Soaring over troubled grounds

After he got to Woodrow Wilson and followed his usual
routine of parking a half block away from his home, Bosch
brought the box inside and placed it on the dining room
table. He lit a cigarette and paced the room, looking down
occasionally at the box. He knew what was in it. He had
the evidence list from the murder book. But he couldn't
overcome a feeling that by opening the box he was
invading some secret privacy, committing a sin that he
didn't understand.

Finally, he took his keys out. There was a small pen
knife on the ring and he used it to slice through the red

tape that sealed the box. He put the knife down and without thinking about it any further lifted the top off the box.

The victim's clothes and other belongings were wrapped individually in plastic bags, which Bosch took out of the box one by one and placed on the table. The clear plastic was yellowed but he could see through it. He did not remove anything from the bags but instead just held each piece of evidence up and studied it in its sterile covering.

He opened the murder book to the evidence list and made sure nothing was missing. It was all there. He held the small bag containing the gold earrings up to the light. They were like frozen tear drops. He put the bag back down and at the bottom of the box he saw the blouse, folded neatly in plastic, the spot of blood exactly where the evidence sheet said it was, on the left breast, about two inches from the center button.

Bosch ran his finger over the plastic where the spot was. It was then that he realized something. There was no other blood. He knew that it was the thing that had bothered him as he read the murder book but he had been unable to get ahold of the thought then. Now he had it. The blood. No blood on the undergarments, the skirt or the stockings, or pumps. Only on the blouse.

Bosch also knew the autopsy had described a body with no lacerations. Then where had the blood come from? He wanted to look at the crime scene and autopsy photos but knew that he couldn't. There was no way he would open that envelope.

Bosch pulled the bag containing the blouse from the box and read the evidence tag and other markings. Nowhere did it mention or give any reference code for any analysis ever being done on the blood.

This invigorated him. There was a good chance that the

blood spot came from the killer, not the victim. He had no idea whether blood that old could still be typed or even submitted for DNA analysis but he intended to find out. The problem, he knew, was comparison. It didn't matter if the blood could still be analyzed if there was nothing to compare it to. To get blood from Conklin or Mittel or anyone, for that matter, he would need a court order. And to get that, he needed evidence. Not just suspicions and hunches.

He had gathered the evidence bags together to replace in the box when he stopped to study one he had not considered closely before. It contained the belt that had been used to strangle the victim.

Bosch studied it a few moments as if it were a snake he was trying to identify before cautiously reaching into the box and picking it up. He could see the evidence tag tied through one of the belt holes. On the smooth silver sea shell buckle there was black powder. He could see that part of the ridge lines from a thumbprint were still there.

He held the belt up to the light. It pained him to look at it but he did. The belt was an inch in width, made of black leather. The sea shell buckle was the largest ornamentation but smaller silver shells were attached along its length. Looking at it brought back the memory. He hadn't really chosen it. Meredith Roman had taken him to the May Co. on Wilshire. She had seen the belt on a rack with many others and told him his mother would like it. She paid for it and allowed him to give it to his mother as a birthday present. Meredith had been right. His mother wore the belt often, including every time she visited him after the court took him away. And including the night she was murdered.

Bosch read the evidence tag but all it said was the case number and McKittrick's name. On the tongue he noticed that the second and fourth holes were imperfect circles, distended by the spoke of the buckle during wear. He guessed that maybe his mother wore it tighter at times, maybe to impress someone, or looser at times, over bulkier clothing. He now knew everything about the belt except who had used it last to kill her.

He realized then that whoever had held this belt, this weapon, before the police had been responsible for taking a life and indelibly changing his own. He carefully replaced it in the box and put the other clothing in on top of it. He then put the lid back on top.

Bosch couldn't stay in the house after that. He felt he had to get out. He didn't bother changing his clothes. He just got in the Mustang and started driving. It was dark now and he took Cahuenga down into Hollywood. He told himself he didn't know or care where he was going but that was a lie. He knew. When he got to Hollywood Boulevard he turned east.

The car took him to Vista, where he turned north and then cut into the first alley. The headlights sliced through the darkness and he saw a small homeless encampment. A man and woman huddled under a cardboard lean-to. Two other bodies, wrapped in blankets and newspapers, lay nearby. A small glow from dying flames came from the rim of a trash can. Bosch cruised by slowly, his eyes further down the alley, to the spot he knew from the crime scene drawing that was in the murder book.

The Hollywood souvenir store was now an adult book and video store. There was an alley entrance for shy customers and several cars were parked alongside the rear of the building. Bosch stopped near the door and killed the lights. He just sat in the car, feeling no need to get out. He had never been to the alley, to the spot, before. He just wanted to sit and watch and feel for a few moments.

He lit a cigarette and watched as a man carrying a bag

walked quickly out the door of the adult shop to a car parked at the end of the alley.

Bosch thought about a time when he was a small boy and still with his mother. They'd had a small apartment on Camrose then and during the summer they'd sit in the back courtyard on the nights she wasn't working or on Sunday afternoons and listen to the music coming over the hill from the Hollywood Bowl. The sound was bad, attacked by traffic and the white noise of the city before it got to them, but the high notes were clear. What he liked about it wasn't the music but that she was there. It was their time together. She always told him that she would take him one day to the bowl to hear 'Scheherazade.' It was her favorite. They never got the chance. The court took him away from her and she was dead before she could get him back.

Bosch finally heard the philharmonic perform 'Scheherazade' the year he spent with Sylvia. When she saw tears welling in the corners of his eyes, she thought it was because of the pure beauty of the music. He never got around to telling her it was something else.

A blur of motion caught his attention and someone banged a fist on the driver's side window. Bosch's left hand instinctively went under his jacket to his waist, but there was no gun there. He turned and looked into the face of an old woman whose years were etched like hash marks on her face. It looked like she was wearing three sets of clothes. When she was done knocking on the window, she opened her palm and held it out. Still startled, Bosch quickly reached into his pocket and pulled out a five. He started the car so he could put the window down and handed the money out to her. She said nothing. She just took it and walked away. Bosch watched her go and wondered how had she ended up in this alley. How had he?

Bosch drove out of the alley and back out to Hollywood Boulevard. He started cruising again. At first aimlessly but soon he found his purpose. He wasn't yet ready to confront Conklin or Mittel but he knew where they were and he wanted to see their homes, their lives, the places they had ended up.

He stayed on the Boulevard until Alvarado and then took that down to Third, where he started west. The drive took him from the Third World poverty of the area known as Little Salvador past the faded mansions of Hancock Park and then to Park La Brea, a huge complex of apartments, condominiums and attendant rest homes.

Bosch found Ogden Drive and cruised slowly down it until he saw the Park La Brea Lifecare Center. There's another irony, he thought. Lifecare. The only thing the place probably cared about was when you were going to die, so your space could be sold to the next one.

It was a nondescript twelve-story building of concrete and glass. Through the glass facade of the lobby Bosch could see a security guard at a post. In this town, even the elderly and infirm weren't safe. He glanced up the front of the building and saw most of the windows were dark. Only nine o'clock and the place was already dead. Someone honked at him from behind and he sped up and away, thinking about Conklin and what his life might be like. He wondered if the old man in his room up there ever gave a thought to Marjorie Lowe after so many years.

Bosch's next stop was Mount Olympus, the gaudy outcropping of modern Roman-style homes above Hollywood. The look was supposed to be neoclassical but he had heard it referred to more than once as neo*crassical*. The huge, expensive homes were jammed side by side as close as teeth. There were ornate columns and statues but the only thing that seemed classic about most of the place was the kitsch. Bosch took Mount Olympus Drive off Laurel

Canyon, turned on Electra and then went to Hercules. He was driving slowly, looking for addresses on curbs to match the one he had written in his notebook that morning.

When he found Mittel's house, he stopped on the street, stunned. It was a house that he knew. He had never been inside it, of course, but everyone knew it. It was a circular mansion that sat atop one of the most recognizable promontories in the Hollywood Hills. Bosch looked at the place with awe, imagining its interior size and its exterior ocean-to-mountain views. Its rounded walls lit from the outside with white lights, it looked like a spaceship that had alighted on a mountaintop and was poised to take to the air once again. Classic kitsch it wasn't. This was a home that bespoke its owner's power and influence.

An iron gate guarded a long driveway that went up a hill to the house. But tonight the gate was open and Bosch could see several cars and at least three limousines parked along one side of the drive. Other cars were parked in the circle at the top. It only dawned on Bosch that there was a party underway at the house when a red blur passed the car window and the door was suddenly sprung open. Bosch turned and looked into the face of a swarthy Latino man in a white shirt and red vest.

'Good evening, sir. We will take your car here. If you could walk up the drive on the left side, the greeters will find you.'

Bosch stared at the man unmoving, thinking.

'Sir?'

Bosch tentatively stepped out of the Mustang and the man in the vest gave him a slip of paper with a number on it. He then slipped into the car and drove away. Bosch stood there, aware that he was about to let events control him, something he knew he should avoid. He hesitated and looked back at the tail lights of the Mustang gliding away. He let the temptation take him.

Bosch fastened his top button and pulled his tie back into place as he walked up the driveway. He passed a small army of men in red vests and as he came all the way up past the limousines, a startling view of the lighted city came into view. He stopped and just looked for a moment. He could see from the moonlit Pacific in one direction to the towers of downtown in the other. The view alone was worth the price of the house, no matter how many millions that was.

The sound of soft music, laughter and conversation came from his left. He followed it down a stone path that curved along the form of the house. The drop-off to the houses down the hill was steep and deadly. He finally came to a flat yard that was lighted and full of people milling about beneath a tent as white as the moon. Bosch guessed there were at least a hundred and fifty well-dressed people sipping cocktails and taking small hors d'oeuvres off trays carried by young women wearing short black dresses, sheer stockings and white aprons. He wondered where the red vests were putting all the cars.

Bosch immediately felt underdressed and was sure he would be identified in seconds as a gate-crasher. But there was something so otherworldly about the scene that he held his ground.

A surfer in a suit approached him. He was about twenty-five, with short, sun-bleached hair and a dark tan. He wore a custom-fitted suit that looked as if it had cost more than every piece of clothing Bosch owned combined. It was light brown but the wearer probably described it as cocoa. He smiled the way enemies smile.

'Yes, sir, how are we doing tonight?'

'I'm doing fine. I don't know about you, yet.'

The surfer in a suit smiled a little more brightly at that.

'I'm Mr Johnson and I'm providing security for the benefit tonight. Might I inquire if you brought your invitation with you?'

Bosch hesitated for only a moment.

'Oh, I'm sorry. I didn't realize I needed to bring that along. I didn't think Gordon would need security at a benefit like this.'

He hoped dropping Mittel's first name would give the surfer pause before he did anything rash. The surfer frowned for only a moment.

'Then could I ask you just to sign in for me?'

'Of course.'

Bosch was led to a table to the side of the entrance area. Taped across the front of it was a red, white and blue banner that said ROBERT SHEPHERD NOW! It told Bosch all he needed to know about the affair.

There was a guest registry on the table and a woman sat behind it in a black crushed-velvet cocktail dress that did little to camouflage her breasts. Mr Johnson seemed more intent on these two items than on Bosch as he signed the name Harvey Pounds in the registry.

As he signed, Bosch noticed a stack of pledge cards and a champagne goblet filled with pencils on the table. He picked up an information sheet and started to read about the unannounced candidate. Johnson finally pulled his eyes away from the table hostess and checked the name Bosch had written.

'Thank you, Mr Pounds. Enjoy yourself.'

He disappeared into the crowd then, probably to check on whether a Harvey Pounds was on the list of invitees. Bosch decided he'd stay a few minutes, see if he could spot Mittel and then leave before the surfer came looking for him.

He stepped away from the entrance and out from beneath the tent. After crossing a short lawn to a retainer wall, he tried to act like he was just enjoying the view. And it was a view; the only higher one would have been from a jet coming in to LAX. But on the jet you wouldn't have the breadth of vision, the cool breeze, or the sounds from the city below.

Bosch turned around and looked back at the crowd under the tent. He studied the faces but could not spot Gordon Mittel. There was no sign of him. There was a large knot of people beneath the center of the tent and Bosch realized that it was a grouping of people trying to reach their hands toward the unannounced candidate, or at least the man Bosch assumed was Shepherd. Harry noticed that while the crowd seemed to exhibit solidarity in terms of wealth, it cut across all age lines. He guessed that many were there to see Mittel as much as Shepherd.

· One of the women in black-and-white came out from under the white canopy and toward him with a tray of champagne glasses. He took one, thanked her, and turned back to the view. He sipped at it and supposed that it was top quality, but he wouldn't be able to tell the difference. He decided he should gulp it and go when a voice from his left interrupted.

'Wonderful view, isn't it? Better than a movie. I could stand here for hours.'

Bosch turned his head to acknowledge the speaker but didn't look at him. He didn't want to get involved.

'Yeah, it's nice. But I'll take the mountains I have.'

'Really? Where is that?'

'The other side of the hill. On Woodrow Wilson.'

'Oh, yes. There are some very nice properties there.'

Not mine, Bosch thought. Unless you like neoearthquake classic.

'The San Gabriels are brilliant in the sun,' the conversationalist said. 'I looked there but then I bought here.'

Bosch turned. He was looking at Gordon Mittel. The host put out his hand.

'Gordon Mittel.'

Bosch hesitated but then figured Mittel was used to people losing a step or stuttering in his presence.

'Harvey Pounds,' Bosch said, taking his hand.

Mittel was wearing a black tuxedo. He was as over-dressed for the crowd as Bosch was underdressed. His gray hair was cropped short and he had a smooth machine tan. He was as trim and tight as a rubber band stretched around a stack of hundreds and looked at least five to ten years younger than he was.

'Glad to meet you, glad you could come,' he said. 'Did you meet Robert yet?'

'No, he's kind of in the middle of the pack there.'

'Yes, that's true. Well, he'll be happy to meet you when he gets the chance.'

'I guess he'll be happy to take my check as well.'

'That, too.' Mittel smiled. 'Seriously, though, I hope you can help us out. He's a good man and we need people like him in office.'

His smile seemed so phony that Harry wondered if Mittel had already pegged him as a crasher. Bosch smiled back and patted the right breast of his jacket.

'I've got the checkbook right here.'

Doing that, Bosch remembered what he really had in his pocket and got an idea. The champagne, though only a single glass, had emboldened him. He suddenly realized he wanted to spook Mittel and maybe get a look at his real colors.

'Tell me,' he said, 'is Shepherd the one?'

'I don't quite follow.'

'Is he going all the way to the White House someday? Is he the one that's going to take you?'

Mittel sloughed off a frown or maybe it was a glimmer of annoyance.

'I guess we shall see. We've got to get him into the Senate first. That's the important thing.'

Bosch nodded and made a show of scanning the crowd.

'Well, it looks like you have the right people here. But, you know, I don't see Arno Conklin. Are you still tight with him? He was your first, wasn't he?'

Mittel's forehead creased with a deep furrow.

'Well …' Mittel seemed to be uncomfortable, but then it quickly passed. 'To tell the truth, we haven't spoken in a long time. He's retired now, an old man in a wheelchair. Do you know Arno?'

'Never spoken to him in my life.'

'Then tell me, what prompts a question about ancient history?'

Bosch hiked his shoulders.

'I guess I'm just a student of history, that's all.'

'What do you do for a living, Mr Pounds? Or are you a full-time student?'

'I'm in law.'

'We have something in common then.'

'I doubt it.'

'I'm a Stanford man. How about you?'

Bosch thought a moment.

'Vietnam.'

Mittel frowned again and Bosch saw the interest go out of his eyes like water down a drain.

'Well, I tell you, I ought to mingle a little more. Watch the champagne, and if you decide you don't want to drive, one of the boys on the driveway can get you home. Ask for Manuel.'

'The one in the red vest?'

'Uh, yes. One of them.'

Bosch held up his glass.

'Don't worry, this is only my third.'

Mittel nodded and disappeared back into the crowd. Bosch watched him cross beneath the tent, stop to shake a few hands, but eventually make it to the house. He entered through a wall of French doors into what looked like a living room or some sort of viewing area. Mittel walked to a couch and bent down to speak quietly to a man in a suit. This man looked to be about the same age as Mittel but with a harder appearance. He had a sharp face and, though sitting, clearly had a much heavier body. As a younger man he had probably used his strength, not his brain. Mittel straightened up and the other man just nodded. Mittel then disappeared into the further recesses of his house.

Bosch finished his glass of champagne and started moving through the crowd under the tent toward the house. As he got near the French doors, one of the black-and-white women asked if he needed help finding something. He said he was looking for the bathroom and she directed him to another door to the left. He went where he was told and found the door was locked. He waited for a few moments and the door finally opened, emitting a man and a woman. They giggled when they saw Bosch waiting and headed back to the tent.

Inside the bathroom Bosch opened his jacket and took a folded piece of paper from the inside pocket on the left. It was the photocopy of the Johnny Fox story that Keisha Russell had given him. He unfolded it and took out a pen. He circled the names Johnny Fox, Arno Conklin and Gordon Mittel, then, under the story, wrote, 'What prior work experience got Johnny the job?'

He refolded the page twice and ran his fingers tightly over the creases. Then, on the outside, he wrote, 'For Gordon Mittel Only!'

Back under the tent, Bosch found a black-and-white woman and gave her the folded paper.

'You have to find Mr Mittel right away,' he told her. 'Give him this note. He's waiting on it.'

He watched her go and then made his way back out through the crowd to the sign-in table at the entry area. He quickly bent over the guest registry and wrote his mother's name down. The table hostess protested that he had already signed in.

'This is for somebody else,' he said.

For an address, he wrote Hollywood and Vista. He left the line for a telephone number blank.

Bosch scanned the crowd again and saw neither Mittel nor the woman he had given the note to. Then he looked into the room beyond the French doors and Mittel appeared with the note in his hand. He walked slowly into the room, studying it. Bosch could tell by the direction of his eyes that he was studying the note scribbled on the bottom. Even with his phony tan, he seemed to Bosch to go pale.

Bosch took a step back into the entrance alcove and watched. He could feel his heart beating at a quicker pace. He felt like he was watching some secret play on a stage.

There was a look of perplexed anger on Mittel's face now. Bosch saw him hand the page to the rough man who still sat in the cushioned chair. Then Mittel turned to the glass panels and looked out at the people under the tent. He said something and Bosch thought he could read his lips.

'Son of a bitch.'

Then he started talking more quickly, barking orders. The man on the chair rose and Bosch knew instinctively that it was his cue to leave. He walked quickly back out to the driveway and trotted down to the group of men in red vests. He handed his valet ticket and a ten-dollar bill to one of them and said in Spanish that he was in a great hurry.

Still, it seemed to take forever. As he waited nervously, Bosch kept his eyes on the house, waiting for the rough man to appear. He had watched which direction the valet had gone for his car and he was ready to bolt that way if necessary. He began to wish he had his gun. Whether he really needed it or not did not matter. In this moment he knew it gave him a sense of security that he felt naked without.

The surfer in a suit appeared at the top of the driveway and strode down toward Bosch. At the same time, Bosch saw his Mustang approaching. He walked out into the street, ready to take it. The surfer got to him first.

'Hey, buddy, hold on a sec –'

Bosch turned from his approaching car and hit him in the jaw, sending him backward onto the driveway. He moaned and rolled onto his side, both hands clutching his jaw. Bosch was sure the jaw was dislocated if not broken. He shook away the pain in his hand as the Mustang screeched to a stop.

The man in the red vest was slow in getting out. Bosch pulled him away from the open door and jumped in. As he settled in behind the wheel he looked up the driveway and saw the rough man was now coming. When he saw the surfer on the ground, he started running but his steps were unsteady on the downgrade of the driveway. Bosch saw his heavy thighs pressing the fabric of his pants and suddenly he slipped and fell. Two of the red vests went to help him up but he angrily shoved them away.

Bosch gunned the car and sped away. He worked his way up to Mulholland and turned east toward home. He could feel adrenaline surging through him. Not only had he gotten away, but it was clear he had struck a nerve with a hammer. Let Mittel think about that for a while, he thought. Let him sweat. Then he yelled out loud in the car, though no one could hear except himself.

'Spooked ya, didn't I, you fuck!'

He banged his palm triumphantly on the steering wheel.

❖ ❖ ❖ ❖ ❖ ❖ ❖

He dreamed of the coyote again. The animal was on a mountain path where there were no homes, no cars, no people. It was moving very quickly through the dark as if it was trying to get away. But the path and place were his. He knew the land and knew he would escape. What it was he fled from was never clear, never seen. But it was there, behind him in the dark. And the coyote knew by instinct it must get away.

The phone woke Bosch, breaking into the dream like a knife stabbed through paper. Bosch pulled the pillow off his head, rolled to his right and his eyes were immediately assaulted by the light of dawn. He had forgotten to close the blinds. He reached for the phone on the floor.

'Hold on,' he said.

He put the phone down on the bed, sat up and rubbed a hand across his face. He squinted at the clock. It was ten minutes after seven. He coughed and cleared his throat, then picked the phone back up.

'Yeah.'

'Detective Bosch?'

'Yeah.'

'It's Brad Hirsch. I'm sorry to call so early.'

Bosch had to think a moment. Brad Hirsch? He had no idea who it was.

'Yeah, it's okay,' he said while he continued to search his mind for the name.

A silence followed.

'I'm the one ... In Latents? Remember, you –'

'Hirsch? Yeah, Hirsch. I remember. What's up?'

'I wanted to tell you I made the AFIS run you wanted. I came in early and ran it with another search I'm doing for Devonshire Homicide. I don't think anybody will know.'

Bosch kicked his legs over the side of the bed, opened a drawer in the bed table and took out a pad and a pencil. He noticed that he had taken the pad from the Surf and Sand Hotel in Laguna Beach. He remembered he had spent a few days with Sylvia there the year before.

'Yeah, you made the run? What'd you get?'

'Well, that's the thing. I'm sorry but I got nothing.'

Bosch threw the pad back into the open drawer and threw himself backward on the bed.

'No hits?'

'Well, the computer came up with two candidates. I then did a visual comparison and it was no good. No matches. I'm sorry. I know this case means ...'

He didn't finish.

'You took it through all the data bases?'

'Every one on our network.'

'Let me ask you something. All those data bases, do they include DA's employees and LAPD personnel?'

There was silence as Hirsch must have been mulling over what the question might mean.

'You there, Hirsch?'

'Yes. The answer is yes.'

'How far back? You know what I mean? These bases have prints going how far back?'

'Well, each data base is different. The LAPD's is extensive. I'd say we have prints on everybody who's worked here since World War II.'

Well, that clears Irving and the rest of the cops, Bosch

165

thought. But that didn't bother him much. His sights were definitely somewhere else.

'What about people working for the DA?'

'The DA's office would be different,' Hirsch said. 'I don't think they started printing employees until the middle sixties.'

Conklin had been there during that time, Bosch knew, but he would already have been elected DA. It would seem that he would not have submitted his own prints, especially if he knew there was a print card in a murder book somewhere that could possibly be matched to him.

He thought of Mittel. He would have been out of the DA's office by the time employees' prints were taken as a matter of course.

'What about the federal base?' he asked. 'What if some guy worked for a president and got the kind of clearance you need to go visit the White House, would those prints be in that base?'

'Yes, they'd be in twice. In the federal employees base and in the FBI's. They keep prints on record of everyone they do background investigations on, if that's what you mean. But remember, just because somebody visits the president, it doesn't mean they get printed.'

Well, Mittel isn't a scratch but it's close, Bosch thought.

'So what you're saying,' Bosch said, 'is that whether or not we have complete data files going back to 1961, whoever belongs to those prints I gave you hasn't been printed since then?'

'That's not one hundred percent but it's close. The person who left these prints probably hasn't been printed – at least by any contributor to the data banks. We can only reach so far with this. One way or another we can pull prints on one out of about every fifty or so people in the country. But I just didn't get anything this time. Sorry.'

'That's okay, Hirsch, you tried.'

'Well, I guess I'll be getting back to work now. What do you want me to do with the print card?'

Bosch thought a moment. He wondered if there was any other avenue to chase down.

'Tell you what, can you just hold on to it? I'll come by the lab and pick it up when I can. Probably be by later today.'

'Okay, I'll put it in an envelope for you in case I'm not here. Good-bye.'

'Hey, Hirsch?'

'Yeah?'

'It feels good, don't it?'

'What's that?'

'You did the right thing. You didn't get a match but you did the right thing.'

'Yeah, I guess.'

He was acting like he didn't understand because he was embarrassed, but he understood.

'Yeah, I'll see you Hirsch.'

After hanging up, Bosch sat on the side of the bed, lit a cigarette and thought about what he was going to do with the day. The news from Hirsch was not good but it wasn't daunting. It certainly didn't clear Arno Conklin. It might not even have cleared Gordon Mittel. Bosch wasn't sure whether Mittel's work for presidents and senators would have required a fingerprint check. He decided his investigation was still intact. He wasn't changing any plans.

He thought about the night before and the wild-ass chance he had taken confronting Mittel the way he had. He smiled at his own recklessness and thought about what Hinojos might make of it. He knew she'd say it was a symptom of his problem. She wouldn't see it as a tactful way of flushing the bird from the bush.

He got up and started the coffee and then showered, shaved and got ready for the day. He took his coffee and the box of cereal from the refrigerator out to the deck, leaving the sliding door open so he could hear the stereo. He had KFWB news on.

It was cool and crisp outside but he could tell it would get warmer later. Blue jays were swooping in and out of the arroyo below the deck and he could see black bees the size of quarters working in the yellow flowers of the primrose jasmine.

There was a story on the radio about a building contractor making a fourteen-million-dollar bonus for completing the rebuilding of the 10 freeway three months ahead of schedule. The officials who gathered to announce the engineering feat likened the fallen freeway to the city itself. Now that it was back upright, so, too, was the city. The city was on the move again. They had a lot to learn, Bosch thought.

Afterward, he went in and got out the yellow pages and started working the phone in the kitchen. He called the major airlines, shopped around and made arrangements to fly to Florida. But flying on one day's notice, the best deal he could get was still seven hundred dollars, a shocking amount to him. He put it on a credit card so that he could pay it off over time. He also reserved a rental car at Tampa International Airport.

When he had that finished he went back out to the deck and thought about the next project he had to tackle:

He needed a badge.

For a long time he sat on the deck chair and contemplated whether he needed it for his own sense of security or because it was a bona fide necessity to his mission. He knew how naked and vulnerable he had felt this week without the gun and the badge, extremities he had carried on his body for more than twenty years. But he had avoided the temptation to carry the backup gun that he knew was in the closet next to the front door. That he could do, he knew. But the badge was different. More so than the gun, the badge was the symbol of what he was. It opened doors better than any key, it gave him more authority than any words, than any weapon. He decided the badge was a necessity. If he was going to Florida and was going to scam McKittrick, he had to look legit. He had to have a badge.

He knew his badge was probably in a desk drawer in Assistant Chief Irvin S. Irving's office. There was no way he could get to it and not be discovered. But he knew where there was another one that would work just as well.

Bosch looked at his watch. Nine-fifteen. It was forty-five minutes until the daily command meeting at Hollywood Station. He had plenty of time.

❖ ❖ ❖ ❖ ❖ ❖ ❖

Bosch pulled into the rear parking lot of the station at five minutes after ten. He was sure that Pounds, who was punctual about everything he did, would already have gone down the front hall to the captain's office with the overnight logs. The meeting was held every morning and included the station's CO, patrol captain, watch lieutenant and detective commander, who was Pounds. They were routine affairs and never lasted longer than twenty minutes. The members of the station's command staff simply drank coffee and went through the overnight reports and ongoing problems, complaints or investigations of particular note.

Bosch went in the back door by the drunk tank and then up the hallway to the detective bureau. It had been a busy morning. There were already four men handcuffed to benches in the hallway. One of them, a drug hype Bosch had seen in the station before and used as an unreliable informant on occasion, asked Bosch for a smoke. It was illegal to smoke in any city-owned building. Bosch lit a cigarette anyway and put it in the man's mouth because both his needle-scarred arms were cuffed behind his back.

'What is it this time, Harley?' Bosch asked.

'Shit, a guy leaves his g'rage open, he's asking me to come in. Isn't that right?'

'Tell that one to the judge.'

As Bosch walked away one of the other lockdowns yelled at him from down the hallway.

'What about me, man? I need a smoke.'

'I'm out,' Bosch said.

'Fuck you, man.'

'Yeah, that's what I thought.'

He came into the detective bureau through the rear door. The first thing he did was confirm that Pounds's glass office was empty. He was at the command meeting. Then he checked the coatrack up at the front and saw he was in business. As he walked down the aisle formed by the separation of the investigation tables, he exchanged nods with a few of the other detectives.

Edgar was at the homicide table sitting across from his new partner, who was in Bosch's old chair. Edgar heard one of the 'Hi, Harry' greetings and turned around.

'Harry, wassup?'

'Hey, man, just came in to get a couple things. Hang on a sec, it's hot outside.'

Bosch walked to the front of the bureau, where old Henry of the Nod Squad sat at the desk behind the counter. He was working on a crossword puzzle and Bosch could see several erasure marks had turned the grid gray.

'Henry, howzit hanging? You getting anywhere with that?'

'Detective Bosch.'

Bosch slipped his sport coat off and hung it on a hook on the rack next to a jacket with a gray cross-hatch pattern. It was on a hanger and Bosch knew it belonged to Pounds. As he put his coat on the hook with his back to Henry and the rest of the bureau, he snaked his left hand inside the other coat, felt for the interior pocket and then pulled out Pounds's badge wallet. He knew it would be there. Pounds was a creature of habit and Bosch had seen the badge wallet in the suit coat once before. He put the wallet into his pants pocket and turned around as Henry continued talking. Bosch had only a momentary tinge of hesitation at the seriousness of what he was doing. Taking another cop's badge was a crime, but Bosch looked at Pounds as being the reason he did not have his own badge. In the inventory of his morality, what Pounds had done to him was equally wrong.

'If you want to see the lieutenant, he's down the hall at a meeting,' Henry said.

'No, I don't want to see the lieutenant, Henry. In fact, don't even tell him I was here. I don't want his blood pressure to go up, you know. I'm just going to get a few things and get out of here, okay?'

'That's a deal. I don't want him cranky, either.'

Bosch didn't have to worry about anyone else in the bureau telling Pounds he had been in. He gave Henry a friendly clasp on the shoulder as he walked behind him, sealing the agreement. He went back to the homicide table and as he approached, Burns began to rise from Bosch's old spot.

'You need to get in here, Harry?' he asked.

Bosch thought he could detect nervous energy in the other man's voice. He understood his predicament and wasn't going to make it a difficult time for him.

'Yeah, if you don't mind,' he said. 'I figured I'd get my personal stuff out of there so you can move in the right way.'

Bosch came around and opened the drawer at the table. There were two boxes of Junior Mints on top of old paperwork that had been shoved in long ago.

'Oh, those are mine, sorry,' Burns said.

He reached in for the two boxes of candy and stood next to the table, holding them like a big kid in a suit while Bosch went through the paperwork.

It was all a show. Bosch took some of the paperwork and dumped it in a manila file and then pointed with his hand, signaling to Burns he could put his candy back.

'Be careful, Bob.'

'It's Bill. Careful of what?'

'Ants.'

Bosch went to the bank of file cabinets that ran along the wall to the side of the table and opened one of the drawers with his business card taped to it. It was three up from the bottom, waist-high, and it was one he knew was almost empty. With his back to the table again, he pulled the badge wallet out of his pocket and put it in the drawer. Then, with his hands in the drawer and out of sight, he opened the wallet and took out the gold badge. He then put it in one pocket and the wallet back in the other. For good measure, he pulled a file out of the drawer and closed it.

He turned around and looked at Jerry Edgar.

'Okay, that's it. Just some personal stuff I might need. Anything going on?'

'Nah, quiet.'

Back at the coatrack, Bosch turned his back on the bureau again and used one hand to reach for his coat while using the other to take the badge wallet from his pocket and slip it back into Pounds's coat. He then put his coat on, said good-bye to Henry and went back to the homicide table.

'I'm outta here,' he said to Edgar and Burns while picking up the two files he had pulled. 'I don't want Ninety-eight to see me and throw a fit. Good luck, boys.'

On the way out, Bosch stopped and gave the hype another cigarette. The lockdown who had complained before was no longer on the bench or Bosch would have given him one, too.

Back in the Mustang, he dumped the files on the

backseat and took his empty badge wallet out of his briefcase. He slipped Pounds's badge into place next to his own ID card. It would work, he decided, as long as no one looked too closely at it. The badge said LIEUTENANT across it. Bosch's ID card identified him as a detective. It was a minor discrepancy and Bosch was happy with it. Best of all, he thought, there was a good chance Pounds would not notice that the badge was missing for some time. He rarely left the station to go to crime scenes and so rarely had to open the wallet or show his badge. There was a good chance its disappearance would go unnoticed. All he had to do was get it back into place when he was done with it.

✦ ✦ ✦ ✦ ✦ ✦ ✦

Bosch ended up outside the door of Carmen Hinojos's office early for his afternoon session. He waited until exactly three-thirty and knocked. She smiled as he entered her office and he noticed that the late-afternoon sun came through the window and splashed light directly across her desk. He moved toward the chair he usually took but then stopped himself and sat on the chair to the left of the desk. She noticed this and frowned at him as if he were a schoolboy.

'If you think I care which chair you sit in, you are wrong.'

'Am I? Okay.'

He got up and moved to the other chair. He liked being near the window.

'I might not be here for Monday's session,' he said after settling in.

She frowned again, this time more seriously.

'Why not?'

'I'm going away. I'll try to be back.'

'Away? What happened to your investigation?'

'It's part of it. I'm going to Florida to track down one of the original investigators. One's dead, the other one's in Florida. So I've got to go to him.'

'Couldn't you just call?'

'I don't want to call. I don't want to give him the chance to put me off.'

She nodded.

'When do you leave?'

'Tonight. I'm taking a red-eye to Tampa.'

'Harry, look at you. You practically look like the walking dead. Can't you get some sleep and take a plane in the morning?'

'No, I've gotta get out there before the mail arrives.'

'What's that mean?'

'Nothing. It's a long story. Anyway, I wanted to ask you something. I need your help.'

She contemplated this for several seconds, apparently weighing how far she wanted to go into the pool without knowing how deep it was.

'What is it you want?'

'Do you ever do any forensic work for the department?'

She narrowed her eyes, not seeing where this was going.

'A little. From time to time somebody will bring me something, or maybe ask me to do a little profiling of a suspect. But mostly the department uses outside contractors. Forensic psychiatrists who have experience with this.'

'But you've been to crime scenes?'

'Actually, no. I've only looked at photos brought to me and worked from them.'

'Perfect.'

Bosch pulled his briefcase onto his lap and opened it. He took out the envelope of crime scene and autopsy photos that had been in the murder book and gently placed them on her desk.

'Those are from this case. I don't want to look at them. I can't look at them. But I need someone to do it and tell me what's there. There's probably nothing but I'd like another opinion. The investigation these two guys did on this case was … well, it was almost like there was no investigation.'

'Oh, Harry.' She shook her head. 'I'm not sure this is wise. Why me?'

'Because you know what I'm doing. And because I trust you. I don't think I can trust anybody else.'

'Would you trust me if there was no ethical constraint on me telling others about what we've talked about here?'

Bosch studied her face.

'I don't know,' he finally said.

'I thought so.'

She slid the envelope to the side of the desk.

'Let's put these aside for now and go on with the session. I really have to think about this.'

'Okay, you can take them. But let me know, okay? I just want your feel for them. As a psychiatrist and as a woman.'

'We'll see.'

'What do you want to talk about?'

'What is happening with the investigation?'

'Is that a professional question, Dr Hinojos? Or are you just curious about the case?'

'No, I'm curious about you. And I'm worried about you. I'm still not convinced that what you are doing is safe – either psychologically or physically. You're mucking around in the lives of powerful people. And I'm caught in the middle. I know what you're doing but am almost powerless to make you stop. I'm afraid you tricked me.'

'Tricked you?'

'You pulled me into this. I bet you've wanted to show me these pictures since you told me what you're doing.'

'You're right, I have. But there was no trick. I thought this was a place where I could talk about anything. Isn't that what you said?'

'Okay, I wasn't tricked, just led down the path. I should've seen it coming. Let's move on. I want to talk more about the emotional aspect of what you are doing. I want to know more about why finding this killer is so important to you after so many years?'

'It should be obvious.'

'Make it more obvious for me.'

'I can't. I can't put it into words. All I know is that everything changed for me after she was gone. I don't know how things would have been if she hadn't been taken away but ... everything changed.'

'Do you understand what you're saying and what it means? You're looking at your life in two parts. The first part is with her, which you seem to have imbued with a happiness I'm sure was not always there. The second part is your life after, which you acknowledge has not met expectations or is in some way unsatisfactory. I think you've been unhappy for a long time, possibly all of that time. This recent relationship you had may have been a highlight but you were still and, I think, have always been, an unhappy man.'

She rested a moment but Bosch didn't speak. He knew she wasn't done.

'Now, maybe the traumas of the last few years – both personally for you and for your community at large – have made you take stock of yourself. And I fear that you believe, whether subconsciously or not, that by going back and bringing some form of justice to what happened to your mother, you will be righting your life. And there's the problem. Whatever happens with this private investigation of yours, it's not going to change things. It just can't be done.'

'You're saying that I can't blame what happened then for what I am now?'

'No, listen to me, Harry. All I'm saying is you are the sum of many parts, not the sum of one. It's like dominoes. Several different blocks must click together for you to arrive at the end, at the point you are at now. You don't jump from the first domino to the last.'

'So I should just give it up? Just let it go?'

'I'm not saying that. But I am finding it hard to see the emotional benefit or healing you will get from this. In fact, I think there is the possibility that you may do yourself more damage than repair. Does that make any sense?'

Bosch stood up and went to the window. He stared out but didn't compute what he saw. He felt the warmth of the sun on him. He didn't look at her as he spoke.

'I don't know what makes sense. All I know is that on every level it seems to make sense that I do this. In fact, I feel … I don't know what the word is, maybe ashamed. I feel ashamed that I haven't done this long before now. A lot of years have gone by and I just let them go. I feel like I let her down somehow … that I let myself down.'

'That's understa –'

'Remember what I told you the first day? Everybody counts or nobody counts. Well, for a long time she didn't count. Not with this department, this society, not even with me. I have to admit that, not even with me. Then I opened that file this week and I could see that her death was just put away. It was buried, just like I had buried it. Somebody put the fix in because she didn't count. They did it because they could. And then when I think about how long I've let it go … it makes me want to … I don't know, just hide my face or something.'

He stopped, unable to put into words what he wanted to say. He looked down and noticed there were no ducks in the butcher shop window.

'You know,' he said, 'she might've been what she was but sometimes I feel like I didn't even deserve that … I guess I got what I deserved in life.'

He stayed at the window, not looking at her. It was several moments before Hinojos spoke.

'I guess this is the point where I should tell you that you're being too hard on yourself, but I don't think that would help much.'

'No, it wouldn't.'

'Could you come back here and sit down? Please?'

Bosch did as he was asked. Finally, after he was seated, his eyes met hers. She spoke first.

'What I want to say is that you are mixing things up. Putting the cart before the horse. You can't take the blame because this case may have been covered up. First of all, you had nothing to do with that, and secondly, you didn't even realize that until you read through the file this week.'

'But don't you see? Why didn't I look at it before? I'm not new here. I've been a cop twenty years. I should've been there before this. I mean, so what that I didn't know the details. I knew she was killed and nothing was ever done about it. That was enough.'

'Look, Harry, think about this, okay? On the plane over tonight, just give it some thought. You've engaged yourself in a noble pursuit but you have to safeguard against damaging yourself further. The bottom line is that it is not worth that. It's not worth the toll you may have to pay.'

'Not worth it? There's a killer out there. He thinks he made it away free. For years, he has thought that. Decades. And I'm going to change that.'

'You're not understanding what I'm saying. I don't want any guilty person to get away, especially with murder. But what I am talking about here is you. You are my only concern here. There is a basic rule of nature. No living thing sacrifices itself or hurts itself needlessly. It's the will of survival and I fear the circumstances of your life may have blunted your own survival skills. You may be throwing it to the wind, not caring what happens to you emotionally, physically, in every way, in this pursuit. I don't want to see you hurt.'

She took a breather. He said nothing.

'I have to say,' she continued quietly, 'I'm very nervous about this. I've never had this situation come up before and I've counseled a lot of cops in nine years here.'

'Well, I got bad news for you.' He smiled. 'I went and crashed a party last night at Mittel's. I think I may have spooked him. At least, I spooked myself.'

'Shit!'

'Is that some new psychiatric term? I'm not familiar with it.'

'This isn't funny. Why'd you do that?'

Bosch thought a moment.

'I don't know. It was kind of a whim type of thing. I was just driving by his house and there was a party. It kind of ... it just made me angry for some reason. Him having a party and my mother ...'

'Did you speak to him about the case?'

'No. I didn't even tell him my name. We just kind've sparred around for a few minutes but then I left him something. Remember that newspaper clip I showed you Wednesday? I left that for him. I saw him read it. I think it struck a nerve.'

She exhaled loudly.

'Now, step outside yourself and look as an uninvolved observer at what you did. If you can. Was that a smart thing to do, going there like that?'

'I already have thought about it. No, it wasn't smart. It was a mistake. He'll probably warn Conklin. They'll both know somebody's out there, coming for them. They'll close ranks.'

'You see, you are proving my point for me. I want you to promise me you won't do anything foolish like that again.'

'I can't.'

'Well, then I have to tell you that a patient-doctor relationship can be broken if the therapist believes the patient is endangering himself or others. I told you I was almost powerless to stop you. Not completely.'

'You'd go to Irving?'

'I will if I believe you are being reckless.'

Bosch felt anger as he realized she had ultimate control over him and what he was doing. He swallowed the anger and held up his hands, surrendering.

'All right. I won't go crashing any parties again.'

'No. I want more than that. I want you to stay away from these men that you think may have been involved.'

'What I'll promise you is that I won't go to them until I have the whole thing in the bag.'

'I mean it.'

'So do I.'

'I hope so.'

They were silent for nearly a minute after that. It was a cooling-off period. She turned slightly in her chair, not looking at him, probably thinking what to say next.

'Let's move on,' she finally said. 'You understand that this whole thing, this pursuit of yours, has eclipsed what we're supposed to be doing here?'

'I know.'

'So we're prolonging my evaluation.'

'Well, that doesn't bother me as much anymore. I need the time off the job for this other thing.'

'Well, as long as you are happy,' she said sarcastically. 'Okay, then I want to go back to the incident that brought you to me. The other day you were very general and very short in your description of what happened. I understand why. I think we were both feeling each other out at that point. But we are far past that now. I'd like a fuller story.

You said the other day that Lieutenant Pounds set things into motion?'

'That's right.'

'How?'

'First of all, he's a commander of detectives who has never been a detective himself. Oh, technically, he probably spent a few months on a table somewhere along the line so he'd have it on his résumé, but basically he's an administrator. He's what we call a Robocrat. A bureaucrat with a badge. He doesn't know the first thing about clearing cases. The only thing he knows about it is how to draw a line through the case on this little chart he keeps in his office. He doesn't know the first thing about the differences between an interview and an interrogation. And that's fine, the department is full of people like him. I say let them do their job and let me do mine. The problem is Pounds doesn't realize where he's good and where he's bad. It's led to problems before. Confrontations. It finally led to the incident, as you keep calling it.'

'What did he do?'

'He touched my suspect.'

'Explain what that means.'

'When you've got a case and you bring someone in, he's all yours. Nobody goes near him, understand? The wrong word, the wrong question and it could spoil a case. That's a cardinal rule; don't touch somebody else's suspect. It doesn't matter if you're a lieutenant or the damn chief, you stay clear until you check first with the guys with the collar.'

'So what happened?'

'Like I told you the other day, my partner Edgar and I brought in this suspect. A woman had been killed. One of these ones who puts ads in the sex tabs you can buy on the Boulevard. She gets called to one of those shithole motel rooms on Sunset, has sex with the guy and ends up stabbed to death. That's the short story. The stab wound's to the upper right chest. The john, he plays it cool, though. He calls the cops and says it was her knife and she tried to rob him with it. He says he turned her arm and put it into her. Self-defense. Okay, so that's when me and Edgar show up and right away we see some things don't fit with that story.'

'Like what?'

'First of all, she's a lot smaller than he is. I don't see her coming at him with a knife. Then there's the knife itself. It's a serrated steak knife, 'bout eight inches long, and she had one of those little purses without a strap.'

'A clutch.'

'Yeah, I guess. Anyway, that knife wouldn't've fit in it, so how'd she bring it in? As they say on the street, her clothes fit tighter than the rubbers in her purse, so she wasn't hiding it on her, either. And there was more. If her purpose was to rip the guy off, why have sex first? Why not pull the knife, take his shit and go? But that didn't happen. His story was that they did it first, then she came at him, which explained why she was still naked. Which, of course, raised another question. Why rob the guy when you're naked? Where you going to run like that?'

'The guy was lying.'

'Seemed obvious. Then we got something else. In her purse – the clutch – was a piece of paper on which she had written down the motel's name and the room number. It was consistent with a right-handed person. Like I said, the stab was to the upper right chest of the victim. So it doesn't add up. If she came at him, the chances are the knife would be in her right hand. If the john then turns it into her, it's likely the wound would be on the left side of the chest, not the right.'

Bosch made a motion of pulling his right hand toward

his chest, showing how awkward it would be for it to stab his right side.

'There was all kinds of stuff that wasn't right. It was a downward-grade wound, also inconsistent with it being in her hand. That would have been upward-grade.'

Hinojos nodded that she understood.

'The problem was, we had no physical evidence contradicting his story. Nothing. Just our feeling that she wouldn't have done it the way he said. The wound stuff wasn't enough. And then, in his favor, was the knife. It was on the bed, we could see it had fingerprints in the blood. I had no doubt they'd be hers. That's not hard to do once she's dead. So while it didn't impress me, that didn't matter. It's what the DA would think and then what a jury would think after that. Reasonable doubt is a big black hole that swallows cases like this. We needed more.'

'So what happened?'

'It's what we call a he-said-she-said. One person's word against the other, but only the other is dead in this case. Makes it even harder. We had nothing but his story. So what you do in a case like that is you sweat the guy. You turn him. And there's a lot of ways to do it. But, basically, you gotta break him down in the rooms. We –'

'The rooms?'

'The interrogation rooms. In the bureau. We took this guy into a room. As a witness. We didn't formally arrest him. We asked if he'd come down, said that we had to straighten a few things out about what she did, and he said sure. You know, Mr Cooperative. Still cool. We stuck him in a room and then Edgar and I went down to the watch office to get some of the good coffee. They've got good coffee there, one of those big urns that was donated by some restaurant that got wrecked in the quake. Everybody goes in there to get coffee. Anyway, we're takin' our time, talkin' about how we're going to go at this guy, which one of us wanted him first, and so on. Meantime, fuckin' Pounds – excuse me – sees the guy in the room through the little window and goes in and informs him. And –'

'What do you mean, informs him?'

'Reads him his rights. This is our goddamn witness and Pounds, who doesn't know what the hell he's doing, thinks he's gotta go in there and give the guy the spiel. He thinks like we forgot or something.'

Bosch looked at her with outrage on his face but immediately saw she didn't understand.

'Wasn't that the right thing to do?' she asked. 'Aren't you required by law to inform people of their rights?'

Bosch struggled to contain his anger, reminding himself that Hinojos might work for the department, but she was an outsider. Her perceptions of police work were likely based more on the media than on the actual reality.

'Let me give you a quick lesson on what's the law and what's real. We – the cops – have the deck stacked against us. What *Miranda* and all the other rules and regs amount to is that we have to take some guy we know is, or at least think is, guilty and basically say, 'Hey, look, we think you did it and the Supreme Court and every lawyer on the planet would advise you not to talk to us, but, how about it, will you talk to us?' It just doesn't work. You gotta get around that. You gotta use guile and some bluffing and you gotta be sneaky. The rules of the courts are like a tightrope that you're walking on. You have to be very careful but there is a chance you can walk on it to get to the other side. So when some asshole who doesn't know shit walks in on your guy and informs him, it can pretty much ruin your whole day, not to mention the case.'

He stopped and studied her. He still saw skepticism. He knew then that she was just another citizen who would be scared shitless if she ever got a dose of the way things really were on the street.

'When someone is informed, that's it,' he said. 'It's over. Me and Edgar came back in from coffee and the john sits there and says he thinks he wants his lawyer. I said, "What lawyer, who's talking about lawyers? You're a witness, not a suspect," and he tells us that the lieutenant just read him his rights. I don't know at that moment who I hated more, Pounds for blowing it or this guy for killing the girl.'

'Well, tell me this, what would have happened if Pounds had not done what he did?'

'We would've made friendly with the guy, asked him to tell his story in as much detail as possible and hoped there would be inconsistencies when compared to what he'd told the uniforms. Then we would have said, "The inconsistencies in your statements make you a suspect." *Then* we would have informed him and hopefully clubbed the shit out of him with the inconsistencies and the problems we found with the scene. We would have tried, and maybe succeeded, in finessing a confession. Most of what we do is just get people to talk. It's not like the stuff on TV. It's a hundred times harder and dirtier. But just like you, what we do is get people to talk … Anyway, that's my view. But we'll never know now what could've happened because of Pounds.'

'Well, what did happen after you found out he'd been informed?'

'I left the room and walked straight into where Pounds was in his office. He knew something was wrong because he stood up. I remember that. I asked him if he'd informed my guy and when he said yes, we got into it. Both of us, screaming … then I don't really remember how it happened. I'm not trying to deny anything. I just don't remember the details. I must've grabbed him and pushed him. And his face went through the glass.'

'What did you do when that happened?'

'Well, some of the guys came running in and pulled me out of there. The station commander sent me home. Pounds had to go to the hospital to fix his nose. IAD took a statement from him and I was suspended. And then Irving stepped in and changed it to ISL. Here I am.'

'What happened with the case?'

'The john never talked. He got his lawyer and waited it out. Edgar went with what we had to the DA last Friday and they kicked it. They said they weren't going into court with a no-witness case with a few minor inconsistencies ... Her prints were on the knife. Big surprise. What it came down to is that she didn't count. At least not enough for them to take the chance of losing.'

Neither of them spoke for a few moments. Bosch guessed that she was thinking about the corollaries between this case and his mother's.

'So what we've got,' he finally said, 'is a murderer out there on the street and the guy who allowed him to go free is back behind his desk, the broken glass already replaced, business as usual. That's our system. I got mad about it and look what it got me. Stress leave and maybe the end of my job.'

She cleared her throat before going into her appraisal of the story.

'As you have set down the circumstances of what happened, it is quite easy to see your rage. But not the ultimate action you took. Have you ever heard the phrase, "a mad minute?"'

Bosch shook his head.

'It's a way of describing a violent outburst that has its roots in several pressures on an individual. It builds up and is released in a quick moment – usually violently, often against a target not wholly responsible for the pressure.'

'If you need me to say Pounds was an innocent victim, I'm not going to say it.'

'I don't need that. I just need you to look at this situation and how it could happen.'

'I don't know. Shit just happens.'

'When you physically attack someone, don't you feel that you lower yourself to the same level as the man who was set free?'

'Not by a long shot, Doctor. Let me tell you something, you can look at all parts of my life, you can throw in earthquakes, fires, floods, riots and even Vietnam, but when it came down to just me and Pounds in that glass room, none of that mattered. You can call it a mad minute or whatever you want. Sometimes, the moment is all that matters and in that moment I was doing the right thing. And if these sessions are designed to make me see I did something wrong, forget it. Irving buttonholed me the other day in the lobby and asked me to think about an apology. Fuck that. I did the right thing.'

She nodded, adjusted herself in her seat and looked more uncomfortable than she had through his long diatribe. Finally, she looked at her watch and he looked at his. His time was up.

'So,' he said, 'I guess I've set the cause of psychotherapy back a century, huh?'

'No, not at all. The more you know of a person and the more you know of a story, the more you understand how things happen. It's why I enjoy my job.'

'Same here.'

'Have you spoken to Lieutenant Pounds since the incident?'

'I saw him when I dropped off the keys to my car. He had it taken away. I went into his office and he practically got hysterical. He's a very small man and I think he knows it.'

'They usually do.'

Bosch leaned forward, ready to get up and leave, when he noticed the envelope she had pushed to the side of her desk.

'What about the photos?'

'I knew you'd bring that up one more time.'

She looked at the envelope and frowned.

'I need to think about it. On several levels. Can I keep them while you go to Florida? Or will you need them?'

'You can keep 'em.'

❖ ❖ ❖ ❖ ❖ ❖ ❖

At four-forty in the morning California time the air carrier landed at Tampa International Airport. Bosch leaned bleary-eyed against a window in the coach cabin, watching the sun rising in the Florida sky for the first time. As the plane taxied, he took off his watch and moved the hands ahead three hours. He was tempted to check into the nearest motel for some real sleep but knew he didn't have the time. From the AAA map he had brought with him, it looked like it was at least a two-hour drive down to Venice.

'It's nice to see a blue sky.'

It was the woman next to him in the aisle seat. She was leaning over toward him, looking out the window herself. She was in her mid-forties with prematurely gray hair. It was almost white. They had talked a bit in the early part of the flight and Bosch knew she was heading back to Florida rather than visiting as he was. She had given LA five years but had had enough. She was going home. Bosch didn't ask who or what she was coming home to, but had wondered if her hair was white when she had first landed in LA five years before.

'Yeah,' he replied. 'These night flights take forever.'

'No, I meant the smog. There is none.'

Bosch looked at her and then out the window, studying the sky.

'Not yet.'

But she was right. The sky had a quality of blue he rarely saw in LA It was the color of swimming pools, with billowing white cumulus clouds floating like dreams in the upper atmosphere.

The plane cleared out slowly. Bosch waited until the end, got up and rolled his back to relieve the tension. The joints of his backbone cracked like dominoes going down. He got his overnighter out of the compartment above and headed out.

As soon as he stepped off the plane into the jetway, the humidity surrounded him like a wet towel with an incubating warmth. He made it into the air-conditioned terminal and decided to scratch his plan to rent a convertible.

A half hour later he was on the 275 freeway crossing Tampa Bay in another rented Mustang. He had the windows up and the air conditioning on but he was sweating as his body still had not acclimated to the humidity.

What struck him most about Florida on this first drive was its flatness. For forty-five minutes not a hillrise came in sight until he reached the concrete-and-steel mountain called the Skyway Bridge. Bosch knew that the steeply graded bridge over the mouth of the bay was a replacement for one that had fallen but he drove across it fearlessly and above the speed limit. After all, he came from postquake Los Angeles, where the unofficial speed limit *under* bridges and overpasses was on the far right side of the speedometer.

After the skyway the freeway merged with the 75 and he reached Venice two hours after landing. Cruising along the Tamiami Trail, he found the small pastel-painted motels inviting as he struggled with fatigue, but he drove on and looked for a gift shop and a pay phone.

He found both in the Coral Reef Shopping Plaza. The

Tacky's Gifts and Cards store wasn't due to open until ten and Bosch had five minutes to waste. He went to a pay phone on the outside wall of the sand-colored plaza and looked up the post office in the book. There were two in town so Bosch took out his notebook and checked Jake McKittrick's zip code. He called one of the post offices listed in the book and learned that the other one catered to the zip code Bosch had. He thanked the clerk who had provided the information and hung up.

When the gift shop opened, Bosch went to the cards aisle and found a birthday card that came with a bright red envelope. He took it to the counter without even reading the inside or the outside of the card. He picked a local street map out of a display next to the cash register and put that on the counter as well.

'That's a nice card,' said the old woman who rang up the sale. 'I'm sure she'll just love it.'

She moved as if she were underwater and Bosch wanted to reach over the counter and punch in the numbers himself, just to get it going.

In the Mustang, Bosch put the card in the envelope without signing it, sealed it and wrote McKittrick's name and post office box number on the front. He then started the car and got back on the road.

It took him fifteen minutes working with the map to find the post office on West Venice Avenue. When he got inside, he found it largely deserted. An old man was standing at a table slowly writing an address on an envelope. Two elderly women were in line for counter service. Bosch stood behind them and realized that he was seeing a lot of senior citizens in Florida and he'd only been here a few hours. It was just like he had always heard.

Bosch looked around and saw the video camera on the wall behind the counter. He could tell by its positioning it was there more for recording customers and possible robbers than for surveilling the clerks, though their workstations were probably fully in view as well. He was undeterred. He took a ten-dollar bill out of his pocket, folded it cleanly and held it with the red envelope. He then checked his loose change and came up with the right amount. It seemed like an excruciatingly long time as the one clerk waited on the women.

'Next in line.'

It was Bosch. He walked up to the counter where the clerk waited. He was about sixty and had a perfect white beard. He was overweight and his skin seemed too red to Bosch. As if he was mad or something.

'I need a stamp for this.'

Bosch put down the change and the envelope. The ten-dollar bill was folded on top of it. The postman acted like he didn't see it.

'I was wondering, did they put the mail out yet in the boxes?'

'They're back there doin' it now.'

He handed Bosch a stamp and swiped the change off the counter. He didn't touch the ten or the red envelope.

'Oh, really?'

Bosch picked up the envelope, licked the stamp and put it on. He then put the envelope back down on top of the ten. He was sure the postman had observed this.

'Well, jeez, I really wanted to get this to my Uncle Jake. It's his birthday today. Any way somebody could run it back there? That way he'd get it when he came in today. I'd deliver it in person but I've got to get back to work.'

Bosch slid the envelope with the ten underneath it across the counter, closer to white beard.

'Well,' he said, 'I'll see what I can do.'

The postman shifted his body to the left and turned slightly, shielding the transaction from the video camera. In one fluid motion he took the envelope and the ten off the counter. He quickly transferred the ten to his other hand and it dove for cover in his pocket.

'Be right back,' he called to the people still in line.

Out in the lobby, Bosch found Box 313 and looked through the tiny pane of glass inside. The red envelope was there along with two white letters. One of the white envelopes was upside down and its return address was partially visible.

City of
Departm
P.O. Bo
Los Ang
90021–3

Bosch felt reasonably sure the envelope carried McKittrick's pension check. He had beaten the mail to him. He walked out of the post office, bought two cups of coffee and a box of doughnuts in the convenience store next door and then returned to the Mustang to wait in the day's growing heat. It wasn't even May yet. He couldn't imagine what a summer must be like here.

Bored with watching the post office door after an hour, Bosch turned on the radio and found it tuned to a channel featuring a southern evangelical ranter. It took several seconds before Harry realized that the speaker's subject was the Los Angeles earthquake. He decided not to change the station.

'And ah ask, is it a coincidence that this cata-clysmic calamity was centered in the very heart of the ind'stry that poe-loots this entarh nation with the smut of pone-ography? I think not! I believe the Lahd struck a mighty blow to the infidels engaged in this vile and mul-tie-billyon-dollah trade when he cracked the uth asundah. It is a sign, mah frens, a sign of things that ah to come. A sign that all is not right in –'

Bosch turned it off. A woman had just come out of the post office holding a red envelope among other pieces of mail. Bosch watched her cross the parking lot to a silver Lincoln Town Car. Bosch instinctively jotted the plate number down, though he had no law enforcement contact in this part of the state who would run it for him. The woman was in her mid-sixties, Bosch guessed. He had been waiting for a man, but her age made her fit. He started the Mustang and waited for her to pull out.

She drove north on the main highway toward Sarasota. Traffic moved slowly. After about fifteen minutes and maybe two miles, the Town Car took a left on Vamo Road and then almost immediately took a right on a private road camouflaged by tall trees and green growth. Bosch was only ten seconds behind her. As he came up to the drive, he slowed but didn't turn in. He saw a sign set back in the trees.

WELCOME TO
PELICAN COVE
Condominium Homes, Dockage

The Town Car passed by a guard shack with a red-and-white-striped gate arm coming down behind it.

'Shit!'

Bosch hadn't anticipated anything like a gated community. He assumed that such things were rare outside of Los Angeles. He looked at the sign again, then turned around and headed out to the main road. He remembered seeing another shopping plaza right before he had turned on to Vamo.

There were eight homes in Pelican Cove listed in the For Sale section of the *Sarasota Herald-Tribune*, but only three were for sale by owner. Bosch went to a pay phone in the plaza and called the first one. He got a tape. On the second call the woman who answered said her husband was golfing for the day and she felt uncomfortable showing the property without him. On the third call, the woman who answered invited Bosch to come over right away and even said she'd have fresh lemonade prepared when he got there.

Bosch felt a momentary pang of guilt about taking advantage of a stranger who was just trying to sell her home. But it passed quickly as he considered that the woman would never know she had been used in such a way, and he had no other alternative for getting to McKittrick.

After he was cleared at the gate and got directions to the lemonade lady's unit, Bosch drove through the densely wooded complex, looking for the silver Town Car. It didn't take him long to see that the complex was mostly a retirement community. He passed several elderly people in cars or on walks, almost all of them with white hair and skin browned by the sun. He quickly found the Town Car, checked his location against the map given to him at the guard shack and was about to make a cursory visit to the lemonade lady to avoid suspicion. But then he saw another silver Town Car. It was a popular car with the older set, he guessed. He took out his notebook and checked the plate number he had written down. Neither car had been the one he had followed earlier.

He drove on and finally found the right Town Car in a secluded spot in the far reaches of the complex. It was parked in front of a two-story building of dark wood siding surrounded by oak and paper trees. It looked to Bosch as if there were six units in the building. Easy enough, he thought. He consulted the map and got back on course to the lemonade lady. She was on the second floor of a building on the other side of the complex.

'You're young,' she said when she answered the door. Bosch wanted to say the same thing back to her but held his tongue. She looked like she was in her mid- to late thirties, which put her three decades behind anyone Bosch had seen around the complex so far. She had an attractive and evenly tanned face framed in brown shoulder-length hair. She wore blue jeans, a blue oxford shirt and a black vest with a colorful pattern in the front. She didn't bother with much makeup, which Bosch liked. She had serious green eyes, which he also didn't disagree with.

'I'm Jasmine. Are you Mr Bosch?'

'Yes. Harry. I just called.'

'That was quick.'

'I was nearby.'

She invited him in and started the rundown.

'It's three bedrooms, like the paper said. Master suite has a private bath. Second bath off the main hall. The view is what makes the place, though.'

She pointed Bosch toward a wall of sliding glass doors that looked out on a wide expanse of water dotted with mangrove islands. Hundreds of birds perched in the branches of these otherwise untouched islands. She was right, the view was beautiful.

'What is that?' Bosch asked. 'The water.'

'That's – you're not from around here, are you? That's Little Sarasota Bay.'

Bosch nodded while computing the mistake he had made by blurting out the question.

'No, I'm not from around here. I'm thinking of moving here though.'

'Where from?'

'Los Angeles.'

'Oh, yes, I've heard. A lot of people are bailing out. Because the ground won't stop shaking.'

'Something like that.'

She led him down a hallway to what must have been the master suite. Bosch was immediately struck by how the room didn't seem to fit this woman. It was all dark and old and heavy. A mahogany bureau that looked like it weighed a ton, matching bedside tables with ornate lamps and brocaded shades. The place smelled old. It couldn't be where she slept.

He turned and noticed on the wall next to the door an oil painting that was a portrait of the woman standing next to him. It was a younger likeness of her, the face much gaunter, more severe. Bosch was wondering what kind of person hangs a painting of herself in her bedroom when he noticed that the painting was signed. The artist's name was Jazz.

'Jazz. Is that you?'

'Yes. My father insisted on hanging that in here. I actually should have taken it down.'

She went to the wall and began to lift the painting off.

'Your father?'

He moved to the other side of the painting to help her.

'Yes. I gave this to him a long time ago. At the time I was thankful he didn't hang it out in the living room where his friends would see it but even here is a little too much.'

She turned the painting so the back faced outward and leaned it against the wall. Bosch put together what she had been saying.

'This is your father's place.'

'Oh, yes. I've just been staying here while the ad ran in the paper. You want to check out the master bath? It has a Jacuzzi tub. That wasn't mentioned in the ad.'

Bosch moved closely by her to the bathroom door. He looked down at her hands, a natural instinct, and saw no rings on any of her fingers. He could smell her as he passed and the scent he picked up was the same as her name: Jasmine. He was beginning to feel some kind of attraction to her but wasn't sure if it was the titillation of being there under false pretenses or an honest pull. He was exhausted, he knew, and decided that was it. His defenses were down. He gave the bathroom a quick once-over and stepped out.

'Nice. Did he live here alone?'

'My father? Yes, alone. My mother died when I was little. My father passed away over Christmas.'

'I'm sorry.'

'Thank you. What else can I tell you?'

'Nothing. I was just curious about who had been living here.'

'No. I mean, what else can I tell you about the condo?'

'Oh, I … nothing. It's very nice. I'm still in the looking-around stage, I guess, not sure what I'm going to do. I –'

'What are you really doing?'

'Excuse me?'

'What are you doing here, Mr Bosch? You're not looking to buy a condo in here. You're not even looking at the place.'

There was no anger in her voice. It was a voice full of the confidence she had in reading people. Bosch felt himself turning red. He had been found out.

'I'm just … I'm just here to look at places.'

It was a terribly weak comeback and he knew it. But it was all he could think of to say. She sensed his predicament and let him off the hook.

'Well, I'm sorry if I embarrassed you. Do you want to see the rest of the place?'

'Yes – uh, well, did you say it was three bedrooms? That's really too big for what I'm looking for.'

'Yes, three. But it said that in the newspaper ad, too.'

Luckily, Bosch knew he probably couldn't get any redder than he already was.

'Oh,' he said. 'I must've missed that. Uh, thanks for the tour, though. It's a very nice place.'

He moved quickly through the living room toward the

door. As he opened it he looked back at her. She spoke before he could say anything.

'Something tells me it's a good story.'

'What's that?'

'Whatever it is you're doing. If you ever feel like telling it, the number's in the paper. But you already know that.'

Bosch nodded. He was speechless. He stepped through the door and closed it behind him.

✦ ✦ ✦ ✦ ✦ ✦ ✦

B y the time he drove back to where he had seen the
Town Car, his face had returned to its normal color
but he still felt embarrassed about being cornered by
the woman. He tried to dismiss it and concentrate on the
task at hand. He parked and went to the first-floor door
that was nearest the Town Car and knocked. Eventually,
an old woman opened the door and stared at him with
frightened eyes. One hand clasped the handle of a small
two-wheeled cart that carried an oxygen bottle. Two clear
plastic tubes snaked over her ears and across both cheeks
to her nose.

'I'm sorry to disturb you,' he said quickly. 'I was looking
for the McKittricks.'

She raised a frail hand, formed a fist with the thumb out
and jerked it up toward the ceiling. Her eyes went up that
way, too.

'Upstairs?'

She nodded. He thanked her and headed for the stairs.

The woman who had picked up the red envelope
answered the next door he knocked on and Bosch exhaled
as if he had spent a lifetime looking for her. It almost felt
that way.

'Mrs McKittrick?'

'Yes?'

Bosch pulled out his badge case and flipped it open.

He held the wallet so that his first two fingers crossed most of the badge, obscuring the LIEUTENANT.

'My name's Harry Bosch. I'm a detective with the LAPD. I was wondering if your husband was here. I'd like to talk to him.'

An immediate concern clouded her face.

'LAPD? He hasn't been out there in twenty years.'

'It's about an old case. I was sent out to ask him about it.'

'Well, you could've called.'

'We didn't have a number. Is he here?'

'No, he's down with the boat. He's going fishing.'

'Where's that? Maybe I can catch him.'

'Well, he doesn't like surprises.'

'I guess it will be a surprise whether you tell him or I tell him. Doesn't make any difference to me. I just have to talk to him, Mrs McKittrick.'

Maybe she was used to the no-debate tone that cops can put into their voice. She gave in.

'You walk around the building here and go straight back past the next three buildings. Go left, you'll see the docks after that.'

'Where's his boat?'

'It's slip six. It says *Trophy* in big letters on the side. You can't miss it. He hasn't left yet because I'm supposed to bring his lunch down.'

'Thanks.'

He had started away from the door to the side of the building when she called after him.

'Detective Bosch? Are you going to be a while? Should I make you a sandwich, too?'

'I don't know how long I'll be but that would be nice of you.'

As he headed toward the docks, he realized that the

woman named Jasmine had never offered him the lemonade she had promised.

❖ ❖ ❖ ❖ ❖ ❖ ❖

It took Bosch fifteen minutes to find the little inlet where the docks were. After that, McKittrick was easy enough to spot. There were maybe forty boats in slips but only one of them was occupied. A man with a deep tan set off by his white hair stood in the stern bending over the outboard engine. Bosch studied him as he got closer but saw nothing recognizable about the man. He did not fit with the image Bosch had in his mind's eye of the man who had pulled him from the pool so long ago.

The cover was off the boat engine and the man was doing something with a screwdriver. He wore khaki shorts and a white golf shirt that was too old and stained for golf but was fine for boating. The boat was about twenty feet long, Bosch guessed, and had a small cabin near the bow, where the helm was. There were fishing rods erected in holders along the sides of the boat, two rods per side.

Bosch stopped on the dock at the bow of the boat on purpose. He wanted to be at a distance from McKittrick when he showed the badge. He smiled.

'Never thought I'd see somebody from the Hollywood homicide table so far away from home,' he said.

McKittrick looked up but showed no surprise. He showed nothing.

'Nope, you're wrong. This is home. When I was over there, that's when I was far away.'

Bosch gave a that's-fair-enough nod and showed the

badge. He held it the same way as when he'd showed it to McKittrick's wife.

'I'm Harry Bosch, from Hollywood homicide.'

'Yeah, that's what I heard.'

Bosch was the one who showed surprise. He could not think of who in LA would have tipped McKittrick to his arrival. No one knew. He had only told Hinojos and he could not fathom that she would betray him.

McKittrick relieved him by gesturing to the portable phone on the dashboard of the boat.

'The wife called.'

'Oh.'

'So what's this all about, Detective Bosch? When I used to work there, we did things in pairs. It was safer that way. You folks that understaffed, you're going singleton?'

'Not really. My partner's chasing down another old case. These are such long shots, they're not wasting money sending two.'

'I assume you're going to explain that.'

'Yeah. As a matter of fact, I am. Mind if I come down there?'

'Suit yourself. I'm fixing to shove off as soon as the wife comes with the food.'

Bosch began walking along the finger dock to the side of McKittrick's boat. He then stepped down into the craft. It wobbled on the water with the added weight but then steadied. McKittrick lifted the engine cover and began snapping it back in place. Bosch felt grossly out of place. He wore street shoes with black jeans, an Army green T-shirt and a black light-weight sport jacket. And he was still hot. He took the jacket off and folded it over one of the two chairs in the cockpit.

'What are you going for?'

'Whatever's biting. What are you going for?'

He looked directly at Bosch when he asked this and Harry saw that his eyes were brown like beer-bottle glass.

'Well, you heard about the earthquake, didn't you?'

'Sure, who didn't? You know, I've been through quakes and 'canes and you can keep the quakes. At least with a hurricane, you see it coming. You take Andrew, he left a lot of devastation, but think how much it woulda been if nobody knew he was about to hit. That's what you get with your earthquakes.'

It took Bosch a few moments to place Andrew, the hurricane that had slammed the South Florida coast a couple of years earlier. It was hard to keep track of all the disasters in the world. There were enough just in LA. He looked out across the inlet. He saw a fish jump and its reentry create a stampede of jumping among the others in the school. He looked at McKittrick and was about to tell him when he realized it was probably something McKittrick saw every day of his life.

'When'd you leave LA?'

'Twenty-one years ago. I got my twenty in and *pffft*, I was gone. You can have LA, Bosch. Shit, I was out there for the Sylmar quake in seventy-one. Knocked down a hospital and a couple freeways. At the time we were living in Tujunga, a few miles from the epicenter. I'll always remember that one. It was like God and the devil meetin' in the room and you were there with 'em playin' referee. Goddamn ... So what's the quake got to do with you being here?'

'Well, it's kind of a strange phenomenon but the murder rate's fallen off. People are being more civil, I guess. We –'

'Maybe there's nothing left there worth killing for.'

'Maybe. Anyway, we're usually running seventy, eighty murders a year in the division, I don't know what it was like when you –'

'We'd do less than half that. Easy.'

'Well, we're running way below the average this year. It's given us time to go back through some of the old ones. Everybody on the table's taken a share. One of the ones I've got has your name on it. I guess you know your partner from back then passed away and –'

'Eno's dead? Goddamn, I didn't know that. I thought I would've heard about that. Not that it would've mattered a whole hell of a lot.'

'Yeah, he's dead. His wife gets the pension checks. Sorry, you hadn't heard.'

'That's okay. Eno and me … well, we were partners. That's about it.'

'Anyway, I'm here because you're alive and he isn't.'

'What's the case?'

'Marjorie Lowe.' He waited a moment for a reaction from McKittrick's face and got none. 'You remember it? She was found in the trash in an alley off –'

'Vista. Behind Hollywood Boulevard between Vista and Gower. I remember them all, Bosch. Cleared or not, I remember every goddamn one of them.'

But you don't remember me, Bosch thought but didn't say.

'Yeah, that's the one. Between Vista and Gower.'

'What about it?'

'It was never cleared.'

'I know that,' McKittrick said, his voice rising. 'I worked sixty-three cases during seven years on the homicide table. I worked Hollywood, Wilshire, then RHD. Cleared fifty-six. I'll put that up against anybody. Today they're lucky if they clear half of 'em. I'll put it up against you blind.'

'And you'd win. That's a good record. This isn't about you, Jake. It's about the case.'

'Don't call me Jake. I don't know you. Never seen you before in my life. I – wait a minute.'

Bosch stared at him, astonished that he might actually remember the pool. But then he realized that McKittrick had stopped because of his wife's approach along the dock. She was carrying a plastic cooler. McKittrick waited silently for her to put it down on the dock near the boat and he hoisted it aboard.

'Oh, Detective Bosch, you'll be way too hot in that,' Mrs McKittrick said. 'Do you want to come back up and borrow a pair of Jake's shorts and a white T-shirt?'

Bosch looked at McKittrick, then up at her.

'No, thanks, ma'am, I'm fine.'

'You are going fishing, aren't you?'

'Well, I haven't exactly been invited and I –'

'Oh, Jake, invite him fishing. You're always looking for somebody to go out with you. Besides, you can catch up on all that blood-and-guts stuff you used to love in Hollywood.'

McKittrick looked up at her and Bosch could see the horses fighting against the restraints. He was able to get it under control.

'Mary, thanks for the sandwiches,' he said calmly. 'Now, could you go back up to the house and leave us be?'

She threw him a frown and shook her head as if he were a spoiled boy. She went back the way she had come without another word. The two of them left on the boat let some time go by before Bosch finally spoke and tried to recover the situation.

'Look, I'm not here for any reason other than to ask you a few questions about this case. I'm not trying to suggest there was anything wrong with the way it was handled. I'm just taking another look at it. That's all.'

'You left something out.'

'What's that?'

'That you're full of shit.'

Bosch could feel the horses rearing up in himself. He was angry at this man's questioning his motives, even though he was right to do so. He was on the verge of shedding the nice-guy skin and going at him. But he knew better. He knew that for McKittrick to act this way, there must be a reason. Something about the old case was like a pebble in his shoe. He had worked it over to the side where it didn't hurt when he walked. But it was still in there. Bosch had to make him want to take it out. He swallowed his own anger and tried to stay level.

'Why am I full of shit?' he said.

McKittrick's back was to him. The former cop was reaching down under the steering console. Bosch couldn't see what he was trying to do, except he guessed he was maybe looking for a hidden set of boat keys.

'Why are you full of shit?' McKittrick answered as he turned around. 'I'll tell you why. Because you come here flashing that bullshit badge around when we both know you don't have a badge.'

McKittrick was pointing a Beretta twenty-two at Bosch. It was small but it would do the job at this distance, and Bosch had to believe that McKittrick knew how to use it.

'Jesus, man, what's the problem with you?'

'I had no problem until you showed up.'

Bosch held his hands chest-high in a nonthreatening pose.

'Just take it easy.'

'You take it easy. Put your fucking hands down. I want to see that badge again. Take it out and toss it over here. Slowly.'

Bosch complied, all the while trying to look around the docks without turning his head more than a few inches. He didn't see anyone. He was alone. And unarmed. He threw the badge wallet down on the deck near McKittrick's feet.

'Now I want you to walk around the bridge to the bow up there. Stand against the bow rail where I can see you. I knew somebody would try to fuck with me someday. Well, you picked the wrong guy and the wrong day.'

Bosch did as instructed and went up to the bow. He grabbed the railing for support and turned around to face his captor. Without taking his eyes off Bosch, McKittrick bent and picked up the wallet. Then he moved into the cockpit and put the gun down on top of the console. Bosch knew if he tried for it McKittrick would get there first. McKittrick reached down and turned something and the engine kicked over.

'What are you doing, McKittrick?'

'Oh, now it's McKittrick. What happened to the friendly "Jake"? Well, what's doing is, we're going fishing. You wanted to fish, that's what we'll do. You try to jump and I'll shoot you in the water. I don't care.'

'I'm not going anywhere. Just take it easy.'

'Now, reach down to that cleat and unhook that line. Throw it up on the dock.'

When Bosch had finished completing the order, McKittrick picked up the gun and stepped back three paces into the stern. He untied the other line and pushed off from a pylon. He returned to the helm and gently put the boat in reverse. It glided out of the slip. McKittrick then put it in forward and they started moving through the inlet toward the mouth of the canal. Bosch could feel the warm salt breezes drying the sweat on his skin. He decided he would jump as soon as they got to some open water, or where there were other boats with people on them.

'Kind of surprised you're not carrying. What kind of guy says he's a cop, then doesn't carry a piece?'

'I am a cop, McKittrick. Let me explain.'

'You don't have to, boy, I already know. Know all about you.'

McKittrick flipped open the badge wallet and Bosch watched him study the ID card and the gold lieutenant's badge. He threw it on the console.

'What do you know about me, McKittrick?'

'Don't worry, I still have a few teeth left, Bosch, and I still have a few friends in the department. After the wife called, I made a call. One of my friends. He knew all about you. You're on leave, Bosch. Involuntary. So I don't know about this bullshit story about earthquakes you were spinning. Makes me think maybe you picked up a little freelance work while you're off the job.'

'You got it wrong.'

'Yeah, well, we'll see. Once we get out into some open water, you're gonna tell me who sent you or you're gonna be fish food. Makes no difference to me.'

'Nobody sent me. I sent myself.'

McKittrick slapped his palm against the red ball on the throttle lever and the boat surged forward. Its bow rose and Bosch grabbed the railing to hold on.

'Bullshit!' McKittrick yelled above the engine noise. 'You're a liar. You lied before, you're lying now.'

'Listen to me,' Bosch yelled. 'You said you remember every case.'

'I do, goddamnit! I can't forget them.'

'Cut it back!'

McKittrick pulled the throttle back and the boat evened off and the noise reduced.

'On the Marjorie Lowe case you pulled the dirty work. You remember that? Remember what we call the dirty work? You had to tell the next of kin. You had to tell her kid. Out at McClaren.'

'That was in the reports, Bosch. So –'

He stopped and stared at Bosch for a long moment.

Then he flipped open the badge case and read the name. He looked back at Bosch.

'I remember that name. The swimming pool. You're the kid.'

'I'm the kid.'

❖ ❖ ❖ ❖ ❖ ❖ ❖

McKittrick let the boat drift in the shallows of Little Sarasota Bay while Bosch told the story. He asked no questions. He simply listened. At a moment where Bosch paused, he opened the cooler his wife had packed and took out two beers, handing one to Bosch. The can felt ice-cold in Bosch's hand.

Bosch didn't pull the tab on his beer until he finished the story. He had told everything he knew to McKittrick, even the nonessential part about his run-in with Pounds. He had a hunch, based on McKittrick's anger and bizarre behavior, that he had been wrong about the old cop. He had flown out to Florida believing he was coming to see either a corrupt or a stupid cop and he wasn't sure which he would dislike more. But now he believed that McKittrick was a man who was haunted by memories and the demons of choices made badly many years ago. Bosch thought that the pebble still had to come out of the shoe and that his own honesty was the best way to get to it.

'So that's my story,' he said at the end. 'I hope she packed more than two of these.'

He popped the beer and drank nearly a third of it. It tasted delicious going down his throat in the afternoon sun.

'Oh, there's plenty more where that came from,' McKittrick replied. 'You want a sandwich?'

'Not yet.'

'No, what you want is my story now.'

'That's what I came for.'

'Well, let's get out there to the fish.'

He restarted the engine and they followed a trail of channel markers south through the bay. Bosch finally remembered he had sunglasses in the pocket of his sport coat and put them on.

It seemed like the wind was cutting in on him from all directions and on occasion its warmth would be traded for a cool breeze that would come up off the surface of the water. It was a long time since Bosch had been on a boat or had even been fishing. For a man who had had a gun pointed at him twenty minutes earlier, he realized he felt pretty good.

As the bay tapered off into a canal, McKittrick pulled back on the throttle and cut their wake. He waved to a man on the bridge of a giant yacht tied up outside a waterside restaurant. Bosch couldn't tell if he knew the man or was just being neighborly.

'Take it on a line even with the lantern on the bridge,' McKittrick said.

'What?'

'Take it.'

McKittrick stepped away from the wheel and into the stern of the boat. Bosch quickly stepped behind the wheel, sighted the red lantern hanging at center point beneath the span of a drawbridge a half mile ahead and adjusted the wheel to bring the boat into line. He looked back and saw McKittrick pull a plastic bag of small dead fish out of a compartment in the deck.

'Let's see who we've got here today,' he said.

He went to the side of the boat and leaned well over the gunwale. Bosch saw him start slapping an open palm on the side of the boat. McKittrick then stood up, surveyed the water for about ten seconds and repeated the banging.

'What's going on?' Bosch asked.

Just as he said it, a dolphin crested the water off the port stern and reentered no more than five feet from where McKittrick was standing. It was a slippery gray blur and Bosch wasn't exactly sure at first what had happened. But the dolphin quickly resurfaced next to the boat, its snout out of the water and chattering. It sounded like it was laughing. McKittrick dropped two of the fish into its open mouth.

'That's Sergeant, see the scars?'

Bosch took a quick look back at the bridge to make sure they were still reasonably on line and then stepped back to the stern. The dolphin was still there. McKittrick pointed down into the water beneath its dorsal fin. Bosch could see three white stripes slashed across its smooth gray back.

'He got too close to a prop one time and it cut him up. The people up at Mote Marine took care of him. But he was left with those sergeant's stripes.'

Bosch nodded as McKittrick fed the dolphin again. Without looking up to see if they were off course, McKittrick said, 'You better get the wheel.'

Bosch turned and saw that they had drifted far off line. He went back to the wheel and corrected the course. He stayed there while McKittrick remained in the back, throwing fish to the dolphin, until they passed under the bridge. Bosch decided he could wait him out. Whether it was while they were going out or coming in didn't matter. He was going to get McKittrick's story. He was not going to leave without it.

Ten minutes after the bridge they came to a channel that took them out to the Gulf of Mexico. McKittrick dropped lures from two of the poles into the water and put out about a hundred yards of line on each one. He took the wheel back from Bosch then, yelling into the wind and engine noise.

'I want to take it out to the reefs. We'll troll until we're there and then we'll do some drift fishing in the shallows. We'll talk then.'

'Sounds like a plan,' Bosch yelled back.

Nothing hit either of the lures, and about two miles from the shore McKittrick killed the engines and told Bosch to bring in one line while he handled the other. It took Bosch, who was left handed, a few moments to get himself coordinated on the right-handed reel but then he started smiling.

'I don't think I've done this since I was a kid. At McClaren every now and then they'd put us on a bus and take us out to the Malibu Pier.'

'Jesus, that pier still there?'

'Yeah.'

'Must be like fishing in a cesspool by now.'

'I guess.'

McKittrick laughed and shook his head.

'Why do you stay there, Bosch? Doesn't sound like they particularly want you.'

Bosch thought a moment before answering. The comment was on point but he wondered if it was on point from McKittrick or whoever the source was he had called.

'Who'd you call back there about me?'

'I'm not telling you. That's why he talked to me, because he knew I wouldn't tell you.'

Bosch nodded, signaling he'd let it go.

'Well, you're right,' he said. 'I don't think they particularly want me back there. But I don't know. It's kind've like the more they push one way, the more I push the other. I feel like if they'd stop asking or trying to make me leave, then I'd probably want to do it.'

'I guess I know what you mean.'

McKittrick stowed the two rods they had used and set

to work outfitting the other two with hooks and buckshot weights.

'We're going to use mullet.'

Bosch nodded. He didn't know the first thing about it. But he watched McKittrick closely. He thought it might be a good time to start.

'So you punched out after your twenty in LA. What'd you do after that?'

'You're looking at it. I moved back here – I'm from Palmetto, up the coast, originally. I bought a boat and became a fishing guide. Did that another twenty, retired and now I fish for my own damned self.'

Bosch smiled.

'Palmetto? Isn't that the name of those big cockroaches?'

'No. Well, yeah, but it's also the name of a scrub palm. That's what the town's named for, not the bug.'

Bosch nodded and watched as McKittrick opened a bag of mullet strips and hooked pieces on each line. After opening fresh beers, they cast on separate sides of the boat and then sat on the gunwales, waiting.

'Then how'd you end up in LA?' Bosch asked.

'What was that somebody said about going west young man? Well, after Japan surrendered I passed through LA on my way back home and I saw those mountains going all the way up from the sea to the sky ... Damn, I ate dinner at the Derby my first night in town. I was going to blow my whole wallet and you know who saw me there in uniform and picked up the tab? Goddamn Clark Gable. I'm not kidding you. I fuckin' fell in love with that place and it took me almost thirty years to see the light ... Mary's from LA, you know. Born and raised. She likes it out here fine.'

He nodded to reassure himself. Bosch waited a few moments and McKittrick was still looking off at distant memories.

'He was a nice guy.'

'Who's that?'

'Clark Gable.'

Bosch crunched the empty beer can in his hand and got another.

'So tell me about the case,' he said after popping it. 'What happened?'

'You know what happened if you read the book. It was all in there. It got dumped. One day we had an investigation, the next we were writing 'No leads at this time.' It was a joke. That's why I remember the case so well. They shouldn't've done what they did.'

'Who's they?'

'You know, the big shots.'

'What did they do?'

'They took it away from us. And Eno let them. He cut some deal with them himself. Shit.'

He shook his head bitterly.

'Jake,' Bosch tried. He got no protest this time over using the first name. 'Why don't you start at the beginning. I need to know everything I can from you.'

McKittrick was quiet while he reeled in. His bait hadn't been touched. He recast it, put the rod in one of the gunwale pipes and got another beer. From beneath the console he grabbed a Tampa Bay Lightning cap and put it on. He leaned on the gunwale with his beer and looked at Bosch.

'Okay, kid, listen, I got nothin' against your mother. I'm just gonna tell you this the way it fell, okay?'

'That's all I want.'

'You want a hat? You're gonna get burned.'

'I'm fine.'

McKittrick nodded and finally started.

'Okay, so we got the call out from home. It was a Saturday morning. One of the footbeat guys had found her. She hadn't been killed in that alley. That much was clear. She'd been dropped off. By the time I got down there from Tujunga, the crime scene investigation was already underway. My partner was there, too. Eno. He was the senior man, he was there first. He took charge of it.'

Bosch put his rod in a pipe and went to his jacket.

'You mind if I take notes?'

'No, I don't mind. I guess I've been waiting for somebody to care about this one since I walked away from it.'

'Go ahead. Eno was in charge.'

'Yeah, he was the man. You've got to understand something. We'd been a team maybe three, four months at that time. We weren't tight. After this one, we'd never be tight. I switched off after about a year. I went in for the transfer. They moved me to Wilshire dicks, homicide table. Never had much to do with him after that. He never had much to do with me.'

'Okay, what happened with the investigation?'

'Well, it was like anything else that you'd expect. We were going through the routine. We had a list of her KAs – got it mostly from the vice guys – and were working our way through it.'

'The known associates, did they include clients? There was no list in the murder book.'

'I think there were a few clients. And the list didn't go into the book because Eno said so. Remember, he was the lead.'

'Okay. Johnny Fox was on the list?'

'Yeah, he was at the top of it. He was her … uh, manager and –'

'Her pimp, you mean.'

McKittrick looked at him.

'Yeah. That's what he was. I wasn't sure what you, uh –'

'Forget it. Go on.'

'Yeah, Johnny Fox was on the list. We talked to about everybody who knew her and this guy was described by everybody as one mean guy. He had a history.'

Bosch thought of Meredith Roman's report that he had beaten her.

'We'd heard that she was trying to get away from him. I don't know, either to go out on her own or maybe go straight. Who knows? We heard –'

'She wanted to be a straight citizen,' Bosch interrupted. 'That way she could get me out of the hall.'

He felt foolish for saying it, knowing his saying it was not convincing.

'Yeah, whatever,' McKittrick said. 'Point is, Fox was none too happy about that. That put him at the top of our list.'

'But you couldn't find him. The chrono says you watched his place.'

'Yeah. He was our man. We had prints we had taken off the belt – the murder weapon – but we had no comparisons from him. Johnny had been pulled in a few times in the past but never booked. Never printed. So we really needed to bring him in.'

'What did it tell you, that he'd been picked up but never booked?'

McKittrick finished his beer, crunched it in his hand and walked the empty over to a large bucket in the corner of the deck and dropped it.

'To be honest, at the time it didn't hit me. Now, of course, it's obvious. He had an angel watching over him.'

'Who?'

'Well, on one of the days we were watching Fox's place, waiting for him to show up, we got a message on the radio to call Arno Conklin. He wanted to talk about the case. ASAP. Now this was a holy shit kind of call. For two reasons. One, Arno was going great guns then. He was running the city's moral commandos at the time and had a lock on the DA's office, which was coming open in a year. The other reason was that we'd only had the case a few days and hadn't come near the DA's office with anything. So now all of a sudden the most powerful guy in the agency wants to see us. I'm thinking … I don't really know what I was thinking. I just knew it – hey, you got one!'

Bosch looked at his pole and saw it bend from a violent jerk on the line. The reel started spinning as the fish pulled against the drag. Bosch grabbed the pole out of the pipe and jerked it back. The hook was set well. He started reeling but the fish had a lot of fight and was pulling out more line than he was reeling in. McKittrick came over and tightened the drag dial, which immediately put a more pronounced bend in the pole.

'Keep the pole up, keep the pole up,' McKittrick counseled.

Bosch did as he was told and spent five minutes battling the fish. His arms started to ache. He felt a strain on his lower back. McKittrick put on gloves and when the fish finally surrendered and Bosch had it alongside the boat, he bent over and hooked his fingers into the gills and brought it on board. Bosch saw a shiny blue-black fish that looked beautiful in the sunlight.

'Wahoo,' McKittrick said.

'What?'

McKittrick held the fish up horizontally.

'Wahoo. Over there in your fancy LA restaurants I think they call it Ono. Here, we just call it wahoo. Meat cooks up white as halibut, you wanna keep it?'

'No, put it back. It's beautiful.'

McKittrick roughly pulled the hook from the gulping mouth of the fish and then held the catch out to Bosch.

'You want to hold it? Must be twelve, thirteen pounds.'

'Nah, I don't need to hold it.'

Bosch stepped closer and ran his finger along the slick skin of the fish. He could almost see himself in the reflection of its scales. He nodded to McKittrick and the fish was thrown back into the water. For several seconds it remained motionless, about two feet below the surface. Post-traumatic stress syndrome, Bosch thought. Finally, the fish seemed to come out of it and darted down into the depths. Bosch put the hook through one of the eyelets on his pole and put the pole back in its pipe. He was done fishing. He got another beer out of the cooler.

'Hey, you want a sandwich, go ahead,' McKittrick said.

'No. I'm fine.'

Bosch wished the fish hadn't interrupted them.

'You were saying that you guys got the call from Conklin.'

'Yeah, Arno. Only I had it wrong. The request for a meeting was only for Claude. Not me. Eno went alone.'

'Why only Eno?'

'I never knew and he acted like he didn't know, either. I just assumed it was because he and Arno had a prior relationship of some kind.'

'But you don't know what.'

'No. Claude Eno was about ten years older than me. He'd been around.'

'So what happened?'

'Well, I can't tell you what happened. I can only tell you what my partner said happened. Understand?'

He was telling Bosch that he didn't trust his own partner. Bosch had known that feeling himself at times and nodded that he understood.

'Go ahead.'

'He came back from the meeting saying Conklin asked him to lay off Fox because Fox was clear on this case and Fox was working as an informant on one of the commando investigations. He said Fox was important to him and he didn't want him compromised or roughed up, especially over a crime he didn't commit.'

'How was Conklin so sure?'

'I don't know. But Eno told me that he told Conklin that assistant DAs, no matter who they are, didn't decide whether someone was clear or not for the police, and that we weren't backing off until we talked to Fox for ourselves. Faced with that, Conklin said he could deliver Fox to be interviewed and fingerprinted. But only if we did it on Conklin's turf.'

'Which was ... ?'

'His office in the old courthouse. That's gone now. They built that big square thing right before I left. Horrible-looking thing.'

'What happened in the office? Were you there for that?'

'Yeah, I was there but nothing happened. We interviewed him. Fox was there with Conklin, so was the Nazi.'

'The Nazi?'

'Conklin's enforcer, Gordon Mittel.'

'He was there?'

'Yup. I guess he was sort of watching out for Conklin while Conklin was watching out for Fox.'

Bosch showed no surprise.

'Okay, so what did Fox tell you?'

'Like I said, not much. At least, that's how I remember it. He gave us an alibi and the names of the people who could verify it. I took his prints.'

'What'd he say about the victim?'

'He said pretty much what we'd already heard from her girlfriend.'

'Meredith Roman?'

'Yeah, I think that's it. He said she went to a party, was hired as kind of a decoration to be on some guy's arm. He said it was in Hancock Park. He didn't have the address. He said he had nothing to do with setting it up. That didn't make sense to us. You know, a pimp not knowing where … not knowing where one of his girls was. It was the one thing we had and when we started leaning on him about it, Conklin stepped in like a referee.'

'He didn't want you leaning on him.'

'Craziest thing I ever saw. Here was the next DA – everybody knew he was going to run. Here he was taking this bastard's side against us … Sorry about that bastard comment.'

'Forget it.'

'Conklin was trying to make it seem like we were out of line, while all the time this big-piece-of-shit Fox was sitting there smiling with a toothpick in the side of his mouth. It's what, thirty-somethin' years ago and I can still remember that toothpick. Galled the Jesus out of me. So to make a long story short, we never did get to brace him on having set up the date she went on.'

The boat rocked on a high wake and Bosch looked around and didn't see any other boat. It was weird. He looked out across the water and for the first time realized how different it was from the Pacific. The Pacific was a cold and forbidding blue, the Gulf a warm green that invited you.

'We left,' McKittrick continued. 'I figured we'd have another shot at him. So we left and started to work on his alibi. It turned out to be good. And I don't mean it was good because his own witnesses said it was. We did the work. We found some independent people. People that didn't know him. As I remember it, it was rock solid.'

'You remember where he was?'

'Spent part of the night in a bar over there on Ivar, place a lot of the pimps hung around. Can't remember the name of it. Then later he drove out to Ventura, spent most of the rest of the night in a card room until he got a phone call, then he split. The other thing about this was that it didn't smack of an alibi set up for this particular night. This was his routine. He was well known in all of these places.'

'What was the phone call?'

'We never knew. We didn't know about it until we started checking his alibi and somebody mentioned it. We never got to ask Fox about it. But to be honest, we didn't care too much at that point. Like I said, his alibi was solid and he didn't get the call until later in the morning. Four, five o'clock. The vic – your mother had been dead a good long while by then. TOD was midnight. The call didn't matter.'

Bosch nodded but it was the kind of detail he would not have left open if it had been his investigation. It was too curious a detail. Who calls a poker room that early in the morning? What kind of call would make Fox up and leave the game?

'What about the prints?'

'I had 'em checked anyway and they didn't match those on the belt. He was clean. The dirtbag was clear.'

Bosch thought of something.

'You did check the prints on the belt against the victim's, right?'

'Hey, Bosch, I know you highfalutin' guys think you're the cat's ass now but we were known for having a brain or two back in those days.'

'Sorry.'

'There were a few prints on the buckle that were the victim's. That's it. The rest were definitely the killer's because of their location. We got good direct lifts and partials on two other spots where it was clear the belt had

226

been grasped by the full hand. You don't hold a belt that way when you're putting it on. You hold it that way when you're putting it around someone's neck.'

They were both silent after that. Bosch couldn't figure out what McKittrick was telling him. He felt deflated. He had thought that if he got McKittrick to open up, the old cop would point the finger at Fox or Conklin or somebody. But he was doing none of that. He really wasn't giving Bosch anything.

'How come you remember so many details, Jake? It's been a long time.'

'I've had a long time to think about it. When you finish up, Bosch, you'll see, there'll always be one. One case that stays with you. This is the one that stayed with me.'

'So what was your final take on it?'

'My final take? Well, I never got over that meeting at Conklin's office. I guess you had to be there but it just ... it just seemed that the one that was in charge of that meeting was Fox. It was like he was calling the shots.'

Bosch nodded. He could see that McKittrick was struggling for an explanation of his feelings.

'You ever interview a suspect with his lawyer there jumpin' in and out of the conversation?' McKittrick asked. 'You know, "Don't answer this, don't answer that." Shit like that.'

'All the time.'

'Well, it was like that. It was like Conklin, the next DA for Chrissake, was this shitheel's lawyer, objecting all the time to our questions. What it came down to was that if you didn't know who he was or where we were, you'd've sworn he was working for Fox. Both of them, Mittel, too. So, I felt pretty sure Fox had his hooks into Arno. Somehow he did. And I was right. It was all confirmed later.'

'You mean when Fox died?'

'Yeah. He got killed in a hit and run while working for the Conklin campaign. I remember the newspaper story on it didn't say nothin' about his background as a pimp, as a Hollywood Boulevard hoodlum. No, he was just this guy who got run down. Joe Innocent. I tell ya, that story must've cost Arno a few dollars and made a reporter a little richer.'

Bosch could tell there was more so he said nothing.

'I was in Wilshire dicks by then,' McKittrick continued. 'But I got curious when I heard about it. So I called over to Hollywood to see who was on it. It was Eno. Big surprise. And he never made a case on anybody. So that about confirmed what I was thinking about him, too.'

McKittrick stared off across the water to where the sun was getting low in the sky. He threw his empty beer can at the bucket. It missed and bounced over the side into the water.

'Fuck it,' he said. 'I guess we should head in.'

He started reeling in his line.

'What do you think Eno got out of all of this?'

'I don't know exactly. He might've just been trading favors, something like that. I'm not saying he got rich, but I think he got something out of the deal. He wouldn't do it for nothing. I just don't know what it was.'

McKittrick started taking the rods out of the pipes and stowing them on hooks along the sides of the stern.

'In 1972 you checked the murder book out of archives, how come?'

McKittrick looked at him curiously.

'I signed the same checkout slip a few days ago,' Bosch explained. 'Your name was still on it.'

McKittrick nodded.

'Yeah, that was right after I put in my papers. I was leaving, going through my files and stuff. I'd hung on to the prints we took off the belt. Kept the card. Also hung on to the belt.'

'Why?'

'You know why. I didn't think it would be safe in that file or in the evidence room. Not with Conklin as DA, not with Eno doing him favors. So I kept the stuff. Then a bunch of years went by and it was there when I was cleaning shit out and going to Florida. So right before I decided to punch out, I put the print card back in the murder book and went down and put the belt back in the evidence box. Eno was already in Vegas, retired. Conklin had crashed and burned, was out of politics. The case was long forgotten. I put the stuff back. I guess maybe I hoped someday somebody like you would take a look at it.'

'What about you? Did you look at the book when you put the card back?'

'Yeah, and I saw I had done the right thing. Somebody had gone through it, stripped it. They pulled the Fox interview out of it. Probably was Eno.'

'As the second man on the case you had to do the paper, right?'

'Right. The paperwork was mine. Most of it.'

'What did you put on the Fox interview summary that would have made Eno need to pull it?'

'I don't remember anything specific, just that I thought the guy was lying and that Conklin was out of line. Something like that.'

'Anything else you remember that was missing?'

'Nah, nothing important, just that. I think he just wanted to get Conklin's name out of it.'

'Yeah, well, he missed something. You'd noted his first call on the Chronological Record. That's how I knew.'

'Did I? Well, good for me. And here you are.'

'Yeah.'

'All right, we're heading in. Too bad they weren't really biting today.'

'I'm not complaining. I got my fish.'

McKittrick stepped behind the wheel and was about to start the engine when he thought of something.

'Oh, you know what?' He moved to the cooler and opened it. 'I don't want Mary to be disappointed.'

He pulled out the plastic bags that contained the sandwiches his wife had made.

'You hungry?'

'Not really.'

'Me neither.'

He opened the bags and dumped the sandwiches over the side. Bosch watched him.

'Jake, when you pulled out that gun, who'd you think I was?'

McKittrick didn't say anything as he neatly folded the plastic bags and put them back in the cooler. When he straightened up, he looked at Bosch.

'I didn't know. All I knew was that I thought I might have to take you out here and dump you like those sandwiches. Seems like I've been hiding out here all my life, waiting for them to send somebody.'

'You think they'd go that far over time and distance?'

'I don't have any idea. The more time that goes by, the more I doubt it. But old habits die hard. I always keep a gun nearby. Doesn't matter that most times I don't even remember why.'

They rode in from the Gulf with the engine roaring and the soft spray of the sea in their faces. They didn't talk. That was done with. Occasionally, Bosch glanced over at McKittrick. His old face fell under the shadow of his cap brim. But Bosch could see his eyes in there, looking at something that had happened a long time before and no longer could be changed.

❖ ❖ ❖ ❖ ❖ ❖ ❖

After the boat trip Bosch felt the onset of a headache from the combination of too much beer and too much sun. He begged off an invitation to dinner from McKittrick, saying he was tired. Once in his car, he took a couple of Tylenol caplets out of his overnighter, downed them without any liquid chaser and hoped they would do the job. He took out his notebook and reviewed some of the things he had written about McKittrick's story.

He had come to like the old cop by the end of the fishing trip. Maybe he saw some of himself in the older man. McKittrick was haunted because he had let the case go. He had not done the right thing. And Bosch knew he was guilty of the same during all the years he had ignored the case that he knew was there waiting for him. He was making up for that now, and so was McKittrick by talking to him. But both of them knew it might be too little too late.

Bosch wasn't sure what he would do next when he got back to Los Angeles. It seemed to him that his only move was to confront Conklin. He was reluctant to do this because he knew he would go into such a confrontation soft, with only his suspicions and no hard evidence. Conklin would have the upper hand.

A wave of desperation came over him. He did not want the case to come to this. Conklin hadn't flinched in almost thirty-five years. He wouldn't with Bosch in his face now. Harry knew he needed something else. But he had nothing.

He started the car but left it in Park. He turned the air conditioner on high and added what McKittrick had told him into the stew of what he already knew. He began formulating a theory. For Bosch, this was one of the most important components of homicide investigation. Take the facts and shake them down into hypothesis. The key was not to become beholden to any one theory. Theories changed and you had to change with them.

It seemed clear from McKittrick's information that Fox had a hold on Conklin. What was it? Well, Bosch thought, Fox dealt in women. The theory that emerged was that Fox had gotten a hook into Conklin through a woman, or women. The news clips at the time reported Conklin was a bachelor. The morals of the time would have dictated then as now that as a public servant and soon-to-be candidate for top prosecutor, Conklin needed not necessarily to be celibate but, at least, not to have succumbed privately to the very vices he was publicly attacking. If he had done that and was exposed, he could kiss his political career good-bye, let alone his position as commander of the DA commandos. So, Bosch concluded, if this was Conklin's flaw and it was through Fox that such dalliances were arranged, then Fox would hold an almost unbeatable hand when it came to having juice with Conklin. It would explain the unusual circumstances of the interview McKittrick and Eno conducted with Fox.

The same theory, Bosch knew, would work to an even greater degree if Conklin had done more than succumb to the vice of sex but had gone further: if he had killed a woman Fox had sent to him, Marjorie Lowe. For one thing, it would explain how Conklin knew for sure that Fox was in the clear on the murder – because he was the killer himself. For another, it would explain how Fox got Conklin to run interference for him and why he was later hired as a Conklin campaign worker. The bottom line was, if Conklin was the killer, Fox's hook would be set even deeper and it would be set for good. Conklin would be like that wahoo at the end of the line, a pretty fish unable to get away.

Unless, Bosch knew, the man at the other end of the line and holding the rod were to go away somehow. He thought about Fox's death and saw how it fit. Conklin let some time separate one death from the other. He played like a hooked fish, even agreeing to Fox's demand for a straight job with the campaign, and then, when all seemed clear, Fox was run down in the street. Maybe a payoff to a reporter kept the victim's background quiet – if the reporter even knew it, and a few months later Conklin was crowned district attorney.

Bosch considered where Mittel would fit into the theory. He felt it was unlikely that all of this had transpired in a vacuum. It was Bosch's guess that Mittel, as Conklin's right-hand man and enforcer, would know what Conklin knew.

Bosch liked his theory but it angered him, largely because that was all it was, theory. He shook his head as he realized he was back to ground zero. All talk, no evidence of anything.

He grew weary thinking about it and decided to put the thoughts aside for a while. He turned the air down because it was too cool against his sunburned skin and put the car in gear. As he slowly cruised through Pelican Cove toward the gatehouse, his thoughts drifted to the woman who was trying to sell her dead father's condo. She had signed the name Jazz on the self-portrait. He liked that.

He turned the car around and drove toward her unit. It was still daylight and no lights shone from behind the building's windows when he got there. He couldn't tell if she was there or not. Bosch parked nearby and watched for a few minutes, debating what he should do, if anything at all.

Fifteen minutes later, when it seemed that indecisiveness had paralyzed him, she stepped out the front door. He was parked nearly twenty yards away, between two other cars. His paralytic affliction eased enough for him to slide down in his seat to avoid detection. She walked out into the parking lot and behind the row of cars which included Bosch's rental. He didn't move or turn to follow her movement. He listened. He waited for the sound of a car starting. Then what, he wondered. Follow her? What are you doing?

He jerked upright at the sound of sharp rapping on the window next to him. It was her. Bosch was flustered but managed to turn the key so he could lower the window.

'Yes?'

'Mr Bosch, what are you doing?'

'What do you mean?'

'You've been sitting out here. I saw you.'

'I …'

He was too humiliated to finish.

'I don't know whether to call security or not.'

'No, don't do that. I, uh, I was just – I was going to go to your door. To apologize.'

'Apologize? Apologize for what?'

'For today. For earlier, when I was inside. I – you were right, I wasn't looking to buy anything.'

'Then what were you doing?'

Bosch opened the car door and stepped out. He felt disadvantaged with her looking down at him in the car.

'I'm a cop,' he said. 'I needed to get in here to see someone. I used you and I'm sorry. I am. I didn't know about your father and all of that.'

She smiled and shook her head.

'That's the dumbest story I've ever heard. What about LA, was that part of the story?'

'No. I'm from LA. I'm a cop there.'

'I don't know if I'd go around admitting that if I were you. You guys've got some bad PR problems.'

'Yeah, I know. So …' He felt his courage rising. He told himself he was flying out in the morning and it didn't matter what happened because he'd never see her or this state again. 'You said something before about lemonade but I never got any. I was thinking, maybe I could tell you the story, apologize and have some lemonade or something.'

He looked over toward the door of the condo.

'You LA cops are pushy,' she said but she was smiling. 'One glass and the story better be good. After that, we both gotta go. I'm driving up to Tampa tonight.'

They started walking toward the door and Bosch realized he had a smile on his face.

'What's in Tampa?'

'It's where I live and I miss it. I've been down here more than up there since I put the condo on the market. I want to spend a Sunday at my own place and in my own studio.'

'That's right, a painter.'

'I try to be.'

She opened the door for him and allowed him in first.

'Well, that's okay by me. I have to get to Tampa sometime tonight. I fly out in the morning.'

While nursing a tall glass of lemonade, Bosch explained his scam of using her to get into the complex to see another resident and she didn't seem upset. In fact, he could tell she admired the ingenuity of it. Bosch didn't tell her how it had backfired anyway when McKittrick had pulled a gun on him. He gave her a vague outline of the

235

case, never mentioning its personal connection to himself and she seemed intrigued by the whole idea of solving a murder that happened thirty-three years earlier.

The one glass of lemonade turned into four and the last two were spiked nicely with vodka. They took care of what was left of Bosch's headache and put a nice bloom on everything. Between the third and the fourth she asked if he would mind if she smoked and he lit cigarettes for both of them. And as the sky darkened over the mangroves outside, he finally turned the conversation toward her. Bosch had sensed a loneliness about her, a mystery of some sort. Behind the pretty face there were scars. The kind that couldn't be seen.

Her name was Jasmine Corian but she said that friends called her Jazz. She spoke of growing up in the Florida sun, of never wanting to leave it. She had married once but it was a long time ago. There was nobody in her life now and she was used to it. She said she concentrated most of her life on her art and, in a way, Bosch understood what she meant. His own art, though few would call it that, took most of his life as well.

'What do you paint?'

'Portraits mostly.'

'Who are they?'

'Just someone I know. Maybe I'll paint you, Bosch. Someday.'

He didn't know what to say to that so he made a clumsy transition to safer ground.

'Why don't you give this place to a realtor to sell? That way you could stay in Tampa and paint.'

'Because I wanted the diversion. I also didn't want to give a realtor the five percent. This is a nice complex. These units sell pretty well without realtors. A lot of Canadian investment. I think I'll sell it. This was only the first week I've run the ad.'

Bosch just nodded and wished he had kept the conversation on her painting instead of realtors. The clumsy change seemed to have clogged things up a bit.

'I was thinking, you want to have dinner?'

She looked at him solemnly, as if the request and her answer had far deeper implications. They probably did. At least, he thought they did.

'Where would we go?'

That was a stall but he played along.

'I don't know. It's not my town. Not my state. You could pick a place. Around here or on the way up to Tampa. I don't care. I'd like your company, though, Jazz. If you want to.'

'How long has it been since you were with a woman? I mean on a date.'

'On a date? I don't know. A few months, I guess. But, look, I'm not a hard-luck case. I'm just in town and alone and thought maybe you'd –'

'It's okay, Harry. Let's go.'

'To eat?'

'Yes, to eat. I know a place on the way up. It's above Longboat. You'll have to follow me.'

He smiled and nodded.

She drove a Volkswagen Beetle convertible that was powder blue with one red fender. He couldn't lose her in a hailstorm let alone the slow-moving Florida highways.

Bosch counted two drawbridges that they had to stop for before they got to Longboat Key. From there they headed north for the length of the island, crossed a bridge onto Anna Maria Island and finally stopped at a place called the Sandbar. They walked through the bar and sat on a deck overlooking the Gulf. It was cool and they ate crabs and oysters chased with Mexican beer. Bosch loved it.

They didn't talk much but didn't need to. It was always in the silences that Bosch felt most comfortable with the women who had moved through his life. He felt the vodka and beer working on him, warming him toward her, sanding off any sharp edges to the evening. He felt a desire for her growing and tugging at him. McKittrick and the case had somehow been pushed into the darkness at the back of his mind.

'This is good,' he said when he was finally nearing his capacity for food and drink. 'It's great.'

'Yeah, they do it right. Can I tell you something, Bosch?'

'Go ahead.'

'I was only kidding about what I was saying about LA cops before. But I have known some cops before … and you seem different. I don't know what it is but it's like you've got too much of yourself left, you know?'

'I guess.' He nodded. 'Thanks. I think.'

They both laughed and then in a hesitant move, she leaned over and kissed him quickly on the lips. It was nice and he smiled. He could taste garlic.

'I'm glad you're already sunburned or you'd be turning red again.'

'No, I wouldn't. I mean, that was a nice thing to say.'

'You want to come home with me, Bosch?'

Now he hesitated. Not because there was any deliberation in his answer. But he wanted her to have the chance to withdraw it in case she had spoken too quickly. After a moment of silence from her he smiled and nodded.

'Yes, I would like that.'

They left then and cut inland to the freeway. Bosch wondered as he tailed the Volkswagen if she would change her mind as she drove alone. He got his answer at the Skyway bridge. As he pulled up to the tollbooth with his dollar already in hand, the tolltaker shook his head and waved off the money.

'Nope. That lady in the bug got ya covered.'

'Yeah?'
'Yeah. You know her?'
'Not yet.'
'I think you're goin' to. Good luck.'
'Thanks.'

＊ ＊ ＊ ＊ ＊ ＊ ＊

Now Bosch couldn't lose her in a blizzard. As the drive grew longer, he found himself in a growing sense of an almost adolescent euphoria of anticipation. He was captured by the directness of this woman and he was wondering how and what that would translate to when they were making love.

She led him north to Tampa and then into an area called Hyde Park. Overlooking the bay, the neighborhood consisted of old Victorian and Craftsman-style houses with sweeping front porches. Her home was an apartment above the three-car garage set behind a gray Victorian with green trim.

As they got to the top of the steps and she was putting the key into the knob, Bosch thought of something and didn't know what to do. She opened the door and looked at him. She read him.

'What's wrong?'

'Nothing. But I was thinking, maybe I should go find a drugstore or something and then come back.'

'Don't worry, I've got what you'll need. But can you stand out here for a second? I just want to make a mad dash inside and clean up a few things.'

He looked at her.

'I don't care about that.'

'Please?'

'Okay. Take your time.'

He waited for about three minutes and then she opened the door and pulled him in. If she had cleaned up, she had done it in the dark. The only light came from what Bosch could see was the kitchen. She took his hand and led him away from the light to a darkened hallway that gave way to her bedroom. Here she turned on the light, revealing a sparely furnished room. A wrought-iron bed with a canopy was the centerpiece. There was a night table of unfinished wood next to it, a matching unfinished bureau and an antique Singer sewing machine table on which stood a blue vase with dead flowers in it. There was nothing hung on any of the walls, though Bosch saw a nail protruding from the plaster above the vase. Jasmine noticed the flowers and quickly took the vase off the table and headed out the door.

'I have to go dump this. I haven't been here in a week and forgot to change them.'

Moving the flowers raised a slightly acrid smell in the room. While she was gone Bosch looked at the nail again and thought he could see the delineation of a rectangle on the wall. Something had hung there, he decided. She hadn't come in to clean up. If she had, she would have gotten rid of the flowers. She'd come in to take down a painting.

When she came back into the room, she put the empty vase back on the table.

'Would you like another beer? I have some wine, too.'

Bosch moved toward her, intrigued even more by her mysteries.

'No, I'm fine.'

Without further word they embraced. He could taste beer and garlic and cigarette smoke as he kissed her but didn't care. He knew she was getting the same from him. He pressed his cheek against hers and with his nose he came across the spot on her neck where she had dabbed perfume. Night-blooming jasmine.

They moved onto the bed, each taking pieces of clothing off between hard kisses. Her body was beautiful, the tan lines distinct. He kissed her lovely small breasts and gently pushed her back on the bed. She told him to wait and she rolled to the side and from the drawer of the bed table extracted a strip of three condom packages and handed it to him.

'Is this wishful thinking?' he asked.

They both burst out laughing and it seemed to make things all the better.

'I don't know,' she said. 'We'll see.'

For Bosch, sexual encounters had always been a question of timing. The desires of two individuals rose and subsided on their own courses. There were emotional needs separate from physical needs. And sometimes all of those things clicked together in a person and then clicked in tandem with those of the other person. Bosch's encounter with Jasmine Corian was one of those times. The sex created a world without intrusion. One so vital that it could have lasted an hour or maybe only a few minutes and he wouldn't have known the difference. At the end, he was above her, looking into her open eyes, and she clutched his upper arms as if she were holding on for her life. Both of their bodies shuddered in unison and then he lay still on top of her, catching his breath from the hollow between her neck and shoulder. He felt so good he had the urge to laugh out loud but he didn't think she'd understand. He stifled it and made it sound like a muffled cough.

'Are you okay?' she asked softly.

'I've never felt better.'

Eventually, he moved off her, backing down over her body. He kissed both of her breasts, then sat up with her legs on either side of him. He removed the condom while using his body to shield her view of the process.

He got up and walked to the door he hoped was the bathroom and found it was a closet. The next door he tried was the bathroom and he flushed the condom down the toilet. He absentmindedly wondered if it would end up somewhere in Tampa Bay.

When he came back from the bathroom she was sitting up with the sheet bunched around her waist. He found his sport coat on the floor and got out his cigarettes. He gave her one and lit it. Then he bent over and kissed her breasts again. Her laugh was infectious and it made him smile.

'You know, I like it that you didn't come equipped.'

'Equipped? What are you talking about?'

'You know, that you offered to go to the drugstore. It shows what kind of man you are.'

'What do you mean?'

'If you had come over here from LA with a condom in your wallet, that would've been so ... I don't know, premeditated. Like some guy just on the make. The whole thing would have had no spontaneity. I'm glad you weren't like that, Harry Bosch, that's all.'

He nodded, trying to follow her line of thought. He wasn't sure he understood. And he wondered what he should think of the fact that she *was* equipped. He decided to drop it and lit his cigarette.

'How'd you hurt your hand like that?'

She had noticed the marks on his fingers. Bosch had taken the Band-Aids off while flying over. The burns had healed to the point that they looked like red welts on two of his fingers.

'Cigarette. I fell asleep.'

He felt he could tell her the truth about everything about himself.

'God, that's scary.'

243

'Yeah. I don't think it will happen again.'

'Do you want to stay with me tonight?'

He moved closer to her and kissed her on the neck.

'Yes,' he whispered.

She reached over and touched the zipper scar on his left shoulder. The women he was with in bed always seemed to do this. It was an ugly mark and he never understood why they were drawn to touch it.

'You got shot?'

'Yeah.'

'That's even scarier.'

He hiked his shoulders. It was history and he never really thought about it anymore.

'You know, what I was trying to say before is that you're not like most cops I've known. You've got too much of your humanity left. How'd that happen?'

He shook his shoulders again like he didn't know.

'Are you okay, Bosch?'

He stubbed out his cigarette.

'Yeah, I'm fine. Why?'

'I don't know. You know what that guy Marvin Gaye sang about, don't you? Before he got killed by his own dad? He sang about sexual healing. Said it's good for the soul. Something like that. Anyway, I believe it, do you?'

'I suppose.'

'I think you need healing in your life, Bosch. That's the vibe I'm getting.'

'You want to go to sleep now?'

She lay down again and pulled the sheet up. He walked around the room naked, turning out the lights. When he was under the sheet in the dark, she turned on her side so her back was to him and told him to put his arm around her. He moved up close behind her and did. He loved her smell.

'How come people call you Jazz?'

'I don't know. They just do. Because it goes with the name.'

After a few moments she asked him why he had asked that.

'Because. You smell like both your names. Like the flower and the music.'

'What does jazz smell like?'

'It smells dark and smoky.'

They were silent for a long while after that and eventually Bosch thought she was asleep. But he still could not make it down. He lay with his eyes open, looking at the shadows of the room. Then she spoke softly to him.

'Bosch, what's the worst thing you've ever done to yourself?'

'What do you mean?'

'You know what I mean. What's the worst thing? What's the thing that keeps you awake at night if you think about it too hard?'

He thought for a few moments before answering.

'I don't know.' He forced an uneasy and short laugh. 'I guess I've done a lot of bad things. I suppose a lot of them are to myself. At least I think about them a lot ...'

'What's one of them? You can tell me.'

And he knew that he could. He thought he could tell her almost anything and not be judged harshly.

'When I was a kid – I grew up mostly in a youth hall, like an orphanage. When I was new there, one of the older kids took my shoes, my sneakers. They didn't fit him or anything but he did it because he knew he could do it. He was one of the rulers of the roost and he took 'em. I didn't do anything about it and it hurt.'

'But you didn't do it. That's not what I –'

'No, I'm not done. I just told you that because you had to know that part. See, when I got older and I was one of the big shots in the place, I did the same thing. I took this new kid's shoes. He was smaller, I couldn't even put 'em on. I just took them and I … I don't know, I threw them out or something. But I took them because I could. I did the same thing that was done to me … And sometimes, even now, I think about it and I feel bad.'

She squeezed his hand in a way he thought was meant to be comforting but said nothing.

'Is that the kind of story you wanted?'

She just squeezed his hand again. After a while he spoke.

'I think the one thing I did that I regret the most, though, was maybe letting a woman go.'

'You mean like a criminal?'

'No. I mean like we lived – we were lovers and when she wanted to go, I didn't really … do anything. I didn't put up a fight, you know. And when I think about it, sometimes I think that maybe if I had, I could've changed her mind … I don't know.'

'Did she say why she was leaving?'

'She just got to know me too well. I don't blame her for anything. I've got baggage. I guess maybe I can be hard to take. I've lived alone most of my life.'

Silence filled the room again and he waited. He sensed that there was something more she wanted to say or be asked. But when she spoke he wasn't sure if she was talking about him or herself.

'They say when a cat is ornery and scratches and hisses at everybody, even somebody who wants to comfort it and love it, it's because it wasn't held enough when it was a kitten.'

'I never heard that before.'

'I think it's true.'

He was quiet a moment and moved his hand up so that it was touching her breasts.

'Is that what your story is?' he asked. 'You weren't held enough.'

'Who knows.'

'What was the worst thing you ever did to yourself, Jasmine? I think you want to tell me.'

He knew she wanted him to ask it. It was true confessions time and he began to believe that the whole night had been directed by her to arrive at this one question.

'You didn't try to hold on to someone you should have,' she said. 'I held on to someone I shouldn't have. I held on too long. Thing is, I knew what it was leading to, deep down I knew. It was like standing on the tracks and seeing the train coming at you but being too mesmerized by the bright light to move, to save yourself.'

He had his eyes open in the dark still. He could barely see the outline of her shoulder and cheek. He pulled himself closer to her, kissed her neck and in her ear whispered, 'But you got out. That's what's important.'

'Yeah, I got out,' she said wistfully. 'I got out.'

She was silent for a while and then reached up under the covers and touched his hand. It was cupped over one of her breasts. She held her hand on top of it.

'Good night, Harry.'

He waited a while, until he heard the measured breathing of her sleep, and then he was finally able to drift off. There was no dream this time. Just warmth and darkness.

❖ ❖ ❖ ❖ ❖ ❖ ❖

In the morning Bosch awoke first. He took a shower and borrowed Jasmine's toothbrush without asking. Then he dressed in the clothes he'd worn the day before and went out to his car to retrieve his overnight bag. Once he was dressed in fresh clothes he ventured into the kitchen to see about coffee. All he found was a box of tea bags.

Leaving the idea behind, he walked around the apartment, his steps creaking on the old pine floors. The living room was as spare as the bedroom. A sofa with an off-white blanket spread on it, a coffee table, an old stereo with a cassette but no CD player. No television. Again, nothing on the walls but the telltale indication that there had been. He found two nails in the plaster. They weren't rusted or painted over. They hadn't been there very long.

Through a set of French doors the living room opened up to a porch enclosed in windows. There was rattan furniture out here and several potted plants, including a dwarf orange tree with fruit on it. The entire porch was redolent with its smell. Bosch stepped close to the windows and by looking south down the alley behind the property, he could see the bay. The morning sun's reflection on it was pure white light.

He walked back across the living room to another door on the wall opposite the French doors. Immediately upon opening this door, he could smell the sharp tang of oils and turpentine. This was where she painted. He hesitated but only for a moment, then walked in.

The first thing he noticed was that the room had a window that gave a direct view of the bay across the backyards and garages of three or four houses down the alley. It was beautiful and he knew why she chose this room for her art. At center on a paint-dappled drop cloth was an easel but no stool. She painted standing. He saw no overhead lamp or artificial light source anywhere else in the room. She painted only by true light.

He walked around the easel and found the canvas on it had been untouched by the painter. Along one of the side walls was a high work counter with various tubes of paint scattered about. There were palette boards and coffee cans with brushes stacked in them. At the end of the counter was a large laundry sink for washing up.

Bosch noticed more canvases leaning against the wall under the counter. They were faced inward and appeared to be unused pieces like the one on the easel, waiting for the artist's hand. But Bosch suspected otherwise. Not with the exposed nails in the walls in the other rooms of the apartment. He reached under the counter and slid a few of the canvases out. As he did this he almost felt as if he was on some case, solving some mystery.

The three portraits he pulled out were painted in dark hues. None were signed though it was obvious all were the work of one hand. And that hand was Jasmine's. Bosch recognized the style from the painting he had seen at her father's house. Sharp lines, dark colors. The first one he looked at was of a nude woman with her face turned away from the painter and into the shadows. The sense Bosch felt was that the darkness was taking the woman, rather than her turning to the darkness. Her mouth was completely in shadow. It was as if she was mute. The woman, Bosch knew, was Jasmine.

The second painting seemed to be part of the same study as the first. It was the same nude in shadow, though she was now facing the viewer. Bosch noted that in the portrait Jasmine had given herself fuller breasts than in reality and he wondered if this was done on purpose and had some meaning, or was perhaps a subliminal improvement made by the painter. He noticed that beneath the veneer of gray shadow over the painting there were red highlights on the woman. Bosch knew little about the art, but he knew this was a dark portrait.

Bosch looked at the third painting he had pulled out and found this to be unattached to the first two, save for the fact that again it was a nude portrait of Jasmine. But this piece he clearly recognized as a reinterpretation of 'The Scream' by Edvard Munch, a painting that had always fascinated Bosch but that he had only seen in books. In the piece before him, the figure of the frightened person was Jasmine. The location had been transferred from Munch's horrific, swirling dreamscape, to the Skyway bridge. Bosch clearly recognized the bright yellow vertical piping of the bridge's support span.

'What are you doing?'

He jumped as if stabbed in the back. It was Jasmine, at the door of the studio. She wore a silk bathrobe she held closed with her arms. Her eyes were puffy. She had just woken up.

'I'm looking at your work, is that okay?'

'This door was locked.'

'No, it wasn't.'

She reached to the doorknob and turned it, as if that could disprove his claim.

'It wasn't locked, Jazz. I'm sorry. I didn't know you didn't want me in here.'

'Could you put those back under there, please?'

'Sure. But why'd you take them off the walls?'

'I didn't.'

'Was it because they're nudes, or is it because of what they mean?'

'Please don't ask me about this. Put them back.'

She left the doorway and he put the paintings back where he found them. He left the room and found her in the kitchen filling a tea kettle with water from the sink. Her back was to him and he walked in and lightly put a hand on her back. Even so, she started slightly at his touch.

'Jazz, look, I'm sorry. I'm a cop. I get curious.'

'It's okay.'

'Are you sure?'

'Yes, I'm sure. You want some tea?'

She had stopped filling the kettle but did not turn around or make a move to put it on the stove.

'No. I was thinking maybe I could take you out for breakfast.'

'When do you leave? I thought you said the plane's this morning.'

'That was the other thing I was thinking about. I could stay another day, leave tomorrow, if you want me to. I mean, if you'll have me. I'd like to stay.'

She turned around and looked at him.

'I want you to stay, too.'

They embraced and kissed but she quickly pulled back.

'It's not fair, you brushed your teeth. I have monster breath.'

'Yeah, but I used your toothbrush, so it evens out.'

'Gross. Now I have to get a new one.'

'That's right.'

They smiled and she gave him a tight hug around the neck, his trespass in her studio seemingly forgotten.

'You call the airline and I'll get ready. I know where we can go.'

When she pulled away he held her in front of him. He wanted to bring it up again. He couldn't help it.

'I want to ask you something.'

'What?'

'How come those paintings aren't signed?'

'They're not ready to be signed.'

'The one at your father's was signed.'

'That was for him, so I signed it. Those others are for me.'

'The one on the bridge. Is she going to jump?'

She looked at him a long time before answering.

'I don't know. Sometimes when I look at it, I think she is. I think the thought is there, but you never know.'

'It can't happen, Jazz.'

'Why not?'

'Because it can't.'

'I'll get ready.'

She broke away from him then and left the kitchen.

He went to the wall phone next to the refrigerator and dialed the airline. While making the arrangements to fly out Monday morning, he decided on a whim to ask the airline agent if it was possible to route his new flight back to Los Angeles through Las Vegas. She said not without a three-hour-and-fourteen-minute layover. He said he'd take it. He had to pay fifty dollars on top of the seven hundred they already had from him in order to make the needed changes. He put it on his credit card.

He thought about Vegas as he hung up. Claude Eno might be dead but his wife was still cashing his checks. She might be worth the fifty-dollar layover.

'Ready?'

It was Jasmine calling from the living room. Bosch stepped out of the kitchen and she was waiting for him in cut-off jeans and a tank top beneath a white shirt she left open and tied above her waist. She already had on sunglasses.

252

She took him to a place where they poured honey on top of the biscuits and served the eggs with grits and butter. Bosch hadn't had grits since basic training at Benning. The meal was delicious. Neither of them spoke much. The paintings and the conversation they had before falling asleep the night before were not mentioned. It seemed that what they had said was better left for the dark shadows of night, and maybe her paintings, too.

When they were done with their coffee, she insisted on picking up the check. He got the tip. They spent the afternoon cruising in her Volkswagen with the top down. She took him all over the place, from Ybor City to St Petersburg Beach, burning up a tank of gas and two packs of cigarettes. By late in the afternoon they were at a place called Indian Rocks Beach to look at the sunset over the Gulf.

· 'I've been a lot of places,' Jasmine told him. 'I like the light here the best.'

'Ever been out to California?'

'No, not yet.'

'Sometimes the sunset looks like lava pouring down on the city.'

'That must be beautiful.'

'It makes you forgive a lot, forget a lot … That's the thing about Los Angeles. It's got a lot of broken pieces to it. But the ones that still work, really do work.'

'I think I know what you mean.'

'I'm curious about something.'

'Here we go again. What?'

'If you don't show your paintings to anybody, how do you make a living?'

It was from out of left field but he had been thinking about it all day.

'I have money from my father. Even before he died. It's not a lot but I don't need a lot. It's enough. If I don't feel the need to sell my work when it is finished, then as I am doing it, it won't be compromised. It will be pure.'

It sounded to Bosch like a convenient way of explaining away the fear of exposing oneself. But he let it go. She didn't.

'Are you always a cop? Always asking questions?'

'No. Only when I care about someone.'

She kissed him quickly and walked back to the car.

After stopping by her place to change, they had dinner in a Tampa steak house where the wine list was actually a book so thick it came on its own pedestal. The restaurant itself seemed to be the work of a slightly delusional Italian decorator, a dark blend of gilded rococo, garish red velvet and classical statues and paintings. It was the kind of place he would expect her to suggest. She mentioned that this meateater's palace was actually owned by a vegetarian.

'Sounds like somebody from California.'

She smiled and was quiet for a while after that. Bosch's mind wandered to the case. He had spent the entire day without giving it a thought. Now a pang of guilt thrummed in his mind. It was almost as if he felt he was shunting his mother aside to pursue the selfish pleasure of Jasmine's company. Jasmine seemed to read him and to know he was privately debating something.

'Can you stay another day, Harry?'

He smiled but shook his head.

'I can't. I gotta go. But I'll be back. As soon as I can.'

Bosch paid for dinner with a credit card he guessed was reaching its limit and they headed back to her apartment. Knowing their time together was drawing to a close, they went right to the bed and made love.

The feel of her body, its taste and its scent seemed perfect to Bosch. He didn't want the moment to end. He'd had immediate attractions to women before in his life and had even acted on them. But never one that felt so fully engaging and complete. He guessed that it was because of all he did not know about her. That was the hook. She was a mystery. Physically, he could not get any closer than he was to her during these moments, yet there was so much of her hidden, unexplored. They made love in gentle rhythm and held each other in a deep, long kiss at the end.

Later, he lay on his side, next to her, his arm across the flatness of her belly. One of her hands traced circles in his hair. The true confessions began.

'Harry, you know, I haven't been with a lot of men in my life.'

He didn't respond because he didn't know what the proper response could be. He was well past caring about a woman's sexual history for anything other than health reasons.

'What about you?' she asked.

He couldn't resist.

'I haven't been with a lot of men, either. In fact, none, as far as I know.'

She punched him on the shoulder.

'You know what I mean.'

'The answer is no. I haven't been with a lot of women in my life. Not enough, at least.'

'I don't know, the men that I've been with, most of them, it's like they wanted something from me I didn't have. I don't know what it was but I just didn't have it to give. Then I either left too soon or stayed too long.'

He propped himself up on one elbow and looked at her.

'Sometimes I think that I know strangers better than I know anybody else, even myself. I learn so much about people in my job. Sometimes I think I don't even have a life. I only have their life … I don't know what I'm talking about.'

'I think you do. I understand. Maybe everybody's like this.'

'I don't know. I don't think so.'

They were quiet for a while after that. Bosch leaned down and kissed her breasts, holding a nipple between his lips for a long moment. She brought her hands up and held his head to her chest. He could smell the jasmine.

'Harry, have you ever had to use your gun?'

He pulled his head up. The question seemed out of place. But through the darkness he could see her eyes on him, watching and waiting for an answer.

'Yes.'

'You killed someone.'

It wasn't a question.

'Yes.'

She said nothing else.

'What is it, Jazz?'

'Nothing. I was just wondering how that would be. How you would go on.'

'Well, all I can tell you is that it hurts. Even when there was no choice and they had to go down, it hurts. You just have to go on.'

She was silent. Whatever she had needed to hear from him he hoped she had gotten. Bosch was confused. He didn't know why she had asked such questions and wondered if she was testing him in some way. He lay back on his pillow and waited for sleep but confusion kept it away from him. After a while she turned on the bed and put her arm over him.

'I think you are a good man,' she whispered close to his ear.

'Am I?' he whispered back.

'And you will come back, won't you?'

'Yes. I'll come back.'

❖ ❖ ❖ ❖ ❖ ❖ ❖

Bosch went to every rental counter in McCarran International Airport in Las Vegas but none had a car left. He silently chastised himself for not making a reservation and walked outside the terminal into the dry crisp air to catch a cab. The driver was a woman and when Bosch gave the address, on Lone Mountain Drive, he could clearly see her disappointment in the rearview mirror. The destination wasn't a hotel, so she wouldn't be picking up a return fare.

'Don't worry,' Bosch said, understanding her problem. 'If you wait for me, you can take me back to the airport.'

'How long you gonna be? I mean, Lone Mountain, that's way out there in the sand pits.'

'I might be five minutes, I might be less. Maybe a half hour. I'd say no longer than a half hour.'

'You waiting on the meter?'

'On the meter or you. Whatever you want to do.'

She thought about it a moment and put the car in drive.

'Where are all the rental cars, anyway?'

'Big convention in town. Electronics or something.'

It was a thirty-minute ride out into the desert northwest of the strip. The neon-and-glass buildings retreated and the cab passed through residential neighborhoods until these, too, became sparse. The land was a ragged brown out here and dotted unevenly with scrub brush. Bosch knew the roots of every bush spread wide and sucked up what little

257

moisture was in the earth. It made for a terrain that seemed dying and desolate.

The houses, too, were few and far between, each one an outpost in a no-man's-land. The streets had been gridded and paved long ago but the boomtown of Las Vegas hadn't quite caught up yet. It was coming, though. The city was spreading like a patch of weeds.

The road began to rise toward a mountain the color of cocoa mix. The cab shook as a procession of eighteen-wheel dump trucks thundered by with loads of sand from the excavation pits the driver had mentioned. And soon the paved roadway gave way to gravel and the cab sent up a tail of dust in its wake. Bosch was beginning to think the address the smarmy supervising clerk at City Hall had given him was a phony. But then they were there.

The address to which Claude Eno's pension checks were mailed each month was a sprawling ranch-style house of pink stucco and dusty white tile roof. Looking past it, Bosch could see where even the gravel road ended just past it. It was the end of the line. Nobody had lived farther away than Claude Eno.

'I don't know about this,' the driver said. 'You want me to wait? This is like the goddamn moon out here.'

She had pulled into the driveway behind a late 1970s-model Olds Cutlass. There was a carport where another car was parked hidden beneath a tarp that was blue in the further recesses of the carport but bleached nearly white along the surfaces sacrificed to the sun.

Bosch took out his fold of money and paid the driver thirty-five dollars for the ride out. Then he took two twenties, ripped them in half and handed one side of each over the seat to her.

'You wait, you get the other half of those.'

'Plus the fare back to the airport.'

'Plus that.'

Bosch got out, realizing it would probably be the quickest forty bucks ever lost in Las Vegas if nobody answered the door. But he was in luck. A woman who looked to be in her late sixties opened the door before he could knock. And why not, he thought. In this house, you could see visitors coming for a mile.

Bosch felt the blast of air conditioning escaping through the open door.

'Mrs Eno?'

'No.'

Bosch pulled out his notebook and checked the address against the black numbers tacked on the front wall next to the door. They matched.

'Olive Eno doesn't live here?'

'You didn't ask that. I'm not Mrs Eno.'

'Can I please speak with Mrs Eno then?' Annoyed with the woman's preciseness, Bosch showed the badge he had gotten back from McKittrick after the boat ride. 'It's police business.'

'Well, you can try. She hasn't spoken to anybody, at least anybody outside her imagination, in three years.'

She motioned Bosch in and he stepped into the cool house.

'I'm her sister. I take care of her. She's in the kitchen. We were in the middle of lunch when I saw the dust come up on the road and heard you arrive.'

Bosch followed her down a tiled hallway toward the kitchen. The house smelled like old age, like dust and mold and urine. In the kitchen a gnome-like woman with white hair sat in a wheelchair, barely taking up half of the space it gave for an occupant. There was a slide-on tray in front of it and the woman's gnarled pearl-white hands were folded together on top of it. There were milky blue cataracts on both eyes and they seemed dead to the world outside the body. Bosch noticed a bowl of applesauce on the nearby table. It only took him a few seconds to size up the situation.

'She'll be ninety in August,' said the sister. 'If she makes it.'

'How long has she been like this?'

'Long time. I've been taking care of her for three years now.' She then bent into the gnome's face and loudly added, 'Isn't that right, Olive?'

The loudness of the question seemed to kick a switch and Olive Eno's jaw started working but no sound that was intelligible issued. She stopped the effort after a while and the sister straightened up.

'Don't worry about it, Olive. I know you love me.'

She wasn't as loud with that sentence. Maybe she feared Olive might actually muster a denial.

'What's your name?' Bosch asked.

'Elizabeth Shivone. What's this about? I saw that badge of yours says Los Angeles, not Las Vegas. Aren't you off the beat here a bit?'

'Not really. It's about her husband. One of his old cases.'

'Claude's been dead going on five years now.'

'How did he die?'

'Just died. His pump went out. Died right there on the floor, about where you're standing.'

They both looked down at the floor as if maybe his body was still there.

'I came to look through his things,' Bosch said.

'What things?'

'I don't know. I was thinking maybe he kept files from his time with the police.'

'You better tell me what you're doing here. This doesn't sound right to me.'

'I'm investigating a case he worked back in 1961. It's still open. Parts of the file are missing. I thought maybe he'd taken it. I thought maybe there might be something important that he kept. I don't know what. Anything. I just thought it was worth a try.'

He could see that her mind was working and her eyes suddenly froze for a second when her memory snagged on something.

'There is something, isn't there?' he said.

'No. I think you should go.'

'It's a big house. Did he have a home office?'

'Claude left the police thirty years ago. He built this house in the middle of nowhere just to be away from all of that.'

'What did he do when he moved out here?'

'He worked casino security. A few years at the Sands, then twenty at the Flamingo. He was getting two pensions and took good care of Olive.'

'Speaking of which, who's signing those pension checks these days?'

Bosch looked at Olive Eno to make his point. The other woman was silent a long moment, then went on the offense.

'Look, I could get power of attorney. Look at her. It wouldn't be a problem. I take care of her, mister.'

'Yeah, you feed her applesauce.'

'I have nothing to hide.'

'You want somebody to make sure or do you want to let it end right here? I don't really care what you're doing, lady. I don't really care if you're even her sister or not. If I was betting, I'd say you're not. But I don't really care right now. I'm busy. I just want to look through Eno's things.'

He stopped there and let her think about it. He looked at his watch.

'No warrant then, right?'

'I don't have a warrant. I've got a cab waiting. You make me get a warrant and I'm going to stop being such a nice guy.'

Her eyes went up and down his body as if to measure how nice and how not nice he could be.

'The office is this way.'

She said the words as if they were bites out of wood planks. She swiftly led him down the hall again and then off to the left into a study. There was an old steel desk as the room's centerpiece, a couple of four-drawer file cabinets, an extra chair and not much else.

'After he died, Olive and I moved everything into those file cabinets and haven't looked at it since.'

'They're all full?'

'All eight. Have at it.'

Bosch reached his hand into his pocket and took out another twenty-dollar bill. He tore it in half and gave one side to Shivone.

'Take that out to the cab driver. Tell her I'm going to be a little longer than I thought.'

She exhaled loudly, snatched the half and left the room. After she was gone Bosch went to the desk and opened each of the drawers. The first two he tried were empty. The next contained stationery and office supplies. The fourth drawer contained a checkbook that he quickly leafed through and saw it was an account covering household expenses. There was also a file containing recent receipts and other records. The last drawer in the desk was locked.

He started with the bottom file drawers and worked his way up. Nothing in the first few seemed even remotely connected with what Bosch was working on. There were files labeled with the names of different casinos and gaming organizations. The files in another drawer were labeled by people's names. Bosch looked through a few of these and determined they were files on known casino cheats. Eno had built a library of home intelligence files. By this time, Shivone had come back from her errand and had taken the seat opposite the desk. She was watching Bosch and he threw a few idle questions at her while he looked.

'So what did Claude do for the casinos?'

'He was a bird dog.'

'What's that?'

'Kind've an undercover thing. He mingled in the casinos, gambled with house chips, watched people. He was good at picking out the cheats and how they did it.'

'Guess it takes one to know one, right?'

'What's that crack supposed to mean? He did a good job.'

'I'm sure he did. Is that how he met you?'

'I'm not answering any of your questions.'

'Okay by me.'

He had only the two top drawers left. He opened one and found it contained no files at all. Just an old, dust-covered Rolodex and other items that had probably sat on the top of the desk at one point. There was an ashtray, a clock and a pen holder made of carved wood that had Eno's name carved on it. Bosch took the Rolodex out and put it on top of the cabinet. He blew the dust off it and then began turning it until he came to the Cs. He looked through the cards but found no listing for Arno Conklin. He met with similar failure when he tried to find a listing for Gordon Mittel.

'You're not going to look through that whole thing, are you?' Shivone asked in exasperation.

'No, I'm just going to take it with me.'

'Oh, no you don't. You can't just come in here and –'

'I'm taking it. If you want to make a complaint about it, be my guest. Then I'll make a complaint about you.'

She went quiet after that. Bosch went on to the next drawer and found it contained about twelve files on old LAPD cases from the 1950s and early 1960s. Again, he didn't have the time to study them, but he checked all the labels and none was marked Marjorie Lowe. By randomly pulling out a few of the files it became clear to him that Eno had made copies of files on some of his cases to take with him when he left the department. Of the random selections, all were murders, including two of prostitutes. Only one of the cases was closed.

'Go get me a box or a bag or something for these files,' Bosch said over his shoulder. When he sensed the woman in the room had not moved, he barked, 'Do it!'

She got up and left. Bosch stood gazing at the files and thinking. He had no idea if these were important or not. He had no idea what they meant. He only knew he should take them in case they turned out to be important. But what bothered him more than what the files that were in the drawer could mean was the feeling that something was certainly missing. This was based on his belief in McKittrick. The retired detective was sure his former partner, Eno, had some kind of hold on Conklin, or at the very least, some kind of deal with him. But there was nothing here about that. And it seemed to Bosch that if Eno was holding something on Conklin, it would still be here. If he kept old LAPD files, then he kept whatever he had on Conklin. In fact, he would have kept it in a safe place. Where?

The woman came back and dropped a cardboard box on the floor. It was the kind a case of beer had come in. Bosch put a foot-thick stack of files in it along with the Rolodex.

'You want a receipt?' he asked.

'No, I don't want anything from you.'

'Well, there is still something I need from you.'

'This doesn't end, does it?'

'I hope it does.'

'What do you want?'

'When Eno died, did you help the old lady – uh, your

264

sister, that is – did you help her clear out his safe deposit box?'

'How'd –'

She stopped herself but not soon enough.

'How'd I know? Because it's obvious. What I'm looking for, he would have kept in a safe place. What did you do with it?'

'We threw everything away. It was meaningless. Just some old files and bank statements. He didn't know what he was doing. He was old himself.'

Bosch looked at his watch. He was running out of time if he was going to make his plane.

'Get me the key for this desk drawer.'

She didn't move.

'Hurry up, I don't have a lot of time. You open it or I'll open it. But if I do it, that drawer isn't going to be much use to you anymore.'

She reached into the pocket of her house dress and pulled out the house keys. She reached down and unlocked the desk drawer, pulled it open and then stepped away.

'We didn't know what any of it was, or what it meant.'

'That's fine.'

Bosch moved to the drawer and looked in. There were two thin manila files and two packs of envelopes with rubber bands holding them together. The first file he looked through contained Eno's birth certificate, passport, marriage license and other personal records. He put it back in the drawer. The next file contained LAPD forms and Bosch quickly recognized them as the pages and reports that had been removed from the Marjorie Lowe murder book. He knew he had no time to read them at the moment and put the file in the beer box with the other files.

The rubber band on the first package of envelopes

snapped when he tried to remove it and he was reminded of the band that had been around the blue binder that contained the case files. Everything about this case was old and ready to snap, he thought.

The envelopes were all from a Wells Fargo Bank branch in Sherman Oaks and each one contained a statement for a savings account in the name of McCage Inc. The address of the corporation was a post office box, also in Sherman Oaks. Bosch randomly took envelopes from different spots in the pack and studied three of them. Though separated by years in the late 1960s, each statement was basically the same. A deposit of one thousand dollars was made in the account on the tenth of each month and on the fifteenth a transfer of an equal amount was made to an account with a Nevada Savings and Loan branch in Las Vegas.

Without looking further, Bosch concluded that the bank statements might be the records of some kind of payoff account Eno kept. He quickly looked through the envelopes at the postmarks looking for the most recent one. He found none more recent than the late 1980s.

'What about these envelopes? When did he stop getting them?'

'What you see is what you get. I have no idea what they mean and Olive didn't know either back when they drilled his box.'

'Drilled his box?'

'Yeah, after he died. Olive wasn't on the safe deposit box. Only him. We couldn't find his key. So we had to have it drilled.'

'There was money, too, wasn't there?'

She waited a moment, probably wondering if he was going to demand that, too.

'Some. But you're too late, it's already spent.'

'I'm not worried about that. How much was there?'

She pinched her lips and acted like she was trying to remember. It was a bad act.

'C'mon. I'm not here for the money and I'm not from the IRS.'

'It was about eighteen thousand.'

Bosch heard a horn honk from outside. The cabdriver was getting restless. Bosch looked at his watch. He had to go. He tossed the envelope packs into the beer box.

'What about his account at Nevada Savings and Loan? How much was in it?'

It was a scam question based on his guess that the account that the money from Sherman Oaks was transferred to was Eno's. Shivone hesitated again. A delay punctuated by another horn blast.

'It was about fifty. But most of that's gone, too. Taking care of Olive, you know?'

'Yeah, I bet. Between that and the pensions, it's gotta be rough,' Bosch said with all the sarcasm he could put into it. 'I bet your accounts aren't too thin, though.'

'Look, mister, I don't know who you think you are but I'm the only one in the world that she has and who cares about her. That's worth something.'

'Too bad she doesn't get to decide what it's worth instead of you. Answer one question for me and then I'm out of here and you can go back to taking whatever you can off her ... Who are you? You're not her sister. Who are you?'

'It's none of your business.'

'That's right. But I could make it my business.'

She put on a look that showed Bosch what an affront he was to her delicate sensibilities but then seemed to gain a measure of self-esteem. Whoever she was, she was proud of it.

'You want to know who I am? I was the best woman he ever had. I was with him for a long time. She had his wedding band but I had his heart. Near the end, when they were both old and it didn't matter, we dropped the pretension and he brought me in here. To live with them. Take care of them. So don't you dare tell me I don't deserve something out of it.'

Bosch just nodded. Somehow, as sordid as the story seemed, he found a measure of respect for her for just having told the truth. And he felt sure it was.

'When did you meet?'

'You said one question.'

'When did you meet?'

'When he was at the Flamingo. We both were. I was a dealer. Like I said, he was a bird dog.'

'He ever talk about LA, about any cases, any people from back there?'

'No, never. He always said that was a closed chapter.'

Bosch pointed to the envelope stacks in the box.

'Does the name McCage mean anything?'

'Not to me.'

'What about these account statements?'

'I never saw any of those things until the day we opened that box. Didn't know he even had an account over at Nevada Savings. Claude had secrets. He even kept secrets from me.'

❖ ❖ ❖ ❖ ❖ ❖ ❖

At the airport Bosch paid off the cabdriver and struggled into the main terminal with his over-nighter and the beer box full of files and other things. In one of the stores along the main terminal mall he bought a cheap canvas satchel and transferred the items he had taken from Eno's office into it. It was small enough so he didn't have to check it. Printed on the side of the bag was LAS VEGAS – LAND OF SUN AND FUN! There was a logo depicting the sun setting behind a pair of dice.

At his gate he had a half hour before they loaded the plane, so he found a section of open seats as far away as possible from the cacophony of the rows of slot machines set in the center of the circular terminal.

He began going through the files in the satchel. The one he was most interested in was the one containing records stolen from the Marjorie Lowe murder book. He looked through the documents and found nothing unusual or unexpected.

The summary of the McKittrick-Eno interview of Johnny Fox with Arno Conklin and Gordon Mittel present was here and Bosch could sense the contained outrage at the situation in McKittrick's writing. In the last paragraph it was no longer contained.

Interview with suspect was regarded by the under-signed as fruitless because of the intrusive behavior of A. Conklin and G. Mittel. Both 'prosecutors' refused to allow 'their' witness to answer questions fully or in the undersign's opinion with the whole truth. J. Fox remains suspect at this time until verification of his alibi and fingerprint analysis.

Nothing else in the documents was of note and Bosch realized that they were probably removed from the file by Eno solely because they mentioned Conklin's involvement in the case. Eno was covering up for Conklin. When Bosch asked himself why Eno was doing this, he immediately thought of the bank statements that had been in the safe deposit box with the stolen documents. They were records of the deal.

Bosch took out the envelopes and, going by the postmarks, began putting them in chronological order. The earliest one he could find was mailed to the McCage Inc. postal drop in November 1962. That was one year after the death of Marjorie Lowe and two months after the death of Johnny Fox. Eno had been on the Lowe case and then, according to McKittrick, he had investigated the Fox killing.

Bosch felt in his gut that he was right. Eno had squeezed Conklin. And maybe Mittel. He somehow knew what McKittrick didn't, that Conklin had been involved with Marjorie Lowe. Maybe he even knew Conklin had killed her. He had enough to put Conklin on the line for a thousand bucks a month for life. It wasn't a lot. Eno wasn't greedy, though a thousand a month in the early sixties probably more than matched what he was making on the job. But the amount didn't matter to Bosch. The payment did. It was an admission. If it could be traced to Conklin, it was hard evidence. Bosch felt himself getting excited. The records hoarded by a corrupt cop dead five years now might be all he needed to go head to head with Conklin.

He thought of something and looked around for the usual bank of phones. He checked his watch and looked over at the gate. People were milling about, ready to board and getting anxious. Bosch put the file and envelopes back into the satchel and carried his things to the phone.

Using his AT&T card, he dialed information in Sacramento and then dialed the state offices and asked for the corporate records unit. In three minutes he knew that McCage Inc. was not a California corporation and never was, at least in records going back to 1971. He hung up and went through the same process again, this time calling the Nevada state offices in Carson City.

The phone clerk told him the incorporation of McCage Inc. was defunct and asked if he was still interested in what information the state had. He excitedly said yes and was told by the clerk that she had to switch to microfiche and it would take a few minutes. While he waited, Bosch got out a notebook and got ready to take notes. He saw the gate door had been opened and people were just starting to board the plane. He didn't care, he'd miss it if he had to. He was too juiced to do anything but hang on to the phone.

Bosch studied the rows of slot machines in the center of the terminal. They were crowded with people trying their last chance at luck before leaving or their first chance after stepping off planes from all over the country and the world. Gambling against the machines had never appealed much to Bosch. He didn't understand it.

As he watched those milling about, it was easy to pick who was winning and who wasn't. It didn't take a detective to study the faces and know. He saw one woman with a stuffed teddy bear clamped under her arm. She was working two machines at once and Bosch could see that all she was doing was doubling her losses. To her left was a man in a black cowboy hat who was filling the machine with coins and pulling the arm back as quickly as he could. Bosch could see he was playing a dollar machine and was going to the five-dollar max on every roll. Bosch figured that, in the few minutes he watched, the man had spent sixty dollars with no return. At least he wasn't carrying a stuffed animal.

Bosch turned back to check the gate. The line of boarders had thinned to a few stragglers. Bosch knew he was going to miss it. But that was okay. He hung on and stayed calm.

Suddenly there was a shout and Bosch looked over and saw the man with the cowboy hat waving it as his machine was paying off a jackpot. The woman with the stuffed animal stepped back from her machines and solemnly watched the payoff. Each metallic *ching* of the dollars dropping in the tray must have been like a hammer pounding in her skull. A steady reminder that she was losing.

'Take a look at me now, baby!' the cowboy whooped.

It didn't appear that the exclamation was directed at anyone in particular. He stooped down and started scooping the coins into his hat. The woman with the teddy bear went back to work on her machines.

Just as the gate door was being closed, the clerk came back on the phone. She told Bosch the immediately available records showed McCage was incorporated in November 1962 and was dissolved by the state twenty-eight years later when a year went by without renewal fees or taxes being paid to keep the incorporation current. Bosch knew this had occurred because Eno had died.

'Do you want the officers?' the clerk asked.

'Yes, I do.'

'Okay, president and chief executive officer is Claude Eno. That's E-N-O. Vice president is Gordon Mittel with two Ts. And the treasurer is listed as Arno Conklin. That first name's spelled –'

'I got it. Thanks.'

Bosch hung up the phone, grabbed his overnighter and the satchel and ran to the gate.

'Just in time,' the attendant said with a tone of annoyance. 'Couldn't leave those one-armed bandits alone, huh?'

'Yeah,' Bosch said, not caring.

She opened the door and he went down the hallway and onto the plane. It was only half filled. He ignored his seat assignment and found an empty row. While he was pushing his luggage into the overhead storage bin, he thought of something. Once in his seat he took out his notebook and opened it to the page where he had just written the notes of his conversation with the incorporation clerk. He looked at the abbreviated notations.

> Prez., CEO – C.E.
> VP – G.M.
> Treas. – A.C.

He then wrote only the initials in a line.

CE GM AC

He looked at the line for a moment and then smiled. He saw the anagram and wrote it on the next line.

MC CAGE

Bosch felt the blood jangling through his body. It was the feeling of knowing he was close. He was on a roll those people out there at the slot machines and all the casinos in the desert could never understand. It was a high they would never feel, no matter how many sevens came up on the dice or how many black jacks they were dealt. Bosch was getting close to a killer and that made him as juiced as any jackpot winner on the planet.

❖ ❖ ❖ ❖ ❖ ❖ ❖

D riving the Mustang out of LAX an hour later, Bosch rolled the windows down and bathed his face in the cool, dry air. The sound of the breeze through the grove of eucalyptus trees at the airport gateway was always there like a welcome home. Somehow, he always found it reassuring when he came back from his trips. It was one of the things he loved about the city and he was glad it always greeted him.

He caught the light at Sepulveda and used the time to change the time on his watch. It was five minutes after two. He decided that he would have just enough time to get home, change into fresh clothes and grab something to eat before heading to Parker Center and his appointment with Carmen Hinojos.

He drove quickly under the 405 overpass and then took the curving on-ramp up onto the crowded freeway. As he turned the wheel to negotiate the turn, he realized that his upper arms ached deep in the biceps and he wasn't sure if it was from his fight with the fish on Saturday or from the way Jasmine had gripped his arms while they made love. He thought about her for a few more minutes and decided he would call her at the house before heading downtown. Their parting that morning already seemed long ago to him. They had made promises to meet again as soon as possible and Bosch hoped the promises would be kept. She was a mystery to him, one in which he knew he had not yet even begun to scratch the surface.

The 10 wasn't set to reopen until the following day, so Bosch bypassed the exit and stayed on the 405 until it rose over the Santa Monica Mountains and dropped into the Valley. He took the long way because he bet it would be faster, and because he had a mail drop in Studio City that he had been using since the post office refused to deliver mail to a red-tagged structure.

He transferred onto the 101 and promptly hit a wall of traffic inching its way along the six lanes. He stayed with it until impatience got the better of him. He exited Coldwater Canyon Boulevard and started taking surface streets. On Moorpark Road he passed several apartment buildings that still hadn't been demolished or repaired, the red tags and yellow tape bleached near-white by the months in the sun. Many of the condemned buildings still had signs like $500 MOVES YOU IN! and NEWLY REMODELED. On one red-tagged structure with the telltale crisscross stress fractures running along its entire length, someone had spray-painted a slogan that many took as the epitaph of the city in the months since the earthquake.

THE FAT LADY HAS SUNG

Somedays it was hard not to believe it. But Bosch tried to keep the faith. Somebody had to. The newspaper said more people were leaving than coming. But no matter, Bosch thought, I'm staying.

He cut over to Ventura and stopped at the private mailbox office. There was nothing but bills and junk mail in his box. He stopped at a deli next door and ordered the special, turkey on wholewheat with avocado and bean sprouts, to go. After that, he stayed on Ventura until it became Cahuenga and then took the turn off to Woodrow

Wilson Drive and the climb up the hill to home. On the first curve he had to slow on the narrow road to squeeze by an LAPD squad car. He waved but he knew they wouldn't know him. They would be out of North Hollywood Division. They didn't wave back.

He followed his usual practice of parking a half block away from his house and then walking back. He decided to leave the satchel in the trunk because he might need the files downtown. He headed down the street to his house with his overnighter in one hand and the sandwich bag in the other.

As he got to the carport, he noticed a patrol car coming up the road. He watched it and noticed it was the same two patrolmen he had just passed. They had turned around for some reason. He waited at the curb to see if they would stop to ask him for directions or maybe an explanation of his wave, and because he didn't want them to see him enter the condemned house. But the car drove by with neither of the patrolmen even looking at him. The driver had his eyes on the road and the passenger was talking into the radio microphone. It must be a call, Bosch thought. He waited until the car had gone around the next curve and then headed into the carport.

After opening the kitchen door, Bosch stepped in and immediately felt that something was amiss. He took two steps in before placing it. There was a foreign odor in the house, or at least the kitchen. It was the scent of perfume, he realized. No, he corrected, it was cologne. A man wearing cologne had either recently been in the house or was still there.

Bosch quietly placed his overnighter and the sandwich bag on the kitchen floor and reached to his waist. Old habits died hard. He still had no gun and he knew his backup was on the shelf in the closet near the front door. For a moment he thought about running out to the street in hopes of catching the patrol car but he knew it was long gone.

Instead, he opened a drawer and quietly withdrew a small paring knife. There were longer blades in there but the small knife would be easier to handle. He stepped toward the archway that led from the kitchen to the house's front entry. At the threshold, still hidden from whoever might be out there, he stopped, tilted his head forward and listened. He could hear the low hiss of the freeway down the hill behind the house, but nothing from within. Nearly a minute of silence passed. He was about to step out of the kitchen when he heard a sound. It was the slight whisper of cloth moving. Maybe the crossing or uncrossing of legs. He knew someone was in the living room. And he knew by now that they would know that he knew.

'Detective Bosch,' a voice said from the silence of the house. 'It is safe for you. You can come out.'

Bosch knew the voice but was operating at such an acute level of intensity, he couldn't immediately compute it and place it. All he knew was that he had heard it before.

'It's Assistant Chief Irving, Detective Bosch,' the voice said. 'Could you please step out? That way you don't get hurt and we don't get hurt.'

Yes, that was the voice. Bosch relaxed, put the knife down on the counter, the sandwich bag in the refrigerator and stepped out of the kitchen. Irving was there, sitting in the living room chair. Two men in suits whom Bosch didn't recognize sat on the couch. Looking around, Bosch could see his box of letters and cards from the closet sitting on the coffee table. He saw the murder book that he had left on the dining room table was sitting on the lap of one of the strangers. They had been searching his house, going through his things.

Bosch suddenly realized what had happened outside.

'I saw your lookout. Anybody want to tell me what's going on?'

'Where've you been, Bosch?' one of the suits asked.

Bosch looked at him. Not a single glimmer of recognition hit him.

'Who the fuck are you?'

He bent down and picked the box of cards and letters up off the coffee table, where it had been in front of the man.

'Detective,' Irving said, 'This is Lieutenant Angel Brockman and this is Earl Sizemore.'

Bosch nodded. He recognized one of the names.

'I've heard of you,' he said, looking at Brockman. 'You're the one who sent Bill Connors to the closet. That must've been good for IAD man of the month. Quite an honor.'

The sarcasm in Bosch's voice was unmistakable, as he intended it to be. The closet was where most cops kept their guns while off duty; going to the closet was department slang for a cop killing himself. Connors was an old beat cop in Hollywood Division who had killed himself the year before while he was under IAD investigation for trading dime bags of heroin to runaway girls for sex. After he was dead, the runaways had admitted making up the complaints because Connors was always hassling them to move off his beat. He had been a good man but saw everything stacked against him and decided to go to the closet.

'That was his choice, Bosch. And now you've got yours. You want to tell us where you've been the last twenty-four?'

'You want to tell me what this is about?'

He heard a clunking sound coming from the bedroom.

'What the hell?' He walked to the door and saw another suit in his bedroom, standing over the open drawer of the

278

night table. 'Hey, fuckhead, get out of there. Get out now!'

Bosch stepped in and kicked the drawer closed. The man stepped back, raised his hands like a prisoner and walked out to the living room.

'And this is Jerry Toliver,' Irving added. 'He's with Lieutenant Brockman, IAD. Detective Sizemore has joined us here from RHD.'

'Fantastic,' Bosch said. 'So everybody knows everybody. What's going on?'

He looked at Irving as he said this, believing if he was going to get a straight answer from anyone here, it would be him. Irving was generally a straight shooter when it came to his dealings with Bosch.

'De – Harry, we have got to ask you some questions,' Irving said. 'It would be best if we explain things later.'

Bosch could tell this one was serious.

'You got a warrant to be in here?'

'We'll show it to you later,' Brockman said. 'Let's go.'

'Where are we going?'

'Downtown.'

Bosch had had enough run-ins with the Internal Affairs Division to know things were being handled differently here. Just the fact that Irving, the second-highest-ranking officer in the department, was with them was an indication of the gravity of the situation. He guessed it was more than their simply finding out about his private investigation. If it was just that, Irving wouldn't have been here. There was something terribly wrong.

'All right,' Bosch said, 'who's dead?'

All four looked at him with faces of stone, confirming that in fact someone was dead. Bosch felt his chest tighten and for the first time he began to be scared. The names and faces of people he had involved flashed through his mind. Meredith Roman, Jake McKittrick, Keisha Russell, the two women in Las Vegas. Who else? Jazz? Could he have possibly put her in some kind of danger? Then it hit him. Keisha Russell. The reporter had probably done what he told her not to. She had gone to Conklin or Mittel and asked questions about the old clip she had pulled for Bosch. She had walked in blindly and was now dead because of her mistake.

'Keisha Russell?' he asked.

He got no reply. Irving stood up and the others followed. Sizemore kept the murder book in his hand. He was going to take it. Brockman went into the kitchen, picked up the overnighter and carried it to the door.

'Harry, why don't you ride with Earl and I?' Irving said.

'How 'bout I meet you guys down there.'

'You ride with me.'

It was said sternly. It invited no further debate. Bosch raised his hands, acknowledging he had no choice, and moved toward the door.

Bosch sat in the back of Sizemore's LTD, directly behind Irving. He looked out the window as they went down the hill. He kept thinking of the young reporter's face. Her eagerness had killed her but Bosch couldn't help but share the blame. He had planted the seed of mystery in her mind and it had grown until she couldn't resist it.

'Where'd they find her?' he asked.

He was met only with silence. He couldn't understand why they said nothing, especially Irving. The assistant chief had led him to believe in the past that they had an understanding, if not a liking, between each other.

'I told her not to do anything,' he said. 'I told her to sit on it a few days.'

Irving turned his body so that he could partially see Bosch behind him.

'Detective, I don't know who or what you're talking about.'

'Keisha Russell.'

'Don't know her.'

He turned back around. Bosch was puzzled. The names and faces went through his mind again. He added Jasmine but then subtracted her. She knew nothing about the case.

'McKittrick?'

'Detective,' Irving said and again struggled to turn around to look at Bosch. 'We are involved in the investigation of the homicide of Lieutenant Harvey Pounds. These other names are not involved. If you think they are people that should be contacted, please let me know.'

Bosch was too stunned to answer. Harvey Pounds? That made no sense. He had nothing to do with the case, didn't even know about it. Pounds never left the office, how could he have gotten into danger? Then it came to him, washing over him like a wave of water that brought with it a chill. He understood. It made sense. And in the moment that he saw that it did, he also saw his own responsibility as well as his own predicament.

'Am I ... ?'

He couldn't finish.

'Yes,' Irving said. 'You are currently considered a suspect. Now maybe you will be quiet until we can set up a formal interview.'

Bosch leaned his head against the window glass and closed his eyes.

'Ah, Jesus ...'

And in that moment he realized he was no better than Brockman was for having sent a man to the closet. For Bosch knew in the dark part of his heart that he was responsible. He didn't know how or when it had happened but he knew.

He had killed Harvey Pounds. And he carried Pounds's badge in his pocket.

❖ ❖ ❖ ❖ ❖ ❖ ❖

Bosch was numb to most of what was going on around him. After they reached Parker Center he was escorted up to Irving's office on the sixth floor and then placed in a chair in the adjoining conference room. He was in there alone for a half hour before Brockman and Toliver came in. Brockman sat directly across from Bosch, Toliver to Harry's right. It was obvious to Bosch by their being in Irving's conference room instead of an IAD interview room that Irving wanted to keep a tight control on this one. If it turned out to be a cop-killed-cop case, he'd need all the control he could muster to contain it. It could be a publicity debacle to rival those of the Rodney King days.

Through his daze and the jarring images of Pounds being dead, a pressing thought finally got Bosch's attention: he was in serious trouble himself. He told himself he couldn't retreat into a shell. He must be alert. The man sitting across from him would like nothing better than to hang a killing on Bosch and he was willing to go to any extreme to do it. It wasn't good enough that Bosch knew in his own mind that he had not, at least physically, killed Pounds. He had to defend himself. And so he resolved that he would show Brockman nothing. He would be just as tough as anybody in the room. He cleared his throat and began before Brockman got the chance.

'When did it happen?'

'I'm asking the questions.'

'I can save you time, Brockman. Tell me when it happened and I'll tell you where I was. We'll get this over with. I understand why I'm a suspect. I won't hold it against you but you're wasting your time.'

'Bosch, don't you feel anything at all? A man is dead. You worked with him.'

Bosch stared at him a long moment before answering in an even voice.

'What I feel doesn't matter. Nobody deserves to be killed, but I'm not going to miss him and I certainly won't miss working for him.'

'Jesus.' Brockman shook his head. 'The man had a wife, a kid in college.'

'Maybe they won't miss him, either. You never know. The guy was a prick at work. No reason to expect him to be anything else at home. What's your wife think about you, Brockman?'

'Save it, Bosch. I'm not falling for any of your –'

'Do you believe in God, Brickman?'

Bosch used Brockman's nickname in the department, awarded to him for his methodical way of building cases against other cops, like the late Bill Connors.

'This isn't about me or what I believe in, Bosch. We're talking about you.'

'That's right, we're talking about me. So, I'll tell you what I think. I'm not sure what I believe. My life's more than half over and I still haven't figured it out. But the theory I'm leaning toward is that everybody on this planet has some kind of energy that makes them what they are. It's all about energy. And when you die, it just goes somewhere else. And Pounds? He was bad energy and now it's gone somewhere else. So I don't feel too bad about him dying, to answer your question. But I'd like to know where that bad energy went. Hope you didn't get any, Brickman. You already have a lot.'

He winked at Brockman and saw the momentary confusion in the IAD detective's face as he tried to interpret what the jibe had meant. He seemed to shake it off and go on.

'Enough of the bullshit. Why did you confront Lieutenant Pounds in his office on Thursday? You know that was off limits while you are on leave.'

'Well, it was kind've like one of those Catch-22 situations. I think that's what they call 'em. It was off limits to go there but then Pounds, my commanding officer, called me up and told me I had to turn in my car. See, it was that bad energy working. I was already on involuntary leave but he couldn't leave well enough alone. He had to take my car, too. So I brought him in the keys. He was my supervisor and it was an order. So going there broke one of the rules but not going would have broken one, too.'

'Why'd you threaten him?'

'I didn't.'

'He filed an addendum to the assault complaint of two weeks earlier.'

'I don't care what he filed. There was no threat. The guy was a coward. He probably felt threatened. But there was no threat. There is a difference.'

Bosch looked over at the other suit. Toliver. It looked as if he was going to be silent the whole time. That was his role. He just stared at Bosch as if he were a TV screen.

Bosch looked around the rest of the room and for the first time noticed the phone on the banquette to the left of the table. The green light signaled a conference call was on. The interview was being piped out of the room. Probably to a tape recorder. Probably to Irving in his office next door.

'There is a witness,' Brockman said.

'To what?'

'The threat.'

'I'll tell you what, Lieutenant, why don't you tell me exactly what the threat was so I know what we're talking about. After all, if you believe I made it, what's wrong with me knowing what it was I said?'

Brockman gave it some thought before answering.

'Very simple, as most are, you told him if he ever, quote, fucked with you again, you'd kill him. Not too original.'

'But damning as hell, right? Well, fuck you, Brockman, I never said that. I don't doubt that that asshole wrote up an addendum, that was just his style, but whoever this wit is you got, they're full of shit.'

'You know Henry Korchmar?'

'Henry Korchmar?'

Bosch had no idea whom he was talking about. Then he realized Brockman meant old Henry of the Nod Squad. Bosch had never known his last name and so hearing it in this context had confused him.

'The old guy? He wasn't in the room. He's no witness. I told him to get out and he did. Whatever he told you, he probably backed Pounds because he was scared. But he wasn't there. You go ahead with it, Brockman. I'll be able to pull twelve people out of that squadroom who watched the whole thing through the glass. And they'll say Henry wasn't in there, they'll say Pounds was a liar and everybody knew it, and then where's your threat?'

Brockman said nothing into the silence so Bosch continued.

'See, you didn't do your work. My guess is that you know everybody who works in that squadroom thinks people like you are the bottom feeders of this department. They've got more respect for the people they put in jail.

And you know that, Brickman, so you were too intimidated to go to them. Instead, you rely on some old man's word and he probably didn't even know Pounds was dead when you talked to him.'

Bosch could tell by the way Brockman's eyes darted away that he had nailed him. Empowered with the victory, he stood up and headed toward the door.

'Where are you going?'

'To get some water.'

'Jerry, go with him.'

Bosch paused at the door and looked back.

'What, do you think I'm going to run, Brockman? You think that and you don't know the first thing about me. You think that and you haven't prepared for this interview. Why don't you come over to Hollywood one day and I'll teach you how to interview murder suspects. Free of charge.'

Bosch walked out, Toliver following. At the water fountain down the hall, he took a long drink of water and then wiped his mouth with his hand. He felt nervous, frayed. He didn't know how long it would be before Brockman could see through the front he was putting up.

As he walked back to the conference room, Toliver stayed a silent three paces behind him.

'You're still young,' Bosch said over his shoulder. 'There might be a chance for you, Toliver.'

Bosch stepped back into the conference room just as Brockman stepped through a door from the other side of the room. Bosch knew it was a direct entrance to Irving's office. He had once worked an investigation of a serial killer out of this room and under Irving's thumb.

Both men sat down across from each other again.

'Now, then,' Brockman started. 'I'm going to read you your rights, Detective Bosch.'

He took a small card from his wallet and proceeded to

read to Bosch the Miranda warning. Bosch knew for sure the phone line was going to a tape recorder. This was something they would want on tape.

'Now,' Brockman said when he was finished. 'Do you agree to waive those rights and talk to us about this situation?'

'It's a situation now, huh? I thought it was a murder. Yeah, I'll waive.'

'Jerry, go get a waiver, I don't have one here.'

Jerry got up and left through the hallway door. Bosch could hear his feet moving quickly on the linoleum, then a door open. He was taking the stairs down to IAD on the fifth.

'Uh, let's start by –'

'Don't you want to wait until you have your witness back? Or is this being secretly recorded without my knowledge?'

This immediately flustered Brockman.

'Yes, Bosch it's being sec – it's being recorded. But not secretly. We told you before we started that we'd be taping.'

'Good cover-up, Lieutenant. That last line, that was a good one. I'll have to remember that one.'

'Now, let's start with –'

The door opened and Toliver came in with a sheet of paper. He handed it to Brockman, who studied it a moment, made sure it was the correct form and slid it across the table to Bosch. Harry grabbed it and quickly scribbled a signature on the appropriate line. He was familiar with the form. He slid it back and Brockman put it off to the side of the table without looking at it. So he didn't notice the signature Bosch had written was 'Fuck You.'

'All right, let's get this going. Bosch, give us your whereabouts over the last seventy-two hours.'

'You don't want to search me first, do you? How 'bout you, Jerry?'

Bosch stood up, opening his jacket so they could see he was not armed. He thought by taunting them like this they would do the exact opposite and not search him. Carrying Pounds's badge was a piece of evidence that would probably put him in the ground if they discovered it.

'Siddown, Bosch!' Brockman barked. 'We're not going to search you. We're trying to give you every benefit of the doubt but you make it damn hard.'

Bosch sat back down, relieved for the time being.

'Now, just give us your whereabouts. We don't have all day.'

Bosch thought about this. He was surprised by the window of time they wanted. Seventy-two hours. He wondered what had happened to Pounds and why they hadn't narrowed time of death to a shorter span.

'Seventy-two hours ago. Well, about seventy-two hours ago it was Friday afternoon and I was in Chinatown at the Fifty-One-Fifty building. Which reminds me, I'm due over there in ten minutes. So, boys, if you'll excuse me …'

He stood up.

'Siddown, Bosch. That's been taken care of. Sit down.'

Bosch sat down and said nothing. He realized, though, that he actually felt disappointed he would miss the session with Carmen Hinojos.

'Come on, Bosch, let's hear it. What happened after that?'

'I don't remember all the details. But I ate over at the Red Wind that night, also stopped at the Epicentre for a few drinks. Then I got to the airport about ten. I took a red-eye to Florida, to Tampa, spent the weekend there and got back about an hour and a half before I found you people illegally inside my home.'

'It's not illegal. We had a warrant.'

'I've been shown no warrant.'

'Never mind that, what do you mean you were in Florida?'

'I guess I mean I was in Florida. What do you think it means?'

'You can prove this?'

Bosch reached into his pocket, took out his airline folder with the ticket receipt and slid it across the table.

'For starters there's the ticket receipt. I think there's one in there for a rental car, too.'

Brockman quickly opened the ticket folder and started reading.

'What were you doing there?' he asked without looking up.

'Dr Hinojos, that's the company shrink, said I should try to get away. And I thought, how 'bout Florida? I'd never been there and all my life I've liked orange juice. I thought, what the hell? Florida.'

Brockman was flustered again. He wasn't expecting something like this. Bosch could tell. Most cops never realized how important the initial interview with a suspect or witness was to an investigation. It informed all other interviews and even court testimony that followed. You had to be prepared. Like lawyers, you had to know most of the answers before you asked the questions. The IAD relied so much on its presence as an intimidating factor that most of the detectives assigned to the division never really had to prepare for interviews. And when they hit a wall like this, they didn't know what to do.

'Okay, Bosch, uh, what did you do in Florida?'

'You ever heard that song Marvin Gaye sang? Before he got killed? It's called –'

'What are you talking about?'

'– "Sexual Healing." It says it's good for the soul.'

'I've heard it,' Toliver said.

Both Brockman and Bosch looked at him.

'Sorry,' he offered.

'Again, Bosch,' Brockman said. 'What are you talking about?'

'I'm talking about that I spent most of the time with a woman I know there. Most of the other time I spent with a fishing guide on a boat in the Gulf of Mexico. What I'm talking about, asshole, is that I was with people almost every minute. And the times I wasn't weren't long enough for me to fly back here and kill Pounds. I don't even know when he was killed but I'll tell you right now you don't have a case, Brockman, because there is no case. You're looking in the wrong direction.'

Bosch had chosen his words carefully. He was unsure what, if anything, they knew about his private investigation and he wasn't going to give them anything if he could help it. They had the murder book and the evidence box but he thought that he might be able to explain all of that away. They also had his notebook because he had stuffed it into his overnighter at the airport. In it were the names, numbers and addresses of Jasmine and McKittrick, the address of the Eno house in Vegas, and other notes about the case. But they might not be able to put together what it all meant. Not if he was lucky.

Brockman pulled a notebook and pen from the inside pocket of his jacket.

'Okay, Bosch, give me the name of the woman and this fishing guide. I need their numbers, everything.'

'I don't think so.'

Brockman's eyes widened.

'I don't care what you think, give me the names.'

Bosch said nothing, just stared down at the table in front of him.

'Bosch, you've told us your whereabouts, now we need to confirm them.'

'I know where I was at, that's all I need.'

'If you're in the clear, as you claim, let us check it out, clear you and move on to other things, other possibilities.'

'You've got the airlines and the car rental right there. Start with that. I'm not dragging people into this who don't need to be. They're good people and unlike you, they like me. I'm not going to let you spoil that by having you come in with your concrete block feet and step all over the relationships.'

'You don't have a choice, Bosch.'

'Oh, yes, I do. Right now, I do. You want to try to make a case against me, do it. If it gets to that point, I'll bring these people out and they'll blow your shit away, Brockman. You think at the moment you've got PR problems in the department over sending Bill Connors to the closet? You'll end this case with worse PR than Nixon had. I'm not giving you the names. If you want to write something down there in your notebook, just write that I said "Fuck you." That ought to cover it.'

Brockman's face got kind of blotchy with pinks and whites. He was quiet a moment before speaking.

'Know what I think? I still think you did it. I think you hired somebody to do it and you went waltzing off to Florida so you'd be nowhere near here. A fishing guide. If that doesn't sound like a conjured-up piece of shit I don't know what does. And the woman? Who was she, some hooker you picked up in a bar? What was she, a fifty-dollar alibi? Or did you go a hundred?'

In one explosive move, Bosch shoved the table toward Brockman, catching him completely by surprise. It slid under his arms and crashed into his chest. His chair tipped back against the wall behind him. Bosch kept the pressure on his end and pinned Brockman against the wall. Bosch pushed back on his own chair until it was against the wall behind him. He raised his left leg and put his foot against the table to keep the pressure on it. He saw the blotches of color on Brockman's face become more pronounced as he went without air. His eyes bugged. But he had no leverage and couldn't move the table off himself.

Toliver was slow to react. Stunned, he seemed to look at Brockman for a long moment as if awaiting orders before jumping up and moving toward Bosch. Bosch was able to fend off his first effort, shoving the younger man back into a potted palm tree that was in the corner of the room. While Bosch did this, he saw in his peripheral vision a figure enter the room through the other door. Then his chair was abruptly knocked over and he was on the ground with a heavy weight on top of him. By turning his head slightly he could see it was Irving.

'Don't move, Bosch!' Irving yelled in his ear. 'Settle down right now!'

Bosch went limp to signify his compliance and Irving got off him. Bosch stayed still for a few moments and then put a hand up on the table to pull himself up. As he got up, he saw Brockman hacking and trying to get air into his lungs while holding both hands against his chest. Irving held one hand out to Bosch's chest as a calming gesture and a means of stopping him from taking another run at Brockman. With his other hand, he pointed at Toliver, who was trying to right the potted palm. It had become uprooted and wouldn't stand up. He finally just leaned it against the wall.

'You,' Irving snapped at him. 'Out.'

'But, sir, the –'

'Get out!'

Toliver quickly left through the hallway door as Brockman was finally finding his voice.

'Buh … Bosch, you sonova bitch, you … you're going to jail. You –'

'Nobody's going to jail,' Irving said sternly. 'Nobody's going to jail.'

Irving stopped to gulp down some air. Bosch noticed that the assistant chief seemed just as winded as anybody in the room.

'There will be no charges on this,' Irving finally continued. 'Lieutenant, you baited him and got what you got.'

Irving's tone invited no debate. Brockman, his chest still heaving, put his elbows on the table and began running his fingers through his hair, trying to look as if he still had some composure but all he had was defeat. Irving turned to Bosch, anger bunching the muscles of his jaw into hard surfaces.

'And you. Bosch, I don't know how to help you. You're always the loose cannon. You knew what he was doing, you've done it yourself. But you couldn't sit there and take it. What kind of man are you?'

Bosch didn't say anything and he doubted Irving wanted a spoken answer. Brockman started coughing and Irving looked back at him.

'Are you all right?'

'I think.'

'Go across the street, have one of the paramedics check you out.'

'No, I'm all right.'

'Good, then go down to your office, take a break. I have someone else I want to have talk to Bosch.'

'I want to continue the inter –'

'The interview is over, Lieutenant. You blew it.' Then, looking at Bosch, he added, 'You both did.'

❖ ❖ ❖ ❖ ❖ ❖ ❖

I rving left Bosch alone in the conference room and in a
few moments Carmen Hinojos walked in. She took the
same seat that Brockman had sat in. She looked at
Bosch with eyes that seemed filled with equal parts anger
and disappointment. But Bosch didn't flinch under her
gaze.

'Harry, I can't believe –'

He held a finger up to his mouth, silencing her.

'What is it?'

'Are our sessions still supposed to be private?'

'Of course.'

'Even in here?'

'Yes. What is it?'

Bosch got up and walked to the phone on the counter.
He pushed the button that disconnected the conference
call. He returned to his seat.

'I hope that was left on unintentionally. I'm going to
speak to Chief Irving about that.'

'You're probably speaking to him right now. The
phone was too obvious. He's probably got the room
wired.'

'C'mon, Harry, this isn't the CIA.'

'No, it's not. Sometimes it's even worse. All I'm saying
is Irving, the IAD, they still might be listening somehow.
Be careful what you say.'

Carmen Hinojos looked exasperated.

'I'm not paranoid, Doctor. I've been through this before.'

'All right, never mind. I really don't care who's listening or not. I can't believe what you just did. It makes me very sad and disappointed. What have our meetings been about? Nothing? I'm sitting in there hearing you resort to the same type of violence that brought you to me in the first place. Harry, this isn't some joke. This is real life. And I have to make a decision that could very well decide your future. This makes it all the more difficult to do.'

He waited until he was sure she was done.

'You were in there with Irving the whole time?'

'Yes, he called and explained the situation and asked me to come over and sit in. I have to say –'

'Wait a minute. Before we go any further. Did you talk to him? Did you tell him about our sessions?'

'No, of course not.'

'Okay, for the record, I just want to reiterate that I do not give up any of my protections under the patient-doctor relationship. We okay on that?'

For the first time she looked away from him. He could see her face turning dark with anger.

'Do you know what an insult that is for you to tell me that? What, do you think I'd tell him about our sessions just because he may have ordered me to?'

'Did he?'

'You don't trust me at all, do you?'

'Did he?'

'No, he didn't.'

'That's good.'

'It's not just me. You don't trust anyone.'

Bosch realized that he had been out of line. He could see, though, that there was more hurt than anger in her face.

'I'm sorry, you're right, I shouldn't have said that. I'm

just … I don't know, I've got my back to the corner here, Doctor. When that happens, sometimes you forget who's on your side and who isn't.'

'Yes, and as a matter of course you respond with violence against those who you perceive are not on your side. This is not good to see. It's very, very disappointing.'

He looked away from her and over to the potted palm in the corner. Before leaving the room, Irving had replanted it, getting his hands dirty with black soil. Bosch noticed it was still slightly tilted to the left.

'So what are you doing up here?' he asked. 'What does Irving want?'

'He wanted me to sit in his office and listen to your interview on the conference line. He said he was interested in my evaluation of your answers as to whether I believed you could have been responsible for the death of Lieutenant Pounds. Thanks to you and your attack on your interviewer, he didn't need any evaluation from me. It's clear at this point you are prone to and quite capable of violence against fellow police officers.'

'That's bullshit and you know it. Damn it, what I did in here to that guy masquerading as a cop was a lot different than what they think I did. You're talking about things that are worlds apart and if you don't see that, you're making your living in the wrong business.'

'I'm not so sure.'

'Have you ever killed anyone, Doctor?'

Saying the question reminded him of his true confessions conversation with Jasmine.

'Of course not.'

'Well, I have. And believe me it's a lot different than roughing up some pompous ass in a suit with a shine on its ass. A lot different. If you or they think that doing one means you can do the other, you all have a lot to learn.'

They were both quiet for a long while, letting their anger ebb away.

'All right,' he finally said. 'So what happens now?'

'I don't know. Chief Irving just asked me to sit in with you, to calm you. I guess he's figuring out what to do next. I guess I'm not doing a very good job of calming you.'

'What did he say when he first asked you to come up here and listen?'

'He just called me and explained what happened and said he wanted my take on the interview. You have to understand something, despite your problems with authority, he is one person who I think is in your court on this. I don't think he honestly believes you're involved in the death of your lieutenant – at least directly. But he realizes that you are a viable suspect who needs to be questioned. I think if you had held your temper during the interview this all might've been over for you soon. They would've checked your story in Florida and that would have been the end of it. I even told them that you told me you were going to Florida.'

'I don't want them checking my story. I don't want them involved.'

'Well, it's too late. He knows you're up to something.'

'How?'

'When he called to ask me to come over he mentioned the file on your mother's case. The murder book. He said it was found at your house. He also said they found the stored evidence from the case there ...'

'And?'

'And he asked if I knew what you were doing with all of it.'

'So he did ask you to reveal what we've talked about in our sessions.'

'In an indirect way.'

'Sounds pretty direct to me. Did he say specifically that it was my mother's case?'

'Yes, he did.'

'What did you tell him?'

'I told him that I was not at liberty to discuss anything that was talked about in our sessions. It didn't satisfy him.'

'I'm not surprised.'

Another wave of silence washed between them. Her eyes wandered the room. His stayed on hers.

'Listen, what do you know about what happened to Pounds?'

'Very little.'

'Irving must have told you something. You must've asked.'

'He said Pounds was found in the trunk of his car Sunday evening. I guess he had been there a while. A day maybe. The chief said he … the body showed signs of torture. Particularly sadistic mutilation, he said. He didn't go into detail. It had happened before Pounds was dead. They do know that. He said that he'd been in a lot of pain. He wanted to know if you were the type of man who could've done that.'

Bosch said nothing. He was imagining the crime scene in his mind. His guilt came crushing back down on him and for a moment he thought he might even get nauseous.

'For what it's worth, I said no.'

'What?'

'I told him you weren't the type of man who could've done that.'

Bosch nodded. But his thoughts were already a great distance away again. What had happened to Pounds was becoming clear and Bosch carried the guilt of having set things in motion. Though legally innocent, he knew he was morally culpable. Pounds was a man he despised, had less respect for than some of the murderers he had known.

But the weight of the guilt was bearing down on him. He ran his hands hard over his face and through his hair. He felt a shudder move through his body.

'Are you all right?' Hinojos asked.

'I'm fine.'

Bosch took out his cigarettes and started to light one with his Bic.

'Harry, you better not. This isn't my office.'

'I don't care. Where was he found?'

'What?'

'Pounds! Where was he found?'

'I don't know. You mean where was the car? I don't know. I didn't ask.'

She studied him and he noticed the hand that held his cigarette was shaking.

'All right, Harry, that's it. What's the matter? What is going on?'

Bosch looked at her for a long moment and nodded.

'Okay, you want to know? I did it. I killed him.'

Her face immediately reacted as if perhaps she had seen the killing firsthand, so close that she had been spattered with blood. It was a horrible face. Repulsed. And she moved back in her chair as if even a few more inches of separation from him were needed.

'You ... you mean this story about Florida was –'

'No. I don't mean I killed him. Not with my hands. I mean what I've done, what I've been doing. It got him killed. I got him killed.'

'How do you know? You can't know for sure that –'

'I know. Believe me, I know.'

He looked away from her to a painting on the wall over the banquette. It was a generic depiction of a beach scene. He looked back at Hinojos.

'It's funny ... ,' he said but didn't finish. He just shook his head.

'What is?'

He got up and reached to the potted palm and stubbed the cigarette out in the dark soil.

'What is funny, Harry?'

He sat back down and looked at her.

'The civilized people in the world, the ones who hide behind culture and art and politics ... and even the law, they're the ones to watch out for. They've got that perfect disguise goin' for them, you know? But they're the most vicious. They're the most dangerous people on earth.'

❖ ❖ ❖ ❖ ❖ ❖ ❖

It seemed to Bosch that the day would never end, that he would never get out of the conference room. After Hinojos left, it was Irving's turn. He came in silently, took the Brockman seat and folded his hands on the table and said nothing. He looked irritated. Bosch thought maybe he smelled the smoke. Bosch didn't care about that but he found the silence discomforting.

'What about Brockman?'

'He's gone. You heard me tell him, he blew it. So did you.'

'How's that?'

'You could've talked your way out of it. Could've let him check your story and be done with it. But you had to make another enemy. You had to be Harry Bosch.'

'That's where you and I differ, Chief. You oughta get out of the office and come out on the street again sometime. I didn't make Brockman an enemy. He was my enemy before I even met him. They all are. And, you know, I'm really getting tired of everybody analyzing me and sticking their noses up my ass. It's getting real old.'

'Somebody's got to do it. You don't.'

'You don't know a thing about it.'

Irving waved Bosch's pale defense away like cigarette smoke.

'So what now?' Bosch continued. 'Why are you here?

You going to try to break my alibi now? Is that it? Brockman's out and you're in?'

'I don't need to break your alibi. It's been checked and it looks like it holds. Brockman and his people have already been instructed to follow other avenues of investigation.'

'What do you mean, it's been checked?'

'Give us some credit here, Bosch. The names were in your notebook.'

He reached into his coat and pulled out the notebook. He tossed it across the table to Bosch.

'This woman that you spent some time with over there, she told me enough to the point that I believed it. You might want to call her yourself, though. She certainly seemed confused by my call. I was rather circumspect in my explanation.'

'I appreciate that. So, then, I guess I'm free to split?' Bosch stood up.

'In a technical sense.'

'And the other senses?'

'Sit down for a minute, Detective.'

Bosch held his hands up. He'd gone this far. He decided he might as well go all the way and hear it all. He sat back down in his chair with a meager protest.

'My butt's getting sore from all this sitting.'

'I knew Jake McKittrick,' Irving said. 'Knew him well. We worked Hollywood together many years ago. But you know that already. As nice as it is to touch base with an old colleague, I can't say I enjoyed anything about the conversation I had with my old friend Jake.'

'You called him, too.'

'While you were in here with the doctor.'

'So then what do you want from me? You got the story from him, what's left?'

Irving drummed his fingers on the tabletop.

'What do I want? What I want is for you to tell me that what you are doing, what you have been doing, is in no way connected to what has happened to Lieutenant Pounds.'

'I can't, Chief. I don't know what happened to him, other than that he's dead.'

Irving studied Bosch for a long moment, contemplating something, deciding whether to treat him as an equal and tell him the story.

'I guess I expected an immediate denial. Your answer already suggests that you think there might be a correlation. I can't tell you how much that bothers me.'

'Anything is possible, Chief. Let me ask you this. You said Brockman and his crew were out chasing other leads – I guess avenues is what you said. Are any of these avenues viable? I mean, did Pounds have a secret life or are they just out there chasing their tails?'

'There's nothing that stands out. I'm afraid you were the best lead. Brockman still thinks so. He wants to pursue the theory that you hired a hitman of some sort and then flew to Florida to establish an alibi.'

'Yeah, that's a good one.'

'I think it stretches credibility some. I told him to drop it. For the moment. And I'm telling you to drop what you are doing. This woman in Florida sounds like the kind of person you could spend some time with. I want you to get on a plane and go back to her. Stay a couple weeks. When you come back, we'll talk about going back on the homicide table at Hollywood.'

Bosch was unsure whether there was a threat in all that Irving had just said. If not a threat, then maybe a bribe.

'And if I don't?'

'If you don't, then you are stupid. And you deserve whatever happens to you.'

'What is it that you think I'm doing, Chief?'

'I don't *think*, I *know* what you're doing. It's easy. You pulled the book on your mother's homicide. Why at this particular point in time you've done this, I don't know. But you're out running a freelance investigation and that's a problem for us. You have to stop it, Harry, or I'll stop you. I'll shut you down. Permanently.'

'Who are you protecting?'

Bosch saw the anger move into Irving's face as his skin turned from pink to an intense red. His eyes seemed to grow smaller and darker with fury.

'Don't you ever suggest such a thing. I've dedicated my life to this depart –'

'It's yourself, isn't it? You knew her. You found her. You're afraid of being dragged into this if I put something together on it. I bet you already knew everything McKittrick told you on the phone.'

'That's ridiculous, I –'

'Is it? Is it? I don't think so. I've already talked to one witness who remembers you from those days on the Boulevard beat.'

'What witness?'

'She said she knew you. She knows my mother knew you, too.'

'The only person I am protecting is you, Bosch. Can't you see that? I'm *ordering* you to stop this investigation.'

'You can't. I don't work for you anymore. I'm on leave, remember? Involuntary leave. That makes me a citizen now, and I can do whatever I goddamn want to do as long as it's legal.'

'I could charge you with possession of stolen documents – the murder book.'

'It wasn't stolen. Besides, what if you bullshit a case, what's that, a misdemeanor? They'll laugh you out of the city attorney's office on your ass with that.'

'But you'd lose your job. That would be it.'

'You're a little late with that one, Chief. A week ago that would've been a valid threat. I'd have to consider it. But it doesn't matter anymore. I'm free of all of that bullshit now and this is all that matters to me and I don't care what I have to do, I'm doing it.'

Irving was silent and Bosch guessed that the assistant chief was realizing that Bosch had moved beyond his reach. Irving's hold over Bosch's job and future had been his leverage before. But Bosch had finally broken free. Bosch began again in a low, calm voice.

'If you were me, Chief, could you just walk away? What does doing what I do for the department matter if I can't do this for her … and for me?'

He stood up and put the notebook into his jacket pocket.

'I'm going. Where's the rest of my stuff?'

'No.'

Bosch hesitated. Irving looked up at him and Bosch saw the anger was gone now.

'I did nothing wrong,' Irving said quietly.

'Sure you did,' Bosch said just as quietly. He leaned over the table until he was only a few feet away. 'We all did, Chief. We let it go. That was our crime. But not anymore. At least, not with me. If you want to help, you know how to reach me.'

He headed toward the door.

'What do you want?'

Bosch looked back at him.

'Tell me about Pounds. I need to know what happened. It's the only way I'll know if it's connected.'

'Then sit down.'

Bosch took the chair by the door and sat down. They both took some time to calm down before Irving finally spoke.

'We started looking for him Saturday night. We found

305

his car Sunday noon in Griffith Park. One of the tunnels closed after the quake. It was like they knew we'd be looking from the air, so they put the car in a tunnel.'

'Why'd you start looking before you knew he was dead?'

'The wife. She started calling Saturday morning. She said he'd gotten a call Friday night at home, she didn't know who. But whoever it was managed to convince Pounds to leave the house and meet him. Pounds didn't tell his wife what it was about. He said he'd be back in an hour or two. He left and never came back. In the morning she called us.'

'Pounds is unlisted, I assume.'

'Yes. That gives rise to the probability it was someone in the department.'

Bosch thought about this.

'Not necessarily. It just had to be someone with connections to people in the city. People that could get his number with a phone call. You ought to put out the word. Grant amnesty to anyone who comes forward and says they gave up the number. Say you'll go light in exchange for the name of the person they gave it to. That's who you want. Chances are whoever gave out the number didn't know what was going to happen.'

Irving nodded.

'That's an idea. Within the department there are hundreds who could get his number. There may be no other way to go.'

'Tell me more about Pounds.'

'We went to work right there in the tunnel. By Sunday the media had wind that we were looking for him, so the tunnel worked to our advantage. No helicopters flying over, bothering us. We just set up lights in the tunnel.'

'He was in the car?'

Bosch was acting like he knew nothing. He knew that if

he expected Hinojos to respect his confidences, he must in turn respect hers.

'Yes, he was in the trunk. And, my God, was it bad. He ... He'd been stripped of his clothes. He'd been beaten. Then – then there was the evidence of torture ...'

Bosch waited but Irving had stopped.

'What? What did they do to him?'

'They burned him. The genitals, nipples, fingers ... My God.'

Irving ran his hand over his shaven scalp and closed his eyes while he did it. Bosch could see that he could not get the images out of his mind. Bosch was having trouble with it, too. His guilt was like a palpable object in his chest.

'It was like they wanted something from him,' Irving said. 'But he couldn't give it. He didn't have it and ... and they kept at him.'

Suddenly, Bosch felt the slight tremor of an earthquake and reached for the table to steady himself. He looked at Irving for confirmation and realized there was no tremor. It was himself, shaking again.

'Wait a minute.'

The room tilted slightly then righted itself.

'What is it?'

'Wait a minute.'

Without another word Bosch stood up and went out the door. He quickly went down the hall to the men's room by the water fountain. There was someone in front of one of the sinks shaving but Bosch didn't take the time to look at him. He pushed through one of the stall doors and vomited into the toilet, barely making it in time.

He flushed the toilet but the spasm came again and then again until he was empty, until he had nothing left inside but the image of Pounds naked and dead, tortured.

'You okay in there, buddy?' a voice said from outside the stall.

'Just leave me alone.'

'Sorry, just asking.'

Bosch stayed in the stall a few more minutes, leaning against the wall. Eventually, he wiped his mouth with toilet paper and then flushed it down. He stepped out of the stall unsteadily and went to the sink. The other man was still there. Now he was putting on a tie. Bosch glanced at him in the mirror but didn't recognize him. He bent over the sink and rinsed his face and mouth out with cold water. He then used paper towels to dry off. He never looked at himself once in the mirror.

'Thanks for asking,' he said as he left.

Irving looked as if he hadn't moved while Bosch was gone.

'Are you all right?'

Bosch sat down and took out his cigarettes.

'Sorry, but I'm gonna smoke.'

'You already have been.'

Bosch lit up and took a deep drag. He stood up and walked to the trash can in the corner. There was an old coffee cup in it and he took it to use as an ashtray.

'Just one,' he said. 'Then you can open the door and air the place out.'

'It's a bad habit.'

'In this town so is breathing. How did he die? What was the fatal injury?'

'The autopsy was this morning. Heart failure. The strain on him was too much, his heart gave way.'

Bosch paused a moment. He felt the beginning of his strength coming back.

'Why don't you tell me the rest of it?'

'There is no rest of it. That's it. There was nothing there. No evidence on the body. No evidence in the car. It had been wiped clean. There was nothing to go on.'

'What about his clothes?'

'They were there in the trunk. No help. The killer kept one thing, though.'

'What?'

'His shield. The bastard took his badge.'

Bosch just nodded and averted his eyes. They were both silent for a long time. Bosch couldn't get the images out of his mind and he guessed Irving was having the same problem.

'So,' Bosch finally said, 'looking at what had been done to him, the torture and everything, you immediately thought of me. That's a real vote of confidence.'

'Look, Detective, you had put the man's face through a window two weeks earlier. We had gotten an added report from him that you had threatened him. What –'

'There was no threat. He –'

'I don't care if there was or wasn't. He made the report. That's the point. True or false, he made the report, therefore, he felt threatened by you. What were we supposed to do, ignore it? Just say, "Harry Bosch? Oh, no, there's no way our own Harry Bosch could do this," and go on? Don't be ridiculous.'

'All right, you're right. Forget it. He didn't say anything at all to his wife before leaving?'

'Only that someone called and he had to go out for an hour to a meeting with a very important person. No name was mentioned. The call came in about nine Friday night.'

'Is that exactly how she said he said it?'

'I believe so. Why?'

'Because if he said it in that way, then it sounds like two people may be involved.'

'How so?'

'It just sounds as though one person called him to set up a meeting with a second person, this very important person. If that person had made the call, then he would have told the wife that so and so, the big important guy, just called and I have to go meet him. See what I mean?'

'I do. But whoever called could have also used the name of an important person as bait to draw Pounds out. That actual person may not have been involved at all.'

'That's also true. But I think that whatever was said, it would have to have been convincing to get Pounds out at night, by himself.'

'Maybe it was someone he already knew.'

'Maybe. But then he probably would have told his wife the name.'

'True.'

'Did he take anything with him? A briefcase, files, anything?'

'Not that we know of. The wife was in the TV room. She didn't see him actually go out the door. We've been over all of this with her, we've been all over the house. There's nothing. His briefcase was in his office at the station. He didn't even take it home with him. There's nothing to go on. To be honest, you were the best candidate and you're clear now. It brings me back to my question. Could what you've been doing have had anything to do with this?'

Bosch could not bring himself to tell Irving what he thought, what he knew in his gut had happened to Pounds. It wasn't the guilt that stopped him, though. It was the desire to keep his mission to himself. In that moment he realized that vengeance was a singular thing, a solo mission, something never to be spoken of out loud.

'I don't know the answer,' he said. 'I told Pounds nothing. But he wanted me to go down. You know that. The guy's dead but he was an asshole and he wanted me to go down. So he'd have had his ear to the ground for anything about me. A couple people have seen me around in the last week. Word could've gotten back to him and he could've blundered into something. He wasn't much of an investigator. He could've made a mistake. I don't know.'

Irving looked at him through dead eyes. Bosch knew he was trying to determine how much was true and how much was bullshit. Bosch spoke first.

'He said he was going to meet someone important.'

'Yes.'

'Look, Chief, I don't know what McKittrick told you about the conversation I had out there with him, but you know there were important people involved back … you know, with my mother. You were there.'

'Yes, I was there, but I wasn't part of the investigation, not after the first day.'

'Did McKittrick tell you about Arno Conklin?'

'Not today. But back then. I remember once when I asked him what was happening with the case, he told me to ask Arno. He said Arno was running interference for someone on it.'

'Well, Arno Conklin was an important person.'

'But now? He's an old man if he's even still alive.'

'He's alive, Chief. And you have to remember something. Important men surround themselves with important men. They're never alone. Conklin may be old but there could be someone else who isn't.'

'What are you telling me, Bosch?'

'I'm telling you to leave me alone. I have to do this. I'm the only one who can. I'm telling you to keep Brockman and everybody else away from me.'

Irving stared at him a long moment and Bosch could tell he didn't know which way to go with this. Bosch stood up.

'I'll keep in touch.'

'You're not telling me everything.'

'It's better that way.'

He stepped through the door into the hallway, remembered something and then stepped back into the room with Irving.

'How am I going to get home? You brought me here.'

Irving reached over to the phone.

✤ ✤ ✤ ✤ ✤ ✤ ✤

Bosch went through the fifth-floor door to the Internal Affairs Division and found no one behind the counter. He waited a few moments for Toliver to show up since Irving had just ordered him to drive Bosch home, but the young IAD detective never showed. Bosch figured it was just one more mind game they were trying to play with him. He didn't want to walk around the counter and have to find Toliver so he just yelled his name out. Behind the counter was a door that was slightly ajar and he was reasonably sure Toliver heard the call.

But the person who stepped through the door was Brockman. He stared at Bosch for a long moment without saying anything.

'Look, Brockman, Toliver is supposed to run me home,' Bosch said to him. 'I don't want anything else to do with you.'

'Yeah, well, that's too bad.'

'Just get Toliver.'

'You better watch out for me, Bosch.'

'Yeah, I know. I'll be watching.'

'Yeah, and you won't see me coming.'

Bosch nodded and looked past him to the door where he expected Toliver to step out any moment. He just wanted to diffuse the situation and get his ride home. He considered walking out and catching a cab, but he knew in rush hour it would probably cost him fifty bucks. He didn't have it on him. Plus, he liked the idea of having an IAD shine chauffeur him home.

'Hey, killer?'

Bosch looked back at Brockman. He was getting tired of this.

'What's it like to fuck another killer? Must really be something, to go all the way to Florida for it.'

Bosch tried to stay cool but he felt his face betray himself. For he suddenly knew who and what Brockman was talking about.

'What are you talking about?'

Brockman's face lit up with a bully's delight as he read Bosch's surprised look.

'Oooh, baby! She didn't even bother telling you, did she?'

'Tell me what?'

Bosch wanted to reach over the counter and drag Brockman across it but at least outwardly he maintained his cool.

'Tell you what? I'll tell you what. I think your whole story stinks and I'm going to bust it open. Then Mr Clean upstairs isn't going to be able to protect you.'

'He said you were told to leave me alone, that I was clear.'

'Fuck him and fuck you. When I come in with your alibi in a bag, he's not going to have a choice but to cut you loose.'

Toliver stepped through the doorway behind the counter. He was holding a set of car keys in his hands. He stood silently behind Brockman with his eyes down.

'First thing I did was run her on the computer,' Brockman said. 'She's got a record, Bosch. You didn't know that? She's a killer, just like you. Takes one to know one, I guess. Nice couple.'

Bosch wanted to ask a thousand questions but he

wouldn't ask any of this man. He felt a deep void opening inside as he began jettisoning his feelings for Jazz. He realized that she had left all the signs out for him but he hadn't read them. Even so, the feeling that descended on him with the strongest grip was one of betrayal.

Bosch pointedly ignored Brockman and looked at Toliver.

'Hey, kid, you going to give me a ride or what?'

Toliver moved around the counter without answering.

'Bosch, I already got you on an association beef,' Brockman said. 'But I'm not satisfied.'

Bosch went to the hallway door and opened it. It was against LAPD regulations to associate with known criminals. Whether Brockman could make a charge like that stick was the least of Bosch's worries. He headed out the door with Toliver following. Before it closed Brockman yelled after them.

'Give her a kiss for me, killer.'

❖ ❖ ❖ ❖ ❖ ❖ ❖

At first, Bosch sat silently next to Jerry Toliver on the ride back to his house. He had a waterfall of thoughts dropping through his mind and decided to simply ignore the young IAD detective. Toliver left the police scanner on and the sporadic chatter was the only thing resembling conversation in the car. They had caught the crest of the evening commute out of downtown and were moving at an excruciatingly slow pace toward the Cahuenga pass.

Bosch's guts ached from the wracking convulsions of nausea of an hour earlier and he kept his arms crossed in front of him as if he were cradling a baby. He knew he had to compartmentalize his thoughts. As much as he was confused and curious about what Brockman had alluded to in regard to Jasmine, he knew he had to put it aside. At the moment, Pounds and what had happened to him were more important.

He tried to piece together the chain of events and the conclusion he drew was obvious. His stumbling into the party at Mittel's and delivery of the photocopy of the *Times* clip had set off a reaction that ended with the murder of Harvey Pounds, the man whose name he had used. Though he had given Mittel only the name at the party, it was somehow traced back to the real Pounds, who was then tortured and killed.

Bosch guessed that it was the DMV calls that had

doomed Pounds. Fresh from receiving the threatening news clip at the fund-raiser from a man who had introduced himself as Harvey Pounds, Mittel likely would have put his lengthy arm out to find out who this man was and what his purpose was. Mittel had connections from LA to Sacramento to Washington, DC. He could have quickly found out that Harvey Pounds was a cop. Mittel's campaign financing work had put a good number of legislators in seats in Sacramento. He would certainly have the connections in the capital city to find out if anyone was running traces on his name. And if he had that done, then he would have learned that Harvey Pounds, an LAPD lieutenant, had inquired not only about him but about four other men who would be of vital interest to him as well. Arno Conklin, Johnny Fox, Jake McKittrick and Claude Eno.

True, all the names were involved in a case and conspiracy almost thirty-five years old. But Mittel was at the center of that conspiracy and the snooping around by Pounds would be more than enough, Bosch believed, for someone of his position to take some kind of action to find out what Pounds was doing.

Because of the approach the man he thought was Pounds had made at the party, Mittel had probably concluded he was being set upon by a chiseler, an extortionist. And he knew how to eliminate the problem. Like Johnny Fox had been eliminated.

That was the reason Pounds had been tortured, Bosch knew. For Mittel to make sure the problem went no further than Pounds, he had to know who else knew what Pounds knew. The problem was that Pounds didn't know anything himself. He had nothing to give. He was tormented until his heart could take it no longer.

A question that remained unanswered in Bosch's mind was what Arno Conklin knew of all this. He had not yet been contacted by Bosch. Did he know of the man who approached Mittel? Did he order the hit on Pounds or was it solely Mittel's reaction?

Then Bosch saw a bump in his theory that needed refining. Mittel had come face to face with him posing as Harvey Pounds at the fund-raiser. The fact that Pounds was tortured before he died indicated that Mittel was not present at the time, or he would have seen that they were brutalizing the wrong man. Bosch wondered now if they understood that they had, in fact, killed the wrong man, and if they would be looking for the right one.

He mulled over the point that Mittel could not have been there and decided that it fit. Mittel was not the type to get involved in the blood work. He'd have no problem calling the shots, he just wouldn't want to see them fired. Bosch realized the surfer in a suit had also seen him at the party and, therefore, could not have been directly involved in the killing of Harvey Pounds, either. That left the man Bosch had seen through the French doors at the house. The man with the wide body and thick neck whom he had seen Mittel show the newspaper clip to. The man who had slipped and fallen while coming down the driveway for Bosch.

Bosch realized that he didn't know how close he had come to being where Pounds was now. He reached into his jacket pocket for his cigarettes and started to light one.

'Do you mind not smoking?' Toliver asked, his first words of the thirty-minute journey.

'Yeah, I do mind.'

Bosch finished lighting the smoke and put his Bic away. He lowered the window.

'There. You happy? The exhaust fumes are worse than the smoke.'

'It's a nonsmoking vehicle.'

Toliver tapped his finger on a plastic magnet that was on

the dashboard ashtray cover. It was one of the little doodads that were distributed when the city passed a widespread antismoking law that forbade the practice in all city buildings and allowed for half of the department's fleet to be declared nonsmoking vehicles. The magnet showed a cigarette in the middle of a red circle with a slash through it. Beneath the circle it said THANK YOU FOR NOT SMOKING. Bosch reached over, peeled the magnet off and threw it out the open window. He saw it bounce once on the pavement and stick on the door of a car one lane over.

'Now it's not. Now it's a smoking car.'

'Bosch, you're really fucked, you know that?'

'Write me up, kid. Add it to the association beef your boss is working on. I don't care.'

They were silent for a few moments and the car crept further away from Hollywood.

'He's bluffing you, Bosch. I thought you knew that.'

'How so?'

He was surprised that Toliver was turning.

'He's just bluffing, that's all. He's still hot about what you did with that table. But he knows it won't stick. It's an old case. Voluntary manslaughter. A domestic violence case. She walked on five years probation. All you have to do is say you didn't know and it gets shitcanned.'

Bosch could almost guess what the case was about. She had practically told him during true confessions. She stayed too long with someone. That was what she had said. He thought of the painting he had seen in her studio. The gray portrait with the highlights red like blood. He tried to pull his mind away from it.

'Why're you telling me this, Toliver? Why are you going against your own?'

'Because they're not my own. Because I want to know what you meant by what you said to me in the hallway.'

Bosch couldn't even remember what he said.

'You told me it wasn't too late. Too late for what?'

'Too late to get out,' Bosch said, recalling the words he had thrown as a taunt. 'You're still a young guy. You better get yourself out of IAD before it's too late. You stay too long and you'll never get out. Is that what you want, spend your career busting cops for trading hookers dime bags?'

'Look, I want to work out of Parker and I don't want to wait ten years like everybody else. It's the easiest and fastest way for a white guy to get in there.'

'It's not worth it, is what I'm telling you. Anybody stays in IAD more than two, three years, they're there for life because nobody else wants 'em, nobody else trusts 'em. They're lepers. You better think about it. Parker Center isn't the only place in the world to work.'

A few moments of silence passed as Toliver tried to muster a defense.

'Somebody's got to police the police. A lot of people don't seem to understand that.'

'That's right. But in this department nobody polices the police who police the police. Think about that.'

The conversation was interrupted by the sharp tone he recognized as his mobile phone. On the back seat of the car were the items the searchers had taken from his apartment. Irving had ordered it all returned. Among them was his briefcase and inside it he heard his phone. He reached back, flipped the briefcase open and grabbed the phone.

'Yeah. It's Bosch.'

'Bosch, it's Russell.'

'Hey, I got nothing to tell you yet, Keisha. I'm still working on it.'

'No, I have something to tell you. Where are you?'

'I'm in the soup. The 101 coming up to Barham, my exit.'

'Well, I have to talk to you, Bosch. I'm writing a story for tomorrow. You will want to comment, I think, if only in your defense.'

'My defense?'

A dull thud went through him and he felt like saying, What now? But he held himself in check.

'What are you talking about?'

'Did you read my story today?'

'No, I haven't had the time. What –'

'It's about the death of Harvey Pounds. Today I have a follow … It concerns you, Bosch.'

Jesus, he thought. But he tried to keep calm. He knew that if she detected any panic in his voice she would gain confidence in whatever it was she was about to write. He had to convince her she had bad information. He had to undermine that confidence. Then he realized Toliver was sitting next to him and would hear everything he said.

'I have a problem talking now. When is your deadline?'

'Now. We have to talk now.'

Bosch looked at his watch. It was twenty-five minutes until six.

'You can go to six, right?'

He'd worked with reporters before and knew that was the deadline for the *Times*'s first edition.

'No, I can't go to six. If you want to say something, say it now.'

'I can't. Give me fifteen minutes and then call back. I can't talk now.'

There was a pause and then she said, 'Bosch, I can't push it far past then. You better be able to talk then.'

They were at the Barham exit now and they'd be up to his house in ten minutes.

'Don't worry about it. In the meantime, you go warn your editor that you might be pulling the story.'

'I will not.'

321

'Look, Keisha, I know what you're going to ask me about. It's a plant and it's wrong. You have to trust me. I'll explain in fifteen minutes.'

'How do you know it's a plant?'

'I know. It came from Angel Brockman.'

He flipped the phone closed and looked over at Toliver.

'See, Toliver? Is that what you want to do with your job? With your life?'

Toliver said nothing.

'When you get back, you can tell your boss that he can shove tomorrow's *Times* up his ass. There isn't going to be any story. See, even the reporters don't trust IAD guys. All I had to do was mention Brockman. She'll start backpedaling when I tell her I know what's going on. Nobody trusts you guys, Jerry. Get out of it.'

'Oh, and like *everybody* trusts you, Bosch.'

'Not everybody. But I can sleep at night and I've been on the job twenty years. Think you'll be able to? What have you got in, five, six years? I'll give you ten, Jerry. That's all for you. Ten and out. But you'll look like one of these guys who puts in thirty.'

His prediction was met with a stony silence from Toliver. Bosch didn't know why he even cared. Toliver was part of the team trying to put him in the dirt. But something about the young cop's fresh face gave him the benefit of the doubt.

They made the last curve on Woodrow Wilson and Bosch could see his house. He could also see a white car with a yellow plate parked in front of it and a man wearing a yellow construction helmet standing in front holding a toolbox. It was the city building inspector. Gowdy.

'Shit,' Bosch said. 'This one of IAD's tricks, too?'

'I don't – if it is, I don't know anything about it.'

'Yeah, sure.'

Without a further word Toliver stopped in front of the

house and Bosch got out with his returned property. Gowdy recognized him and immediately came over as Toliver pulled away from the curb.

'Listen, you're not living in this place, are ya?' Gowdy asked. 'It's been red-tagged. We gotta call said somebody bootlegged the electric.'

'I gotta call, too. See anybody? I was just going to check it out.'

'Don't bullshit me, Mr Bosch. I can see you've made some repairs. You gotta know something, you can't repair this place, you can't even go in. You gotta demolition order and it's overdue. I'm gonna put in a work order and have a city contractor do it. You'll get the bill. No use waitin' any longer. Now, you might as well get out of here because I'm going to pull the electric and padlock it.'

He bent down to put the toolbox on the ground and proceeded to open it up and retrieve a set of stainless steel hinges and hasp locks he would apply to the doors.

'Look, I've got a lawyer,' Bosch said. 'He's trying to work it out with you people.'

'There's nothing to work out. I'm sorry. Now if you go in there again, you're subject to arrest. If I find these locks have been tampered with, you're also subject to arrest. I'll call North Hollywood Division. I'm not fooling with you anymore.'

For the first time it occurred to Bosch that it might be a show, that the man might want money. He probably didn't even know Bosch was a cop. Most cops couldn't afford to live up here and wouldn't want to if they could. The only reason Bosch could afford it was he had bought the property with a chunk of money he had made years earlier on a TV movie deal based on a case he had solved.

'Look, Gowdy,' he said, 'just spell it out, okay? I'm slow about these things. Tell me what you want and you've got it. I want to save the house. That's all I care about.'

Gowdy looked at him for a long moment and Bosch realized he had been wrong. He could see the indignation in Gowdy's eyes.

'You keep talking like that and you could go to jail, son. I'll tell you what I'm going to do. I'm going to forget what you just said. I –'

'Look, I'm sorry …' Bosch looked back at the house. 'It's just like, I don't know, the house is the only thing I've got.'

'You've got more than that. You just haven't thought about it. Now, I'm going to cut you a break here. I'll give you five minutes to go inside and get what you need. After that, I'm putting the locks on it. I'm sorry. But that's the way it is. If that house goes down the hill on the next one, maybe you'll thank me.'

Bosch nodded.

'Go on. Five minutes.'

Bosch went inside and grabbed a suitcase from the top shelf of the hallway closet. First he put his second gun in it, then he dumped in as much of the clothing from the bedroom closet as he could. He walked the overstuffed suitcase out to the carport, then came back inside for another load. He opened the drawers of his bureau and dumped them on the bed, then wrapped everything in the bedclothes and carried that out as well.

He went past the five-minute mark but Gowdy didn't come in after him. Bosch could hear him working with a hammer on the front door.

After ten minutes he had a large stack of belongings gathered in the carport. Included there was the box in which he kept his keepsakes and photos, a fireproof box containing his financial and personal records, a stack of unopened mail and unpaid bills, the stereo and two boxes containing his collection of jazz and blues LPs and CDs. Looking at the pile of belongings, he felt forlorn. It was a lot to fit into a Mustang, but he knew it wasn't much to show for almost forty-five years on the planet.

'That it?'

Bosch turned around. It was Gowdy. He was holding a hammer in one hand and a steel latch in the other. Bosch saw a keyed lock was hooked through one of the belt loops on his pants.

'Yeah,' Bosch said. 'Do it.'

He stepped back and let the inspector go to work. The hammering had just begun when his phone rang. He had forgotten about Keisha Russell.

He had the phone in his jacket pocket instead of his briefcase now. He took it out and flipped it open.

'Yeah, it's Bosch.'

'Detective, it's Dr Hinojos.'

'Oh … Hi.'

'Something wrong?'

'No, uh, yeah, I was expecting somebody else. I've got to keep this line open for a few minutes. I've got a call coming in. Can I call you back?'

Bosch looked at his watch. It was five minutes until six.

'Yes,' Hinojos said. 'I'll be at the office until six-thirty. I want to talk to you about something, and to see how you fared on the sixth floor after I left.'

'I'm fine, but I'll call you back.'

As soon as he flipped the phone closed, it rang again in his hand.

'Bosch.'

'Bosch, I'm up against it and don't have time for bullshit.' It was Russell. She also didn't have time to identify herself. 'The story is that the investigation into the killing of Harvey Pounds has turned inward and detectives spent several hours with you today. They searched your home and they believe you are the prime suspect.'

'Prime suspect? We don't even use those words, Keisha.

Now I *know* you're talking to one of those squints in IAD. They wouldn't know how to run a homicide investigation if the doer came up and bit them on their shiny ass.'

'Don't try to deflect what we're talking about here. It's really simple. Do you or don't you have a comment on the story for tomorrow's paper? If you want to say something, I have just enough time to get it in the first run.'

'On the record, I have no comment.'

'And off?'

'Off the record, not for attribution or any use at all, I can tell you that you're full of shit, Keisha. Your story is wrong. Flat-out wrong. If you run it as you have just summarized it for me, you will have to write another one tomorrow correcting it. It will say I am not a suspect at all. Then, after that, you'll have to find another beat to cover.'

'And why is that?' she asked haughtily.

'Because this is a smear orchestrated by Internal Affairs. It's a plant. And when it is read tomorrow by everybody else in the department they'll know it is and they'll know you fell for it. They won't trust you. They'll think you're just a front for people like Brockman. No one that it is important for you to have a source relationship with will want to have that relationship with you. Including me. You'll be left covering the police commission and rewriting the press releases out of media relations. And then, of course, whenever Brockman wants to cream somebody else, he'll pick up the phone and call.'

There was silence on the line. Bosch looked up at the sky and saw it turning pink with the start of sunset. He looked at his watch. It was one minute until her deadline.

'You there, Keisha?'

'Bosch, you're scaring me.'

'You should be scared. You got about a minute to make a big decision.'

'Let me ask you this. Did you attack Pounds two weeks ago and throw him through a window?'

'On or off the record?'

'It doesn't matter. I just need an answer. Quick!'

'Off the record, that's more or less accurate.'

'Well, that would seem to make you a suspect in his death. I don't see –'

'Keisha, I've been out of the state for three days. I got back today. Brockman brought me in and talked to me for less than an hour. My story checked and I was kicked free. I'm not a suspect. I'm talking to you from the front of my house. You hear that hammering? That's my house. I've got a carpenter here. Are prime suspects allowed to go home at night?'

'How can I confirm all of this?'

'Today? You can't. You've got to pick. Brockman or me. Tomorrow, you can call Assistant Chief Irving and he'll confirm – if he is willing to talk to you.'

'Shit! Bosch, I can't believe this. If I go to my editor at deadline and tell him a story that they had budgeted for the front page since the three o'clock meeting is not a story … I might be looking for a new beat and a new paper to cover it for.'

'There's other news in the world, Keisha. They can find something for the front page. This will pay off for you in the long run, anyway. I'll spread the word about you.'

There was a brief silence while she made her decision.

'I can't talk. I have to get in there and grab him. Good-bye, Bosch. I hope I'm still working here the next time we talk.'

She was gone before he could say good-bye.

He walked up the street to the Mustang and drove it down to the house. Gowdy had finished with the latches and both doors now had locks on them. The inspector was out at his car using the front hood as a desk. He was writing on a clipboard and Bosch guessed he was moving slowly so as to make sure Bosch left the property. Bosch started loading his pile of belongings into the Mustang. He didn't know where he was going to take himself.

He put the thought of his homelessness aside and began thinking about Keisha Russell. He wondered if she would be able to stop the story so late in the game. It had probably taken on a life of its own. Like a monster in the newspaper's computer. And she, its Dr Frankenstein, would likely have little power over stopping it.

When he had everything in the Mustang, he waved a salute to Gowdy, got in and drove down the hill. Down at Cahuenga he didn't know which way to turn because he still didn't know where he should go. To the right was Hollywood. To the left was the Valley. Then he remembered the Mark Twain. In Hollywood, only a few blocks from the station on Wilcox, the Mark Twain was an old residence hotel with efficiencies that were generally clean and neat – a lot more so than the surrounding neighborhood. Bosch knew this because he had stashed witnesses there on occasion. He also knew that there were a couple of units that were two-room efficiencies with private baths. He decided he would go for one of them and turned right. The phone rang almost as soon as he had made the decision. It was Keisha Russell.

'You owe me big time, Bosch. I killed it.'

He felt relief and annoyance at the same time. It was typical thinking for a reporter.

'What are you talking about?' he countered. 'You owe me big time for saving your ass.'

'Well, we'll see about that. I'm still going to check this out tomorrow. If it falls the way you said, I'm going to Irving to complain about Brockman. I'll burn him.'

'You just did.'

Realizing she had just confirmed Brockman as the source, she laughed uneasily.

'What did your editor say?'

'He thinks I'm an idiot. But I told him there's other news in the world.'

'Good line.'

'Yeah, I'm going to keep that one in my computer. So what's going on? And what's happening with those clips I got you?'

'The clips are still percolating. I can't really talk about anything yet.'

'Figures. I don't know why I keep helping you, Bosch, but here goes. Remember you asked about Monte Kim, the guy who wrote that first clip I gave you?'

'Yeah. Monte Kim.'

'I asked about him around here and one of the old rewrite guys told me he's still alive. Turns out that after he left the *Times* he worked for the DA's office for a while. I don't know what he's doing now but I got his number and his address. He's in the Valley.'

'Can you give it to me?'

'I guess so, since it was in the phonebook.'

'Damn, I never thought of that.'

'You might be a good detective, Bosch, but you wouldn't make much of a reporter.'

She gave him the number and address, said she'd be in touch and hung up. Bosch put the phone down on the seat and thought about this latest piece of information as he drove into Hollywood. Monte Kim had worked for the district attorney. Bosch had a pretty good idea which one that would be.

❖ ❖ ❖ ❖ ❖ ❖ ❖

The man behind the front desk at the Mark Twain didn't seem to recognize Bosch, though Harry was reasonably sure he was the same man he had dealt with before while renting rooms for witnesses. The counterman was tall and thin and had the hunched-over shoulders of someone carrying a heavy burden. He looked like he'd been behind the desk since Eisenhower.

'You remember me? From down the street?'

'Yeah, I remember. I didn't say anything 'cause I didn't know if this was an undercover job or not.'

'No. No undercover. I wanted to know if you have one of the big rooms in the back open. One with a phone.'

'You want one?'

'That's why I'm asking.'

'Who you going to put in there this time? I don't want no gangbangers again. Last time, they –'

'No, no gangbangers. Only me. I want the room.'

'You want the room?'

'That's right. And I won't paint on the walls. How much?'

The desk man seemed nonplussed by the fact that Bosch wanted to stay there himself. He finally recovered and told Bosch he had his choice: thirty dollars a day, two hundred a week or five hundred a month. All in advance. Bosch paid for a week with his credit card and waited anxiously while the man checked to make sure the charge would clear.

'Now, how much for the parking space in the loading zone out front?'

'You can't rent that.'

'I want to park out front, make it harder for one of your other tenants to rip my car off.'

Bosch took out his money and slid fifty dollars across the counter.

'If parking enforcement comes by, tell them it's cool.'

'Yeah.'

'You the manager?'

'And owner. Twenty-seven years.'

'Sorry.'

Bosch went out to get his things. It took him three trips to bring everything up to room 214. The room was in the back and its two windows looked across an alley to the back of a one-story building that housed two bars and an adult film and novelties store. But Bosch had known all along it would be no garden spot. It wasn't the kind of place where he would find a terry cloth robe in the closet and mints on the pillow at night. It was just a couple of notches up from the places where you slid your money to the clerk through a slot in the bulletproof glass.

One room had a bureau and a bed, which had only two cigarette burns in the bedspread, and a television mounted in a steel frame that was bolted to the wall. There was no cable, no remote and no courtesy *TV Guide*. The other room had a worn green couch, a small table for two and a kitchenette that had a half refrigerator, a bolted-down microwave and a two-coil electric range. The bathroom was off the hallway that connected the two rooms and came complete with white tile that had yellowed like old men's teeth.

Despite the drab circumstances and his hopes that his

stay would be temporary, Bosch tried his best to transform the hotel room into a home. He hung some clothes in the closet, put his toothbrush and shaving kit in the bathroom and set the answering machine up on the phone, though nobody knew his number. He decided that in the morning he'd call the telephone company and have a forwarding tape put on his old line.

Next he set up the stereo on the bureau. For the time being he just placed the speakers on the floor on either side of the bureau. He then rummaged through his box of CDs and came across a Tom Waits recording called 'Blue Valentine.' He hadn't listened to it in years so he put it on.

He sat down on the bed near the phone and listened and thought for a few minutes about calling Jazz in Florida. But he wasn't sure what he could say or ask. He decided it might be better to just let it go for now. He lit a cigarette and went to the window. There was nothing happening in the alley. Across the tops of the buildings he could see the ornate tower of the nearby Hollywood Athletic Club. It was a beautiful building. One of the last in Hollywood.

He closed the musty curtains, turned around and studied his new home. After a while he yanked the spread off the bed along with the other covers and then remade it with his own sheets and blanket. He knew it was a small gesture of continuity but it made him feel less lonely. It also made him feel a little bit as though he knew what he was doing with his life at that point and it made him forget for a few more moments about Harvey Pounds.

Bosch sat on the newly made bed and leaned back on the pillows propped against the headboard. He lit another cigarette. He studied the wounds on his two fingers and saw that the scabs had been replaced with hard pink skin. They were healing nicely. He hoped the rest of him would, too. But he doubted it. He knew he was responsible. And he knew he had to pay. Somehow.

He absentmindedly pulled the phone off the bed table and placed it on his chest. It was an old one with a rotary dial. Bosch lifted the receiver and looked at the dial. Who was he going to call? What was he going to say? He replaced the receiver and sat up. He decided he had to get out.

❖ ❖ ❖ ❖ ❖ ❖ ❖

M onte Kim lived on Willis Avenue in Sherman Oaks in the midst of a ghost town of apartment buildings red-tagged after the quake. Kim's apartment building was a gray-and-white Cape Cod affair that sat between two empties. At least they were supposed to be empty. As Bosch pulled up he saw lights go out in one of the buildings. Squatters, he guessed. Like Bosch had been, always on alert for the building inspector.

Kim's building looked as though it had been either completely spared by the quake or already completely repaired. Bosch doubted it was the latter. He believed the building was more a testament to the serendipitous violence of nature, and maybe a builder who didn't cut corners. The Cape Cod had stood up while the buildings around it cracked and slid.

It was a common, rectangular building with apartment entrances running down each side of it. But to get to one of the doors, you had to be buzzed through a six-foot-tall electronic gate. The cops called them 'feel good' gates because they made the dwellers inside feel safer, but they were worthless. All they did was put up a barrier for legitimate visitors to the building. Others could simply climb over, and they did, all over the city. Feel good gates were everywhere.

He said only that it was the police when Kim's voice sounded on the intercom and he was buzzed in. He took the badge wallet out of his pocket as he walked down to apartment eight. When Kim opened up, Bosch shoved the open badge wallet through the door and about six inches from his face. He held it so his finger was across the badge and obscured the marking that said LIEUTENANT. He then pulled the wallet back quickly and put it away.

'I'm sorry, I didn't catch the name on there,' Kim said, still blocking the way.

'Hieronymus Bosch. But people call me Harry.'

'You're named for the painter.'

'Sometimes I feel old enough that I think he was named for me. Tonight's one of those nights. Can I come in? This shouldn't take long.'

Kim led him into the living room with a confused look on his face. It was a decent-sized and neat room with a couch and two chairs and a gas fireplace next to the TV. Kim took one of the chairs and Bosch sat on the end of the couch. He noticed a white poodle sleeping on the carpet next to Kim's chair. Kim was an overweight man with a wide, florid face. He wore glasses that pinched his temples and what was left of his hair was dyed brown. He wore a red cardigan sweater over a white shirt and old khakis. Bosch guessed Kim wasn't quite sixty. He had been expecting an older man.

'I guess this is where I ask, "What's this all about?" '

'Yeah, and I guess this is where I tell you. Problem is I'm not sure how to begin. I'm investigating a couple of homicides. You can probably help. But I wonder if you'd indulge me and let me ask you some questions going a while back? Then, when we're done, I'll explain why.'

'Seems unusual but ...'

Kim raised his hands and waved off any problems. He made a movement in his chair as if to get more comfortable. He checked the dog and then squinted his eyes as if that might better help him understand and answer the questions. Bosch could see a film of sweat developing in the defoliated landscape that had once been his scalp.

'You were a reporter for the *Times*. How long did that last?'

'Oh, boy, that was just a few years in the early sixties. How do you know that?'

'Mr Kim, let me ask these questions first. What kind of reporting did you do?'

'Back then they called us cub reporters. I was on the crime beat.'

'What do you do now?'

'Currently, I work out of my home. I'm in public relations. I have an office upstairs in the second bedroom. I had an office in Reseda but the building was condemned. You could see daylight through the cracks.'

He was like most people in LA. He didn't have to preface his remarks by saying he was talking about earthquake damage. It was understood.

'I have several small accounts,' he continued. 'I was a local spokesman for the GM plant in Van Nuys until they closed it down. Then I went out on my own.'

'What made you quit the *Times* back in the sixties?'

'I got – Am I a suspect in something?'

'Not at all, Mr Kim. I'm just trying to get to know you. Indulge me. I'll get to the point. You were saying why you quit the *Times*.'

'Yes, well, I got a better job. I was offered the position of press spokesman for the district attorney at the time, Arno Conklin. I took it. Better pay, more interesting than the cop beat and a brighter future.'

'What do you mean, brighter future?'

'Well, actually I was wrong about that. When I took the job I thought the sky would be the limit with Arno. He was a good man. I figured I'd eventually – you know, if I stayed with him – ride with him to the governor's mansion, maybe the Senate in Washington. But things didn't turn out. I ended up with an office in Reseda with a crack in the wall I could feel the wind come through. I don't see why the police would be interested in all –'

'What happened with Conklin? Why didn't things turn out?'

'Well, I'm not the expert on this. All I know is that in sixty-eight he was planning on running for attorney general and the office was practically his for the taking. Then he just … dropped out. He quit politics and went back to practice law. And it wasn't to harvest the big corporate bucks that sit out there when these guys go into private practice. He opened a one-man law firm. I admired him. As far as I heard, sixty percent or better of his practice was pro bono. He was working for free most of the time.'

'Like he was serving a penance or something?'

'I don't know. I guess.'

'Why'd he drop out?'

'I don't know.'

'Weren't you part of the inner circle?'

'No. He didn't have a circle. He had one man.'

'Gordon Mittel.'

'Right. You want to know why he didn't run, ask Gordon.' Then it clicked in Kim's brain that Bosch had introduced the name Gordon Mittel to the conversation. 'Is this about Gordon Mittel?'

'Let me ask the questions first. Why do you think Conklin didn't run? You must have some idea.'

'He wasn't officially in the race in the first place, so he didn't have to make any public statement about dropping out. He just didn't run. There were a lot of rumors, though.'

'Like what?'

'Oh, lots of stuff. Like he was gay. There were others.

337

Financial trouble. Supposedly there was a threat from the mob that if he won, they'd kill him. Just stuff like that. None of it was ever more than backroom talk amongst the town politicos.'

'He was never married?'

'Not as far as I know. But as far as him being gay, I never saw anything like that.'

Bosch noted that the top of Kim's head was slick now with sweat. It was already warm in the room but he kept the cardigan on. Bosch made a quick change of tracks.

'Okay, tell me about the death of Johnny Fox.'

Bosch saw the quick glimmer of recognition pass behind the glasses but then it disappeared. But it was enough.

'Johnny Fox, who's that?'

'C'mon, Monte, it's old news. Nobody cares what you did. I just need to know the story behind the story. That's why I'm here.'

'You're talking about when I was a reporter? I wrote a lot of stories. That was thirty-five years ago. I was a kid. I can't remember everything.'

'But you remember Johnny Fox. He was your ticket to that brighter future. The one that didn't happen.'

'Look, what are you doing here? You're not a cop. Did Gordon send you? After all these years, you people think I …'

He stopped.

'I am a cop, Monte. And you're lucky I got here before Gordon did. Something's coming undone. The ghosts are coming back. You read in the paper today about that cop found in his trunk in Griffith Park?'

'I saw it on the news. He was a lieutenant.'

'Yeah. He was my lieutenant. He was looking into a couple old cases. Johnny Fox was one of them. Then he ended up in his trunk. So you'll have to excuse me if I'm a little nervous and pushy, but I need to know about Johnny

Fox. And you wrote the story. You wrote the story after he got killed that made him out to be an angel. Then you end up on Conklin's team. I don't care what you did, I just want to know what you did.'

'Am I in danger?'

Bosch hiked his shoulders in his best who-knows-and-who-cares gesture.

'If you are, then we can protect you. You don't help us, we can't help you. You know how it goes.'

'Oh my God! I knew this – What other cases?'

'One of Johnny's girls who got killed about a year before him. Her name was Marjorie Lowe.'

Kim shook his head. He didn't recognize the name. He ran his hand over his scalp, using it like a squeegee to move the sweat into the thicker hair. Bosch could tell he had perfectly primed the fat man to answer the questions.

'So what about Fox?' Bosch asked. 'I don't have all night.'

'Look, I don't know anything. All I did was a favor for a favor.'

'Tell me about it.'

He composed himself for a long moment before speaking.

'Look, you know who Jack Ruby was?'

'In Dallas?'

'Yeah, the guy who killed Oswald. Well, Johnny Fox was the Jack Ruby of LA, okay? Same era, same kind of guy. Fox ran women, was a gambler, knew which cops could be greased and greased them when he needed to. It kept him out of jail. He was a classic Hollywood bottom feeder. When he ended up dead on the Hollywood Division blotter, I saw it but was going to pass. He was trash and we didn't write about trash. Then a source I had in the cop shop told me Johnny had been on Conklin's payroll.'

'That made it a story.'

'Yeah. So I called up Mittel, Conklin's campaign manager, and ran it by him. I wanted a response. I don't know how much you know about that time, but Conklin had this squeaky-clean image. He was the guy attacking every vice in the city and here he had a vice hoodlum on the payroll. It was a great story. Though Fox didn't have a record, I don't think, there were intel files on him and I had access to them. The story was going to do damage and Mittel knew it.'

He stopped there at the edge of the story. He knew the rest but to speak of it out loud he had to be pushed over the edge.

'Mittel knew it,' Bosch said. 'So he offered you a deal. He'd make you Conklin's flak if you cleaned up the story.'

'Not exactly.'

'Then what? What was the deal?'

'I'm sure any kind of statute has passed ...'

'Don't worry about it. Just tell me and only me, you and your dog will ever know it.'

Kim took a deep breath and continued.

'This was mid-campaign so Conklin already had a spokesman. Mittel offered me a job as deputy spokesman after the election. I'd work out of the office in the Van Nuys Courthouse, handle the Valley stuff.'

'If Conklin won.'

'Yeah, but that was a given. Unless this Fox story caused a problem. But I held out, used some leverage. I told Mittel I wanted to be the main spokesman after Arno's election or forget it. He got back to me later and agreed.'

'After he talked to Conklin.'

'I guess. Anyway, I wrote a story that left out the details of Fox's past.'

'I read it.'

'That's all I did. I got the job. It was never mentioned again.'

Bosch sized Kim up for a moment. He was weak. He didn't see that being a reporter was a calling just the same as being a cop. You took an oath to yourself. Kim had seemingly had no difficulty breaking it. Bosch could not imagine someone like Keisha Russell acting the same way under the same circumstances. He tried to cover his distaste and move on.

'Think back now. This is important. When you first called up Mittel and told him about Fox's background, did you get the impression that he already knew the background?'

'Yes, he knew. I don't know if the cops had told him that day or he had known all along. But he knew Fox was dead and he knew who he was. I think he was a little surprised that I knew and he became eager to make a deal to keep it out of the paper ... It was the first time I ever did anything like that. I wish I hadn't done it.'

Kim looked down at the dog and then to the beige rug and Bosch knew it was a screen on which he saw how his life diverged sharply the moment he took the deal. It went from where it was going to where it eventually was.

'Your story didn't name any cops,' Bosch said. 'Do you remember who handled it?'

'Not really. It was so long ago. It would have been a couple guys from the Hollywood homicide table. Back then, they handled fatal accidents. Now there's a division for that.'

'Claude Eno?'

'Eno? I remember him. It might've been. I think I remember that it ... Yes, it was. Now I remember. He was on it alone. His partner had transferred or retired or something and he was working alone, waiting for his next partner to transfer in. So they gave him the traffic cases.

They were usually pretty light, as far as any investigation went.'

'How do you remember so much of this?'

Kim pursed his lips and struggled for an answer.

'I guess … Like I said, I wish I never did what I did. So, I guess, I think about it a lot. I remember it.'

Bosch nodded. He had no more questions and was already thinking of the implications of how Kim's information fit with his own. Eno had worked both cases, Lowe and Fox, and later retired, leaving behind a mail-drop corporation with Conklin's and Mittel's name on it that collected a thousand dollars a month for twenty-five years. He realized that compared to Eno, Kim had settled for too little. He was about to get up when he thought of something.

'You said that Mittel never mentioned the deal you made or Fox again.'

'That's right.'

'Did Conklin ever say anything about either one?'

'No, he never mentioned a thing, either.'

'What was your relationship like? Didn't he treat you as a chiseler?'

'No, because I wasn't a chiseler,' Kim protested but the indignation in his voice was hollow. 'I did a job for him and I did it well. He was always very nice to me.'

'He was in your story on Fox. I don't have it here but in it he said he had never met Fox.'

'Yeah, that was a lie. I made that up.'

Bosch was confused.

'What do you mean? You mean, you made up the lie?'

'In case they went back on the deal. I put Conklin in the story saying he didn't know the guy because I had evidence he did. They knew I had it. That way, if after the election they reneged on the deal, I could dredge up the story again and show Conklin said he didn't know Fox but he did. I could then make the inference that he also knew Fox's background when he hired him. It wouldn't have done much good because he'd have already been elected, but it would do some PR damage. It was my little insurance policy. Understand?'

Bosch nodded.

'What was the evidence you had that Conklin knew Fox?'

'I had photos.'

'What photos?'

'They were taken by the society photographer for the *Times* at the Hollywood Masonic Lodge's St Patrick's Day dance a couple of years before the election. There's two of them. Conklin and Fox are at a table. They were scratches but one day I was –'

'What do you mean, scratches?'

'Photos never published. Outtakes. But, see, I used to look at the society stuff in the photo lab, so I could learn who the big shots in the city were and who they were out with and so on. It was useful information. One day I saw these photos of Conklin and some guy that I recognized but wasn't sure from where. It was because of the social background. This wasn't Fox's turf so at the time I didn't recognize him. Then, when Fox got killed and I was told he worked for Conklin, I remembered the photos and who the other man was. Fox. I went back to the scratch files and pulled them out.'

'They were just sitting there together at this dance?'

'In the photos? Yeah. And they were smiling. You could tell they knew each other. These weren't posed shots. In fact, that's why each was a scratch. They weren't good photos, not for the society page.'

'Anybody else with them?'

'A couple women, that was it.'

'Go get the photos.'

'Oh, I don't have them anymore. I tossed them after I didn't need them anymore.'

'Kim, don't bullshit me, okay? There was never a time you didn't need them. Those photos are probably why you are alive today. Now go get them or I'll take you downtown for withholding evidence, then I'll come back with a warrant and tear this place apart.'

'All right! Jesus! Wait here. I have one of them.'

He got up and went up the stairs. Bosch just stared at the dog. It was wearing a sweater that matched Kim's. He heard a closet door being moved on rollers, then a heavy thud. He guessed a box had been taken off the shelf and dropped to the floor. In a few more moments, Kim's heavy steps were coming down the stairs. As he passed the couch, he handed Bosch a black-and-white eight-by-ten that was yellowed around the edges. Bosch stared at it for a long time.

'I have the other in a safe deposit box,' Kim said. 'It's a clearer shot of the two of them. You can tell it's Fox.'

Bosch didn't say anything. He was still looking at the photo. It was a flashbulb shot. Everybody's face was lit up white as snow. Conklin sat across a table from the man Bosch assumed was Fox. There were a half dozen drink glasses on the table. Conklin was smiling and heavy-lidded – that was probably why the photo was a scratch – and Fox was turned slightly away from the camera, his features indistinguishable. Bosch guessed you would have had to know him to recognize him. Neither of them seemed aware of the photographer's presence. Flashbulbs were probably going off all over the place.

But more so than the men, Bosch studied the two women in the photo. Standing next to Fox and bending over to whisper in his ear was a woman in a dark one-piece dress that was tight around the middle. Her hair was swirled on top of her head. It was Meredith Roman. And

344

sitting across the table and next to Conklin, mostly obscured by him, was Marjorie Lowe. Bosch guessed that if you didn't already know her, she wouldn't have been recognizable. Conklin was smoking and had his hand up to his face. His arm blocked off half of Bosch's mother's face. It almost looked as if she was peeking around a corner at the camera.

Bosch turned the photo over and there was a stamp on the back that said TIMES PHOTO BY BORIS LUGAVERE. It was dated March 17, 1961, seven months before his mother's death.

'Did you ever show this to Conklin or Mittel?' Bosch finally asked.

'Yeah. When I made my case for head spokesman. I gave Gordon a copy. He saw that it was proof the candidate knew Fox.'

Mittel must also have seen that it was proof that the candidate knew a murder victim, Bosch realized. Kim didn't know what he had. But no wonder he got the head spokesman's job. You're lucky you're alive, he thought but didn't say.

'Did Mittel know it was only a copy?'

'Oh yeah, I made that clear. I wasn't stupid.'

'Did Conklin ever mention it to you?'

'Not to me. But I assume Mittel told him about it. Remember, I said he had to get back to me about the job I wanted. Who would he have to clear it with, he was campaign manager? So he must've talked to Conklin.'

'I'm going to keep this.'

Bosch held up the photo.

'I've got the other.'

'Have you stayed in touch with Arno Conklin over the years?'

'No. I haven't spoken to him in, I don't know, twenty years.'

'I want you to call him now and I –'

'I don't even know where he is.'

'I do. I want you to call him and tell him you want to see him tonight. Tell him it has to be tonight. Tell him it's about Johnny Fox and Marjorie Lowe. Tell him not to tell anyone you are coming.'

'I can't do that.'

'Sure you can. Where's your phone? I'll help you.'

'No, I mean, I can't go see him tonight. You can't make –'

'You're not going to see him tonight, Monte. I'm going to be you. Now where's your phone?'

✧ ✧ ✧ ✧ ✧ ✧ ✧

At Park La Brea Lifecare, Bosch parked in a visitor's space in the front lot and got out of the Mustang. The place looked dark; few windows in the upper stories had lights on behind them. He checked his watch – it was only nine-fifty – and moved toward the glass doors of the lobby.

He felt a slight pull in his throat as he made the walk. Deep down he had known as soon as he finished reading the murder book that his sights were set on Conklin and that it would come to this. He was about to confront the man he believed had killed his mother and then used his position and the people he surrounded himself with to walk away from it. To Bosch, Conklin was the symbol of all that he never had in his life. Power, home, content-ment. It didn't matter how many people had told him on the trail that Conklin was a good man. Bosch knew the secret behind the good man. His rage grew with each step he took.

Inside the door a uniformed guard sat behind a desk working on a crossword puzzle torn from the *Times Sunday Magazine*. Maybe he had been working on it since then. He looked up at Bosch as if he was expecting him.

'Monte Kim,' Bosch said. 'One of the residents is expecting me. Arno Conklin.'

'Yeah, he called down.' The guard consulted a clip-board, then turned it around and handed the pen to Bosch.

'Been a long time since he's had any visitors. Sign here, please. He's up in nine-oh-seven.'

Bosch signed and dropped the pen on the clipboard.

'It's kind of late,' the guard said. 'Visitation is usually over by nine.'

'What's that mean? You want me to leave? Fine.' He held his briefcase up. 'Mr Conklin can just roll his wheelchair down to my office tomorrow to pick this stuff up. I'm the one making a special trip here, buddy. For him. Let me up or not, I don't care. He cares.'

'Whoah, whoah, whoah, hold on there, partner. I was just saying it was late and you didn't let me finish. I'm going to let you go up. No problem. Mr Conklin specifically requested it and this ain't no prison. I'm just saying all the visitors are gone, okay? People are sleeping. Just keep it down, is all. No reason to blow a gasket.'

'Nine-oh-seven, you said?'

'That's right. I'll call him and tell him you're on your way up.'

'Thanks.'

Bosch moved past the guard toward the elevators without apology. He was forgotten as soon as he was out of Bosch's sight. Only one thing, one person, occupied his mind now.

The elevator moved about as quickly as the building's inhabitants. When he finally got to the ninth floor, Bosch walked past a nurses' station but it was empty, the night nurse apparently tending to a resident's needs. Bosch headed the wrong way down the hall, then corrected himself and headed back the other way. The paint and linoleum in the hallway were fresh but even top-dollar places like this couldn't completely eliminate the lingering smell of urine, disinfectant and the sense of closed lives behind the closed doors. He found the door to nine-oh-seven and knocked once. He heard a faint voice telling him to enter. It was more like a whimper than a whisper.

Bosch was unprepared for what he saw when he opened the door. There was a single light on in the room, a small reading lamp to the side of the bed. It left most of the room in shadow. An old man sat on the bed propped against three pillows, a book in his frail hands, bifocals on the bridge of his nose. What Bosch found so eerie about the tableau before him was that the bedcovers were bunched around the old man's waist but were flat on the remainder of the bed. The bed was flat. There were no legs. Compounding this shock was the wheelchair to the right of the bed. A plaid blanket had been thrown over the seat. But two legs in black pants and loafers extended from beneath it and down to the chair's footrests. It looked as if half the man was in his bed but he had left his other half in the chair. Bosch's face must have shown his confusion.

'Prosthesis,' said the raspy voice from the bed. 'Lost my legs … diabetes. Almost nothing of me left. Except an old man's vanity. I had the legs made for public appearances.'

Bosch stepped closer to the light. The man's skin was like the back of peeled wallpaper. Yellowish, pale. His eyes were deep in the shadows of his skeletal face, his hair just a whisper around his ears. His thin hands were ribbed with blue veins the size of earthworms under his spotted skin. He was death, Bosch knew. Death certainly had a better grip on him than life did.

Conklin put the book on the table near the lamp. It seemed to be a labor for him to make the reach. Bosch saw the title. *The Neon Rain*.

'A mystery,' Conklin said, a small cackle following. 'I indulge myself with mysteries. I've learned to appreciate the writing. I never did before. Never took the time. Come in, Monte, no need to be afraid of me. I'm a harmless old man.'

Bosch stepped closer until the light was on his face. He saw Conklin's watery eyes study him and conclude that he was not Monte Kim. It had been a long time but Conklin seemed to be able to tell.

'I came in Monte's place,' he whispered.

Conklin turned his head slightly and Bosch saw his eyes fall on the emergency call button on the bed table. He must have figured he had no chance and no strength for another reach. He turned back to Bosch.

'Who are you, then?'

'I'm working on a mystery, too.'

'A detective?'

'Yes. My name's Harry Bosch and I want to ask you about ...'

He stopped. There was a change in Conklin's face. Bosch could not tell if it was fear or maybe recognition but something had changed. Conklin brought his eyes up to Bosch's and Bosch realized the old man was smiling.

'Hieronymus Bosch,' he whispered. 'Like the painter.'

Bosch nodded slowly. He now realized he was as shocked as the old man.

'How do you know that?'

'Because I know of you.'

'How?'

'Through your mother. She told me about you and your special name. I loved your mother.'

It was like getting hit in the chest with a sandbag. Bosch felt the air go out of him and he put a hand down on the bed to hold himself steady.

'Sit. Please. Sit.'

Conklin held out a shaky hand, motioning Bosch onto the bed. He nodded when Bosch did as he had been told.

'No!' Bosch said loudly as he rose off the bed almost as soon as he had sat down on it. 'You used her and you killed her. Then you paid off people to bury it with her.

That's why I'm here. I came for the truth. I want to hear you tell it and I don't want to hear any bullshit about loving her. You're a liar.'

Conklin had a pleading look in his eyes, then he turned them away, toward the dark side of the room.

'I don't know the truth,' he said, his voice like dried leaves blown along the sidewalk. 'I take responsibility and therefore, yes, it could be said I killed her. The only truth I know is that I loved her. You can call me a liar but that is the truth. You could make an old man whole again if you believed that.'

Bosch couldn't fathom what was happening, what was being said.

'She was with you that night. In Hancock Park.'

'Yes.'

'What happened? What did you do?'

'I killed her … with my words, my actions. It took me many years to realize that.'

Bosch moved closer until he was hovering over the old man. He wanted to grab him and shake some sense out of him. But Arno Conklin was so frail that he might shatter.

'What are you talking about? Look at me. What are you talking about?'

Conklin turned his head on a neck no wider than a glass of milk. He looked at Bosch and nodded solemnly.

'You see, we made plans that night. Marjorie and I. I had fallen for her against all better judgment and advice. My own and others. We were going to get married. We'd decided. We were going to get you out of that youth hall. We had many plans. That was the night we made them. We were both so happy that we cried. The next day was Saturday. I wanted to go to Las Vegas. Take the car and drive through the night before we could change our minds or have them changed for us. She agreed and went home to pick up her things … She never came back.'

'That's your story? You expect me –'

'You see, after she had left, I made one call. But that was enough. I called my best friend to tell him the good news and to ask him to stand with me as my best man. I wanted him to go with us to Las Vegas. Do you know what he said? He declined the honor of being my best man. He said that if I married that ... that woman, I'd be finished. He said he wouldn't let me do that. He said he had great plans for me.'

'Gordon Mittel.'

Conklin nodded sadly.

'So what are you saying, Mittel killed her? You didn't know?'

'I didn't know.'

He looked down at his feeble hands and balled them into tiny fists on the blanket. They looked completely powerless. Bosch only watched.

'I did not realize it for many years. It was beyond the pale to consider that he had done it. And then, of course, I must admit I was thinking of myself at the time. I was a coward, thinking only of my escape.'

Bosch was not tracking what he was saying. But it didn't seem that Conklin was talking to him, anyway. The old man was really telling himself the story. He suddenly looked up from his reverie at Bosch.

'You know, I knew someday you would come.'

'How?'

'Because I knew you would care. Maybe no one else. But I knew you would. You had to care. You were her son.'

'Tell me about what happened that night. Everything.'

'I need you to get me some water. For my throat. There's a glass there on the bureau, a fountain in the hallway. Don't let it run too long. It gets too cold and hurts my teeth.'

Bosch looked at the glass on the bureau and then back at Conklin. He was seized with a fear that if he left the room for even a minute the old man might die and take the story with him. Bosch would never hear it.

'Go. I'll be fine. I certainly can't go anywhere.'

Bosch glanced at the call button. Again, Conklin knew his thoughts.

'I am closer to hell than heaven for what I've done. For my silence. I need to tell my story. I think you'd be a better confessor than any priest could be.'

As Bosch stepped into the hallway with the glass, he saw a figure of a man turn the corner at the end of the hall and disappear. He thought the man was wearing a suit. It wasn't the guard. He saw the fountain and filled the glass. Conklin smiled weakly as he took the glass and murmured a thanks before drinking. Bosch then took the glass back and put it on the night table.

'Okay,' Bosch said. 'You said she left that night and never came back. How did you find out what happened?'

'By the next day, I was afraid something had happened. I finally called my office and made a routine check to see what had come in on the overnight reports. Among the things they told me was that there had been a homicide in Hollywood. They had the victim's name. It was her. It was the most horrible day of my life.'

'What happened next?'

Conklin rubbed a hand on his forehead and continued.

'I learned that she had been found that morning. She – I was in shock. I couldn't believe this could have happened. I had Mittel make some inquiries but there was nothing useful coming out. Then the man who had ... introduced me to Marjorie called.'

'Johnny Fox.'

'Yes. He called and he said he had heard the police were looking for him. He said he was innocent. He threatened me. He said if I did not protect him, he would reveal to the police that Marjorie was with me that last night. It would be the end of my career.'

'So you protected him.'

'I turned it over to Gordon. He investigated Fox's claim and confirmed his alibi. I cannot remember it now but it was confirmed. He had been in a card game or somewhere where there had been many witnesses. Since I was confident that Fox was not involved, I called the detectives assigned to the case and arranged for him to be interviewed. In order to protect Fox and thereby protect myself, Gordon and I concocted a story in which we told the detectives that Fox was a key witness in a grand jury investigation. The plan was successful. The detectives turned their attention elsewhere. At one point I spoke to one of them and he told me he believed that Marjorie was the victim of some sort of a sex killer. You see, they were quite rare back then. The detective said the outlook on the case was not good. I'm afraid that I never suspected ... Gordon. Such a horrible thing to do to an innocent person. It was right there in front of my face but I didn't see it for so long. I was a fool. A puppet.'

'You're saying that it wasn't you and that it wasn't Fox. You're saying that Mittel killed her to eliminate a threat to your political career. But that he didn't tell you. It was all his idea and he just went out and did it.'

'Yes, I say that. I told him, I told him that night when I called, I said that she meant more to me than all of the plans he had for me, that I had for myself. He said it would mean the end of my career and I accepted it. I accepted it as long as I started the next part of my life with her. I believe those minutes were the most peaceful of my life. I was in love and I had made a stand.'

He softly pounded a fist onto the bed, an impotent gesture.

'I told Mittel I didn't care what he thought the damage to my career would be. I told him we were going to move away. I didn't know where. La Jolla, San Diego, I threw a few places out. I didn't know where we were going to go but I was defiant. I was mad at him for not sharing the joy of our decision. And in doing so I provoked him, I know now, and I hastened your mother's death.'

Bosch studied him a long moment. His agony seemed sincere. Conklin's eyes looked as haunted as the portholes on a sunken ship. There was only blackness behind them.

'Did Mittel ever admit this to you?'

'No, but I knew. I guess it was a subconscious knowledge but then something he said years later brought it out. It confirmed it in my mind. And that was the end of our relationship.'

'What did he say? When?'

'Many years later. It was at the time I was preparing for a run for attorney general. Do you believe such a charade occurred? Me the liar, the coward, the conspirator being groomed for the office of the state's top law enforcement officer. Mittel came to me one day and said that I needed to take a wife before the election year. He was that blunt about it. He said there were rumors about me that could cost me votes. I said that was preposterous and that I wouldn't take a wife just to assuage some rednecks out in Palmdale or the desert somewhere. Then he made a comment, just a flippant, offhand comment as he was leaving my office.'

He broke off to reach for the glass of water. Bosch helped him and he slowly drank. Bosch noticed the medicinal smell about him. It was horrible. It reminded him of dead people and the morgue. Bosch took the glass when Conklin was done and put it back.

'What was the comment?'

'As he was leaving my office, he said, and I remember it

word for word, he said, "Sometimes I wish I hadn't saved you from that whore scandal. Maybe if I hadn't, we wouldn't have this problem now. People would know you aren't queer." Those were his words.'

Bosch just stared at him for a moment.

'It might've been just a figure of speech. He could have just meant that he had saved you from the scandal of knowing her by taking the steps to keep you out of it. It's not evidence that he killed her or had her killed. You were a prosecutor, you know that's not enough. It wasn't direct evidence of anything. Didn't you ever directly confront him?'

'No. Never. I was too intimidated by him. Gordon was becoming a powerful man. More powerful than I. So I said nothing to him. I simply dismantled my campaign and folded my tent. I left the public life and haven't spoken to Gordon Mittel since that time. More than twenty-five years.'

'You went into private practice.'

'Yes. I took up pro bono work as my self-imposed penance for what I was responsible for. I wish I could say it helped suture the wounds of my soul but it did not. I'm a helpless man, Hieronymus. So tell me, did you come here to kill me? Don't let my story dissuade you from believing I deserve it.'

The question at first startled Bosch into silence. Finally, he shook his head and spoke.

'What about Johnny Fox? He had his hooks into you after that night.'

'Yes, he did. He was very capable as extortionists go.'

'What happened with him?'

'I was forced to hire him as a campaign employee, paying him five hundred dollars a week for practically nothing. You see what a farce my life had become? He

356

was killed in a hit and run before picking up his first paycheck.'

'Mittel?'

'I would assume that he was responsible, though I must admit he's a rather convenient scapegoat for all the bad deeds I've been involved in.'

'You didn't think that it was just a little too coincidental that he got killed?'

'Things are so much clearer in hindsight.' He shook his head sadly. 'At the time I remember being thrilled with my luck. The one thorn in my side had been removed by serendipity. You have to remember, at the time I had no inkling that Marjorie's death was in any way connected to me. I simply saw Fox as being a man on the make. When he was removed through the luck of an automobile mishap, I was pleased. A deal was made with a reporter to keep Fox's background on the QT and everything was fine ... But, of course, it wasn't. It never was. Gordon, genius that he was, didn't plan on me not being able to get over Marjorie. And I'm still not.'

'What about McCage?'

'Who?'

'McCage Incorporated. Your payoffs to the cop. Claude Eno.'

Conklin was quiet a moment while he composed an answer.

'Of course, I knew Claude Eno. I didn't care for him. And I never paid him a dime.'

'McCage was incorporated in Nevada. It was Eno's company. You and Mittel are both listed as corporate officers. It was a payoff scam. Eno was getting a grand a month from somewhere. You and Mittel.'

'No!' Conklin said as forcefully as he could. The word came out as little more than a cough. 'I don't know about McCage. Gordon could have set it up, even signed for me

357

or made me sign unwittingly. As district attorney he took care of things for me. I signed when he told me to sign.'

He said it while looking directly at Bosch and Harry believed him. Conklin had admitted to far worse deeds. Why would he lie about paying off Eno?

'What did Mittel do when you folded your tent, when you told him you were through?'

'By then he was already quite powerful. Politically. His law firm represented the city's upper tier and his political work was branching out, growing. Still, I was the centerpiece. The plan was to take the attorney general's office and then the governor's mansion. Who knows what after that. So Gordon ... he was unhappy. I refused to see him but we talked on the phone. When he could not convince me to change my mind, he threatened me.'

'How?'

'He told me that if I ever attempted to assault his reputation, he would see to it that I was indicted for Marjorie's death. And I had no doubt that he could have done it.'

'From best man to greatest enemy. How'd you ever get hooked up with him?'

'I guess he slipped in the door while I wasn't looking. I never saw the real face until it was too late ... I don't think in my life I've come across anyone as cunningly focused as Gordon. He was – is – a dangerous man. I'm sorry I ever brought your mother into his path.'

Bosch nodded. He had no more questions and didn't know what else to say. After a few moments during which Conklin seemed to be lost in thought, the old man spoke up.

'I think, young man, that you only run into a person that is a perfect fit once in your life. When you find the one that you think fits, then grab on for dear life. And it's no matter what she's done in the past. None of that matters. Only the holding on matters.'

Bosch nodded again. It was all he could think of to do.

'Where did you meet her?'

'Oh … I met her at a dance. She was introduced and, of course, she was younger than me so I didn't think there would be any interest from her. But I was wrong … We danced. We dated. And I fell in love.'

'You didn't know about her past?'

'At the time, no. But she told me eventually. By then I didn't care.'

'What about Fox?'

'Yes, he was the liaison. He introduced us. I didn't know who he was, either. He said he was a business man. You see, for him, it was a business move. Introduce the girl to the prosecutor, sit back and see what happens. I never paid her and she never asked me for money. All the while we fell in love, Fox must have been weighing his options.'

Bosch wondered if he should take the photo from Monte Kim out of his case and show it to Conklin, but he decided not to tempt the old man's memory with the reality of a photo. Conklin spoke while Bosch was still thinking about it.

'I'm very tired now and you never answered my question.'

'What question?'

'Did you come here to kill me?'

Bosch looked at his face and his useless hands and realized he felt the stirring of sympathy.

'I didn't know what I was going to do. I just knew I was coming.'

'You want to know about her?'

'My mother?'

'Yes.'

Bosch thought about the question. His own memories of his mother were dim and fading farther all the time. And he had few recollections about her that came from others.

'What was she like?' he said.

Conklin thought for a moment.

'She is hard for me to describe. I felt a great attraction to her … that crooked smile … I knew she had secrets. I suppose all people do. But hers ran deep. And despite all of that, she was full of life. And, you see, I didn't think I was at the time we met. That's what she gave to me.'

He drank from the glass of water again, emptying it. Bosch offered to get more but Conklin waved off the offer.

'I had been with other women and they wanted to show me off like a trophy,' he said. 'Your mother wasn't like that. She'd rather stay at home or take a picnic basket to Griffith Park than go to the clubs on the Sunset Strip.'

'How did you find out about … what she did?'

'She told me. The night she told me about you. She said she needed to tell me the truth because she needed my help. I have to admit … the shock was … I initially thought of myself. You know, protecting myself. But I admired her courage in telling me and I was in love by then. I couldn't turn away.'

'How did Mittel know?'

'I told him. I regret it to this day.'

'If she … If she was as you described her, why did she do what she did? I've never … understood.'

'I haven't, either. As I told you, she had her secrets. She didn't tell me them all.'

Bosch looked away from him and out the window. The view was to the north. He could see the lights of the Hollywood Hills glimmering in the mist from the canyons.

'She used to tell me that you were a tough little egg,'

Conklin said from behind him. His voice was almost hoarse now. It was probably more talking than he had done in months. 'She once told me that she knew it didn't matter what happened to her because you were tough enough to make it through.'

Bosch said nothing. He just looked through the window.

'Was she right?' the old man asked.

Bosch's eyes followed the crestline of the hills directly north. Somewhere up there the lights glowed from Mittel's spaceship. He was up there somewhere waiting for Bosch. He looked back at Conklin, who was still waiting for an answer.

'I think maybe the jury's still out.'

✧ ✧ ✧ ✧ ✧ ✧ ✧

Bosch leaned against the stainless steel wall of the elevator as it descended. He realized how different his feelings were from those that he held while the elevator had been carrying him up. He had ridden up with hatred pounding in his chest like a cat in a burlap bag. He didn't even know the man he carried it for. Now he looked upon that man as a pitiful character, a half of a man who lay with his frail hands folded on the blanket, waiting, maybe hoping, for death to come and end his private misery.

Bosch believed Conklin. There was something about his story and his pain that seemed too genuine to be dismissed as an act. Conklin was far beyond posing. He was facing his grave. He had called himself a coward and a puppet and Bosch could think of nothing much harsher that a man could put on his own tombstone.

In realizing that Conklin spoke the truth, Bosch knew that he had already met the real enemy face to face. Gordon Mittel. The strategist. The fixer. The killer. The man who held the strings to the puppet. Now they would meet again. But this time, Bosch planned to make it on his terms.

He pushed the L button again as if that might coax the elevator to descend faster. He knew it was a useless gesture but he did it again.

When the elevator finally opened, the lobby seemed

empty and sterile. The guard was there, behind his desk, working on his word puzzle. There wasn't even the sound of a far-off TV. Only the silence of old people's lives. He asked the guard if he needed him to sign out and he was waved off.

'Look, sorry I was an asshole before,' Bosch offered.

'Don't worry about it, partner,' the guard replied. 'It gets to the best of us.'

Bosch wondered what the 'it' was he was talking about but said nothing. He nodded solemnly, as if he got most of his life lessons from security guards. He pushed through the glass doors and headed down the steps into the parking lot. It was getting cool and he turned up the collar of his jacket. He saw the sky was clear and the moon as sharp as a sickle. As he approached the Mustang he noticed the trunk of the car next to it was open and a man was bent over, attaching a jack to the rear bumper. Bosch picked up his pace and hoped he wouldn't be asked to help out. It was too cold and he was tired of talking to strangers.

He passed the crouched man and then, not used to the rental car keys, he fumbled as he tried to get the proper key into the Mustang's door lock. Just as he got the key in the slot, he heard a shoe scuff along the pavement behind him and a voice said, 'Excuse me, fella.'

Bosch turned, trying to quickly think of an excuse for why he couldn't help the man. But all he saw was the blur of the other man's arm coming down. Then he saw an explosion of red the color of blood.

Then all he saw was black.

❖ ❖ ❖ ❖ ❖ ❖ ❖

Bosch followed the coyote again. But this time the animal did not take him on the path through the mountain brush. The coyote was out of his element. He led Bosch up a steep incline of pavement. Bosch looked around and realized he was on a tall bridge over a wide expanse of water that his eyes followed to the horizon. Bosch became panicked as the coyote got too far ahead of him. He chased the animal but it crested the rise of the bridge and disappeared. The bridge was now empty, except for Bosch. He struggled to the top and looked around. The sky was blood red and seemed to be pulsing with the sound of a heartbeat.

Bosch looked in all directions but the coyote was gone. He was alone.

But suddenly he wasn't alone. The hands of someone unseen grabbed him from behind and pushed him toward the railing. Bosch struggled. He swung his elbows wildly and dug his heels in and tried to stop his movement to the edge. He tried to speak, to yell for help, but nothing came from his throat. He saw the water shimmering like the scales of a fish below him.

Then, as quickly as they had taken hold of him, the hands were gone and he was alone. He spun around and no one was there. From behind he heard a door close sharply. He turned again and there was no one. And there was no door.

❖ ❖ ❖ ❖ ❖ ❖ ❖

B osch woke up in darkness and pain to the sound of muffled shouting. He was lying on a hard surface and at first it was a struggle just to move. Eventually, he slid his hand across the ground and determined it was carpet. He knew he was inside somewhere, lying on a floor. Across the expanse of darkness he saw a small line of dim light. He stared at it for some time, using it as a focal point, before realizing that it was the crack of light emitted at the bottom edge of a door.

He pulled himself up into a sitting position and the movement made his interior world slide and melt like a Dalí painting. A feeling of nausea came over him and he closed his eyes and waited for several seconds until equilibrium returned. He raised his hand to the side of his head where the pain came from and found the hair matted with a stickiness he knew by smell was blood. His fingers carefully traced the matted hair to a two-inch-long gash in his scalp. He touched it gingerly and determined that the blood had clotted for now. The wound was no longer bleeding.

He didn't think he could stand so he crawled toward the light. The dream of the coyote broke into his mind and then disappeared in a flash of red pain.

He found the door knob was locked. That didn't surprise him. But the effort exhausted him. He leaned back against the wall and closed his eyes. Inside, his instinct to seek a means of escape and his desire to lay up and mend fought for his attention. The battle was interrupted only by the start of the voices again. Bosch could tell they did not come from the room on the other side of the door. They were farther away, yet near enough to be understood.

'Stupid fuck!'

'Look, I tol' you, you didn't say anything about any briefcase. You –'

'There had to have been one. Use your common sense.'

'You said bring the man. I brang the man. You want, I go back to the car and look for a briefcase. But you dint say nothin' about –'

'You can't go back, you fool! The place will be crawling with cops. They probably have his car and the briefcase already.'

'I didn't see any briefcase. Maybe he didn't have one.'

'And maybe I should have depended on someone else.'

Bosch realized that they were talking about him. He also recognized the angry voice as belonging to Gordon Mittel. It had the crisp delivery and haughtiness of the man Bosch had met at the fund-raiser. The other voice Bosch didn't recognize, though he had a good idea who it was. Though defensive and submissive, it was a gruff voice full of the timbre of violence. Bosch guessed it was the man who had hit him. And he imagined that to be the man he had seen Mittel with inside the house during the fund-raiser.

It took Bosch several minutes to consider the content of what they were arguing about. A briefcase. His briefcase. It wasn't in the car, he knew. Then he realized he must have forgotten it, left it in Conklin's room. He had brought it up with him so he could take out the photo Monte Kim had given him and the bank statements from Eno's safe deposit box and confront the old man with his lies. But the old man hadn't lied. He hadn't denied Bosch's mother.

And so the photo and statements weren't necessary. The briefcase lay at the foot of the bed, forgotten.

He thought about the last exchange he had heard. Mittel told the other man he could not go back, that the police would be there. This made no sense to him. Unless someone had witnessed the attack on him. Maybe the security guard. It gave him hope, then he dashed it himself when he thought of another possibility. Mittel was taking care of all the loose ends and Conklin had to be one of them. Bosch slumped against the wall. He knew he was now the last loose end. He sat there in silence until he heard Mittel's voice once more.

'Go get him. Bring him outside.'

As quickly as he could, not yet formulating a plan, Bosch crawled back toward the spot where he thought he had been when he woke up. He rammed into something heavy, put his hands on it and determined it was a pool table. He quickly found the corner and reached into the pocket. His hand closed on a billiard ball. He pulled it out, quickly trying to think of a way to conceal it. Finally, he shoved it inside his sport coat so that it rolled down the inside of the left sleeve to the crook in his elbow. There was more than enough room. Bosch liked large jackets because they gave him room to grab his gun. That made the sleeves baggy. He believed that by cocking his arm he could conceal the heavy ball in the folds of the sleeve.

As he heard a key hit the door knob, he moved to his right and sprawled on the carpet, closed his eyes and waited. He hoped he was in or close to the spot on the carpet where he had been dropped by his captors. In moments, he heard the door open and then light burned through his eyelids. There was nothing after that. No sound or movement. He waited.

'Forget it, Bosch,' the voice said. 'That only works in movies.'

Bosch didn't move.

'Look, your blood is all over the carpet. It's on the door knob here.'

Bosch realized he must have left a trail to the door and back. His half-hatched plan to surprise his captor and overtake him had no chance now. He opened his eyes. There was a light on the ceiling directly overhead.

'All right,' he said. 'What do you want?'

'Get up. Let's go.'

Bosch slowly got up. It was an actual struggle but he added to it, ad libbing a bit. And when he was all the way up, he saw blood on the green felt bumper of the pool table. He quickly stumbled and grabbed the spot for support. He hoped the man in the room had not seen the blood was already there.

'Get away from there, goddamnit. That's a five-thousand-dollar table. Look at the blood ... shit.'

'Sorry. I'll pay for it.'

'Not where you're going. Let's go.'

Bosch recognized him. It was the man he guessed it would be. Mittel's man from the party. And his face matched his voice. Gruff, strong, he had broken a few boards with it. He had a ruddy complexion set off by two small brown eyes that never seemed to blink.

He wore no suit this time. At least that Bosch could see. He was dressed in a bulky blue jumpsuit that looked brand-new. It was a splatter suit. Bosch knew that professional killers often used them. It was easier to clean up after a job and you didn't mess up your suit. Just zip off the splatter suit, dump it, and you're on your way.

Bosch stood on his own and took a step but immediately bent over and folded his arms across his stomach. He thought this was the best way to conceal the weapon he had.

'You really hit me, man. My balance is shot. I think I might get sick or something.'

'You get sick and I'll make you clean it up with your tongue. Like a fuckin' cat.'

'I guess I won't get sick then.'

'You're a funny guy. Let's go.'

The man backed away from the door and into the room. He then signaled Bosch out. For the first time Bosch saw that he carried a gun. It looked like a Beretta twenty-two and was held down low at his side.

'I know what you're thinking,' he said. 'Only a twenty-two. You think you could take maybe two, three shots and still get to me. Wrong. I got hollow points in here. I'll put you down with one shot. Tear a hole the size of a soup bowl outta your back. Remember that. Walk ahead a'me.'

He was playing it smart, Bosch noticed, not coming closer than five or six feet even though he had the gun. Once Bosch was through the door, the man issued directions. They walked down a hallway, through what looked like a living room and then through another room that Bosch thought would also qualify as a living room. This one Bosch recognized by the French doors and windows. It was the room off the party lawn at Mittel's mansion on Mount Olympus.

'Go out the door. He's waiting for you out there.'

'What did you hit me with, man?'

'Tire iron. Hope it put a splinter in your skull, but it don't matter if it did or didn't.'

'Well, I think it did anyway. Congratulations.'

Bosch stopped at one of the French doors as if he expected it to be opened for him. Outside the party tent was gone. And out near the edge of the overhang he saw Mittel standing with his back turned to the house. He was silhouetted by the lights of the city extending out into infinity from below.

369

'Open it.'

'Sorry, I thought … never mind.'

'Yeah, never mind. Just get out there. We don't have all night.'

Out on the lawn, Mittel turned around. Bosch could see he was holding the badge wallet with his ID in one hand and the lieutenant's badge in the other. The gunman stopped Bosch with a hand on his shoulder, then moved back to his six-foot distance.

'So, then, Bosch is the real name?'

Bosch looked at Mittel. The former prosecutor turned political backdoor man smiled.

'Yes. That's the real name.'

'Well, then, how do you do, Mr Bosch?'

'It's Detective, actually.'

'Detective, actually. You know, I was wondering about that. Because that's what this ID card says but then this badge says something completely different. It says lieutenant. And that's curious. Wasn't that a lieutenant I read about in the papers? The one who was found dead and without his badge? Yes, I'm sure it was. And wasn't his name, Harvey Pounds, the same name that you used when you were parading around here the other night? Again, I think so, but correct me if I am wrong, Detective Bosch.'

'It's a long story, Mittel, but I am a cop. LAPD. If you want to save yourself a few years in prison, you'll get this old fuck with the gun away from me and call me an ambulance. I've got a concussion, at least. It might be worse.'

Before speaking, Mittel put the badge in one of the pockets of his jacket and the ID wallet in the other.

'No, I don't think we'll be making any calls on your behalf. I think things have gone a little too far for humanitarian gestures like that. Speaking of the human existence, it's a shame that your play here the other night cost an innocent man his life.'

'No. It's a fucking crime *you* killed an innocent man.'

'Well, I was thinking more along the lines that it was you who killed him. I mean, of course, you are ultimately responsible.'

'Just like a lawyer, passing the buck. Should've stayed out of politics, Gordie. Stuck to the law. You'd probably have your own TV commercials by now.'

Mittel smiled.

'And what? Given up all of this?'

He spread his arms to take in the house and the magnificent view. Bosch followed the arc of his arm to look at the house but he was really trying to get a bead on the other man, the one with the gun. He spotted him standing five feet directly behind him, the gun at his side. He was still too far away for Bosch to risk making a move. Especially in his condition. He moved his arm slightly and felt the billiard ball nesting in the crook of his elbow. It was reassuring to him. It was all he had.

'The law is for fools, Detective Bosch. But I must correct you. I don't really consider myself to be in politics. I consider myself to be just a fixer. A solver of problems of any kind for anyone. Political problems just happen to be my forte. But now, you see, I have to fix a problem that is neither political nor someone else's. This one is my own.'

He raised his eyebrows as though he could hardly believe it himself.

'And that's why I have invited you here. Why I asked Jonathan to bring you along. You see, I had an idea that if we watched Arno Conklin, our mystery party crasher of the other night would eventually show up. And I wasn't disappointed.'

'You're a clever man, Mittel.'

Bosch turned his head slightly so that he could see

Jonathan in his peripheral vision. He was still out of reach. Bosch knew he had to draw him closer.

'Hold your ground, Jonathan,' Mittel said. 'Mr Bosch is not one to get excited about. Just a minor inconvenience.'

Bosch looked back at Mittel.

'Just like Marjorie Lowe, right? She was just a minor inconvenience. Just a nobody who didn't count.'

'Now, that's an interesting name to bring up. Is that what this is about, Detective Bosch?'

Bosch stared at him, too angry to speak.

'Well, the only thing I can admit to is that I did use her death to my advantage. I saw it as an opportunity, you could say.'

'I know all about it, Mittel. You used her to get control of Conklin. But eventually even he saw through your lies. It's over now. It doesn't matter what you do to me here, my people will be coming. You can count on it.'

'The old give-up-the-place-is-surrounded ploy. I don't think so. This badge business ... something tells me that you've exceeded your bounds on this one. I think maybe this is what they call an unofficial investigation and the fact that you used a false name before and were carrying a dead man's badge tends to bear me out ... I don't think anyone is coming. Are they?'

Bosch's mind raced but he drew a blank and remained silent.

'I think you're just a small-time extortionist who stumbled onto something somehow and wants a payoff to go away. Well, we're going to give you a payoff, Detective Bosch.'

'There are people who know what I know, Mittel,' Bosch blurted. 'What are you going to do, go out and kill them all?'

'I'll take that suggestion under advisement.'

'What about Conklin? He knows the whole story.

Anything happens to me, I guarantee he'll go right to the cops.'

'As a matter of fact, you could say Arno Conklin is with the police right now. But I don't think he's saying much.'

Bosch dropped his head and slumped a little. He had guessed that Conklin was dead but had hoped he was wrong. He felt the billiard ball move in his sleeve and he folded his arms again to cover up.

'Yes. Apparently, the former district attorney threw himself from his window after your visit.'

Mittel stepped aside and pointed out into the lights below. Far off Bosch could see the cluster of lighted buildings that were Park La Brea. And he could see blue and red lights flashing at the base of one of the buildings. It was Conklin's building.

'Must have been a truly traumatic moment,' Mittel continued. 'He chose death rather than give in to extortion. A principled man to the end.'

'He was an old man!' Bosch yelled angrily. 'Goddamnit, why?'

'Detective Bosch, keep your voice down or Jonathan will have to lower it for you.'

'You're not getting away this time,' Bosch said in a lower, tighter, controlled voice.

'As far as Conklin goes, I assume the final declaration will be suicide. He was very sick, you know.'

'Right, a guy with no legs walks over to the window and decides to throw himself out.'

'Well, if the authorities don't believe that, then maybe they will come up with an alternate scenario when they find your fingerprints in the room. I'm sure you obliged us by leaving a few.'

'Along with my briefcase.'

That hit Mittel like a slap across the face.

'That's right. I left it there. And there's enough in it to

373

bring them up this mountain to see you, Mittel. They'll come for you!'

Bosch yelled the last line at him as a test.

'Jon!' Mittel barked.

Almost before the word was out of Mittel's mouth, Bosch was clubbed from behind. The impact came on the right side of the neck and he went down to his knees, careful to keep his arm bent and the heavy ball in place. He slowly, more slowly than was needed, got up. Since the impact had been on the right, he assumed that Jonathan had hit him with his gun hand.

'By providing me with the location of the briefcase, you have answered the most important question I had,' Mittel said. 'The other, of course, was what was in the briefcase and how it would concern me. Now, the problem I have is that without the briefcase or the ability to get it I have no way of checking the veracity of what you tell me here.'

'So I guess you're fucked.'

'No, Detective, I think that would more accurately describe your situation. However, I have one other question before you go off. Why, Detective Bosch? Why were you bothering with something so old and so meaningless?'

Bosch looked at him for a long time before answering.

'Because everybody counts, Mittel. Everybody.'

Bosch saw Mittel nod in the direction of Jonathan. The meeting was over. He had to make his play.

'*Help!*'

Bosch yelled it as loudly as he could. And he knew the gunman would make his move toward him immediately. Anticipating the same swing of the gun to the right side of the neck, Bosch spun to his right. As he moved he straightened his left arm and used the centrifugal force of the move to let the billiard ball roll down his sleeve into his hand. In continuing the move, he swung his arm up and out. And as he turned his face he saw Jonathan inches behind him, swinging his own hand down, the fingers laced around the Beretta. He also saw the surprise on Jonathan's face as he realized his swing would surely miss and that his momentum prevented him from correcting the course.

After Jonathan's arm went by harmlessly and he was vulnerable, Bosch's arm arced downward. Jonathan made a last-second lunge to his left but the billiard ball in Bosch's fist still caught him with a glancing blow to the right side of his head. It made a sound like a lightbulb popping and Jonathan's body followed the momentum of his falling arm. He fell face first on the grass, his body on top of the gun.

Almost immediately, the man tried to get up and Bosch delivered a vicious kick to his ribs. Jonathan rolled off the gun and Bosch came down on his body with his knees, swinging his fist into the back of his head and neck two more times before realizing that he still gripped the billiard ball and that he had hurt the man enough.

Breathing as if he had just come up for air, Bosch glanced around and saw the gun. He quickly grabbed it up and looked for Mittel. But he was gone.

The slight sound of running on grass caught his attention and he looked to the far northern line of the lawn. He caught a glimpse of Mittel then, just as he disappeared into the darkness at the spot where the flat, manicured grass gave way to the rugged brush of the hilltop.

'Mittel!'

Bosch jumped up and followed. At the point where he had last seen Mittel, he found a path worn into the brush. He realized it was an old coyote trail that had been widened over time by human feet. He raced down it, the yawning drop-off to the city below no more than two feet on his right.

He saw no sign of Mittel and followed the trail along the edge of the drop-off until the house was no longer in sight behind him. Finally he stopped after coming across nothing that indicated Mittel was even near or had taken this path.

Breathing heavily, his head pounding where he was wounded, Bosch came upon a steep bluff rising off the side of the trail and saw that it was ringed with old beer bottles and other debris. The bluff was a popular lookout spot. He put the gun in his waistband and then used his hands for balance and purchase as he climbed ten feet to its top. He did a slow three-sixty-degree turn while on top of the bluff but saw nothing. He listened but the hiss of the city's traffic precluded any chance of his hearing Mittel moving in the brush. He decided to give it up, to get back to the house and call out an air unit before Mittel could get away. They'd find him with a spotlight if the chopper could get out here quickly enough.

As he gingerly slid back down the bluff, Mittel suddenly came at him from the darkness to the right. He had been hiding behind a thick growth of brush and Spanish sword plants. He dove into Bosch's midsection, knocking him down onto the trail, his weight on top of him. Bosch felt the man's hands going for the gun still in his waistband. But Bosch was younger and stronger. The surprise attack was Mittel's last card. Bosch closed his arms around him and rolled to his left. Suddenly, the weight was off and Mittel was gone.

Bosch sat up and looked about, then pulled himself over to the edge. He pulled the gun out of his waistband and then leaned over and looked down. There was only darkness when he looked directly down the side of the rugged hill. He could see the rectangular roofs of houses about a hundred and fifty yards down. He knew they were built along the twisting roads that fed off Hollywood Boulevard and Fairfax Avenue. He did another complete turn and then looked down again. He didn't see Mittel anywhere.

Bosch surveyed the scene beneath him in its entirety until his eyes caught the backyard lights flicking on behind one of the houses directly below. He watched as a man came out of the house carrying what looked like a rifle. The man slowly approached a round backyard spa platform, the rifle pointed ahead of him. The man stopped at the edge of the spa and reached to what must have been the outdoor electrical box.

The tub light came on, silhouetting the body of a man floating in a circle of blue. Even from on top of the hill Bosch could see the swirls of blood seeping from Mittel's body. Then the voice of the man with the rifle came up the hillside intact.

'Linda, don't come out! Just call the police. Tell them we got a body in our hot tub.'

Then the man looked up the hillside and Bosch moved back away from the edge. Immediately, he wondered why he'd had the instinctive reaction to hide.

He got up and slowly made his way back to Mittel's house along the path. As he walked, he looked out across the city at the lights shimmering in the night and thought it was beautiful. He thought about Conklin and Pounds and then pushed the guilt out of his mind with thoughts about Mittel, about how his death finally closed the circle begun so long ago. He thought of the image of his mother in Monte Kim's photo. Her looking timidly around the edge of Conklin's arm. He waited for the feeling of satisfaction and triumph that he knew was supposed to come with vengeance accomplished. But none of it ever came to him. He only felt hollow and tired.

When he got back to the perfect lawn behind the perfect mansion, the man called Jonathan was gone.

✤ ✤ ✤ ✤ ✤ ✤ ✤

Assistant Chief Irvin S. Irving stood in the open doorway of the examination suite. Bosch was sitting on the side of the padded table holding an ice pack to his head. The doctor had given it to him after putting in the stitches. He noticed Irving when he adjusted the bag in his hand.

'How do you feel?'

'I'll live, I guess. That's what they tell me, at least.'

'Well, that's better than you can say for Mittel. He took the high dive.'

'Yeah. What about the other one?'

'Nothing on him. We got his name, though. You told the uniforms Mittel called him Jonathan. So that means he's probably Jonathan Vaughn. He's worked for Mittel for a long time. They're working on it, checking the hospitals. Sounds like you might've hurt him enough that he'd come in.'

'Vaughn.'

'We're trying to do a background on him. So far, not much. He's got no record.'

'How long was he with Mittel?'

'That we're not sure of. We've talked to Mittel's people at the law firm. Not what you'd call cooperative. But they say Vaughn has been around forever. He was described by most people as Mittel's personal valet.'

Bosch nodded and put the information away.

'There's also a driver. We picked him up but he isn't saying much. A little surfer punk. He couldn't talk if he wanted to anyway.'

'What do you mean?'

'His jaw is broken. Wired shut. He won't talk about that, either.'

Bosch just nodded again and looked at him. There didn't seem to be anything hidden in what he had said.

'The doctor said you have a severe concussion but the skull is not fractured. Minor laceration.'

'Could've fooled me. My head feels like the Goodyear blimp with a hole in it.'

'How many stitches?'

'I think he said eighteen.'

'He said you'll probably have headaches and keep the knot up there and the eye hemorrhages for a few days. It'll look worse than it is.'

'Well, nice to know he's telling somebody what's going on. I haven't heard anything from him. Just the nurses.'

'He'll be in in a minute. He was probably waiting for you to come out of it a little more.'

'Come out of what?'

'You were a little dazed when we got up there to you, Harry. You sure you want to talk about this now? It can wait. You're hurt and need to take it –'

'I'm okay. I want to talk. You been by the scene at Park La Brea?'

'Yes, I was there. I was there when we got the call from Mount Olympus. I've got your briefcase in the car, by the way. You left it there, didn't you? With Conklin?'

He started to nod but stopped because it made things swirl.

'Good,' he said. 'There's something there I want to keep.'

'The photo?'

'You looked through it?'

'Bosch! You must be groggy. It was found at the scene of a crime.'

'Yeah, I know, sorry.'

He waved off his objection. He was tired of fighting.

'So, the crew working the scene up on the hill already told me what happened. At least, the early version based on the physicals. What I'm not clear about is what got you up there. You know, how all of this figures. You want to run it down for me or wait until maybe tomorrow?'

Bosch nodded once and waited a moment for his mind to clear. He hadn't tried to collect the story into one cohesive thought yet. He thought about it some more and finally gave it a shot.

'I'm ready.'

'Okay, I want to read you your rights first.'

'What, again?'

'It's just a procedure so it doesn't look like we're cutting any slack to one of our own. You've got to remember, you were at two places tonight and at both somebody took a big fall. It doesn't look good.'

'I didn't kill Conklin.'

'I know that and we have the security guard's statement. He says you left before Conklin took the dive. So you're gonna be okay. You're clear but I have to follow procedure. Now, you still want to talk?'

'I waive my rights.'

Irving read them to him from a card anyway and Bosch waived them again.

'Okay, then, I don't have a waive form. You'll have to sign that later.'

'You want me to tell the story?'

'Yes, I want you to tell the story.'

'Okay, here we go.'

But then he stopped as he tried to put it into words.

'Harry?'

'Okay, here it is. In 1961 Arno Conklin met Marjorie Lowe. He was introduced by local scumbucket Johnny Fox, who made his living off making such introductions and arrangements. Usually for money. This initial meeting between Arno and Marjorie was at the St Pat's party at the Masonic Lodge on Cahuenga.'

'That's the photo in the briefcase, right?'

'Right. Now, at that first meeting, according to Arno's story, which I believe, he didn't know that Marjorie was a pro and Fox was a pimp. Fox arranged the introduction because he probably saw the opportunity and had one eye on the future. See, if Conklin knew it was a pay-to-play sort of thing, he would have walked away. He was the top county vice commando. He would have walked away.'

'So he didn't know who Fox was either?' Irving asked.

'That's what he said. He just said he was innocent. If you find that hard to take, the alternative is harder; that this prosecutor would openly consort with these types of people. So, I'm going with Arno's story. He didn't know.'

'Okay, he didn't know he was being compromised. So what was in it for Fox and … your mother?'

'Fox is easy. Once Conklin went with her, Fox had a nice hook into him and he could reel him in whenever he wanted. Marjorie is something else and I've been thinking about it but it still isn't clear. But you can say this, most women in that situation are looking for a way out. She could have played along with Fox's plan because she had her own plan. She was looking for a way out of the life.'

Irving nodded and added to the hypothesis.

'She had a boy in the youth hall and wanted to get him out. Being with Arno could only help.'

'That's right. The thing of it was, Arno and Marjorie did something none of the three of them expected. They fell in love. Or at least Conklin did. And he believed she did, too.'

Irving took a chair in the corner, crossed his legs and stared thoughtfully at Bosch. He said nothing. Nothing about his demeanor indicated he was anything else but totally interested and believing in Bosch's story. Bosch's arm was getting tired of holding the ice pack up and he wished he could lie down. But there was only the table in the examination suite. He continued the story.

'So they fall in love and their relationship continues and somewhere along the line she tells him. Or maybe Mittel did some checking and told him. It doesn't matter. What matters is that at some point Conklin knew the score. And again, he surprises everybody.'

'How?'

'On October twenty-seven, nineteen sixty-one, he proposes marriage to Marj –'

'He told you this? Arno told you this?'

'He told me tonight. He wanted to marry her. She wanted to marry him. On that night back then, he finally decided to chuck it all, to risk losing everything he had to gain the one thing he wanted most.'

Bosch reached into his jacket on the table and took out his cigarettes. Irving spoke up.

'I don't think this is a – nothing, never mind.'

Bosch lit a smoke with his lighter.

'It was the bravest act of his life. You realize that? That took balls to be willing to risk everything like that … But he made a mistake.'

'What?'

'He called his friend Gordon Mittel to ask him to go with them to Vegas to be best man. Mittel refused. He knew it would be the end of a promising political career for Conklin, maybe even his own career, and he wanted no part of it. But then he went further than just refusing to be best man. See, he saw Conklin as the white horse on which he would be able to ride into the castle. He had big plans for himself and Conklin and he wasn't going to sit back and let some ... some Hollywood whore ruin it. He knew from Conklin's call that she had gone home to pack. So Mittel went there and intercepted her somehow. Maybe told her that Conklin had sent him. I don't know.'

'He killed her.'

Bosch nodded and this time he didn't go dizzy.

'I don't know where, maybe in his car. He made it look like a sex crime by tying the belt around her neck and tearing up her clothes. The semen ... it was already there because she had been with Conklin ... After she was dead, Mittel took the body to the alley near the Boulevard and put her in the trash. The whole thing stayed a secret for a lot of years after that.'

'Until you came along.'

Bosch didn't answer. He was savoring his cigarette and the relief of the end of the case.

'What about Fox?' Irving asked.

'Like I said, Fox knew about Marjorie and Arno. And he knew they were together the night before Marjorie was found dead in that alley. That knowledge gave Fox a powerful piece of leverage over an important man, even if the man was innocent. Fox used it. In who knows how many ways. Within a year he was on Arno's campaign payroll. He was hooked on him like a bloodsucking leech. So Mittel, the fixer, finally stepped in. Fox died in a hit and run while supposedly handing out Conklin campaign fliers. Would've been easy to set up, make it look like it was an accident and the driver just fled. But that's no surprise. The same guy who worked the Marjorie Lowe case worked the hit and run. Same result. Nobody ever arrested.'

'McKittrick?'

'No. Claude Eno. He's dead now. Took his secrets with him. But Mittel was paying him off for twenty-five years.'

'The bank statements?'

'Yeah, in the briefcase. You look, you'll probably find records somewhere linking Mittel to the payments. Conklin said he didn't know about them and I believe him … You know, somebody ought to check all the elections Mittel worked on over the years. They'll probably find out he was a rat fucker that could've held his own in the Nixon White House.'

Bosch ground his cigarette out on the side of a trash can next to the table and dropped the butt in. He started to feel very cold and put his jacket back on. It was smudged with dirt and dried blood.

'You look like a mess in that, Harry,' Irving said. 'Why don't you –'

'I'm cold.'

'Okay.'

'You know, he didn't even scream.'

'What?'

'Mittel. He didn't even scream when he went down that hill. I can't figure that out.'

'You don't have to. It's just one of those –'

'And I didn't push him. He jumped me in the brush and when we rolled, he went over. He didn't even scream.'

'I understand. No one is saying –'

'All I did was start to ask questions about her and people started dying.'

Bosch was staring at an eye chart on the far wall of the room. He could not figure out why they would have such a thing in an emergency room examination suite.

'Christ … Pounds … I –'

'Yes, I know what happened,' Irving interrupted.

Bosch looked over at him.

'You do?'

'We interviewed everyone in the squad. Edgar told me that he made a computer run for you on Fox. My only conclusion is that Pounds either overheard or somehow got wind of it. I think he was monitoring what your close associates were doing after you went on ISL. Then he must've taken it a step further and stumbled into Mittel and Vaughn. He ran DMV traces on the parties involved. I think it got back to Mittel. He had the connections that would have warned him.'

Bosch was silent. He wondered if Irving really believed that scenario or if he was signaling to Bosch that he knew what had really happened and was letting it go by. It didn't matter. Whether or not Irving blamed him or took departmental action against him, Bosch's own conscience would be the hardest thing to live with.

'Christ,' he said again. 'He got killed instead of me.'

His body started shuddering then. As if saying the words out loud had started some kind of exorcism. He threw the ice pack into the trash can and wrapped his arms around himself. But the shuddering wouldn't stop. It seemed to him that he would never be warm again, that his shaking was not a temporary affliction but a permanent part of him now. He had the warm salty taste of tears in his mouth and he realized then that he was crying. He turned his face away from Irving and tried to tell him to leave but he couldn't say anything. His jaw was locked as tight as a fist.

'Harry?' he heard Irving say. 'Harry, you okay?'

Bosch managed to nod, not understanding how Irving could not see his body shaking. He moved his hands into the pockets of his jacket and pulled it closed around him. He felt something in his left pocket and started absent-mindedly pulling it out.

'Look,' Irving was saying, 'the doctor said you could get emotional. This knock on the head ... they do weird things to you. Don't wor – Harry, are you sure you're okay? You're turning blue, son. I'm gonna – I'll go get the doctor. I'll –'

He stopped as Bosch managed to remove the object from his jacket. He held his palm upright. Clasped in his shaking hand was a black eight ball. Much of it was smeared with blood. Irving took it from him, having to practically pry his fingers off it.

'I'll go get somebody,' was all he said.

Then Bosch was alone in the room, waiting for someone to come and the demon to leave.

❖ ❖ ❖ ❖ ❖ ❖ ❖

Because of the concussion, Bosch's pupils were dilated unevenly and purple hemorrhages bulged below them. He had a hell of a headache and a one-hundred-degree temperature. As a precaution, the emergency room physician ordered that he be admitted and monitored, not allowed to sleep until four in the morning. He tried to pass the time by reading the newspaper and watching the talk shows but they only seemed to worsen the pain. Finally, he just stared at the walls until a nurse came in, checked on him and told him he could sleep. After that, nurses kept coming into his room and waking him at two-hour intervals. They checked his eyes and temperature and asked if he was okay. They never gave him anything for the headache. They told him to go back to sleep. If he dreamed of the coyote during the short sleep cycles, or anything else, he didn't remember it.

Finally, at noon, he got up for good. He was unsteady on his feet at first but equilibrium quickly came back to him. He made his way into the bathroom and studied his image in the mirror. He burst out laughing at what he saw, though it was not that funny. It was just that he seemed to be about to laugh or cry or do both at any given moment.

He had a small shaved spot on his skull where there was an L-shaped seam of stitches. It hurt when he touched the wound but he laughed about that, too. He managed to comb hair over it with his hand, fairly well camouflaging the injury.

The eyes were another matter. Still dilated unevenly and now cracked with red veins, they looked like the bad end of a two-week bender. Below them, deep purple triangles pointed to the corners of the eyes. A double shiner. Bosch didn't think he'd ever had one before.

Stepping back into the room he saw that his briefcase had been left by Irving next to the bed table. He bent to pick it up and almost lost his balance, grabbing on to the table at the last moment. He got back into bed with the briefcase and began examining its contents. He had no purpose in mind, he just wanted to be doing something.

He leafed through his notebook, finding it hard to concentrate on the words. He then reread the five-year-old Christmas card from Meredith Roman, now Katherine Register. He realized he needed to call her, that he wanted to tell her what happened before she read about it in the paper or heard it on the news. He found her number in his notebook and dialed on the room's phone. He got her answering machine and left a message.

'Meredith, uh, Katherine … this is Harry Bosch. I need to talk to you today when you get a minute. Some things have happened and I think you'll, uh, feel better about things when you hear from me. So, give me a call.'

Bosch left a variety of numbers on the tape, including his mobile, the Mark Twain and the hospital room and then hung up.

He opened the accordion pocket in the lid of the briefcase and slipped out the photo Monte Kim had given him. He studied his mother's face for a long time. The thought that eventually poked through was a question. Bosch had no doubt from what Conklin had said that he had loved her. But he wondered if she really loved Conklin back. Bosch remembered a time when she had visited him at McClaren. She had promised to get him out. At the time, the legal effort was going slowly and he knew that she had no faith in courts. When she made the promise, he knew she wasn't thinking about the law, only ways to get around it, to manipulate it. And he believed she would have found a way to do it if her time hadn't been taken away.

He realized, looking at the photo, that Conklin might simply have been part of the promise, part of the manipulation. Their marriage plan was her way of getting Harry out. From unwed mother with an arrest record to wife of an important man. Conklin would be able to get Harry out, to win back Marjorie Lowe's custody of her son. Bosch considered that love may have had nothing to do with it on her part, that it was only opportunity. In all the visits to McClaren, she had never spoken of Conklin or any man in particular. If she had truly been in love, wouldn't she have told him?

And in considering that question, Bosch realized that his mother's effort to save him was what might ultimately have led to her death.

'Mr Bosch, are you okay?'

The nurse moved quickly into the room and put the food tray down on the table with a rattle. Bosch didn't answer her. He barely noticed her. She took the napkin off the tray and used it to wipe the tears off his cheeks.

'It's okay,' she soothed. 'It's okay.'

'Is it?'

'It's the injury. Nothing to be embarrassed about. Head injuries jumble the emotions. One minute you're crying, the next you're laughing. Let me open these curtains. Maybe that will cheer you up.'

'I think I just want to be left alone.'

She ignored him and opened the curtains and Bosch had a view of another building twenty yards away. It did cheer him up, though. The view was so bad it made him laugh. It also reminded him he was in Cedars. He recognized the other medical tower.

The nurse then closed his briefcase so she could roll the table over the bed. On the tray was a plate containing Salisbury steak, carrots and potatoes. There was a roll that looked as hard as the eight ball he had found in his pocket the night before and some kind of red dessert wrapped in plastic. The tray and its smell made him feel the onset of nausea.

'I'm not going to eat this. Is there any Frosted Flakes?'

'You have to eat a full meal.'

'I just woke up. You people kept me up all night. I can't eat this. It's making me sick.'

She quickly picked up the tray and headed to the door. 'I'll see what I can do. About the Frosted Flakes.'

She looked back at him and smiled before heading out the door.

'Cheer up.'

'Yeah, that's the prescription.'

Bosch didn't know what to do with himself but wait for time to pass. He started thinking about his encounter with Mittel, about what was said and what was meant. There was something about it that bothered him.

He was interrupted by a beeping sound coming from the side panel of the bed. He looked down and found it was the phone.

'Hello?'

'Harry?'

'Yes.'

'It's Jazz. Are you okay?'

There was a long silence. Bosch didn't know if he was ready for this yet, but now it was unavoidable.

'Harry?'

'I'm fine. How'd you find me?'

'The man who called me yesterday. Irving something. He –'

'Chief Irving.'

'Yes. He called and told me you were hurt. He gave me the number.'

That annoyed Bosch but he tried not to show it.

'Well, I'm fine, but I can't really talk.'

'Well, what happened?'

'It's just a long story. I don't want to go through it now.'

Now she was quiet. It was one of those moments when both people try to read the silence, pick up each other's meanings in what they weren't saying.

'You know, don't you?'

'Why didn't you tell me, Jasmine?'

'I …'

More silence.

'Do you want me to tell you now?'

'I don't know …'

'What did he tell you?'

'Who?'

'Irving.'

'It wasn't from him. He doesn't know. It was somebody else. Somebody trying to hurt me.'

'It was a long time ago, Harry. I want to tell you what happened … but not on the phone.'

He closed his eyes and thought for a minute. Just hearing her voice had renewed his sense of connection to her. But he had to question whether he wanted to get into this.

'I don't know, Jazz. I've got to think about –'

'Look, what was I supposed to do? Wear a sign or something to warn you away from the start? You tell me, when was a good time for me to tell you? Was it right after that first lemonade? Should I have said, "Oh, by the way,

392

six years ago I killed the man I was living with when he tried to rape me for the second time in the same night?' Would that have been proper?'

'Jazz, don't ...'

'Don't what? Look, the cops didn't believe my story here, what should I expect from you?'

He could tell she was crying now, not so that he was supposed to hear. But he could tell it in her voice, full of loneliness and pain.

'You said things to me,' she said. 'I thought ...'

'Jazz, we spent a weekend together. You're putting too much –'

'Don't you dare! Don't you tell me it didn't mean anything.'

'You're right. I'm sorry ... Look, this isn't the right time. I've got too much going on. I gotta call you back ...'

She didn't say anything.

'Okay?'

'Okay, Harry, you call me.'

'Okay, good-bye, Jazz.'

He hung up and kept his eyes closed for a while. He felt the numbness of disappointment that comes from broken hopes and wondered if he would ever talk to her again. In analyzing his thoughts he realized how much they seemed to be the same. And so his fear was not of what she had done, whatever the details were. His fear was that he would indeed call her and that he would become entwined with someone with more baggage than himself.

He opened his eyes and tried to put the thoughts aside. But he came back to her. He found himself marveling at the randomness of their meeting. A newspaper want ad. It might as well have said Single White Killer Seeks Same. He laughed out loud but it wasn't funny.

He turned the television on as a distraction. There was a talk show on and the host was interviewing women who stole their best friends' men. The best friends were also on and every question devolved into a verbal cat fight. Bosch turned the sound down and watched for ten minutes in silence, studying the contortions of the women's angry faces.

After a while he turned it off and rang the nurses' station on the intercom to inquire about his cereal. The nurse he spoke to knew nothing about his request for breakfast at lunch time. He tried Meredith Roman's number again but hung up when he got the tape.

Just as Bosch was getting hungry enough to be tempted to call for the return of the Salisbury steak, a nurse finally came back in with another food tray. This one contained a banana, a small glass of orange juice, a plastic bowl with a little box of Frosted Flakes in it and a pint-size carton of milk. He thanked her and began eating the cereal out of the box. The other stuff he didn't want.

He picked up the phone and dialed the main number at Parker Center and asked for Assistant Chief Irving's office. The secretary who eventually answered said Irving was in conference with the police chief and could not be disturbed. Bosch left his number.

Next he dialed Keisha Russell's number at the paper.

'It's Bosch.'

'Bosch, where have you been? You turn your phone off?'

Bosch reached into his briefcase and took the phone out. He checked the battery.

'Sorry, it's dead.'

'Great. That doesn't help me any, does it? The two biggest names in that clip I gave you end up dead last night and you don't even call. Some deal we made.'

'Hey, this is me on the phone, right?'

'So what've you got for me?'

394

'What've you got already? What are they saying about it?'

'They're not saying jack. I've been waiting on you, man.'

'But what are they really saying?'

'I mean it, nothing. They're saying both deaths are being investigated and that there is no clear connection. They're trying to pass it off as a big coincidence.'

'What about the other man? Did they find Vaughn?'

'Who's Vaughn?'

Bosch couldn't figure out what was happening, why there was a cover-up. He knew he should wait to hear from Irving but the anger was growing in his throat.

'Bosch? You there? What other man?'

'What are they saying about me?'

'You? They're not saying anything.'

'The other man's name is Jonathan Vaughn. He was there, too. Up at Mittel's last night.'

'How do you know?'

'I was there, too.'

'Bosch, you were there?'

Bosch closed his eyes but his mind couldn't penetrate the shroud being thrown over the case by the department. He didn't get it.

'Harry, we had a deal. Tell me the story.'

He noted that it was the only time she had ever used his first name. He continued to say nothing while he tried to figure out what was happening and weighed the consequences of talking to her.

'Bosch?'

Back to normal.

'All right. You got your pencil? I'm going to give you enough to get started. You'll have to go to Irving to get the rest.'

'I've been calling him. He won't even take my calls.'

'He will when he knows you have the story. He'll have to.'

By the time he was done telling her the story he was fatigued and his head was hurting again. He was ready to go to sleep, if it would have him. He wanted to forget everything and just sleep.

'That's an incredible story, Bosch,' she said when he was done. 'I'm sorry, you know, about your mother.'

'Thanks.'

'What about Pounds?'

'What about him?'

'Is it connected? Irving was honchoing that investigation. Now he's doing this one.'

'You'll have to ask him.'

'If I can get him on the line.'

'When you call over there, tell the adjutant to tell Irving you're calling on behalf of Marjorie Lowe. He'll call you back when he gets the message. I guarantee it.'

'Okay, Bosch, last thing. We didn't talk about this at the start like we should have. Can I use your name as a source?'

Bosch thought about it but only for a few moments.

'Yeah, you can use it. I don't know what my name's worth anymore but you can use it.'

'Thanks. I'll see you. You're a pal.'

'Yeah, I'm a pal.'

He hung up and closed his eyes. He dozed off but wasn't sure for how long. He was interrupted by the phone. It was Irving and he was angry.

'What did you do?'

'What do you mean?'

'I just got a message from a reporter. She says she's calling because of Marjorie Lowe. Have you talked to reporters about this?'

'I talked to one.'

'What did you tell her?'

'I told her enough so that you won't be able to let this one blow away.'

'Bosch ...'

He didn't finish. There was a long silence and then Bosch spoke first.

'You were going to cover it all up, weren't you? Shove it in the trash with her. You see, after everything that's happened, she still doesn't count, does she?'

'You don't know what you're talking about.'

Bosch sat up. Now he was angry. Immediately, he was hit with vertigo. He closed his eyes until it passed.

'Well, then why don't you tell me what I don't know? Okay, Chief? You're the one who doesn't know what you're talking about. I heard what you people put out. That there may be no connection between Conklin and Mittel. What kind of – you think I'm going to sit here for that? And Vaughn. Not even a mention of him. A fucking mechanic in a splatter suit, he throws Conklin out the window and is ready to put me in the dirt. He's the one who did Pounds and he doesn't even rate a mention by you people. So, Chief, why don't you tell me what the fuck I don't know, okay?'

'Bosch, listen to me. *Listen* to me. Who did Mittel work for?'

'I don't know and I don't care.'

'He was employed by very powerful people. Some of the most powerful in this state, some of the most powerful in the country. And –'

'I don't give a shit!'

'– a majority of the city council.'

'So? What are you telling me? The council and the governor and the senators and all of those people, what, are they all involved now, too? You covering their asses, too?'

'Bosch, would you calm down and make sense? Listen to yourself. Of course, I'm not saying that. What I am trying to explain to you is that if you taint Mittel with this, then you taint many very powerful people who associated with him or who used his services. That could come back to haunt this department as well as you and me in immeasurable ways.'

That was it, Bosch saw. Irving the pragmatist had made a choice, probably along with the police chief, to put the department and themselves ahead of the truth. The whole deal stunk like rotting garbage. Bosch felt exhaustion roll over him like a wave. He was drowning in it. He'd had enough of this.

'And by covering it up, you are helping them in immeasurable ways, right? And I'm sure you and the chief have been on the phone all morning letting each of those powerful people know just that. They'll all owe you, they'll all owe the department a big one. That's great, Chief. That's a great deal. I guess it doesn't matter that the truth is nowhere to be found in it.'

'Bosch, I want you to call her back. Call that reporter and tell her that you took this knock on the head and you –'

'No! I'm not calling anybody back. It's too late. I told the story.'

'But not the whole story. The whole story is just as damaging to you, isn't it?'

There it was. Irving knew. He either outright knew or had made a pretty good guess that Bosch had used Pounds's name and was ultimately responsible for his death. That knowledge was now his weapon against Bosch.

'If I can't contain this,' Irving added, 'I may have to take action against you.'

'I don't care,' Bosch said quietly. 'You can do whatever

you want to me, but the story is coming out, Chief. The truth.'

'But is it the truth? The whole truth? I doubt it and deep in inside I know you doubt it, too. We'll never know the whole truth.'

A silence followed. Bosch waited for him to say more and when there was only more silence, he hung up. He then disconnected the phone and finally went to sleep.

❖ ❖ ❖ ❖ ❖ ❖ ❖

Bosch awoke at six the next morning with dim memories of his sleep having been interrupted by a horrible dinner and the visits of nurses through the night. His head felt thick. He gently touched the wound and found it not as tender as the day before. He got up and walked around the room a bit. His balance seemed back to normal. In the bathroom mirror his eyes were still a colorful mess but the dilation of the pupils had evened out. It was time to go, he knew. He got dressed and left the room, briefcase in hand and carrying his ruined jacket over his arm.

At the nurses' station he pushed the elevator button and waited. He noticed one of the nurses behind the counter eyeing him. She apparently didn't readily recognize him, especially with his street clothes on.

'Excuse me, can I help you?'

'No, I'm fine.'

'Are you a patient?'

'I was. I'm leaving. Room four-nineteen. Bosch.'

'Wait a moment, sir. What are you doing?'

'I'm leaving. Going home.'

'What?'

'Just send me the bill.'

The elevator doors opened and he stepped in.

'You can't do that,' the nurse called. 'Let me get the doctor.'

Bosch raised his hand and waved good-bye.

'Wait!'

The doors closed.

He bought a newspaper in the lobby and caught a cab outside. He told the driver to take him to Park La Brea. Along the way, he read Keisha Russell's story. It was on the front page and it was pretty much an abbreviated account of what he had told her the day before. Everything was qualified with the caveat that it was still under investigation, but it was a good read.

Bosch was mentioned throughout by name as a source and main player in the story. Irving was also a named source. Bosch figured the assistant chief must have decided in the end to throw in with the truth, or a close approximation of it, once Bosch had already let it out. It was the pragmatic thing to do. This way it seemed like he had a handle on things. He was the voice of conservative reason in the story. Bosch's statements were usually followed by those from Irving cautioning that the investigation was still in its infancy and no final conclusions had been made.

The part Bosch liked best about the story were the statements from several statesmen, including most of the city council, expressing shock both at the deaths of Mittel and Conklin and at their involvement in and/or cover-up of murders. The story also mentioned that Mittel's employee, Jonathan Vaughn, was being sought by police as a murder suspect.

The story was most tenuous in regard to Pounds. It contained no mention that Bosch was suspected or known to have used the lieutenant's name or that his using it had led to Pounds's death. The story simply quoted Irving as saying the connection between Pounds and the case was still under investigation but that it appeared that Pounds might have stumbled onto the same trail Bosch had been following.

Irving had held back when he talked to Russell even after threatening Bosch. Harry could only believe it was the assistant chief's desire not to see the department's dirty laundry in print. The truth would hurt Bosch but could damage the department as well. If Irving was going to make a move against him, Bosch knew it would be inside the department. It would remain private.

Bosch's rented Mustang was still in the La Brea Lifecare parking lot. He had been lucky; the keys were in the door lock where he had left them a moment before being attacked by Vaughn. He paid the driver and went to the Mustang.

Bosch decided to take a cruise up Mount Olympus before going to the Mark Twain. He plugged his phone into the cigarette lighter so it would recharge and headed up Laurel Canyon Boulevard.

On Hercules Drive, he slowed outside the gate in front of Mittel's grounded spaceship. The gate was closed and there was yellow police-line tape still hanging from it. Bosch saw no cars in the driveway. It was quiet and peaceful. And soon he knew that a FOR SALE sign would be erected and the next genius would move in and think he was master of all he surveyed.

Bosch drove on. Mittel's place wasn't what he really wanted to see, anyway.

Fifteen minutes later Bosch came around the familiar turn on Woodrow Wilson but immediately found things unfamiliar. His house was gone, its disappearance as glaring in the landscape as a tooth missing from a smile.

At the curb in front of his address were two huge construction waste bins filled with splintered wood, mangled metal and shattered glass, the debris of his home. A mobile storage container had also been placed at the curb and Bosch assumed – hoped – it contained the salvageable property removed before the house was razed.

He parked and walked over to the flagstone path that formerly had led to his front door. He looked down and all that was left were the six pylons that poked out of the hillside like tombstones. He could rebuild upon these. If he wanted.

Movement in the acacia trees near the footings of the pylons caught his eye. He saw a flash of brown and then the head of a coyote moving slowly through the brush. It never heard Bosch or looked up. Soon it was gone. Harry lost sight of it in the brush.

He spent another ten minutes there, smoking a cigarette and waiting, but he saw nothing else. He then said a silent good-bye to the place. He had the feeling he wouldn't be back.

❖ ❖ ❖ ❖ ❖ ❖ ❖

When Bosch got to the Mark Twain, the city's morning was just starting. From his room he heard a garbage truck making its way down the alley, taking away another week's debris. It made him think of his house again, fitted nicely into two dumpsters.

Thankfully, the sound of a siren distracted him. He could identify it as a squad car as opposed to a fire engine. He knew he'd get a lot of that with the police station just down the street. He moved about his two rooms and felt restless and out of it, as if life was passing by while he was stuck here. He made coffee with the machine he had brought from home and it only served to make him more jittery.

He tried the paper again but there was nothing of real interest to him except the story he had already read on the front page. He paged through the thin Metro section anyway and saw a report that the county commission chambers were being outfitted with bulletproof desk blotters that the commissioners could hold up in front of them in the event a maniac came in spraying bullets. He threw the section aside and picked up the front section again.

Bosch reread the story about his investigation and couldn't escape a growing feeling that something was wrong, that something was left out or incomplete. Keisha Russell's reporting had been fine. That wasn't the problem. The problem was in seeing the story in words, in print. It didn't seem as convincing to him as it had been when he recounted it for her or for Irving or even for himself.

He put the newspaper aside, leaned back on the bed and closed his eyes. He went over the sequence of events once more and in doing so finally realized the problem that gnawed at him was not in the paper but in what Mittel had said to him. Bosch tried to recall the words exchanged between them on the manicured lawn behind the rich man's house. What had really been said there? What had Mittel admitted to?

Bosch knew that at that moment on the lawn, Mittel was in a position of seeming invulnerability. He had Bosch captured, wounded and doomed before him. His attack dog, Vaughn, stood ready with a gun to Bosch's back. In that situation, Bosch believed there would be no reason for a man of Mittel's ego to hold back. And, in fact, he had not held back. He had boasted of his scheme to control Conklin and others. He had freely, though indirectly, admitted that he had caused the deaths of Conklin and Pounds. But despite those admissions, he had not done the same when it came to the killing of Marjorie Lowe.

Through the fragmented images of that night, Bosch tried to recall the exact words said and couldn't quite get to them. His visual recollection was good. He had Mittel standing in front of the blanket of lights. But the words weren't there. Mittel's mouth moved but Bosch couldn't get the words. Then, finally, after working at it for a while, it came to him. He had it. Opportunity. Mittel had called her death an opportunity. Was that an acknowledgement of culpability? Was he saying he killed her or had her killed? Or was he simply admitting that her death presented an opportunity for him to take advantage of?

Bosch didn't know and not knowing felt like a heavy

weight in his chest. He tried to put it out of his mind and eventually started drifting off toward sleep. The sounds of the city outside, even the sirens, were comforting. He was at the threshold of unconsciousness, almost there, when he suddenly opened his eyes.

'The prints,' he said out loud.

Thirty minutes later he was shaved, showered and in fresh clothes heading downtown. He had his sunglasses on and he checked himself in the mirror. His battered eyes were hidden. He licked his fingers and pressed his curly hair down to better cover the shaved spot and the stitches in his scalp.

At County-USC Medical Center, he drove through the back lot to the parking slots nearest the rear garage bays of the Los Angeles County medical examiner's office. He walked in through one of the open garage doors and waved to the security guard, who knew him by sight and nodded back. Investigators weren't supposed to go in the back way but Bosch had been doing it for years. He wasn't going to stop until someone made a federal case out of it. The minimum-wage guard was an unlikely candidate to do that.

He went up to the investigators' lounge on the second floor, hoping not only that there would be someone there he knew but, more important, someone Bosch hadn't alienated over the years.

He swung the door open and immediately was hit with the smell of fresh coffee. But the room was bad news. Only Larry Sakai was in the room, sitting at a table with newspapers spread across it. He was a coroner's investigator Bosch had never really liked and the feeling was mutual.

'Harry Bosch,' Sakai said after looking up from the newspaper he held in his hands. 'Speak of the devil, I'm reading about you here. Says here you're in the hospital.'

'Nah, I'm here, Sakai. See me? Where's Hounchell and Lynch? Either of them around?'

Hounchell and Lynch were two investigators who Bosch knew would do him a favor without having to think about it too long. They were good people.

'Nah, they're out baggin' and taggin'. Busy morning. Guess things are picking up again.'

Bosch had heard a rumor through the grapevine that while removing victims from one of the collapsed apartment buildings after the earthquake, Sakai had gone in with his own camera and taken photos of people dead in their beds – the ceilings crushed down on top of them. He then sold the prints to the tabloid newspapers under a false name. That was the kind of guy he was.

'Anybody else around?'

'No, Bosch, jus' me. Whaddaya want?'

'Nothing.'

Bosch turned back to the door, then hesitated. He needed to make the print comparison and didn't want to wait. He looked back at Sakai.

'Look, Sakai, I need a favor. You want to help me out? I'll owe you one.'

Sakai leaned forward in his chair. Bosch could see just the point of a toothpick poking out between his lips.

'I don't know, Bosch, having you owe me one is like having the old whore with AIDS say she'll give me a free one if I pay for the first.'

Sakai laughed at the comparison he had created.

'Okay, fine.'

Bosch turned and pushed through the door, keeping his anger in check. He was two steps down the hall when he heard Sakai call him back. Just as he had hoped. He took a deep breath and went back into the lounge.

'Bosch, c'mon, I didn't say I wouldn't help you out.

Look, I read your story here and I feel for what you're going through, okay?'

Yeah, right, Bosch thought but didn't say.

'Okay,' he said.

'What do you need?'

'I need to get a set of prints off one of the customers in the cooler.'

'Which one?'

'Mittel.'

Sakai nodded toward the paper, which he had thrown back onto the table.

'That Mittel, huh?'

'Only one I know of.'

Sakai was quiet while he considered the request.

'You know, we make prints available to investigating officers assigned to homicides.'

'Cut the crap, Sakai. You know I know that and you know, if you read the paper, that I'm not the IO. But I still need the prints. You going to get them for me or am I just wasting my time here?'

Sakai stood up. Bosch knew that Sakai knew that if he backed down now after making the overture, then Bosch would gain a superior position in the netherworld of male interaction and in all their dealings that would follow. If Sakai followed through and got the prints, then the advantage would obviously go to him.

'Cool your jets, Bosch. I'm gonna get the prints. Why don't you get yourself a cup of coffee and sit down? Just put a quarter in the box.'

Bosch hated the idea of being beholden to Sakai for anything but he knew this was worth it. The prints were the one way he knew to end the case. Or tear it open again.

Bosch had a cup of coffee and in fifteen minutes the coroner's investigator was back. He was still waving the card so the ink would dry. He handed it to Bosch and went to the counter to get another cup of coffee.

'This is from Gordon Mittel, right?'

'Right. That's what it said on the toe tag. And, man, he got busted up pretty good in that fall.'

'Glad to hear it.'

'You know, it sounds to me like that story in the newspaper ain't as solid as you LAPD guys claim if you're sneaking around here gettin' the guy's prints.'

'It's solid, Sakai, don't worry about it. And I better not get any calls from any reporters about me picking up prints. Or I'll be back.'

'Don't give yourself a hernia, Bosch. Just take the prints and leave. Never met anybody who tried so hard to make the person doin' him a favor feel bad.'

Bosch dumped his coffee cup in a trash can and started out. At the door he stopped.

'Thanks.'

It burned him to say it. The guy was an asshole.

'Just remember, Bosch, you owe me.'

Bosch looked back at him. He was stirring cream into his cup. Bosch walked back, sticking his hand in his pocket. When he got to the counter he pulled out a quarter and dropped it into the slotted tin box that was the coffee fund.

'There, that's for you,' Bosch said. 'Now we're even.'

He walked out and in the hallway he heard Sakai call him an asshole. To Bosch that was a sign that all might be right in the world. His world, at least.

When Bosch got to Parker Center fifteen minutes later, he realized he had a problem. Irving had not returned his ID tag because it was part of the evidence recovered from Mittel's jacket in the hot tub. So Bosch loitered around the front of the building until he saw a group of detectives and administrative types walking toward the building from the

City Hall annex. When the group moved inside and around the entry counter, Bosch stepped up behind them and got by the duty officer without notice.

Bosch found Hirsch at his computer in the Latent Fingerprint Unit and asked him if he still had the Lifescan from the prints off the belt buckle.

'Yeah, I've been waiting for you to pick them up.'

'Well, I got a set I want you to check against them first.'

Hirsch looked at him but hesitated only a second.

'Let's see 'em.'

Bosch got the print card Sakai had made out of his briefcase and handed it over. Hirsch looked at it a moment, turning the card so it reflected the overhead light better.

'These are pretty clean. You don't need the machine, right? You just want to compare these to the prints you brought in before.'

'That's right.'

'Okay, I can eyeball it right now if you want to wait.'

'I want to wait.'

Hirsch got the Lifescan card out of his desk and took it and the coroner's card to the work counter, where he looked at them through a magnifying lamp. Bosch watched his eyes going back and forth between the prints as if he were watching a tennis ball go back and forth across a net.

Bosch realized as he watched Hirsch work that more than anything else in the world he wanted the print man to look up at him and say that the prints from the two cards in front of him matched. Bosch wanted this to be over. He wanted to put it away.

After five minutes of silence, the tennis match was over and Hirsch looked up at him and gave him the score.

❖ ❖ ❖ ❖ ❖ ❖ ❖

When Carmen Hinojos opened her waiting room door she seemed pleasantly surprised to see Bosch sitting on the couch.

'Harry! Are you all right? I didn't expect to see you here today.'

'Why not? It's my time, isn't it?'

'Yes, but I read in the paper you were at Cedars.'

'I checked out.'

'Are you sure you should have done that? You look …'

'Awful?'

'I didn't want to say that. Come in.'

She ushered him in and they took their usual places.

'I actually look better than I feel right now.'

'Why? What is it?'

'Because it was all for nothing.'

His statement put a confused look on her face.

'What do you mean? I read the story today. You solved the murders, including your mother's. I thought you'd be quite different than this.'

'Well, don't believe everything you read, Doctor. Let me clarify things for you. What I did on my so-called mission was cause two men to be murdered and another to die by my own hands. I solved, let's see, I solved one, two, three murders, so that's good. But I didn't solve the murder I set out to solve. In other words, I've been running around in circles causing people to die. So, how did you expect me to be during our session?'

'Have you been drinking?'

'I had a couple beers with lunch but it was a long lunch and I think that a minimum of two beers is required considering what I just told you. But I am not drunk, if that is what you want to know. And I'm not working, so what's the difference?'

'I thought we agreed to cut back on –'

'Oh, fuck that. This is the real world here. Isn't that what you called it? The real world? Between now and the last time we talked, I've killed someone, Doc. And you want to talk about cutting back on booze. Like it means anything anymore.'

Bosch took out his cigarettes and lit one. He kept the pack and the Bic on the arm of the chair. Carmen Hinojos watched him for a long time before speaking again.

'You're right. I'm sorry. Let's go to what I think is the heart of the problem. You said you didn't solve the murder you set out to solve. That, of course, is your mother's death. I am only going by what I read, but today's *Times* attributes her killing to Gordon Mittel. Are you telling me that you now know that to be incontrovertibly wrong?'

'Yes. I now know that to be incontrovertibly wrong.'

'How?'

'Simple. Fingerprints. I went down to the morgue, got Mittel's prints and had them compared to those on the murder weapon, the belt. No match. He didn't do it. Wasn't there. Now, I don't want you to get the wrong idea. I'm not sitting here with a guilty conscience over Mittel. He was a man who decided to kill people and then had them killed. Just like that. At least two times I'm sure of, then he was going to have me killed, too. So I say fuck him. He got what he had coming. But I'll carry Pounds and Conklin around with me for a long time. Maybe forever. And one way or another, I'll pay for it. It's just that it would make that weight easier to carry if there had been a reason. Any good reason. Know what I mean? But there isn't a reason. Not anymore.'

'I understand. I don't – I'm not sure how to proceed with this. Do you want to talk some about your feelings in regard to Pounds and Conklin?'

'Not really. I've thought about it enough already. Neither man was innocent. They did things. But they didn't have to die like they did. Especially Pounds. Jesus. I can't talk about it. I can't even think about it.'

'Then how will you go on?'

'I don't know. Like I said, I have to pay.'

'What is the department going to do, any idea?'

'I don't know. I don't care. It's bigger than the department to decide. I have to decide my penance.'

'Harry, what does that mean? That concerns me.'

'Don't worry, I'm not going to the closet. I'm not that type.'

'The closet?'

'I'm not going to stick a gun in my mouth.'

'Through what you've said here today, it is already clear you have accepted responsibility for what happened to these two men. You're facing it. In effect, you are denying denial. That is a foundation you can build on. I am concerned about this talk about penance. You have to go on, Harry. No matter what you do to yourself, it doesn't bring them back. So the best you can do is go on.'

He didn't say anything. He suddenly grew tired of all the advice, of her intervention in his life. He was feeling resentful and frustrated.

'Do you mind if we cut the session short today?' he asked. 'I'm not feeling so hot.'

'I understand. It's no problem. But I want you to

promise me something. Promise me we will talk again before you make any decisions.'

'You mean about my penance?'

'Yes, Harry.'

'Okay, we'll talk.'

He stood up and attempted a smile but it came out more like a frown. Then he remembered something.

'By the way, I apologize for not getting back to you the other night when you called. I was waiting on a call and couldn't talk and then I just kind of forgot. I hope you were just checking on me and it wasn't too important.'

'Don't worry about it. I forgot myself. I was just calling to see how you made it through the rest of the afternoon with Chief Irving. I also wanted to see if you wanted to talk about the photos. It doesn't matter now.'

'You looked at them?'

'Yes. I had a couple of comments but –'

'Let's hear them.'

Bosch sat back down. She looked at him, weighing his suggestion, and decided to go ahead.

'I have them here.'

She bent down to get the envelope out of one of the lower drawers of the desk. She almost disappeared from Bosch's view. Then she was up and placed the envelope on the desk.

'I guess you should take these back.'

'Irving took the murder book and the evidence box. He's got it all now except for those.'

'You sound like you're unhappy about that, or that you don't trust him with it. That's a change.'

'Aren't you the one who said I don't trust anyone?'

'Why don't you trust him?'

'I don't know. I just lost my suspect. Gordon Mittel's clear and I'm starting from ground zero. I was just thinking about the percentages …'

'And?'

'Well, I don't know the numbers but a significant number of homicides are reported by the actual doer. You know, the husband who calls up crying, saying his wife is missing. More often than not, he's just a bad actor. He killed her and thinks calling the cops helps convince everybody he's clean. Look at the Menendez brothers. One of 'em calls up boohooing about mom and dad being dead. Turns out he and the brother were the ones who shotgunned them. There was a case up in the hills a few years back. This little girl was missing. It was Laurel Canyon. It made the papers, TV. So the people up there organized search parties and all of that and a few days later one of the searchers, a teen-aged boy who was one of the girl's neighbors, found her body under a log near Lookout Mountain. It turned out he was the killer. I got him to confess in fifteen minutes. The whole time of the search I was just waiting for the one who would find the body. It was percentages. He was a suspect before I even knew who it was.'

'Irving found your mother's body.'

'Yes. And he knew her before that. He told me once.'

'It seems like a stretch to me.'

'Yeah. Most people probably thought that about Mittel, too. Right up until they fished him out of the hot tub.'

'Isn't there an alternative scenario? Isn't it possible that maybe the original detectives were correct in their assumption back then that there was a sex killer out there and that tracking him was hopeless?'

'There's always alternative scenarios.'

'But you always seem drawn toward finding someone of power, a person of the establishment, to blame. Maybe that's not the case here. Maybe it's a symptom of your larger desire to blame society for what happened to your mother ... and to you.'

Bosch shook his head. He didn't want to hear this.

'You know, all this psychobabble … I don't … Can we just talk about the photos?'

'I'm sorry.'

She looked down at the envelope as if she was seeing right through it to the photos inside it.

'Well, it was very difficult for me to look at them. As far as their forensic value goes, there wasn't a lot there. The photos show what I would call a statement homicide. The fact that the ligature, the belt, was still wrapped around her neck seems to indicate that the killer wanted police to know exactly what he did, that he had been deliberate, that he had had control over this victim. I also think the choice of placement is significant as well. The trash bin had no top. It was open. That suggests that placing the body there may not have been an effort to hide it. It was also a –'

'He was saying she was trash.'

'Right. Again, a statement. If he was just getting rid of a body, he could've put it anywhere in that alley, but he chose the open dumpster. Subconsciously or not, he was making a statement about her. So to make a statement such as that about a person, he would have to have known her to some degree. Known about her. Known she was a prostitute. Known enough to judge her.'

Irving came to Bosch's mind again but he said nothing.

'Well,' he said instead, 'couldn't it have been a statement about all women? Could it be some sick fuck who – excuse me – some nut who hated all women and thought all women were trash? That way he wouldn't have to have known her. Maybe somebody who simply wanted to kill a prostitute, any prostitute, to make a statement about them.'

'Yes, that's a possibility, but like you I'm going with the percentages. The kind of sick fuck you are talking about –

which, incidentally, in psychobabble we call a sociopath –
is much rarer than the one who keys on specific targets,
specific women.'

Bosch shook his head dismissively and looked out the
window.

'What is it?'

'It's just frustrating, that's all. There wasn't much in the
murder book about them taking a hard look at anybody in
her circle, any of the neighbors, nothing like that. To do it
now is impossible. It makes me feel like it's hopeless.'

He thought of Meredith Roman. He could go to her to
ask about his mother's acquaintances and customers, but he
didn't know if he had the right to reawaken that part of
her life.

'You have to remember,' Hinojos said, 'in 1961 a case
like this would probably have seemed impossible to solve.
They wouldn't even have known how to start. It just
didn't happen as often as today.'

'They're almost impossible to solve today, too.'

They sat in silence for a few moments. Bosch thought
about the possibility that the killer was some hit-and-run
nut. A serial killer who was long gone into the darkness of
time. If that was the case, then his private investigation was
over. It was a failure.

'Do you have anything else on the photos?'

'That's really all I had – no, wait. There was one thing.
And you may already have this.'

She picked the envelope up and opened it. She reached
in and began sliding out a photo.

'I don't want to look at that,' Bosch said quickly.

'It's not a photo of her. Actually, it's her clothing, laid
out on a table. Is that okay to look at?'

She paused, her hand holding the photo half in and half
out of the envelope. Bosch waved his hand, telling her to
go ahead.

'I've already seen the clothes.'

'Then you've probably already considered this.'

She slid the photo to the edge of the desk and Bosch leaned forward to study it. It was a color photo that had yellowed with age, even inside the envelope. The same items of clothing he had found in the evidence box were spread out on a table in a formation that outlined a body, in the way a woman might put them out on a bed before dressing. It reminded Bosch of cutouts for paper dolls. Even the belt with the sea shell buckle was there, but it was between the blouse and the black skirt, not at the imaginary neck.

'Okay,' she said. 'What I found odd here was the belt.'

'The murder weapon.'

'Yes. Look, it has the large silver shell as the buckle and there are smaller silver shells as ornamentation. It's rather showy.'

'Right.'

'But the buttons on the blouse are gold. Also, the photos of the body, they show she was wearing gold teardrop earrings and a gold neck chain. Also a bracelet.'

'Right, I know that. They were in the evidence box, too.'

Bosch didn't understand what she was getting at.

'Harry, this is not a universal rule or anything, that's why I hesitate to bring it up. But usually people – women – don't mix and match gold and silver. And it appears to me your mother was well dressed on this evening. That she had jewelry on that matched the buttons of her blouse. She was coordinated and she had style. What I am saying is that I don't think she would have worn this belt with those other items. It was silver and it was showy.'

Bosch said nothing. Something was poking its way into his mind and its point was sharp.

'And lastly, this skirt buttons on the hip. It's a style that

418

is still around and I even have something similar to it myself. What's so functional about it is that because of the wide waistband it can be worn with or without a belt. There are no loops.'

Bosch stared at the photo.

'No loops.'

'Right.'

'So what you're saying is …'

'This might not have been her belt. It might have –'

'But it was. I remember it. The sea shell belt. I gave it to her for her birthday. I identified it for the cops, for McKittrick the day he came to tell me.'

'Well … then that shoots down everything I was going to say. I guess maybe when she came into the apartment the killer was already waiting with it.'

'No, it didn't happen in her apartment. They never found the crime scene. Listen, never mind whether it was her belt or not, what were you going to say?'

'Oh, I don't know, just a theory about it possibly being the property of another woman who may have been the motivating factor behind the killer's action. It's called aggression transference. It doesn't make sense now with this evidence but there are examples of what I was going to suggest. A man takes his ex-girlfriend's stockings and strangles another woman with them. In his mind, he's strangling the girlfriend. Something like that. I was going to suggest it could have happened in this case with the belt.'

But Bosch was no longer listening. He turned and looked out the window but wasn't seeing anything either. In his mind, he was seeing the pieces falling together. The silver and gold, the belt with two of the punch holes worn, two friends as close as sisters. One for both and both for one.

But then one was leaving the life. She'd found a white knight.

And one was staying behind.

'Harry, are you okay?'

He looked over at Hinojos.

'You just did it. I think.'

'Did what?'

He reached for his briefcase and from it withdrew the photo taken at the St Patrick's Day dance more than three decades before. He knew it was a long shot but he needed to check. This time he didn't look at his mother. He looked at Meredith Roman, standing behind the sitting Johnny Fox. And for the first time he saw that she wore the belt with the silver sea shell buckle. She had borrowed it.

It dawned on him then. She had helped Harry pick the belt out for his mother. She had coached him and she chose it not because his mother would like it but because she liked it and knew she would get to use it. Two friends who shared everything.

Bosch shoved the photo back into the briefcase and shut it. He stood up.

'I gotta go.'

❖ ❖ ❖ ❖ ❖ ❖ ❖

Bosch used the same ruse he had earlier to get back into Parker Center. Coming out of the elevator on the fourth floor, he practically ran into Hirsch, who was waiting to go down. He grabbed hold of the young print tech's arm and held him in the hallway as the elevator doors closed.

'You going home?'

'I was trying to.'

'I need one more favor. I'll buy you lunch, I'll buy you dinner, I'll buy you whatever you want if you do it for me. It's important and it won't take long.'

Hirsch looked at him. Bosch could see he was beginning to wish he'd never gotten involved.

'What's that saying, Hirsch? "In for a penny, in for a pound." Whaddaya say?'

'I've never heard it.'

'Well, I have.'

'I'm having dinner with my girlfriend tonight and I –'

'That's great. This won't take that long. You'll make it to your dinner.'

'All right. What is it you need?'

'Hirsch, you're my goddamn hero, you know that?'

Bosch doubted he even had a girlfriend. They went back to the lab. It was deserted, since it was almost five on a slow day. Bosch put his briefcase on one of the abandoned desks and opened it. He found the Christmas card and took it out by holding a corner between two fingernails. He held it up for Hirsch to see.

'This came in the mail five years ago. You think you can pull a print off it? A print from the sender? My prints are going to be on there, too, I'm sure.'

Hirsch furrowed his brow and studied the card. His lower lip jutted outward as he contemplated the challenge.

'All I can do is try. Prints on paper are usually pretty stable. The oils last long and sometimes leave ridge patterns in the paper even when they evaporate. Has it been in its envelope?'

'Yeah, for five years, until last week.'

'That helps.'

Hirsch carefully took the card from Bosch and walked over to the work counter, where he opened the card and clipped it to a board.

'I'm going to try the inside. It's always better. Less chance of you having touched it inside. And the writer always touches the inside. Is it all right if this gets kind of ruined?'

'Do what you have to do.'

Hirsch studied the card with a magnifying glass, then lightly blew over the surface. He reached to a rack of spray bottles over the work table and took down one marked NINHYDRIN. He sprayed a light mist over the surface of the card and in a few minutes it began to turn purple around the edges. Then light shapes began to bloom like flowers on the card. Fingerprints.

'I've got to bring this out some,' Hirsch said, more to himself than Bosch.

Hirsch looked up at the rack and his eyes followed the row of chemical reagents until he found what he was looking for. A spray bottle marked ZINC CHLORIDE. He sprayed it on the card.

'This should bring the storm clouds in.'

The prints turned the deep purple shade of heavy rain clouds. Hirsch then took down a bottle labeled PD, which Bosch knew meant physical developer. After the card was misted with PD, the prints turned a grayish black and were more defined. Hirsch looked them over with his magnifying lamp.

'I think this is good enough. We won't need the laser. Now, look at these here, Detective.'

Hirsch pointed to a print that appeared to have been left by a thumb on the left side of Meredith Roman's signature and two smaller finger marks above it.

'These look like marks left by someone trying to hold the card steady while it was being written on. Any chance that you might've touched it this way?'

Hirsch held his fingers in place an inch over the card in the same position that the hand that left the prints would have been in. Bosch shook his head.

'All I ever did was open it and read it. I think those are the prints we want.'

'Okay. Now what?'

Bosch went to his briefcase and pulled out the print cards Hirsch had returned to him earlier in the day. He found the card containing the lifts from the belt with the sea shell buckle.

'Here,' he said. 'Compare this to what you got on the Christmas card.'

'You got it.'

Hirsch pulled the magnifying glass with the ringed light attachment in front of him and once again began his tennis match eye movement as he compared the prints.

Bosch tried to envision what had happened. Marjorie Lowe was going to Las Vegas to get married to Arno Conklin. The very thought of it must have been absurdly wonderful to her. She had to go home and pack. The plan was to drive through the night. If Arno was planning to bring along a best man, perhaps Marjorie was to bring a maid of honor. Maybe she would have gone upstairs to ask Meredith to come. Or maybe she would have gone to her to borrow back the belt that her son had given her. Maybe she would have gone to say good-bye.

But something happened when she got there. And on her happiest night Meredith killed her.

Bosch thought about the interview reports that had been in the murder book. Meredith told Eno and McKittrick that Marjorie's date on the night she died had been arranged by Johnny Fox. But she didn't go to the party herself because she said Fox had beaten her the night before and she was not presentable. The detectives noted in the report that she had a bruise on her face and a split lip.

Why didn't they see it then, Bosch wondered. Meredith had sustained those injuries while killing Marjorie. The drop of blood on Marjorie's blouse had come from Meredith.

But Bosch knew why they hadn't seen it. He knew the investigators dismissed any thought in that direction, if they ever even had any, because she was a woman. And because Fox backed her story. He admitted he beat her.

Bosch now saw what he believed was the truth. Meredith killed Marjorie and then hours later called Fox at his card game to give him the news. She asked him to help her get rid of the body and hide her involvement.

Fox must have readily agreed, even to the point of his willingness to say he beat her, because he saw the larger picture. He lost a source of income when Marjorie was killed but that would have been tempered by the increased leverage the murder would give him over Conklin and Mittel. Keeping it unsolved would make it even better. He'd always be a threat to them. He could walk into the police station at any time to tell what he knew and lay it on Conklin.

What Fox didn't realize was that Mittel could be as cunning and vicious as he was. He learned that a year later on La Brea Boulevard.

Fox's motivation was clear. Bosch still wasn't sure about Meredith's. Could she have done it for the reasons Bosch had set out in his mind? Would the abandonment of a friend have led to the rage of murder? He began to believe there was still something left out. He still didn't know it all. The last secret was with Meredith Roman and he would have to go get it.

An odd thought pushed through these questions to Bosch. The time of death of Marjorie Lowe was about midnight. Fox didn't get his call and leave his card game until roughly four hours later. Bosch now assumed that the murder scene was Meredith's apartment. Now he wondered, what did she do in that place for four hours with the body of her best friend lying there?

'Detective?'

Bosch looked away from his thoughts to Hirsch, who was sitting at the desk nodding his head.

'You got something?'

'Bingo.'

Bosch just nodded.

It was confirmation of more than just the match of fingerprints. He knew it was a confirmation that all the things he had accepted as the truths of his life could be as false as Meredith Roman.

❖ ❖ ❖ ❖ ❖ ❖ ❖

The sky was the color of a ninhydrin bloom on white paper. It was cloudless and growing dark purple with the aging of dusk. Bosch thought of the sunsets he had told Jazz about and realized that even that was a lie. Everything was a lie.

He stopped the Mustang at the curb in front of Katherine Register's home. There was another lie. The woman who lived here was Meredith Roman. Changing her name didn't change what she had done, didn't change her from guilty to innocent.

There were no lights on that he could see from the street, no sign of life. He was prepared to wait but didn't want to deal with the thoughts that would intrude as he sat alone in the car. He got out, crossed the lawn to the front porch and knocked on the door.

While he waited, he got out a cigarette and was lighting it when he suddenly stopped. He realized that what he was doing was his reflex of smoking at death scenes where the bodies were old. His instincts had reacted before he had consciously registered the odor from the house. Outside the door it was barely noticeable, but it was there. He looked back out to the street and saw no one. He looked back at the door and tried the knob. It turned. As he opened it, he felt a rush of cool air and the odor came out to meet him.

The house was still, the only sound the hum of the air

426

conditioner in the window of her bedroom. That was where he found her. He could tell right away that Meredith Roman had been dead for several days. Her body was in the bed, the covers pulled up to her head on the pillow. Only her face, what was left of it, was visible. Bosch's eyes did not linger on the image. The deterioration had been extensive and he guessed that maybe she had been dead since the day he had visited.

On the table next to the bed were two empty glasses, a half-gone fifth of vodka and an empty bottle of prescription pills. Bosch bent down to read the label and saw the prescription was for Katherine Register, one each night before bed. Sleeping pills.

Meredith had faced her past and administered her own penance. She had taken the blue canoe. Suicide. Bosch knew it wasn't for him to decide but it looked that way. He turned to the bureau because he remembered the Kleenex box and he wanted to use a tissue to cover his tracks. But there on the top, near the photos in gilded frames, was an envelope that had his name on it.

He picked it up, took some tissues and left the room. In the living room, a bit farther away from the source of the horrible odor but not far enough, he turned the envelope over to open it and noticed the flap was torn. The envelope had been opened already. He guessed maybe Meredith had reopened it to read again what she had written. Maybe she'd had second thoughts about what she was doing. He dismissed the question and took the note out. It was dated a week earlier. Wednesday. She had written it the day after his visit.

Dear Harry,
If you are reading this then my fears that you would learn the truth were well founded. If you are reading this then the decision I have made tonight was the correct one and I have no regrets as I make it. You

see, I would rather face the judgment of afterlife than have you look at me while knowing the truth.

I know what I have taken from you. I have known all my life. It does no good to say I am sorry or to try to explain. But it still amazes me how one's life can change forever in a few moments of uncontrolled rage. I was angry at Marjorie when she came to me that night so full of hope and happiness. She was leaving me. For a life with you. With him. For a life we had only dreamed was possible.

What is jealousy but a reflection of your own failures? I was jealous and angry and I struck at her. I then made a feeble effort to cover what I had done. I am sorry, Harry, but I took her from you and with that took any chance you ever had. I've carried the guilt every day since then and I take it with me now. I should have paid for my sin a long time ago but someone convinced me otherwise and helped me get away. There is no one left to convince me now.

I don't ask for your forgiveness, Harry. That would be an insult. I guess all I want is for you to know my regrets and to know that sometimes people who get away don't really get away. I didn't. Not then, not now. Good-bye.

Meredith

Bosch reread the note and then stood there thinking about it for a long time. Finally, he folded it and put it back in its envelope. He walked over to the fireplace, lit the envelope on fire with his Bic and then tossed it onto the grate. He watched the paper bend and burn until it bloomed like a black rose and went out.

He went to the kitchen and lifted the receiver off the phone after wrapping his hand in tissue. He put it on the counter and dialed nine-one-one. As he walked toward the front door, he could hear the tiny voice of the Santa

Monica police operator asking who was there and what the problem was.

He left the door unlocked and wiped the exterior knob with the tissue after stepping out onto the porch. He heard a voice from behind him.

'She writes a good letter, don't she?'

Bosch turned around. Vaughn was sitting on the rattan love seat on the porch. He was holding a new twenty-two in his hand. It looked like another Beretta. He looked none the worse for wear. He didn't have the black eyes that Bosch had, or the stitches.

'Vaughn.'

Bosch couldn't think of anything else to say. He couldn't imagine how he had been found by him. Could Vaughn have been daring enough to hang around Parker Center and follow Bosch from there? Bosch looked out into the street and wondered how long it would take the police operator to dispatch a car to the address the computer gave her for the 911 call. Even though Bosch had said nothing on the line, he knew they would eventually send a car to check it out. He had wanted them to find Meredith. If they took their time about it, they would probably find him as well. He had to stall Vaughn for as long as possible.

'Yeah, nice note,' the man with the gun said. 'But she left something out, don't you think?'

'What's left out?'

Vaughn seemed not to have heard him.

'It's funny,' he said. 'I knew your mother had a kid. But I never met you, never even saw you. She kept you away from me. I wasn't good enough, I guess.'

Bosch continued to stare as things began to fall together.

'Johnny Fox.'

'In the flesh.'

'I don't understand. Mittel ...'

'Mittel had me killed? No, not really. I killed myself, I guess you could say. I read that story you people put in the paper today. But you had it wrong. Most of it, at least.'

Bosch nodded. He knew now.

'Meredith killed your mother, kid. Sorry about that. I just helped her take care of it after the fact.'

'And then you used her death to get to Conklin.'

Bosch didn't need any confirmation from Fox. He was just trying to chew up time.

'Yeah, that was the plan, to get to Conklin. Worked pretty good, too. Got me out of the sewer. Only I found out pretty fast that the real power was Mittel. I could tell. Between the two of them, Mittel could go the distance. So I threw in with him, you could say. He wanted a better hold on the golden boy. He wanted an ace up his own sleeve. So I helped.'

'By killing yourself? I don't get it.'

'Mittel told me that supreme power over someone is the power they don't know you have until you need to use it. You see, Bosch, Mittel always suspected that Conklin was really the one who did your mother.'

Bosch nodded. He saw where the story was going.

'And you never told Mittel that Conklin wasn't the killer.'

'That's right. I never told him about Meredith. So knowing that, look at it from his side. Mittel figured that if Conklin was the doer and he believed I was dead, then he'd think he was home free. See, I was the only loose end, the one who could tie him in. Mittel wanted him to think he was clear. He wanted it because he wanted Conklin at ease. He didn't want him to lose his drive, his ambition. Conklin was going places and Mittel didn't want him to even hesitate. But he also wanted to keep an ace up his sleeve, something that he could always pull out if Conklin tried to step out of line. That was me. I was the ace. So we arranged that little hit and run, me and Mittel. Thing is, Mittel never had to play the ace with Conklin. Conklin gave Mittel a lot of good years after that. By the time he backed out on that attorney general thing, Mittel was well diversified. By then he had a congressman, a senator, a quarter of the local pols on his client list. You could say by then he had already climbed on Conklin's shoulders to the higher ground. He didn't need Arno anymore.'

Bosch nodded again and thought a moment about the scenario. All those years. Conklin believed it had been Mittel who killed her and Mittel believed it had been Conklin. It was neither.

'So who was the one you ran over?'

'Oh, just somebody. It doesn't matter. He was just a volunteer, you could say. I picked him up on Mission Street. He thought he was handing out Conklin fliers. I planted my ID in the bottom of the satchel I gave him. He never knew what hit him or why.'

'How'd you get away with it?' Bosch asked, though he thought he already knew the answer to that as well.

'Mittel had Eno on the line. We set it up so that it happened when he was next up on call. He took care of everything and Mittel took care of him.'

Bosch could see that the setup also gave Fox a share of power over Mittel. And he'd ridden along with him ever since. A little plastic surgery, a nicer set of clothes, and he was Jonathan Vaughn, aid to the wunderkind political strategist and rainmaker.

'So how'd you know I'd show up here?'

'I'd kept tabs on her over the years. I knew she was here. Alone. After our little run-in on the hill the other night, I came here to hide, to sleep. You gave me a headache – what the hell you hit me with?'

'The eight ball.'

'I guess I should have thought of that when I put you in there. Anyway, I found her like that in the bed. I read the note and knew who you were. I figured you'd be back. Especially after you left that message on the phone yesterday.'

'You've been here all this time with ...'

'You get used to it. I put the air on high, closed the door. You get used to it.'

Bosch tried to imagine it. Sometimes he believed that he was used to the smell, but he knew he wasn't.

'What did she leave out of the note, Fox?'

'That was the part about her wanting Conklin for herself. See, I tried her with Conklin first. But it didn't take. Then I set him up with Marjorie and got the fireworks. Nobody expected that he'd want to end up marrying her, though. Least of all Meredith. There was only room on the horse with the white knight for one rider. That was Marjorie. Meredith couldn't handle that. Must've been a hell of a cat fight.'

Bosch said nothing. But the truth stung his face like a sunburn. That's what it had all come down to, a cat fight between whores.

'Let's go to your car now,' Fox said.

'Why?'

'We need to go to your place now.'

'For what?'

Fox never answered. A Santa Monica squad car stopped in front of the house just as Bosch asked his question. Two officers started getting out.

'Be cool, Bosch,' Fox said quietly. 'Be cool if you want to live a little longer.'

Bosch saw Fox turn the aim of his gun toward the approaching officers. They could not see it because of the thick bougainvillea running along the front of the porch. One of them started to speak.

'Did someone here call nine –'

Bosch took two steps and launched himself over the railing to the lawn. As he did it, he yelled a warning.

'*He's got a gun! He's got a gun!*'

On the ground, Bosch heard Fox start running on the wood decking of the porch. He guessed he was going for the door. Then came the first shot. He was sure it came from behind him, from Fox. Then the two cops opened up like the Fourth of July. Bosch couldn't count all the shots. He stayed on the grass with his arms spread wide and his hands up, just hoping they wouldn't send one his way.

It was over in no more than eight seconds. When the echoes died and silence returned, Bosch yelled again.

'*I'm unarmed! I'm a police officer! I am no threat to you! I am an unarmed police officer!*'

He felt the end of a hot gun barrel pressed against his neck.

'Where's the ID?'

'Right inside coat pocket.'

Then he remembered he still didn't have it. The cop's hands grasped him by the shoulders.

'I'm going to roll you over.'

'Wait a minute. I don't have it.'

'What is this? Roll over.'

Bosch complied.

'I don't have it with me. I've got other ID though. Left inside pocket.'

The cop started going through his jacket. Bosch was scared.

'I'm not going to do anything wrong here.'

'Just be quiet.'

The cop got Bosch's wallet out and looked at the driver's license that was behind a clear plastic window.

'Whaddaya got, Jimmy?' the other cop yelled. Bosch couldn't see him. 'He legit?'

'Says he's a cop, got no badge. Got a DL here.'

Then he hunched back down over Bosch and patted the rest of his body in a search for weapons.

'I'm clean.'

'All right, turn back over.'

Bosch did so and his hands were cuffed behind his back. He then heard the man above him call in for backup and an ambulance on his radio.

'All right, get up.'

Bosch did as he was told. For the first time he could see the porch. The other cop stood with his handgun pointing down at Fox's crumpled body at the front door. Bosch was led up the steps to the porch. He could see Fox was still alive. His chest was heaving, he had wounds in both legs and the stomach and it looked like one slug had gone through both cheeks. His jaw hung open. But his eyes seemed even wider as he stared at death coming for him.

'I knew you'd fire, you fuck,' Bosch said to him. 'Just die now.'

'Shut up,' the one called Jimmy ordered. 'Right now.'

The other cop pulled him away from the front door. Out in the street, Bosch could see neighbors joining together in little knots or watching from their own porches. Nothing like gunshots in suburbia for getting people together, he thought. The smell of spent gunpowder in the air does it better than a barbecue any day.

The young cop got right up in Bosch's face. Harry could see that his name plate identified him as D. Sparks.

'Okay, what the fuck's going on here? If you're a cop, tell us what's going on.'

'You two are a couple of heroes, that's what's going on.'

'Tell the story, man. I don't have time for bullshit.'

Bosch could hear approaching sirens now.

'My name's Bosch. I'm with LAPD. This man you shot is the suspect in the killing of Arno Conklin, the former

434

district attorney of this county, and LAPD Lieutenant Harvey Pounds. I'm sure you've heard about these cases.'

'Jim, you hear that?' He turned back to Bosch. 'Where's your badge?'

'Stolen. I can give you a number to call. Assistant Chief Irvin Irving. He'll tell you about me.'

'Never mind that. What's he doing here?'

He pointed to Fox.

'He told me he was hiding out. Earlier today I got a call to come to this address and he was here waiting to ambush me. See, I could identify him. He had to take me out.'

The cop looked down at Fox wondering if he should believe such an incredible story.

'You got here right in time,' Bosch said. 'He was going to kill me.'

D. Sparks nodded. He was beginning to like the sound of this story. Then concern creased his brow.

'Who called 911?' he asked.

'I did,' Bosch said. 'I came here, found the door open and went in. I was calling 911 when he got the jump on me. I just dropped the phone because I knew you people would come.'

'Why call 911 if he hadn't grabbed you yet?'

'Because of what's in the back bedroom.'

'What?'

'There's a woman in the bed. She looks like she's been dead about a week.'

'Who is she?'

Bosch looked at the young cop's face.

'I don't know.'

❖ ❖ ❖ ❖ ❖ ❖ ❖

'Why didn't you reveal that you knew she was your mother's killer? Why did you lie?'

'I don't know. I haven't figured it out. It's just that there was something about what she wrote and what she did at the end that ... I don't know, I just felt like that was enough. I just wanted to let it go.'

Carmen Hinojos nodded her head as if she understood but Bosch wasn't sure he did himself.

'I think that's a good decision, Harry.'

'You do? I don't think anybody else would think it was a good decision.'

'I'm not talking about on a procedural or criminal justice level. I'm just talking about on a human level. I think you did the right thing. For yourself.'

'I guess ...'

'Do you feel good about it?'

'Not really ... You were right, you know.'

'I was? About what?'

'About what you said about me finding out who did it. You warned me. Said it might do me more harm than good. Well, that was an understatement ... Some mission I gave myself, right?'

'I'm sorry if I was right. But as I said in the last session, the deaths of those men can't be –'

'I'm not talking about them anymore. I'm talking about something else. You see, I know now that my mother was

436

trying to save me from that place I was at. Like she had promised me that day out by the fence that I told you about. I think that whether she loved Conklin or not, she was thinking of me. She had to get me out and he was the way to do it. So, ultimately, you see, it was because of me that she died.'

'Oh, please, don't tell yourself that, Harry. That's ridiculous.'

Bosch knew that the anger in her voice was real.

'If you are going to take that form of logic,' she continued, 'you can come up with any reason why she was killed, you can argue that your own birth set circumstances in motion that led to her death. You see how silly that is?'

'Not really.'

'It's the same argument you made the other day about people not taking responsibility. Well, the inverse of that is people who take too much responsibility. And you are becoming one of them. Let that go, Harry. Let it go. Let someone else take some responsibility for some things. Even if that someone else is dead. Being dead does not absolve them of everything.'

He was cowed by the forcefulness of her admonition. He just looked at her for a long moment. He could tell her outburst would signal a natural break in the session. The discussion of his guilt was done. She had ended it and he had his instructions.

'I'm sorry to have raised my voice.'

'No problem.'

'Harry, what do you hear from the department?'

'Nothing. I'm waiting on Irving.'

'What do you mean?'

'He kept my ... culpability out of the paper. Now it's his move. He's either going to come at me with IAD – if he can make a case against me impersonating Pounds – or he's going to let it go. I'm betting he's going to let it go.'

437

'Why?'

'The one thing about the LAPD is that it is not into self-flagellation. Know what I mean? This case is very public and if they do something to me, they know there's always the danger it will get out and it will be one more black eye for the department. Irving sees himself as the protector of the department's image. He'll put that ahead of taking me down. Besides, he'll have leverage on me now. I mean, he thinks he will.'

'You seem to know Irving and the department well.'

'Why?'

'Chief Irving called me this morning and asked me to forward a positive RTD evaluation to his office as soon as possible.'

'He said that? He wants a positive return-to-duty report?'

'Yes, those were his words. Do you think you are ready for that?'

He thought a few moments but didn't answer the question.

'Has he done that before? Told you how to evaluate somebody?'

'No. It's a first time and I'm very concerned about it. It undermines my position here if I simply accede to his wishes. It's quite a dilemma because I don't want you caught in the middle.'

'What if he didn't tell you which way to go, what would your evaluation be? Positive or negative?'

She played with a pencil on the desktop for a few moments while considering the question.

'It's very close, Harry, but I think you need more time.'

'Then don't do it. Don't give in to him.'

'That's quite a change. Only a week ago all you could talk about was getting back to the job.'

'That was a week ago.'

There was a palpable sadness in his voice.

'Stop beating yourself to death with it,' she said. 'The past is like a club and you can only hit yourself in the head with it so many times before there is serious and permanent damage. I think you're at your limit. For what it's worth, I think you are a good and clean and ultimately kind man. Don't do this to yourself. Don't ruin what you have, what you are, with this kind of thinking.'

He nodded as if he understood but he had dismissed her words as soon as he heard them.

'I've been doing a lot of thinking the last couple of days.'

'About what?'

'Everything.'

'Any decisions on anything?'

'Almost. I think I'm going to pull the pin, leave the department.'

She leaned forward and folded her arms on the desk. A serious look creased her brow.

'Harry, what are you talking about? This is not like you. Your job and your life are the same. I think it's good to have some distance but not total separation. I –' She stopped when she seemed to come upon an idea. 'Is this your idea of penance, of making up for what happened?'

'I don't know … I just … For what I did, something has to be paid. That's all. Irving's not going to do anything. I will.'

'Harry, you made a mistake. A serious mistake, yes. But for that you are giving up your career, the one thing that even you readily admit you do well? You're going to throw it all away?'

He nodded.

'Did you pull the papers yet?'

'Not yet.'

'Don't do it.'

'Why not? I can't do this anymore. It's like I'm walking around handcuffed to a chain of ghosts.'

He shook his head. They were having the same debate that he had been having in his mind for the last two days, since the night at Meredith Roman's house.

'Give it some time,' Hinojos said. 'All I'm saying is, think about it. You're on paid leave now. Use it. Use the time. I'll tell Irving he's not getting an RTD from me yet. Meantime, you just give it some time and think hard on it. Go away somewhere, sit on the beach. But think about it before you turn in your papers.'

Bosch raised his hands in surrender.

'Please, Harry. I want to hear you say it.'

'All right. I'll do some more thinking.'

'Thank you.'

She let some silence underline his agreement.

'Remember what you said about seeing the coyote on the street last week?' she asked quietly. 'About it being the last coyote?'

'I remember.'

'I think I know how you felt. I'd hate to think that I was seeing the coyote for the last time, too.'

❖ ❖ ❖ ❖ ❖ ❖ ❖

From the airport Bosch took the freeway to the Armenia exit and then south to Swann. He found that he didn't even need the rent-a-car map. He went east on Swann into Hyde Park and then down South Boulevard to her place. He could see the bay shimmering in the sun at the end of the street.

At the top of the stairs the door was open but the screen door was closed. Bosch knocked.

'Come in. It's open.'

It was her. Bosch pushed through the screen into the living room. She wasn't there but the first thing he noticed was a painting on the wall where before there had been only the nail. It was a portrait of a man in shadows. He was sitting at a table alone. The figure's elbow was on the table and the hand was up against his cheek, obscuring the face and making the deep set of the eyes the focal point of the painting. Bosch stared at it a moment until she called again.

'Hello? I'm in here.'

He saw the door to her studio was open a half foot. He stepped over and pushed it open. She was there, standing in front of the easel, dark earth-tone oils on the palette in her hand. There was a single errant slash of ocher on her right cheek. She immediately smiled.

'Harry.'

'Hello, Jasmine.'

He moved in closer to her and stepped around the side

of the easel. The portrait had only just been started. But she had begun with the eyes. The same eyes in the portrait that hung on the wall in the other room. The same eyes he saw in the mirror.

She hesitantly came closer to him. There was not a glimmer of embarrassment or unease in her face.

'I thought that if I painted you, you would come back.'

She dropped her brush into an old coffee can bolted to the easel and came even closer. She embraced him and they kissed silently. At first it was a gentle reunion, then he put his hand against her back and pulled her tightly against his chest as if she were a bandage that could stop his bleeding. After a while she pulled back, brought her arms up and held his face in her hands.

'Let me see if I got the eyes right.'

She reached up and took off his sunglasses. He smiled. He knew the purple below his eyes was almost gone but they were still red-rimmed and shot with swollen capillaries.

'Jesus, you took the red-eye.'

'It's a long story. I'll tell you later.'

'God, put these back on.'

She hooked the glasses back on and laughed.

'It's not that funny. It hurt.'

'Not that. I got paint on your face.'

'Well, then I'm not alone.'

He traced the slash on her face. They embraced again. Bosch knew they could talk later. For now he just held her and smelled her and looked over her shoulder to the brilliant blue of the bay. He thought of something the old man in the bed had told him. When you find the one that you think fits, then grab on for dear life. Bosch didn't know if she was the one, but for the moment he held on with everything he had left.

available from

THE ORION PUBLISHING GROUP

All Orion/Phoenix titles are available at your local bookshop or from the following address:

Mail Order Department
Littlehampton Book Services
FREEPOST BR535
Worthing, West Sussex, BN13 3BR
telephone 01903 828503, *facsimile* 01903 828802
e-mail MailOrders@lbsltd.co.uk
(Please ensure that you include full postal address details)

Payment can be made either by credit/debit card (Visa, Mastercard, Access and Switch accepted) or by sending a £ Sterling cheque or postal order made payable to *Littlehampton Book Services*.
DO NOT SEND CASH OR CURRENCY.

Please add the following to cover postage and packing

UK and BFPO:
£1.50 for the first book, and 50p for each additional book to a maximum of £3.50

Overseas and Eire:
£2.50 for the first book plus £1.00 for the second book and 50p for each additional book ordered

---

BLOCK CAPITALS PLEASE

name of cardholder ....

address of cardholder ....

delivery address
(if different from cardholder)
....
....
....

postcode ....

postcode ....

☐ I enclose my remittance for £ ....

☐ please debit my Mastercard/Visa/Access/Switch (delete as appropriate)

card number ⬜⬜⬜⬜⬜⬜⬜⬜⬜⬜⬜⬜⬜⬜⬜⬜

expiry date ⬜⬜⬜⬜   Switch issue no. ⬜⬜

signature ....

prices and availability are subject to change without notice